READER'S DIGEST
SELECT EDITIONS

The condensations in this volume
are published with the consent of the authors
and the publishers © 2007 Reader's Digest.

www.readersdigest.co.uk

The Reader's Digest Association Limited
11 Westferry Circus Canary Wharf London E14 4HE

For information as to ownership of
copyright in the material of this book,
and acknowledgments, see last page.

Printed in Germany
ISBN 978 0 276 44225 4

SELECTED AND CONDENSED
BY READER'S DIGEST

THE READER'S DIGEST ASSOCIATION LIMITED, LONDON

CONTENTS

J ack Reacher and Frances Neagley, once members of an elite unit in the US military, have been out of touch for years. And, with his unpredictable life on the road, Reacher knows he's hard to track down. So when Neagley contacts him through a coded message, he knows it's serious. Sure enough, her news is just the beginning of a whole lot of bad luck and trouble—but there's no way Reacher can let his old buddies down. A brand-new gripping adventure for Lee Child's iconic hero.

W hen financier Michael Dormer arrives at a small seaside town in Australia, he anticipates just another business deal. But the area is famous for the whale pods that winter in the surrounding waters, and the locals, including Kathleen Mostyn, owner of the ramshackle Silver Bay Hotel, and her niece Liza, force Mike to question what he hopes to achieve. As he becomes involved with life in Silver Bay, Mike begins to ask what he really wants for himself. A powerful story of love and redemption.

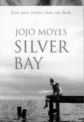

LOSING YOU

NICCI FRENCH

293

With its open marshlands and huge skies, Sandling Island, off the English coast, is a sanctuary, a place where you'd never expect to fear for your child's safety. But one morning Nina Landry is plunged into a deep anxiety, as she realises that her teenage daughter Charlie is not just late home from her paper round—she's missing. Like the rising tide near Nina's home, suspense builds implacably in this mesmerising novel.

Genghis Khan, one of the greatest conquerors of all time, ruled an empire that stretched from the Pacific Ocean to the Caspian Sea. Now, centuries later, a hunger for Khan-like dominance is driving the ambitions of a modern would-be overlord with visions of a similar, seismic shift in the balance of world power. His methods, however, are subtle. And it takes the intrepid Dirk Pitt and his fellow experts at the National Underwater and Marine Agency to unravel what's really going on.

TREASURE OF KHAN

CLIVE CUSSLER

435

BAD LUCK AND TROUBLE

LEE CHILD

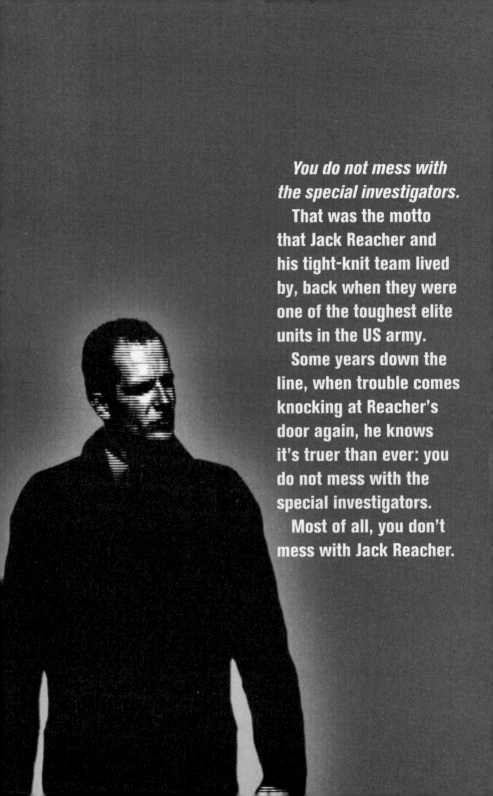

You do not mess with the special investigators. That was the motto that Jack Reacher and his tight-knit team lived by, back when they were one of the toughest elite units in the US army.

Some years down the line, when trouble comes knocking at Reacher's door again, he knows it's truer than ever: you do not mess with the special investigators.

Most of all, you don't mess with Jack Reacher.

CHAPTER ONE

The man was called Calvin Franz and the helicopter was a Bell 222. Franz had two broken legs, so he had to be loaded on board strapped to a stretcher. Not a difficult manoeuvre. The Bell was a roomy aircraft, twin-engined, with space for seven passengers. The rear doors were as big as a panel van's and they opened wide. The middle row of seats had been removed. There was plenty of room for Franz on the floor.

The helicopter was idling. Two men were carrying the stretcher. They ducked low under the rotor wash and hurried, one backwards, one forwards. When they reached the open door the guy who had been walking backwards got one handle up on the sill and ducked away. The other guy stepped forward and shoved hard and slid the stretcher all the way inside. Franz was awake and hurting. He cried out and jerked around a little, but not much, because the straps across his chest and thighs were buckled tight. The two men climbed in after him and got into their seats and slammed the doors.

Then they waited.

The pilot waited. A third man walked across the concrete. He bent low under the rotor and held a hand flat on his chest to stop his necktie whipping in the wind. He got in the seat next to the pilot.

'Go,' he said, then bent to concentrate on his harness buckle.

The pilot goosed the turbines and the Bell lifted straight off the ground, rotated slightly, retracted its wheels and climbed a thousand feet. Then it dipped its nose and hammered north. Below it science parks and small factories slid past, metal sidings blazing red in the late sun.

The man in the forward seat said, 'Know where we're going?'

The pilot nodded and said nothing.

The Bell clattered onwards, turning east of north, heading for darkness. It crossed a highway far below, a river of lights. Low, barren hills gave way to small, rounded mountains. The man in the forward seat twisted round and looked down at Franz. Smiled briefly and said, 'Twenty minutes, maybe.'

Franz didn't reply. He was in too much pain.

Twenty minutes took the Bell almost fifty-four miles, well out over the empty desert. The pilot flared the nose and slowed a little. The man in the forward seat stared down into the darkness. 'Where are we?' he asked.

The pilot said, 'Where we were before.'

'Height?'

'Three thousand feet.'

'What's the air like up here?'

'Still. A few thermals, but no wind.'

'So let's do it.'

The pilot slowed more and came to a stationary hover. The man in the forward seat signalled to the two guys in the back. Both unlocked their safety harnesses. One crouched forward, held his harness tight in one hand and unlatched the door with the other. The pilot tilted the Bell a little so the door fell all the way open under its own weight. Then he put the craft in a slow clockwise rotation that held the door wide. The second guy jacked the stretcher upwards to a forty-five degree slope. Franz was a big guy, and determined. His legs were useless but his upper body was powerful and straining hard. His head was snapping from side to side.

The first guy took out a knife and sawed through the strap round Franz's thighs. He sliced the strap round Franz's chest at the exact same time the second guy jerked the stretcher upright. Franz took an involuntary step forward. Onto his broken right leg. Then his broken left leg. He screamed once, briefly, his arms flailed and his upper body momentum levered him over his locked hips and took him straight out of the open door, into the noisy darkness, into the gale-force rotor wash, into the night.

CHAPTER TWO

Seventeen days later Jack Reacher was in Portland, Oregon, short of money. In Portland, because he had to be somewhere and the bus had stopped there. Short of money, because he had met an assistant district attorney called Samantha in a cop bar, and had twice bought her dinner before twice spending the night. Now she had gone to work and he was heading back to the bus depot, hair still wet from her shower, sated, relaxed, destination as yet unclear, with a very thin wad of bills in his pocket.

The terrorist attacks of September 11, 2001 had changed Reacher's life in two practical ways. Firstly, in addition to his folding toothbrush he now carried his passport. Too many things in the new era required photo ID. Reacher was a drifter, not a hermit, restless, not dysfunctional, and had yielded gracefully.

Secondly, he had changed his banking methods. New worries about terrorist financing had pretty much killed telephone banking, so Reacher had got an ATM card. He used 8197 as his PIN. He considered himself a man of very few talents but some abilities, most of which were related to his abnormal size and strength, but one of which was always knowing what time it was without looking, and another of which was some kind of a savant facility with arithmetics. Hence 8197. He liked 97 because it was the largest two-digit prime number, and he loved 81 because it was absolutely the only number whose square root was also the sum of its digits. No other non-trivial number in the cosmos had that kind of sweet symmetry.

His arithmetic awareness and his inherent cynicism about financial institutions always compelled him to check his balance every time he withdrew cash. He always deducted the ATM fees and every quarter he added in the bank's paltry interest. And despite his suspicions, his balance came up exactly as he predicted every time. Until that morning in Portland, when his balance was a thousand dollars bigger than it should have been.

Exactly one thousand and thirty dollars bigger, according to Reacher's own calculation. A mistake, obviously. By the bank. He pressed another button and requested a mini-statement. A slip of thin paper came out of a slot, listing the last five transactions against his account. Three of them were ATM cash withdrawals. One was the bank's most recent interest payment. The last was a deposit made three days previously. So there it was.

One thousand and thirty dollars. 1030.

Not inherently an interesting number, but Reacher stared at it for a minute. Not prime, obviously. No even number greater than two could be prime. Square root? A hair more than 32. Cube root? A hair less than ten and a tenth. Factors? Not many.

A mistake. Maybe. Or, maybe not a mistake. Reacher took fifty dollars from the machine and dug in his pocket for change.

He found a payphone inside the depot. He dialled his bank's number from memory and spoke to someone who was amazed that a customer would call about a bank error in his own favour. 'Might not be an error,' Reacher said.

'Do third parties make deposits into your account?' she asked.

'No.'

'It's likely to be an error, then. Don't you think?'

'I need to know who made the deposit.'

'May I ask why?' the woman said. 'There are confidentiality issues if a bank error exposes one customer's affairs to another.'

'It might be a message. From the past,' Reacher said.

'I don't understand.'

'I was a military policeman back in the day. If a military policeman needs urgent assistance from a colleague he calls in a ten-thirty radio code. If I do know the person who made the deposit, it might be a call for help.'

'Wouldn't this person just have called you on the phone?'

'I don't have a phone.'

'An email, then? Or a telegram. Or even a letter.'

'I don't have addresses for any of those things.'

'So how do we contact you, usually?'

'You don't,' Reacher said.

'A credit into your bank would be a very difficult way of communicating. Someone would have to trace your account.'

'That's my point. It would take a smart and resourceful person to do it. And if a smart and resourceful person needs to ask for help, there's big trouble somewhere.'

Silence on the phone. Except for the patter of a keyboard.

Reacher said. 'You're looking, aren't you?'

The woman said, 'I really shouldn't be doing this.'

'I won't rat you out.'

The keyboard patter stopped. 'You'll have to help me out. Give me clues. So I don't have to come right out with it. Would it be a man or a woman?'

Reacher smiled, briefly. It was a woman. Had to be. A smart, resourceful woman, capable of imagination and lateral thinking. A woman who knew about his compulsion to add and subtract. 'Let me guess. The deposit was made in Chicago.'

'Yes, by personal cheque through a Chicago bank.'

'Neagley.'

'That's the name we have. Frances L. Neagley.'

'Then forget we ever had this conversation,' Reacher said.

REACHER HAD SERVED thirteen years in the army, all of them in the military police. He had known Frances Neagley for ten of those years. He had been a second lieutenant, a lieutenant, a captain, a major. Neagley had steadfastly refused promotion beyond sergeant. She wouldn't consider Officer Candidate School. Reacher didn't really know why. There was a lot he didn't know about her.

But there was a lot he did know. She was smart and resourceful and thorough. And very tough. And strangely uninhibited. Not in terms of personal relationships. She was intensely private and resisted any kind of closeness, physical or emotional. Her lack of inhibition was professional. If she felt something was right, nothing stood in her way, not politics or practicality or politeness or even what a civilian might call the law. Reacher had recruited her to a special investigations unit. Most people put its occasional spectacular successes down to his leadership, but he put them down to her presence. She impressed him, deeply. Sometimes even came close to scaring him.

She worked for a private security provider in Chicago. He knew that. At least she had four years ago, which was the last time he had come into contact with her. She had left the army a year later than he had and gone into business with someone she knew.

He dug back in his pocket and came out with more quarters. Dialled long-distance information. Asked for Chicago. Gave the company name, as he remembered it, and a robot voice came on the line with a number. Reacher broke the connection, redialled and asked for Frances Neagley. A receptionist put him on hold.

A man's voice came on the line. 'Frances Neagley's office. May I know who's calling?'

'Jack Reacher.'

'Good. Thank you for getting in touch.'

'Who are you?'

'I'm Ms Neagley's assistant.'

'Is she there?'

'She's en route to Los Angeles. In the air right now, I think. She wants to see you as soon as possible.'

'In Chicago?'

'She'll be in LA for a few days. I think you should go there.'

'What's this all about?'

'I don't know. Can't be work-related. She'd have a file.'

'Where is she staying in LA?'

'I don't know that either. She said you'd track her down.'

Reacher asked, 'What is this, some kind of test?'

'She said if you can't find her, she doesn't want you. She's worried about something. But she didn't tell me what.'

Reacher turned and glanced at the departures board. 'Who else is she reaching out to?'

'There's a list of names. You're first to get back to her.'

'Will she call you when she lands?'

'Probably.'

'Tell her I'm on my way.'

HE TOOK A SHUTTLE to Portland Internatioanl Airport and bought a one-way ticket on United to LAX. The one-way walk-up fare was outrageous. Alaska Airlines would have been cheaper, but they put a scripture card on their meal trays. Ruined his appetite. His carry-on baggage amounted to precisely none at all and he had no keys, no cellphone, no watch, so he was through the X-ray hoop in thirty seconds. Then he was on his way to the gate, Neagley on his mind.

Not work-related. Therefore, private business. But as far as he was aware she had no private business. No private life. She never had. So what was her problem? The past, he guessed, which meant the army.

A list of names? Maybe chickens were coming home to roost. The army seemed like a long time ago to Reacher. A different world. Different rules. Maybe some long-delayed internal inquiry had started. His special investigations unit had cut a lot of corners and busted a lot of heads. Someone, maybe Neagley herself, had come up with a catchphrase: You *do not mess* with the special investigators. It had been repeated endlessly, as a promise, and a warning. Deadpan, and deadly serious.

Now maybe someone *was* messing with the special investigators. Maybe subpoenas and indictments were flying around. But in that case why would Neagley contact him? He was as close to untraceable as a human being in America could get.

He gave it up and got on the plane, but he used the flight time figuring out where in LA she would hole up. Back in the day he had been pretty good at finding people. Success depended on empathy. Think like them, feel like them. *Be* them.

Easier with AWOL soldiers, of course. Their aimlessness gave their decisions a special kind of purity. And they were heading away from something.

Neagley was heading *for* something. Her private business, and he didn't know what it was. So, first principles. What did he know about her? Well, she was cheap. She didn't see the point in spending a buck on something she didn't need. And she didn't need much. She didn't need room service or fluffy robes and complementary slippers.

So, scratch downtown. Not Beverly Hills, either. So where?

Reacher asked himself. Where would *I* go?

Hollywood, he answered. A little ways south and east of the good stuff. The wrong stretch of Sunset. That's where I'd go, he thought. And that's where she'll be.

The plane landed at LAX well after lunch and he was hungry. He didn't stop to eat. Just headed out to the taxi line and got a Korean guy in a Toyota minivan, watched the hot, brown afternoon light through the window. Palm trees, movie billboards, traffic lanes. And cars, rivers of cars, floods of cars.

The driver took the 101 north and exited a block from Sunset. Reacher got out and paid the fare. Hiked south, then turned left and faced east. He knew Sunset had a dense knot of cheap places right there, both sides of the boulevard. He had a potential dozen motel desks to canvass. He could see a Denny's sign ahead on the right. A chain diner. He decided to eat first. He cut across the drive-through lane. Walked past a long line of windows. Saw Frances Neagley inside, sitting alone in a booth.

REACHER STOOD for a moment in the parking lot and watched Neagley through the window. She hadn't changed much in the years since he'd seen her. She had to be nearer forty than thirty now, but her hair was still long and dark and shiny. Her eyes were still dark and alive. She was still slim and lithe. Still spending serious time in the gym. That was clear. She was wearing a tight white T-shirt with tiny cap sleeves and it would have taken an electron microscope to find any body fat on her arms.

She was a little tanned, which looked good with her colouring. Her nails were done. Her T-shirt looked like a quality item. Overall she looked richer than he remembered her. Comfortable, successful, accustomed to the civilian life. For a moment he felt awkward about his own cheap clothes and his scuffed shoes and his bad barbershop haircut. Like she was making it, and he wasn't. Then the pleasure of seeing an old friend swamped the thought and he walked on through the door and slid straight into her booth.

She looked up at him and smiled. 'Hello,' she said.

'To you too,' he said.

'Want lunch?'

'That was my plan.'

'So let's order, now you're here. You're about on time.'

'Am I?'

'My office guy traced the caller ID. We figured you'd head straight for the airport, then take United. You must hate Alaskan. Then a cab ride here. Your ETA was easy enough to predict.'

'You knew I would come here? To this diner?'

'Like you taught me.' Neagley smiled again.

'I didn't teach you anything.'

'You did. Think like them, *be* them. So I was being you, being me. You'd figure I'd head for Hollywood. You'd start right here on Sunset. But there's no meal on United, so I figured you'd want to eat first. This place has the biggest sign and you're no gourmet.'

'I thought I was tracking you. Are you staying here?'

'Beverly Hills. The Wilshire. I got here ten minutes ago.'

'The Beverly Wilshire? You've changed.'

'Not really. It's the world that changed. I need email, Internet and FedEx now. Business centres and concierges.'

'You make me feel old-fashioned.'

'You're improving. You use ATMs now.'

'That was a good move. The bank message. But extravagant. Ten dollars and thirty cents would have worked as well.'

Neagley said, 'I thought you might need the air fare.'

Reacher said nothing.

'I found your account, obviously. You're not rich.'

'I don't want to be rich.'

'I didn't want you responding to my ten-thirty on your dime.'

Reacher let it go. Truth was, he was almost poor. His savings had eroded to the point where he was starting to think maybe a couple of months of casual labour were in his future. The waitress came over with menus. Neagley ordered without looking, a cheeseburger and a soda. Reacher matched her, tuna melt and hot coffee.

He said. 'So what was your ten-thirty for exactly?'

Neagley pulled a black three-ring binder out of a tote bag and passed it across. It was a copy of an autopsy report.

'Calvin Franz is dead,' she said. 'I think someone threw him out of an airplane.'

CALVIN FRANZ had been an MP and Reacher's exact contemporary and pretty much his equal through his thirteen years of service. They had met here and there in the way that brother officers tended to, crossing paths in different parts of the world when investigations collided. Then they had done a serious spell together in Panama. It had been very intense, and they had seen things in each other that left them feeling more like real brothers than brother officers. After Reacher had been given the special investigations operation to build, they had spent the next two years together in a real unit-within-a-unit hothouse. They had become fast friends. Then new orders had come in and the special operation had been disbanded and Reacher had never seen Franz again.

Until that moment, in an autopsy photograph punched into a three-ring binder on a sticky laminate table in a cheap diner.

In life Franz had been smaller than Reacher but bigger than most people. Maybe six-three and two-ten. Powerful upper body, short legs. Primitive, in a way. But reasonably handsome. Calm, resolute, capable, relaxing to be around. He looked awful in the photograph, laid out on a stainless-steel tray, his skin bleached pale green.

Reacher asked, 'How did you get this?'

Neagley said, 'I can usually get things.'

Reacher turned the page. The corpse had weighed a hundred and ninety pounds. Cause of death was given as multiple organ failure due to massive impact trauma. Both legs were broken. Ribs were cracked. The bloodstream was flooded with free histamines. The body was severely dehydrated and the stomach held nothing but mucus. Trace evidence from the recovered clothing was unexceptional, apart from unexplained ferrous oxide powder low down on both pant legs.

Reacher asked. 'Where was he found?'

'In the desert about fifty miles north and east, a hundred yards off a road. No footprints coming or going.'

The waitress brought the food and Reacher started his sandwich. Neagley said, 'Two deputies in a car saw buzzards circling. Went to check. They said it was like he had fallen out of the sky. The pathologist agrees.'

Reacher nodded. He was reading the doctor's conclusion, that a free fall from maybe three thousand feet onto hard sand could have caused the internal injuries if Franz landed flat on his back, which was possible if he had been alive and flailing his arms. A dead weight would have fallen on its head.

Neagley said, 'They made the ID through his fingerprints.'

Reacher asked, 'How did you find out?'

'His wife called me. Three days ago. Seems he kept our names in his book. A special page. I was the only one she could find.'

'I didn't know he was married.'

'It was recent. They have a kid, four years old. He was a private eye here in LA, mostly background checks, database stuff.'

'What did his wife want you to do?'

'Nothing. She was just telling me. The cops are on it. Where he was found is outside LAPD jurisdiction, so it's LA County deputies, actually. They're working on the airplane thing. They figure it was maybe out of Vegas. That's happened to them before.'

Reacher said, 'An airplane has a stall speed of what? Eighty? He'd have come out of the door horizontal into the slip-stream. He'd have smashed against the wing or the tail.'

'He had two broken legs.'

'His blood was full of free histamines. That's a massive pain reaction. The broken legs were old. You know what ferrous oxide is?'

'Rust,' Neagley said. 'On iron.'

Reacher nodded. 'Someone broke his legs with an iron bar. Must have hurt like hell.'

Neagley said nothing.

'And they starved him. Didn't let him drink. He was a prisoner, two or three days. Maybe more. They were torturing him.'

Neagley said nothing.

'It was a helicopter. Probably at night. Stationary hover, straight out of the door.' Reacher closed his eyes and pictured his old friend, tumbling in the dark, cartwheeling, flailing, not knowing where the ground was. Not knowing when he would hit. 'It probably wasn't Vegas.' He opened his eyes. 'The trip would be out of range for most helicopters. It was probably LA. The deputies are barking up the wrong tree.'

Neagley sat quiet.

'Coyote food,' Reacher said. 'The perfect disposal. The fall strips away hairs and fibres. No forensics at all. Which is why they threw him out alive. No ballistics.' He was quiet a long moment, then closed the binder. 'But you know all this, don't you? You're testing me. Seeing if my brain still works.'

Neagley said nothing.

Reacher said, 'You're playing me like a violin. Why did you bring me here?'

'Like you said, the deputies are barking up the wrong tree. You have to do something.'

'I will do something. There are dead men walking as of right now. You don't throw my friends out of helicopters and live to tell the tale.'

'No, I want you to do something else,' Neagley said. 'I want you to put the old unit back together.'

CHAPTER THREE

The old unit. It had been a typical US Army invention. About three years after the need for it had become blindingly obvious the Pentagon had started to think about it. After another year of committees, the brass had signed off on the idea. Obviously no sane CO had wanted to touch it with a stick, so a new unit had been carved out of the 110th MP. Failure had to be deniable, so they went looking for a competent pariah to command it.

Reacher had been the obvious choice.

His reward was the chance to do something properly for once. His way. He figured a special-investigations unit needed the best the army had to offer, and he knew who they were. He wanted a small unit, for speed and flexibility, and no clerical support, to prevent leaks.

In the end he settled on eight names: Tony Swan, Jorge Sanchez, Calvin Franz, Frances Neagley, Stanley Lowrey, Manuel Orozco, David O'Donnell and Karla Dixon. Neagley was the only NCO. The others were all captains and majors, but Reacher knew that nine people working closely would operate laterally as a team: no stars, no egos, mutually supportive, and above all ruthlessly effective.

Reacher said, 'That was all a long time ago.'

'We have to do something,' Neagley said. 'All of us. Collectively. You *do not mess* with the special investigators. Remember that? We depended on it.'

'For morale, that was all. It was just bravado. It was whistling in the dark.'

'It was more than that. We had each other's backs.'

'Then.'

'And now and always. It's a karma thing. Someone killed Franz, and we can't just let it go. How would you feel if it was you?'

'If it was me, I wouldn't feel anything. I'd be dead.'

'You know what I mean.'

Reacher closed his eyes and the picture came back: Calvin Franz tumbling through the darkness. Maybe screaming. Maybe not. 'I can handle it. Or you and I together. But we can't go back to how it was. That never works.'

'We have to go back. The others are entitled to participate. They earned that right over two hard years. And we need them. Franz was good. As good as me, as good as you. And yet someone broke his legs and threw him out of a helicopter.'

Reacher opened his eyes. He said, 'The others should have been a lot easier to find than me.'

'I can't raise any of them,' Neagley said.

'How much do you know about the six of them?'

'Five,' Neagley said. 'Stan Lowrey is dead. Car wreck in Montana. Years ago. The other guy was drunk.'

'I didn't know that.'

'Bad things happen.'

'That's for damn sure,' Reacher said.

'Tony Swan is assistant director of corporate security for a defence manufacturer somewhere in Southern California. Some start-up. He's been there about a year.'

Reacher nodded. Tony Swan, short, wide, almost cubic in shape. Affable, intelligent.

Neagley said, 'Orozco and Sanchez run a security business in Vegas, casinos and hotels, on contract. Dave O'Donnell is a private detective in DC. And Karla Dixon is in New York. Forensic accounting.'

Reacher asked, 'Why can't you raise them?'

'I don't know. I put calls out, but nobody's answering.'

'You called the same day you put money in my bank?'

Neagley nodded.

'It's only been three days. Maybe they're all busy. You and I can stand up for Franz. Just the two of us.'

'We were a good team. You were the best leader the army had.'

Reacher said nothing.

Neagley folded her hands together. Slim brown fingers, painted nails, tendons and sinew. 'One question,' she said. 'Suppose I hadn't bothered to try your bank. Suppose you found out years from now that Franz had been

murdered and the six of us had fixed it without you. How would you feel?'
 Reacher shrugged. Paused a beat. 'Bad, I guess. Cheated, maybe. Left out.'
Neagley said nothing.
 'OK, we'll try to find them. But we won't wait for ever.'

NEAGLEY HAD a rental car in the lot. She paid the bill and led Reacher
outside. The car was a red Mustang convertible. They climbed in and
Neagley dropped the top and took a pair of sunglasses from the dash.
Backed out of her slot and headed for Beverly Hills. Reacher sat quiet
beside her and squinted in the afternoon sun.
 Inside a tan Ford Crown Victoria thirty yards west of the restaurant, a
man called Thomas Brant watched them go. He used his cellphone and left
his boss a voicemail.
 Parked five cars behind Brant was a dark blue Chrysler sedan containing
a man in a dark blue suit. He too used a cellphone. He said, 'She just picked
the first one of them up.'
 Then he listened to his boss's reply, and pictured him smoothing his
necktie, one-handed, while he held the phone.

LIKE ITS NAME suggested, the Beverly Wilshire Hotel was on Wilshire
Boulevard, in the heart of Beverly Hills, opposite Rodeo Drive. It was made
up of two large limestone buildings, one old and ornate, the other new and
plain, separated by a valet lane. Neagley nosed the Mustang in close to a
knot of black Town Cars and Reacher said, 'I can't afford to stay here.'
 'I already booked your room. It's on my card.'
 'I won't be able to pay you back.'
 'Get over it. Maybe we'll take some spoils of war down the track if the
bad guys are rich.'
 Neagley left the key in and the motor running and a guy ran up and gave
her a valet stub. She took the steps up to the back of the hotel and Reacher
followed through a crowded corridor to a reception area the size of a baronial
hall. There was a check-in desk, a bell desk, a concierge desk, all separate.
There were pale velvet armchairs with beautifully dressed guests in them.
 Reacher said, 'I look like a bum in here.'
 'Or like a billionaire. Nowadays you can't tell.'
 She checked him in. She had reserved his room under the name Thomas
Shannon, who had been Stevie Ray Vaughan's giant bass player back in the
day, and one of Reacher's favourites. He smiled. He liked to avoid paper

trails. Pure reflex. 'What are you calling yourself here?' he asked.

'My real name. That stuff's too complicated now.'

The clerk handed over a key card and Reacher put it in his shirt pocket. 'Let's make a start,' he said.

They started in Neagley's room, which was actually a two-room suite. The living room was stately and had been done up in blues and golds. It could have been a room in Buckingham Palace. There was a desk in the window with Neagley's two laptops and five printed papers. Names, addresses, telephone numbers. The old unit, less two dead and two already present.

Reacher said, 'Tell me about Stan Lowrey.'

'Not much to tell. He moved to Montana, got hit by a truck.'

'What was he doing in Montana?'

'Raising sheep. Churning butter. They had a lot of acres. No call for private eyes in Montana, where the girlfriend was.'

Reacher nodded. 'Why can't we raise the others?' he asked.

'I don't know,' Neagley said.

'What was Franz working on?'

'Nobody seems to have that information.'

'Didn't the new wife say anything?'

'She was telling me her husband was dead,' Neagley said.

'We're going to have to ask her. She's the obvious starting point here.'

'After we try the others again,' Neagley said.

Reacher picked up the five sheets of paper and gave three to Neagley. She used her cellphone and he used a room phone on a credenza. His numbers were for Dixon and O'Donnell. He got their business office machines and heard their long-forgotten voices. He left them both the same message: 'This is Jack Reacher with a ten-thirty from Frances Neagley at the Beverly Wilshire Hotel in LA. Get off your ass and call her back.' Then hung up. 'Don't you have home numbers?' he asked.

'They're all unlisted. My guy in Chicago is working on it. Phone company computers have got a lot more secure.'

'They must be carrying cellphones. They can call in and check their office voicemail remotely, can't they?'

'Easily.'

'Swan must have a secretary. He's an assistant director.'

'All they're saying is he's temporarily out of the office.'

'Let me try.' He took Swan's number and dialled, heard Swan's phone ring and ring and ring. 'No answer,' he said.

'Someone answered a minute ago. It's his direct line.'

He tried again. Same result. 'Weird,' he said. 'Where the hell is he?' He checked the paper. The address line was blank.

'Where is this place?'

'I'm not sure.'

'Does it have a name?'

'New Age Defense Systems. That's how they've answered.'

'What kind of a name is that? Like they kill you with kindness?' He dialled information. There was no listing for New Age Defense Systems in the United States. He hung up. 'Can corporations be unlisted too?'

Neagley said, 'In the defence business, certainly.'

'We have to find them. They must have an office somewhere, so Uncle Sam can send them cheques.'

So Neagley called her guy in Chicago and told him to track down a physical address for New Age Defense Systems.

'Get cell numbers too,' Reacher called. 'For the others.'

Neagley hung up. 'He's been on that for three days. So now we wait.'

They waited less than twenty minutes and then one of Neagley's laptops pinged to announce an incoming email.

It contained New Age's address, courtesy of UPS's computer. Or actually, New Age's two addresses. One in Colorado, one in East LA.

Neagley opened a map and they checked the East LA address. It was out past Dodger Stadium, somewhere in the no-man's-land between South Pasadena and East LA proper. 'That's a long way,' she said. 'Rush hour has started. Mrs Franz is closer.'

'Where is she?'

'Santa Monica.'

'Franz lived in Santa Monica?'

'Not on the ocean. But still, I bet it's nice.'

IT WAS NICE. Way nicer than it could have been. It was a small bungalow on a small street trapped halfway between the 10 and Santa Monica airport. On the face of it, not a prime location. But it was a beautifully presented house. Neagley drove past it twice, looking for a place to park. It was a tiny symmetrical structure. Two bay windows with the front door between them. Twin rocking chairs on the porch. Some stone, some Arts and Crafts influences, some Spanish tiles. But it worked. And the paint was perfect. The windows shone. The yard was tidy. Green lawn, clipped.

Reacher felt he could see an expression of his old friend's whole thorough and meticulous personality displayed right there in a little piece of real estate.

They parked and walked to Franz's porch. It was late afternoon but still faintly warm. Reacher could smell the ocean. He asked, 'How many widows have we been to see?'

'Too many,' Neagley said.

'What's her name?' Reacher asked.

'Angela,' Neagley said. 'The kid is called Charlie. A boy.'

'OK.'

Neagley found a bell push and laid a fingertip on it, gently, as if the electric circuit could sense deference. Reacher waited. About a minute and a half later the door was opened. Apparently by nobody. Then he looked down and saw a little boy stretching up to the handle. The arc of the door's travel was pulling him off his tiptoes. 'You must be Charlie.' Reacher said.

'I am,' the boy said.

'I was a friend of your dad's.'

'My dad's dead.'

'I know. I'm very sad about that. Is it OK to be opening the door all by yourself?'

'Yes,' the boy said. 'It's OK.'

He looked exactly like Calvin Franz. The resemblance was uncanny. The face was the same. The body shape was the same. The short legs, the long arms. The eyes were Franz's own, dark, cool, calm, reassuring.

Neagley asked, 'Charlie, is your mom home?'

The boy nodded. 'She's in the back,' he said. He let the handle go and stepped away to let them enter. A small living room, a small kitchenette behind it. Everything off-white and pale yellow. Flowers in vases. Windows shaded with white wooden shutters. Reacher closed the door and the street noise disappeared and silence clamped down over the house.

A woman stepped out of the kitchen area. She looked a little younger than Neagley. She was tall, white blonde, like a Scandinavian, and thin. She was made up and her hair was brushed. Perfectly composed, but Reacher could see wild bewilderment around her eyes, like a fright mask worn under the skin.

There was awkward silence and then Neagley stepped forward. 'Angela? I'm Frances Neagley. We spoke on the phone.'

Angela Franz smiled in an automatic way and offered her hand. Neagley shook it briefly. Reacher said, 'I'm Jack Reacher. I'm very sorry for your loss.' Her hand felt cold and fragile in his.

'You've used those words more than a few times,' she said.

'I'm afraid so,' Reacher said.

'You're on Calvin's list. You were an MP just like him.'

'Not just like him. Not nearly as good. I admired him tremendously.'

'He told me about all of you. Many times. Sometimes I felt like a second wife. Like he'd been married to you all.'

'The service was like a family. If you were lucky, that is. I think he got even luckier afterwards.'

Angela smiled again. 'Maybe. But his luck ran out, didn't it?'

'Is there anything we can do for you?' Reacher asked.

Charlie was watching them, Franz's eyes half-open, appraising. Angela said, 'Why are you here?'

'To give you our condolences.'

'But you don't know me. I came later.' Angela moved away, towards the kitchen. Then she changed her mind and sat down. Laid her palms on the arms of her chair. Reacher saw her fingers moving. Just a slight flutter.

'I'm here,' Reacher said, 'because Calvin would have been there for me, if the shoe was on the other foot.'

'Would he have been?'

'I think so.'

'He gave all of that up. No pressure from me, but he wanted to be a father. He gave it all up apart from the easy, safe stuff.'

'He can't have done. What was he working on?'

'I'm sorry. I should have asked you to sit down,' Angela said.

There was no sofa in the room. No space for one. There were two arm-chairs, one either side of a small fireplace, plus a half-sized wooden rocker for Charlie to the left of the chimney. His name had been branded into the wood at the top, seven neat letters. A gift, probably, father to son. Reacher took the chair opposite Angela's and Neagley perched on the arm.

Charlie stepped over Reacher's feet and sat down in his chair.

'What was Calvin working on?' Reacher asked again.

Angela Franz said, 'Charlie, you should go out and play.'

Charlie said, 'Mom, I want to stay here.'

Reacher asked, 'Angela, what was Calvin working on?'

'Since Charlie came along he only did background checks. It was a good business to be in here. Everyone's worried about hiring a thief or a junkie.'

'Where did he work?'

'He had an office in Culver City. I guess I'll have to bring his things home.'

Neagley asked, 'Would you give us permission to search it first?'

'The deputies already searched it.'

'We should search it again.'

'Why?'

'Because he must have been working on something bigger than background checks.'

'Junkies kill people, don't they? And thieves, sometimes,' said Angela.

Reacher glanced at Charlie, and saw Franz looking back at him. 'But that's not the way that it seems to have happened here.'

'OK. Search it again if you want.' Angela got up and stepped to the kitchen. Came back with two unmarked keys on a steel split ring and handed them to Neagley. 'I would like these back. This is his own personal set.'

Reacher asked, 'Did he keep stuff here? Files, anything?'

'Here? He gave up undershirts to save on drawer space.'

'What happened the last time you saw him?'

'He went out in the morning, same as always.'

'Did he ever talk to you about his work?'

Angela said, 'Charlie, do you need a drink?'

Charlie said, 'I'm OK, mom.'

Reacher asked, 'Did Calvin ever talk about his work?'

'Not very much. Sometimes the studios would want an actor checked out. He would give me the showbiz gossip.'

'When we knew him he was a pretty blunt guy. He would say what was on his mind. So would you mind if I was blunt?'

'Go right ahead.'

'I think there's something you're not telling us.'

Angela sat down again. 'You think I'm hiding something?'

'I asked what Calvin was working on, and you sat us down. I asked again, and you told Charlie to go out to play. Not to spare him your answer. To gain time to decide you don't have an answer.'

Angela looked straight at him. 'Are you going to break my arm now? Calvin told me he saw you break someone's arm in an interview. Or was that Dave O'Donnell?'

'Me, probably. O'Donnell was more of a leg breaker.'

'I promise you, I don't know what Calvin was working on.'

Reacher looked into her bewildered blue eyes. She was hiding something, but it wasn't necessarily about Calvin Franz. 'OK,' he said. 'I apologise.'

He and Neagley left, after further brief condolences, with directions to Franz's Culver City office.

THE MAN called Thomas Brant watched them go. He was twenty yards from his Crown Victoria, which was parked forty yards west of Franz's house. He was walking up from a corner bodega with a cup of coffee. He slowed his gait and speed-dialled his boss, Curtis Mauney, one-handed.

At that same moment the man in the dark blue suit was walking back to his dark blue Chrysler in the Beverly Wilshire's valet lane. He was poorer by the fifty bucks that the desk clerk had accepted as a bribe, and correspondingly richer in new information. He called his boss on his cell and said, 'According to the hotel the big guy's name is Thomas Shannon but there was no Shannon on our list.'

His boss said, 'I think it's safe to assume that Thomas Shannon is a phoney name. So let's stay on it.'

REACHER WAITED until they were round the corner and out of Franz's street and said, 'Did you see a tan Crown Vic back there?'

'Parked,' Neagley said. 'Forty yards west of the house, on the opposite kerb. A base model '02.'

'I think I saw the same car outside the Denny's we were in.'

'You sure? Crown Vics are common,' Neagley said. 'It was empty anyway.'

'It wasn't empty outside Denny's. There was a guy in it.'

'If it was the same car. You want to go back?'

Reacher paused a beat. 'No, it was probably nothing.'

The 10 was jammed eastbound. Neither one of them knew enough about LA geography to risk taking surface streets, so they covered the five free-way miles to Culver City slower than walking. Franz's office was a bland storefront in a long, low tan strip mall where Venice Boulevard crossed La Cienega. The door glass and the window had been painted head-high from inside with tan paint banded with a gold coach line edged in black. *Calvin Franz Discreet Investigations* and a telephone number had been written on the door in the same gold-and-black style.

'Sad,' Reacher said. 'From the big green machine to this?'

'It was his choice. This was all he wanted now,' Neagley said.

'But I'm guessing your Chicago place doesn't look like this.'

'No, it doesn't.' Neagley took out the key ring, tripped the lock and pulled the door. But she didn't go in.

Because the whole space was trashed from top to bottom. Computers, telephones, other hardware, all were long gone. The desk and the filing cabinets had been smashed with hammers in a quest for hiding places. The chair had been ripped apart, the wall boards crowbarred off the studs and the insulation shredded. The ceiling had been torn down. The floor had been pulled up and there was wreckage knee-high in the space beneath it.

Reacher said, 'LA County deputies wouldn't be this thorough.'

'Not a chance. This was the bad guys tying up the loose ends days before. Retrieving whatever Franz had on them.'

Reacher backed away on the sidewalk and looked at the neat gold lettering: *Calvin Franz Discreet Investigations.* In his mind he blocked out his old friend's name and tried *David O'Donnell* in its place. *Sanchez & Orozco. Karla Dixon.* 'I wish those guys were answering their damn phones.'

'This thing is not about us as a group,' Neagley said. 'It can't be. It's more than seventeen days old and nobody came after me yet.'

'Or me,' Reacher said. 'But then, if Franz was in trouble, who would he call? Not you, because you're way upscale now and too busy. And not me, because nobody apart from you could find me. But suppose the other guys were all accessible? Suppose they all came running out here to help? Suppose they're all in the same boat now?'

'But what kind of a thing can disappear six of *our* people?'

'I hate to think,' Reacher said, and then he went quiet. In the past he would have put his people up against anyone.

Neagley said, 'No point standing here. We're wasting time. I think we can assume they got what they came for.'

Reacher said, 'I think we can assume they didn't. Normally, when you find what you're looking for, you stop looking. But these guys never stopped.'

'So where is it?'

'I don't know. What would it be?'

'A floppy disk, a CD-ROM, something like that. He didn't take it home. I think he was separating home and work.'

Think like them. Be them. Reacher put his back to Franz's door as if he had just stepped out. He cupped his hand and looked down at his palm. He had never used a computer disk or burned a CD-ROM. But he knew what one was.

Neagley said, 'Maybe it was in his car. In his auto-changer. You know, maybe the fourth slot, after the John Coltrane stuff.'

'Miles Davis,' Reacher said. 'He only listened to Coltrane on Miles Davis albums. But guys this thorough, they'd have checked.'

'So where? A safe deposit box?'

'I don't see a bank here. And I don't think he would have wanted to take too much of a detour. Not with this traffic. Not if there was some kind of urgency.'

'There are two keys on the ring,' Neagley said. 'Although it's possible the smaller one was for the desk.'

Reacher looked down at his empty palm again.

'It's a computer file,' he said. 'Got to be. Because they knew to look for it. Probably they took his computers first,' he said. 'Found some kind of traces that told them he'd been copying files. That happens, right? But maybe that's why they broke his legs. Franz wouldn't tell them where the copies were.'

'So where is it?'

'Not under any old rock. I'd want somewhere structured. Maybe somewhere kind of custodial. Because there's regularity involved here. Isn't there? Isn't that what people do with computers? They back stuff up every night. So this would be a matter of routine. Every night, you need something safe and permanently available.'

'I email stuff to myself,' Neagley said.

Reacher paused a beat. Smiled. 'There you go,' he said.

'You think that's what Franz did?'

'Not a chance. The bad guys would have spent their time trying to break down his password instead of busting up his building.'

'So what did he do?'

Reacher turned and glanced along the row of stores. A dry cleaner's, a nail salon, a pharmacy. A post office.

'Not email,' he said. 'Regular mail. That's what he did. He backed up his stuff and every night he put it in an envelope and addressed to himself. To his post-office box, because that's where he got his mail. There's no slot in his door. Once the envelope was out of his hands it was safe in the system. He must have had three or four disks in rotation. It's not easy to rob a mailbox. USPS bureaucracy is about as safe as a Swiss bank.'

'The small key. Not his desk. Not a safe deposit box.'

Reacher nodded. 'His post-office box,' he said.

CHAPTER FOUR

B ut US Postal Service bureaucracy cut two ways. It was late in the
afternoon. The dry cleaner's was still open. The nail salon was open.
The pharmacy was open. But the post office was closed.

'Tomorrow,' Neagley said. 'We're going to be in the car all day. We have
to get to Swan's place too. Unless we separate.'

'It's going to take two of us here,' Reacher said. 'But maybe one of the
others will show up and do some work.'

'I wish they would. And not because I'm lazy.' For form's sake, like a
little ritual, she pulled out her cellphone and checked the screen. No
messages.

There were no messages at the hotel desk, either. No messages on the
hotel voicemail. No emails on either laptop computer.

Neagley shuffled the five sheets of contact information like a card player
and dealt Reacher Tony Swan and Karla Dixon. He used the land line and
tried Swan first. Thirty, forty rings, no answer. Next, he tried Dixon's New
York City number. Six rings, and straight to a machine. He left the same
message he had left earlier and added: 'Please, Karla. We really need to
hear from you.' Then he hung up.

Neagley was closing her cellphone. 'Not good,' she said.

'They could all be on vacation.'

'At the same time?'

'They could all be in jail. We were a pretty rough bunch.'

'First thing I checked. They're not in jail.'

'What about their businesses?' Reacher asked. 'Is there any good reason
why they should all be out of contact for days at a time?'

'I guess O'Donnell could have to travel overseas. His practice is pretty
general. Marital stuff could take him anyplace. Child abductions, custody
issues. There are lots of possible reasons.'

'But?'

'I'd have to talk myself into really believing one of them.'

'What about Karla?'

'She could be down in the Caymans looking for someone's money, I
guess. But it's not like the money is actually *there*. And Sanchez and Orozco

wouldn't ever have to leave Vegas. Not professionally.'

Reacher stared out of the window. It was getting dark. He said, 'Franz didn't go to his office the morning he disappeared. Angela had his keys. He was going somewhere else.'

Neagley said nothing.

'And the landlord at the strip mall saw the bad guys. Franz's lock wasn't broken, therefore they scammed one from the owner. Therefore we need to find him tomorrow, along with everything else.'

'Franz should have called me,' Neagley said. 'I would have dropped everything.'

They ate dinner in the downstairs restaurant, where a bottle of still water from Norway cost eight dollars. Then they said good night and headed for their rooms. Reacher's was a chintzy cube two floors below Neagley's suite. He stripped and showered and folded his clothes and put them under the mattress to press. He got into bed and stared up at the ceiling. Thought about Calvin Franz for a minute, in random images, but in all of them Franz was moving, talking, laughing, full of drive and energy. Then Karla Dixon joined the parade, petite, dark, sardonic, very pretty, laughing with Franz. Dave O'Donnell was there, tall, fair, handsome, like a stockbroker with a switchblade. And Jorge Sanchez, durable, eyes narrowed, with a hint of a smile that showed a gold tooth. And Tony Swan and Manuel Orozco. Even Stan Lowrey, drumming his fingers on a table to a rhythm only he could hear.

Then Reacher blinked all the pictures away and closed his eyes and fell asleep. Ten thirty in the evening, a long day, over.

TEN THIRTY in the evening in Los Angeles was one thirty the next morning in New York, and the last British Airways flight from London, delayed, had just landed at JFK.

The passengers went through the giant Terminal Four arrivals hall. Third in the visitors' line was a first-class passenger who had napped in seat 2K for most of the trip. He was medium height, medium weight, expensively dressed, and he radiated the kind of expansive courtesy typical of people who know how lucky they are to have been rich all their lives. He was perhaps forty years old. He had thick black hair, shiny, beautifully cut, and the kind of mid-brown skin and regular features that could have made him Indian, or Iranian, or Syrian, or Algerian, or even Israeli or Italian. His passport was British and it passed the agent's scrutiny with no trouble at all, as did its owner's manicured forefingers on the electronic fingerprint pad. Seventeen minutes after unclipping his seat belt the guy was out in the shiny New York night.

THE NEXT MORNING they parked the Mustang outside Franz's trashed office and walked back past the dry cleaner's, the nail salon and the pharmacy. The post office lobby had been open a half-hour, but whatever ritual rush there had been was over.

'We can't do this when it's empty,' Reacher said.

'So let's find the landlord first,' Neagley said.

They asked in the pharmacy. An old man behind the dispensing counter told them the guy who owned the dry cleaner's was the landlord. Reacher and Neagley ducked into the cleaner's and found the right guy immediately. Reacher got straight to the point.

'When did you last see Calvin Franz?'

'Three or four weeks ago, I guess.'

'Just before the guys came round and asked you for his key.'

The dry cleaner shrugged his shoulders. 'I don't remember the guys.'

'They trashed your unit,' Reacher said. 'Whatever they paid you for the key won't cover the damage.'

'Fixing the unit is my problem. It's my building.'

'Suppose it was your pile of smouldering ashes? Suppose I came back tonight and burned the place down?'

'You'd go to prison.'

'I don't think so. A guy with a memory as bad as yours wouldn't have anything to tell the police.'

The guy nodded. 'They were white men. Two of them. Blue suits. A new car. They looked like everybody else I see. Not cops. Too clean and too rich.'

THEY WALKED BACK to the post office. It was a small, dusty place, moderately busy. There was one clerk and a short line of customers. Neagley handed Reacher Franz's keys and joined the line. Reacher stepped to a counter in the back and used a pen on a chain and pretended to fill out a form. Glanced at the mailboxes filling the whole end wall. Six tiers of small boxes then below them four tiers of medium, then three tiers of large. Total, three hundred and thirty. Which one was Franz's?

One of the large ones, for sure. Franz's business would have generated a fair amount of mail. But which large box? There were fifty-four.

No way of telling.

He heard Neagley say, 'Good morning.'

He glanced left and saw her at the counter, leaning forward, commanding attention. Saw the clerk's eyes lock in on hers. He dropped the pen and took Franz's key from his pocket. Tried the first lock on the left. Failure.

He pulled the key out and tried the lock below. Failure. The one below. Failure.

Neagley was asking a complicated question about air rates. He shuffled right, one box over. Failure. Four down, fifty to go. Twelve seconds consumed, odds now improved to two chances in a hundred. He tried the next box down. Failure. He crouched to the floor. Failure.

He shuffled right. Started the next column from the bottom. No luck. No luck. No luck. Nine down, twenty-five seconds elapsed. Neagley was still talking. Then Reacher was aware of a woman on his left. Opening her box, mass of curled junk. *Move*, he begged her. *Step to the trash.* She backed away. He stepped to his right. The key didn't fit the top, middle, bottom.

Twelve down. Odds one in forty-two. The key didn't fit anything in the fifth row. Nor the sixth. One-third gone. Odds improving. He could still hear Neagley. People would be looking round, getting impatient.

He started on the seventh row, at the top. No go. The middle box. The lowest. The clerk was explaining something. Neagley was pretending not to understand. Reacher moved right again. The key didn't fit the top box. The lobby was going quiet. Reacher could feel eyes on his back. He dropped his hand and tried the middle box.

The small metallic sound was very loud. Failure.

Reacher crouched down and tried the lowest box. The lock opened.

He swung the door. The box was stuffed. Padded envelopes, big brown envelopes, letters, catalogues, magazines.

Reacher heard Neagley say, 'Thank you very much for your help.' He heard her footsteps on the tiles. He raked the contents forward into a stack and clamped it under his arm and relocked the box and walked away like the most natural thing in the world.

Neagley was waiting in the Mustang, three doors down.

The man in the dark blue suit watched them go.

NEAGLEY PLUGGED the first flat metal flash memory into a socket on the side of her laptop computer. Nothing happened for a second and then an icon of a small silver object appeared. It was labelled *No Name*. Neagley tapped twice and the icon blossomed into a full-screen demand for a password.

'Damn,' she said. 'My guess is we'll get three tries. Ideas?'

Reacher had busted computer passwords before, back in the day. As always, the technique was to consider the person. Franz had been a relaxed guy, a words guy, a man of enthusiasms, affections and loyalties. Middlebrow tastes. He said, 'Angela, Charlie, Miles Davis, Dodgers, Koufax, Panama, Pfeiffer, Brooklyn, Heidi or Jennifer.'

Neagley wrote them all down in a spiral-bound notebook. 'What's Panama?' she asked.

'Where he was deployed at the end of 1989. I think that was the place he had the most professional satisfaction. Passwords come from down deep.'

'Pfeiffer as in Michelle Pfeiffer?'

'His favourite actress. Miles Davis was his favourite music, the Dodgers were his favourite team and Sandy Koufax was his favourite player.'

'Brooklyn?'

'Where he was born. They moved west when he was little.'

'Heidi?'

'His first serious girlfriend. Terrific in the sack.'

'Only five letters. Most software asks for a minimum of six characters. And he was too much into Angela now anyway. Same for Michelle Pfeiffer. Who was Jennifer?'

'Jennifer was his dog,' Reacher said. 'When he was a kid.'

'Possibility, then. But we've only got three tries.'

'We've got twelve tries. Four envelopes, four flash memories. We can afford to burn the first three. That's old information.'

Neagley clicked the oldest memory unit into the port and waited until the icon appeared. She clicked on it and tabbed the cursor to the password box. 'You want a priority order?'

'Do the people names first.'

'OK. We'll start with music.' She typed *MilesDavis* and hit *Enter*. There was a short pause and then the screen redrew and came back with the box and a note: *Your first attempt was incorrect.* 'One down,' she said. 'Now sports.'

She tried Dodgers. *Incorrect.*

'Two down.' She typed *Koufax.*

The hard drive inside her laptop chattered and the screen went blank. 'What's happening?' Reacher asked.

'It's dumping the data,' she said. 'Erasing it. Three down.'

She pulled the flash memory out and inserted the second unit. Typed *Jennifer. Incorrect.*

She tried *Panama. Incorrect.*

She tried *Brooklyn.* The screen went blank and the hard drive chattered. 'Not his old hood. You're zip for six, Reacher,' she said and plugged in the third. 'Ideas?'

'Your turn. I seem to have lost my touch. It's going to be something talismanic, something that would give him a feeling of warmth.'

'What about "You do not mess with the special investigators"?'

'That would make a hell of a long password,' Reacher said. '"Do not mess"—nine letters.'

Neagley typed *donotmess.* Hit *enter. Incorrect.*

'Damn,' she said. She typed *specialinvestigators.* Held her finger over the enter key. 'Yes or no?'

'Try it?'

Incorrect. Neagley went quiet.

Charlie was still in Reacher's mind. And his tiny chair, with the neat branded name. 'Try Charlie.'

Neagley shrugged and typed *Charlie.* Hit *enter. Incorrect.*

The hard disk spun up and the memory unit erased itself.

'Nine down,' Neagley said. She plugged the fourth unit in. The last one. 'Three to go.'

Reacher asked, 'Who did he love before Charlie?'

'Angela,' Neagley said. 'Way too obvious.'

'Try it.'

'Are you sure?'

'I'm a gambler.'

She typed *Angela.* Hit *enter. Incorrect.*

'What about Angela Franz?'

'That's even worse.'

'What about her unmarried name?'

'I don't know what it was.'

'Call her and ask.'

So Neagley found the number and fired up her cellphone. Small-talked for a moment, then asked the question. Reacher saw her eyes widen which for Neagley was about the same thing as falling on the floor with shock.

She hung up. 'It was Pfeiffer,' she said.

'Interesting. Are they related?'

'She didn't say.'

'So try it. It's a perfect twofer. He feels good twice over.'

Neagley typed *Pfeiffer*. Hit *enter*. *Incorrect*.

The room was hot and stuffy. And it seemed to have got smaller.

'We should take a break, go look for Swan,' Reacher said. 'If we find him, he might have ideas. If not, at least we'll come back fresh.'

STRAIGHT THROUGH MacArthur Park. Then north and east on the Pasadena Freeway. They headed deep into a rats' nest of surface streets bounded by science parks, business parks and strip malls thick with parked cars. There was traffic everywhere, moving slow. A brown sky. Neagley had an austere Rand McNally map in the Mustang's glove box. Reacher squinted and followed the faint grey lines, his thumb on New Age's location.

When they got there they found a sign of chiselled granite and a big, prosperous mirror-glass cube surrounded by a wide lot with specimen trees. The main gate was standing open and Neagley paused to let a photo-copier truck out, then drove to a visitor slot. She and Reacher got out.

The reception entrance had a step up to double glass doors which opened automatically to a large, square lobby which had a slate floor and aluminium walls. There were leather chairs and a long reception counter. Behind the counter was a blonde woman of about thirty with *New Age Defense Systems* embroidered on her corporate polo shirt. 'Can I help you?' she asked.

'We're here to see Tony Swan,' Reacher said. 'Jack Reacher and Frances Neagley. We were friends of his in the service.'

'Then please take a seat.' The woman picked up her desk phone and Reacher and Neagley stepped away to the leather chairs. About four minutes later Reacher heard the click of shoes on slate from a corridor behind the desk and saw a woman step into view. About forty years old, slim, brown hair stylishly cut. She was in a tailored black trouser suit and a white blouse. She held out her hand and said, 'I'm Margaret Berenson.'

Neagley and Reacher said their names and shook hands with her. Up close she had old looping car crash scars under her make up. She was wearing no wedding band.

'We're looking for Tony Swan,' Reacher said.

'I know,' the woman said. 'Let's find somewhere to talk.'

One of the aluminium wall panels was a door that led to a small confer-ence room. Its floor to ceiling windows gave directly onto the parking lot. The front bumper of Neagley's Mustang was about five feet away.

'I'm the New Age human-resources director. I'll get straight to the point, which is that Mr Swan isn't with us anymore.'

Reacher asked, 'Since when?'

'A little over three weeks ago. I'd feel more comfortable talking about it if I knew for sure you have a connection with him.'

'I'm not sure how we could prove it.'

Berenson smiled. 'If I told you he used a piece of stone as a paperweight, could you tell me where it came from?'

'The Berlin Wall,' Reacher said. 'He was in Germany when it came down. He took the train up and got himself a souvenir. And it's concrete, not stone. There's a trace of graffiti on it.'

Berenson nodded. 'That's the story I heard.'

'So what happened?' Reacher asked. 'He quit?'

'Not exactly,' Berenson said. 'You have to understand, this is a new company. It was always speculative, and we're not where we want to be yet. We operated a last-in, first-out policy, and basically had to let the whole assistant-management level go. I lost my own assistant director. If things pick up, we'll beg Mr Swan to come back. But I'm sure he'll have secured another position by then.'

Reacher glanced through the window at the half-empty parking lot. Listened to the quiet of the building. 'OK,' he said.

'Not OK,' Neagley said. 'I've been calling his office and every time I was told he had just stepped out for a minute.'

Berenson nodded again. 'That's a professional courtesy I insist upon with this calibre of management. I do hope you understand. It's the least I can do. Mr Swan is in a far better position if he can approach a new employer as if it were a voluntary move.'

Reacher said, 'I called Swan and nobody answered at all.'

'We had to cut the secretarial pool too. The ones we kept on can't get to every call.'

Reacher asked, 'So what's up with your business?'

'I really can't discuss that. But you were in the army. You know how many weapons systems work straight out of the gate. Ours is taking a little longer than we hoped.'

'Where is it made?'

'Right here.'

'No, it isn't. You've a fence a three-year-old could walk through, no guard shack and an unsecured lobby. Swan wouldn't have let you get away with that if anything sensitive was happening here. Who was his boss?'

'Our director of security? He's a retired LAPD lieutenant.'

'Your last-in-first-out policy didn't do you any favours there.'

'They're all great people. We hated making the cut.'

TWO MINUTES LATER Reacher and Neagley were back in the Mustang. 'Really bad timing,' Reacher said. 'Suddenly Swan is at loose ends, Franz calls him with a problem, what is Swan going to do? He's going to run right over.'

'He'd have gone anyway, unemployed or not.'

'They all would. And I guess they all did.'

'So are they all dead now? *All* of them? I just can't believe it.'

'Hope for the best, plan for the worst. Someone's going to pay.'

'You think? We've got nothing. We've got one last chance with a password. Which we'll be too nervous to take.'

They retraced their route through the surface streets. Reacher pictured Tony Swan making the same drive more than three weeks earlier. Maybe with the contents of his New Age desk and his chip of Soviet concrete. On his way to help his old buddy. Sanchez and Orozco hustling over on the 15. O'Donnell and Dixon coming in on planes. Meeting and greeting.

Running into some kind of a brick wall.

Neagley left the car with the Beverly Wilshire valets and they entered the lobby from the rear corridor. They rode the elevator in silence. Neagley used her key and pushed open her door.

Then she stopped dead. Because sitting in her chair by the window, reading Franz's autopsy report, was a man in a suit. Tall, fair, aristocratic, relaxed. David O'Donnell.

CHAPTER FIVE

O'Donnell looked up, sombre. 'I was going to inquire as to the meaning of all those rude and abusive messages on my answering machine.' Then he raised the report. 'But now I understand.'

Neagley asked, 'How did you get in here?'

O'Donnell just said, 'Oh, please.'

'Where the hell were you?' Reacher asked.

'I was in New Jersey. My sister was very sick.'

'Did she die?'

'No, she recovered.'

'Then you should have been here days ago.'

'Thanks for your concern.'

'We were worried,' Neagley said. 'We thought they got you too.'

O'Donnell nodded. 'You should be worried. It's a worrying situation. I had to wait for a flight. I used the time making calls. No answer from Franz, obviously. No answer from Swan or Dixon or Orozco or Sanchez either. My conclusion was that one of them had got all the others together and they had run into a problem. Not you or Reacher, because you're too high-grade now and who the hell could ever find Reacher? And not me, because I wasn't where I normally am.'

'Except your sister being sick was a stroke of luck for us.'

'But not for her.'

'Stop whining,' Reacher said. 'She's alive, isn't she?'

'Nice to see you too,' O'Donnell said. 'After all these years.'

'How *did* you get in here?' Neagley asked.

O'Donnell took a switchblade from one pocket and a set of brass knuckles from the other. 'A guy who can get these through airport security can get into a hotel room, believe me.'

'How did you get those through an airport?'

'Ceramic,' Reacher said. 'They don't make them any more.'

'Correct. The switchblade spring's steel, but very small.'

'It's good to see you again, David,' Reacher said.

'Likewise. But I wish it was under happier circumstances.'

'The circumstances just got happier now it's three of us.'

'What have we got?'

'Very little. Apart from his autopsy report, two generic white men who tossed his office. We found his mailbox and four flash memories and we're down to the last try at a password.'

O'Donnell took a deep breath and held it longer than seemed humanly possible. Then he exhaled, gently. It was an old habit. 'Tell me what you've tried.'

Neagley handed her notebook over. O'Donnell read and Reacher watched him. He hadn't changed much in eleven years. He had the kind of corn-coloured hair that would never show grey. He had the kind of greyhound's body that would never show fat. His suit was beautifully cut. In the same way as Neagley he looked settled and successful.

'Koufax didn't work?' he asked.

Neagley shook her head. 'That was our third try.'

'Should have been your first. Franz related to icons, gods, performances he idolised. Koufax is the only one that fits the bill.'

'So what would you vote for?' Neagley asked.

'It's tough, with one try. What are we going to find anyway?'

'Something he got his legs broken for,' Reacher said. 'He didn't give anything up. He drove them into a fury.'

'What's our ultimate aim here?'

'Seek and destroy. Is that good enough for you?'

O'Donnell shook his head. 'No,' he said. 'I want to piss on their ancestors' graves.'

'You haven't changed.'

'I've got worse. Have you changed?'

'If I have I'm ready to change back.'

O'Donnell smiled, briefly. 'Neagley, what don't you do?'

Neagley said, 'You don't mess with the special investigators.'

'Correct. You do not. Can we get room-service coffee?'

They drank strong coffee and kept pretty quiet, each of them tracing the same mental circles, trying to find another avenue forward.

Finally O'Donnell put his cup down and said, 'Time to fish or cut bait.'

Reacher said, 'You do it, Dave.'

O'Donnell got out of his chair, stepped over to the laptop and typed seven letters in the box on the screen.

Took a breath and held it.

Paused. Waited. Hit *enter*.

The laptop screen redrew. A file directory appeared. A big, bold table of contents. O'Donnell breathed out.

He had typed: *Reacher*.

Reacher spun away from the computer like he had been slapped and said, 'Ah, man, that ain't fair.'

'He admired you,' O'Donnell said.

'It's like a voice from the grave. Like a call.'

'You were here anyway.'

'It doubles everything. Now I can't let him down. Too much pressure.'

'No such thing as too much pressure. We thrive on pressure.'

Neagley was at the keyboard, staring at the screen. 'Eight separate files,' she said. 'Seven are a bunch of numbers and the eighth is a list of names.'

'Show me the names,' O'Donnell said.

Neagley clicked on an icon and a word-processor page opened. It contained a vertical list. At the top, typed in bold and underlined, was *Azhari Mahmoud*. Then came *Adrian Mount, Alan Mason, Andrew MacBride* and *Anthony Matthews*.

'Top one is Arab,' O'Donnell said.

'Syrian,' Neagley said. 'That would be my guess.'

'Last four names feel English or Scottish.' Reacher said.

'Significance?' O'Donnell asked.

Reacher said, 'At first glance I would say one of Franz's background checks came up with a Syrian guy with four known aliases. And phoney British names with British paperwork get round the kind of scrutiny American paperwork invites here.'

'Possible,' O'Donnell said.

Reacher said, 'Show me the numbers.'

Neagley opened the first of seven spreadsheets. A page-long vertical list of fractions. At the top was *10/12*. At the bottom was *11/12*. In between were twenty or so similar numbers.

'Next,' Reacher said.

The next spreadsheet was essentially identical, starting with *13/14* and ending with *8/9*. Twenty or so similar numbers in between. The third spreadsheet showed more or less the same thing.

'So what are they?' O'Donnell asked Reacher. 'Fractions?'

'Not really. Ten-over-twelve would be five-over-six.'

'They're like scores, then.'

The fourth spreadsheet showed pretty much the same denominators, twelves and tens and thirteens. But the numerators were generally smaller. There was even a *5/14*.

'If these are scores, someone's slumping,' Reacher said.

The trend continued. The fifth sheet had a *3/12*. The best was a *6/11*. The sixth had *5/13* as its best score and *3/13* as its worst. The last was about the same.

Neagley looked at Reacher. 'You're the numbers guy,' she said.

'Can you print them out? I can't think without seeing them on paper.'

'I can print them in the business centre downstairs.' Neagley reopened the word-processor document. *Azhari Mahmoud, Adrian Mount, Alan Mason, Andrew MacBride, Anthony Matthews*.

'So who is this guy?' Reacher said.

THREE TIME ZONES away in New York City the dark-haired forty-year-old man who could have been Indian, or Iranian, or Syrian, or Algerian, or Israeli, or Italian was crouching on a bathroom floor inside an expensive Madison Avenue hotel room. The door was closed. There was no smoke detector in the bathroom but there was an extractor fan. The British passport issued to Adrian Mount was burning over the toilet pan. As always the inside pages went up easily. The stiff red covers burned slower. Page 31 was the laminated ID page. It burned slowest of all. The man used the hair dryer from the bathroom wall at a distance to fan the flames.

Five minutes later Adrian Mount was flushed away and Alan Mason was on his way down to the street in the elevator.

NEAGLEY DETOURED to the Beverly Wilshire's business centre and printed out all eight of Franz's files. Then she joined O'Donnell and Reacher for lunch in the lobby restaurant.

The room was dim and stylish and full of people who could have been movie agents or executives. Neagley and O'Donnell looked right at home. Neagley was wearing black high-waisted pants and a cotton T-shirt that fitted her like a second skin. O'Donnell's suit was grey with a slight sheen to it and his shirt was white and crisp even though he must have put it on three thousand miles away. His tie was striped and regimental and perfectly knotted.

Reacher was in a shirt a size too small with a tear in the sleeve. His hair was long and his jeans were cheap and his shoes were scuffed and he couldn't afford to pay for the dish he had ordered.

Sad, he had said about Franz, when he had seen the strip-mall office. *From the big green machine to this*. What were O'Donnell and Neagley thinking about him?

'Show me the pages with the numbers,' he said.

Neagley passed them across the table. She had marked them in pencil to indicate their order. He scanned them all, one to seven, looking for overall impressions. A total of 183 fractions, the top number was always smaller than the bottom number. Therefore *10/12* and *8/10* were saying *ten times out of twelve* or *eight times out of ten, something happened*. Or didn't happen.

There were twenty-six scores on each page, except for the fourth, where there were twenty-seven. Expressed like a win percentage they hovered between a fine .870 and an excellent .907 for three sheets, then there was a dramatic fall on the fourth, where the average looked like a .574. The fifth, sixth, and seventh got progressively more dismal, with a .368, a .308 and a .307.

'Got it yet?' Neagley asked Reacher.

'No clue. I wish Franz was here to explain it.'

'If he was here, we wouldn't be here.'

'We could have been. We could have all got together from time to time.'

'Like a class reunion?'

O'Donnell raised his glass and said, 'Absent friends.'

They drank to the memory of friends they assumed they'd never see again. But they assumed wrong.

A WAITER BROUGHT their food. Salmon for Neagley, chicken for Reacher, tuna for O'Donnell, who said, 'I assume you've been to Franz's house.'

'Yesterday,' Neagley said. 'Santa Monica.'

'Anything there?'

'A widow and a fatherless child. Nothing else.'

'We should go to Swan's house.'

'We don't have his address,' Neagley said. The New Age lady wouldn't have told us. She was very correct.'

Reacher said, 'We could try that UPS thing again.'

'OK.' Neagley used her cell to call Chicago, right there, and looked more like a movie executive than ever. She listened and wrote on a slip of paper.

'Santa Ana, near the zoo.'

O'Donnell said, 'Let's hit the road.'

They used his car, a Hertz four-door with GPS navigation, and started the slow crawl south and east to the 5.

THE MAN CALLED Thomas Brant watched them go. His Crown Vic was parked a block away and he used his cell and called Curtis Mauney, his boss.

FORTY YARDS WEST the man in the blue suit, slumped low in his blue Chrysler in a hairdresser's lot on Wilshire, dialled his boss too.

AND THREE THOUSAND MILES away in New York City the dark-haired forty-year-old was in the airline offices at Park and 42nd. He was buying an open round-trip ticket to Denver. He was paying for it with a Visa card in the name of Alan Mason.

SANTA ANA was way south and east, past Anaheim, down in Orange County. The township itself was twenty miles west of Santa Ana Mountains, where the infamous winds came from. But that day the air was still and brown and heavy. O'Donnell's rented GPS had a polite, insistent female voice which led them south of the zoo through spacious streets towards the Orange County Museum of Art before it turned them left and right and left again and told them they had arrived at their destination.

Which they clearly had. O'Donnell coasted to a stop next to a mailbox tricked out like a swan and painted bright white.

Behind the box a cast concrete driveway led to a double gate in a four-foot fence and a narrow concrete walkway led to a single gate. Both gates had *Beware of the Dog* signs on them. A garage was attached to a small, plain, stucco bungalow with corrugated metal awnings. The place was quiet and still.

'Feels empty,' Neagley said. 'Like there's nobody home.'

Reacher nodded. 'Let's check it out.'

They got out of the car and walked to the single gate. It wasn't locked or chained. They walked to the door. Reacher pushed the bell. Waited. No response. There was a slab path to a door in the garage. It was locked. A kitchen door in the back of the house was locked too. The top half of it was a single glass panel. Through it was visible a small, old-fashioned kitchen. A small table and two chairs. Empty dog bowls, one for food, one for water, neatly side by side on a green linoleum floor.

A tiny subliminal hum sounded a faint alarm in the back of Reacher's mind. 'Kitchen door?' O'Donnell asked.

Reacher nodded. O'Donnell put his hand in his pocket and came out with his brass knuckles. Ceramic knuckles, technically, made from complex mineral powder molded under tremendous pressure and bound with epoxy adhesives. O'Donnell fitted them to his hand, balled his fist and tapped the door glass quite gently. A triangular shard fell into the kitchen. He tapped twice more, then slipped the knuckles off and unlocked the door from the inside. It sagged open. No alarm.

Reacher went in first. Took two steps and stopped. Inside, the hum was louder. And there was a smell in the air. Both were unmistakable. The hum was a million flies going crazy. The smell was dead flesh.

Neagley and O'Donnell crowded in behind him. 'We knew anyway,' O'Donnell said, maybe to himself. 'This is not a shock.'

'It's a shock,' Neagley said. 'I hope it always will be.'

She covered her mouth and nose. Reacher stepped to the hallway. There were stray flies in the air, big and blue and shiny, buzzing in and out of a partially open door.

'The bathroom,' Reacher said.

The smell filled the house. The air was hot and foul. No sound, except the flies. 'Stay there,' Reacher said.

He walked down the hall. Pushed the bathroom door with his foot. Fanned the air and peered through the buzzing insects.

There was a dog on the floor. Once it had been a big German shepherd. It was lying on its side. Its hair was dead and matted. Reacher stepped right into the bathroom. All the water was gone from the toilet. 'It's his dog,' he said. 'Check the other rooms and the garage.'

There was nothing in the other rooms or the garage. No signs of struggle or disturbance, no sign of Swan himself. They regrouped in the hallway.

'What happened here?' Neagley asked.

'It died of thirst,' Reacher said. 'The toilet is dry. Probably lasted a week.'

'Awful,' Neagley said.

'You bet,' Reacher said. 'I like dogs. If I lived anywhere I'd have three or four. We're going to rent a helicopter, and throw these guys out in little pieces.'

They shoved scraps of paper towel from the kitchen up their noses and settled down to a long and serious search. They found nothing of any significance. There was food in the refrigerator and trash in the kitchen pail. There was a desk and a filing cabinet and a wall of shelves.

They started with the desk. They found nothing. The filing cabinet was full of routine paperwork. Taxes, insurance, paid bills, receipts. There was stuff from a vet. The dog's name had been Maisi. There was stuff from an organisation called People for the Ethical Treatment of Animals. Swan had been a contributor.

They checked the shelves. Found a shoe box full of snaps from Swan's life and career. Maisi the dog was in some of them. Reacher and Neagley and O'Donnell were in others, and Franz, and Karla Dixon, and Sanchez and Orozco, and Stan Lowrey. All of them long ago in the past, younger, different in crucial ways, blazing with youth and vigour and preoccupation.

Reacher stepped to the desk and picked up the phone. Hit redial. There was a rapid sequence of electronic blips, then a purring ring tone. Then Angela Franz answered. He put the phone down. 'The last call he made was to Franz, in Santa Monica.'

'Reporting for duty,' O'Donnell said. 'Doesn't help us.'

'Nothing here helps us,' Neagley said.

'But what isn't here might,' Reacher said. 'His piece of the Berlin Wall isn't here. There's no box of stuff from New Age.'

'How does that help us?'

'No idea,' Reacher said. 'But the more we know the luckier we'll get.'

They left through the kitchen and followed the slab path to the driveway. Headed back to the kerb. It was a quiet neighbourhood. Nothing was moving. Reacher scanned for signs of nosy neighbours and saw none.

But he did see a tan Crown Victoria. A guy behind the wheel, facing them. He said, 'Come to a casual stop and turn like you're taking one last look at the house. Make conversation.'

O'Donnell turned. 'Looks like the married officers' quarters at Fort Hood,' he said.

'Apart from the mailbox,' Reacher said.

Neagley turned. 'I like the mailbox,' she said.

Reacher said, 'There's a tan Crown Vic parked on the kerb forty yards west. It's tailing us. Tailing Neagley, to be precise. It was there when I met her on Sunset and it was outside Franz's place. I think it's time to find out who it is.'

'Like we used to?' O'Donnell asked.

Reacher nodded. 'Exactly like we used to. I'll drive.'

They took one last look at Swan's house and slid into O'Donnell's rental. No seat belts. Reacher started the engine and checked the view ahead, checked the mirror. Nothing coming.

He spun the wheel, stamped on the gas, pulled a fast U-turn and accelerated thirty yards. Jammed on the brakes and O'Donnell jumped out in front of the Crown Vic and Reacher stopped dead level with the driver's door. O'Donnell was already at the passenger window. Reacher jumped out and O'Donnell shattered the glass with his knuckles and chased the driver straight out into Reacher's arms. Reacher hit him in the gut and then again in the face. Fast and hard. The guy slammed back against his car and fell sideways, slowly, like a bulldozed tree. Sprawled on his back, unconscious, bleeding from a broken nose.

'Well, that still works,' O'Donnell said.

Neagley pulled the flap of the guy's sports coat open, looking for a pocket. And then she stopped.

He was wearing a worn black leather shoulder holster. There was a Glock 17 in it. His belt had a pouch for a spare magazine. Another holster with stainless-steel handcuffs.

Reacher glanced inside the Crown Vic. There was a radio mounted under the dash. 'Hell,' he said. 'We just took down a cop.'

Reacher crouched and put his fingers against the guy's neck. His pulse was there, strong and regular. The guy was breathing.

'Why did you hit him so hard?' Neagley asked.

'I was upset about the dog.'

'This guy didn't do that.'

'I know that now.'

Neagley dug through the guy's pockets. Came out with a leather ID folder. There was a chrome-plated badge pinned opposite a card behind a milky plastic window. 'His name is Thomas Brant,' she said. 'He's an LA County deputy.'

'This is Orange County,' O'Donnell said. 'He's outside of his jurisdiction. As he was on Sunset and in Santa Monica.'

'Think that will help us?'

'Not very much. He's working on Franz.'

Reacher said, 'Let's get him comfortable and get out of here.'

O'Donnell took Brant's feet and Reacher took his shoulders and they left him in the rear seat of his car in what medics call the recovery position, on his side, one leg drawn up, unlikely to choke. There was plenty of fresh air coming in through the broken window.

They got back in O'Donnell's rental. The polite voice inside the GPS set about guiding them back towards the freeway.

'We should return this car,' Neagley said. 'Right now. And then my Mustang. He'll have got both the plate numbers.'

'And then do what for transport?' Reacher asked.

'Your turn to rent something.'

'I don't have a driver's licence.'

'Then we'll have to take cabs. Change hotels. So be it.'

LAX was a gigantic, sprawling mess. Permanently half-finished. O'Donnell threaded through construction zones and perimeter roads and made it to the Hertz returns bay. He parked and a guy in a company jacket scanned a bar code in the rear window. That was it, rental over.

'Now what?' O'Donnell said.

Neagley said, 'Now we take the shuttle bus to the terminal and we find a cab. Then we check out of the hotel and come back with my Mustang. Reacher can find a new hotel. OK?'

But Reacher didn't reply. He was staring across the lot, through the rental office's plate-glass windows.

He was smiling.

'What?' Neagley said. 'Reacher, what?'

'In there,' Reacher said. 'Fourth in line. See her?'

'Who?'

'Small woman, dark hair? I'm pretty sure that's Karla Dixon.'

Reacher and Neagley and O'Donnell hurried across the lot, getting surer with every step. By the time they were ten feet from the office windows they were absolutely certain. It was Karla Dixon. Dark and pretty and comparatively small, she was right there now, third in line. As always she looked relaxed but never quite still, always burning energy. She was dressed in black jeans and a black leather jacket. Her thick black hair was cut short.

Then as if she felt their gazes on her back she turned and looked straight at them, nothing much in her face, as if she had last seen them minutes ago instead of years ago. She smiled a brief smile. The smile was a little sad, as if she already knew what was happening. Reacher held up four fingers and mouthed, *Get a four-seat car*. She nodded and turned again to wait.

Finally she received a fat yellow packet and a key, hoisted her black leather briefcase and grabbed her luggage. She stepped out to the sidewalk and looked at each of them in turn. Said, 'Sorry I'm late to the party. But it's not much of a party, is it?'

'What do you know so far?' Reacher asked her.

Dixon said, 'I only just got your messages. First flight out was through Vegas, so I did some checking. And I found out Sanchez and Orozco are missing. It seems that about three weeks ago they just vanished off the face of the earth.'

CHAPTER SIX

Hertz had given Dixon a Ford 500, a decent-sized four-seat sedan. She put her bags in the trunk and climbed into the driver's seat. Neagley sat next to her, and Reacher and O'Donnell got in the back. Dixon started up and left the airport heading north on Sepulveda. She talked for the first five minutes. She had been working under cover as a new hire at a Wall Street brokerage house, which meant she could afford no contact with her regular life, but eventually she had checked her machine from a Port Authority payphone and found the long string of desperate 10-30s.

So she had ditched her job and headed straight for JFK. When she had called Sanchez and Orozco from the Vegas airport, their voicemail was full, so she had cabbed over to their office and found them deserted with weeks of mail backed up behind the door. Their neighbours hadn't seen them in a long time.

'So that's it,' Reacher said. 'Now it's just the four of us left.'

Then Neagley covered all the hard intelligence and all the speculation from Angela Franz's first phone call onwards. The autopsy report, the small house in Santa Monica, the trashed Culver City office, the flash memories, the New Age building, the dead dog, the unfortunate attack on the LA County deputy.

'Conclusions?' Reacher asked.

'One, mainly,' Dixon said. 'This wasn't about Franz calling only some of us because he assumed only some of us would be available. Look at who's here and who isn't. I think this was about Franz calling only those of us who could get to him real fast. Swan and Sanchez and Orozco. So this is about speed and panic and urgency.'

There was quiet in the car for a moment. Traffic was moving OK. Dixon slid onto the 405, heading north. 'Where are we going?' she asked.

Neagley said, 'Let's go to the Chateau Marmont. It's out of the way and discreet.'

'And expensive,' Reacher said.

Something in his tone made Dixon take her eyes off the road and glance behind her. Neagley said, 'Reacher's broke.'

'I'm not surprised,' Dixon said. 'He hasn't worked in nine years.'

'He didn't do much when he was in the army, either,' O'Donnell said. 'Why change the habit of a lifetime?'

'He's sensitive about people paying for him,' Neagley said.

'Poor baby,' Dixon said.

Reacher said, 'I'm just trying to be polite.'

Dixon stayed on the 405 until Santa Monica Boulevard. Then she struck out north and east. 'Mission statement,' she said. 'You do not mess with the special investigators. The four of us have to make that stick. On behalf of the four who aren't here. So we need a command structure, a plan and a budget.'

Neagley said, 'I'll take care of the budget. This year there's seven billion dollars of Homeland Security money washing round the private system. Some comes our way in Chicago.'

'So are you rich?'

'Richer than I was when I was a sergeant.'

'So are we agreed on Neagley staking the budget?' Dixon asked.

'What is this, a democracy?' Reacher said.

'Temporarily. Are we agreed?'

Four raised hands. Two majors and a captain, letting a sergeant pick up the tab. 'OK, command structure,' Dixon said. 'I nominate Reacher for CO.'

'Me too,' O'Donnell said.

'Like it always was,' Neagley said.

'Can't do it,' Reacher said. 'I hit that cop. If it comes to it, I have to put my hands up. Can't have a CO in that position.'

O'Donnell said, 'If it comes to it, you get out of town.'

'Then they'll come after you and Neagley as accessories.'

Nobody spoke.

Reacher said, 'Neagley should be CO.'

'I decline,' Neagley said.

Dixon said, 'Reacher until he goes to jail. Then Neagley. All in favour?' Three hands went up.

'You'll regret this,' Reacher said. 'I'll make you regret it.'

'So what's the plan, boss?' Dixon asked, and the question sent Reacher spinning nine years into the past, to the last time he had heard anyone ask it.

'Same as ever,' he said. 'We find them, we take them down, and then we piss on their ancestors' graves.'

THE CHATEAU MARMONT was a bohemian old pile on Sunset near the foot of Laurel Canyon. All kinds of movie stars and rock stars had stayed there. There were plenty of photographs on the walls. Clark Gable, Greta Garbo, James Dean, John Lennon, Bob Dylan, Jim Morrison. John Belushi had died in there, speedballing heroin and cocaine. There were photographs of him.

The desk clerk wanted IDs, so they all checked in under their real names. No choice. Then the guy told them there were only three rooms available. Neagley had to be alone, so Reacher and O'Donnell bunked together, then O'Donnell drove Neagley in Dixon's car to pick up their bags and take the Mustang back to LAX. It would be a three-hour hiatus. Reacher and Dixon would work on the numbers.

They set up in Dixon's room. Reacher laid the seven spreadsheets side by side on the bed and watched Dixon scan them.

'Two key issues,' she said immediately. 'There are no hundred-per-cent scores. And the first three sheets have twenty-six numbers, the fourth has twenty-seven, and the last three all have twenty-six again.'

'Which means what?'

'I don't know. But none of the sheets is full. Therefore the twenty-six and twenty-seven thing must mean something. It's seven separate categories, and the scores get worse quite suddenly.'

'But what can be measured like that, repetitively?'

'Anything can, I guess. It could be that errors are being recorded, in which case the numbers are actually getting better, not worse.' Dixon shrugged. Walked to the window and pulled a faded drape aside and looked up at the hills. 'I like LA,' she said.

'Me too, I guess,' Reacher said.

'I like New York better. But the contrast is nice.'

'I guess.'

'Lousy circumstances, but it's great to see you, Reacher. Really great.'

Reacher nodded. 'Likewise. We thought we'd lost you. Didn't feel good.'

'Can I hug you?'

'You want to hug me?'

'I wanted to hug all of you at the Hertz office. But I didn't, because Neagley wouldn't have liked it.'

'She shook Angela Franz's hand. And the dragon lady's at New Age.'

'That's progress,' Dixon said.

'A little,' Reacher said.

'She was abused way back. That was always my guess.'

'She'll never talk about it,' Reacher said.

'It's sad.'

'You bet.'

She turned to him and Reacher took her in his arms and hugged her. She was fragrant. Her hair smelt of shampoo. He lifted her off her feet and spun her round, a complete slow circle. She was wearing a black silk shirt, and her skin felt warm underneath it. He set her back and she stretched up tall and kissed his cheek.

'I've missed you,' she said. 'Missed you all, I mean.'

'Me too,' he said. 'I didn't realise how much.'

'You like life after the army?' she asked.

'Yes, I like it fine.'

'I don't. But maybe you're reacting better than me.'

'I don't know whether I'm reacting at all. I look at you people and I feel like I'm just treading water.'

'Are you really broke?'

'Almost penniless.'

'Me too,' she said. 'I earn three hundred grand a year and I'm practically on the breadline. That's life. You're well out of it.'

'I feel that way, usually. Until I have to get back in it. Neagley put a thousand and thirty bucks in my account.'

'Like a ten-thirty radio code? Smart girl.'

'And for my air fare. Without that I'd be hitchhiking.'

'Nobody in their right mind would pick you up.'

Reacher glanced at himself in an old spotted mirror. Six-five, two-fifty, hands as big as frozen turkeys, hair all over the place, unshaven, torn shirt cuffs up on his forearms like Frankenstein's monster.

A bum. *From the big green machine to this.*

Dixon said, 'Can I ask you a question?'

'Go ahead.'

'I always wished we had done more than just work together.'

'Who?'

'You and me. Did you feel the same way?'

'Honestly? Yes, I did.'

'So why didn't we do more?'

'It would have wrecked the unit. The others would have been jealous.'

'We could have kept it a secret.'

Reacher said, 'Dream on.'

'We could keep it a secret now. We've got three hours.'

Reacher said nothing.

Dixon said, 'I'm sorry. It's just that all of this bad stuff makes me feel that life is so short.'

'Don't you have a boyfriend back east?'

'Not right now.'

Reacher stepped back to the bed. Karla Dixon came over and stood next to him. The paper sheets were still laid out in a line.

'Want to look at these some more?' Reacher asked.

'Not right now,' Dixon said.

'Me neither.' He gathered them up and placed them on the night stand.

AFTERWARDS they lay in bed together and Dixon said, 'We need to get back to work.' Reacher rolled over to take the papers off the stand but Dixon said, 'No, let's do it in our heads. We'll see more that way. Total of one hundred and eighty-three numbers,' she said. 'Tell me about one hundred and eighty-three, as a number.'

'Multiply it by two and you get three hundred and sixty-six, which is the number of days in a leap year.'

'So is this half a leap year?'

'Not with seven lists,' Reacher said. 'Half of any kind of a year would be six months and six lists.'

Dixon went quiet.

Reacher thought: *Half a year. Half. Twenty-six, twenty-seven.*

He said, 'How many weeks in a year?'

'Fifty-two.'

'How many working days?'

'Two hundred and sixty for five-day weeks, three hundred and twelve for six-day weeks.'

'So how many days would there be in seven months' worth of six-day working weeks?'

Dixon thought for a second. 'Depends on which seven months you pick. Depends on where the Sundays fall. Depends on what day of the week January first is.'

'Run the numbers, Karla. There are two possible answers.'

Dixon paused a beat. 'One hundred and eighty-two or one hundred and eighty-three.'

'Exactly,' Reacher said. 'Those seven sheets are seven months' worth of six-day working weeks.'

Dixon slid out from under the sheet and walked naked to her briefcase and came back with a leather Filofax diary. She opened it out on the bed and arranged the papers in a line below.

'It's this year,' she said. 'It's the last seven calendar months. Right up to the end of last month.'

'There you go,' Reacher said. 'Some kind of six-day-a-week figures got worse and worse over the last seven months.'

'Now tell me what the figures mean.'

'I don't know.' Reacher said.

'Me neither,' Dixon said.

'We should shower and get dressed.'

'After.'

'After what?'

Dixon pinned him to the pillow and kissed him again.

TWO THOUSAND horizontal and seven vertical miles away the dark-haired forty-year-old calling himself Alan Mason was in a United Airlines Boeing 757, en route to Denver. He was in seat 3A, with a glass of sparkling mineral water beside him on the armrest tray and a newspaper open on his lap. But he was gazing out of the window at the bright white clouds below.

And eight miles south the man in the dark blue suit in the dark blue Chrysler tailed O'Donnell and Neagley from the LAX Hertz lot to the hotel. He called it in. 'They moved to the Chateau Marmont. And there's four of them now. Karla Dixon showed up. So they are all present and correct.'

O'DONNELL SAID, 'We're nowhere at all,' and Neagley said, 'The trail is stone cold and we have virtually no data.'

They were in Karla Dixon's bedroom. The bed was made. Reacher and Dixon were showered and dressed and their hair was dry.

The seven spreadsheets were laid out on the dresser with the diary next to them. No one disputed that they represented the last seven calendar months. But no one saw how that information helped.

Dixon looked at Reacher. 'What do you want to do, boss?'

'Take a break,' Reacher said. 'We're not thinking straight.'

'We never used to take breaks.'

'We used to have five more pairs of eyes.'

REACHER WENT for a walk west on Sunset, alone. Solitude was still his natural condition. He took his money out of his pocket and counted it. Not much left. He ducked into a souvenir store and found a rail of discounted shirts. On the end of the rail was a bunch of blue items with white patterns, shiny, some kind of a man-made material. He picked the largest one out, found a mirror and jammed the hanger up under his chin. The shirt was probably wide enough in the shoulders, and the short sleeves would accommodate his arms. His arms were like a gorilla's, only longer and thicker.

With tax the garment cost nearly twenty one dollars. Reacher paid the guy at the register.

'Barbershop near here?' he asked.

'Two blocks north,' the guy said. 'Up the hill. Shoeshines and haircuts in the corner of the grocery store.'

THE GROCERY STORE sold beer and coffee. Reacher took a medium cup of house blend, black, and headed for the barber's chair. It was an old-fashioned thing covered in red speckled vinyl. A thin guy was sitting on it. He had needle tracks up and down his arms.

'Let me guess,' he said. 'Shave and a haircut.'

Thirty minutes later Reacher was down to his last dollar but his face was smooth and his head was shaved almost as close.

Reacher checked the guy's arms again, then asked, 'Where can a person score round here?'

'You're not a user.'

'For a friend.'

The guy shrugged. 'There's usually a crew behind the wax museum.'

Reacher walked back to the hotel on the low canyon streets, and along the way he passed a dark blue Chrysler 300C parked on the kerb. A guy in a dark blue suit was behind the wheel. The suit matched the sheet metal. The engine was off and Reacher assumed it was a livery car. He figured some enterprising car-service owner had dressed the drivers in matching suits, looking for an edge. LA was a tough market, in the limousine business. He had read about it somewhere.

Dixon and Neagley were polite about his new shirt but O'Donnell laughed at it. They all laughed at his haircut. Reacher didn't care. He had to agree it was a little extreme. A real whitewall. And he was happy to provide a moment of levity. They weren't going to get any light relief anyplace else, that was for sure.

There was a new page next to the spreadsheets in Dixon's handwriting. She had extrapolated the numbers out to three hundred and fourteen days and 3,766 events in a complete year. But the rest of the page was blank. Nobody had come up with anything.

'There must be more than this,' O'Donnell said.

Reacher nodded. 'It ain't much. The bad guys got his computers, his Rolodex, his phone book. All we've got is the tip of the iceberg. Fragments. Like archaeological remains. But it's all we're going to get.'

'So what do we do?'

'Break the habit.'

'What habit?'

'Asking me what to do. I imagine those deputies are gearing up right now. I might not be here tomorrow.'

'Until then what do we do?'

'Take another break, then we'll go and get some dinner. My treat. I'll see you in the lobby in an hour.'

REACHER GOT Dixon's Ford from the valets and drove east on Hollywood Boulevard until he was two blocks west of Hollywood and Vine, which was where the bad stuff had traditionally been. Now it seemed to have migrated, which was usually the way.

He pulled into the kerb. There was a wide alley behind the wax museum that had been colonised by dealers into a drive-through facility. The operation was organised in the conventional triangulated manner. A buyer would drive in and slow up. A kid, not more than eleven years old, would approach. The driver would place his order and hand over his cash. The kid would run the cash to the bag man then continue to a stash man and pick up the product. Meanwhile the driver would be crawling through a slow half circle, ready to meet the kid again on the other side of the lot when the transfer would be made and the driver would leave.

A smart system. A system Reacher had seen before.

Reacher waited.

A black Mercedes ML pulled in to the lot. The kid ran up and picked up a folded wad. The Mercedes eased forward and the kid ran over to the bagman. The wad went into the bag and the kid headed for the stashman.

Reacher put the Ford in gear, hit the gas and turned the wheel and slammed into the lot. Headed straight for the centre of the space. Straight for the bag man. The bag man froze.

Ten feet before hitting him Reacher did three things. He twitched the wheel. He stamped on the brake. And he opened his door. The car slewed right, the front wheels washed into the loose stones then the door swung out through a moving arc and caught the guy like a full-on punch. He went over backwards and the car stopped dead. Reacher leaned over and grabbed the vinyl duffle bag left-handed from the floor. Pitched it into the passenger seat and hit the gas. Slammed his door shut. Roared back out of the lot and bounced over the kerb onto Highland. In the mirror he saw dust in the air and confusion and the bag man flat on his back. Two guys running. Then he was through the light, back on Hollywood Boulevard.

Twelve seconds, beginning to end.

No reaction. No gunshots. No pursuit.

Reacher slowed and caught his breath and drove a complete counter-clockwise circle. Nobody was behind him. He stopped on a deserted hairpin up high and emptied the bag. Two AMT Hardballers, stainless-steel copies of Colt M1911 .45 automatics. Then he counted the money. Close to nine hundred dollars. Enough for dinner. Even with a tip.

IN THE EVENT, dinner cost Reacher way less than nine hundred bucks. Either out of taste or deference to his economic predicament the others opted for a noisy hamburger barn on Sunset. Tap and domestic beer and thick, juicy patties, a round table, conversation stopping and starting as the centre of attention bounced between them. After thirty minutes of reminiscence and catch-up, the talk turned back to Franz.

O'Donnell said, 'If we believe his wife, he quit everything except routine database mining. So why would he suddenly launch into something this serious?'

Dixon said, 'Because someone asked him to.'

'Exactly,' O'Donnell said. 'This thing starts with his client. So who was it? He went the extra mile here. Kind of broke faith with his wife and son.'

Neagley said, 'It could have been a big payer.'

'Or someone he was obligated to somehow,' Dixon said.

Reacher listened. Something stirred in the back of his mind. Something Dixon had said, hours ago, in the car leaving LAX. He closed his eyes, but he couldn't get it. 'We should ask Angela if he had some kind of a long-standing big-deal client.'

'I'd like to meet Charlie,' O'Donnell said.

'We'll go tomorrow,' Reacher said. 'Unless the deputies come for me.'

They walked back to the hotel and split up in the lobby to get some sleep and start work again early. Reacher and O'Donnell headed up together. Didn't talk much.

Reacher woke up at seven in the morning. Early sun was coming in the window. David O'Donnell was coming in through the door. In a hurry, cardboard cups of coffee in both hands.

'I went for a walk,' he said. 'And you're in trouble. That deputy. He's parked a hundred yards from here.'

'The same guy? Just sitting there?'

'Like he's waiting. He's got a metal splint on his face and a garbage bag taped across his window.'

They ordered breakfast in Dixon's room. First rule, learned a long time ago: eat when you can, especially when you're about to disappear into the system. Reacher shovelled eggs and bacon and toast down his throat and followed it with plenty of coffee.

'How did they find us so fast?' Dixon asked.

'Computers,' Neagley said. 'Homeland Security and the Patriot Act. They can search hotel registers any time they want now. This is a police state.'

'I wish we still were the police,' O'Donnell said. 'You'd hardly have to break a sweat any more.'

'You guys get going,' Reacher said. 'I don't want you snarled up in this so don't let the deputy see you. Go chase the client. I'll get back when I can.'

He headed back to his room. Put his folding toothbrush in his pocket and hid his passport and his ATM card and eight hundred dollars in O'Donnell's suit carrier. Because certain things can go missing after an arrest. Then he took the elevator down to the lobby. No need to turn the whole thing into a big drama, running up and down hotel corridors. Because, second rule, learned from a lifetime of bad luck and trouble: maintain a little dignity.

He just sat in an armchair and waited.

Thirty minutes. Sixty. The lobby had three morning papers, and he read them all. Every word. Sports, features, editorials, national, international. And business. Ninety minutes.

Nothing happened.

At the two-hour point Reacher put the papers back on the rack. Stepped to the door and looked out. A fine day. The nineteenth day Calvin Franz hadn't been around to see. Same for Tony Swan and Jorge Sanchez and Manuel Orozco, presumably.

There are dead men walking. You don't throw my friends out of helicopters and live to tell the tale.

Reacher stepped outside. The sidewalk was quiet. No parked vehicles. No surveillance. He turned left on Sunset. Left again on Laurel Canyon Boulevard. Kept close to hedges and plantings. Turned left again on the winding canyon road.

The tan Crown Vic was dead ahead. It was parked on the far kerb a hundred yards away. Still, inert, engine off. Like O'Donnell had said, its broken window was taped over with a black garbage bag. The driver wasn't moving, except for regular turns of his head. Rearview mirror, straight ahead, door mirror. Reacher caught a flash of an aluminium splint.

Just watching and waiting. But for what?

Reacher turned round and backtracked to the lobby. Sat down again, with the germ of a new theory in his mind. *His wife called me. She was just telling me. Just telling me,* Neagley had said.

And then Reacher had asked Charlie: *Is it OK to be opening the door all by yourself?* And the little boy had said: *Yes, it's OK.*

And then: *Charlie, you should go out and play.*

Reacher sat in the velvet armchair, thinking, waiting to be proved right or wrong by whoever came through the door first, his old unit or a bunch of fired-up LA County deputies.

HIS OLD UNIT came through the door first. What was left of it, anyway. Fast and anxious, they stopped dead in surprise when they saw him.

'You're still here,' O'Donnell said.

'No, I'm an optical illusion.'

'Outstanding.'

'What did Angela Franz say?'

'Nothing. She doesn't know anything about his clients.'

'Why are you still here?' Dixon said.

'That's a very good question,' Reacher said. 'Is the deputy still out there?'

She nodded. 'We saw him from the end of the street.'

They went up to Reacher and O'Donnell's room. The first thing Reacher did was retrieve his money, his passport and his ATM card.

O'Donnell said, 'Looks like you think you're sticking around.'

'I think I am,' Reacher said.

'Why?'

'Because Charlie opened the door all by himself.'

'Which means?'

'Seems to me that Angela is a pretty good mom. Normal, at worst. Yet she let the kid open the door to a couple of complete strangers. Charlie's all she's got left, yet she told him to go out to play. In a yard on a busy street. Why would she do that?'

'I don't know,' Dixon said.

'Because she knew that deputy was watching the house.'

'You think?'

'Why did she wait fourteen days before calling Neagley?'

'She was distracted,' Dixon said.

'Possibly,' Reacher said. 'But maybe she wasn't going to call us at all. We were ancient history. The bad old days, rough, dangerous, uncouth. But from the deputies' point of view, they find a dead guy in the desert, they ID him and they get nowhere. No clues, no leads. So after two weeks of frustration they get an idea. Angela has told them all about the unit and the loyalty and the old slogan, so they prompt her to call us. Because they know that's the exact same thing as winding up the Energiser Bunny. They know they can just stay in the shadows and watch us look for answers.'

'That's ridiculous,' O'Donnell said.

'But I think it's exactly what happened,' Reacher said. 'Police work by proxy. That's what Angela wasn't telling us. And that's why I'm still here. They figure a busted nose is the price of doing business. Take a walk round the block and talk to the deputy.'

'You think?'

'Dixon should go. She wasn't with us in Santa Ana. So if I'm wrong the guy probably won't shoot her.'

CHAPTER SEVEN

Dixon went. She left the room without a word. O'Donnell said, 'I don't think Angela was hiding anything today. So I don't think Franz had a client at all.'

'How hard did you press her?' Reacher asked.

'We didn't need to press her. It was all right out there. She had nothing to tell us. It's inconceivable he could have had such a guy without Angela at least hearing a name.'

Reacher smiled, briefly. He liked his old team. He could rely on them, absolutely. No second-guessing.

Neagley asked, 'What next?'

'Let's talk to the deputies first,' Reacher said.

Dixon came back. Said, 'He didn't shoot me.'

'That's good,' Reacher said. 'Is he mad about his face?'

'Livid.'

'So what's the story? Did he 'fess up to anything?'

'He called his boss. Curtis Mauney. They want to meet with us here an hour from now.'

'OK,' Reacher said. 'We'll see what the guy has got.'

They waited in the lobby. No stress, no strain. Military service teaches a person how to wait. O'Donnell sprawled on a sofa and cleaned his fingernails with his switchblade. Dixon read the seven spreadsheets over and over. Neagley sat alone in a chair against a wall. Reacher sat under an old framed photograph of Raquel Welch. The picture had been taken outside the hotel, late in the afternoon, and the light was as golden as her skin.

THE DARK-HAIRED forty-year-old calling himself Alan Mason was waiting, too. He was waiting to hold a clandestine meeting in his hotel room in downtown Denver. He was uncharacteristically nervous and out of sorts. He had a suitcase stacked against the wall. It was a dark grey, hard-shell Samsonite, expensive but not ostentatious. Inside it were bearer bonds and cut diamonds and Swiss bank access codes worth sixty-five million US dollars, and the people he was meeting were not the kind a prudent person would trust around portable and untraceable assets.

FIRST IN through the Chateau Marmont's lobby door was the banged-up deputy himself, Thomas Brant. He had a vivid bruise on his forehead and the metal splint was taped so tight that the skin around his eyes was distorted. He was walking like he hurt. He was followed in by an older guy who had to be his boss. Curtis Mauney looked to be approaching fifty. He was short and solid and had the worn look of a guy in the same line of work too long. His hair was dyed a dull black that didn't match his eyebrows. He was carrying a battered briefcase. He asked, 'Which one of you jerks hit my guy?'

'Does it matter?' Reacher said.

'I'm saying you don't come here and start hitting cops.'

Reacher said. 'He was outside of his jurisdiction, and he was acting in a suspicious manner. He was asking for it.'

'Why are you here anyway?'

'For our friend's funeral.'

'The body hasn't been released yet.'

'So we'll wait.'

'Was it you who hit my guy?'

Reacher nodded. 'I apologise. But all you had to do was ask for our help.'

Mauney looked blank. 'You think we brought you to help? We brought you as bait.' He sat down and tucked his briefcase between his ankles. 'Let's get a couple of things straight. We're not hicks from the sticks. We knew within twelve hours that Calvin Franz was one of eight survivors of an elite military unit. And within twenty four hours we knew that three other members of that unit were missing.'

Reacher said, 'Your thesis is someone's hunting all of us?'

'I don't know what my thesis is. But that's certainly a possibility. Therefore flushing you four out was a win-win for me.'

'How do you know the two from Vegas are missing?'

'Because I called,' Mauney said. 'We work with the Nevada State Police a lot, and they work with the Vegas cops a lot, and your guys Sanchez and Orozco went missing three weeks ago and both their apartments have been royally trashed.'

'Trashed as bad as Franz's office?'

'Similar handiwork.'

'They miss anything?'

'Did they miss something at Franz's place? Did we?'

Mauney looked like a pretty good cop but maybe playable, so Reacher said, 'Franz was mailing computer files to himself for security. We got them.'

'From out of his post-office box? That's a federal crime, you should have got a warrant.'

'I couldn't have,' Reacher said. 'I'm retired. So what did they miss in Vegas?'

'Are we trading here?'

Reacher nodded. 'But you go first.'

'OK. They missed a napkin with writing on it. It was balled up in Sanchez's kitchen trash. The kind of paper napkin you get with Chinese delivery. And ordering that Chinese seems to be about the last thing Sanchez ever did in Las Vegas.'

'What does the note say?'

Mauney hauled his battered briefcase up on his knees and clicked the latches. Lifted the lid. Took out a clear plastic page protector with a colour photocopy showing creases and grease stains and paper texture. And a half-line scrawled with a blue fibre-tipped pen in Sanchez's bold handwriting: *650 at $100k per.*

Mauney asked, 'What does it mean?'

Reacher said, 'Your guess is as good as mine.'

'I think it's an offer or a bid,' Mauney said.

'Or a market report,' O'Donnell said.

'What did you get from Franz's post-office box?' Mauney asked.

'A flash memory chip,' Reacher said. 'For a computer. We can't break the password.'

'We could try,' Mauney said. 'There's a lab we use.'

'I don't know. We're down to the last attempt.'

'Actually it's evidence, and therefore it's ours.'

'Will you share the information?'

Mauney nodded. 'We're in sharing mode, apparently.'

'OK. Good luck.' Reacher nodded to Neagley. She put her hand in her tote bag and came out with the silver plastic sliver. Passed it to Mauney.

'Pointers?' Mauney asked.

'It'll be numbers. Franz was a numbers type of guy.'

'OK.'

'It wasn't an airplane, you know.'

'I know,' Mauney said. 'You know how many private helicopters there are within range of the place we found him? More than nine thousand.'

'Did you check Swan's office?'

'He was canned. He didn't have an office.'

'Did you check his house?'

'Through the windows. It hadn't been tossed.'

'So why didn't you check on the rest of us?'

'Because at that point I was dealing with what I had. Franz, Swan, Sanchez and Orozco. I had all four of them on tape. Video surveillance, the night before Franz went out and didn't come back.'

Mauney raised the lid of his briefcase again and took out another page protector. In it was a copy of a black-and-white still frame. Four men, shoulder to shoulder in front of some kind of a store counter. He said, 'I made the IDs by comparing old snapshots from a shoe box in Franz's bedroom closet.' Then he passed the photograph counterclockwise, to Neagley, Dixon, O'Donnell and Reacher.

Manuel Orozco was on the left, glancing right, caught by the camera in his perpetual state of restlessness. Then came Calvin Franz, hands in his pockets, patience on his face. Then came Tony Swan looking straight ahead. On the right was Jorge Sanchez, in a buttoned-up shirt, no tie.

They all looked older. Orozco's hair was grey at the temples and his eyes were weary. Franz had maybe lost a little weight. Swan, wide as ever, was thicker in the gut. Sanchez's scowl had settled into a permanent tracery of lines. Older, but maybe a little wiser, too. There was a lot of experience and capability right there in the picture. Four tough guys. In Reacher's opinion, four of the best eight in the world.

Who or what had beaten them?

Behind them, running away from the camera, were narrow store aisles that looked familiar. 'Where is this?' Reacher asked.

Mauney said, 'The pharmacy next to Franz's office. Swan was buying aspirin for his dog's arthritis. He gave it a quarter-tab a day.'

'How much aspirin did he buy?'

'The economy bottle. Ninety-six pills, generic.'

'At a quarter-tab a day, that's a year and nineteen days' worth.' Reacher looked at the picture again. 'Can I keep this?'

Mauney nodded. 'Keep it. It's a copy.'

'What next?'

'Stay visible.' Mauney clicked the latches of his case. 'And call me if you see anyone sniffing round. No more independent action, OK?'

'We're just here for the funeral,' Reacher said. As he stood he looked in the reflective glass and he saw the others stand behind him.

Mauney turned towards the door and Neagley, O'Donnell and Dixon stepped towards the hotel interior. But Thomas Brant moved the other way.

Reacher kept his eye on the glass. He knew instantly what was going to happen. Brant stepped closer. His left hand snaked forward and his right hand eased back in a fist. He tapped Reacher on the shoulder. Reacher turned fast and caught the incoming straight right in his left palm just in front of his face.

Then it was all about superhuman self-control. Reacher looked into Brant's eyes, breathed out, and shook his head.

'I apologised once,' he said. 'And I apologise again. If that's not good enough, wait until this is all over, and jump me three-on-one, OK?'

'Maybe I'll do that,' Brant said.

Mauney came over and said. 'No fighting. Not now, not ever.' He hauled Brant away by the collar. Reacher waited until they were both out of the door, grimaced and shook his left hand wildly.

'Damn, that stings,' he said.

'Put some ice on it,' Neagley said.

'Wrap it round a cold beer,' O'Donnell said.

'Get over it and let me tell you about six hundred and fifty,' Dixon said.

THEY WENT UP to Dixon's room and she arranged the spreadsheets neatly on her bed. Said, 'OK, what we have here is some kind of a performance analysis. For simplicity's sake let's call them hits and misses. The first three months are pretty good, then we get worse.'

'We know that already,' Neagley said.

'So for the sake of argument, let's take the first three months as a baseline. We know they can hit ninety per cent, give or take. Let's say they could have continued that level of performance indefinitely, but they didn't. What's the result?'

Neagley said, 'More misses later than earlier.'

'If they had continued their baseline success rate through the final four months they would have saved themselves exactly six hundred and fifty extra misses,' Dixon said.

'Really?'

'Really. Six hundred and fifty.'

Reacher nodded. 'I wish we knew what we were looking at.'

'Sabotage,' O'Donnell said. 'Someone got paid to screw something up.'

'At a hundred grand a time?' Neagley said.

'But it ties in,' Dixon said. 'Doesn't it? There was a definite mathematical relationship between what Franz knew and what Sanchez knew.'

Reacher stepped to Dixon's window and looked out at the view. 'So assuming Orozco knew whatever Sanchez knew, we're missing what Swan knew. We've got nothing from him.'

'His house was clean. Nothing there.'

'So it's at his office.'

'He didn't have an office. He was canned.'

'But only recently. So his office is just sitting there mothballed. They're shedding staff, not hiring. I think we have to see the dragon lady again.'

THE MAN in the dark blue suit in the dark blue Chrysler tailed them east on Sunset, hunting the 101. Outside the KTLA studios, just before the freeway, he dialled his boss.

His boss said, 'I'm still in Colorado. Watch them for me.'

DIXON TURNED IN through New Age's open gate and parked head-on against the shiny corporate cube. The lot was still half empty. The same receptionist was on duty. 'Help you?' she said.

'We need to see Ms Berenson again,' Reacher said.

'I'll see if she's available,' the receptionist said.

When Berenson arrived she shook hands all round and opened the aluminium door. Everyone filed past her into the conference room.

'How may I help you today?' she said. There was a little irritation in her voice.

'Tony Swan is missing,' Reacher said.

'Missing? I don't understand.'

'It's not a difficult concept to grasp.'

'But he could be anywhere. A new job, out of state. Or a vacation. People sometimes do that, in Mr Swan's circumstances. Like a silver lining.'

O'Donnell said, 'His dog died of thirst in his house. No silver lining there. Swan didn't go anywhere he planned to go.'

'His dog? How awful,' Berenson said. 'Mr Swan left here more than three weeks ago. Isn't this a matter for the police?'

'They're working on it,' Reacher said. 'We're working on it too.'

'I don't see how I can help.'

'We'd like to see his desk. And his computer. And there might be notes. Or information, or appointments.'

'There are no notes here, no paper at all. No pens or pencils. This is a completely paperless environment. It's a rule. Basic security. Everything is done on computers here. We have an in-house network with secure firewalls and automatic random data monitoring.'

'Can we see his computer, then?' Neagley asked.

'Someone leaves here,' Berenson said, 'within thirty minutes their desktop hard drive is destroyed. Smashed. It's another security rule. Data can be recovered otherwise.'

'So there's no trace of him left?'

'None at all, I'm afraid.'

'You've got some pretty heavy rules here.'

'I know. Mr Swan designed them himself. They were his first contribution. He had to play a cop's role here to be effective.'

'What about his boss?' O'Donnell said. 'What's his name?'

'I can't tell you that.'

'You're very discreet.'

'Mr Swan insisted on it. His procedures are still in place.'

'Was Swan upset or worried the week he left?'

'Not that I saw.'

'What do you think might have happened to him?'

'Me?' Berenson said. 'I really have no idea. I walked him to his car, and that was the last I saw of him.'

They got back in Dixon's car and reversed away from the mirror glass.

O'Donnell said, 'They were using him there. They picked his brains for a year and then kicked him out.'

'Sure looks that way,' Neagley said.

'They're not making anything there. It's an unsecured building.'

'Obviously. They must have a remote plant somewhere.'

'I'd like to know what they make.'

'So go ahead and find out,' Reacher said.

'I don't know anyone to ask.'

'I do,' Neagley said. 'I know a guy in Pentagon procurement.'

IN HIS ROOM in his Denver hotel the dark-haired forty-year-old calling himself Alan Mason was concluding his meeting. His guest had shown up exactly on time and had been accompanied by a single bodyguard. Mason appreciated punctuality in business. And being outnumbered only two to one was a luxury.

So, a good start. It had been followed by substantive progress. No lame excuses about late delivery or lowered numbers. Just the sale as previously discussed, six hundred and fifty units at a hundred thousand dollars each.

Mason had opened his suitcase and his client had started the long process of totalling the consideration inside. The Swiss bank balances and the bearer bonds were uncontroversial. They had reliable face values. The diamonds were more subjective, of course, but Mason's guest had pronounced himself entirely satisfied.

At which point Mason received a key and a piece of paper.

The key was small, old, scratched and worn, the key to a padlock currently securing a shipping container at the Los Angeles docks. The piece of paper was a bill of lading, describing the container's contents as six hundred and fifty DVD players.

Mason's guest and his bodyguard left, and Mason stepped into the bathroom and set fire to his passport over the toilet pan. Half an hour later, Andrew MacBride left the hotel and headed back to the airport.

FRANCES NEAGLEY called Chicago from the back of Dixon's car. She told her assistant to email her contact at the Pentagon and explain that she was away from a secure phone and had an inquiry about New Age's product. She knew her guy would feel better about responding by email than talking on an unsecured cell network.

O'Donnell asked, 'Who's the guy?'

'Just a guy,' Neagley said. 'Who owes me big.'

'Big enough to deliver?'

'Always.'

Dixon came off the 101 at Sunset and headed west to the hotel. The traffic was slow. Less than three miles, but a jogger could have covered them faster. When they eventually arrived they found a Crown Vic waiting out front. Not Thomas Brant's.

Curtis Mauney climbed out as soon as Dixon parked. He walked over, short, solid, worn, tired. He asked, 'Did one of your friends have a tattoo on his back?'

A gentle tone of voice. Quiet. Sympathetic.

MANUEL OROZCO had gone through college on army money and had assumed he would wind up a combat infantry officer. His baby sister had assumed he would wind up KIA with serious disfiguring wounds. She would never know what had happened to him. He told her about dog tags. She said they might get blown off. He told her about dental identification. She said his jaw might get exploded. Later he realised she was worrying on a deeper level but at the time he thought the answer to her fears was to get a big black tattoo across his upper back that said *Orozco, M.* with his service number below. He had got home and peeled off his shirt in triumph and had been mystified when the kid had cried even harder.

Ultimately he had ended up a key part of the 110th MP, where Reacher rechristened him Kit Bag because his broad olive back looked like a GI duffle with its stencil. Now fifteen years later Reacher stood in the Chateau Marmont's sun-blasted parking lot and said, 'You found another body.'

'I'm afraid we did,' Mauney said. 'Same area. In a gully.'

'Orozco,' Reacher said.

'That's the name on his back. Who's the next of kin?'

'He has a sister somewhere. Younger.'

'So you should make the formal ID. If you would.'

They got back in the car and followed Mauney to a county facility north of Glendale. Nobody spoke. Reacher sat in the back and ran through a long involuntary sequence of remembered Orozco moments. The guy had been a comedian, part unwitting. He had called everyone *mate*. His command skills had been first rate, but he had never really issued orders. He would wait until a junior officer or a grunt had grasped the general consensus and then he would say, *If you wouldn't mind, mate, please.*

O'Donnell said, 'We knew already. This is not a surprise.'

Nobody answered him.

THE COUNTY FACILITY turned out to be a brand new hospital with a state-of-the-art receiving station for townships without morgues of their own.

Everyone parked and got out. Mauney led the way to a personnel elevator and pressed four.

The fourth floor was as cold as a meat locker. Mauney passed a public viewing area and headed through a door to a storage area. Three walls showed the fronts of refrigerated stainless-steel drawers. The air was bitter with cold and heavy with smells. Mauney pulled a drawer. It came out easily on ball-bearing runners. Full length.

Inside was a refrigerated corpse. Male. Hispanic. The ankles were tied with rough twine that had bitten deep. The arms were tied behind the back. The head and shoulders were grievously damaged.

'He fell head first,' Reacher said, softly. 'He would, I guess, tied up like that. If you're right about the helicopter.'

'No tracks to or from,' Mauney said.

Further medical details were hard to discern. Decomposition was well advanced and the body was shrunken, collapsed, leathery.

Mauney asked, 'Do you recognise him?'

'Not really,' Reacher said.

'Check the tattoo.'

Reacher just stood there.

Mauney shook his head and put a hand under the corpse's icy shoulder. Lifted. The body rolled awkwardly, all of a piece. It settled face down. The tattoo was creased and faded but unmistakable: *Orozco, M.*, and a service number.

'It's him,' Reacher said. 'It's Manuel Orozco.'

Mauney said, 'I'm very sorry.'

There was silence for a moment. Reacher asked, 'Are you still searching the area?'

'Not actively. It's not like we've got a missing child.'

'Is Franz in here too? In one of these damn drawers?'

'You want to see him?' Mauney asked.

'No,' Reacher looked back at Orozco. 'When is the autopsy?'

'Soon.'

'Do we have an estimate on when he died?'

'Before Franz, we think. But we may never know.'

'We will,' Reacher said. 'I'll ask whoever did it. And he'll tell me. By that point he'll be begging to.'

'No independent action, remember?'

'In your dreams.'

Mauney stayed to process paperwork and Reacher and Neagley and Dixon and O'Donnell took the elevator back down to warmth and sunlight. They stood in the lot, saying nothing. Doing nothing. Just crackling and trembling with suppressed rage. It was a given that soldiers contemplate death. They live with it, they expect it. Some of them even want it. But deep down they want it to be *fair*. They want it to arrive with significance.

A soldier dead with his arms tied behind him was the worst kind of outrage. It was about helplessness and submission and abuse. It was about powerlessness. It took away all the illusions.

'Let's go,' Dixon said. 'We're wasting time.'

THEY WENT BACK to Dixon's room at the hotel. They were dead-ended. They had nothing to go on. Those feelings didn't improve any when they transferred to Neagley's room and found an email response from her Pentagon contact: *Sorry, no way. New Age is classified.*

'Seems he doesn't owe you all that big,' O'Donnell said.

'He does,' Neagley said. 'Bigger than you could imagine.' She scrolled on through her inbox. There was another message from the same guy. Different version of his name, different email address. 'That's a one-time free account,' she said.

The message said: *Frances, great to hear from you. We should get together. Dinner and a movie? And I need to return your Hendrix CDs. Thanks so much. I loved them all. The sixth track on the second album is dynamically brilliant. Let me know when you're next in Washington. Please call soonest.*

Reacher said, 'You own CDs?'

'No,' Neagley said. 'I especially don't own Jimi Hendrix CDs. I don't like him.'

O'Donnell said, 'So he's confusing you with some other woman.'

'Unlikely,' Reacher said.

'It's coded,' Neagley said. 'That's what it is. It's the answer to my question. Something to do with the sixth track on the second album.'

Reacher said, 'What was the second Hendrix album?'

O'Donnell said, '*Electric Ladyland*?'

'That was later,' Dixon said.

Reacher said, '*Axis: Bold As Love* was the second album.'

'What was the sixth track?' Dixon asked.

'I have no idea.'

O'Donnell said, 'When the going gets tough, the tough go shopping.'

They walked a long way on Sunset, and they found a Tower Records. They went inside and found young people and loud music and the H section in the Rock/Pop aisles. There was a dense foot-and-a-half of Jimi Hendrix CDs. *Axis: Bold As Love* was right there, three copies. Reacher pulled one. It was wrapped in plastic and the bar-code label was stuck over the second half of the track listings.

Same for the second copy. Same for the third.

'Rip off the plastic,' O'Donnell said.

'Can't do that. It's not ours.'

'You smack cops around but you won't damage a wrapper?'

'It's different. Cars have CD players, right?'

'For the last hundred years,' Dixon said.

Reacher took the CD and lined up behind a girl with more metal punched through her face than a grenade victim. He peeled off thirteen of his remaining eight hundred dollars and for the first time in his life became the owner of a digital product.

It was wrapped tight. Reacher used his fingernails to scrape a corner and his teeth to tear the plastic. He ran his finger down the track list. '"Little Wing",' he said.

O'Donnell shrugged. Neagley looked blank.

'Doesn't help,' Dixon said.

'I know the song,' Reacher said.

'Please don't sing it,' Neagley said.

'So what does it mean?' O'Donnell said.

Reacher said, 'It means New Age makes a weapons system called Little Wing. Sounds like a drone phone or something.' He tried to open the CD box but had to pick at the title label until it came off in sticky fragments. 'No wonder the record business is in trouble,' he said.

Dixon asked, 'What are we going to do?'

'What did the email say?'

'You know what it said. Find the sixth track on the second Hendrix album.'

'And?'

'And nothing.'

'No, it said please call soonest.'

'That's ridiculous,' Neagley said. 'If he won't tell me by email, why would he tell me on the phone?'

'It didn't say please call *me*. There must be somebody he knows you know can help. Maybe from Washington, since every word counts?'

Neagley opened her mouth to say *nobody*. But then she paused. 'There's a woman, Diana Bond. We both know her. She's a staffer for a guy on the House Defense Committee.'

'There you go. Who's the guy?'

Neagley said a familiar but unloved name. 'He's her boss. He's signing the cheques, so he'll have been briefed, and if he knows, she knows too. But she's not going to tell me.'

'She is. Because you're going to call her and tell her that Little Wing's name is out here, and you're about to tell the papers that the leak came from her boss's office, and the price of your silence is everything she knows about it.'

'That's dirty.'

'That's politics. She can't be unfamiliar with the process.'

'Do we really need to do this? I don't want to involve her.'

'Your Pentagon buddy wants you to,' O'Donnell said. 'He could have just said the sixth track was great. Or amazing. But he said dynamically brilliant, which is the letters *d* and *b*. Like this Diana Bond woman's initials.'

CHAPTER EIGHT

Neagley insisted on making the call to Diana Bond alone. When they got back to the hotel she parked herself in a far corner of the lobby and did a whole lot of dialling and redialling. Then some serious talking. She came back twenty minutes later.

'Turns out she's not far away,' she said. 'She's up at Edwards Air Force Base for a few days. Some big presentation.'

O'Donnell said, 'That's why your guy said call her soonest.'

'What did she say?' Reacher asked.

'She's coming down here,' Neagley said. 'Just as soon as she can get away. Little Wing must be important.'

'Feel bad about the call?'

Neagley nodded. 'I feel bad about everything.'

They went up to her room and looked at maps and figured out Diana Bond's earliest possible arrival time. Edwards was about seventy miles, on the other side of the San Gabriel Mountains. A two-hour wait, minimum.

'I'm going for a walk,' Reacher said.

O'Donnell said, 'I'll come with you.'

They headed east on Sunset to where West Hollywood met Hollywood. It was early afternoon and Reacher felt the sun burning through his shaved hair. 'I should buy a hat,' he said.

'You should buy a better shirt,' O'Donnell said.

'Maybe I will.'

They saw a store, some kind of a popular chain, that sold cotton stuff, jeans, chinos and shirts. And baseball caps. They were brand new but looked like they had been worn and washed a thousand times already. Reacher picked one out and tried it on.

'What do you think?' he asked.

O'Donnell said. 'Find a mirror.'

'Doesn't matter what I see. You're the one laughing at how I look.'

'It's a nice hat.'

Reacher kept it on and moved across to a table with T-shirts and a mannequin torso wearing two of them, one showing underneath at the hem and the sleeves and the collar.

He picked two XXLs, took off the hat and carried the three items to the register. Refused a bag, bit off the tags and stripped off his shirt right there in the store, tossed it in the trash and put his new shirts on. Jammed the cap on his head and headed back to the street.

O'Donnell asked, 'What are you running from?'

'I'm not running from anything.'

'You could have kept the old shirt.'

'Slippery slope,' Reacher said. 'I carry a spare shirt, pretty soon I'm carrying spare pants. Then I'd need a suitcase. Next thing I know, I've got a house and a car and a savings plan and I'm filling out all kinds of forms.'

'People do that.'

'Not me.'

'So like I said, what are you running from?'

'From being like people, I guess. From being different than I used to be.'

'We're all different than we used to be.'

'We don't all have to like it.'

'I don't like it,' O'Donnell said. 'But I deal with it.'

Reacher nodded. 'You're doing great, Dave. I mean it. It's me that I worry about. I've been looking at you and Neagley and Karla and feeling like a loser.'

'Really? All that we've got that you don't is suitcases.'

'But what have I got that you don't?'

O'Donnell didn't answer.

WHEN THEY STEPPED through the hotel door, Curtis Mauney was waiting in the lobby. Still tired, still carrying his battered briefcase. He sat down and balanced it on his knees and asked, 'Who is Adrian Mount?'

Azhari Mahmoud, Adrian Mount, Alan Mason, Andrew MacBride, Anthony Matthews. The Syrian and his four aliases. Information Mauney didn't know they had. 'No idea,' Reacher said.

'You sure?'

'Pretty much.'

Mauney opened the briefcase and took out a sheet of paper. Handed it over. It was blurred and indistinct, like a fax of a copy of a copy of a fax. At the top it said *Department of Homeland Security*. It related to a booking Adrian Mount had for a flight three days ago. First class, one way, Heathrow to JFK, seat 2K, last departure of the evening. Booked through the British Airways website, although it was impossible to say exactly where in the world the mouse had been physically clicked.

Mauney said, 'I got the Vegas PD to check Sanchez and Orozco's office. This was stored in their fax machine's memory. It came in two weeks ago. The machine was out of paper. But we know Sanchez and Orozco weren't around two weeks ago. Therefore this must be a response to a request they made at least a week earlier. We think that they put a bunch of names on an unofficial watch list.'

'A bunch of names?'

'We found what we think is the original request. They had notes circulating in the mail, just like Franz.' From his case Mauney pulled a photocopy of a sheet of paper with Manuel Orozco's spidery handwriting all over it. *Adrian Mount, Alan Mason, Andrew MacBride, Anthony Matthews, check w. DHS for arrival.* Fast untidy scrawl.

Azhari Mahmoud's name wasn't there.

'The Department of Homeland Security,' Mauney said. 'You know how hard it is for a civilian to get cooperation out of DHS? Your pal Orozco must have called in a load of favours. I need to know why.'

'Casino business, maybe.'

'Possible. Although Vegas security doesn't necessarily worry if bad guys show up in New York.'

'Did this Adrian Mount guy actually arrive in New York?'

Mauney nodded. 'The immigration computer has him entering through Terminal Four. He checks in at a Madison Avenue hotel, then disappears. No further trace. But Alan Mason flies to Denver, Colorado.'

'And then?'

'We don't know yet. We're still checking.'

'But you think they're all the same guy?'

'Obviously the same. The initials are a dead giveaway.'

Reacher asked. 'So who is he?'

'I have no idea. We're working on getting the immigration photo. We started a watch list of our own. You ever hear of those names?'

'Not that I recall.'

'Did Orozco know anyone with those initials?'

'I haven't spoken to Orozco in ten years. I don't know.'

'No problem. I'm sorry for your loss.'

THE MAN in the blue suit in the blue Chrysler dialled his cellphone. 'They're back in the hotel,' he said. 'All four of them.'

'Are they getting close to us?' his boss asked.

'Gut feeling? Yes, I think they're getting close.'

'OK, it's time we made our move to take them down.'

THEY WENT UP to Dixon's room. No real reason. They were still dead-ended, but they had to be somewhere.

O'Donnell checked over the captured Hardballers, clean, oiled and fully loaded. Then he walked to Dixon's windows and asked, 'What have we got?'

It was a routine question from the past, a part of standard operating procedure. Reacher had always insisted on constant recaps, on combing through accumulated information in the light of what had come after. But this time nobody answered, except Dixon, who said, 'All we've got is four dead friends.' The room went quiet.

'Let's get dinner,' Neagley said. 'No point in us starving.'

Dinner. Reacher recalled the burger barn, twenty-four hours previously. The thick beef patties, the cold beer. The round table, the rotating conversation. One talker, three listeners.

One talker, three listeners. 'Mistake,' he said.

Neagley said, 'Eating is a mistake?'

'No, my mistake. I jumped to a false conclusion. Why can't we find Franz's client?'

'I don't know.'

'Because Franz didn't have a client. His was the first body found, so we just assumed he had to have been the prime mover. Like he was the talker and the other three were the listeners. But suppose he was a listener? Suppose this whole thing is basically Orozco's deal? For one of *his* clients? Or Sanchez's? If *they* needed help, who were they going to call?'

'Franz and Swan.'

'Exactly. We need to reverse the paradigm. Suppose Franz got a panic call from Orozco or Sanchez? Not a client, but he's got to help, no matter what.' Silence in the room.

Reacher said, 'Orozco contacted Homeland Security. It's more than Franz seems to have done. But let's not make the same mistake twice. It could have been Swan.'

'Swan wasn't working,' Dixon said.

'Could those numbers be something to do with casinos?' Neagley asked.

'Possibly,' Dixon said. 'They could be house-win percentages taking a hit after someone worked out a system.'

'What gets played nine or ten or twelve times a day. Cards?'

O'Donnell nodded. 'Six hundred and fifty winning hands at a hundred grand a time would get anyone's attention.'

'So maybe it's more than one guy. Maybe it's a cartel.'

Neagley said, 'We have to go to Vegas.'

Then Dixon's room phone rang. She answered it and handed the receiver to Reacher. 'Curtis Mauney,' she said.

Reacher took the phone. Mauney said: 'Andrew MacBride just got on a plane in Denver. He's heading for Las Vegas. I'm telling you as a courtesy. No independent action, remember?'

THEY DECIDED TO DRIVE to Vegas, not fly. No way could they take the Hardballers on a plane, anyway. And they had to assume that firepower would be necessary sooner or later. They headed east and fought through the tangle of clogged freeways until they found the 15. It would run them north through the mountains and all the way to Vegas.

It would also run them close to where they knew a helicopter had hovered at least twice, three thousand feet up, dead of night, its doors open. Reacher had made up his mind not to look, but he did. After the road brought them out of the hills he found himself looking west towards the flat, tan badlands. He saw O'Donnell doing the same thing. And Neagley. Dixon stared left for seconds at a time, her face creased against the setting sun and her lips clamped down at the corners.

THE DARK-HAIRED forty-year-old calling himself Andrew MacBride stepped out of the jetway inside the Las Vegas airport and the first thing he saw was a bank of slot machines. Bulky black and silver and gold boxes, with winking neon fascias. Maybe twenty of them. Each machine had a vinyl stool in front of it. Men and women, perhaps twelve of them, staring at the screens with a peculiar fatigued concentration.

Andrew MacBride decided to try his luck. He decided to designate the result as a harbinger of his future success. If he won everything would be fine.

He sat on a stool and took out a change purse. There weren't many quarters. They made satisfying metallic sounds as they fell through the slot. A red LED showed five credits. There was a large touchpad, worn and greasy from a million fingers. He pressed it, again and again.

The first four times, he lost. The fifth time, he won.

A muted bell rang and a quiet *whoop-whoop* siren sounded. A hundred quarters rattled down a chute and clattered into a metal dish near his knee.

THEY STOPPED for dinner in a roadside diner in Barstow. At night on the 15, Las Vegas was going to take a little over three hours. O'Donnell dozed in the back. Reacher stared out of the window. Neagley said, 'Damn, we forgot all about Diana Bond.'

'Doesn't matter now,' Dixon said.

'I should call her,' Neagley said. But she couldn't get a signal.

They arrived in Vegas at midnight. Reacher had been there before. In daylight, Las Vegas looked absurd. Inexplicable, trivial, tawdry, exposed. But at night with the lights full on it looked like a gorgeous fantasy. Dixon pulled in at one of the glittering palaces, and a swarm of valets and bellmen came at them. The lobby was full of tiles and pools and fountains and loud with the chatter of slot machines.

Neagley headed to the desk.

'Expensive,' Reacher said.

'But a possible short cut,' Neagley said back. 'Maybe they gave Orozco and Sanchez their security contract.'

Reacher nodded. The whole place dripped money, literally. The pools and the fountains in the desert spoke of breathtaking extravagance. The cash flow must have been immense. It had been quite something if Sanchez and Orozco had been safeguarding this kind of massive enterprise.

Neagley handed out the key cards and they arranged to freshen up and meet again in ten minutes to start work. It was after midnight, but in Vegas time had no relevance. There were famous clichés about the lack of windows and clocks in the casinos, and they were all true, as far as Reacher knew. There was nothing better than a tired guy who kept on losing all night.

Reacher's room was on the seventeenth floor. It was a dark concrete cube tricked out to look like a centuries-old salon in Venice. Altogether it was fairly unconvincing. Reacher had been to Venice, too. He opened his folding toothbrush and stood it upright in a glass in the bathroom. He splashed water on his face and went back down to look around.

Even in such an upmarket joint most of the ground-floor real estate was devoted to slot machines. Patient, tireless, microprocessor-controlled, they skimmed a small but relentless percentage off a torrent of cash. Plenty of people were winning, but slightly more were losing. There was very light security. He moved on to huge rooms in the back where roulette and poker and blackjack were being played. The way he understood it, roulette was really no different than a slot. Assuming the wheel was honest. He moved to the card games which were the only casino components he figured, where human intelligence could be truly engaged. And where crime came soon after. But major crime would need more than a player's input. A player with self discipline and a great memory and a rudimentary grasp of statistics could beat the odds. But beating the odds wasn't a crime. And beating the odds didn't earn a guy sixty-five million in a few months.

Still, there were plenty of cameras aimed at the players and dealers, some obvious, some small and discreet. There were men and women patrolling in evening wear, with earpieces and wrist microphones, like Secret Service agents. And others, in plain clothes. Reacher made five within a minute.

He threaded his way back to the lobby. Found Karla Dixon waiting by the fountains. She had showered and changed into a black trouser suit. Her hair was wet and slicked back. Her suit coat was buttoned and she had no blouse under it. She looked pretty good.

Then O'Donnell showed up. Same suit, different tie, maybe a fresh shirt. His shoes shone in the lights. Maybe he had found a polishing cloth in his bathroom. Neagley stepped out of the elevator, dressed the same as Dixon in a severe black suit.

'I called Diana Bond,' she said. 'She got there and waited an hour and went back again.'

'Was she pissed at us?' Reacher asked.

'She's worried. She doesn't like Little Wing's name out there.'

'Let's make a start,' O'Donnell said.

So they started at the concierge desk, where they asked to see the duty security manager. There was a long wait before the man showed up. He was about fifty years old, still trim in Italian shoes and a thousand-dollar suit. He said his name was Wright and shook hands all round.

They found a quiet corner. No chairs, of course. No comfortable place to sit away from the action. O'Donnell showed his DC PI licence and Dixon matched it with her licence. Neagley had a card from the FBI. Reacher produced nothing.

Wright said to Neagley, 'I was with the FBI, once upon a time.'

Reacher asked him, 'Did you know Manuel Orozco and Jorge Sanchez?'

'Did I?' Wright said. 'Or do I?'

'Did you,' Reacher said. 'Orozco's dead for sure, and we figure Sanchez is, too.'

'Dead when?'

'Three, four weeks ago.'

'Friends of yours?'

'From the army.'

'I'm very sorry,' Wright said. 'I knew them pretty well. Everyone in the business knew them.'

'Did you use them? Professionally?'

'Not here. We don't contract out. We're too big. Same with all the larger places. Everything's in-house.'

'So how did you know them?'

'Because the places they look after are like training camps. Someone gets a new idea, they don't try it out here. So we keep people like Orozco and Sanchez sweet, hook up once in a while, dinners, casual drinks.'

'Were they busy? Are you busy?'

'Like one-armed paperhangers.'

'You ever heard the name Azhari Mahmoud?'

'No. Who is he?'

'We don't know. But we think he's here under an alias. Somewhere in Vegas. Can you check hotel registrations?'

'I can check ours, obviously. And I can call round.'

'Try Andrew MacBride and Anthony Matthews.'

'Subtle.'

O'Donnell said, 'Sanchez had a piece of paper with a number written on it. Sixty-five million dollars. A hundred grand, times six hundred and fifty separate occasions, over a four-month period. Are those the kind of numbers you'd recognise as a rip-off?'

'What's that in a year? Almost two hundred million?'

'Hundred and ninety five,' Reacher said.

'Conceivable,' Wright said. 'We try to keep wastage below eight percent so we lose way more than two hundred million in a year. But two hundred million in one scam would be a hell of a large proportion. Unless it was something new, over and above. In which case you're starting to worry me.'

'It worried them,' Reacher said. 'We think it killed them.'

'It would be a very big deal,' Wright said. 'They'd need to recruit dealers and pit bosses and security people. They'd need to jinx cameras and erase tapes. Keep the cashiers quiet. It would be industrial-scale scamming.'

'It might have happened.'

'So why aren't the cops talking to me?'

'We're a little way ahead of them.'

'The Vegas PD? The Gaming Board? What does that mean?'

Reacher said nothing. Wright was quiet for a beat. Then he looked at each face in turn. 'Wait,' he said. 'Don't tell me. The army? You're the special investigators. Their old unit. They talked about it all the time.'

Reacher said, 'In which case you understand our interest.'

'If you find something, will you cut me in?'

'Earn it,' Reacher said.

'There's a girl,' Wright said. 'She works in some bar with a fire pit, near where the Riviera used to be. She's tight with Sanchez. She'll know more than I do.'

REACHER CHECKED with the concierge as to where the Riviera had been. He got directions to the cheap end of the Strip. They walked. It was a warm, dry desert night. The stars were out, on the far horizon, beyond the wash of the street lights. They turned into a mess of curving streets flanked by one-storey tan stucco motels, restaurants and bars. All had the same kind of signs, the same permanent low prices. They walked past five or six before they found a sign that said: *Fire Pit*.

The sign was outside a plain stucco shoe box short on windows. But inside it was definitely a Vegas bar. Five hundred people drinking, shouting, laughing, purple walls, dark red banquettes. The bar was long and curved into an S-shape round a sunken pit with a round fake fireplace. Jagged flames of orange silk swayed in beams of bright red light. Music played from hidden speakers. Waitresses in abbreviated outfits threaded through the crowds with trays held high.

'Lovely,' O'Donnell said.

'Call the taste police,' Dixon said.

They couldn't find the girl. Reacher asked at the bar for Jorge Sanchez's friend and a woman said she had gone home at midnight after a twelve-hour shift. She said the girl's name was Milena. For safety's sake Reacher asked two waitresses the same question. Nobody would tell him where home was.

They fought their way out to the sidewalk. Vegas was lit up and humming, but after the inside of the bar it felt as quiet as the cold, grey surface of the moon.

'Plan?' Dixon said.

'We get here at eleven thirty in the morning,' Reacher said.

'Until then?'

'Nothing. We take the rest of the night off.'

They walked back to the Strip four abreast on the sidewalk. Forty yards behind them a dark blue Chrysler sedan swerved across four lanes of traffic and stopped in a side street.

LAS VEGAS HAD more hotel rooms per square inch than any other place on the planet, but Azhari Mahmoud wasn't in any of them. He was in a house in a suburb three miles from the Strip, leased two years ago for an operation that had been planned but not executed.

Mahmoud was in the kitchen, with the Yellow Pages open on the counter, leafing through the truck-rental section, trying to figure out how big a U-Haul he was going to need.

THE STRIP had a permanent redevelopment tide which slopped back and forth like water in a bathtub. Once upon a time the Riviera had anchored the glamour end. Investment had raced down the street block by block, the stakes had been raised high and the Riviera had suddenly looked old and dowdy by comparison. So the investment had bounced back in the reverse direction. The result was a perpetually moving block-long construction site which separated the brand-new stuff that had just been built from the slightly older stuff that was just about to be demolished again. The new lanes were straight, but the old route looped through rubble. The city felt quiet and deserted there, and that was exactly where the man in the blue suit came up on foot behind his targets. Collectively, across the width of the sidewalk, they made a target maybe nine feet wide.

The man in the suit took his gun out of his pocket, a Daewoo DP51, unregistered and untraceable. Its magazine held thirteen 9mm Parabellums. It was being carried in what its owner's long training had taught him was the only safe-transport mode: chamber empty, safety on.

He dry-fired against the locked trigger and rehearsed the sequence. Biggest targets first, four shots, maybe three seconds, from twenty feet. Maximum traverse a little more than twenty degrees. A simple task.

He glanced all around. Clear. Looked behind. Clear.

He pushed the safety down, gripped the barrel in his left hand and racked the slide with his right. The first fat shell pushed neatly into the chamber.

There was a lot of urban ambient noise. Traffic on the Strip, rooftop condensers, the muted rumble of a hundred thousand people playing hard. But Reacher heard the rack of the slide twenty feet behind him. It was the kind of complex split-second sound he had trained himself never to miss.

His life and his history lacked many things. He had never known stability or comfort or convention. He had never counted on anything except unpredictability and danger. He took things exactly as they came, for exactly what they were. Therefore he heard the slide rack back and felt no disabling shock. It seemed entirely reasonable that he should be listening to a man preparing to shoot him in the back. There was just a purely mechanical problem, then there was reaction. He knew the first shot would be aimed at him. Or at O'Donnell.

Better safe than sorry.

He used his right arm and shoved O'Donnell hard and set him sprawling into Dixon, then fell away in the opposite direction and crashed into Neagley. As he was going down he heard the gun fire and felt the bullet pass through the void of empty air where he had been a split second before.

He had his hand on his Hardballer before he hit the sidewalk, calculating trajectories. The gun had two safeties. Before he had either one set to fire he had decided not to shoot. Not immediately, anyway.

He had fallen on top of Neagley towards the inside edge of the sidewalk. Their attacker was in the centre of the sidewalk. Any angle vectoring from the inside of the sidewalk through the centre would launch a bullet out towards the roadway. If he missed the guy he could hit a passing car. Even if he hit their attacker, he could still hit a passing car. A jacketed .45 could go right through flesh and bone.

He made a split-second decision to wait for O'Donnell. He had fallen towards the kerb. His line of sight was inward. A miss or a through-and-through would do no harm at all.

Reacher twisted as he hit the ground. He was in that zone where his mind was fast but the physical world was slow. He saw O'Donnell's left arm moving with painful slowness. Saw his thumb dropping the Hardballer's safety lever.

Their attacker fired again, into empty air where O'Donnell's back had been. Reacher saw O'Donnell's gun move up, up, up. Saw O'Donnell fire.

Too low, Reacher thought. *That's a leg wound at best.*

But a leg wound from a high-velocity jacketed .45 was not a pretty thing. The guy took the slug in the lower thigh and his femur exploded. Immense trauma. Instant catastrophic blood loss.

The guy stayed vertical but his gun hand dropped and O'Donnell was instantly on his feet. He covered the twenty feet full tilt and slammed the guy with his knuckles.

Game over, right there.

CHAPTER NINE

Reacher helped Dixon up. Neagley got up on her own. O'Donnell was scooting round the big welling puddle of blood. A human heart was a powerful pump and this guy's femoral artery was wide open.

Reacher put a finger on the pulse in his neck and felt an irregular thready beat. The guy was turning blue. 'He's on the way out,' Reacher said.

He grabbed the guy's collar and pulled him backwards. He checked through his pockets. No wallet, no ID, no nothing. Just car keys and a remote clicker, on a plain steel ring.

'Nobody shot us in LA,' Dixon said. 'We must be getting close.'

Reacher broke down a section of construction fence and hauled the guy through the gap past piles of gravel until he found a wide trench built up with plywood formwork. The trench was about eight feet deep. Reacher rolled the guy in.

'Good shooting, Dave,' Dixon said.

'Left-handed, too,' O'Donnell said. 'I was falling on my right arm.'

'Outstanding,' Reacher said.

'What did you hear?'

'The slide. It's an evolution thing. Like a predator stepping on a twig.'

'So there's an advantage in being closer to the cavemen than the rest of us.'

'You bet there is.' Reacher looked down. 'I think I recognise him. I think I saw the suit. I can't remember where. Find shovels, we need to cover him with gravel.'

Between them they had to make several trips to the gravel pile before the guy was adequately hidden. Neagley found a standpipe and unrolled a hose and rinsed the blood into the gutter, then followed the others out backwards and hosed away their footprints. Reacher pulled the fence back into shape. He knew there was nothing that would attract anyone's attention in the short term. For a few hours, at least.

'OK,' he said. '*Now* we take the rest of the night off.'

They dusted themselves down and resumed their walk down the Strip.

Wright was waiting for them in the hotel lobby. For a Vegas guy he didn't have a great poker face.

He hurried them over to the same quiet corner of the lobby they had used before. 'Azhari Mahmoud isn't in any Las Vegas hotel,' he said. 'Also negative on Andrew MacBride and Anthony Matthews.'

Reacher nodded. 'Thanks for checking,' he said.

'And I made a few panic calls to my opposite numbers, and you know what? You guys are completely full of it. We ran emergency cash-flow audits. No way is this town down sixty-five million dollars. It just isn't happening. I'm going to send you my Prozac bill. I practically overdosed tonight.'

Wright walked off and they found a bar off the lobby and bought each other beers and sat in a line in front of four idle slots. Reacher's was simulating a big jackpot win, over and over.

Dixon said, 'Wright already figured it would have to be industrial-scale scamming. It's not much more of a leap to imagine that apparent cash flow could be massaged. They could have installed a phoney program that makes everything look kosher for as long as they need it to.'

Reacher asked. 'When would they find out?'

'When they do their books at the end of the financial year.'

'How would Sanchez and Orozco find that out?'

'Maybe they tapped in lower down the food chain.'

'Who would need to be involved?'

'Key people. Like Wright himself.'

O'Donnell said, 'We talked to him and a half-hour later someone was trying to shoot us in the back.'

'Should we move hotels?' Dixon said.

'No point. Wright will have buddies all over town,' Reacher said. 'Just lock your door.'

REACHER FOLLOWED his own advice when he got back to his room. He clicked the security lever and put the chain on. He put the Hardballer in the bedside drawer. Put his clothes under the mattress to press and took a long, hot shower. Then he started thinking about Karla Dixon.

She was alone. Maybe she didn't like that. Maybe she would appreciate a little safety in numbers.

He wrapped a towel round his waist and padded over to the phone. But before he got to it there was a knock at his door. He changed course, undid the chain and the extra lock. Opened the door.

Karla Dixon. Black suit, no shirt. 'Can I come in?' she said.

'I was just about to call you,' Reacher said.

'Why?'

'Lonely.'

'You?'

'Me for sure. You, I hoped.'

'So can I come in?'

He held the door wide. Within a minute he discovered a shirt wasn't the only thing she wasn't wearing under the suit.

AN HOUR AFTER BREAKFAST they were back on the Strip, heading for the bar with the fire pit. Vegas in the morning looked flat and small under the hard desert sun. This time they knew exactly where they were going and found a short cut. The bar wasn't open yet. They sat on a low wall and waited.

By the time the clock in Reacher's head hit twenty to twelve people started showing up for work. As they came down the street in loose knots, Reacher asked all the women if they were called Milena. They all said no. Then the sidewalk went quiet again.

The clock in Reacher's head ticked round. One minute to twelve. Neagley checked her watch. 'Worried yet?' she asked.

'No,' Reacher said, because beyond her shoulder he had seen a girl he knew had to be the one. She was short and slim and dark, dressed in low-rider blue jeans and a short white T-shirt. She had a winking jewel in her navel and long, jet-black hair which framed a pretty face.

She looked unhappy.

Reacher got up when she was ten feet away and said, 'Milena?' Accosted by a giant of a stranger, she slowed with sudden wariness and glanced at the bar door.

Reacher said, 'We're friends of Jorge's.'

She looked at him, and then at the others, and then back at him. Some kind of slow realisation dawned on her face. 'You're from the army,' she said. 'He told me you'd come.'

'When?'

'All the time. He said if he ever had trouble, you'd show up.'

'And here we are. Where can we talk?'

'Just let me tell them I'm going to be late today.' She smiled a little shyly and headed inside the bar. Came out again with her shoulders straighter.

'Let me guess,' she said. She turned to Neagley. 'You must be Neagley.' Then she moved on to Dixon and said, 'Which makes you Karla.' She turned to Reacher and O'Donnell and said, 'Reacher and O'Donnell, right? The big one and the handsome one.' O'Donnell smiled at her.

Reacher said, 'We wanted to talk to you about Jorge.'

Milena took a breath and swallowed. 'He's dead, isn't he?'

'Probably,' Reacher said. 'We know Manuel Orozco is.'

Milena said, 'No.'

'I'm sorry,' Reacher said. 'Where can we go to talk?'

'We should go to Jorge's place,' Milena said. 'You should see it. It was wrecked. I cleaned it up a little. We can walk.'

They walked back down the Strip, all five of them. Milena asked twice more whether Sanchez was dead. Both times Reacher answered, 'Probably.'

'But you don't know for sure?'

'His body hasn't been found.'

'But Orozco's has?'

'Yes. We saw it. And Franz is dead. Swan too, probably.'

'But not Jorge for sure?'

'Not for sure. But probably.'

'OK.' She walked on, refusing to give up hope. They passed the high-end hotels, then they saw apartment buildings. Milena stopped under an awning that led to the lobby of a building. 'This is it,' she said. 'I have a key.'

A doorman greeted her in the lobby. She led them to the elevator. They went up to the tenth floor and stopped outside a door. She used her key.

Inside, the apartment was two bedrooms, a living room, a kitchen. Plain decor, mostly white. A man's place, simple, unadorned.

It was a real mess.

It had been through the same kind of trauma as Calvin Franz's office. The walls and the floor and the ceiling were solid concrete, but all the furniture was ripped and torn apart. Books and papers had been dumped. A TV set and stereo equipment had been smashed. CDs were littered everywhere. The kitchen had been almost demolished.

Milena's cleaning up had been limited to piling some of the debris. Apart from that, there hadn't been much she could do.

Reacher found the kitchen trash, where Curtis Mauney said the crumpled napkin had been found. The pail had been torn off its mounting under the sink and booted across the room. 'This was more about anger than efficiency,' he said.

'I agree,' Neagley said.

Reacher moved on to the master bedroom. The bed was wrecked. The mattress had been destroyed. The closet rails had been torn down, the shelves smashed. There was nothing left of Sanchez in his apartment.

Reacher asked, 'When did you last see Jorge?'

'We had dinner here his last night in Vegas,' Milena said. 'Chinese take-out. It was just the two of us.'

'He wrote something on a napkin. Because someone called him?'

Milena nodded.

'Who called him?'

Milena said, 'Calvin Franz.'

Milena was looking shaky so Reacher used his forearm to clear shards of broken china off the kitchen countertop. She boosted herself up and sat, palms trapped under her knees.

Reacher said, 'We need to know what Jorge was working on. We need to know what caused all this trouble. What was on his mind?'

'Business was slow. That was on his mind. Years ago, they had a lot of contracts. But the big places all set up in-house operations once they reach a certain size.'

'We met a guy at our hotel who said Jorge was still busy.'

Milena smiled. 'Jorge put a brave face on it. Manuel Orozco, too. They were too proud to beg.'

'So what are you saying? They were going down the tubes?'

'Fast. They did a bit of muscle work here and there. Doorman at some of the clubs, running cheats out of town.'

'Did you see what Jorge wrote on the napkin?'

'Of course. I cleared dinner away. He wrote numbers.'

'What did they mean?'

'I don't know. But he was very worried about them. He called Manuel Orozco right away. Orozco was worried too.'

'How did it all start? Who was their client?'

Milena looked straight at him. 'You're not listening to me,' she said. 'They didn't really have clients any more.'

'Someone must have come to them with a problem. Jorge didn't say?'

'No. One day they were sitting around, the next they were busy. Orozco's wife might know.'

The wrecked apartment went very quiet. 'Orozco was married?'

Milena nodded. 'They have three children.'

Reacher looked at Neagley and asked, 'Why didn't we know that? We told Mauney the next of kin was the sister.'

'I don't know everything,' Neagley said.

MILENA LED THEM another quarter of a mile away from the centre of town to Orozco's apartment house. It was very similar to Sanchez's. Same age, same style. Reacher asked, 'What is Mrs Orozco's name?'

'Tammy,' Milena said. 'We're going to have to wake her up. She works nights in the casinos, gets the children on the bus and goes right to bed.'

But it was the doorman who woke her up. He called upstairs on the house phone. There was a long wait, then the doorman announced their names, and there was another long wait. 'Please go on up,' the doorman said.

They rode the elevator to the eighth floor. A door was standing open. Milena led them inside.

Tammy Orozco was a small hunched figure on a sofa. Wild black hair, pale skin, a patterned housecoat. She ignored Reacher and O'Donnell and Dixon and Neagley completely. She looked directly at Milena and said, 'Manuel is dead, isn't he?'

Milena sat beside her. 'These guys say so. I'm very sorry.'

Tammy asked, 'Jorge too?'

Milena said, 'We don't know yet.'

The two women hugged and cried. Reacher knew to wait it out. The apartment was larger than Sanchez's. The whole place was battered and untidy, maybe because it had been tossed three weeks ago. Reacher guessed Orozco's children were young, from the toys and clothing he saw lying around.

Eventually Tammy Orozco looked up. 'How did it happen?'

Reacher said, 'The police have all the details.'

'Did he suffer?'

'It was instantaneous,' Reacher said, as he had been trained to long ago. All service KIAs were said to have been killed instantly, unless it could be proven otherwise. And in Orozco's case it was technically true. After the mistreatment and the starvation and the thirst and the helicopter ride and the writhing, screaming, twenty-second free fall.

'Why did it happen?' Tammy asked.

'That's what we're trying to find out. It's why we're here.'

'But there are no answers here.'

'There must be,' Reacher said. 'Someone must have come to them with a problem, at their office, or out in one of the casinos.'

'That didn't happen,' Tammy said.

'Then they stumbled over the problem on their own.'

There was a long silence. 'This was nothing to do with Vegas.'

'It wasn't?'

'They got a call for help, out of the blue. That's how it started. From one of you guys in California. One of their precious old army buddies.'

AZHARI MAHMOUD dropped Andrew MacBride's passport in a Dumpster and became Anthony Matthews on his way to the U-Haul depot. He had a wad of active credit cards and a valid driver's licence in that name.

He had decided to rent a medium-size truck. Clerks remembered people who demanded the biggest or the smallest of anything. And a medium truck would do the job. He knew that volume was calculated by multiplying height by width by length, therefore a pile containing six hundred and fifty boxes could be constructed by stacking them ten wide and thirteen deep and five high. He'd stack them on their edges. It would all work out. He was still carrying the hundred quarters he had won in the airport.

THEY GAVE their condolences and Curtis Mauney's name to Tammy Orozco and left her. Then they walked Milena back to the bar. The sun was high. She had a living to earn and was already three hours down on the day.

'Tammy's angry,' Milena said. 'I'm sorry about that.'

'It's to be expected,' Reacher said.

'She was asleep when the bad guys came to search. They hit her on the head. She was unconscious for a week. She doesn't remember anything. Now she blames whoever called for her troubles.'

'Understandable,' Reacher said.

'But I don't blame you,' Milena said. 'It wasn't any of you that called.' She ducked inside the bar without looking back. The door closed behind her.

Reacher sat down on the wall where they had waited that morning. 'I'm sorry, people. We just wasted a lot of time,' he said. 'Neagley should take over. I'm losing my touch.'

'Mahmoud came here,' Dixon said. 'Not LA.'

'He probably made a connection. He's probably in LA now. He's cautious, whoever he is. He lays false trails.'

'We were attacked here,' Dixon said. 'Makes no sense.'

Reacher heard a siren on the Strip. A cop car, moving fast. He glanced towards the construction zone, shading his eyes and watching the short length of the Strip he could see. If some construction foreman had showed up for work and found something, there would be a whole convoy.

He waited. No more sirens. Just a routine traffic stop, maybe. He took one step to widen his view, to be certain. Saw a wink of blue beyond the corner of a grocery store. A car, parked in the sun.

Dark blue paint.

He said, 'I know where I saw that guy before.'

THEY STOOD ROUND the Chrysler at a cautious distance. A 300C, dark blue, California plates, locked up and cold. Reacher took the keys and pressed the remote button. The lights flashed and the doors unlocked with a *thunk*.

'It was behind the Chateau Marmont,' he said. 'That guy's suit matched the sheet metal exactly. I took it for a car service with a gimmick.'

'The others told them we would come,' O'Donnell said. 'So they sent the guy to take us out. He spotted us on the sidewalk, I guess, just after he hit town. He got lucky.'

'May all our enemies have the same good fortune,' Reacher said. He opened the driver's door, slid in and stretched a long arm over to the glove box. A wallet and a cellphone were all that was in there. The wallet had a wad of cash in the money clip. More than seven hundred dollars. Reacher took it all. 'That's two more weeks before I need to find a job,' he said.

He turned to the credit-card section. There was a current California driver's licence and two Visas, an Amex and a MasterCard, all made out to a guy by the name of Saropian. The address on the licence had a Los Angeles street name and zip. He dropped the wallet on the passenger seat.

The cellphone was small and silver. Reacher handed it to Neagley, who scrolled through menus and selected options. 'All the calls in and out are to and from the same number. A 310 area code. Los Angeles.'

'A grunt calling his boss and vice versa. Could your guy in Chicago get a name and address for the boss?'

'Eventually.'

'Get him started on it. The licence plate on this car, too.'

Neagley used her own cell and called her office. Then she handed the dead guy's phone back to Reacher. He scrolled through the call log to the last call made and pressed the green button, cupped the phone to his ear and waited. He had never owned a cellphone but he knew how they were used.

The phone was answered in a real hurry. A voice said, 'Where the hell have you been?' The voice was deep. A man, not young. Not small. Behind the exasperation and the urgency there was a West Coast accent, professional. Reacher listened hard for background sounds, but there were none.

The voice said, 'Hello? Where the hell are you? What's happening?'

'Who's this?' Reacher asked, like he had every right to know. Like he had gotten an accidental wrong number.

But the guy didn't bite. He had seen the caller ID. 'No, who are you?'

Reacher paused a beat. 'Your boy failed last night. He's dead and buried. Now we're coming for you.'

There was a long silence. Then the voice said, 'Reacher?'

'You know my name. Doesn't seem fair I don't know yours.'

'Nobody ever said life was fair.'

'Enjoy what's left of it. You've got about two days, max.'

'You're nowhere.'

'Look out of your window.'

Reacher heard the rustle of jacket tails, the oiled grind of a swivel chair. An office. 'You're nowhere,' the voice said again.

'We'll see you soon. We're going to take a helicopter ride together. Just like you did before. My friends were reluctant, presumably. But you'll be begging to jump out.'

Reacher closed the phone. 'First impressions?' Neagley asked.

'An executive,' Reacher said. 'A solo office with a window and a closed door. And he didn't seem too worried that we have his phone number.'

'So what now?'

'We head back to LA. We should never have left. We need to talk to Swan's old boss, so set up the thing with Diana Bond again. We need a bargaining chip.'

THEY STOLE THE CHRYSLER. Reacher drove it round to the hotel and waited in the drop-off lane while the others went to pack. He quite liked the car. It was quiet and powerful. It was square and bluff and as subtle as a hammer. His kind of machine.

Dixon came out of the lobby first, trailing a bellboy carrying her luggage. Then came Neagley and O'Donnell together.

'We got a hit on the licence plate,' Neagley said. 'A shell corporation called Walter at a downtown LA mail drop.'

'Cute,' Reacher said. 'Walter for Walter Chrysler. I bet the phone comes back to a corporation called Alexander, for Graham Bell.'

Dixon said she would drive O'Donnell back in her rental. So Reacher popped the Chrysler's trunk and Neagley heaved her bags in and then slid in beside him.

'Where are we holing up?' Dixon asked, through the window.

'Somewhere different,' Reacher said. 'We need a place they won't think to look. Let's try the Dunes on Sunset.'

'What is that?'

'A motel. My kind of place.'

'How bad is it?'

'It's fine. It has beds and doors that lock.'

REACHER AND NEAGLEY took off first. Traffic was slow out of town and then the 15 emptied and Reacher settled in for the cruise across the desert. Neagley spent the first thirty minutes playing phone tag round Edwards Air Force Base before her cell coverage failed. Reacher concentrated on the road. He was an adequate driver, but not great. He had learned in the army and had never held a civilian licence. Neagley finished her calls and fidgeted with impatience. Kept glancing over at the speedometer.

'Drive it like you stole it,' she said. 'Which you did.'

So he accelerated a little. Started passing people, including a medium-sized U-Haul truck lumbering west in the right lane.

Barstow and the diner they had used before, Victorville, Lake Arrowhead. Then the mountains reared in front of them. They passed through an active cell area and Neagley's phone rang. Diana Bond, all set to leave Edwards at a moment's notice. Reacher said, 'Tell her to meet us at that Denny's on Sunset.'

Neagley arranged the rendezvous. He kicked the transmission down and climbed onto Mount San Antonio's first low slopes. Less than an hour later they were checking in at the Dunes Motel.

The Dunes was the kind of place where guests were required to leave a security deposit for the TV remote. Reacher paid cash from his stolen wad for all four rooms, which got round the necessity for ID. They parked the cars out of sight and regrouped in a dark, battered lounge, as anonymous as four people could get in Los Angeles County. Reacher's kind of place.

THEY WALKED a short stretch of Sunset and stepped into the Denny's neon lobby and found a tall blonde woman waiting for them. She was dressed all in black. Serious East Coast style, seriously out of place in a Denny's on the West Coast. She was slim, attractive, somewhere in her late thirties.

She looked a little irritated and a little worried.

Neagley introduced her all round. 'This is Diana Bond. From Washington DC via Edwards Air Force Base.'

They led her through the shabby restaurant and found a table in the back and ordered coffee. The waitress came back with five heavy mugs and a flask, and poured. They each took a preliminary sip, in silence. Then Diana Bond said, 'I could have you all arrested.'

'I'm kind of surprised you haven't,' Reacher said.

Bond said, 'One call to the Defense Intelligence Agency would have done it. But I'm trying to be civilised. I really would urge you not to pursue this. I'm appealing to your patriotism. This is a question of national security.'

Reacher said. 'Between the four of us here we've got sixty years in uniform. How many have you got?'

'None.'

'How many has your boss got?'

'None.'

'Then you're not qualified about patriotism and national security, OK?'

'Why on earth do you need to know about Little Wing?'

'We had a friend who worked for New Age. We're trying to complete his obituary.'

'I'm very sorry. But again, I appeal to you not to press this.'

'No deal.'

Diana Bond paused a long moment. 'I'll trade,' she said. 'I'll give you outline details, and in return you swear on those sixty years in uniform that they'll go no further.'

'Deal.'

'And after I talk this one time, I never hear from you again.'

'Deal.'

Another long pause. Like Bond was wrestling with her conscience. 'Little Wing is a new type of torpedo,' she said. 'For the Navy's Pacific submarine fleet. It's fairly conventional apart from an enhanced control capability.'

Reacher smiled. 'Good try, but we don't believe you. New Age was a clean-sheet start up, and if they were working for the Navy they'd have built in San Diego or Connecticut or Newport News, Virginia. The closest places to East LA are Air Force places, including Edwards, and the name is Little Wing, so it's an airborne device.'

Diana Bond shrugged. 'I had to try,' she said.

Reacher said, 'Try again.'

Another pause. 'It's an infantry weapon. Army, not Air Force. New Age is in East LA to be near Fort Irwin. It's a man-portable shoulder-launched surface-to-air missile. The next generation.'

'What does it do?'

Diana Bond shook her head. 'I can't tell you that.'

'You'll have to. Or your boss goes down.'

'That's not fair.'

'Compared to what?'

'All I'll say is that it's a revolutionary advance.'

'What does it do?'

'You're not going to call the newspapers. You'd be selling your country out.'

'Try us.'

'I don't believe this.'

'Suck it up. Or your boss needs a new job tomorrow.'

'The newspapers wouldn't publish.'

'Dream on.'

Bond was quiet for a minute more. 'It's complicated,' she said. 'You know the Stinger? The current generation?'

Reacher nodded. 'I've seen them in action. We all have. They chase the heat signature of jet exhaust.'

'But from below. They have to climb and manoeuvre at the same time. Which makes them relatively slow and cumbersome. They show up on downward-looking radar. And they're vulnerable to countermeasures, like decoy flares. Little Wing completely ignores its target on the way up. It does all its work on the way down.'

'I see,' Reacher said.

Bond nodded. 'Going up, it's very, very fast. It reaches about eighty thousand feet and then it slows, stops and topples. Then the electronics switch on and it starts hunting its target. It has boosters to manoeuvre with and because gravity is doing most of the work the manoeuvring can be incredibly precise.'

'It falls on its prey from above, like a hawk.'

Bond nodded again. 'At unbelievable speed. Way supersonic. It can't miss. And it can't be stopped. That's why this is so sensitive. We've got about a two-year window in which our surface-to-air capability will be completely unbeatable. Maybe longer.'

'The speed will make countermeasures difficult.'

'Almost impossible,' Bond said. 'Human reaction times will be too slow, so defences will have to automated. Potentially it will be chaos. Civilian airlines will want protection because of terrorism worries, but the skies above civilian airports are thick with stacked planes. They'd have to turn off their protection for take-off and landing, which makes them totally vulnerable just when they can't afford to be.'

'But Little Wing isn't working well,' O'Donnell said.

'The prototypes were fine,' Bond said. 'The beta testing was excellent. But they ran into problems with production.'

'Rockets or electronics or both?'

'Electronics. The rocket technology is more than forty years old. They do the rocket production in their sleep up in Denver. It's the electronics packs that are giving them problems down here in LA. They haven't even started mass production. Their bench assembly is screwed up.'

Reacher nodded and said nothing. He stared out of the window for a moment and then took a stack of napkins out of the dispenser and butted them into a neat pile. Weighted them down with the sugar container. The restaurant had pretty much emptied out. There were two guys in separate booths at the end of the room.

'So Little Wing is the same old story,' O'Donnell said. 'A Pentagon pipe dream that does nothing but burn dollars.'

Diana Bond said, 'It wasn't supposed to be like that.'

'It never is.'

'It's not a total failure. Some units work. It will be perfected eventually. You know, Little Wing could take out Air Force One without breaking a sweat.'

'Bring it on,' O'Donnell said. 'Easier than voting.'

'Read the Patriot Act. You could be arrested for even thinking that.'

'Jails aren't big enough,' O'Donnell said.

DIANA BOND LEFT and Reacher neatened his stack of napkins and placed the sugar container on top of it.

He sat in silence for a moment, staring out of the window. Then he moved suddenly and pointed at the sugar container and asked Neagley, 'You know what that is?'

'Sugar,' she said.

'No, it's a paperweight. Who carries a gun with the chamber empty?'

'Someone trained that way.'

'Like a cop. Or an ex-cop. Ex-LAPD, maybe. The dragon lady at New Age lied to us. People take notes, they doodle. There are no completely paperless environments.'

O'Donnell said, 'Things might have changed since you last held a job.'

'She told us Swan used his piece of the Berlin Wall as a paperweight. It's hard to use a paperweight in a completely paperless environment, isn't it?'

O'Donnell said, 'It could have been a figure of speech. Paperweight, desk ornament, is there a difference?'

'First time we were there, we had to wait to get in the lot.'

Neagley nodded. 'There was a truck coming out of the gate.'

'What kind of a truck?' Reacher asked.

'A photocopier truck. Repair or delivery.'

'Kind of hard to use a photocopier in a paperless environment. If she lied about that, she lied about a whole bunch of stuff.'

Nobody spoke.

Reacher said, 'New Age's director of security is ex-LAPD. I bet his foot soldiers are, too. Safeties on, chambers empty.'

Nobody spoke.

Reacher said, 'Call Diana Bond. Get her back here now.'

'She's only just left,' Neagley said.

'She can turn round. Tell her if she doesn't there'll be a whole lot more than her boss's name in the newspaper.'

DIANA BOND was angry. 'We had a deal,' she said, standing beside the table. 'I talk to you one time, you leave me alone.'

'Six more questions,' Reacher said. 'Then we leave you alone. This is important.'

'Go to hell. It's not important to me.'

'You could have kept driving. You could have called the DIA. But you didn't. So quit pretending. You're going to answer.'

Silence in the room. Bond sat down.

'First question.' Reacher said. 'Does New Age have a rival? A competitor somewhere with similar technology?'

Bond said. 'No. New Age's proposition was unique.'

'OK. Does the government really want Little Wing to work without defence capabilities in place? Suppose it's captured and copied?'

'We would never do anything if we thought like that. The Manhattan Project, supersonic fighters, everything.'

'OK. Now tell me about New Age's bench assembly.'

'Is this the third question?'

'Yes. Tell me what it is, basically.'

'It's assembled by hand. Women at laboratory benches using magnifying glasses and soldering irons. Averaging a dozen units a day, six days a week.'

'When did they start bench assembly?'

'They started about seven months ago.'

'How did it go?'

'Is this the fifth question?'

'No, it's a follow-up.'

'It went fine for three months. They hit their targets.'

'Six days a week, right?'

'Yes. After assembly the units are tested. More and more of them weren't working.'

'Who tests them?'

'They have a quality-control director, the original development engineer. At this stage he's the only one who knows how they're supposed to work.'

'What happens to the rejects?'

'They get destroyed. Now I really have to go.'

'Last question,' Reacher said. 'Did you cut their funding?'

'Are you nuts? We have to make this thing work.'

DIANA BOND LEFT for the second time and O'Donnell said, 'We should celebrate. We know what happened now.'

'Should we?' Reacher said. 'Lay it out and see for yourself.'

'OK, Swan was investigating his own company. He was checking why the success rate fell away so badly after three months. He was worried about insider involvement, therefore he recruited Franz and Sanchez and Orozco. Who else would he trust?'

'And?'

'First they analysed the production figures. Then they ruled out sabotage. New Age had no rivals, what else was there? They figured the quality-control guy had falsely condemned six hundred and fifty working units and the firm was booking them in as destroyed but actually selling them out of the back door for a hundred grand a piece to Azhari Mahmoud, a.k.a. whoever.'

'And?'

'They confronted New Age prematurely and got killed for it. The firm cooked up a story and the dragon lady fed it to you.'

'So now we should celebrate?'

'We know what happened. We always used to celebrate.'

Reacher said nothing.

'It's a home run,' O'Donnell said. 'Isn't it? And you know what? I think we already talked to Swan's old boss. On that cellphone? That was New Age's director of security.'

'Probably.'

'So what's the problem?'

'You said you wanted to piss on their ancestors' graves.'

'And I will.'

'You won't,' Reacher said. 'And neither will I, or any of us.'

'They're right here in town. They're sitting ducks.'

'They sold working electronics packs out of the back door. Which has implications. Somebody buys the electronics here, they're buying the rockets and launch tubes in Colorado. That's what we've got to face. Some guy called Azhari Mahmoud now owns six hundred and fifty latest-generation SAMs and we can guess what he wants them for. We have to tell someone, folks.'

Nobody spoke.

'And a thin minute after we drop that dime, we're buried in federal agents. We won't be able to cross the street without permission, let alone go get these guys. They'll get lawyers and eat three squares a day for ten years while they run through appeals.'

Nobody spoke.

'So that's why we can't celebrate. They messed with the special investigators and we can't lay a glove on them.'

CHAPTER TEN

Reacher didn't sleep a wink that night. He lay awake, hour after hour. His eyes were jammed wide open but fevered images flooded him. Calvin Franz, talking, laughing, full of drive and sympathy. Jorge Sanchez, the narrowed eyes, the hint of a smile, the gold tooth. Tony Swan, short, wide, sincere, decent. Manuel Orozco, the absurd tattoo, the jokes.

Friends all. Friends unavenged. Friends abandoned.

Then others swam into sight. Angela Franz, carefully dressed, eyes wide with panic. The boy Charlie, rocking in his little wooden chair. Milena, slipping into the darkness of the bar. Tammy Orozco on her sofa. Even Swan's mailbox was there, blinding in the Santa Ana light.

Reacher gave it up at five in the morning and got dressed and went out for a walk. He turned west on Sunset and stamped his way through a whole angry mile, hoping against hope that he could snarl and yell at someone in his way, but the sidewalks were deserted. Nobody walked in LA, especially not at five in the morning near a giant in an obvious rage.

Up ahead he saw a vacant corner lot fenced with wire. At a bus bench in the side street was a small crowd of day labourers, waiting for work, tiny brown men with tired, stoic faces. They were drinking coffee from a mission cart outside some kind of a community centre. Reacher paid a hundred stolen dollars for a cup. He said it was a donation.

The coffee was good. He sipped it slowly and leaned on the fence. The wire gave slightly and supported his bulk like a trampoline. He floated there, not quite upright, coffee in his mouth, fog in his brain. Then the fog cleared, and he started thinking.

About Neagley, and her mysterious contact at the Pentagon.

He owes me, she had said. *Bigger than you could imagine.*

By the time he finished the coffee and tossed the cup he had a faint glimmer of new hope, and the outline of a new plan. Odds of success, about fifty-fifty. Better than roulette.

He was back at the motel by six. He couldn't raise the others. No answer from their rooms. So he headed on down Sunset and found them in Denny's. He slid into the unoccupied seat and ordered coffee, pancakes, bacon, sausage, eggs, toast.

'You're hungry,' Dixon said. 'Where were you?'

'Walking.'

'Didn't sleep?'

'Not even close.'

The others were picking at their food. They looked tired and dispirited. O'Donnell asked, 'When do we drop the dime?'

Reacher said. 'Maybe we don't.'

Nobody spoke.

'Ground rules,' Reacher said. 'If Mahmoud has got the missiles, this thing is bigger than we are. We have to suck it up and move on. Either he wants to turn the whole Middle East into a no-fly zone, or he's going to make the Twin Towers look like a day at the beach. We're looking at thousands of KIA. Maybe tens of thousands. Those numbers trump any interest of ours. Agreed?'

Dixon and Neagley nodded and looked away.

'We have to assume he has the missiles,' O'Donnell said.

'No. We have to assume he's either collected the rockets first, or the electronics. It's fifty-fifty. He's got to have both before we drop the dime.'

'How do we find out?'

'Neagley hits up her Pentagon guy. She calls in whatever markers she's holding. He organises some kind of audit out in Colorado. If anything is missing up there, then it's game over for us. But if everything is accounted for, then it's game on.'

Neagley checked her watch. Just after six in the west, just after nine in the east. She took out her phone and dialled.

NEAGLEY'S BUDDY wasn't dumb. He insisted on calling back and was smart enough to realise that any payphone within a mile radius of the Pentagon would be continuously monitored. So there was a whole hour's delay while he got himself across town to a wall phone outside a New York Avenue bodega. Then the fun began.

Neagley told him what she wanted. He gave her all kinds of reasons why it wasn't possible. One by one, she started calling in heavy-duty favours owed her. Reacher felt a certain amount of sympathy for the guy. Neagley suggested Army CID should roll up unannounced and match the books with inventory. He asked for a week. Neagley gave him four hours. Four hours later Neagley had news.

The news was that New Age had no physical plant in Colorado, just an office, and contracted out their raw missile production to a Denver aerospace manufacturer whose Little Wing assemblies an army CID officer had counted, and his final tally was precisely what the books said it should be. Except that six hundred and fifty units currently stored in a separate secure warehouse were awaiting transport to a Nevada facility to be decommissioned and destroyed.

'They're junking what's left of the Mark Ones,' Neagley said. 'Current production is specified as Mark Two. Mark Twos have a small fluorescent arrow painted on to make loading in the dark easier.'

'That's the only difference?' O'Donnell asked.

'Yes. It's a scam. But it's a way of making the paperwork look legal when Mahmoud's people drive them through the factory gate.'

Reacher nodded. He'd seen the Pentagon junk stuff for less. 'How do the electronics packs fit on?'

'In,' Neagley said. 'There's an access port in the side. Then there's testing and calibration. In the field it's going to be a specialist's job. We have to assume Mahmoud's got a guy.'

'Can we cancel that transport order?'

'Not without dropping the dime.'

'You still got any markers left on your guy?'

'A couple.'

'Tell him to have someone call you the second those units roll out.'

At that moment it became a race against time. When the warehouse door opened in Colorado, a door of a different kind would slam shut in LA. But there was still a lot to discover. Including exact locations. Clearly, New Age's glass cube wasn't the centre of anything. For one thing, there was no helicopter there.

And they needed to know who knew, and who flew. 'I want them all,' Reacher said.

'Including the dragon lady?' Neagley asked.

'Starting with the dragon lady. She lied to me.'

They needed equipment, clothing, communications, and alternative vehicles. And cash. Lots of it.

AZHARI MAHMOUD had time for a leisurely lunch. He took it in a sidewalk café in Laguna Beach. He was staying in a rented townhouse a short walk away. The development had a large transient population. It wasn't unusual to see U-Haul trucks parked overnight.

His contacts at New Age had insisted that Little Wing must not be used inside the United States. He had readily agreed. He had said he planned to use the weapon in Kashmir, on the border, against the Indian Air Force. He had lied, of course. Hence the temporary inconvenience of the dockside shipping container. But Southern California was full of day labourers. Loading the U-Haul would take them a little less than thirty minutes.

REACHER DROVE NEAGLEY in the captured Chrysler and waited outside a bank in Beverly Hills. Fifteen minutes later she came out with fifty thousand dollars in a brown sandwich bag. Ninety minutes later they had clothes and phones. The phones were pay-as-you-go cells with chargers and earpieces. The clothes were grey denim shirts and pants and black canvas windcheaters, plus gloves and woollen caps and boots. They bought four three-cell Maglites too.

They changed at the motel and spent ten minutes in the lounge storing numbers and learning how to set up conference calls. Then, wired and blending in, they headed north and west to Van Nuys Boulevard and hit the used car lots until they found two used Civics and two beat-up Preludes. Two silver and two white. No one would give them a second glance.

They planned via a mobile conference call and went out for dinner in Pasadena. They found a burger bar and sat at a table for four, two opposite two, shoulder to shoulder in their new grey denims. A uniform, of sorts. Nobody admitted it but Reacher knew they all felt good. Focused, energised, up against high stakes. They talked about the past. Escapades, scandals, capers. The old unit, back together. Almost.

The next morning O'Donnell and Neagley took first watch at New Age. Reacher and Dixon were left with the task of buying guns. The Hardballers and the Daewoo were not nearly enough. They thought it out over breakfast and dismissed the notion of buying legally. Neither knew the exact details relevant to California, but assumed there would be registration and an ID requirement and maybe some kind of cooling-off period involved. So Dixon proposed driving south into neighbouring Orange County heavy with Republican voters, then finding pawn shops and having Reacher use Neagley's cash plus local respect for the Second Amendment to get round whatever lesser regulations might apply down there.

They left for Orange County right after breakfast, Reacher driving one of the Preludes.

Dixon asked, 'What are you going to do when this is over?'

'Depends if I survive.'

'You think you won't?'

'We're not what we used to be. The others weren't, for sure.'

'I think we'll be OK.'

'I hope so.'

'Feel like dropping by New York afterwards?'

'I'd like to.'

'But?'

'I don't make plans, Karla.'

'Why not? People make plans.'

'I know. People like Calvin Franz. And Sanchez and Orozco. And Tony Swan. He planned to give his dog an aspirin every day for the next fifty-four and a half weeks.'

THIRTY MILES AWAY north of west Azhari Mahmoud was standing in the sun, sweating lightly, and watching as his shipping container emptied. The boxes were smaller than he had imagined. Inevitable, he supposed. The units were no bigger than cigarette packs. To book them down as home-theatre components had been foolish. Unless they could be passed off as personal DVD players. The kind of thing people took on airplanes.

Airplanes. He smiled to himself.

SEVEN GLOCKS. One a 19, the other six 17s. In terms of visual condition they ranged from good to mint. From Reacher's kind of place, in the cheapest part of town. He'd pulled most of Neagley's wad from his pocket and fanned the bills out and dropped them on the counter. Total choice, thirteen suitable pistols from a stock of about three hundred. Four and a third per cent.

They stopped at a legitimate firearms dealer and bought ammunition, then headed back north. Traffic was slow. About level with Anaheim they took a call from O'Donnell in East LA.

'Nothing's happening here,' he said.

'Nothing?'

'No activity at all. You shouldn't have made that call from Vegas. It was a bad mistake. You threw them into a panic. They've gone into full-on lockdown mode. We've been here since five a.m. and nobody's gone in.'

'Not even the dragon lady?'

'Negative.'

'I was hoping to follow someone over to the manufacturing plant.'

'Not going to happen.'

'Enough,' Reacher said. 'Back to base. Last one buys lunch.'

Reacher wasn't a fast driver. The other two Hondas were in the lot when he and Dixon got there. They walked down to Denny's. First thing he saw inside the restaurant was Curtis Mauney, sitting at a round table with Neagley and O'Donnell. Reacher sat down with Dixon and there was a moment of tense silence and then Mauney said, 'Hello again.'

A gentle tone of voice. Quiet. Sympathetic.

Reacher asked, 'Sanchez or Swan?'

Mauney didn't answer.

Reacher said, 'What, both of them?'

'We'll get to that. First tell me why you're hiding.'

'Who says we're hiding?'

'You're in a West Hollywood dive under false names. The clerk gave you up. As a group you're fairly distinctive, physically. It wasn't hard to find you. And it was an easy guess that you'd come in here for lunch.'

Reacher said, 'Jorge Sanchez or Tony Swan?'

Mauney said, 'Tony Swan.'

'Where?'

'Same general area.'

'When?'

'Some time ago.'

'No doubt about the ID?'

'His hands were tied behind him. His fingerprints were preserved. His wallet was in his pocket. I'm very sorry.'

The waitress came over, sensed the mood and went away again.

Mauney asked, 'So why the false names?'

'You brought us here as bait. Whoever they are, we don't want to make it easy for them.'

'Don't you know who they are yet?'

'Do you?'

'No independent action, OK?'

'We're on Sunset Boulevard here,' Reacher said. 'Which is LAPD turf. Are you speaking for them?'

'Friendly advice,' Mauney said. 'Andrew MacBride disappeared in Vegas. But Anthony Matthews rented a U-Haul.'

'The last name on Orozco's list.'

Mauney nodded. 'Endgame.'

'Where did he take it?'

'I have no idea.' Mauney placed four business cards on the table. His name and two phone numbers were printed on them. 'Call me. You might need help. Tony Swan looked like a real tough guy. What was left of him.'

Mauney left and the waitress came over. Reacher guessed no one was hungry anymore, but they ordered anyway. Swan would have approved. Swan ate anywhere, all the time. Autopsies, exhumations, crime scenes.

Nobody talked at all. The sun was bright outside the window. Reacher ate mechanically without the slightest idea of what was on his plate.

'Should we move?' Dixon asked.

'I don't like it that the clerk gave us up,' O'Donnell said. 'We should steal his damn TV remotes.'

'We don't need to move,' Reacher said. 'Mauney is no danger to us. And I want to know about it when they find Sanchez.'

'So what next?' Dixon asked.

'We rest up. We go out again after dark. We pay New Age a visit. It's time to go proactive,' Reacher said.

He left ten bucks for the waitress and paid the bill at the register. Then they headed back to the Dunes.

Reacher fetched the Glocks from the Prelude and they gathered in his room and checked them over. Dixon took the 19 and said she was happy with it. O'Donnell picked out the best three among the 17s and paired them with the magazines from the rejects.

Reacher asked, 'What kind of security can we expect?'

'State-of-the-art locks,' Neagley said. 'An intruder alarm on the gate. I imagine the door opener at reception will be wired as a proximity sensor at night. Plus another intruder alarm. Plus motion sensors all over inside, maybe intruder alarms on office doors, all hard-wired out through the phone lines.'

'How long will we have inside after we breach the gate?'

'Two minutes,' Neagley said. 'A situation like that, the two-minute rule is the only thing we can rely on.'

'OK,' Reacher said. 'We'll go at one in the morning. Dinner at six. Get some rest.'

The others headed for the door. Reacher followed them out with the Chrysler keys. Neagley looked at him, quizzically. 'We don't need it any more,' he said. 'I'm going to give it back. But first I'm going to have it washed. We should try to be civilised.'

THEY COULDN'T FACE Denny's again for dinner. They called out to Domino's instead, for pizzas, and ate them in the battered lounge.

Then Reacher went up to his room and brushed his teeth and took a long, hot shower. He stretched out on the bed and took a nap. The clock in his head woke him at half past midnight. Grey denim pants, grey shirt, black windcheater zipped all the way up. Boots, tightly laced. Gloves on. The Chrysler keys, the spare Glock mag. The captured Vegas cell, his own phone, the Maglite, the Glock. Nothing else.

He walked out to the lot. The others were already there, a shadowy trio standing well away from any pools of light.

'OK,' he said. He turned to O'Donnell and Neagley. 'You guys drive your Hondas.' He turned to Dixon. 'Karla, you drive my car. Park it close, facing west, and leave the keys in for me. Then you ride back with Dave.'

Dixon said, 'Are you really leaving the Chrysler there?'

'We don't need it.'

'It's full of our prints and hair and fibre.'

'Not any more. A bunch of car-wash guys on Van Nuys just made sure of that. Two treatments inside and out. Now let's go.'

They bumped fists like ballplayers, and then they dispersed to their cars. Reacher slid into the Chrysler and started it up. He heard the Hondas start, headed for the exit and swung east on Sunset. Saw the others in his mirror, following in the light night-time traffic.

The great city went quiet after they passed MacArthur Park and hit the 110. Then Dodger Stadium was huge and dark and empty. They plunged into the difficult surface streets to the east, but Reacher figured he could spot the turns, and he did.

He led the others through a wide two-block pass. New Age's glass cube looked dark and deserted. The ornamental trees in the lot were up-lit with spots and the light reflected a little off the building's mirror siding, but the razor wire on the fence looked dull grey in the darkness. Reacher slowed next to the closed gate and dropped his window and stuck his arm out and made a circular gesture with his gloved finger. He led them three-quarters of the way round, then pointed at the kerb where he wanted them to park. They shut their motors down and climbed out. O'Donnell detoured to the gate and came back and said, 'It's a very big lock.'

Reacher said, 'The bigger they are, the harder they fall.'

'We doing this stealthily?'

'Not very,' Reacher said. 'I'll meet you at the gate.'

They walked ahead and he put the Chrysler in gear and followed them, slowly. New Age's gate was set in a curved scallop maybe twenty feet deep, so that arriving vehicles could pull off the roadway and wait. Reacher turned ninety degrees into the scallop and brought the Chrysler's front bumper to within an inch of the gate. Then he reversed straight back until he felt the rear tyres touch the far kerb. He put his foot hard on the brake and slotted the transmission back into drive and dropped all four windows.

'Start the clock,' he called. 'Two minutes.'

He hit the gas until the transmission was wound up tight and the whole car was bucking and straining. Then he slipped his foot off the brake. The car shot forward forty-two feet with the rear tyres smoking and howling and smashed head on into the gate. The lock ruptured instantly and the gate flung back and about a dozen air bags exploded inside the Chrysler. Reacher was driving one-handed and had his other arm up in front of his face. The open windows saved his eardrums. Ahead on the front wall of the building a blue strobe started flashing.

He kept his foot hard down. The car laid rubber all the way through the lot. He lined up the steering and aimed for the reception area doors.

He was doing close to fifty when the front wheels hit the shallow step and the whole car launched and smashed through the doors about a foot off the ground. Glass shattered and the door frames tore right out of the walls. The car hit the slate floor and skidded straight on and demolished the reception counter, ending up buried in rubble up to the windshield.

Reacher unclipped his belt, forced his door open and spilled out onto the lobby floor. All around him tiny white alarm strobes were flashing. A loud siren was sounding. He got to his feet and saw the others hurdling the wreckage in the doorway. Dixon was heading straight for the back of the lobby and O'Donnell and Neagley were heading for the corridor. Their flashlights were on, bright cones of light jerking through clouds of white dust. He pulled his own flashlight out and followed them.

Twenty one seconds gone, he thought.

There were two elevators halfway down the corridor, but he flung open an adjacent door and hit the stairs, two steps at a time. The sound of the siren was unbearable in the stairwell. He burst out into the corridor. The alarm strobes were lighting the place up like the disco from hell. It was lined with maple doors. Offices. The doors had name plates on them. Neagley was busy kicking down a door labelled *Margaret Berenson*. The door wouldn't give. She pulled out her Glock, fired three shots into the lock and kicked again. The door sagged open. She went inside.

Reacher moved on. *Fifty two seconds gone*, he thought.

He passed a door labelled *Allen Lamaison*. Farther on he saw *Anthony Swan*. He braced himself against the opposite wall and delivered a mighty kick just above the lock. The maple splintered and he finished the job with a sharp blow from the flat of his gloved hand. *Sixty three seconds gone*.

He stood stock still and played his flashlight beam all around his dead friend's office. It was like Swan had just stepped out for lunch. There was a coat hanging on a hat stand. There were file cabinets, phones. A computer on the desk. And pens, and pencils.

And a paperweight, holding down papers. A lump of Soviet concrete, the size of a fist, grey with faint traces of blue and red graffiti. Reacher put it in his pocket. Rolled the papers tight and put them in his other pocket.

Eighty nine seconds gone, he thought. *Thirty one to go*.

He stepped to the window. Saw Karla Dixon far below in the darkness, on her way out of the lot. Her pants and jacket were coated with wall-board dust. She was carrying papers and a white three-ring binder. She was lit up in short blue strobe pulses.

Twenty six seconds to go.

He saw O'Donnell run out like he was escaping from a burning house, taking giant strides, carrying stuff clutched to his chest. And then Neagley, running hard, long dark hair streaming out behind her, a thick wad of file folders gripped in each hand. *Nineteen seconds to go*.

He crossed the office and touched the jacket on the hat stand, gently, on the shoulder, like Swan was still in it. Then he stepped behind the desk and sat in the chair. *Twelve seconds to go*.

He looked out at the manic flashing in the corridor and knew he could just wait. Sooner or later, the men who had killed his friends would show up. He could sit right where he was and take them down. *Five seconds*.

Except that he couldn't, of course. There was no way to be sure of putting the right guys down before he lost to tear gas and reinforcements.

One second to go.

He exploded out of the chair and jinked left into the corridor and right into the stairwell. He hit the first floor about ten seconds over budget, dodged round the Chrysler and was out in the lot fifteen seconds late. Out in the street forty seconds late, running towards the Prelude a hundred yards away. He hurled himself inside in twenty seconds. He slammed his door and saw a set of headlights in the far distance, moving very fast, coming towards him.

CHAPTER ELEVEN

Altogether three cars showed up. They came in fast and stopped short outside the wrecked gate, engines running, headlights blazing. They were brand new Chrysler 300Cs, dark blue, pretty much identical to the one already parked in New Age's lobby.

Five guys got out. Reacher was dazzled by the headlights, so he couldn't make out much detail. But the slight man wearing a raincoat seemed to be in charge. He was gesturing the others away from the breached gate, as if it was somehow dangerous. *An ex-cop*, Reacher thought. *Reluctant to contaminate a crime scene.*

Then the five backtracked behind their cars. The engines shut down and the headlight beams shut off and the scene went dark.

They figure this could be an ambush, Reacher thought. He watched them until his night vision came back, then took out the cellphone from Vegas and beeped his way through the menus to the last number dialled. He hit the call button.

None of the five guys reacted. The ring tone in Reacher's ear went on and on and then cut to voicemail. He clicked off, redialled, and nobody moved a muscle. It was inconceivable that a director of security would be out on an emergency alert without his cellphone switched on. Therefore the guy in the raincoat was the third man on the totem pole, at best, allowing for Swan's number-two spot. And he was acting like a guy in third place. Slow and ponderous.

Civilians, Reacher thought. He waited. Eventually the guy in the raincoat ordered everyone back in their cars and they burst into the lot at high speed. Reacher started the Honda and headed west.

THEY REGROUPED in O'Donnell's room dead on three o'clock in the morning. The captured paperwork was laid out on the bed in three neat piles. Reacher unrolled Swan's stuff and added it to the line. It wasn't very interesting. Most of it was a memorandum about overtime requirements.

O'Donnell's collection wasn't very interesting either, but it proved that the glass cube was relatively unsecured because it contained very little worth stealing. Some minor design work happened there, and some component sourcing, but most of the square footage was given over to management functions.

Which made it all the more important to find the plant.

Which was where Dixon's stuff made all the difference. She had dug through the wreckage of the reception area under the crashed Chrysler and come up with solid gold. In the shattered remains of a locked drawer she had found New Age's internal phone directory, a thick wad of loose-leaf pages in a three-ring binder printed with the corporate logo. Right at the front was a block diagram detailing the company divisions down through the various hierarchies. The security division was headed by Allen Lamaison. His number two had been Tony Swan. Below Swan two lines led to two other guys, and five more lines fanned out to five more, one of whom had the name Saropian, and was as dead as Tony Swan, in a Vegas hotel foundation. A total staff of nine, two down, seven survivors.

'Turn to the back,' Dixon said.

The last section had account numbers for FedEx and UPS and DHL. Plus street addresses and phone numbers for the East LA glass cube and the Colorado contracting office.

And then, bizarrely, a third address, with a note printed in bold and underlined: *No deliveries to this location.*

The third address was for the electronics manufacturing plant. It was in Highland Park, halfway between Glendale and South Pasadena, nine miles east of where they were standing. Close enough to taste.

Neagley had personnel files on the whole security division. Nine folders. Reacher started with the top boy, Allen Lamaison. There was a Polaroid photograph. Lamaison was a bulky, thick-necked man with dark, blank eyes and a mouth too small for his jaw. His personal information showed he had done twenty years inside the LAPD, twelve in Robbery-Homicide. He was forty-nine years old.

The first of the guys sharing the third spot was called Lennox. Forty-one, ex-LAPD, grey buzz cut, heavy build, meaty red face. The second was the guy in the raincoat. His name was Parker. Forty-two, ex-LAPD, tall, slim.

'They're all ex-LAPD,' Neagley said. 'According to the data they all quit round the same time.'

'Could your guy in Chicago get their histories?'

Neagley shrugged. 'We might be able to get into their computer.' She dialled her Chicago guy's voicemail and Reacher checked the photographs of the four remaining foot soldiers, then piled their files on top of Parker's.

'I saw these five tonight,' he said.

'What were they like?' O'Donnell asked.

'Lousy. Really stupid and slow.'

Reacher opened Tony Swan's file, but he didn't get past the Polaroid. It was much clearer than Curtis Mauney's video-surveillance still. Ten years after the army Swan's hair had thinned and he had changed to an all-over half-inch crew cut. Chestnut brown, was now dusty grey. His eyes were pouched and his neck was wider than ever. Reacher was amazed that anyone made shirts with collars that size. Like car tyres.

'What next?' Dixon asked, in the silence. Reacher knew she was just trying to spare his feelings. He closed the file. 'Who knew, and who flew,' he said. 'Anyone else can live a little longer. You and Dave can go scope out Highland Park. Neagley and I are going back to East LA.'

THEY LEFT THE MOTEL at five in the morning, in separate Hondas, talking to each other on the phone like commuters. Reacher said he guessed that when the alarm call came in Lamaison and Lennox had headed straight for Highland Park, the more sensitive location, and would make for the real crime scene around dawn. Neagley agreed, and grasped the next part of the plan without having to ask, which was one of the reasons why Reacher liked her so much.

They parked a hundred yards apart on different streets, hiding in plain sight. The sun was over the horizon and the dawn was grey. Fifty yards from New Age, Reacher's car was anonymous. There was a flat-bed truck backed up to the wrecked reception area. The guy called Parker was still there in his raincoat, directing operations. He had one foot soldier he had dispatched to the smashed gate as sentry. Reacher guessed the other three had been sent up to Highland Park to relieve Lamaison and Lennox.

The flat-bed's steel cable jerked and tightened and started hauling. The blue Chrysler came out of the lobby backwards, a lot slower than it had gone in. It had scars on the paint and some front-end damage, but overall was in excellent shape. It came to rest on the flat-bed and as soon as it was out of the lot its undamaged twin drove in. Another blue 300C, fast and confident. Allen Lamaison stopped and climbed out to inspect the gate.

Reacher recognised him instantly from his photograph. In the flesh he was about six feet tall and two hundred and forty pounds. Big shoulders, thin legs. He was dressed in a grey suit and held a red necktie flat against his white shirt, even though the weather wasn't windy. He climbed back in his car and drove just short of the shattered doors and got out.

Just to be sure Reacher took out the Vegas phone and redialled. Lamaison's hand went straight to his pocket and came out with a phone. He glanced at the screen and froze.

Got you, Reacher thought.

He wasn't expecting an answer. But Lamaison flicked the phone open and brought it up to his face and said, 'What?'

'How's your day going?' Reacher asked.

'It only just started,' Lamaison said.

'How was your night?'

'I'm going to kill you. Where are you?'

'We got out of town. But we'll be back. Next week, next month. You better get used to looking over your shoulder.' Reacher clicked off.

Ten minutes later Lennox showed up in another blue 300C. Grey buzz cut, heavy build, meaty red face. The other number three, Parker's equal. He was carrying a cardboard tray of coffee and disappeared into the building. Fifty minutes after that Margaret Berenson showed up in a silver Toyota. The dragon lady. She parked neatly in a slot close to the door, then picked her way through the wreckage. Two more managers showed up and Parker checked them in at the door.

Then the scene went quiet for more than two hours.

Halfway through the wait Dixon called in. She and O'Donnell had been at Highland Park since six. They had seen the foot soldiers show up. Had seen Lamaison and Lennox leave. They had driven a two-block radius, for a fuller picture.

'It's the real deal,' Dixon said. 'Multiple buildings, serious fence. And it's got a helicopter. A white Bell 222.'

At half past nine the dragon lady headed back to her Toyota. Reacher's cellphone rang. 'Both of us go?' Neagley asked.

'Absolutely,' Reacher said. 'Time to rock and roll.'

He pulled his gloves on and started his Honda at the same time that Berenson started her Toyota. He eased off the kerb, U-turned in the mouth of the next side street and came back along New Age's fence. Berenson was hustling through the lot. A block away he could see Neagley's Honda, riding low. Berenson made a left through the wrecked gate without pausing. Neagley fell in twenty yards behind her. Reacher slowed and then tucked in about seventy yards behind Neagley.

The Prelude was a low-slung coupé, and therefore Reacher didn't have the best angle in the world, but most of the time he got a decent view of the silver Toyota up ahead. Berenson was driving well under the speed limit. Maybe the car-crash scars were more vivid in her memory than they were on her face. She made a right onto a road called Huntingdon Drive, headed north and east, then made a left for South Pasadena.

His phone rang. Neagley. 'I've been behind her too long,' she said. 'I'm taking three sides of the next block. You move up for a spell.'

He turned into Van Horne Avenue and accelerated about fifty yards behind Berenson. He couldn't see her. The road curved too much. He accelerated again and eased off round a final curve and spotted her about forty yards ahead. In his mirror he saw Neagley swing back on the road behind him.

Monterey Hills gave way to South Pasadena and low hills, curving streets, trees, perpetual blossom. Berenson made a left and then a right and pulled into a quiet cul-de-sac. Small, smug houses basking in the morning sun. Reacher didn't follow. The beat-up Prelude was not anonymous in a street like that. He braked and came to a stop thirty yards farther on. Neagley pulled in behind him. 'Now?' she asked, on the phone.

'Now,' Reacher said.

They slid out and ran. Together, as if they were jogging buddies. They made it into the cul-de-sac and through a curve in time to see a garage door opening next to a house on the right. Berenson's Toyota was waiting on a blacktop driveway. The house was small and neat. Faced with brick. There was a basketball hoop over the garage. A bike, a skateboard and a Little League bat were stacked against a wall inside.

The Toyota's brake lights went off and it crept forward. Neagley sprinted. She made it inside the garage just as the door started back down. Reacher arrived about ten seconds after her and used his foot to trip the safety mechanism, then ducked inside.

Margaret Berenson was already out of her car. Neagley had one gloved hand in her hair and other clamped round her wrists from behind. Berenson was struggling, and Neagley forced her face against the Toyota's hood. She started yelling. Neagley straightened her up and Reacher popped her in the solar plexus just enough to drive the air out of her lungs.

Reacher hit the button and the door started down again. A bulb in the ceiling replaced the sunlight with a dim glow. At the rear of the garage there was a door.

An alarm pad was next to it. 'Is it set?' Reacher asked.

'Yes,' Berenson said, breathlessly.

'No,' Neagley said. 'The kid is about twelve years old. Mom was out early this morning. The kid made the school bus on his own. Setting the alarm won't be a part of his routine.'

'Maybe Dad set it.'

'Dad is long gone. Mom isn't wearing a ring.'

'Boyfriend?'

'You must be kidding.'

Reacher tried the door. It was locked. He pulled the keys out of the Toyota's ignition and one fitted the lock. The door opened. No warning beeps. 'You tell a lot of lies, Ms Berenson,' he said.

They bundled her into a kitchen. There was a table and two chairs. Neagley forced Berenson down into one and Reacher rooted around until he found a roll of duct tape and a kitchen knife. He taped Berenson tight to the chair.

'We were in the army,' he said to her. 'We mentioned that, right? When we needed information, our first port of call was the company clerk. That's you. So start talking.'

'You're crazy,' Berenson said back.

'Tell me about the car wreck. Your scars.'

'It was a long time ago. It was bad.'

'This could be much worse.' Reacher put the knife on the table and followed it with the Glock and Tony Swan's lump of concrete. 'I'll let you choose.'

Berenson started to cry. Hopeless, helpless sobs. Her shoulders shook and tears dripped into her lap.

'Not helping, you're crying at the wrong guy. Start talking,' Reacher said.

'I can't,' Berenson said. 'He'll hurt my son.'

'Who will? Lamaison?'

'I can't say.'

'It's time to make your mind up. We want to know who knew and who flew. You've got some serious talking to do.'

'He'll hurt my son.'

'Look at it from our side. If in doubt, we'll take you out.'

Berenson said nothing.

'Be smart, Margaret,' Reacher said. 'Whoever is threatening your son, you make a good case against him, he'll be dead.'

'I can't rely on that.'

Reacher stepped to the refrigerator and opened it up. Took out a plastic bottle of Evian water. He unscrewed the top and emptied the water in the sink and used the kitchen knife to saw an oval hole in the bottom of the bottle. He fitted it over the Glock's muzzle so that the neck lined up.

'A home-made silencer.' he said, holding the gun a foot and a half from Berenson's face. 'The neighbours won't hear a thing.'

IN RETROSPECT it was a tale that Reacher could have scripted in advance. The original development engineer up at the Highland Park plant, now the quality-control manager, had started showing signs of severe stress. His name was Edward Dean. By chance his annual performance review was scheduled and Margaret Berenson pursued the matter.

At first Dean claimed his move north was the root of his problem. He had bought land out in the desert south of Palmdale and the commute was killing him. Berenson didn't buy that. All Angelinos had the commute from hell. So then Dean said there were outlaw bikers and meth labs close by, but a pained echo in a chance remark led her to believe that his daughter was in some way the problem. Berenson figured maybe the fourteen-year-old was hanging with the bikers or experimenting with crystal.

Then Tony Swan disappeared. He just vanished. One day he was there, the next day he wasn't. Margaret Berenson followed up. Swan had classified knowledge. There were national security implications. She asked all kinds of questions. Then one day she got home and found Allen Lamaison playing basketball with her son.

Berenson was afraid of Lamaison. How much, she hadn't realised until she saw him tousle her twelve-year-old's hair with a hand big enough to crush his skull. He suggested the kid stay outside and practise throws while he went inside for a chat with Mom.

The chat started with a confession. Lamaison told Berenson exactly what had happened to Swan. Every detail. And by and by he revealed that Dean was cooperating with a special project, because if he didn't his daughter would disappear and be found weeks later with a happy band of bikers.

Then he said the same thing could happen to her son. Most outlaw bikers had been in prison, and prison distorted a person's tastes.

He issued a warning, and two instructions. The warning was that old friends from Swan's service days would show up and start asking questions. The first instruction was that they were to be deflected firmly. The second was that nothing of this current conversation was ever to be revealed.

Then he went outside and sank a few more baskets with her son. Then he drove away.

Reacher believed her. He believed the basketball part, the prison reference. People like Margaret Berenson didn't make that kind of stuff up. Their frames of reference weren't wide enough. He cut the duct tape and helped her to her feet. 'So who knew?' he asked.

'Lamaison,' Berenson said. 'Lennox, Parker and Saropian.'

'What about the other four ex-LAPD?'

'They're from a different era. He wouldn't trust them.'

'Is there somewhere you can go until this is over?'

'You don't know Lamaison. You can't beat him.'

Reacher looked at Neagley. 'Can we beat him?'

'Like a drum,' she said.

Berenson said, 'But there are four of them.'

'Three,' Reacher said. 'Saropian is already down.'

Berenson was quiet for a long moment. 'I could go to a hotel, I'll go get my son out of school.'

Reacher nodded. 'Who flew?'

'Lamaison, Lennox and Parker. Just the three of them.'

'Plus the pilot,' Reacher said. 'That's four.'

Berenson went to pack her bags and Reacher put Swan's rock in his pocket and pulled the Evian bottle off the Glock.

'Would that really have worked?' Neagley asked.

'I doubt it,' Reacher said. 'But it looked good, didn't it?'

His phone rang. It was Dixon. She and O'Donnell were in Highland Park and they were starting to feel conspicuous.

'Head home,' Reacher said. 'We've got what we need.'

Then Neagley's phone rang. Her personal cell. Her Chicago guy. She listened, then clicked off. 'From the LAPD grapevine,' she said. 'Lamaison fought eighteen Internal Affairs investigations and won all of them.'

'Charges?'

'You name it. He's a bad guy but smart.'

Berenson came downstairs with two bags. She loaded them into the Toyota's trunk. Reacher and Neagley walked down to get their cars and formed up into a close protection convoy. Berenson stopped at a school and came back out with a small, brown-haired boy. Then she drove a little way on the 110 and came off in Pasadena and headed for an inn on a quiet street.

Reacher and Neagley stayed on site to give them time to settle in. They used the time getting lunch, in a bar off the lobby.

Reacher's phone rang as he was finishing up his coffee. Dixon again. She was back at the motel, with O'Donnell. There was an urgent message at the desk from Curtis Mauney.

'He wants us up at that place north of Glendale,' she said.

'Where we went for Orozco?'

'Yes. Right now.'

'Because they found Sanchez?'

'He didn't say. But Reacher, he said to meet him at the hospital, not the morgue. So if it's Sanchez, he's still alive.'

REACHER EXPECTED that he and Neagley would get there first but the 210 was jammed. Within a hundred yards of the slip road it was completely static. A river of cars curved ahead into the distance, winking in the sun, burning gas, going nowhere. A classic LA panorama. Reacher checked his mirror and saw Neagley's white Honda Civic behind him. He called her on the phone.

'Accident up ahead,' she said. 'I heard it on the radio.'

'Terrific.'

'If Sanchez made it this far, he can make it a few minutes more.'

Reacher asked, 'Where did they go wrong?'

'I don't know. This wasn't the toughest thing they ever faced.'

'So something tripped them up. Something unpredictable. Where would Swan have started?'

'With Dean,' Neagley said. 'The quality-control guy. His behaviour must have been the trigger.'

'Did he get the whole story out of Dean?'

'Probably not. But enough to join the dots. He'd have talked to the local cops. Asked for protection.'

Reacher paused a beat. 'Which actually means Swan didn't talk to anyone, because that's Curtis Mauney's kingdom, and he didn't know anything about Dean or New Age.'

'Swan wouldn't leave Dean unprotected.'

'So maybe Swan didn't know about him. Maybe he found a different way in. Maybe Sanchez will tell us.'

'You think he's alive?'

'Hope for the best.'

'But plan for the worst.'

They clicked off. Their lane moved a little. In the next five minutes of silence they covered about ten cars' lengths, six times slower than walking.

Reacher's pay-as-you-go rang. Neagley again. 'More from Chicago. We're into the LAPD mainframe. Lennox and Parker were partners. They resigned rather than face their twelfth IA inquiry about a week before Lamaison hired them.'

Two hundred yards later in the far haze they saw the source of the delay, a broken-down car in the left lane. Reacher called Dixon. 'You there yet?'

'Maybe ten minutes away.'

'We're stuck in traffic. Call us if there's good news. Call us if there's bad news, too, I guess.'

It took another quarter of an hour to reach the stalled car, then the flow freed up and Reacher and Neagley were at the county facility ten minutes later. They parked in the hospital's visitor lot and walked to the main entrance. Reacher saw O'Donnell's Honda, then Dixon's.

The lobby was fairly quiet. There was no sign of Dixon or O'Donnell. Or Curtis Mauney. Reacher asked the desk clerk for Mauney and got no response. He asked for Jorge Sanchez and got no response. He asked about emergency John Doe admissions and got redirected to another desk.

The new desk reported no recent John Doe admissions and knew nothing about a patient named Jorge Sanchez. Reacher stepped out to the lot and called Dixon. No reply.

He tried O'Donnell's number. No reply.

Neagley said, 'Maybe they're switched off or something.'

'This feels wrong,' Reacher said.

Neagley took Mauney's card out of her pocket. Reacher dialled Mauney's cell number. No answer. His land line. No answer.

Then Neagley's personal phone rang. She answered. Listened. Her face went literally bloodless, like wax.

'Curtis Mauney was Allen Lamaison's partner in the LAPD,' she said.

Something tripped them up. Something unpredictable. Reacher closed his eyes and saw Swan talking to Dean, extracting the story, then driving straight to some dusty sheriff's office, talking to Mauney. Saw Mauney picking up a phone, sealing Swan's fate right there and then. And Franz's and Orozco's and Sanchez's.

Reacher opened his eyes and said, 'We're not going to lose another two. Not while I live and breathe.'

THEY ABANDONED Neagley's Civic at the hospital and used Reacher's Prelude. They had nowhere to go. They were just moving for the sake of moving.

'Plan?' Neagley asked.

'No plan,' Reacher said.

The 210 was flowing fast and free, so they pieced together half-remembered fragments of the manufacturing plant's Highland Park address and headed in that direction.

They found Highland Park easily enough. It was full of streets and business parks and small hi-tech manufacturing enterprises. It was harder to find New Age's location. They looked for unmarked buildings and serious fences and found several.

'Dixon called the helicopter a Bell 222,' Reacher said. 'Could you recognise one of those if you saw one?'

'I've seen three in the last five minutes,' Neagley said.

'She said it was white.'

'Two in the last five minutes. No names, no signs.'

Reacher said, 'We need the exact address.'

'We don't have time. The Dunes is a long way from here.'

'But Pasadena isn't.'

They made the short hop east on the 110 to the inn and told Margaret Berenson what they needed. Fifteen minutes later they were cruising past the place. The fence was appalling. Brutal. It was at least eight feet tall and four feet thick, two faces of tight barbed wire with giant coils of razor wire heaped between them. A main battle tank might have breached it. No way through on wheels. And no way through on foot with a bolt cutter. And no way over the huge loose concertinas piled on top, either.

Reacher drove all the way round the block. The whole facility occupied a couple of acres. It was roughly a hundred yards a side. Four buildings, one large, three small. Dried brown grass and cinder footpaths between them. A small parking lot full of cars. The fence had no weak spots and only one gate, a wide steel assembly which slid sideways on wheels. Welded to its top rail was more concertina wire. Flanking it was a guard hut.

'No way through,' Reacher said.

'Are they even in there?'

'Must be. It's like a private jail. Safer than stashing them anywhere else.'

Reacher drove on, turned a corner and parked a quarter of a mile away. Didn't speak. Because he had nothing to say.

Neagley's personal phone rang again. She answered. Listened. Clicked off. 'My Pentagon guy,' she said. 'The missiles just rolled out of the gate in Colorado.'

CHAPTER TWELVE

If Mahmoud has got the missiles, this thing is bigger than we are. We have to suck it up and move on. Reacher looked at Neagley. 'How much do they weigh?' he asked.

'I don't know. Crated, with launch tubes and spare parts, say fifty pounds each.'

'That's sixteen and a quarter tons.'

'A semitruck,' Neagley said.

'Average speed on the Interstates, fifty miles an hour?'

'Probably.'

'North on I-25 to I-80, then southwest to Nevada, that's about nine hundred miles. So we've got eighteen hours. Call it twenty-four, because the driver will take a rest period.'

'They're not going to Nevada,' Neagley said.

'Wherever. Anywhere significant is eighteen hours.'

'This is insane. We can't wait twenty-four hours. Or eighteen. You said it yourself, there could be ten thousand KIAs.'

'But not yet.'

'We can't wait,' Neagley said again. 'Easier to stop the truck on the way out of Denver. It could be headed anywhere. To New York. JFK or LaGuardia. Or Chicago. You want Little Wing deployed at O'Hare? We have to tell someone.'

Reacher said nothing.

'We have to, Reacher.'

'They might not listen. They didn't listen about September eleventh.'

'You're clutching at straws. They've changed. We have to tell someone.'

'We will,' said Reacher. 'But not yet.'

'Karla and Dave will have a better chance with a couple of SWAT teams on their side.'

'You're kidding. They'll wind up as collateral damage in a heartbeat.'

Neagley said, 'We can't even get through the fence. Dixon will die, O'Donnell will die, ten thousand other people will die, and we'll die.'

'Look on the bright side. Maybe none of the bad stuff will happen. Maybe we'll win. You and me.'

'Here? Maybe. But later? Dream on. We have no idea where that truck is going.'

'We can find out later. It's what we're good at.'

'Good enough to gamble ten thousand lives against two?'

'I hope so,' Reacher said. 'What's their security like?'

'Normally?' Neagley said. 'Motion detectors on the fence and big locks on all the doors and a twenty-four-hour sentry. But today the whole of New Age security is going to be here, locked and loaded. And we're going to be outside the fence.'

'Let me worry about the fence.'

'There's no way through it.'

'There's a gate. What time does it get full dark?'

'Say nine o'clock, to be safe.'

'They won't fly before dark. We've got seven hours. Seven out of our twenty-four.'

'We never had twenty-four.'

'You elected me CO. We've got what I say we've got.'

'This is insane.'

'I'm not going to lose another two,' Reacher said.

They drove round New Age's block one more time, and fixed the geography in their minds. The gate was in the centre of the front face of the square. The main building was behind it at the end of a short driveway. At the back of that the three outbuildings were scattered, one close to the helipad. All four buildings had grey galvanised siding. There were no trees, just the uneven brown grass and the parking lot.

'Where are the Chryslers?' Reacher asked.

'Out,' Neagley said. 'Looking for us.'

They headed back to the hospital in Glendale. Neagley collected her car from the lot. They stopped at a supermarket. Bought a pack of wooden kitchen matches and two six-pack cases of Evian water shrink-wrapped in plastic. They stopped at an auto parts store. Bought a five-gallon gasoline can and a bag of polishing rags. Then they stopped at a gas station and filled the can.

They headed southwest out of Glendale and found a roundabout route back to the motel. They parked a block away and headed for O'Donnell's room by different routes, just in case.

O'Donnell's lock was broken. The room was completely trashed, searched and wrecked. All the New Age paperwork was gone, the reject Glock 17s were gone, the spare ammunition was gone, the AMT Hardballers were gone, Saropian's Daewoo DP 51 was gone, the Maglites were gone.

Dixon's room was trashed. And Neagley's. And Reacher's.

'Bastards,' he said.

Neagley said, 'They're all waiting for us in Highland Park.'

Reacher nodded. Between them they had two Glocks, plus their recent purchases in the Prelude's trunk.

Two against seven or more. No time. No element of surprise. A fortified position with no way in. A hopeless situation.

'We're good to go,' Reacher said.

They parked in a quiet street three blocks from New Age's factory, opposite sides of the street. They both had a view of the place. Things had changed behind the fence. The workers' cars were gone from the lot. In their place were six blue Chrysler 300Cs. Beyond the cars they could see the helicopter in the distance, a small white shape.

Reacher had both his phones set to vibrate. Neagley buzzed him. 'You made a will?' she asked.

'No point,' Reacher said. 'Now they broke my toothbrush I don't own anything.'

'How does that feel?'

'Bad. I liked that toothbrush. It's been with me a long time.'

'No, I mean the rest of it.'

'It feels OK. I don't see that Karla or Dave are really any happier than me.'

'Right now they're not, for sure.'

'They know we're coming,' Reacher said.

A BIG WHITE semitruck laboured west on I-70 in Colorado, heading for the state of Utah. It was less than half full. So it was running light, but it was running slow, because of the mountains. It would run a little easier down I-15 to California. Its driver had calculated an average of fifty miles an hour for the trip. Eighteen hours, door-to-door. He wasn't going to take a rest period. How could he? He was a man on a mission.

AZHARI MAHMOUD checked his map for the third time. He figured he needed three hours. Or maybe more. He had to cross just about the whole of Los Angeles, south to north. The U-Haul was slow and a pig to drive, and he was sure that the traffic was going to be awful. He decided to give himself four hours. He set his alarm and laid down on the bed and tried to will himself to sleep.

REACHER STARED straight ahead at the horizon, trying to judge the light. The tint on the windshield didn't help. He buzzed his window down. There was still at least an hour of daylight. Then maybe an hour of dusk. He buzzed the window up and rested. Slowed his breathing and relaxed.

He stayed relaxed until Allen Lamaison called him.

He called on Reacher's pay-as-you-go. The caller ID showed he was using Karla Dixon's phone at his end. There was smug satisfaction in his voice. 'Reacher?' he said. 'We need to talk.'

'So talk,' Reacher said.

'You're useless. You've lost every round so far.'

'Except Saropian.'

'True,' Lamaison said. 'And I'm very unhappy about that. But we're going to make a deal.'

'Dream on.'

'The terms are excellent. Want to hear them? You can save your friends a world of hurt.'

'How?'

'You and Ms Neagley come in now, we'll hold you all for a week. Until the heat dies down. Then we'll let you all go.'

'Or?'

'We'll break O'Donnell's arms and legs and use his switchblade all over Dixon. Then we'll put them both in the helicopter.'

Reacher said nothing.

'Don't worry about Little Wing, that's a done deal. They're going to Kashmir, anyway. It's a dump. Why should you care?'

Reacher said nothing.

Lamaison said, 'Do we have a deal?'

'Why would I trust you? I'll walk in and you'll shoot me.'

'I agree, it's a risk. But I think you'll take it. Because you're responsible for your people's situation. You're their leader, and you screwed up. I've heard a lot about you. In fact I'm sick of hearing your name. You'll do what it takes to help them.'

'Where are you?' Reacher asked.

'I'm sure you know.'

Reacher glanced through the windshield, factored in the window tint and tried to judge the light. 'We're two hours away,' he said, with a little tension in his voice.

'Where are you?'

'South of Palmdale. We're going to visit with Dean.'

'Turn round, right now. For Ms Dixon's sake. I bet she's a screamer. I'll put her on the phone and let you listen.'

Reacher paused. 'Two hours. We'll talk again.'

He clicked off and dialled Neagley. 'We go in sixty minutes,' he said. Then he leaned back and closed his eyes.

SIXTY MINUTES LATER the sky was a dark navy blue, almost black. Reacher dialled Neagley and clicked off after one ring. Her window dropped and she waved. A small, pale hand in the darkness. He started his car and eased away east and made a right. Three blocks later he was skirting New Age's back fence. He made another right and coasted to a stop two thirds of the way down the side of their lot.

He got out and listened. New Age's place was part of a commercial zone. The work day was over. People were gone. The streets were dark and quiet.

He opened the Prelude's trunk. Used his thumbnail to slit the plastic round the one-litre Evian bottles. He took one out and unscrewed the top and poured the water away in the gutter. Stood the empty bottle upright in the trunk. He repeated the process eleven more times.

Then he took out the gas can. He filled the bottles carefully. When the twelfth bottle was full he put the can on the ground, almost two gallons still in it. He tore open the bag of polishing rags. They were foot-square pieces of white cotton jersey. He rolled them tight, like cigars, and eased them down the necks of the bottles. The gasoline soaked upwards, pale and colourless.

He rolled a thirteenth rag, laid it on the ground and dripped gas on it until it was soaked. He found the box of wooden kitchen matches and jammed them in his pocket. Lifted the twelve Molotov cocktails out of the trunk, one by one, and stood them upright six feet behind the Prelude's rear bumper. Then he trapped the thirteenth rag in the trunk lid, three quarters out.

Showtime, he thought.

He struck a match and held it against the trapped rag until the rag was burning bright. Then he lit the first Molotov cocktail off the burning rag and hurled it high over the fence. It tumbled through a lazy blazing arc and burst against the base of the main building's end wall. Gas exploded and flared and settled into a small burning pool.

He threw the second bomb. Same procedure. The bottle hit the same place and burst. There was a brief white-hot flare and then the pool of flames started to lick upwards against the siding.

He threw the third bomb directly into the fire. And the fourth. He aimed the fifth a little to the left. It started a brand new fire. He followed it with the six and the seventh. His shoulder started to ache from the effort of the giant throws. The grass all round the building's end wall started to burn. The eighth bottle fell short and burst about eight feet out. Now there was a large irregular four-foot-high patch of flames.

He threw the ninth bottle harder, and further to the left. It exploded near the building's door. The tenth bottle rolled and leaked and flames raced through the dry grass. He used the eleventh bottle to fill the gap on the building's corner. The last bottle hit the siding high up, burst into flames and spattered the whole end wall.

He knocked the burning rag out and stamped on it, then peered through the fence. Flames were leaping high all along the front wall as far as the door. The metal building was resisting. But it would be getting warm inside.

He screwed the lid on the gas can and wound up and hurled it like a discus thrower. It soared up over the fence and spun and landed dead in the flames. There was a split second's pause and then a huge white fireball. For a time it looked like the whole place was on fire. The flames were twice as high as before and the paint on the siding was starting to burn.

Reacher got back in the Prelude and started up and pulled a ragged U-turn. Three blocks later he killed his motor behind Neagley's Civic and watched out of his window. He could see the glow in the distance, clouds of billowing smoke up-lit by bright, leaping flames. A decent blaze, getting worse by the minute. Impressive.

The fire department showed up inside four minutes.

Clearly New Age had an alarm system hard-wired straight into the precinct house. Far to his right in the distance Reacher heard the faint bass bark of sirens and saw flashing blue lights. He saw Neagley start her car and put it in gear. He started his own. And then he waited. The sirens grew louder. They changed to a manic continuous shriek, and the blue lights got brighter. The trucks were two blocks away. Neagley eased off the kerb, drove ahead and waited on the stop line. Reacher was right behind her. The fire trucks were a block away, bearing down fast. Neagley swooped left and Reacher followed, just yards in front of the lead truck. Its siren blared at him angrily. One block, two, following the fence along the front of New Age's property. The sirens were yelping furiously. Then Neagley pulled over, like a good citizen. Reacher tucked in behind her. The three trucks roared past them, braked hard and turned and headed for New Age's gate.

The gate was rolling back.

Neagley slammed her car into a side street and was out of her seat and running hard through the darkness. Reacher followed. They caught up with the last truck as it slowed to turn in. They ran hard on its left, on the blind side, away from the guard shack. Its siren still sounding, its engine deafening, the truck roared straight ahead. Neagley turned a hard left and ran down the inside face of the fence. Reacher headed half-left through the grass, ten long seconds, then rolled and crammed himself flat in the dirt.

A minute later he raised his head.

He was sixty yards from the fire. Beyond the trucks he could see flames. He could see people over by the far fence, trying to see what had started the fire. New Age security. Firemen were running everywhere, hauling equipment, unrolling hoses.

It took them eight minutes to put out the fire. Then they spent another thirty dousing the ashes and following up in one way or another. Reacher spent the time surveying the buildings from as close as he dared to get, then crawling back as far as he could go. By the time the trucks rolled out of the gate he was in the far back corner of the property, a hundred and fifty yards from the action.

The closest thing to him was the helicopter, on its pad, maybe seventy yards away. Beyond it was the closest of the outbuildings. The pilot's office, Reacher guessed. He had seen a guy in a leather jacket run out of the door. Thirty yards south was the parking lot. Six blue Chryslers.

Beyond the pilot's office was the second outbuilding. A store room of some kind, Reacher guessed. The fire chief had been allowed to take a fast look inside. Then came the main building, the assembly line. All around it people were still moving out in the open. Reacher was pretty sure he recognised Lamaison, by his size and his shape, stamping around in the last of the smoke. Lennox and Parker were there, too. Plus others. Three at least.

The third outbuilding was set far back, directly opposite Reacher's corner. Its door had not opened at any point, and nobody had gone anywhere near it. That was the prison, Reacher guessed.

The main gate had rolled back into place with an impact that had sent a shudder through the roll of concertina wire. The light above the guard in the shack was spilling out from the windows in a soft twenty-foot circle.

Beyond the main building Lamaison had formed up four security guys for a briefing. He split them into pairs and sent them off to check the fence, one pair clockwise, the other counterclockwise, scuffing the grass with their feet. A hundred and fifty yards away Reacher rolled onto his back. Checked the sky. It was close to full dark. There was no moon. No light at all, except a little orange scatter from the city's lights.

Reacher rolled onto his front again. The security guys were moving slow. The clockwise guys were Neagley's. The counterclockwise guys were his. They had a little over four minutes, at their current pace, before they got anywhere near him. They were concentrating on the fence. They had no flashlights. They would have to fall over something to find it. Reacher crawled twenty yards inwards. Found a dip behind a hummock in the grass, pressed himself down into it and dialled Dixon's cell.

More than a hundred yards away, Lamaison answered the call. Reacher kept his thumb over the phone's bright LCD window. He spoke as normally as he dared. 'We're stuck on the 210,' he said. 'There's a stalled car up ahead.'

'Like hell,' Lamaison said. 'You've been throwing gasoline bombs over my fence.' Over the cellular circuits his angry voice came through penetrating and edgy. Reacher slipped the pad of his index finger over the earpiece perforations. The searchers were a hundred and twenty yards away.

'What bombs?' he said. 'We're on the freeway.'

'You heard me.'

'I have no idea what you're talking about.'

'Like hell, Reacher. You're right here. You started a fire. But it was pathetic. I'm sure you saw them put it out.'

Reacher said nothing. Just watched his pair of searchers.

'The deal is off,' Lamaison said.

'Wait, I'm still thinking about the deal. But I want a proof of life. You could have shot them already.'

'They're still alive.'

'Prove it.' The searchers were ninety yards away.

'How?'

'I'll call you when we're through this traffic. Bring them to the gate.'

'No way. They stay where they are.'

'Then we can't do business.'

'Think of a question only they can answer. We'll ask them and call you back.'

'I'll call you. I don't answer the phone when I'm driving.'

'You're not driving. What's the question?'

Reacher said, 'Ask them who they were with before they joined the 110th MP.' Then he clicked the phone off. He crawled another twenty yards inwards, slow and cautious. The searchers were now forty yards away, five feet apart, scuffing the grass.

Reacher saw the door open at the front of the main building. A tall shape stepped out. Parker, probably. He headed for the distant shack thirty yards away. He unlocked the door and went in and less than a minute later came back out again. *The prison*, Reacher thought. *Thank you.*

The searchers were twenty yards away. Reacher shuffled ahead a little. Now on a diagonal, they were maybe ten yards to his left.

His phone vibrated in his pocket.

He hauled it out and cupped it in his hand. The caller ID said Dixon, which meant Lamaison. *I said I'd call you. Can't talk.*

He jammed the phone back in his pocket. The searchers were almost dead level, eight yards to his left. They moved on. Reacher squirmed round a silent half-circle on the ground. The searchers walked on. Reacher got silently to his feet. Stepping high to keep his soles from brushing the grass, he fell in behind them, ten feet back, then eight, then six. They were a decent size. Maybe six-two, two-ten. Broad shoulders, thick necks.

He hit the first guy with a massive straight right in the back of the neck, two hundred and fifty pounds and days of rage behind the blow. The guy's skull snapped back and he went straight down in a heap and his buddy turned towards him in shock and Reacher danced through a short shuffle step and head-butted him full in the face. The sound was the unmistakable crunch of serious bone damage. The guy went down unconscious.

Reacher checked their pockets. The first guy had a cellphone and a gun and a wallet full of cash and credit cards. Reacher took the 9mm SIG P226 and the two hundred dollars. The second guy had another phone, another SIG, another wallet. Plus Dave O'Donnell's ceramic knuckle-duster.

Reacher put it in his own pocket and jammed the SIGs in his waistband and the cash in his back pocket. Then he wiped his hands on the second guy's jacket and crawled away, low and fast. He had heard nothing from Neagley, but he wasn't worried. Neagley against two guys in the dark was about as reliable as the sun setting in the west.

He found another broad dip in the grass and lay down on his elbows and pulled out his phone. Called Dixon's number.

'Where the hell were you?' Lamaison asked.

'I told you, I don't pick up when I'm driving.'

'You're not driving.'

'So why didn't I pick up?'

'Whatever,' Lamaison said. 'Before the 110th Dixon was with the 53rd MP and O'Donnell was with the 131st.

'OK. I'll call you back in ten. When we arrive.'

Reacher clicked off and sat up. He had his proof-of-life answers. Only problem was, neither one was true.

He crawled south through the grass, fifty fast yards. He blundered right into Neagley. She was lying on her side, propped up on one elbow.

'You OK?' he whispered.

'Feeling good,' she whispered back.

Reacher turned. 'Any problems?' he asked.

'Easy,' she said. 'And quieter than you. I heard that head butt all the way over here.'

'Lamaison thinks we're on the outside,' Reacher said. 'He's trying to scam us with a deal. I asked for a proof of life. Personal questions. Dixon says she was with the 53rd MP and O'Donnell says he was with the 131st.'

'But there was no 53rd. And Dave was posted to the 110th straight out of officer candidate school.'

'They're talking to us,' Reacher said. 'Fifty three. Karla knew I'd pick up on a prime number. Five and three make eight. She's telling us there are eight hostiles.'

'Four left, then. Lennox, Parker and Lamaison. Who's the fourth?'

'That's Dave's message. One-three-one. Thirteenth letter of the alphabet, first letter of the alphabet. M and A. Mauney is here.'

'Excellent,' Neagley said. 'Saves hunting him down later.'

Then cellphones started to ring. Loud and piercing. Two of them, different tones, behind them to the right. Reacher had no doubt the same thing was happening fifty yards away. Lamaison was touching base with his foot patrol. *Something unpredictable.*

The phones rang six times each and stopped. 'What would you do now?' Reacher asked. 'If you were Lamaison?'

Neagley said, 'I'd get guys in those Chryslers and turn the headlights on bright. I'd run us down in less than a minute.'

Reacher nodded. He glanced at the fence. 'What are they going to do if they don't find us?'

'How are they not going to find us?'

'Suppose.'

'They're going to assume we got out and panic. They're going to kill Karla and Dave and hunker down.'

Reacher nodded. 'That's my guess too,' he said.

He got up and ran. Reacher ran straight for the helicopter. Neagley followed. It was sixty yards away, large and luminous in the city's night-time glow. Reacher got there just as the main building's door burst open and light and men spilled out. He dodged left and kept the chopper between him and them. Neagley crowded in at his elbow. Three guys were heading for the parking lot, fast and urgent. Parker and Lennox. And Lamaison. For every yard they covered, Reacher and Neagley moved a corresponding inch round the Bell.

Thirty yards away three Chryslers started up. Three pairs of headlights flicked on, then switched to high beam. Reacher and Neagley slid round the Bell's long pointed nose and hugged the other flank. The cars separated like a shell burst and accelerated in random directions.

Within ten seconds they slewed to a stop fifty yards apart, and threw long grotesque shadows off the four humped shapes. Three distant figures ran around, moving through the beams.

'We can't stay here,' Neagley said. 'They're going to come back this way and light us up like we're on stage at the Hollywood Bowl.'

'How long have we got?'

'They're going to check the fence. Four minutes, maybe.'

'Start counting.' Reacher ran for the main building.

The door had been left ajar. Lights had been left on. Reacher walked straight in, very quietly, with his hand on his Glock in his pocket. The place seemed deserted. There were offices on the right and a big open-plan work area on the left, behind a floor-to-ceiling plate-glass screen. The work area had long laboratory benches and complex extraction ducts. One office door was labelled *Edward Dean*. The next door was labelled *Margaret Berenson*. The next door was Tony Swan's.

The next was Allen Lamaison's. It was standing open.

Reacher took a breath. Took out his Glock. Stepped into the doorway. Saw a desk, chair, phones, file cabinets. Nothing unusual or out of place.

Except for Curtis Mauney and a suitcase.

Neagley stepped into the room. 'Sixty seconds,' she said.

Mauney just sat there at the desk, immobile. 'Lamaison was my partner,' he said, like an excuse.

Reacher nodded. 'Loyalty, it's a bitch, ain't it?'

The suitcase was a dark grey hard-shell Samsonite.

Mauney asked, 'What are you going to do?'

'With you?' Reacher asked. 'Nothing yet.'

Neagley aimed her gun at Mauney's face and Reacher knelt down and tried the latches. They were locked. He put his Glock on the floor and jammed the tips of his index fingers under the tips of the latches and braced his thumbs and heaved. The locks broke instantly.

He lifted the lid. 'Payday,' he said.

The case was full of fancy engraved paper certificates and letters from foreign banks and small suede drawstring bags.

'Sixty-five millions dollars,' Neagley said.

'At a guess,' Reacher said.

'Ninety seconds gone,' Neagley said.

Reacher handed the paperwork to Neagley. He followed it with the bags. Neagley slid everything into her pockets. Reacher picked up his gun.

'Two minutes gone,' Neagley said.

'Your friends are here,' Mauney said.

'I know,' Reacher said. 'Do they know you're here?'

'I've been here before,' Mauney said. 'Many times.'

'Pick up the phone or I'll shoot you in the head.'

'You will anyway.'

'You gave up six of my friends. Pick up the phone.'

'And what?'

'Tell the gate guard to open up exactly one minute from now.'

Mauney hesitated. Reacher put the Glock's muzzle against his temple. Mauney picked up the phone. Dialled. 'This is Mauney. Open the gate one minute from now.'

Reacher turned to Neagley. 'Am I your CO?' he asked.

'Yes,' she said. 'You are.'

'Listen up. We get out of here as fast as we possibly can. We have to really go for it. You're a lot faster, so don't wait for me. Don't even look back. We can't afford to lose a yard, either one of us.'

'Understood,' she said. 'Three minutes gone.'

Reacher grabbed Mauney's collar and hauled him to his feet. Dragged him out of the office, down the hallway, over to the main doorway. And then a yard outside, into the night. The three Chryslers were turning tight circles in the distance, their headlights sweeping the fence like searchlights in a prison movie.

'Wait for the starting gun,' Reacher said to Neagley.

He watched the guard in his booth, saw the gate start to move. He put the Glock to Mauney's temple and pulled the trigger. Then he and Neagley took off at full speed.

Neagley was ahead after half a step. She flew through the pool of light from the guard hut, dodged the end of the moving gate, raced to the street and was lost to sight. Reacher turned and ran in the opposite direction. Fifteen seconds later he was back behind the Bell's long nose.

CHAPTER THIRTEEN

Maybe they had seen Neagley go, and assumed Reacher was ahead of her. Or maybe they had just seen the gate move. Certainly they must have heard the gunshot. Possibly they imagined the rest, but they took the bait. They reacted instantly. All three cars accelerated and headed for the street, fishtailing like crazy. They went out through the gate like stock cars through a turn. Reacher watched them go.

He waited for the night to go quiet again. Then he counted to ten and moved slowly along the Bell's starboard flank to the rear door and tried the handle. It was unlocked.

He glanced over his shoulder at the pilot's hut. No movement there. The door opened. He climbed inside and closed the latch with one decisive click. He knelt on the cabin floor in the darkness. From the inside the Bell looked like a swelled-up version of a minivan. A little more contoured. There would have been seven seats, except that the centre row was missing. The seats were all bulky high-backed recliners, faced with black leather. They had safety harnesses. The bulkheads were padded with black quilted vinyl.

There was a space behind the two rearmost seats. For bags, Reacher guessed. It wasn't a huge space. But it was big enough. He flopped the seat backs forward, climbed over and sat down on the floor with his back jammed against the side bulkhead. He took the captured SIGs out of his waistband and laid them next to his knees. He hauled the seat backs upright, then slumped down to keep his head out of sight.

He waited. Five minutes. Ten.

Then the misted windows lit up. Three sets of headlight beams played on the glass for a moment, then stopped. The cars, back in the lot. Parked.

Reacher strained to hear. Slow footsteps and low voices, unmistakable sound of failure. The search was over.

He waited and grew cold and cramped. He waited twenty long minutes.

Then a door opened up in the front and the helicopter dipped as its undercarriage compressed. The door closed. A seat creaked. A harness buckle clicked. Switches clicked. Faint orange light from instrument faces threw sudden shadows on the roof. Reacher leaned forward between the seats and saw the pilot's leather sleeve. His hand was dancing over switches as he ran through preflight checks.

Then there was an incredibly loud noise, the starter mechanism, forcing the rotor round. The engines fired up and gears meshed and the rotor caught and settled to a lazy *whop-whop* idle. The torque rocked and twisted the whole craft on its wheels, just a little, rhythmically, like it was dancing. The interior was filled with a loud thrumming noise.

A minute later the rear door was wrenched open. A blast of louder noise flooded in. After the noise came Karla Dixon, dumped on the floor like a log, facing away on her side. Her wrists and ankles were tied with rope. Two minutes later O'Donnell was wrestled in, tied up the same way as Dixon. He rolled face down alongside her. They lay there struggling against the ropes.

Then the wheels bounced again and Lennox and Parker climbed in the rear seats. Allen Lamaison dumped himself in the front seat opposite the pilot and said, 'Go.' The turbines spun up and vibration filled the cabin and the rotor note changed to an urgent *whip-whip-whip*.

Then they were airborne. Reacher felt the floor come up at him. He heard the wheels pull upwards into their wells. He felt rotation and drift and a long steady climb and then the nose went down for speed. He braced himself against spread fingers to stop himself sliding into the seats in front of him.

For twenty minutes, with his head well down, he kept his arms and legs moving through silent fractions of an inch and kept his muscles tensing and relaxing. There was no conversation.

Until the helicopter slowed down.

He bent forward to the gap between the seats and saw Lamaison leaning over with his forehead pressed against his window. Saw him lean towards the pilot. Heard him speak. Or maybe he only imagined that he heard him speak. He had reconstructed the orders in his head a thousand times. He felt that he knew them, word for word, in all their cruel inevitability.

'Where are we?' Lamaison asked.

'The badlands,' the pilot said.

'Height?'

'Three thousand feet.'

'What's the air like up here?'

'Still. A few thermals, but no wind.'

'So let's do it.'

Reacher felt the helicopter come to a stationary hover. Lamaison turned and nodded to Parker and Lennox. Reacher heard the click of safety-harness catches and then the weight came up off the seats in front of him. Parker and Lennox were both in half-crouches, arms thrust out for balance. One of them was going to die easy and one of them was going to die hard.

Lennox half-turned and grabbed his trailing safety harness. Then he crabbed sideways and groped for the door release. He unlatched it and pushed. The pilot put the craft into a slow clockwise rotation so that motion and inertia and air pressure held the door wide open against its hinge.

Lennox turned back. Big, red-faced, meaty, his left hand tight on his harness, his right pawing the air like a man on ice.

Reacher leaned forward and used his left hand to find the release lever and force the seat back horizontal. He brought the Glock up in his right and twisted from the waist and laid his forearm flat. Closed one eye and picked a spot an inch above Lennox's navel.

And pulled the trigger. The bullet hit Lennox low in the midriff. An instant through-and-through from a range of four feet, it went straight out of the open door. A bloom of blood haloed the hole in his shirt. It looked black in the orange light. His left hand came off the harness and pawed the air, a perfect mirror image of his right. Lennox balanced there, a foot from the door sill, catastrophic physical shock on his face.

Reacher moved the Glock a small fraction and shot him again, this time through the sternum. Lennox's upper body mass pitched backwards and took him right out of the door into the night. The last Reacher saw of him was the soles of his shoes, whipping away into the windy darkness.

By that point it was much less than two seconds since he had dropped the seat but to Reacher it seemed like two lifetimes. Franz's and Orozco's, maybe. He felt infinitely fluent and languid. He was floating in a state of grace and torment, planning his moves like chess, minutely aware of potentials and threats. The pilot was half-turned in his seat.

Reacher stood up. He dropped the second seat and climbed out over it like a nightmare apparition, a sudden giant figure from nowhere. Then he stood still, his head jammed up hard against the roof, his feet a yard apart. His left hand held a SIG, pointing straight at Parker's face. His right held his Glock, pointing straight at Lamaison's.

The time of maximum danger. Reacher could not afford to fire forward and chance hitting some essential cockpit avionics. He couldn't take Parker down hand to hand, because O'Donnell and Dixon were occupying all the floor space. Whereas Lamaison and the pilot were still strapped in their seats. All the pilot had to do was throw the Bell all over the sky until everyone else fell out.

Stalemate if they understood. Or victory, if they seized the moment.

They didn't understand. They didn't seize the moment. Instead O'Donnell got his head and his feet off the floor and desperately porpoised six inches closer to Reacher, and Dixon rolled back and a precious foot of space opened up. Reacher stepped into it and smashed Parker in the gut with the SIG's muzzle. The breath punched out of Parker's lungs and he staggered, straight into the channel O'Donnell and Dixon had created. Reacher dodged past him like a bullfighter, shoved hard with the sole of his boot and sent him stumbling blindly out of the door. Before his scream had died Reacher had his left arm round Lamaison's throat and the Glock jammed into his neck with the SIG pointing straight at the pilot.

After that, it got easier.

The Bell hung there in its noisy hover. The door stayed open, wide and inviting, pinned back by the airflow. Reacher hauled back on Lamaison's neck and pulled until his shoulder straps went tight. Then he put the Glock on the floor and fished in his pocket for O'Donnell's knuckle-duster. He extended his arm and pushed Dixon onto her front and used the knuckle-duster's wicked spines to rub at the bonds on her wrists. She tensed her arms and the sisal fibres ruptured slowly. Lamaison started to struggle and Reacher tightened his elbow, which had the disadvantage of aiming the SIG behind the pilot. But the pilot just sat there, keeping the Bell turning slow.

Reacher kept on sawing away, blindly. Dixon kept on moving her arms. Lamaison struggled harder. He was a big guy, strong and powerful. But Reacher was bigger, and Reacher was stronger, and Reacher was angry. Reacher tightened his arm, but he wanted him conscious. Suddenly a whole skein of fibres unravelled and Dixon's wrists came free. Reacher gave her the knuckle-duster and his Glock.

Dixon did the smart thing, which was to haul herself to Lamaison's pockets, where she found another SIG and O'Donnell's switchblade. Two seconds later her feet were free, and five seconds after that O'Donnell was free. He grabbed the pilot's collar in one fist and jammed a SIG's muzzle up under his chin. The pilot stayed passive. Reacher leaned towards him and asked, 'Height?'

The pilot swallowed. 'Three thousand feet.'

'Take it up a little,' Reacher said. 'Try five thousand feet.'

THE CLIMB took the Bell out of its slow rotation and the open door slammed shut. The cabin went quiet. Lamaison hauled down listlessly on Reacher's forearm. He had gone strangely passive and inert. Like he couldn't really believe what was going to happen.

Like Swan couldn't, Reacher thought. *Like Orozco couldn't, and Franz couldn't, and Sanchez couldn't.*

He felt the Bell top out and level off. 'More,' he said. 'Let's do another two hundred and eighty feet. Let's make it a whole mile.'

The craft moved upwards again, slowly, precisely. It turned a little and came back to a hover. The pilot said, 'One mile.'

Reacher turned to Dixon and said, 'Open the door.'

Lamaison found some new energy. He bucked and thrashed in his seat and said, 'No, please, please, no.'

Reacher tightened his elbow and asked, 'Did my friends beg?'

Lamaison just shook his head.

'They wouldn't,' Reacher said. 'Too proud.'

Dixon moved back in the cabin and grabbed Lennox's seat harness and clicked the door release. She pushed hard and the door swung open. The pilot set up the rotation. Shattering noise and cold night air poured in. The mountains showed black on the horizon. Beyond them the glow of Los Angeles was visible, then rotated away.

Dixon sat down on Parker's folded seat. O'Donnell tightened his hold on the pilot's collar. Reacher used the SIG's muzzle to hit Lamaison's harness release, pulled him all the way over the top of the seat and dumped him on the floor. Wrestled him down and got a knee between his shoulder blades and jammed the SIG against the top of his spine. Lamaison's head was up and Reacher knew he was staring out into the void. He was screaming. Reacher could hear him clearly over the noise.

Too late, Reacher thought. *You reap what you sow.*

He swapped the SIG into his left hand and looped his right over

Lamaison's neck and squeezed hard. Lamaison's arteries compressed and his brain craved oxygen. Reacher rolled him over and sat him up like a drunk. Pushed him across the floor, feet first.

He got him as far as the door sill and held him there, arms pinned behind him. The helicopter turned, slowly. The engines whined and the rotor beat out thumps of sound. Reacher felt every one of them in his chest, like heartbeats. Minutes passed and Lamaison came round to find himself sitting on the edge with his feet hanging over the void. A mile above the desert floor.

Reacher had rehearsed a speech. He had perfected it over the previous days. It was full of fine phrases about loyalty and retribution, but when it came to it he didn't say much. Lamaison was crazy with terror and there was too much noise. Reacher just put his mouth close to his ear and said, 'You messed with the wrong people. Now it's time to pay.'

Then he bent his legs, put his heel flat against the small of Lamaison's back and pushed.

THERE WAS NOTHING the pilot could do to them without killing himself also, so they left him alone in the cockpit. Dixon and O'Donnell sat down in the rear seats. Reacher lay on his back with his arms and legs flung wide. He was tired and dispirited. Lamaison was gone, but no one had come back.

'Where's Neagley? O'Donnell asked.

'Working, I hope. The missiles rolled out of the gate in Colorado eight hours ago. And we don't know where they're going.'

'Where would you take six hundred and fifty SAMs?'

'The Middle East,' Dixon said. 'And I'd send them by sea.'

Reacher raised his head. 'Lamaison said they were going to Kashmir.'

'I think he didn't want to know the truth.'

'Which is?'

'Terrorism here in the States. Got to be. Kashmir is a squabble between governments. Governments don't run around with Samsonite suitcases full of bearer bonds and diamonds.'

Dixon asked, 'Is that what you found?'

'Highland Park. Sixty-five millions dollars' worth. Neagley's got it all. You're going to have to convert it for us, Karla.'

'If I survive. My plane back to New York might get blown up. Eight hours at, say, fifty miles an hour is already a radius of four hundred miles. Which is a half-million-square-mile circle.'

'Five hundred and two thousand, seven hundred and twenty. But that's the bargain we made. We could stop them when the circle was small, or we could come for you guys.'

'Thanks,' O'Donnell said. 'So how do we do this?'

'Mahmoud isn't dumb,' Reacher said. 'He just spent sixty-five million dollars on what are basically just components. He must have insisted that part of the deal was that someone would show him how to screw the damn things together.'

'Who?'

'Diana Bond told us New Age's engineer does the quality-control tests because he's the only guy in the world who knows how Little Wing works. Well, Lamaison had him on a string. He was threatening the guy's daughter.'

O'Donnell said, 'So Lamaison was going to take him somewhere. And you threw Lamaison out of the damn helicopter.'

Reacher shook his head. 'Lamaison said the whole thing was a done deal. He wasn't taking anyone anywhere.'

'So who?'

'Not who,' Reacher said. 'The question is, where?'

Dixon said, 'If Lamaison wasn't planning to take him somewhere, they'll have to bring the missiles to him. The guy lives in the middle of nowhere.'

Reacher pulled out his pay-as-you-go. Got cell reception. Found Neagley's number. Hit the green button.

'Dean's place?' he asked.

'Dean's place,' she said. 'For sure. I'm twenty minutes away.'

THE BELL HAD A GPS system that produced a pair of always-changing latitude and longitude readings. Reacher told the pilot to get himself somewhere south of Palmdale and wait.

Then Reacher called Neagley back. She had got Dean's address from Margaret Berenson, but she had no GPS either. Reacher told her to find Dean's spread and drive in tight circles with her lights on bright.

Reacher took Lamaison's seat up front. Dixon and O'Donnell took side windows in the back. Between them they covered a one-eighty panorama.

They saw nothing. Nothing at all, except vast featureless blackness and occasional pinpoints of light. Gas stations, maybe. Reacher tried his phone again. No service.

'Highway on the left,' Dixon called.

Reacher looked down. Two cars heading south and three north. He closed his eyes and pictured maps he had looked at. 'We shouldn't see a north–south highway. We're too far west.'

The Bell tilted and swung east on a long, fast curve. Way far ahead in the distance a tiny grid of lights winked and twinkled. Palmdale, presumably.

'Turn south,' Reacher said. 'And climb. We need a better angle.'

The Bell climbed a couple of hundred feet. The pilot turned a wide circle, like he was hosing the horizon with an imaginary searchlight. They saw nothing. There was no cell coverage. 'Higher,' Reacher said.

He closed his eyes again and pictured the map. Berenson had said Dean had complained about the commute from hell. He had two choices, Route 138 or Route 2. Route 2 was smaller and twistier, and it joined the 210 at Glendale, which probably made it more hellish. Which meant Dean was starting due south of Palmdale, not southeast. Reacher waited until the distant grid of lights slid back into view. 'Now pull a one-eighty and head back,' he said.

The craft turned. Dipped its nose and clattered onwards.

Sixty seconds later they found Neagley.

A mile in front and four hundred feet down, a cone of light turning and pulsing like a beacon. It looked like Neagley had the Civic on maximum lock and was driving a thirty-foot circle, flashing between dipped and brights as she went. The effect was spectacular. Like a lighthouse on a rocky shore. There were small hills and rises thrown into dramatic relief, and a forty-foot-wide gully. 'Land there,' Reacher said. 'In the ditch.'

The pilot dropped a couple of hundred feet and turned to line up with the gully. Then he took the Bell down like an elevator. Through the windows Reacher could see Neagley's lights coming towards them through a sandstorm kicked up by the rotor wash.

Reacher was first out of the door. He sent Dixon and O'Donnell ahead to meet Neagley and then turned back to the pilot. 'Nice landing,' he said.

The pilot said, 'Thanks.'

'That thing with the rotation. The way it kept the door open. Smart move. But then, you had plenty of practice.'

The pilot said nothing.

'Four times,' Reacher said. 'That I know about, at least. Those men were my friends.'

'Lamaison told me I had to do it. I'd lose my job. It was wrong, I know.'

'But you did it anyway.'

'What choice did I have?'

Reacher shook his head. 'Lots of choices,' he said.

NEAGLEY'S LIGHTS were still on bright when Reacher got to the car. She and Dixon and O'Donnell were standing together in a tight group of three.

'We OK?' Reacher asked.

Dixon and O'Donnell nodded. Neagley didn't.

'You mad with me?' Reacher asked her.

'Not really,' she said. 'I would have been if you'd screwed up.'

'I needed you to work out where the missiles were headed.'

'You already knew.'

'I wanted a second opinion. Let's go see Mr Dean.'

Dean opened up on the first knock. He didn't look much like a rocket scientist. He was tall and maybe forty years old and had a shock of sandy hair. He was barefoot and dressed in tracksuit bottoms and a T-shirt. It was close to midnight. 'Who are you people?' he asked.

Reacher explained who they were, and why they were there.

Dean had no idea what he was talking about.

Reacher had been expecting some kind of a denial, but Dean's denial seemed genuine. The guy was puzzled, not evasive. 'Let's start at the beginning. We know what you did with the electronics packs, and why you had to do it. We know about the threat against your daughter. Where is she?'

'Away. Her mother, too.'

'You sent them away. That was smart.' Reacher nodded. 'Lamaison is dead. I threw him out of the helicopter.'

Dean said nothing.

Reacher said, 'Show him, Karla.'

Dixon pulled out the wallet she had taken from Lamaison's pocket. Dean took it and shuffled through the contents. Driver's licence, credit cards, a New Age photo ID. He handed the wallet back.

'Doesn't prove you got him.'

'I can show you the pilot. He's dead, too. I just killed him.'

'You're crazy.'

'And you're off the hook. Get used to it. But we need to know who's coming, and when.'

'Nobody's coming. That was never the deal.'

'Wasn't it? Someone has to be.'

'Tell me again,' Dean said. 'Lamaison's dead?'

'He killed four of my friends,' Reacher said. 'If he wasn't dead, I sure as hell wouldn't be wasting time with you.'

Dean nodded, slowly. 'But I still don't know what you're talking about. OK, I signed off on phoney paperwork, which is terrible, but that was all I did. There was never anything about me assembling units or showing anyone else how to do it.'

'Nine hours,' Neagley said.

'Another hundred and thirty thousand square miles,' Dixon said.

A hundred and thirty three thousand, five hundred and thirty five, Reacher thought. The increase alone was more than half of Texas. 'They're coming here,' he said. 'They have to be.'

Nobody answered. Dean led them inside.

His house was a long, low shack built from concrete and timber. There was a big living room with Navajo rugs and worn furniture and a fireplace heaped with last winter's ash. There were plenty of books. There was a stereo with CDs piled everywhere. The place looked like a city refugee's dream.

Dean went to make coffee in the kitchen and Dixon said, 'Nine hours and twenty-six minutes.' Neagley and O'Donnell didn't get the point, but Reacher did. Assuming three decimal places for *pi* and a speed of fifty, exactly seven hundred thousand square miles.

Dean served coffee and nobody spoke for a while. Then Reacher asked him, 'Did you do your own electrical work?'

Dean said, 'Some of it.'

'Got any plastic cable ties?'

'Lots of them. Workshop out back.'

'You should drive north,' Reacher said. 'Head for Palmdale, get some breakfast.'

'Now?'

'Now. Stay for lunch. Don't come back until the afternoon.'

'Why? What's going to happen here?'

'I'm not sure yet. But whatever, you shouldn't be around.'

Dean sat still for a moment. Then he got up, found his keys and left. They heard his car start up. The house went quiet again.

Dixon said, 'Nine hours and forty-six minutes.' The circle was now three-quarters of a million square miles in size.

'He's coming,' Reacher said.

Eighteen hours from Denver, if the driver didn't rest, made six in the morning a likely rendezvous time. Ideal, from Mahmoud's point of view. Lamaison would have told him about the threat against the daughter, and he would figure the kid would be home at six in the morning. A perfect reminder of Dean's vulnerability.

Reacher got up and went for a stroll. Three bedrooms, a den, a kitchen. One of the bedrooms was the daughter's. There were inkjet prints of photographs pinned up on a board. Groups of teenage girls, three or four at a time. Reacher worked out which girl appeared in every picture. A tall blonde girl, maybe fourteen. A hostage to fortune. Reacher wished Lamaison had screamed a little more on the way down.

By FIVE in the morning the sky in the east was lightening. By five thirty Reacher took another walk. Dean had no neighbours. He was living in the middle of thousands of empty acres. Worthless, sun-blasted land. A stony driveway from the southeast was at least a mile long, maybe more.

Reacher moved Neagley's Civic behind the garage, and a hundred yards out he saw a flat rock the size and shape of a coffin. He walked over and took Tony Swan's lump of concrete out of his pocket and rested it on the slab, like a monument. He walked back and ducked into the workshop. The black plastic cable ties were about two feet long, thick and stiff. He took eight of the biggest, then went back inside the house to wait.

Six o'clock arrived, and Mahmoud didn't. Now the circle measured more than two and a half million square miles. Six fifteen came and went, two-point-six million.

Then, at six thirty-two, the telephone bell dinged, just once.

'Here we go,' Reacher said. 'Someone cut the phone line.'

They moved to the windows. They waited. South and east, they saw a tiny white dot winking in the early sun, trailing a cloud of dust backlit by the dawn like a halo.

THEY WAITED in the living room, tense and silent. Five minutes later they heard the crunch of stones under tyres and the wet muffled beat of a worn V-8 engine. The crunching stopped and the engine died and a minute after that, they heard a knock at the door.

Reacher counted to twenty and walked down the hall. Opened the door. Saw a man on the step, with a mid-size panel truck parked behind him. A rented U-Haul, white and red. The man was medium height, medium weight, expensively dressed but a little rumpled. He was maybe forty years old. He had thick black hair, shiny, beautifully cut, and the kind of mid-brown skin and regular features that could have made him Indian, or Iranian, or Algerian, or even Israeli or Italian.

In turn Azhari Mahmoud saw a dishevelled giant of a white man, wrists as wide as two-by-fours, dressed in dusty grey denims and work boots. *A crazy scientist*, he thought. *Right at home in a desert shack.* 'Edward Dean?' he said.

'Yes,' Reacher said. 'Who are you?'

'No cell coverage here, I notice. And I took the precaution of cutting your land line down the road.'

'Who are you?'

'I'm a friend of Allen Lamaison's. You are to extend me the same courtesies you would extend to him.'

'I don't extend Allen Lamaison courtesies. So get lost.'

Mahmoud nodded. 'Let me put it another way. The threat that Lamaison made is still operative against your daughter.'

Reacher said nothing.

'You're going to show me how to arm Little Wing.'

Reacher glanced at the U-Haul. 'All you have are electronics.'

'The missiles will be here very soon.'

'Where are you going to use them?'

'Here and there.'

'Inside the US?'

'It's a target-rich environment.'

'I won't do it.'

'You will. Like you did before. For the same reason.'

Reacher paused a beat and said, 'You better come in.'

He stepped aside. Mahmoud was accustomed to deference, so he walked ahead into the hallway. Reacher hit him hard in the back of the head and sent him stumbling towards the living-room door, where Frances Neagley dropped him with a neat uppercut. A minute later he was hog-tied on the floor with cable ties. The ties were zipped hard and the flesh around them was already swelling. Mahmoud was moaning. Reacher stepped back into the living room and waited.

The truck from Denver was a white eighteen-wheeler. Its driver was hog-tied next to Mahmoud a minute after climbing down from the cab. Then Reacher dragged Mahmoud out of the house and left him next to his U-Haul. Mahmoud's eyes were full of fear. Reacher figured he would prefer to die, which was why he left him there alive. They all crammed themselves into Neagley's Civic and headed south, fast. As soon as cell coverage kicked in Neagley called her Pentagon buddy. Reacher watched out of the back window and before they even hit the mountains he saw a whole squadron of choppers heading west on the horizon. Bell AH-1s, from some nearby Homeland Security base, he assumed. The sky was thick with them.

After the mountains they talked about money. Neagley gave Dixon the financial documents and the diamonds to carry to New York and convert to cash. First call would be to repay Neagley's expense budget, second call would be to set up trust funds for Angela and Charlie Franz, Tammy Orozco and her children, and Sanchez's friend Milena, and the third call would be to make a donation to People for the Ethical Treatment of Animals, in the name of Tony Swan.

Then it got awkward. Neagley was OK for salary, but Reacher sensed that Dixon and O'Donnell were hurting, though sensitive about asking. So he suggested they take whatever little margin was left over and divide it up four ways. Everyone agreed.

After that, they didn't talk much at all. And Reacher got to ask himself the big question: If the stalled car on the 210 had not delayed his arrival at the hospital, would he have performed any better than Dixon or O'Donnell? Truth was, he didn't know the answer, and he hated not knowing.

TWO HOURS LATER they were at LAX. They abandoned the Civic in a fire lane, and before they split up they stood on the sidewalk and said good-byes they promised would be temporary. Neagley headed inside to American. Dixon went looking for America West. O'Donnell went to search for United. Reacher stood in the heat and watched them walk away.

He left California with close to two thousand dollars in his pocket. As a result he didn't run low on cash for almost four weeks. Finally he stopped by an ATM in the bus depot in Santa Fe, New Mexico. As always he worked out his balance first, then checked the bank's.

For the second time in his life, it didn't match.

The machine told him that his account balance was a hundred and eleven thousand, eight hundred and twenty-two dollars and eighteen cents more than he was expecting.

111,822.18. Dixon, obviously. The spoils of war.

At first he was disappointed. Not with the amount. He was disappointed with himself, because he couldn't perceive any message in the number. It had hundreds of factors. Its reciprocal was boring. Its square root was a long messy string of digits. Its cube root was worse.

111,822.18. Dixon's head wasn't in the game.

She had let him down. Maybe. Or maybe not.

He pressed the button for the mini-statement. A slip of thin paper came out of a slot. Neagley's original deposit from Chicago. His fifty-dollar withdrawal at the Portland bus depot. His airfare from Portland to LAX.

Then a new deposit in the sum of one hundred and one thousand, eight hundred and ten dollars and eighteen cents. Then, on the same day, another deposit, ten thousand and twelve dollars exactly.

101,810.18. 10,012.

He smiled. Dixon's head was in the game, after all. Totally in the game. The first deposit was 10-18, repeated. Military police radio code for mission accomplished, twice over. Herself and O'Donnell, rescued. Lamaison and Mahmoud, beaten.

Nice, Karla, he thought.

The second deposit was her zip code: 10012. Greenwich Village. Where she lived. A geographic reference. A hint.

She had asked: *Feel like dropping by New York afterwards?*

He smiled again and balled up the slip of paper and dropped it in the trash. Took a hundred dollars from the machine and headed inside the depot and bought a ticket for the first bus he saw. He had no idea where it was going.

He had answered: *I don't make plans, Karla.*

LEE CHILD

Born: Coventry, England, 1954
Homes: New York and the South of France
Motto: Do it once and do it right

RD: Reacher is usually a loner but in this book he works with his old team. Was there a particular reason behind the change?

LC: I started thinking about the book in 2005, ten years after I left Granada Television, where I worked as part of a tight-knit team. I suppose I was daydreaming about going back to a team situation. Writing, by contrast is a lonely job. The idea seemed interesting for Reacher too. He's a loner, but suppose he had a good reason to get back together with his old colleagues? It felt like a good platform for some emotion.

RD: He seems to be questioning some of the choices he's made. Does this herald a new direction for Reacher?

LC: I felt it was time for him to examine his lifestyle. I like the way that he's very sure of himself but too much of that might be unrealistic. I think the availability of direct comparisons with his old team would raise questions for him. But I don't know what his future direction will be. I'll have to wait and see.

RD: Reacher's interest in numbers is fun, where did that idea come from?

LC: I like to confound expectations. Reacher is a rough, tough guy but he can also think. In earlier books, crucial clues came from punctuation marks—Reacher doesn't do it with his fists alone.

RD: In the novel he seems very cynical about gambling, do you share his views?

LC: Not cynical, just realistic. The house will always win overall. Otherwise they'd all go out of business.

RD: Did you visit Las Vegas?

LC: I visited it in 2004. Loved it by night, wasn't so sure by day. Reacher's views are pretty much my own.

RD: When you start a new novel, how do you go about it?

LC: I get an idea for a theme, plus maybe an idea for an opening scene, plus maybe a crucial line of dialogue. In this case it was Frances Neagley saying, 'I want you to put the old unit back together.' That seemed like a great hook.

RD: What sort of writing regime do you have and where do you write?

LC: I write between September and March, five or six days a week, five or six hours a day. When I'm in the South of France I have a separate house in town that I use as an office. It's a fourteenth-century building in the Arab quarter. In New York, I have a separate apartment on the twenty-fifth floor of my block, overlooking the Empire State Building.

RD: When you first introduced readers to Reacher, in *Killing Floor*, I understand that you were surprised that it appealed to women as much as to men?

LC: Yes. I thought it was going to appeal to the rough tough male market. That women would hate it because he's too rough, too dirty, too uncivilised. I thought that was a drag because women buy a lot of books. But, as it turned out, women loved it from the start, more than men probably. That shows how much I know about women!

RD: And, of course, he does have a strong male following.

LC: Yes. He's unencumbered, which seems to be a fantasy that appeals to men especially: men who have mortages and responsibilities. The idea that you can just wander from place to place with nothing but the clothes on your back is very appealing.

RD: How do you relax?

LC: With music or sport. Football in France and baseball in America.

RD: What are you most proud of?

LC: My daughter Ruth.

THE JACK REACHER FILE

Name: Jack Reacher (no middle name)

DOB: October 29, 1960

Birthplace: Berlin, Germany

Height: 6'5" **Weight:** 220–250 lbs

Education: West Point Military Academy, New York.

Employment status: Retired US Army Military Policeman.

Military rank: Major

Service Awards: Silver Star, the Defense Superior Service medal, the Legion of Merit, the Bronze Star, the Purple Heart.

Famous fans: Author Stephen King and former US President Bill Clinton.

Book appearances: *Killing Floor*, *Die Trying*, *Tripwire*, *The Visitor*, *Echo Burning*, *Without Fail*, *Persuader*, *The Enemy*, *One Shot*, *The Hard Way*, *Bad Luck and Trouble*.

Did you know? Reacher does not have a driving licence, a telephone or an email account. As a drifter, he likes to be almost untraceable.

Websites:

www.leechild.com/reacher.html

www.booksattransworld.co.uk/leechild

Silver Bay
Jojo Moyes

High above the sparkling waters of
Silver Bay, stands a quaint old family-run
hotel. It offers simple hospitality to guests
and the whale-boat crews who take
tourists to marvel at the winter migration
of the whales.
Into this timeless haven strides smartly
dressed City banker Michael Dormer.
From the cut-and-thrust of London. With
a plan. To change the bay for ever.

PROLOGUE

My name is Kathleen Whittier Mostyn, and when I was seventeen I became famous for catching the biggest shark New South Wales had ever seen: a grey nurse with an eye so mean it still looked like it wanted to rip me in two several days after we'd laid it out. That was back in the days when all of Silver Bay was given over to game fishing, and for three straight weeks all anyone could talk about was that shark. A newspaper reporter came from Newcastle and took a picture of me standing next to it (I'm the one in the bathing-suit).

What you can see is a tall, rather stern-seeming girl, better-looking than she knew and with a waist trim enough that she never needed a corset. There I am, unable to hide my pride, not yet aware that I would be tied to that beast for the rest of my days as surely as if we had been married.

For years I was known as the Shark Girl, even when my girlhood was well over. But my success, my father always said, made the Silver Bay Hotel. Two days after that picture appeared we were booked solid, and stayed booked solid until the west wing of the hotel burned down in 1962. Men came because they wanted to beat my record. Or because they assumed that if a *girl* could land a creature like that, why, what was possible for a *proper* fisherman? A few came to ask me to marry them, but my father always sent them packing. Women came because until then they had never thought it possible that they could catch game fish. And families came because Silver Bay, with its protected bay, endless dunes and calm waters, was a fine place to be.

Two more jetties were hurriedly built to cope with the extra boat traffic, and every day the air was filled with the sound of outboard motors as the bay and the sea around it was virtually dredged of aquatic life. There was a time, during the 1950s, when it is not too fanciful to say that we were *the* place to be.

We still have our boats, and our jetties, although we only use one now, and what people are chasing is pretty different. We're fairly quiet, even in the summer. Most of the holiday traffic heads to the clubs and high-rise hotels, the more obvious delights of Coffs Harbour or Byron Bay and, to tell the truth, that suits most of us just fine.

I still hold that record. It's noted in one of those doorstop-sized books that sell in huge numbers and no one you know ever buys. Occasionally the local schoolchildren stop by to tell me they've found me in the library, and I always act surprised, just to keep them happy. I'm telling you this not out of any desire to boast, or because I'm a seventy-six-year-old woman and it's nice to feel I once did something of note, but because when you're surrounded by as many secrets as I am, it feels good to get things straight out in the open occasionally.

PART ONE
Hannah

Yoshi reckoned that if you'd paid nearly $150 to go out chasing dolphins, the least you could expect was a decent biscuit. So she bought all-butter Anzacs—thick, oaty, double-layered with chocolate—Scotch Fingers and Mint Slices wrapped in foil. Lance, the skipper, said she got decent biscuits because they were pretty well all she had to eat. I stared at the biscuits, as *Moby One* headed out into Silver Bay, holding up the tray as Yoshi offered the passengers tea and coffee. I was hoping they wouldn't eat all the Anzacs before I had a chance to take one.

'*Moby One* to *Suzanne*, how many beers did you sink last night? You're steering a course like a one-legged drunk.'

Lance was on the radio. As we went into the cockpit, I dropped my hand straight into the biscuit jar and pulled out the last Anzac. The ship-to-ship radio crackled, and a voice muttered something I couldn't make out. He tried again: '*Moby One* to *Sweet Suzanne*. Look, you'd better straighten up, mate . . . you've got four passengers up front hanging over the rails.' Lance's voice sounded like it had been rubbed down with wire wool.

Yoshi gave him a mug of coffee.

'Greg's so done in he can't steer straight.' Lance pointed out of the window towards the smaller boat. 'I tell you, Yoshi, his passengers will be asking for refunds. What the hell's got into him?' It was then that Lance had caught sight of me. 'What are you doing here, Squirt? Your mum'll have my guts for garters.'

'She'll stay out of sight,' Yoshi said. 'She just wanted to see the dolphins.'

'You gonna wear a life jacket? And not get under my feet?'

I nodded.

'Be nice to her,' said Yoshi. 'She's been ill twice already.'

'It's nerves,' I said. 'My tummy always does it.'

'Ah . . . Hell. Look, just make sure your mum knows it was nothing to do with me, OK?'

It was, Yoshi said, as we headed back out, a good day to be on the water. The sea was a little choppy, but the winds were mild, and the air so clear that you could see the white horses riding the little breakers miles into the distance. I followed her to the main restaurant deck.

While the passengers sat up on the top deck, enjoying the crisp May day, Yoshi, the steward, was laying out the buffet, offering drinks and, if the water was choppy, which it was most days now that winter was coming, preparing the disinfectant and bucket for seasickness. It didn't matter how many times you told them, she grumbled, glancing at the well-dressed Asians who made up most of the morning's custom, they *would* stay below decks, and they *would* eat and drink too quickly.

'Tea? Coffee? Biscuits? Tea? Coffee? Biscuits?'

I followed her out onto the foredeck, pulling my windcheater up round my neck. The wind had dropped a little but I could still feel the chill in the air, biting at my nose and the tips of my ears. Most of the passengers didn't want anything—they were chatting loudly, to be heard above the engines, gazing out at the distant horizon and taking pictures of each other.

I helped Yoshi put the tea- and coffee-pots back in their holders, then stepped back out onto the narrow side deck, where we gazed across the sea to where the smaller boat was still making its uneven path across the waves. Even from this distance we could see that more people now were hanging over *Suzanne*'s rails, their heads lower than their shoulders.

'We can take ten minutes now. Here.' Yoshi cracked open a can of cola and handed it to me as we felt the engines slow.

The engines stopped and *Moby One* quieted, the sea growing silent around us. I loved it out here, loved watching my house become a white dot against the narrow strip of beach, then disappear behind the endless coves. Perhaps my pleasure was made greater because I knew I was breaking the rules.

Lance appeared beside us. 'Can't believe he'd take tourists out like that.' He lifted his binoculars better to study *Sweet Suzanne* scudding along some distance away.

Yoshi gestured at him to pass them on. 'He was so drunk this morning—'

We were interrupted by the excited yells of the tourists on the upper deck. They were jostling towards the pulpit at the front.

'Here we go,' muttered Lance, grinning at me. 'There's our pocket money, Squirt. Time to get back to work.'

Sometimes, Yoshi said, they could run the whole bay but the bottlenoses would refuse to show, and a boat full of unsatisfied dolphin-watchers was a boat full of free second trips and fifty-per-cent refunds.

At the bow, a group of tourists were pressed together, cameras whirring as they tried to catch the glossy grey shapes that were now riding the breaking waves below. I checked the water to see who had come to play. Below decks, Yoshi had covered a wall with photographs of the fins of every dolphin in the area. She had given them all names.

'Looks like Polo and Brolly,' Yoshi said, leaning over the side.

'Is that Brolly's baby?'

The dolphins were silent grey arcs, circling the boat as if they were the sightseers. Every time one broke the surface the air was filled with the sound of clacking camera shutters. What did they think of us gawping at them? I knew they were as smart as humans. I used to imagine them meeting up by the rocks afterwards, laughing in dolphin language about us.

Lance's voice came over the PA system: 'Ladies and gentlemen, please do not rush to one side to see the dolphins. I will turn the ship so that everyone can get a good view. If you rush to one side we are likely to capsize.'

As *Moby One* slowly shifted position, I leaned over the side, sticking my feet under the bottom rail to see my new trainers. Yoshi had promised she'd let me sit in the boom nets when the weather got warmer, so that I could touch the dolphins, perhaps even swim with them. But only if my mother agreed. And we all knew what that meant.

I stumbled as the boat moved unexpectedly. It took me a second to register that the engines had started up. Startled, I grabbed the handrail. I knew there was a way of doing things around dolphins. Shut down engines if you want them to play. Yoshi frowned at me as the catamaran lurched. My confusion was mirrored in her face as a sudden acceleration sent the boat shooting forward and, above, squealing tourists collapsed onto their seats.

Lance was on the radio as we clambered into the cockpit behind him.

'Lance! What are you doing?' Yoshi grabbed at a rail.

'See you there, bud . . . Ladies and gentlemen—' Lance reached for the PA system button. 'We have something a bit special for you this morning. We've had a sighting of the first whales of the season, a little farther out to sea. These are the humpback whales that come past our waters every year on their long migration north from the Antarctic. Now, please hold on tight. I want to make sure we get you there in time to see them.'

He spun the wheel and nodded to Yoshi, who took the PA system. She repeated what he had said in Japanese, then in Korean for good measure.

'How far?' Yoshi scanned the glinting waters.

'Four, five miles? Dunno. The tourist helicopter said they'd seen two a couple of miles off Torn Point. It's a little early in the season, but . . .'

'Fourteenth of June last year. We're not that far out,' said Yoshi. 'Bloody hell! Look! Greg's going to lose passengers if he carries on at that pace.'

'He doesn't want us to get there before him.' Lance shook his head. 'Full throttle. Let's make sure *Moby One*'s first this year.'

There was magic in the first whale sighting of the migration season. It was as if, until that creature had been seen, it was impossible to believe they would be back. To be the first to see one didn't mean much—once the whales were known to be out there, all five boats that operated off Whale Jetty would switch their business from dolphins to whale watching—but it was of importance to the crews.

'Look at that great idiot. Funny how he can hold a straight course now,' Lance spat. Greg was portside of us, but seemed to be gaining.

'Am I really going to see a whale?' I asked. Beneath our feet, the hull smacked noisily against the waves, forcing me to hang on to the side.

'Fingers crossed.' Yoshi's eyes were trained on the horizon.

A real whale. I had only once seen a whale, with my aunt Kathleen.

'There . . . There! No, it's just spray.' Yoshi had lifted the binoculars. 'Watch out for the blow.'

'Yeah. And the little flag that says, "Whale".'

'Just trying to help, Lance.'

'There!' he cried. I could just make out the shape, like a distant black pebble dipping below the water. 'North-northeast. Heading behind Break Nose Island. Just dived.' A plume of water rose joyously above the horizon. Yoshi squealed. Lance glanced towards Greg, who hadn't seen it. 'We got her!' Lance hissed. All whales were 'her' to Lance, just as all kids were 'squirt'.

'We're going to be first,' muttered Yoshi, excitedly.

I watched Lance swing the wheel, counting under his breath to mark the number of times the whale blew. More than thirty seconds apart and it was likely to dive deep. Then we would have lost it. Closer together meant it had already dived, and we would have a chance to follow.

'Seven . . . eight . . . She's up. *Yessss*.' Lance grabbed the PA system. 'Ladies and gentlemen, if you look over to your right, you might make out the whale, which is headed behind that piece of land there.'

'Greg's realised where we're headed.' Yoshi grinned. 'He'll never catch us now. His engine isn't powerful enough.'

I saw the headland grow, and wondered whether the whale would slow there, allow us to come closer. Perhaps it would lift its head and eye us. Perhaps it would swim up to the side of the boat and reveal its calf.

'Come on, girlie. Give us a good show.' Yoshi was talking to herself, binoculars still raised.

Whale, I told it silently, *wait for us, whale*.

'I don't—bloody—believe—it.' Lance was scowling. '*Look!*'

I followed their gaze. As *Moby One* came round the headland, all of us fell silent. A short distance from the scrub-covered landmass, half a mile out to sea in aquamarine waters, the stationary *Ishmael* sat, its newly painted sides glinting under the midday sun. At the helm stood my mother, her hair whipping around her face under the bleached cap she insisted on wearing out to sea. Milly, our dog, lay—apparently asleep—across the wheel. She looked as if she had been there, waiting for this whale, for years.

'How the hell did she do that?'

'She's always there first.' Yoshi's response was half amused, half resigned.

'Beaten by a bloody Pom. It's as bad as the cricket.' Lance lit a cigarette, then tossed away the match in disgust.

I stepped out onto the deck and at that moment the whale emerged. As we gasped, it lobtailed, sending a huge spray of water towards *Ishmael*. The tourists on *Moby One*'s top deck cheered. It was enormous, close enough that we could see the barnacled growths along its body, the corrugated white belly; near enough that I could look briefly into its eye.

My breath had stalled in my throat. One hand clutching the lifelines, I lifted the binoculars with the other and gazed not at the whale but at my mother, forgetting briefly that I should not allow myself to be seen. Even from that distance I could make out that Liza McCullen was smiling. It was an expression she rarely, if ever, wore on dry land.

AUNT KATHLEEN WALKED to the end of the verandah to put a large bowl of prawns and some lemon slices on the bleached wooden table with a large basket of bread. She's actually my great-aunt but she says that makes her feel like an antique, so most of the time I call her Auntie K. Behind her the white weatherboard of the hotel's frontage glowed softly in the evening sun.

'What's this for?' Greg lifted his head from the bottle of beer he'd been nursing. The shadows under his eyes betrayed the events of the previous evening.

'I heard you needed your stomach lined,' she said, thwacking a napkin in front of him. 'Hannah, you dig in now. I'll bet you never had a bite to eat for lunch. I'm going to fetch the salad.'

We were gathered, as the Whale Jetty crews were most evenings, outside the hotel kitchens. There were few days when the crews wouldn't share a beer or two before they headed home.

As I bit into a juicy tiger prawn, I noticed that the burners were outside. Few guests at the Silver Bay Hotel wanted to sit out in May or June, but in winter the whale-watching crews congregated here to discuss events on the water, no matter the weather. Their members changed from year to year, as people moved on to different jobs or went to uni, but Lance, Greg, Yoshi and the others had been a constant in my life for as long as I had lived there. Aunt Kathleen usually lit the burners about now and they stayed on most evenings until September or even October.

'Did you have many out?' She had returned with the salad. 'I've had no one at the museum.'

'*Moby One* was pretty full. Lot of Koreans.' Yoshi shrugged. 'Greg nearly lost half of his over the side.'

'They got a good sight of the whale.' Greg reached for a piece of bread. 'No complaints.'

'You see it, Hannah?'

'It was enormous. I could see its barnacles.'

Greg narrowed his eyes. 'If she'd been out on her mother's boat she could have brushed its teeth.'

'Yes, well, the least said about that . . .' Aunt Kathleen shook her head. 'Not a word,' she mouthed at me. 'That was a one-off.'

I nodded dutifully. It was my third one-off that month.

'That Mitchell turn up? I heard he's joining those Sydney-siders with the big boats.'

They all looked up.

'Thought the National Parks and Wildlife Service had frightened them off,' said Lance.

'When I went to the fish market,' Aunt Kathleen said, 'they told me they'd seen one all the way out by the heads. Music at top volume, people dancing on the decks. Ruined the night's fishing. By the time the Parks and Wildlife people got there they were long gone. Impossible to prove a thing.'

The balance in Silver Bay was delicate: too few whale-watching tourists and the business would be unsustainable; too many, and it would disturb the creatures it wanted to display. Lance and Greg had come up against the over-crowded triple-decker catamarans from round the bay, often blaring loud music. 'They'll be the death of us all, that lot,' Lance said. 'Irresponsible. Money-mad. Should suit Mitchell down to the ground.'

I hadn't realised how hungry I was. I ate six of the huge prawns in quick succession, chasing Greg's fingers around the empty bowl. He grinned and waved a prawn head at me. I stuck out my tongue at him.

'Aye aye, here she is. Princess of Whales.'

'Very funny.' My mother dumped her keys on the table and gestured to Yoshi to move down so that she could squeeze in next to me. She dropped a kiss on to my head. 'Good day, lovey?' She smelt of suncream and salt air.

'Fine.' I bent to fondle Milly's ears, grateful that my mother could not see the pinking in my face.

'What have you been doing?' my mother asked.

'Yeah. What have you been doing, Hannah?' Greg winked at me.

'She helped me with the beds this morning.' Aunt Kathleen glared at him. 'Heard *you* had a good afternoon.'

'Not bad.' My mother downed a glass of water. 'God, I'm thirsty.' Her English accent was still pronounced, even after so many years in Australia.

'How many did you see?'

'Just the one. Big girl. Lobtailed half a bath of water into my bag. Look.' She held up her cheque book, its edges frilled and warped.

'Well, there's an amateur's mistake.' Aunt Kathleen sighed in disgust. 'Didn't you have anyone out with you?'

My mother shook her head. 'I wanted to try out that new rudder, see how well it worked in choppier waters. The boatyard warned me it might stick.'

'And you just happened on a whale,' said Lance.

She took another swig of water. 'Something like that.' Her face had closed. *She* had closed. It was as if the whale thing had never happened.

For a few minutes we ate in silence, as the sun sank towards the horizon.

'Come out with me Friday?' Greg asked my mother. He looked as if he hadn't shaved for a week.

'Nope.' My mother stood up, checked her watch. 'That rudder's still not right. I've got to ring the yard before they head off. Don't stay out without your sweater, Hannah. The wind's getting up.'

I watched as she strode away, pursued by the dog.

We were silent until we heard the slam of the screen door. Then Lance leaned back in his chair to gaze out at the darkening bay. 'Our first whale of the season, Greg's first knockback of the season. Got a nice kind of symmetry to it, don't you think?'

He ducked as a piece of bread bounced off the chair behind him.

Kathleen

The Whalechasers Museum had been housed in the old processing plant, a few hundred yards from the Silver Bay Hotel, since commercial whaling was abandoned off Port Stephens in the early 1960s. It didn't have much to recommend it as a modern tourist attraction.

Our centrepiece was a section of the hull of *Maui II*, a commercial whalechaser, a hunting vessel that had broken clean in two in 1935 when a minke had taken exception to it and had risen beneath the boat, lifting it on its tail until it flipped and snapped. Mercifully, a nearby fishing trawler had saved the hands. For years local people had come to see the evidence of what nature could wreak on man when it felt man had harvested enough.

I had kept the museum open since my father died in 1970, and had always allowed visitors to climb over the remains of the hull. I had posed for pictures when the sharp-eyed recognised me as the Shark Girl of the framed newspaper reports, and talked them through the stuffed game fish that adorned the glass wall cases. But there weren't too many interested tourists now.

That day, standing behind the counter, I thought perhaps I couldn't blame them. *Maui II* was more like a heap of driftwood, and there were only so many times people wanted to handle a whalebone. For years people had been telling me to modernise, but what was the point? Half the people who walked around the museum looked a little uncomfortable to be celebrating something that is now illegal. Sometimes even I didn't know why I stayed open.

I adjusted *Maui II*'s old harpoon on its hooks on the wall. Then, from below it, I took a rod, ran my duster up its length and wound the reel, to confirm that it still worked.

'Won't catch much in here.'

I spun round. 'Nino Gaines! You nearly made me drop my rod.'

'Fat chance.' He removed his hat and smiled, revealing a row of crooked teeth. 'I got a couple of cases of wine in the truck. Thought you might like to crack open a bottle with me over some lunch.'

The lines on his face told of years spent in his vineyards, and a touch of pink around his nose hinted at the evenings afterwards.

'I've got to get a room ready for a guest coming tomorrow.'

'How long's it going to take you to tuck in a sheet, woman?'

I saw the disappointment in his face and relented. 'I should be able to spare a few minutes, long as you don't expect too much in the way of food to go with it. I'm waiting on my grocery delivery.'

'Thought of that.' He lifted up a paper bag. 'Got a couple of pies, and a couple of tamarillos for after. I know what you career girls are like. It's all work, work, work . . . Someone's got to keep your strength up.'

I couldn't help laughing. Nino Gaines had always got me like that, as long ago as the war, when he'd first come and announced his intention to set up here. The bay had been taken over by Australian and American servicemen, and my father had had to make pointed references to his accuracy with a shotgun when the young men whooped and catcalled at me behind the bar. Nino had been more gentlemanly: he had always removed his cap while he waited to be served, and he had never failed to call my mother 'ma'am'. 'Still don't trust him,' my father had muttered.

Out at sea it was bright and calm and, as we sat down, I watched *Moby One* and *Two* heading out for the mouth of the bay. It looked like they had a good number of passengers.

'You shutting this place up for the winter?' Nino asked me.

I shook my head, and took a bite of my pie. 'Nope. The *Moby*s are going to try out a deal with me—bed, board and a whale trip for a fixed sum, plus museum admission. Like I do with Liza. They've printed some leaflets and they're going to put something on a New South Wales tourism website.'

He said. 'Good idea. I sell maybe forty cases a month online now.'

'You're on the Internet?' I gazed at him over the top of my spectacles.

He lifted a glass, unable to hide his satisfaction at having surprised me. 'I've been out there in cyberspace for a good eighteen months now.' He gestured at my glass—he wanted me to taste the wine.

I felt wrong-footed, unable to admit quite how thrown I was by Nino's apparent ease with technology. I tried to concentrate on the wine, letting the flavour flood my mouth. 'This is very nice, Nino. A hint of raspberry there.'

'Thought you'd pick up on that.' He nodded, pleased. 'You know you get a mention? The Shark Girl—picture and all. From newspaper archives.'

'There's a picture of *me* on the Internet?'

'In your bathing-suit. You always did look fetching in it. You should put up a picture of Liza and her boat. You might get a few more visitors. A fine-looking girl like her could be quite a draw. Bed, board and a trip on the *Ishmael* with Liza. She'd get enquiries from all over the world.'

'No.' I began to tidy up. 'I don't think it's for us. Liza likes to pick who she takes out.'

'No way to run a business. And, you never know, she might find herself a bloke. About time she was courting.'

It was a while before he saw something in my expression that gave him pause. 'Hey, didn't mean to offend you, Kate.'

'You haven't.'

'Well, something's wrong. You're all twitchy. What's the matter?'

'If you'll excuse me, Nino, I've already wasted half the day.'

'You're not going in? Aw, come on, Kate.' He was trying to work out what he'd said that had been so wrong. 'Is it what I said about your picture?'

No one except Nino calls me Kate, and for some reason this intimacy just about finished me. 'I have a room to make up, Nino. I'll see you soon.' I brushed some imaginary crumbs from my trousers. 'Thank you for lunch.'

He watched as I—the woman he had loved and been perplexed by for more than half a century—stood up, less heavily than age should have allowed, and began to walk briskly towards the house, leaving him with two half-eaten pies and a barely touched glass of his best vintage.

'Kathleen Whittier Mostyn—you're the most contrary woman I ever met,' he yelled after me.

To my shame, I didn't even bother to turn my head.

A LONG TIME AGO, back when my parents died and I was left in charge of the Silver Bay Hotel, plenty of people told me I should modernise, install en-suite bathrooms and satellite television, as they had at Port Stephens and Byron Bay, and that I should advertise more to spread the word about the beauty of our little stretch of coast. I paid them heed for all of two minutes.

We had watched our neighbours up and down the coast grow fat on their profits, but then have to live with the unexpected results of success: heavy traffic, drunken holidaymakers, endless updating, the loss of peace.

In Silver Bay I liked to think we had the balance about right—enough visitors to make a living, not so many for anyone to start getting ideas. For years I had watched the bay's population double in the summer, drifting down in the winter. The growth of interest in whale watching had caused the odd peak now and then, but in general the business was steady, likely neither to make us rich nor cause many upsets. It was just us, the dolphins and the whales.

When my father had built our hotel, my family lived in quarters separate from the rest of the Silver Bay Hotel. My mother didn't like to be seen by guests in what she called 'domestic mode'—I think that meant without her hair done—while my father liked to know there were limits on how much access my sister and I had to the world outside. Not that this stopped Norah: she was off to England before she hit twenty-one.

Since the west wing burned down, I had lived in what remained as if it were a private house and our guests were boarders. Guests slept in the rooms off the main corridor, while we had the rooms on the other side of the stairs, and anyone was welcome to use the lounge. Only the kitchen was sacred, a rule we made when the girls first came to live with me a few years ago. When Liza was not outside with the crews, she spent all her time in the kitchen. She disliked casual conversation and avoided the lounge and the dining room. Hannah, with the conviviality of youth, spent most of her time draped across the sofa in the lounge, watching television, reading or, more often now, on the telephone to her friends.

'Mum? Have you ever been to New Zealand?' As she entered the kitchen, I saw a deep indent running down the side of her cheek from the binding of the sofa cushion where her face must have been resting on it.

Liza reached out absently to try to smooth it away. 'No, sweetheart.'

'I have,' I said. I was darning an old pair of socks. 'I went to Lake Taupo on a fishing trip, about twenty years ago.'

'Why do you ask, Hannah?' Liza said.

'There's a school trip to Wellington. After Christmas. I was wondering if I could go.' Hannah looked from one of us to the other, as if she'd guessed what we would say. 'It's not that expensive. We'll be staying in hostels.'

It's a terrible thing to watch the face of a child who knows she is asking the impossible.

'I don't think so.' Liza reached out a hand. 'I'm really sorry, lovey.'

'Everyone else is going.' She was too good a child to get angry. It was more a plea than a protest. '*Please.*'

'We don't have the money.'

'But there's ages to go. We could all save up.'

'We'll see,' Liza said, in a tone that suggested even to me that she wouldn't.

'I'll make a deal with you, Hannah.' I put down my darning. 'I've got some investments that are due to come in next year. I thought I might pay for us all to take a trip up to the Northern Territory. I've always fancied a look round Kakadu National Park. What do you think?'

I could see from her face what she thought: that she didn't want to be travelling around Australia with her mum and an old woman, that she would rather be headed for a foreign country with her friends.

'That would be nice,' she said eventually, and then added, 'I'm going next door. My programme's on in a minute.'

Liza looked at me. Her eyes said everything we both knew: Silver Bay is a beautiful little town, but even a stretch of Paradise will become ugly if you're never allowed to leave it.

'There's no point blaming yourself,' I said, when I was sure Hannah couldn't hear. 'There's nothing you can do. She'll get over it.' I laid a hand on hers, and she squeezed it gratefully.

I'm not sure either of us was convinced.

Mike

Tina Kennedy was wearing a violet brassière, edged with lace and mauve rosebuds. It was not something I wanted to think about— and especially not now. But as she paused by my boss's shoulder to hand him the file of documents he had requested, she bent low and looked straight at me in a manner I could only describe as challenging.

That brassière was sending me a message. That, and the moisturised, lightly tanned flesh it contained, was a souvenir of my promotion night two and a half weeks previously. It was terrifying.

I felt in my pocket for my phone. Vanessa, my fiancée, had texted me three times in the past half-hour, even though I had told her that this meeting was of vital importance and not to be interrupted. I had read the first message—Swtie pls call me we need 2 talk about seat plans—and tried to ignore the insistent vibration of those that followed.

The phone buzzed against my thigh, and I wondered absently if it was audible over the sound of Dennis Beaker's voice. I had to hand it to Nessa. She wouldn't give in. She'd seemed barely to hear me this morning when I explained that calling her would be difficult. But, then, she didn't seem to hear much these days, except 'wedding'.

Below, Liverpool Street stretched away towards the City. I could just see the figures on the pavement below: men and women dressed in blue, black or grey, marching smartly along. Some people thought of it as a rat-race, but I had never felt like that: I had always felt comforted by the uniformity, the shared sense of purpose. Even if that purpose was money. On quiet days, Dennis would point out of the window and demand, 'What do you think he earns, eh, or her?' And we would value them, depending on such variables as cut of jacket and type of shoes. Dennis Beaker says that nothing and nobody on God's earth is without a monetary value. After four years' working with him, I'm inclined to agree.

On the table in front of me sat the bound proposal, its glossy pages testament to the weeks Dennis, the other partners and I had spent clawing this deal back from the brink. Nessa had complained last night, as I checked it yet again, that I was devoting far more energy to that one document than to what she considered our more pressing concerns. I protested, but mildly. I was far more comfortable with revenue streams and income projections than with her ever-shifting desires for this or that colour-coordinated outfit. I couldn't tell her I preferred to leave the wedding to her.

'So, I'd like to get my colleague to make a short presentation, to give you a flavour of what we consider a very exciting opportunity.'

Tina stood next to the coffee-table, her stance deceptively relaxed. I could still glimpse that violet strap. I closed my eyes, trying to force away a sudden memory of her breasts, pushed up against me in the men's toilets at Bar Brazilia, the fluid ease with which she had removed her blouse.

'Mike?' There was the faintest edge to Dennis's voice. I rose from my seat, shuffling my notes. 'Yes,' I said. I took hold of the remote-control device for my presentation, and raised a smile for the row of Vallance Equity's flint-eyed venture capitalists round the table. 'Tina? Lights?'

She responded with a slow smile, her eyes dropping to my groin.

'Right,' I said, refusing resolutely to look at her. 'I'd like to show you lucky gentlemen a few images of what we modestly consider to be the investment opportunity of the decade.' There was a low rumble of amusement. They liked me. There they sat, primed by Dennis's enthusiasm, ready for my facts and figures. My father often said I was ideally suited to a business environment. He meant business in the grey-suited sense, rather than the hyper-sexy mega-deal sense. Because, although I had somehow ended up at the latter end, I had to admit that I was not a natural risk-taker. I was Mr Due Diligence, one of life's careful, considered deliberators.

None of this meant I was unambitious. I knew exactly where I wanted to be, and had long since learned that taking the quiet path was the key to my success. While colleagues' more incendiary careers crashed and burned, I had become financially secure, due to my dogged monitoring of interest rates and investments. Now, six years into my tenure at Beaker Holdings— my promotion to junior partner apparently nothing to do with my engagement to the boss's daughter—I was valued as someone who would accurately assess the benefits of any choice before making it. Another seven years until Dennis retired, and I would be ready to step into his shoes.

Which was why my behaviour that night had been so out of character.

'I think you're having your teenage rebellion late,' my sister Monica had observed, two days previously. I had taken her to lunch, in the smartest restaurant I knew, as a birthday treat. She worked as a journalist on a national newspaper but earned less per month than I spent in expenses.

'I don't even like the girl,' I said.

'Since when did sex have anything to do with liking someone?' She sniffed. 'It's a reaction against the wedding. You should tell Vanessa you're not ready.'

'But I'll never be ready. I'm not that kind of bloke.'

'So you'd rather she made the decisions?'

'In our personal life, yes. It works well for us like that.'

'So well that you felt the need to shag someone else?'

'Keep your voice down, OK? What if she says something to Dennis?'

'Then you're in big trouble—but you must have known that when you copped off with his secretary. Come on, Mike, you're thirty-four years old, hardly an innocent.'

I held my head in my hands. 'I don't know what the hell I was doing.'

Monica had been buoyant. 'God, you don't know how cheering it is for me to know that *you* can cock up your life just like the rest of us.'

Distracted by the flashback of my sister's triumph, I had to glance at my notes. I took a breath and looked up again at the expectant faces around me.

'As Dennis has explained,' I continued, 'the emphasis in this project is on the quality end of the market. The consumers we'll be targeting are time-poor, possession-rich. They are searching for ways to spend their money. The growth area, according to our research, is in their sense of well-being. To that end, this luxury development will offer a variety of leisure opportunities suited to the surroundings.' I clicked the remote control, bringing up images. 'It will have a state-of-the-art spa, with six different pools, a full-time therapeutic staff and a range of the newest holistic treatments. And for those who prefer something a little more active—and, let's face it, that's usually the men'—here I paused for the amused nods of recognition—'we have the *pièce de résistance*—an integrated centre devoted entirely to watersports. This will include jet-skis, waveboards, speedboats and water-skiing. There will be game fishing. There will also be trained instructors to take clients on tailor-made diving trips farther out to sea. We believe a combination of top-class equipment with a highly skilled team will give clients a never-to-be-forgotten trip and offer them the chance to learn new skills.'

'I heard you lost the site for this.' The voice had come from the back.

Oh Christ, I thought.

'Tina, bring up the lights.' It was Dennis's voice, and I wondered if he was about to answer, but he was looking at me.

I made my expression bland. I'm good at that. 'I'm sorry, I didn't catch that, Neville. Did you have a question?'

'I heard this was planned for South Africa and that you lost your site. There's nothing on this document about where it's going to be now.'

The flicker in Dennis's jaw betrayed his own surprise. How the hell had they found out about South Africa?

My voice cut through the air even before I knew what I was saying: 'South Africa was only ever an option for us. Having examined our potential location there in some detail, we decided that it couldn't provide our clients with the kind of holiday we had in mind. We—'

'Why? My understanding is that it's one of the fastest-growing holiday destinations in the world.'

'Politics,' interjected Dennis. 'It would have been an hour-and-a-half transfer from the airport to the resort. And whatever route we took would have brought us through some of the . . . shall we say, less . . . *affluent* areas? Our research tells us that when they have paid a premium for a luxury holiday, clients don't want to be confronted by abject poverty. It makes them uncomfortable. And that is the last emotion we want them to feel.'

'So you have an alternative site in mind?'

'Not just in mind but signed and sealed,' I said. 'It is, I can truly say, one of the most beautiful spots I have ever seen. I can't go into more detail,' I said smoothly. 'But I can tell you that there were other things we discovered about the South African site that suggested much lower future revenues.'

In truth, I knew almost nothing about the new site. Out of desperation we had used a land agent, some old mate of Dennis's, and the deal had been closed only two days previously.

'No one cares about the profit margins more than us, but—'

Dennis held up a pudgy hand. 'Tim. No. Not a word—because there's something else I'd like to show you before we go any further. Gentlemen, if you'd like to follow me through to the next room, we have a bit of fun lined up before we tell you exactly where it is.'

Having come in half an hour late, I wasn't sure what Dennis had in mind. But, venture capitalists, I mused as I walked behind them, didn't look as though fun was a high priority on their agenda.

Boardroom Two had been emptied of its table and chairs. In the centre of the floor was a large piece of machinery, surrounded by inflatable blue tubing, its centrepiece a florid yellow surfboard.

We were all stunned by the sheer unlikeliness of the thing.

'It's a simulator,' Dennis announced, when nobody said anything. 'You can all have a go.'

The room was silent, bar the low hum of the surf simulator, its flashing buttons gamely advertising that their surf experience could be accompanied by a Beach Boys tune.

'I just want to give you gentlemen an idea of how irresistible our proposal is. I had a little go earlier,' he said, kicking off his shoes. 'It really is quite good fun. You stand on here and . . .' He had removed his jacket and the barely restrained bulk of his stomach hung over the waistband of his trousers. 'I'll start off with some little waves. See? It's easy.'

To the strains of 'I Get Around', my boss stood on the surfboard.

'Switch it on, Mike.'

I glanced at the men behind me, and tried to smile. I wasn't sure that this was a good idea, but I flicked the switch and turned the speed dial.

'Come on, Tim, Neville, you can't pretend you don't want to have a go.' With a low whine, the surfboard jolted into life. 'What—I—haven't— told—you, gentlemen, is that simulators will also—be—whoops!' Dennis struggled to keep his balance. 'There we go . . . The simulators will be on site for guests to learn on before they go out on the water.'

Even those who had never been on the water in their lives, he said, gasping with the effort, would be able to practise in private before exposing themselves to the gaze of their fellow holidaymakers. I don't know if it was the bizarre improbability of this machine forming part of the proposal, or Dennis's evident enjoyment, but within minutes he was winning them over. Tim and Neville's finance man had already taken off his shoes and two junior members of their team were quoting at each other from pages of a surfing slang booklet that Tina had prepared.

Dennis had imagination, I had to hand it to him.

Neville took off his jacket and handed it to his secretary. 'What level will you go to, Dennis?' He was, as I had guessed, one of nature's competitors.

But so was Dennis. 'Any you want, Nev. Turn her up,' he cried, his face beaded with sweat. 'We'll see who can catch the biggest wave, eh?'

'Go on, Mike,' Neville urged. I smiled and then turned the dial again. The simulator had turned their attention from the South African rumours.

'I've always fancied a bit of the old surf,' said Tim, removing his jacket too. 'What level you on there, old chap?'

'He's on three,' I said, glancing at the dial. 'I really don't think—'

'Come on, turn him up, Mike. Let's see who can stay on longest.'

'Yes, turn him up,' the grey suits of Vallance Equity chanted.

I looked at Dennis, who nodded. 'Come on, Mike, bring on the waves.' He was now sweating profusely and, despite his apparent gaiety, I saw desperation in his eyes as he struggled to stay aloft the now rapidly undulating board.

'I'm not—' I began.

Afterwards, no one was sure how it had happened, but somehow Dennis's balance failed him. With a terrible cry he was hurled across the boardroom, to land heavily on his hip. It broke, of course.

There was pandemonium. Everyone crowded round. Over the cries of 'Call an ambulance!' the surfboard gyrated and the Beach Boys sang on.

'Australia, eh?' said Neville, as Dennis was stretchered towards the lift. 'Unforgettable presentation. We're definitely interested.'

'Mike will send you a copy of the site report. Won't you, Mike?' Dennis spoke through clenched teeth, his face grey with pain.

'Sure.' I tried to look as confident as he had sounded.

As he was loaded into the ambulance, he beckoned me closer. 'I know what you're thinking,' he whispered. 'You'll have to compile one.'

'But the timing—the wedding—'

'I'll square it with Vanessa. Book yourself a flight.'

Kathleen

It's hard to believe now, given the size of our land, but whaling was once one of Australia's primary industries. From way back in the nineteenth century, whaling ships would come from Britain, unload a few convicts on us, then load up with some of our whales and sell them back to us at our ports. The Aussies got wise in the end and caught their own. After all, you could use a whale for just about anything—the oil for lamp fuel, candles and soap, the whalebone for corsets, furniture, umbrellas and whips.

Whales are protected now, of course. What remains of them. Here on the east coast, there hadn't been the whaling madness that we'd heard of out west—except in our little corner. Perhaps because the whales came so close that you could see them from dry land, this bay became a base for whale-chasers. (Our whale-watching crews have inherited their nickname.) When I was a girl, they had killed them from small boats. But then they got greedy. Between 1950 and 1962 some 12,500 humpbacks were killed and processed. Whale oil and meat made people rich, and the whalechasers used more and more sophisticated weaponry to increase their catch. The ships became bigger and faster, and by the time humpback whaling was banned they were using sonars, guns and cannon-launched harpoons.

Of course, they killed too many. They swept those oceans and put themselves out of business in the process. One by one the whaling operations closed and the area sank back slowly into shabby solitude. My father, who had loved the romanticism of early whaling, bought Silver Bay's own whale-processing plant and turned it into the museum. Nowadays the scientists reckon there might be fewer than 2,000 humpbacks that come past us on their annual migration, and some say the numbers will never recover.

I tell this story to the crews, occasionally, when they talk about getting a bigger fleet, or trying to up their passenger numbers, or of whale watching as the tourist attraction of the future and the way to rejuvenate Silver Bay.

There's a lesson in there for us all. But I'm darned if anyone's listening.

'GOOD AFTERNOON.'

'Afternoon?' Michael Dormer hovered in the doorway, wearing the dazed expression of someone whose body clock was in a different hemisphere.

'I knocked earlier and left a cup of coffee outside your room, but when I found it stone cold an hour later I figured I'd let you sleep.' I motioned to him to sit at the table. I don't normally let people sit in the kitchen, but I'd just finished preparing the dining room for that evening. 'They say it usually takes a week to sleep through properly. Did you wake up much?'

He rubbed at his hair. He was unshaven, and wearing a shirt and casual trousers—still smarter than we were used to in Silver Bay, but a good step forward from the formal get-up he'd arrived in.

'Only once.' He smiled. 'But that was for about three hours.'

I laughed, and poured him a coffee. He had a good face, Mr Michael Dormer, the kind that suggested a little self-knowledge. 'Like some breakfast? I'm happy to fix you something.'

'At a quarter to one?' He glanced at the clock.

'We can call it lunch.' I still had some pancake batter in the fridge. I'd serve them with blueberries, and a side order of eggs and bacon.

He stared at his coffee for a bit, stifling a yawn. I said nothing, but pushed the newspaper towards him, recognising that his disorientation would ease off after a mug or two of caffeine. I moved quietly, distantly calculating the food I needed to prepare for supper that evening. Hannah was at a friend's house after school, and Liza ate barely enough to feed a fly, so it was only the guests I had to worry about.

Mr Dormer perked up a bit when I put a plate in front of him. 'Wow,' he said, staring at the stack. 'Thank you.' I'd bet he didn't get much in the way of home cooking. They're always the most grateful.

While he had his head down I had the chance to look him over. We don't get many men of his age on their own; usually the single ones stick to the busier resorts. I'm a little embarrassed to admit that I looked at him in the way I always look at men who might be suitable for Liza. No matter how hard she protests, I've not yet given up hope of pairing her off. Though the one time I'd remarked that it would be good for Hannah to have a father-figure, she'd glared at me with such anguish and reproach that I'd felt instantly ashamed. But I still lived in hope.

'That was delicious. Really.'

'A pleasure, Mr Dormer.'

He smiled. 'Mike. Please.'

Not as formal as he seemed, then. I sat down opposite him, giving myself a coffee break as I refilled his mug. 'Got any plans for today?'

He looked down at his coffee. 'Just thought I'd get my bearings, really.

My hire car should arrive later so there's not much I can do till then.'

'Oh, there's lots of places you can go when you've got wheels. You're right. The bus goes to Port Stephens from up the road, but apart from that you'd be pretty stuck. Did you say you were here on holiday?'

A curious thing: he flushed a little. 'Something like that,' he said.

I left it there. I know not to pursue someone who doesn't want to talk. Mike Dormer had paid me for a week in advance, thanked me for his breakfast, and those two things alone entitled him to my professional courtesy.

'I'll leave you to it, then, Miss Mostyn,' he said, rising from the table.

'Kathleen.'

I went to clear his plates without another thought.

I had other guests to worry about that week—namely a middle-aged couple here for their twenty-fifth wedding anniversary. The man complained about everything. The room wasn't big enough, the furnishings were shabby. To cap it, he complained that Liza had set off late on their whale-watching trip, even though they'd arrived late at the jetty. His wife, an elegant woman, followed him around apologising under her breath to everyone he rubbed up the wrong way. The breathless, conspiratorial ease with which she did this suggested it was not a new experience for her.

'He was a bully,' Liza said, when she came in. 'If it hadn't been for her I wouldn't have taken them.'

We exchanged a look. 'Bet you made her day, though.'

'Not really. Not a whale anywhere. I gave them an extra hour but it was like the seas were empty.'

'Perhaps they knew.'

Sometimes I can see her mother, my little sister Norah, in Liza. She's there in the way Liza tilts her head when she's thinking, in her smile when she sees her daughter. That's when I know their presence here is a blessing. That there is an elemental pleasure in seeing the continuation of a family line, a joy that we who are childless might not otherwise experience. I have been grateful for this knowledge, these last five years. Those glimpses of familial brow, frown or giggle have made up, in some small way, for the loss of my sister.

Liza, however, has other features—her watchfulness, the ever-present sadness, the faded white scar where her cheekbone meets her left ear—that are entirely her own.

I SUPPOSE IT SHOULD have been of no surprise to me that Nino Gaines hadn't called by for a few days—not after the way I'd sent him packing. But I didn't like the idea that he might be sitting at Barra Creek thinking badly of me.

After lunch I packed up a lemon cake in greaseproof paper, sat it on the passenger seat of my car and headed out to his place. It was a beautiful day, the air so clear you could see the distant mountains. It had been an especially dry summer, and as I drove inland I glanced at the reddish earth, the bony horses with no grass to graze. The air was different out here, the atmosphere unfiltered and sullen. I don't understand how people can live inland. I find that endless brown depressing.

Nino was just headed indoors when I pulled up outside. He turned at the sound of my engine, and touched one hand to the brim of his hat.

I hesitated before I got out of the car. We had rarely fallen out, and I was not entirely sure of my reception. 'Afternoon,' I said.

'Come for your order?' he asked, but there was a twinkle in his eye that made me relax. A twinkle that, if I'm honest, I didn't deserve.

'I brought you a cake,' I said, reaching back into the car to get it.

'I hope it's lemon.'

'Well, I don't remember you as picky, Nino Gaines. Stubborn, greedy and rude, yes. Picky, no.'

'You've got lipstick on.'

'Over-familiar, too.'

He grinned at me, and I couldn't quite keep the smile from my face.

'Come on in, Kathleen. I'll make us both a cup of tea. You look very nice, by the way.'

The first time Nino Gaines asked me to marry him I was nineteen years old. The second time I was nineteen and two weeks. The third time was forty-two years later. In the intervening years, having given up on me, he was married to Jean. He met her two months after I'd turned him down for the second time, and she had a ring firmly on her finger before another two months were out. He brought her to his newly purchased vineyard at Barra Creek and they were together until she died at the age of sixty-seven from cancer. They used to fight like billy-oh, but it didn't take a fool to see that, for all their arguments, they were a good match.

Nino Gaines, it was widely acknowledged back then, was one of the handsomest men in Silver Bay. The first time I laid eyes on him I was serving at the hotel bar. He strode in wearing his air-force uniform, appraised me hard enough to make me blush, saw the framed newspaper picture, and asked, 'Do *you* bite?'

It wasn't the words that got my father's back up, but the wink that went with them. I was such an innocent that it all flew as swiftly over my head as the war planes that stacked up over at Tomaree Point.

'No,' my father said, from behind the till. 'But her father does.'

'You stay away from him, you hear?' he said later. 'Got a mouth as smart as a whip cut.'

Back in those days, I thought my father's word was gospel. I kept my exchanges with Nino Gaines to the minimum, tried not to blush too hard when he complimented me on my dresses, stifled my giggles when he cracked secret jokes at me from across the bar. I tried not to notice that he came in every night that he wasn't on duty. My sister Norah was just four at the time, and she used to gaze up at him like he was a god.

And then Nino asked me to marry him. Knowing my father's views on servicemen, I had to refuse. We might have been all right, I sometimes think, if the second time he'd asked me he hadn't done it in front of my father.

When Jean died, nearly fifteen years ago now, I thought Nino Gaines might collapse into himself and fade away. I've seen it before with men of that age—they have a lost quality about them. It was how that generation of men was raised, you see. They never learned to do anything for themselves. But his sons, Frank and John John, kept him busy, made sure their father was not alone, set up new projects with this grape and that blend. Yes, Nino Gaines did better than any of us had expected. After a year or so, one night, he confided in me that Jean had told him she'd celestially box his ears if he moped around by himself when she was gone.

'She was quite right,' I said, avoiding his eyes. 'Make sure you get out and about. Best thing for you.'

There were other things he said, later, but we didn't talk about those any more. For many years now Nino had accepted that he and I would never be more than good friends. I treasured his friendship—probably more than he knew—but it was some years since he had talked to me with any intimacy.

'Frank was in town yesterday, and bumped into Cherry Dawson,' he said.

'She still working for the council?'

'Sure is. She told him the Bullens have sold the old oyster farm. There's a lot of cloak-and-dagger stuff in the town hall about what'll go there.'

I took a sip of my tea. 'Land as well?'

'A good stretch of the beachfront, including the old hatchery. But it's the oyster beds I'm curious about.'

'What can they do with an underwater stretch like that?'

'That's what I'm curious about.' He looked at his watch. Every evening he climbed onto his quad bike to ride around the estate, checking his vines.

'The bay's not suitable for much. It could only be another oyster farm.'

'I don't think so.' Nino shook his head.

I got the feeling he knew more than he was telling. 'Well,' I said, when I realised he wasn't going to elucidate, 'they'll have to keep the deep-water channel open for the boats to get in and out, so I don't see how it will make too much difference to the crews.' I glanced at the clock and stood up.

'Good to see you, Kate.' When I made to leave he leaned forward to kiss my cheek and I held his arm, which might have been a sign of my affection—or a way to keep him at a distance.

My dad had thought he was like all the rest, you see. He swore they were only after my fame and the hotel. It's only now I wonder at a man who couldn't let his daughter believe she was good enough to be loved for herself.

WHEN I GOT back they were already out at the tables. Liza must have served them, and they sat along the bench, cradling their beer and packets of chips. Yoshi and Lance were playing cards, and all were wrapped in fleeces and hats, muffled against the wind. No one had thought to turn on the burners.

'The butcher's delivery arrived,' Liza said. 'I wasn't sure what you wanted out so I stuck it all in the fridge.'

'I'd better make sure he brought the right order. Last time he got it all wrong,' I said. 'Afternoon, all. You're back early.'

'One pod, too far off for the punters to see much. Been off with your fancy man, Miss M?'

Greg glanced at my niece as he spoke, but Liza was ignoring him.

A few days ago it had been Hannah's eleventh birthday and at her party Greg had handed her a little parcel. She had ripped it open, flanked by her friends. 'It's a key,' she'd said, puzzled, as she held it aloft. 'I don't get it.'

'A key?' he'd replied, looking confused. 'That's the key to my lockup. Darn—I must have left your present in there. You and your mates might want to scoot down and check.'

They'd gone before he could say another word, feet kicking up in the sand, all squeals and sneakers. I'd gazed at him quizzically.

Within minutes they'd come sprinting back up the path. 'Is it the boat? Is it the little boat?'

'Did you check the name?' he'd said.

'*Hannah's Glory*.' She'd turned to me. 'It's a blue dinghy and it's called *Hannah's Glory*. Is it really for me, Greg?'

'Sure is, Princess,' he'd said.

She'd thrown her arms round him, beaming. 'Can I take it out? Can I take it out, Auntie K?'

'Not right now, sweetheart. You've got your cake to cut. But I'm sure you can sit in it in the lockup.' I'd heard her excited chatter the whole way down the path.

I'd turned to Greg, one eyebrow arched. 'You talk to Liza about this?'

'Ah . . . not yet. But I think I'm about to get my chance.'

Liza was striding towards us, holding a plate with the birthday cake on it. 'Hi.' She'd nodded a greeting at Greg. 'Where are the kids off to?'

'You might want to talk to Greg about that,' I'd said.

'They're—ah—checking out my present.'

She'd put the plate on the table. 'Oh yes? What did you get?'

'Old Carter was selling it. Little sculling craft. I've rubbed it down, given it a lick of paint. It's in perfect nick.'

It had taken her a minute to register what he'd said. 'You bought my daughter a boat? My daughter who isn't allowed out on the water? What the hell did you think you were doing?' Her voice was blistering.

He'd stared back at her, unable to believe she was so mad. 'I was giving the kid a birthday treat. She lives by the water. All her mates have little boats. Why shouldn't she have one?'

'Because I've told her she can't.'

'Why? What harm can it do? She's got to learn, hasn't she?' When she hadn't answered, he'd gestured towards Hannah, who was standing at the door of the lockup. 'Look at her—she's pleased as punch. I heard her telling her mates it was the best birthday present she'd ever had.'

'Yes! So now I've got to be the wicked witch who tells her she can't accept it. Thanks a bunch, Greg.'

'So don't. Let her have it. We'll mind her.'

'We? I've told you a dozen times I don't want a bloody relationship with you, and you sucking up to my daughter isn't going to change that.'

'Mum?'

Hannah had returned and was standing beside Liza, her birthday smile wiped clean off her face. She'd looked from me to her mum and back again.

'Why are you shouting at Greg?' Her voice, when it came again, had been sad. 'I suppose it means I'm not allowed to keep the boat?'

Liza had taken a deep breath. 'We'll talk about it, lovey,' she'd said.

'Liza,' Greg had said, 'I never meant to—'

'I'm not interested,' she'd cut in. 'Hannah. Tell your friends it's time for the cake.' When Hannah hadn't moved, she'd waved an arm. 'Go on.'

Greg had put his hand on the little girl's shoulder. 'Your boat will be waiting for you in the lockup whenever you're ready,' he'd said, and then walked stiffly away.

Now, as I looked at my niece, I guessed she probably hadn't spoken to Greg since, and I felt sorry. He had meant well.

When I reached the door I found Mike Dormer in the hallway, flicking through the newspaper I leave out for guests. He looked up when I entered.

'Did you get your car?' I asked him.

'Yup. A Holden.' He pulled the keys from his pocket.

'That'll do. You feeling any more human?' He looked weary still.

'I'll get there. I was wondering . . . would it be possible to eat here this evening?'

'Eat now, if you want. I'm about to put some soup out for the crews. Grab your jacket and join us.'

I saw his hesitation. I don't know why I pushed him. Perhaps it was because I suddenly couldn't face the thought of laying out a whole meal for one guest. Perhaps I wanted Liza to see a male face that wasn't Greg's . . .

'This is Mike. He'll be eating with us this evening.' They murmured hello. Greg's glance was more assessing than the others', and his voice carried a little farther after Mike had sat down, his jokes a little more hearty.

I took the food out on two trays. Each man reached for a bowl and a hunk of bread, hardly looking up. But Mike stood and climbed out of the bench. 'Let me help you,' he said, taking the second tray.

'Strewth,' said Lance, grinning. 'Can tell you're not from round here.'

Liza looked up then, and I saw her glance at him.

He sat down, looking somehow out of place in his ironed shirt. He was probably no younger than Greg, but in comparison his skin was curiously unlined. All that time cooped up in an office, I thought.

'Are you not cold in just a shirt?' said Yoshi, leaning forward.

'It feels quite warm to me,' Mike said.

'You were like that when you first came, Liza.' Lance waved a finger at her. 'Now she wears her thermals for sunbathing.'

'Where do you come from originally?' he asked, but Liza didn't appear to have heard him.

'What do *you* do, Mike?' I said.

'I work in finance,' he said.

'Finance,' I said a little louder, because I wanted Liza to hear that.

'How are you finding Silver Bay?' Yoshi was smiling at Mike. 'Did you get out at all today?'

He paused while he finished a mouthful of bread. 'Didn't get much farther than Miss Mostyn—Kathleen's kitchen. What I've seen seems very . . . nice. So . . . ah . . . do you all work on cruise boats?'

'We're modern-day whalechasers,' said Lance.

Mike looked surprised. 'I thought that was illegal.'

'Whale watching,' I butted in. 'They take tourists out to look at them. Between now and November the humpbacks travel north to warmer waters then back to the Antarctic, passing by not far from here. I thought that was why you were staying,' I said to Mike. 'Most people only stop here for the whale watching.'

He glanced down. 'Well, I'll certainly . . . It sounds like a good thing to do.'

'Careful if you go out with Greg, though,' said Yoshi. 'He tends to lose the odd passenger. Unintentionally, of course.'

'That girl jumped. Bloody madwoman,' Greg expostulated. 'I had to throw a lifebelt overboard.'

'Ah. But why did she jump?' said Lance. 'She was afraid she was about to get—ahem—harpooned by Greg.'

Greg glanced at Liza. 'Not true.'

'Then how come I saw you taking her number later?'

'I gave her my number,' he said slowly, 'because she said she might want me to take out a private party.'

The table burst into noisy laughter.

Mike was gazing at my niece. She was saying little, as was common, but her stillness marked her out in the exact opposite way that she had intended. I tried to see her through his eyes: a still-beautiful woman, who was both older and younger than her thirty-two years, her hair scraped back as if she had long since stopped caring what she looked like.

'And you?' he said quietly, leaning towards her. 'Do you chase whales?'

'I don't chase anything,' she said, and her face was unreadable, even to me. 'I go to where they might be and keep my distance. I find that's generally the wisest course of action.'

As their eyes locked, I noticed Greg was watching. His eyes followed her as she rose from the table, saying she needed to pick up Hannah. Then he turned to Mike. 'Yup. Generally the best course of action when it comes to Liza,' he said, his smile as wide and friendly as a shark's. 'Keep your distance.'

Mike

The bay stretches around an area of four miles between Taree Point and the outlying Break Nose Island, a short drive north from Port Stephens. The waters are clear and protected, perfectly suited to watersports. There is little in the way of a tidal system, making it safe for bathing, and there is a thriving but low-level cottage industry in cetacean watching.

Silver Bay is three to four hours' drive from Sydney. As a bay, the name is misleading for the seafront is actually made up of two half-bays, separated by Whale Jetty, which sticks out on the piece of land that cuts through them. The seafront at the northernmost point is virtually undeveloped, the other, home to Silver Bay proper, is a short drive away. This town supports a number of small accommodation units and retail outlets, whose business comes mainly from residents of Sydney and Newcastle. There is an existing operation ripe for redevelopment, and numerous buildings with little economic worth. It is highly likely that the owners would see a fair financial settlement as advantageous both to themselves and the local economy.

As far as competition is concerned, the only hotel located within the bay farthest from the town is half its original size, having suffered a fire decades ago. It is run on a bed-and-breakfast basis. There are no recreational facilities, and it would be unlikely to create a problem in terms of competition should the owner be unwilling to sell.

I couldn't present anyone with this, I thought. It didn't matter how many facts and figures I had gleaned from the local planning department and chamber of commerce, I still felt as though I was writing about something I knew nothing about.

I was used to square footage in the City; executive apartments, prestige headquarters. On such jobs I could go in, look around unobserved and work out the local rental yields against the disposable income of nearby residents. Here, I was acutely aware of my visibility. Even in a sweatshirt and jeans I felt as if my lack of a salt crust gave away my intentions.

I consulted my watch. I had been sitting there for almost two hours and had strung together three paragraphs. It was time for another tea break.

Kathleen Mostyn had given me what she described as her 'good' room and the previous night had brought up a tray with tea- and coffee-making equipment. She was the kind of woman who made you think 'Age shall not wither her': sharp-eyed, fiercely busy, wit undimmed. I liked her. I had realised pretty quickly that I was her only long-term guest. The hotel had the air of somewhere that might once have been smart, but had long since settled for pragmatic, then decided it didn't want much company anyway.

My room was not luxurious but comfortable; the polar opposite to most of the executive-class hotel rooms I stayed in. The walls were whitewashed, and the wood-framed double bed was made up with white linen and a blue-and white-striped blanket. There was an aged leather armchair and a Persian rug that might once have been valuable. I would work at a small scrubbed-pine desk, sitting on a kitchen chair.

While the kettle boiled, I stood at the window, which looked straight out across the bay. There was no road between the house and the beach. The previous night I had slept with the window open, the sound of the waves lulling me into my first decent night's sleep for months. I had been only dimly aware, as dawn broke, of the whalers' trucks and the fishermen heading back and forth across the shingle to the jetty.

When I'd told Nessa about the setting, she had accused me of being a jammy bugger and said she'd given her father an earful for sending me away. 'You wouldn't believe how much I've got to organise,' she'd said.

'You know, we could do this differently,' I'd ventured. 'We could fly off somewhere and get married on a beach.'

'After all the planning I've done?' Her voice had been disbelieving.

'Yes, sorry. Forget I said anything. You know I didn't ask to be here. I'm working on this deal as hard as I can and I'll be back before you know it.'

But it was hard to work in an environment that conspired to tell even me to do the opposite. The beach with its elegant curve and white sand, demanded to be walked on. The wooden jetty called out to be sat on, bare legs dangling into the sea. The long bleached table where the whale crews relaxed on their return spoke of ice-cold beers and hot chips.

I made a cup of tea and took it back to my desk, then opened an email and began to type: Dennis, hope you're feeling OK. Went to the planning dept yesterday and met Mr Reilly, as you suggested. He seemed to like the look of the plans and said the only possible problems were—

I jumped at the sound of a knock at the door and shut my laptop. I got up and opened it to find Hannah, Liza McCullen's daughter. She was holding out a sandwich on a plate. 'Auntie K thought you might be hungry.'

I took it from her. How could it be lunchtime already? 'That was kind. Tell her thank you.'

She peered round the door and caught sight of my computer.

'Is that connected to the Internet?'

'Just about.'

'I'm desperate for a computer. Loads of my friends at school have them.' She hovered on one leg. 'Did you know my aunt is on the Internet? I heard her telling my mum. She doesn't like to talk about it now, but she used to be famous round here for catching sharks.'

I tried to imagine the old lady wrestling with some *Jaws*-like creature. Oddly, it wasn't so difficult.

The child was hovering in the doorway. She had that light, gangly look that girls get just before they burst into adulthood. 'Mr Dormer?'

'Mike.'

'Mike. When you're not too busy one day, may I have a go on your computer? I'd really like to see that picture of Auntie K.'

Since I'd arrived, I'd felt like a fish out of water. It was nice to have someone ask me to do something familiar. 'We could have a look now,' I said.

Hannah and I sat there for almost an hour, during which time I decided she was a sweet kid. A little young for her age in some ways—she was much less interested in her appearance than the London kids I knew, or pop culture, music, all that stuff—yet she carried an air of wistfulness, and a maturity that sat awkwardly on such a young frame.

She asked me about London, about my house, whether I had any pets. She found out pretty quickly that I was due to get married, and asked, with some gravity, 'Are you sure she's the right person?'

I was a little taken aback. 'I think so. We've been together a long time. We know each other's strengths and weaknesses.'

'Are you nice to her?'

I thought for a minute. 'I hope I'm nice to everyone.'

'You do *seem* quite nice,' she conceded. Then we turned to the important business of the computer and printed out two different photographs and a couple of pieces on the young woman in the bathing-suit with the shark. Then we visited a website for a string of facts and figures about humpback whales.

'Do you go out with your mum much to see the whales?'

'I'm not allowed,' she said. 'My mum doesn't like me going out on the water.' She shrugged, as if to convince herself she didn't care. 'She's trying to make sure I'm safe. Can we find some pictures of England?'

'We certainly can. What was it you wanted to look at?'

'I was wondering where you were.' Liza McCullen stood in the open doorway. The way she looked from one of us to the other made me feel as if I had been doing something wrong. A second later, I felt really pissed off.

'Hannah brought me a sandwich,' I said, a little pointedly. 'Then she asked if she could look at my computer.'

'There are twenty-three thousand one hundred web pages for humpback whales on the Internet,' Hannah said triumphantly.

Liza softened. 'And I suppose she wanted to check out every one.' There was the hint of an apology in her voice. 'Hannah, lovey, come and leave Mr Dormer alone now.'

She was wearing the same outfit she'd had on the last two times I had seen her: dark green canvas jeans, a fleece and a yellow storm jacket. Her hair, as then, was scraped back into a ponytail. The ends were bleached white, although her natural colour was darker. I thought of Nessa, who, for the first year of our relationship, used to get up half an hour earlier than me to do her hair and put on her make-up before I could see her.

'I'm sorry if she's been bothering you,' she said.

'She hasn't bothered me in the slightest. If you want, Hannah, I'll bring the computer downstairs and set it up for you to use when I'm out.'

Hannah's eyes widened. 'Really? By myself? Mum! I could do all the stuff for my project.'

I didn't look at her mother. I just unhooked the computer, having first closed all my password-protected files.

'Are you going out now?'

A thought had occurred to me. Something Kathleen had mentioned earlier that morning.

'I am,' I said. 'If your mother will take me.'

I thought that Liza McCullen would jump at the chance to take out a private charter. Especially when I offered to pay the equivalent of four fares— the minimum the boats needed allegedly to make a trip economically viable.

'I'm not going out this afternoon,' she said, hands deep in her pockets.

'Why? I'm offering you almost a hundred and eighty dollars. That's got to be worth your while.'

'I'm not going out this afternoon.'

'Is there a storm coming?'

'Auntie K said it was set fair,' said Hannah. 'Go on, Mum. Then I can use Mike's computer.'

I couldn't quite suppress a smile.

She wouldn't look at me. 'I'm not taking you out. Find someone else.'

'The others are big boats, right? Full of tourists. Not my scene.'

'I'll give you a ticket for Monday,' Liza said. 'I've got three other people going out then. You'll have a better time.'

For some reason I had started to enjoy myself. 'No, I won't,' I said. 'I'm antisocial. And I want to go this afternoon.'

Finally she looked directly at me and shook her head. 'No,' she said.

Hannah was giggling.

I'm not sure what had got hold of me. Perhaps it was because Greg had attempted to warn me off. But I was going out in that boat if it killed me.

'OK . . . five hundred dollars,' I said, pulling the money out of my wallet. 'That's a full boat, right?' I heard Hannah's sharp intake of breath.

Liza stared at me.

'And I'll expect a lot of coffee and biscuits.'

'Your money,' said Liza, eventually. 'You'll need soft-soled shoes and a warm jumper. And I'll be leaving in fifteen minutes.' She took the money and stuffed it into her jeans pocket. Her sideways glance at me said she thought I was insane. But I knew what I was doing. As Dennis always says, everyone and everything has its price.

LIZA'S BOAT WAS the only one on Whale Jetty. She walked ahead of me, not indulging in small talk, except with the dog, Milly, so I had a chance to look around as we approached it. There was little in Silver Bay, even around the jetty: a café, a souvenir shop whose turnover was obviously slow—the window display was dusty—and a seafood market, situated towards the main town and housed in the most modern building in the bay. It had its own car park, and was a short walk away, which meant that the customers who stopped for fish were unlikely to walk back to use the other facilities—a poorly thought-out decision. I would have placed it opposite the jetty.

Although it was a Saturday, few people were about. The tourists, if there were any, must have been out in the other whale-watching boats. The bay had the air of a place that did not expect much out of season. That said, neither did it look particularly troubled. The bright sunshine lent it a jovial air, while its few inhabitants seemed uncommonly cheerful.

Except Liza. She ordered me aboard, made me stand and watch while she ran through a safety checklist in a flat monotone, then rather grudgingly, I thought, asked me if I wanted her to put on the coffee.

'Point me towards it and I'll do it,' I said.

'Bend your knees when you walk around and when you come up,' she said, turning her back to me. Then, bounding up the stairs, she was gone.

The lower deck had two tables and chairs, some plastic-covered benches and a glass case, with chocolate, whale videos and tapes, and seasickness tablets for sale. I found the tea and coffee area and made two coffees. Then the engines started, and I had to hold on to the side to keep steady. We were headed out to sea at some pace.

I made my way unsteadily up the flight of stairs to the back of the boat. Liza was standing at the wheel, her little dog draped across the helm behind it. I handed her a mug and felt the wind on my face.

'How long have you been doing this?' I had to shout to be heard.

'Five years.'

'Is it a good business?'

'It does for us.'

'So what's a boat this size worth?'

'Does everything for you revolve round money?'

It wasn't said in an unfriendly manner, but it gave me pause. I took a sip of my coffee and tried again. 'You come from England?'

She thought for a moment. 'Yes. We used to live there.'

'Did you come out here specially? To do whale watching?'

'Not really.'

Was she like this with all her customers? Bad divorce, I speculated.

'Is it a good way of life?'

She faced me, suspicious. 'You ask a lot of questions.'

I was determined not to bite back. I had the feeling she was not a naturally antagonistic person. 'You're a rarity. I don't imagine there are many female English skippers around here.'

'How would you know? There could be thousands of us.' She allowed a small smile. 'Actually, Port Stephens is famous for them.' This, I guessed, was the closest she would come to humour. 'OK, a question for you. Why did you spend so much money just to go on a boat trip?'

Because it was the only way I could get you to take me. But I didn't say it aloud. 'Would you have done it for less?' I asked, changing tack.

She grinned. 'Of course.'

After that something changed. Liza McCullen relaxed, or perhaps decided that I wasn't as objectionable as she had initially thought, and the froideur that had hung over our trip out of the bay dissipated.

We didn't say much. I sat on the wooden bench behind her and gazed out to sea. She spun the wheel, checked the dials, radioed one of the other boats. Sometimes she would point at a stretch of land or a creature that held some interest. But I couldn't tell you now what she said. Because although she was not the most beautiful woman I had ever seen, I found Liza McCullen oddly compelling. If I hadn't already worked out that she would have been sensitive to it, I would have stared at her. That's not like me at all.

'Lance says they've sighted a female about three miles on,' she said, after we had been at sea for about half an hour. 'You happy to keep going?'

'Sure,' I said. I'd forgotten we were meant to be searching for whales.

'That's where we're headed,' she said, spinning the wheel. I could just make out some sea birds, dive-bombing. 'That means there are fish. And where there are fish there are often whales.'

She pointed out Greg's boat, about the same size as hers, and farther away what she described as *Moby Two*.

'There!' she said. 'Blow!'

'Blow what?' I queried. That made her laugh.

'*There.*' She was pointing. 'We'll go a bit closer.'

This was a Liza McCullen I had not yet seen. A wide, ready smile, a lift in her voice. 'Oh, she's a beauty. I bet you there's a calf too.'

I heard her on the radio: '*Ishmael* to *Moby Two*—our girl is portside to you, about a mile and a half ahead. She may have a calf with her.'

'*Moby Two* to *Ishmael*. Spotted her, Liza. Giving her a wide berth.'

'We stay at least a hundred metres away,' she explained. 'We make that three hundred when calves are involved. It all depends on the mother. Some are curious—they'll bring the babies right up to see us, and that's different. But I don't like to encourage it. You can't guarantee that the next boat they meet is going to be as friendly.'

The three boats moved closer together. The engines were turned off and we waited for the whale to show herself again.

When that great head come out of the water, not thirty feet from us, an involuntary '*whoa*' escaped me. Meeting a creature so huge, so unlikely, in its own environment, threw me in a way I found hard to convey.

'Look!' Liza was shouting. 'There it is!' And, just visible, sheltered half under its mother, I saw a flash of grey or blue, which was the calf. They went past our boat twice, then shouts from the other boats told us she had gone to look at them too.

I was grinning like an idiot. When Liza smiled back at me, there was something triumphant in it, as if she were saying, 'You see?' When its weirdly long fin appeared, she laughed. 'She's waving. She's belly up—it means she's comfortable with us.'

As we sat, Liza spotted two more humpbacks in the distance. I was dimly aware of the radio conversation between the three boats, the exclamations of pleasure at this unexpected haul. 'Want to hear something magic?' she said suddenly, her face illuminated. She nipped down into the galley and emerged with a strange-looking thing on a cable. She plugged one end into a box on the side, then threw it into the water. 'Listen,' she said. 'Hydrophone. There might be escorts nearby.'

For several minutes, I stared out to sea, hearing nothing but the sound of the water meeting the sides of the boat, the wheeling birds overhead, and occasionally, brought over on a soft wind, the other boats' passengers. Then there was a low, drawn-out moan, almost eerie. It sent shivers up my spine.

'Beautiful, isn't it?'

I stared at her. 'That's a whale?'

'A male. They all sing the same song, you know. It's normally fifteen minutes long and each year all the whales in the pod sing the same one. If a new whale comes along with a new song, they pick it up instead. Can you imagine them down there, teaching each other?'

I had been wrong when I said Liza McCullen wasn't such a beauty: when she smiled she was stunning.

Suddenly the smile evaporated. 'What the—'

It was a thumping sound, regular, insistent. Then it grew louder. A large catamaran came round the headland, packed with passengers. Loud music emanated from four oversized speakers on the top deck, and even from our distance away, the clink of glasses and the hysterical laughter of the well lubricated were audible.

'Not again,' said Liza. 'The noise destroys them. They get confused . . . especially the babies. She'll be frightened.' She got onto the radio. '*Ishmael* to *Disco Ship*, or whatever your name is. Turn your music down. You are too loud. Do you hear me? You're too loud.'

I stared at the water. Nothing broke the surface now. No sound could be heard above the insistent thud of the beat, drawing closer.

Her brow wrinkled as she realised the speed at which the boat was approaching. '*Ishmael* to unidentified large cat, east-north-east of Break Nose Island. Turn off your engines and your music. You are close to a whale cow and calf. You are going too fast, putting you at risk of collision, and your noise is likely to cause them distress. Do you read me?'

She tried twice more to contact them. It was unlikely, I thought, that they could hear anything above the noise of that bass.

'*Ishmael* to *Suzanne*—Greg, can you call the coastguard? The police? See if they can send out a speedboat.'

'Got you, Liza. *Moby Two* is headed round to see if they can steer them off course.'

'What can I do?' I said. The anxiety in the atmosphere was clear.

'Hold this,' she said, and handed me the wheel. She started the engines. 'Now, steer for *Disco Billy* over there, and I'll tell you when to turn. I'm going to make sure we don't hit anything as we go.'

She ran downstairs, then came up with a load of things under her jacket. I was busy focusing on the wheel. It felt unfamiliar in my hands, and it was daunting to be going at such speed, the waves bouncing under us.

We were about a hundred feet from the ship when Liza instructed me to keep a parallel course. Then she ran to the front, a loudhailer in her hand. '*Night Star Two*, you are too loud and travelling too fast. Please turn your music down. You are in an area inhabited by migrating whales. We have alerted the coastguard and the National Parks and Wildlife Service. Leave the area at once.'

If there was a skipper, he wasn't listening. One of the stewards gave Liza the finger and disappeared. A moment later the music was noticeably louder. I could no longer see what Liza was doing. I stared at the name on the side of the big boat. Then it hit me.

I pulled out my phone as the radio hissed into life: 'Liza? It's Greg. The Parks people are on their way. C'mon, let's head back. The fewer of us moving around the better for the whales. *Suzanne* to *Ishmael,* do you read me?'

I put my phone back into my pocket, then I picked up the receiver. I squeezed it tentatively. 'Hello? It's—ah—Mike Dormer.'

There was a brief silence, then Greg said, 'What's she doing up front?'

'I don't know,' I confessed.

Then there was an explosion. I leapt to the side of the boat just in time to see a huge flare headed into the air angled at no more than twenty feet above the disco ship. Liza was standing at the prow, loading something long and thin into some kind of launcher. I saw people backing away rapidly from the top deck of the other ship and heard a man screaming abuse at her. The dog was barking wildly. Then I saw Liza load another flare, point it high into the air and stumble backwards as, with a huge *crack*, she sent it into the sky not quite high enough above them.

As the disco ship's engines finally swung it round and propelled it the other way, I heard a gravelly voice come over the radio: '*Moby Two* to *Ishmael*. Jesus Christ, Liza. You've really gone and done it now.'

Liza

B y the time we reached the jetty, Kathleen was already shouting at me, her upright body bristling with indignation. I secured *Ishmael*, helped Milly ashore and walked briskly towards her. 'I know,' I said.

'Do you realise what you've done? Are you totally insane, girl?'

I stopped and pushed the hair off my face. 'I wasn't thinking.'

The anxiety on her face mirrored my own. In fact, I could have kicked myself. I had thought of nothing else for the twenty minutes it had taken us to come back to the bay.

'They were straight onto the Water Police, Liza. For all we know they're on their way over here now. Apparently, you let the second flare off while they were on the marine radio.'

I was a fool and I knew it. Against every rule of marine safety and common sense, I had positioned those two distress flares into their launchers, and aimed them just close enough to scare the boat's passengers. But flares were notoriously unpredictable. If one had misfired . . . If Search and Rescue had caught sight of the other . . .

I closed my eyes. It was only when I opened them again that I remembered I hadn't waited for Mike Dormer to disembark. The crunch of his shoes heralded his arrival next to us. He looked shaken. Kathleen's face softened. 'Why don't you go inside, Mike? I'll make some tea.'

He began to protest.

There was something steely in her tone. 'We need a few moments alone.'

I felt his eyes on me. Then he took a few reluctant paces away and stroked Milly, as if unwilling to go altogether.

'What do I do?' I whispered. 'They'll want to take down my details. There might be some kind of database . . .'

I felt a rising swell of panic in my chest. I glanced behind me to where the *Suzanne* and *Moby Two* were berthing. Then the sound of an engine drew my attention to the other coast road, where, bearing its distinctive logo, I saw a white pick-up truck of the New South Wales Police.

'Oh Christ,' I said.

'Smile,' Kathleen said. 'Just smile and say it was an accident.'

Two officers climbed out of the cab with the relaxed air that belies serious intent, their badges glinting in the late-afternoon sun.

'Afternoon, ladies,' said the taller man, tipping his cap as he approached.

'Officer Trent,' said my aunt, and smiled. 'Beautiful afternoon.'

'It is,' he agreed. He gestured towards *Ishmael*. 'That yours?'

'It certainly is,' said my aunt, before I could speak. '*Ishmael*. Registered to me. Has been for seventeen years.'

He looked at her then back at me. 'Had a call from two other vessels who say distress flares were fired at them from a boat matching her description this afternoon. Could you tell me anything about that?'

I wanted to speak, but the sight of that blue uniform had stuck my tongue to the roof of my mouth. 'I . . .'

Greg was beside me. 'Yes, mate,' he said firmly. 'That'd be my fault.'

The officer turned to him.

'I was out with a group of whale watchers. I knew the kids would be trouble, but I wasn't watching them close enough. While I had my back turned, searching for the whales, the little buggers let off two flares.'

'Kids?' the policeman said sceptically.

'I knew I shouldn't have let them on,' Greg said, and paused to light a cigarette. 'Liza here said they'd be trouble. But we like to let all the kids see the whales and dolphins. Educate them, you know.' He met my eye briefly, and what I saw in it filled me with gratitude, and a little shame.

'Why didn't you let Marine Rescue know what had happened?'

'I'm sorry, mate. I just wanted to get back here soon-as, so they couldn't do anything else. I had other passengers aboard, you know.'

'Which boat is yours again, Greg?'

Greg gestured. Our boats were both forty-eight-foot cruisers. They bore a band of the same colour.

'OK, so what were the kids' names?' The policeman took out a notebook.

Kathleen broke in, 'We don't keep records. If we wrote down the details of every person we took out on our boats we'd never get out on the water.'

'Why weren't your flares secured, Greg? They should be in a locked box.'

Greg shook his head. 'Little buggers had my keys from my pocket. I always carry a spare set, see? Just to be on the safe side.'

I was sure the policeman didn't believe a word of it: he frowned at the three of us in turn. 'The caller said a woman was firing at them.'

'Long hair,' said Greg, quick as you like. 'You can't tell them apart, these days. Bloody hippies. Look, Officer, it was my fault. I was minding the wheel and I guess I took my eye off the ball. No harm done, though, eh?'

'You realise the use of a distress flare as a weapon is an offence under the Firearms and Dangerous Weapons Act, leading to a charge of assault under the NSW Crimes Act? That's two thousand dollars and/or twelve months in jail. And you could be charged under the Maritime Services Act.'

Greg appeared penitent. I had never seen him so conciliatory. Suddenly I ached for him. I sensed his humiliation—and I was responsible for it.

'Tell you what,' said Kathleen, 'why don't I get some tea and you can decide what you want to do while it's brewing? Officer Trent, do you still take sugar?'

At that point Mike Dormer approached. My heart leapt into my mouth. Go away, I told him silently. He had no idea what we'd told them. If he opened his mouth and blurted out the truth we'd all be sunk.

'Actually,' he said, 'can I say something?'

'Not now, Mike,' said Kathleen, briskly. 'We're a bit busy.'

'I just want to tell the police something,' Mike said. I thought, with horror, that I had no idea how he felt about what I'd done. I hadn't spoken to him on the way back, my brain humming with the reality of what I'd done.

The same thought had occurred to Kathleen, I could tell.

'I don't think this is anything you can help with, Mike,' she said, firmly. But it was too late. He was pulling something from his pocket.

'While we were out on the water,' he said, 'some kind of party boat came close by. It was making enough noise and commotion to frighten the whales. I believe there are regulations about such things.'

The first policeman crossed his arms. 'That'd be right,' he said.

Mike held up his mobile phone. The Englishness in his voice gave him a kind of gentle authority. 'Well, I filmed it all on my phone. You can hear the level of noise.' As we gaped, his little mobile phone displayed a clip of the *Night Star*, showing the speed at which it had been travelling, revealing the outline of the revellers on deck. You could hear the thump of the music. 'The whales seemed distressed by it. Not that I'm an expert or anything.'

'We did try to radio the coastguard,' I said, 'but they didn't get out there in time.' My voice was squeaky with relief.

'I can send you a copy,' offered Mike, 'in case you want to use it to prosecute anyone.'

The two policemen examined the image. 'Not sure what you'd send it to,' said one, 'but give us your number and we'll let you know. Who are you?'

'Oh, I'm just a guest,' Mike said. 'Michael Dormer. Here on holiday from England. I can get my passport, if you like.' He held out his hand. I'm not sure that many people offer to shake hands with the police out here. The stunned faces that accompanied the handshake suggested not.

'That won't be necessary just now. Well, we'll be getting on. But make sure you lock up your flares securely, people, or you'll be getting another visit. A less friendly one.'

'Two locks,' said Greg, waving his keys.

'Thank you, Officers,' said Kathleen. 'You take care, now.'

I couldn't speak. As they climbed back into the truck, a long, quivering breath escaped from somewhere high in my chest and I realised my legs were shaking. 'Thank you,' I mouthed at Greg, and nodded at Mike.

THERE ARE MANY things I love about Australia. It's not the usual things—the weather, the light, or the wide-open spaces—although they're a bonus. It's not the scenery, or the leisurely pace of life, although those things have made bringing up my daughter here more of a pleasure. For me it's that, in a quiet corner like Silver Bay, you can live out your life without anyone paying you the slightest attention.

From almost the day I pitched up at Kathleen's, with my exhausted daughter in tow, with the barest of explanations, we were drawn into the Silver Bay community. Nobody asked too many questions. And if you chose not to answer those that were asked, well, that seemed OK, too. In five years, only Greg had grilled me over why I'd left England, and then I'd been so drunk that, to my shame, I couldn't remember what I'd told him.

I'd guessed instinctively that Mike Dormer would upset that. I overheard him asking Kathleen who worked in the bay, how long people tended to stick around, how long we'd lived there. He'd said he was on holiday, but I'd never known a tourist ask so many focused questions. When I take a group out on *Ishmael*, they talk to each other. When it's just me and one other, they want to talk to me. They ask questions. So, I don't generally take people out alone.

As Greg well knew. 'So, what was your cosy little trip for two about, then, huh?' We were sitting on the bench, watching, as Hannah made Milly chase bits of bladderwrack up and down the shore in the fading light. Mike Dormer was in his room and Kathleen had gone for more beers. He spoke quietly so that Lance and Yoshi couldn't hear.

'Money, mainly.' I pulled the wad of notes from my jeans pocket. 'Five hundred,' I said. 'For one trip.'

He stared at it. 'Why would he pay that much to go out with you? He turns up here, throws his money around . . . What's it all about?'

I shrugged. 'I don't know and I don't care. He'll be gone soon enough.'

'He'd better be. I don't like him.'

Hannah ran up, breathless and giggling. Milly flopped down at my feet. 'Have you got homework?' I reached out to push her hair off her face. Every time I looked at her now she seemed to have grown a little, her face taking on new aspects.

'Just revision. We've got a science test on Tuesday.'

'What's your test about?' asked Yoshi. 'I'll help you, if you like.'

Over the years I had discovered that the crews had enough skills between them to provide a whole education for Hannah. Yoshi, for example, had an advanced degree in biology and marine science. She sat with Hannah and, as night fell around us, they ploughed through something to do with osmosis, Yoshi explaining things far better than I ever could.

Greg seemed to recognise that I'd been shaken by the day's events, and tried to make me laugh with stories of the warring couple he'd had on board.

'You fancy coming to my place tonight? I got a whole load of videos off one of the guys at the boatyard. New comedies. Might be something you'd like.' He made it sound casual.

'No,' I said, 'but thanks.'

'It's just a film,' he said.

'It's never just a film, Greg.'

'One day,' he said, his eyes lingering on mine.

'One day,' I conceded.

Mike Dormer came out as the last of the light disappeared. The burners were on, and Kathleen had made bacon sandwiches. Hannah was squashed next to me, wrapped in a muffler against the colder air. Kathleen had handed Mike a plate, and he walked round the side of the table to get to the remaining seat. He glanced at me, then at the others, muttering, 'Evening.'

Hannah leaned forward. 'Did you see what I wrote?'

He tilted his head.

'On your computer. I left you a note. I did that thing you said for looking people up and there's a picture of you. Of your face. And your company.'

He seemed uncomfortable. Mind you, I sympathise with people who don't like to have their lives dug into, so I admonished Hannah.

'So what is it, mate?' said Lance. 'Drugs? White-slave trade? We can sell you Squirt here at a good price. Throw in the dog, if you like.'

Hannah poked Lance's arm. 'Actually, it looks a bit boring,' she said, grinning. 'I don't think I'd like to work in a city.'

'What is it you actually do?' said Greg aggressively.

Mike took a big bite of his sandwich. 'It's research, mainly. Background information for financial deals.' His voice was muffled with food.

'Oh,' said Greg, dismissively. 'The boring stuff.'

'Is it your own company?' asked Hannah.

Mike shook his head, his mouth apparently too full to talk.

I waited until Hannah had gone in before I spoke to Mike again. 'Listen, I'm sorry about earlier. If I gave you a fright, I mean. I just couldn't work out how to get rid of those boats. But it was stupid.'

He had had a few beers and was leaning back in his chair, staring at the black nothing where the sea should have been.

'It was a bit of a surprise,' he said. I could just make out his smile from the porch light. 'I thought you were going to harpoon them.'

That smile made me wonder how I had ever suspected he would talk to the police about me. 'Not this time,' I said, and he grinned.

He was all right, Mike. And it was a long time since I'd thought that about a man.

MY ROOM WAS at the back of the hotel, at the farthest end of the corridor. Hannah's room was next door, and in the small hours still, more frequently than either of us cared to admit, she would pad along the corridor and crawl into my bed as she had when she was small. I only slept soundly when I could feel her against me. But I would never have told her so; she had enough burdens to carry.

From the day I had arrived I had slept with the window open, lulled by the sound of the sea, comforted by the endless stars in the uninterrupted sky. There, two storeys up, I could be alone with my thoughts, and, when alone, cry without anyone hearing. Those were the only times when I closed my window, so that any sound I uttered did not carry down to the whale crews below. But the gentle breeze from the west carried their words, their laughter, straight up to me. Which was how, as I hauled my fleece over my head, I heard Greg's voice. It was lubricated by drink, its warmth gone. 'You won't get anywhere with her,' he was saying emphatically. 'I've been waiting four years for her and, I tell you, no one's got closer than me.'

It was several seconds before I grasped that he was talking about me. I was so mad that he could dare to presume any kind of ownership over me that I had to fight the urge to go down and say as much. But I didn't. I was too shaken by the day's events to pick another fight. I just lay awake, cursed Greg Donohoe, and tried not to think about things that could be brought back by an English accent.

It was a good hour before I realised I hadn't heard Mike Dormer's reply.

Kathleen

He thought I couldn't tell. He didn't realise it shone out of him like a beacon every time he looked at her. I could have warned him, but what would have been the point? I've never yet met a man who didn't think he could turn the world on its axis if he wanted something badly enough.

That said, the prospect of him making a move on my niece made me look a little harder at Mr Michael Dormer of London, England. He seemed kind, was unfailingly polite, always had time to indulge Hannah, no matter how trivial the query, and all these things were in his favour. He was handsome, at least to my eyes, and despite his quiet, easy-going manner, he was no pushover, as I had observed when, one late evening recently, Greg had tried to warn him off my niece. 'Thank you for your advice,' he had replied. 'You won't mind if I ignore it, since my private life is none of your business.'

He still looked like a fish out of water, even after three weeks in Silver Bay. He had bought himself a storm jacket, but sitting with the whalers, as he did most evenings, he was still no more at home than I would have been in the City. Oh, he tried: he responded good-naturedly to their jokes, bought more than his share of drinks. But something about Mike told me he wasn't being straight with us. He had told me one morning that he wasn't married, and then politely changed the subject. Why would a single young man spend so long in a quiet little resort like ours?

Then there was the afternoon I saw him at the council offices. As I stood outside the bank, I saw him coming down the steps, a big folder under his arm. The expression on his face when he caught sight of me . . . I know when someone feels they have been discovered. He recovered pretty quickly, came striding across the road and made small talk with me. But I felt, suddenly, that Mike had something to hide.

Nino told me I'd made too much of it. He knew a little of Liza's history—as much as he needed to know—and thought me overprotective. 'She's a very different character from the one who arrived here,' he said. 'And she's thirty-two, you know.' He was right. In fact, I can chart the truth of Nino's words in the photographs she sent me over the years.

After her mother, my sister Norah, died, Liza was wearing dark make-up that presumably gave her something to hide behind. It was hard to believe that the child who had visited here and turned cartwheels along the jetty, the girl who had written me rambling letters about ponies, was under all that camouflage. Then, a few years later, I saw something new: the softening and vulnerability that comes with motherhood. After she met Steven the pictures had stopped coming. In the only one I have from that period he looks smug, apparently proud to be a father, but her eyes are veiled.

We have no pictures of the time when she arrived here. But now, five years on, what would a photograph of her show? A wiser, stronger woman. A courageous, loving person. That's what it would show. If she'd let us take one.

THE DAY THAT Liza and Hannah arrived here, I drove the three hours to Sydney airport to pick them up, and when we got back to the hotel Liza lay down on my bed and didn't get up for nine days. I was so frightened by day three that I called the doctor. She didn't eat, she didn't sleep, she took only occasional sips of the sweet tea that I placed on the bedside table, and declined to answer any of my questions. Most of the time she lay on her side and stared at the wall, her pale hair lank, a cut on her face and a huge bruise down the side of her arm. Dr Armstrong pronounced her basically healthy and said that she should be left to rest.

Hannah was only six, anxious and clingy, and prone to tearful outbursts. It was unsurprising, considering she had travelled for a day and two nights to a place she didn't know, to be looked after by an old lady she had never met before. It was high summer, and she couldn't understand why I wouldn't let her run around outside. I was afraid of the sun on her fair skin, afraid of letting her too close to the water, afraid of her not coming back. If I wasn't watching her, she would creep upstairs and cling onto her mother. The way she cried at night broke your heart. I remember calling up to my sister in the heavens, asking her what I was meant to do.

By day nine I had had enough. I was exhausted from looking after the guests and this tearful child, who had not been able to explain what was going on, just as I, in return, could explain nothing to her. I wasn't used to the chaos that children bring, their endless needs and demands, and I got snappy. I wanted my bed back and a moment's peace.

'Get up,' I yelled at Liza, opening the window. When she didn't respond, I pulled back the covers. 'C'mon, it's a beautiful day and it's time for you to get up. Your daughter needs you, Liza, and I have to get on.'

I recall how she turned her head, her eyes dark with remembered horrors, and how my resolve vanished. I sat down on my bed, taking her hands in mine. 'What is it, Liza?' I said softly. 'What's going on?'

When she told me, I held her to me, white-knuckled, as she wept.

IN THE AFTERNOON of the day after Liza had been questioned by the Water Police, Yoshi had called me on the radio to tell me they had seen a female humpback in distress, swimming up and down at the mouth of the bay. The creature bore no obvious signs of illness, she just kept swimming, following some strange irregular path. It was abnormal behaviour for a migrating whale. At ten o'clock that evening we got a call that a baby whale had beached. It had been discovered by a boatload of office workers out for a party.

'It's the one we saw before,' said Liza, as she hung up. 'I just know it.'

'Can I help?' Mike said, when he saw us in the main hallway, pulling on our jackets and boots.

'Could you stay here so that Hannah's not alone? Don't tell her what's going on if she happens to wake up.'

I was surprised that Liza asked him. She had never so much as employed a sitter since she'd been here. 'We may be a while,' I said, patting his arm. 'Don't wait up. And whatever you do, don't let Milly out. The poor whale will have enough on its plate without a dog running round it.'

THERE ARE FEW more heartbreaking sights than a beached calf. The baby lay in the sand, maybe six feet long, alien and vulnerable.

Greg was already there. 'I've called the authorities,' he said. It was illegal to try to move a whale without official help: if it was sick you could do more harm than good. If well-wishers turned it towards the sea, it might call in an entire pod: the next day whales would be beaching themselves in terrifying numbers, as if in sympathy. 'He might be sick. He'll still be nursing, and he's not going to last long without milk. Reckon he could have been here a few hours already.'

The calf lay on his side, his nose pointed towards the shore, his eyes half closed as if in contemplation of his misery.

'He didn't beach because he's sick. It's those bloody boats,' hissed Liza, grabbing her bucket and heading to the sea to fill it. 'They play music so loud it disorientates the whales. The little ones haven't got a chance.'

We worked for almost an hour as we waited for the National Parks people to arrive. The light from our torches swung backwards and forwards as we walked down to the sea and back again, trying to keep the calf wet.

'Come on, baby boy,' whispered Liza, kneeling in the sand. 'Hang on in there while we get you a stretcher. Your mum's out there, waiting for you.'

We suspected this was true. Every half an hour or so we heard a distant splash—the sound, perhaps, of her searching the seas, judging how close she could come. I was afraid that the mother, in her desperation and anguish, would beach herself.

It was past midnight before two National Parks and Wildlife rangers reached us. Apparently the wrong location had been reported.

'We'll try to float him,' one of them said. They rolled the baby onto a stretcher, then, grunting with the effort, walked with it into the shallows. Even half elevated by water, a baby whale is awesomely heavy. From the shore, Yoshi at my side, I watched as Greg, Liza and the rangers tried to will the calf into swimming back to its mother. After an hour or so, they went deeper, but still the baby didn't move.

By that time it was getting on for 2 a.m. and it was obvious that the calf was in a bad way. Its breathing was irregular, its eye closing periodically. I don't know how long they all stood there, the hours creeping along in a fug of cold and growing despair. At one point Yoshi and I made coffee on the berthed *Moby One*, then she and Lance stepped in so that each helper could break for fifteen minutes and warm themselves with a hot drink.

Then we heard it: a faint, terrible sound from out at sea, a strange keening and lowing, the rare sound of whalesong above water.

'It's his mother!' cried Liza. 'She's calling him.'

Yoshi shook her head. 'It's far more likely to be a male accompanying the mother and child at a distance. Like an escort, looking out for them.'

'Doesn't seem to have done this little fellow much good,' said one of the National Parks men. 'He doesn't appear to have the energy to fight.'

Next to me, Liza shook her head. 'He's got to. He's just disorientated.'

But to me the poor thing looked half dead, and I was no longer sure who they were holding it in the water for.

Finally, as the sun broke over the headland, casting a pale blue light over our little group, one of the National Parks guys announced that there was no hope. 'We should euthanise,' he said. 'Leave it any longer and we'll risk the mother coming in and beaching herself.'

'But he's still alive,' said Liza. The pale light revealed her to be grey and exhausted. 'Surely while there's life . . .'

Greg placed his arm round her shoulders and squeezed. His eyes were rimmed with red and his face was dark with stubble. 'We've done everything we can, Liza. We can't risk the mother too.'

'But if we can get him out to his mother, he'll be OK,' she cried.

I had to look away. I couldn't bear what I heard in her voice.

'No, he won't.' The National Parks man laid a hand on the baby's back. 'We've had him here for eight hours and he's barely moved. He's too frail to get back out there. If we take him deeper he'll drown.'

I left then, partly to be with Hannah when she woke for school, and partly to escape a scene I knew I would find unbearable. I'm glad I didn't see the anguish of the National Parks man as he placed a gun to the whale's head. Yoshi told me later that they had all wept when the calf died.

But Liza had sobbed so hard that she had almost hyperventilated, and Greg had held on to her for fear that she was not herself. She had half waded into the water, her arms outstretched, crying out an apology to the mother, as if she, personally, had failed.

It was then, Yoshi said, that Greg had given Liza a large brandy—he had a bottle in his truck. After a few more, as the sun rose over Silver Bay, illuminating the body on the beach, Liza had calmed down a little and climbed unsteadily into the truck and headed off to Greg's.

Mike

Curse that jet lag. I was uncomfortably awake, thinking about the conversation I had just had with Dennis in England, trying to tell myself I wasn't feeling the things I shouldn't be feeling.

I had woken shortly after four, and had lain awake for some time, my thoughts humming malevolently in the dark. In Silver Bay, for the most part, I had managed to forget my own actions . . . things I had not told

Vanessa. But in the silent hours before dawn there was little way of escaping the truth about myself. Eventually I had got up and wandered through the deserted rooms. It seemed that the hotel was still empty, but for myself and Hannah. I had returned to my room with a pair of Kathleen's binoculars and focused them out of the bay window. I'd just been able to make out the flickering of torchlight, and in flashing pools of light I'd seen Greg and the others wading in and out of the water. Some time later, I'd recognised Liza and two guys talking beside what looked like a tarpaulin.

Then Dennis had rung, apparently heedless of the time difference, explosive with barely suppressed fury at his enforced bedridden state, and had insisted on me detailing every step I had taken towards the progression of the development. He was hard to reassure at the best of times, but nigh on impossible when he was in this mood.

'Have you secured the planning permission?' he demanded.

'It doesn't work that quickly here.' I wondered why this man could bring me out in a sweat even at a distance of thousands of miles.

'You know I need it to be a done deal, Mike.'

'There may be a few problems with . . . the ecological side of things.'

'What the hell does that mean?'

'The watersports might . . . be considered to impact negatively on the local sea life. We may get a bit of resistance from the whale watchers.'

'Whale watchers? What are they? Greenpeace-loving lentil-eaters?'

'They're the most important tourism attraction in the bay.'

'So what the hell do they watch the whales in? Yachts? Rowing boats?'

'Motorboats.' I could see where he was going.

When I looked out of the window again everyone, even the whale, was gone.

At around six I heard the screen door, and arrived at the bottom of the stairs to find Kathleen peeling off her wet coat in the hall. She looked done in.

'Let me take your coat,' I said.

She brushed me aside. 'Don't fuss,' she said, and from her tone I guessed the fate of the baby whale. 'Where's Hannah?'

'Still asleep.'

Kathleen nodded. 'Thank you,' she said. She was stooped. It was the first time I had seen her as an old woman. 'I'm going to make a pot of tea.'

I guessed that the death of the baby whale was unusual enough to have shaken her. While I was pondering this, sitting at the kitchen table because Kathleen insisted on making the tea herself, I realised I was waiting for the sound of Liza's oilskin to swish against the door as she came in.

'Poor creature,' Kathleen said, when she finally sat down. 'Didn't have a chance. We should have shot it at the beginning.'

I tried to sound casual. I observed that Liza had obviously decided to go out early on *Ishmael*, but almost before the words had left my mouth, Kathleen gave me a look. 'She's with Greg,' she said.

The words hung in the air.

'I didn't realise they were an item.' My voice sounded high and false.

'They're not,' she said wearily. And then, apparently apropos of nothing, 'She took the calf dying very personally.'

'But surely there wasn't anything she could have done,' I said. I couldn't understand how a dead whale meant she had to sleep with Greg.

'Look, Mike, Liza lost a child five years ago. This is her way of dealing with it.' She took a sip of tea. 'Unfortunately, it means that once or twice a year that poor fool thinks he has a hope.'

While I was digesting this news, she stood up and announced that she had better get Hannah up. Her abrupt change of subject told me she didn't want to discuss the matter any further.

'I'll drive her to school if you want,' I said. Suddenly I knew I needed a task to stop me thinking. I wanted to get out of this house.

'You sure?' The look of gratitude told me just how tired Kathleen was.

IT IS POSSIBLE that I appear, as my sister Monica would say, to be more of a player than I am. In fact, during the four years of my relationship with Vanessa, until the night with Tina at the office party, I had never so much as kissed another girl. Even as I'd held Tina's slim body to me, some part of me had wanted to laugh out loud at the fact that it was happening at all.

I met Vanessa Beaker at Beaker Holdings, and we had been dating for several weeks before I discovered who she was. At that point, I considered ending the relationship; the possibility of jeopardising my career over someone I was unsure about seemed not worth the risk. But she told me not to be ridiculous, informed her father about us in front of me, adding that whether we stayed together or not was no concern of his, then announced to me afterwards that she knew I was The One. She gave me the kind of smile that said the possibility that such a statement might alarm me was not even worth considering.

And I suppose I hardly did consider it. Monica said I was lazy in relationships; I was happy for attractive women to chase me, and had had to end a relationship myself only once. Vanessa was pretty, confident and clever, and spent endless amounts of energy worrying about my appearance and well-being. I didn't mind. I trusted Vanessa's opinion. She was clever, as I've said, and she had her father's aptitude for business.

I didn't know why I had to defend my relationship to my sister, but I did. She said I'd probably marry anyone who made the same efforts as Vanessa, who made my life that easy. She told me I had never been truly in love because I had never been hurt.

'What do you want?' she said, when I telephoned her.

'Hello, brother dear. I've missed you,' I said. 'How's life on the other side of the planet? How's your deal shaping up?'

'Are you ringing me to tell me you're emigrating? Buy me a club-class ticket and I'll tell Mum and Dad for you.' I heard a cigarette being lit. 'So, what *do* you want?' she said, exhaling noisily.

The truth was, I didn't know. 'Just to talk to someone, I guess.'

'You OK?'

'Yeah, fine. Just . . . just had an odd night. A baby whale beached itself outside the hotel and died. It . . . threw me a little.'

'Wow. A baby whale. Were you all trying to get it back in the water?'

'Not me personally.'

'Didn't want to get those designer trousers dirty, huh?'

Suddenly I felt irritated by her inability ever to be nice and straightforward with me. 'Oh, forget it. I'd better go.'

'Hey—hey—OK, Mike. Sorry.'

'Look, we'll speak another time.' I should have rung Vanessa. But I knew why I hadn't.

I SPIED HER walking down the coast road after I had returned from dropping Hannah. When she saw me sitting at the beach end of the jetty, she stopped a few feet away from me on the sand, one hand raised against the morning sun. I looked at her differently now, knowing what I knew.

'You want to drive to the market with me?' she said.

Silhouetted as she was, I could barely see her face. 'You're driving?'

'I guess you could drive me. Kathleen's too tired to go grocery shopping.'

I figured it was as close to an invitation as I was going to get. I went inside to get my car keys.

To the British eye, Australian supermarkets are a cornucopia, with an abundance of brightly coloured fruit and vegetables punctuated by alien delights such as Violet Crumbles and Green's Pancake Shake. Liza marched up and down the aisles, lobbing items into the oversized trolley.

'Anything you want in particular?' she called over her shoulder.

'I'm easy,' I said, putting a packet of crackers back onto the shelf, and thought of the myriad ways in which that statement was true.

As I watched, I found myself piecing things together, considering what now made sense. Her inability to let her surviving child out on the water. Her melancholy. Perhaps the other child had drowned. Perhaps she had lost her husband at the same time. I realised how few questions I had asked her.

We had been on the road for almost twenty minutes before we spoke again, although I sat in the driver's seat acutely aware of Liza beside me. We passed the council offices, and I thought about the development and my conversation with Dennis. I knew I should have said something to Kathleen by now. Part of it, I guess, was cowardice. I knew how she—any of them—was likely to respond. I liked these people, and the thought of them not liking me . . . got to me. And now, after Liza, the distress flares and the baby whale, I was no longer convinced of the development plan's rightness. There must be a way, I thought, to tie in the two sets of needs—those of our proposed hotel and those of the whalechasers.

Two boats were moored at Whale Jetty: *Moby One* and *Ishmael*. The sun, high in the sky, glinted off the blue water behind them as I drove past, and the dense pines that covered the hills were an unnatural lush green. Every time I looked at this setting, I imagined it in a brochure.

'I guess you know what happened last night,' Liza said.

'It's none of my business,' I said.

'No,' she agreed, 'it's not.'

I indicated left and headed slowly up the track to the hotel.

'I've known Greg a long time. He . . . well, I know him well enough to know that it doesn't matter for him. That it doesn't have to mean anything.'

I pulled up beside the hotel. We sat in silence as we pondered the weighty realisation that she had deemed it necessary to say anything to me at all.

'Your aunt told me about your child. I'm sorry.'

Her head snapped round. Her eyes, I saw, were red-rimmed. It might have been lack of sleep, or the result of endless tears. 'She shouldn't have.'

I didn't know what to say.

So I leaned forward, took Liza McCullen's exhausted, beautiful face in my hands and kissed her. God only knows why. The really surprising thing was that she kissed me back.

Hannah

My friend Lara took me out on her boat *Baby Dreamer*, which was rigged with a mainsail and a jib. She taught me how to tack and gybe, the most important things in sailing. I didn't tell Mum. But Lara's mum watched from their house and I wore her spare life jacket. My mum never says much to the other mums, so I guessed I was pretty safe.

Lara has done a sailing course at Salamander Bay. She said that when my mum agrees to let me use *Hannah's Glory* we can go and do the course together. They run them in the school holidays and it's quite cool if you bring your own boat. I had asked Mum once about Greg's dinghy, since my party, and she just said a flat no, in the way that meant she wasn't going to discuss it. But Auntie K said Mum will come round.

The sea was calm and we were allowed to go between the two nearest buoys and up the coast as long as we didn't go out as far as the shipping lane. The dolphins came out to see us near the point. I recognised Brolly and Brolly's baby. This was the third time I had been out with Lara and the dolphins always came to us. They always look like they're smiling. We spent about an hour talking to them and watching them play.

Dolphins were Letty's favourite animals. She had four on pieces of coloured crystal that she got for her fourth birthday. I used to rearrange them on her dressing table and she got cross. We used to fight quite a lot. Sometimes I still think about when we used to fight and I feel really bad because if I'd known what was going to happen to her I would have tried to be nice to her every day. I still have the crystal dolphins, but I keep them in a box now.

Once, when I had them out, Lara said, picking them up carefully, 'Do you think about your sister a lot?'

I was under my bed trying to find a magazine that I wanted to show her, so I don't think she could see me nodding. 'I don't really talk about her because Mum gets too upset,' I said, as I backed out, 'but I still miss her.' I couldn't really say more than that. It still felt too difficult.

'I hate my sister,' Lara said. 'She's a witch. I'd love to be an only.'

I couldn't explain it properly to her—but I'll always have a sister. Letty not being alive any more doesn't make me an only, just half of what I was.

ON THURSDAY, MUM asked me to take Mike his breakfast for the third time in a week.

'Can't you do it?' I said, as I wanted to plait my hair before school.

'No,' she said. Like, that was that. And she left his tray outside my room.

She was being quite weird. I didn't know if it was because she didn't like Mike, but she won't sit out in the evenings any more, even though he sits out every night like he was waiting for her.

'Are you cross with Mike?' I asked Mum in the end.

She was a bit shocked. 'No, I'm not cross, sweetheart.' She started to fiddle with her hair. 'I just don't think it's a good idea to get too close to the guests.' Later I heard her and Auntie K talking in the kitchen, when they thought I was watching telly.

'Liza, love, you can't hide for ever,' Auntie K was saying.

'Why? We're happy, aren't we? It's just not a good idea.'

'And Greg is?'

Greg doesn't like Mike. He called him a 'sonofabitch' when Aunt Kathleen was talking to him and he thought nobody could hear.

Mum's voice was all stressed when she said, 'I just think it's better all round if Hannah and I steer clear of getting . . . involved.'

I looked up 'involved' in the dictionary. It said, 'participating in a romantic or sexual relationship/complicated or difficult to follow'. I showed it to Auntie K to see which one it was, but she stuck her finger on both and said that about summed it up.

AT SCHOOL, they were all talking about the school trip, even though it was months away. Katie Taylor asked me if I was coming, and I said I might not be. She's the kind who twists everything you say, so she stood there in front of everyone and said, 'Why? Haven't you got enough money?'

'It's not because of money,' I said, and went pink.

'Why, then? Everyone else in our year is coming.'

'I'm not coming because we're going somewhere else.' I'd spoken before I'd thought about what I would say. 'We're . . . we're going on a trip.'

'Back to England?'

'Maybe. Or we might go to the Northern Territory.'

'Don't be such a stickybeak, Katie,' said Lara. She can put on this voice that says not to mess with her. 'It's none of your business where they go.'

Later, Lara put her arm through mine when we walked back to hers. My mum was picking me up from there after tea. I like the way her family is all noisy and happy even when they're shouting at each other.

'Hannah,' Lara said, and her voice was really kind. 'Is it really about money? The reason why you can't come to New Zealand?'

I chewed my nail. 'It's a bit complicated.'

'You're my best friend,' she said. 'I wouldn't tell anyone, whatever it is.'

'I know.' I squeezed her arm. I would really have liked to talk to her about it. But Mum had told me that we couldn't ever leave Australia and that I mustn't talk to anyone about it.

'Katie Taylor's a stupid bitch,' said Lara. 'Don't pay her any attention.' Suddenly I felt mad with my mum. Because all I wanted was to do what everyone else did. Why was it always me who had to say no?

Mum picked me up and I almost said something, but she was so busy thinking about something else that she didn't notice how quiet I was.

'Do you have any homework?' she said, when we pulled up at the hotel.

'No,' I said, then climbed out of the car before she could check.

When I was going to my room, I saw that Mike's door was open. He was on the phone and I hovered for a minute. I think he felt me there because he spun round. 'OK—can't talk now, Dennis. I'll ring you back.' Then he put down the phone and smiled a great big smile at me. 'Hello there. How are you doing?'

'Terrible,' I said, dropping my bag on the floor. 'I hate everyone.'

He just nodded. 'I have days like that. Here,' he motioned at me to sit down, 'would one of these cheer you up? I've made it my mission to try every Australian biscuit there is.'

When he pulled open his drawer, I saw he had all my favourites: Anzacs, chocolate Tim Tams and Arnott's Mint Slices. 'You'll get fat,' I warned him.

'Nope. I go running most mornings,' he said. 'I have a good metabolism.'

Then he let me go on his computer. He showed me a programme that lets you change pictures, so we pulled up another picture of Aunt Kathleen and the shark and I drew a big smile on its face.

Just as I was finishing, I felt him looking at me. 'Did you have a brother or a sister?' he said. 'The one who died, I mean.'

I was shocked to hear someone say that out loud. Aunt Kathleen has this kind of pained look whenever I say Letty's name, and Mum's so sad when I talk about her that I don't like to.

'A sister,' I said, after a minute. 'Her name was Letty. She died when she was five, in a car crash.'

He shrugged a bit. 'That's really tough,' he said. 'I'm sorry.'

Suddenly I wanted to cry. No one has ever said that to me. No one has ever thought about what it was like for me to lose my sister. They say, 'Thank goodness she can't remember too much.' But they never say, 'OK, Hannah. Let's talk about Letty. Let's talk about all the things you miss about her, and all the things that make you sad.' But I didn't feel I could say that to Mike. So when the tears came I pretended I was upset about the school trip and about the money and how I was the only one in my class who couldn't go.

Mike passed me his handkerchief and pretended to be interested in something outside while I pulled myself together. Then he leaned forward and said, 'OK, Hannah. I'm going to make you a business proposition.'

He asked me to take photographs around the bay. He had bought three disposable cameras and he said he would pay me a dollar for every good shot. He said he wasn't much of a photographer so I should take pictures of Silver Bay so he could show his friends back home. Then he asked me to write him a list of all the things that were good about my school, and a list of all the things that would improve it. And the same for Silver Bay. 'I want a really professional job,' he said. 'Do you think you're up to it?'

I nodded, because I was so excited at the idea of earning some money. Mike said if I worked hard enough there was no reason why I shouldn't be able to afford to go to New Zealand with my friends.

'But how long are you staying?' I asked him. I was trying to work out how much time I had to earn the money and whether, if I showed Mum I had enough, she'd feel she couldn't say no. He said his departure date was one of life's imponderables.

LANCE HAD HAD a win on the horses and bought everyone pizza. He told Aunt Kathleen that for once she should put her feet up, and Mike might be her guest but he was part of the ruddy furniture now so she didn't have to worry about him. And Mike had this little smile like he didn't want anyone to see but he was pleased to be part of the furniture.

Mr Gaines stopped by with some wine that Auntie K said was far too good for the likes of us, but she opened both bottles anyway, and they started on about the Old Days, which is what they talk about a lot.

Greg wasn't there. The others said he hadn't been out on his boat for four days. Auntie K said he was probably at the bottom of a bottle somewhere.

It was a cold evening, but all the burners were lit and we were squashed up on the bench, apart from Auntie Kathleen and Mr Gaines, who were on two wicker chairs with cushions. Mum was sitting on the other side of me and when I finished my drink I told her about Mike's business proposition and her face did that thing it does when she's about to stop me doing something.

'You're paying her to take photographs? You're as bad as Greg,' she said, not in a good way.

Mike took a sip of his wine. 'I'm nothing like Greg. And you know it.'

'Don't use her, Mike,' she whispered, as if I couldn't hear. 'Don't use her to try to get close to me, because it won't work.'

But Mike didn't look bothered. 'I'm not doing it for you. I'm doing it because I need some jobs done. If I hadn't asked Hannah, I'd only have had to ask someone else.' He bit off a piece of his pizza. 'Anyway,' he said, as he chewed. 'Who says I want to get close to you?'

There was a short silence, then I saw Mum's mouth quiver, like she didn't want to smile but couldn't help it, and I relaxed because if she was going to stop me earning the money she would have said so there and then.

'What are these photographs for?' she said, staring at her fingers.

Just as he was about to answer we saw headlights appear along the coast road. We were quiet as they drew closer, trying to see who it was.

It was a taxi. As it pulled up, Auntie K got up. 'I've got no food left,' she said. 'I hope they won't want feeding.'

'Well?' said Mum, turning to Mike. 'You haven't answered my question.'

I was waiting too, because I wanted to know. But Auntie K, who was walking back up the drive carrying a suitcase, distracted me. Behind her was a young woman with straight blonde hair and a soft pink cardigan wrapped round her shoulders. She was wearing high-heeled shoes with sequins, like she was going to a party. Auntie K came up to Mike, eyebrows raised, and dropped the case in front of him. 'Someone to see you,' she said.

'Dad gave me the time off,' the girl said. Mike stood up beside me. 'I've come to give you a hand. I thought we could have our honeymoon early.'

Mike

It was weird. Think of all the ways you're meant to greet your lover after a long separation—the slow-mo running together, the endless kisses, the desperate holding and touching—and all I felt on seeing Vanessa was this sensation I used to get when I was a kid, like when you're at a friend's house and your mum comes to get you before you're ready.

'I thought you'd be glad,' she said, as we lay next to each other later that night. That was the other weird thing: we weren't touching.

'I am glad,' I said. 'It's just I've never been great with surprises.'

In truth it had probably been the most awkward twenty minutes of our entire relationship. She had stood there in front of the whalechasers, dressed like something from a fashion magazine, her carefully prepared smile fading. Kathleen had gone inside to fetch her a drink. Mr Gaines had made a show of offering her his chair. Lance had joked about me being a dark horse, going on about it so long that I had seen Vanessa start calculating how small a presence in my life she had been while I was in Australia.

Liza had sat on my other side, her eyes coolly registering this unforeseen element. I had wanted to take her aside, to explain, but it had been impossible. After about ten minutes, she announced that she and Hannah had to go in as Hannah had to get ready for school the next day.

It was strange having Vanessa in that room. Her endless shoes, the rows of unguents—her very presence—changed things. It reminded me of my life in London. It made me wonder whether I had been as happy there as I'd believed.

I felt mean even thinking it. 'Look,' I said, trying to reassure her, 'it's just been a bit odd, with them not knowing about the development plans. I guess you being here makes it a little more complicated.'

'You seem to have got yourself quite . . . involved,' she said, shifting beside me in the bed. 'It felt really strange walking up to you in the middle of all those people, with your fisherman's jacket or whatever it is. I felt like an outsider.' She sat up and swung her legs over the side of the bed, so that her back was towards me. 'I thought you'd phone more often.'

'It's night here when it's day in England—you know that.'

'You could have rung me any time.'

'It's business, Ness. You know what I'm like.'

She turned away. 'I do. I'm sorry. I don't know what's wrong with me.'

'It's the jet lag,' I said, a bit shaken by her uncharacteristic wobble. Vanessa was sure of everything. 'I felt odd for days after I arrived.'

I didn't like the idea that I might be more responsible for Vanessa's happiness than I'd realised. I reached for her, to persuade her to lie down, thinking that perhaps if we made love we'd start to feel less like strangers. But she rose and walked round the bed to the window. The moon was high and the night clear so you could see the whole bay.

'It's beautiful,' she said quietly. 'You said it was.'

'You're beautiful,' I said. She was silhouetted against the moonlight, the curves of her body visible through the filmy fabric of her nightdress. It's OK, I told myself silently. If I can feel like this about her it's OK.

She half turned towards me. This is the woman who is going to be my wife, I told myself. This is the woman I will love until I die.

'So, where are we with the planning permission?' she asked.

As I TOLD VANESSA, there had been a few difficulties with the development plan. The day before I had spent hours in the council planning department with Mr Reilly, who was on the highest rung of the planning ladder. Together we had gone through the various forms that needed filling in.

In several meetings over the previous weeks, he had said he liked the design and the employment opportunities. He also liked the benefits for local shops and traders, and I had emphasised the positive impact of similar developments on the local economy along the east Australian coast.

What Mr Reilly didn't like was the development's potential impact on the environment. It wasn't just the disruption of the building work, he said, but the residents of Silver Bay had strong opinions about restriction of their waters.

'This area has a growing awareness of its whale and dolphin population, and people round here don't want to do anything to harm them. On a purely economic level, they're a growing tourist attraction in themselves. Your development would occupy some of the waterfront.'

'Only with the kind of activities that tourists normally take part in.'

'But that's it. We don't get those kind of tourists round here—not in Silver Bay, anyway. They might swim or paddle out in dinghies, but wet-bikes, jet- or waterskiing are much noisier, much more intrusive activities.'

'Mr Reilly, you know as well as I do that in a place like this, development is only a matter of time. If it's not us, it'll be some other corporation.'

He looked at me with a mixture of belligerence and sympathy. 'Look, mate, we're all for anything that will help the local community. We know we need the employment and the infrastructure. But our sea creatures are not an afterthought. You won't win over this town unless you can sort out the environmental stuff.'

'That's fine, Mr Reilly,' I said, pulling my papers together. 'But I'd have more sympathy with your argument if this week I hadn't watched two whales bullied half to death by a disco boat that didn't seem to be policed by anyone. The threat to the whales is already out there, and, as far as I can see, no one is doing anything about it. We're willing to be as sympathetic as we can be to environmental concerns, but you can't tell me your area's a model for environmental excellence when I saw what prompted the death of a whale.'

'I'll discuss it,' he said. 'But don't be surprised if it goes to a public inquiry. People are getting wind of these plans and a few are already antsy.'

I had arrived home in a foul mood and had rung Dennis. I outlined the results of my meeting. 'It's complicated, Dennis. But I've had a radical thought. What if we abandon the watersports angle and make it more of a spa experience? *Vogue*-type thing. Where celebrities go.'

'But watersports are the development's Unique Selling Point,' Dennis barked. 'That's why the venture capitalists are interested. It's *meant* to be about sport, about keep-fit. You're not making sense.'

'Dennis, we'd have an easier ride from the planners if there was no risk of anything happening to the sea creatures. When you're out here, you get a sense of the'—I ran a hand through my hair—'the importance of the whales.'

There was a pause before he spoke again. I braced myself.

'Mike, this is *not* what I want to hear. We need the permissions secured, and we need them superfast. We have to start building in a matter of months. So, you talk to your bloody crusty whale friends and go and throw some money at Mr Reilly—whatever it takes!—but come back to me in the next forty-eight hours with a concrete plan that I can present to Vallance Equity when they turn up on Monday. OK?' He took a deep, shaking breath. 'Look, you wanted to be a partner—prove you're up to it. Or, even though I love you like a son, you may find your arse imprinted with my metaphorical left boot. Along with your employment prospects. You get me?'

It certainly didn't need spelling out any more clearly than that. I sat back in my chair and thought about everything I'd worked for over the past years. Then I thought of what Hannah had told me about her school bus. The lack of a library. 'OK,' I said. 'There's one possible way through this. There's a document called an S94.'

As Mr Reilly had explained it to me, it worked like this: for every tourist development in the Silver Bay area, the council generally expected a fifty per cent financial contribution from the developers towards the extra strain on local services, such as roads, car parking, emergency services. We had come across similar provisions in other developments, and I had found there was usually some clause that allowed for a waiver if the development was deemed of sufficient benefit to the community.

Studying the S94 document, I had seen that we could turn this one on its head: what if our company brought with it, for example, a new library for the Silver Bay School or a new school bus? Beaker Holdings would not, like most developers, try to provide the *minimum* material public benefit to build its resort. Instead it would provide over and above what was needed, and show itself to be a model for responsible development.

VANESSA SLEPT TILL after eleven the next morning. I lay beside her for some time after daybreak, glancing at her face. Eventually, when my thoughts became too complicated, I got out of bed. Some time after 7.30, I crept downstairs and ran five miles along the coast road and back, enjoying the damp chill of the morning air, the sense of quiet and isolation.

Twice, people whose faces I now recognised—dog-walkers, fishermen—lifted a hand in greeting, and I wondered what they would think of my plans. As I headed back, I tried not to look at the Silver Bay Hotel. If the development were to go ahead it would be at best overshadowed, at worst demolished.

I now saw that my first concerns were no longer money and ambition, but something far more difficult: successful compromise. I wanted Kathleen and Liza to be as happy with this outcome as the flint-eyed venture capitalists. I wanted the whales and dolphins to continue their lives as unaffected by the development as any creature can be when it lives in close proximity to man.

I arrived back at the hotel at 8.30, half hoping I could shower and have breakfast without bumping into anyone. I had timed my return, I am ashamed to say, to coincide with Liza and Hannah's school run—my best chance of finding an empty house.

But Kathleen was still sitting at the kitchen table, her own breakfast long finished. She had set me a place, with coffee and cereal. Another place setting sat ostentatiously beside it. 'You kept that one quiet,' she observed, from behind her newspaper, as I sat down.

How could I tell her it was as if I had forgotten?

Liza

Del, the owner of MacIver's Seafood Bar and Grill, was happy to host the meeting. He'd told me beforehand that he didn't oppose the development. Sited where he was, within a few feet of it, he said, he stood to make a killing. But he knew he'd get a few extra all-day breakfasts out of the locals who came along.

Greg had put the word around, and a few neighbouring hotel owners, local fishermen, whalechasers, people who were likely to be affected by it all, were coming. We sat waiting for people to straggle in. A few clutched copies of the newspaper with the front-page story under the headline: MAJOR TOURIST BOOST FOR TOWN. It said that a multi-million-dollar development had been approved for the land along the bay from the Silver Bay Hotel. A major international corporation had got planning permission after an unprecedented series of offers to safeguard the nature of the town and the sea life around it.

'We're hoping that this is just the beginning of a fruitful partnership with the local community,' said Dennis Beaker of Beaker Holdings, one of the British-based developers. 'We want to take the relationship further to provide a benchmark for responsible building in the area.'

Mayor of Silver Bay Don Brown said: 'We deliberated long and hard about the appropriateness of this development. But after a lengthy planning process we are happy to welcome both the employment and infrastructure benefits that the new hotel complex will bring. But most of all we welcome the company's responsible and thoughtful attitude towards our waters.'

Some people murmured to each other, while a few chatted normally, as if the town weren't about to be changed completely.

'Will all the dolphins move away?' Hannah asked me. She had come to join me at one of the tables.

Kathleen had also arrived, and sat down beside Hannah. She had heard the question and put a hand on her shoulder. 'I'm sure they've seen worse than this,' she said. 'In the war we had warships in the bay, bombers going overhead, submarines . . . but we still had dolphins. Don't you worry.'

'They're smart, aren't they? They'll know to keep out of everyone's way.'

Lance got up and began to speak. He said he appreciated that the development would have some economic benefits for the town, but the water-sports school would run the risk of destroying the town's one area for tourist growth: the whales and dolphins. 'This is the one thing that marks out Silver Bay from a lot of the other destinations.'

There was a murmur of agreement.

'This development is foreign money,' he continued. 'Yes, there will be a few jobs, but you can bet your life the profits won't stick around in Silver Bay. Foreign investment means returns to foreigners. Besides, we don't even know the full nature of this development. If it has its own cafés and bars, well, hell, you guys will lose as much as you gain.'

'It might boost the winter trade,' came a voice from the back.

'At what cost? If the whales and dolphins go, there isn't going to be any winter trade,' said Lance.

There was silence.

Beside me Hannah was reading the paper. 'Mum,' she said, frowning.

'What is it, sweetheart?' I whispered.

'That's Mike's company.' Her finger was on a bit of the print. 'Beaker Holdings. That's the one that has his picture on their website.'

It took me a minute or two to work out what she was saying. 'Beaker Holdings,' I read. 'You sure, sweetheart?'

'I remembered it because it was like a bird beak. Does that mean Mike's bought Silver Bay?'

I could barely see straight for the rest of that meeting. I just about held it together while Lance organised a petition. And then, as everyone drifted away, I asked Kathleen if she knew whether Mike was at the hotel.

'He's in his room,' she said. 'I think his fiancée's gone shopping.' She sniffed. 'She likes shopping.' She looked up at me. 'You OK?'

As IT TURNED OUT, Mike was sitting in the kitchen. When I appeared in the doorway he looked up. Just the sight of him made me want to smack him. I slammed the newspaper onto the kitchen table.

'That how you do your research, is it?'

He looked at the headline and went white.

'Sit in our hotel for the best part of a month making friends, asking questions, chatting up my daughter, and all the while you're planning to ruin us? How could you do that?'

He stood up. 'Liza, let me explain—'

'Explain? Explain what? That you came here pretending to be on holiday and all the while you've been plotting with the council to destroy us?'

'It's not going to destroy you or the whales. I've been working on putting all these safeguards in place.'

I laughed then. 'Safeguards. How is a bloody watersports park bang in the middle of our bay any kind of safeguard? There'll be speedboats whizzing around pulling skiers, jet-skis, you name it. Do you know what this is going to do to the whales?'

'How is it worse than what you do? It's just boat engines. They'll know to steer clear of the migration path. There will be rules.'

'Rules? You think an eighteen-year-old boy with a jet-ski wants to talk about rules?' I was shaking with rage. 'You saw us try to save that baby whale, and now you stand there and say your watersports park won't affect anything? Worse, you got my daughter to tell you what was most needed so you could suck up to the planning department and win them over.'

'She said they were things they needed. I've been doing my best to make this thing work for everybody.'

'You've been doing your best to line your own pockets,' I said. I moved a step closer to him. 'Everything you said you were is a lie. *Everything.*'

'No,' he said urgently, reaching out a hand. 'Not everything. I wanted to talk to you. I'm sorry. I wanted to say something about the development, but I had to get it worked out first. Once I realised what the whales meant to you all, I wanted to find a way to keep everyone happy.'

'Well, congratu-bloody-lations,' she spat. 'I hope you're pleased, because this thing's going to destroy us, and it'll destroy the whales.'

PART TWO

Kathleen

Newcastle Observer, April 11, 1939

A grey nurse shark has been landed in a fishing community north of Port Stephens—by a seventeen-year-old girl. Miss Kathleen Whittier Mostyn, daughter of Angus Mostyn, proprietor of the Silver Bay Hotel, hauled in the creature on Wednesday afternoon out in waters near Break Nose Island. She landed it unaided from a small sculling craft. A fisheries spokesman confirmed it was the largest shark of its kind ever netted in the area.

Mr Mostyn plans to have it mounted and placed in the hotel as a record of his daughter's estimable catch. 'We just have to find a wall strong enough,' he joked.

I dusted the glass frame and put the yellowing newspaper cutting back against the wall, alongside the photographs of the stuffed shark. The taxidermy hadn't been particularly successful and the creature had fallen apart when it was moved into the museum, stuffing oozing from the seams round the fins. Eventually we admitted defeat and put it out with the bins. I ran the duster lightly over the other objects.

They were all up at the hotel, discussing their ideas to fight the planning decision over beer and chips. I hadn't wanted to be among them. My own reservations were quite different from theirs.

I heard the door creak and turned. Mike Dormer stood there.

'I haven't been in here before,' he said. His hands were shoved in his pockets, his normally straight-backed posture stooped and apologetic.

'Nope,' I agreed. 'You haven't.'

He walked around slowly. 'I recognise this,' he said, stopping in front of the newspaper cutting.

'Yes, well . . . One thing we do know about you, Mike, is that you certainly do your research.'

It came out harder than I'd intended, but I was tired and I still felt unbalanced because I'd had him under my roof for so long yet failed to get the measure of him.

'I'm sorry,' he said. 'I deserved that.'

I sniffed and began to dust the souvenirs on the trestle table. All of a sudden they seemed tacky: whale key rings, dolphins suspended in plastic balls, tea towels featuring grinning sea creatures.

'Look, Kathleen, I know you might not want to talk to me right now but I do have to say something to you. It's important to me that you understand.'

'Oh, I understand, all right.'

'No, you don't,' he said. 'Really. I came out here expecting it to be a straightforward development job. I thought I was building in an area that no one would be fussed about. Once I realised that wasn't the case, I began trying to work out a solution that would keep my boss happy in England and you lot happy out here.'

'You could have shared that with us. We might have been able to contribute something.'

'I know that now. But once I got to know you all it was impossible.'

'Especially Liza,' I said. Call it a wild guess.

'Yes,' he said. 'Yes, and Liza.'

We were silent for a few minutes, as I worked with my back to him.

'Anyway,' he said, coughing, 'I've been ringing around. There's a place up the coast that will have me—us. We'll go this afternoon. I just wanted to say how sorry I was, and that if there's anything I can do to—well, to mitigate the effects of this development, you should let me know.'

I turned to him. 'How do you mitigate killing off a seventy-year-old family business, Mike?' I asked. 'You know I'm not that fussed about the bay. I'm hoping that the busybodies who look out for the whales and dolphins now will see they're OK. But when you destroy this place, you destroy Hannah's safety. This is the one place she can be safe in all the world. I can't explain more than that, but you should know it. Your actions will have an impact on our little girl. And for that I can't forgive you.'

'But—but why would you have to leave here?'

'How can we afford to live in a hotel with no customers?'

'Who says you'll have no customers? Your hotel is completely different from what's planned. There'll always be customers for a place like yours.'

'When there are a hundred and fifty rooms with en-suites and satellite television next door? And winter three-for-two offers and a heated pool indoors? I don't think so. The one thing we had going for us here was isolation. The kind of people who came here wanted to be able to hear the sea at night and the whisper of the grass on the dunes and nothing else. They didn't want to hear karaoke night in the Humpback Lounge, and the sound of forty-eight cars reversing in and out of the car park. Come on, Mike, you deal in hard figures. You tell me how an operation like this stays afloat.'

He made as if to speak, then mutely shook his head.

I was close to tears and this made me so furious that I had to turn away and start dusting again, so he couldn't see my face. I couldn't help it. Every time I thought about Liza and Hannah having to settle somewhere far from here, having to start over, I got short of breath.

I had half expected him to leave, but when I turned he was still there.

'I'll get it changed,' he said. 'I'm not sure how, Kathleen, but I'll put it right. I promise you, Kathleen. I'll put it right.'

THE FOLLOWING DAY I dropped Hannah at school, then took the inland road to see Nino Gaines. He was one of the few people with whom I could have an honest discussion about money.

'So, how much have you got?' We were sitting in his office. Through the window I could see rows of vines, bare now, under an unusually grey sky. Behind him there were books on wine and a framed poster of the first supermarket promotion that had included his shiraz.

I scribbled some figures on the pad in front of me and shoved it towards him. 'That's the pre-tax profits. And that's the rough turnover. We get by. But if I had to put on a new roof, or anything like it, I'd have to sell the boat.'

'That tight, eh?'

As I explained to him, it was fifty years since the hotel's heyday. And ten years since the Silver Bay had had anything like a constant stream of guests. Taxes, building repairs and the cost of looking after two extra people had put paid to what little I had set aside.

'Do you want me to invest in the hotel so you could do a bit of renovation? Smarten up the rooms? Put in some satellite TV? I'd be glad to sink a few quid into something new.'

'What's the point, Nino? Once that monster goes up by the jetty, we'll be little better than a shed at the end of their garden.'

'Could you survive on the whale-watching money? Surely Liza will be taking out more trips with more people around. Perhaps you could invest in another boat. Get someone to run it for you.'

'But that's just it. Liza won't stay if there are more people. She—she gets nervous. She needs to be somewhere quiet.'

We sat quietly, as Nino digested this. Then he leaned forward over the desk. 'OK, Kate. You know I've never stuck my nose in, but I'm going to ask you now.' His voice dropped. 'What the hell is Liza running from?'

It was then that the tears came and I realised, in horror, that I couldn't stop them. I wanted so badly to protect my girls, but Mike Dormer and his plans had brought home to me how vulnerable they were.

When I had composed myself a little I looked at him.

His smile was sympathetic, his eyes concerned. 'Can't tell me, huh?'

'You mustn't think badly of Liza,' I mumbled, through my fingers. A soft, worn handkerchief was thrust into them, and I mopped inelegantly at my eyes. 'No one has suffered more than she has.'

'Don't you go fretting. I know what I've seen of your girls, and I know there isn't a malicious hair on either of their heads. I won't ask again, Kate.'

I reached out then, and took his strong old hand. He held mine tightly, his huge knuckles atop mine, and I took great comfort from it. I realised I didn't want to go home. I didn't have the strength to reassure Liza. I didn't want to be nice to Mike Dormer and his fashion-plate girlfriend. I just wanted to sit in this room and have someone look after me.

'You could come here.' His voice was gentle. 'You and the girls. Plenty of room. Close enough for Hannah to stay at her school. Look at this big old house. These rooms would love to see youngsters again.'

I said nothing. My head was swimming.

He was gazing at me intently. 'It would make us both happy, I know. And

I'd help to protect the girls from whatever it is you're so worried about. Hell, I'm in the middle of bloody nowhere, you know that. Even the ruddy mailman can't find us half the time.'

I laughed, despite myself.

Then his hold on my hand became tighter. 'I know you love me, Kathleen.' When I said nothing, he continued, 'I still remember that night. Every minute of it. And I know what it meant.'

My head jerked up. 'Don't talk about that night,' I snapped.

'Is that why you won't marry me? Is it because you feel guilty? Jeez, Kate, it was just one night—one night we agreed wouldn't be repeated. And it wasn't, was it? I was a good husband to Jean, and you know it.'

Oh, I knew it. I'd spent more than half my life thinking about it.

'Jean told me, Kate, with her dying words . . . she as good as told me that we should be together. What the hell is stopping you?'

I had to get up to leave. I couldn't tell him the truth. That what Jean had told him was a message, all right, but it was a message for me. She was telling me, through him, that for all those years afterwards she'd known. And she'd understood that knowing this would fill me with guilt for the rest of my days.

THAT NIGHT I DIDN'T go out to the crews. I let Liza serve them and pleaded a headache. Then I sat in my little office at the back of the kitchen. After a while, I looked up at the photograph of my mother and father, solemn in their wedding clothes, and wondered what they would have thought of my predicament. Nino had told me I could probably sell this place to the hotel people. Maybe get enough to start somewhere new. But my life was in these walls. I realised I needed this house more than I had admitted.

It was almost a quarter past ten when Liza knocked on the door. 'How's your head?' she said, closing the door behind her.

'Fine.' I closed the accounts book.

'Mike Dormer has just walked in and gone straight upstairs. He acted like he's not going anywhere. I thought you should probably have a word.'

'I said he could stay,' I told her quietly.

'You said *what?*'

'You heard.'

'But why? We don't want him anywhere near us.'

'You think I can throw that sort of money away?' I snapped at her. 'We're going to need every last penny, and that means every last guest who wants to stay here is going to get a welcome from me.'

She was shocked. 'But he's going to destroy us.'

'What's done is done, Liza. Whether that hotel goes ahead or not is out of our hands. We need to think about making the most of our income while we still have one. We can't afford principles. Not if we want to keep Hannah in school shoes.'

I knew what she was really saying, what neither of us could bear to say out loud. How could I willingly harbour the man who had broken what remained of her heart? How could I put her through the ache of having to watch him and that girl float around her home, flaunting their relationship?

We glared at each other. Her lips were tight with hurt and indignation. 'You know what, Kathleen? I really don't understand you sometimes.'

'Well, you don't have to understand,' I said curtly, making as if to tidy my desk. 'You just get on with your business and let me run my hotel.'

Mike

The dog-walkers along the coast road had stopped waving to me. But on the second morning when I lifted my hand in greeting and they turned away their faces, I realised that in parts of Silver Bay I was now public enemy number one.

'Oh, you're always going to ruffle a few feathers,' Vanessa said dismissively. 'Remember that school development in east London? The people in the flats opposite were funny about it until they discovered how much it would push up the value of their properties.'

But that had been different, I wanted to say to her. I didn't care what those people thought of me. And, besides, Vanessa wasn't having to confront Liza, who managed to behave as if I were no longer in existence.

On the one occasion I had found her alone in the kitchen I'd said, 'I've told your aunt that I'm going to try to stop it. I'm sorry.'

'Sorry about what, Mike? That you've been living here under false pretences, that you're about to ruin us, or that you're a duplicitous pig?'

'You told me you didn't want a relationship.'

'You didn't tell me you were already in one.' As soon as she said this her expression closed, as if she felt she had given too much away. But I knew what she had felt. I had rerun that moment in the car as if it were on a spool tape inside my head. I could have recited our conversation word for word.

I told Vanessa why I thought the development was no longer right as the plans stood. She didn't believe me, so I took her out on *Moby One* with several tourists and showed her the dolphins. Yoshi and Lance were courteous, but I felt discomfort at the lack of good-humoured conversation.

Vanessa told me I was being oversensitive. 'Why should you care what they think?' she said. 'You'll never have to see any of them again.'

'I care because I want to get this right,' I said. 'And I think we *can* get it right. Ethically and commercially.' I knew it was vital to have Vanessa on side if we were to convince Dennis to alter the plans.

Then, as if in answer to my prayers, Yoshi's voice came over the PA system. 'Ladies and gentlemen,' she said, 'if you look out of your portside windows you can just make out a humpback. We're going to turn off the engines and hope she comes close.'

There was a swell of excited chatter on the top deck. I pointed to where I'd caught sight of a blow, then watched Vanessa's face, praying that the whale would impress her.

As if on cue, the creature breached not forty feet away from us, its huge, prehistoric head turning as it splashed back into the water. Vanessa couldn't help gasping, and her face softened with a childlike joy. For a moment, I saw in her the girl I had loved before I had come here. I squeezed her hand.

'You see what I mean?' I said. 'You see why I don't want to feel responsible for spoiling something here?'

We stood and watched as the whale breached again, farther away this time, then disappeared under the waves, no longer diverted by curiosity, compelled to continue its journey north. The tourists around us hung over the rails, hoping it might re-emerge. I stood, taking in the distant coastline, the series of small, uninhabited islands that stood like sentries to the greater expanse of land. Above us birds swooped and dived: ospreys, gannets, white-breasted sea eagles. Around us the sea rose and fell, glinting on one side, darker and apparently less amenable on the other. I no longer felt alien out here. Despite their insecure lifestyle, I envied the whalechasers.

It was then that Vanessa spoke. 'Mike?'

I turned to her. She was wearing the diamond earrings I had bought her for her thirtieth birthday.

'I know something's gone on,' she said carefully. 'I know I've lost a bit of you. But I'm going to pretend that you and I are still OK, and that this is some kind of weird reaction to the shock that you're getting married.'

My heart skipped a beat. 'Nessa—' but she waved a hand to stop me.

'I don't want you to explain,' she said. 'If you think we can be OK, that you can love me and be faithful to me, I just want us to carry on as we were. I want us to get married, forget this and get on with our lives.'

The engines started up again. I felt the vibrations under my feet and then, as the boat swung round, the wind picked up.

She turned back to the sea. 'OK?' she said, pulling her collar up.

'OK,' I said, and stepped forward to hug her.

IN THE FIVE DAYS that remained before we travelled back to Sydney, Vanessa and I spent most of our time locked in our room, hunched over my laptop, working out how to alter the plans in a way that would satisfy her father and the venture capitalists. It was not an easy task.

'If we can get the Unique Selling Proposition, we can crack it,' she said. I thanked God that she had marketing skills. 'Without the watersports, the whales are the USP. We just have to work out a way of involving them that isn't going to alienate all the whale-watching people. That means not setting up our own operation, which would be my immediate choice. There has to be some other way of making the sea creatures accessible.' She had contacted the National Parks and Wildlife people, but they had said they wouldn't encourage tourists to have greater contact with the animals than they already allowed. 'Perhaps some kind of undersea viewing area at the mouth of the bay.'

'Too expensive. And the shipping people would probably object. We could build a new jetty with a restaurant on top and a viewing area below.'

'But how much are you going to see that close to land?' She sucked the end of her pen. 'I just can't picture the hotel, in the present scheme, without the watersports. There's just nothing else to mark it out from what's available in the luxury market.'

'Tennis?' I said. 'Horse riding?'

'A new site,' she said. 'We've got five days to find a new waterfront site for a one-hundred-and-thirty-million-pound development.'

We looked at each other and started to laugh: saying it out loud made it sound even more ridiculous than it actually was. But Vanessa Beaker wasn't her father's daughter for nothing. Within four hours she had spoken to almost every land agent between Cairns and Melbourne.

'Can you email me some pictures?' Between calls on my own phone, I heard the same request time and time again, then the other questions. 'Are the waters designated a protected area? Do you have sea mammals or other indigenous creatures that are likely to be affected by a development? Would they be interested in selling?'

By the end of the following day we had earmarked two possible sites. One was an hour south of Brisbane. Its plus points included its own protected bay, which had been used without complaint for watersports. But it wasn't as beautiful as Silver Bay. The other, half an hour from Bundaberg, was almost a third again in price.

'Dad's not going to like that,' she said, then smiled brightly at me. 'But everything's doable, right? I mean, look what we've achieved already.'

'You,' I said fondly, pushing her hair back from her face, 'are a star.'

THAT NIGHT we made love for the first time since she had come to Silver Bay. Given our previous physical appetite for each other, I can't explain what had happened until that point—but neither of us had felt our old confidence in the other's response.

We had gone out to eat in the town, and then walked back along the bay holding hands. The wine, the moonlight, and the fact that I might have saved Silver Bay from the fate I had almost inflicted on it conspired to smooth over the resistance I felt when Vanessa and I now held each other.

I had nearly messed it up, I told myself, but not quite. We would save this development, we would save the whales and we would save our relationship. I had been given a second chance.

Afterwards we lay quiet as something heavy and melancholy settled in the dark around us.

'You OK?' I said, reaching across her for her hand.

'Fine,' she said, after a pause. 'Lovely.'

I stared up into the dark, listening to the waves breaking on the sand, thinking about what the core of me knew had been missing. Thinking about what I had lost.

WE LEFT ON the Saturday. I went downstairs early and settled up with Kathleen. 'I'll be in touch,' I said. 'I won't let you down. Things are happening fast. Really.'

She looked at me steadily. 'I hope so,' she said.

'Is Liza around?' I asked, when I realised she wasn't going to volunteer.

'She's out on *Ishmael*,' she said.

'Say goodbye to her for me.' I tried not to sound as awkward as I felt. I was acutely aware of Vanessa, who had come downstairs behind me.

Kathleen said nothing, but shook Vanessa's hand. 'Goodbye,' she said. 'I wish you luck with the wedding.'

There was more than one way you could interpret that, I thought, as I went upstairs for the bags, and none reflected well on me. When I passed the family corridor, I heard music. Hannah was still there. She had barely spoken to me since the development had come to light.

I stood at the door and knocked. Eventually she opened it.

'I thought I'd say goodbye,' I said. 'And give you this.' I held out an envelope. 'Your wages. The pictures were very good.'

She glanced at it. 'My mum says I'm not allowed to accept your money.'

'OK,' I said, trying to look less disconcerted than I felt. 'Well, I'm going to leave it on the hall table, and if you really aren't allowed to take it I hope you'll give it to a charity for the dolphins. I know you love them.'

Hannah stood in the doorway, studying me. 'Why did you lie, Mike?'

I took a step back towards her. 'I don't know,' I said. 'I made a big mistake and I'm trying to put it right.'

I saw suddenly that what I had done had merely reinforced her sense of adult fallibility. I took a breath, and then, almost as if by instinct, I held out a hand. After the longest pause, she shook it.

THE FLIGHT BACK was as much of a pleasure as a twenty-four-hour flight ever is. We swapped unwanted items from our trays of food, and watched several films. At some point I slept, and when I woke, I was dimly aware of Vanessa going through a list of figures next to me. I was thankful again for her willingness to back me.

Heathrow was crowded, chaotic and grey, even at six in the morning and at the height of summer. Everyone feels bad when they get back from abroad, I told myself, as we headed for the baggage carousel.

'I could murder a coffee,' said Vanessa.

'I need to find a loo,' I said. She looked exhausted, even with her carefully refreshed hair and make-up. She never slept well on flights. 'The coffee shops don't start till after Customs. You watch for the bags.'

Spending a week joined at the hip to Vanessa had been hard, and the short walk by myself was quite a relief. But I have done the right thing, I told myself, feeling bad about such disloyal thoughts.

I returned several minutes later. Oddly, Vanessa had not collected our luggage although I could see it travelling its lonely, squeaking path along the conveyor belt. She was looking at her mobile phone.

'Not your dad,' I said wearily. 'Not already.' I was dreading what I knew would be a confrontational meeting.

'No,' she said, her face uncharacteristically pale. 'No, it's *your* phone. It's a text. From Tina.' Then, thrusting the message under my nose, she walked out of the airport, leaving her baggage slowly travelling round the carousel.

THE NEXT TIME I saw her was almost twenty-eight hours later, when I arrived at the office for the crunch meeting with Dennis.

The office felt alien to me, the City so loud and crowded. When I closed my eyes I could see the serene horizon of Silver Bay. When I opened them I saw grey pavements, filthy gutters and buses belching fumes. Beaker Holdings, once so familiar to me, seemed monolithic and forbidding.

And then there was Dennis.

'What's going on, then? Feeling good about your big coup? The VCs are happy boys, I can tell you.' His time immobilised had brought him extra weight, and he was oversized, florid, compared to the lean, wind-whipped figures with whom I had spent the past month. 'Let's organise some coffee. I'll get one of the girls to go out and get us some. None of that instant swill.'

After he left the boardroom, I sat down next to Vanessa. She had failed resolutely to meet my eye, and was wearing what she called her power suit.

'I'm sorry,' I murmured. 'It's not what it seems. Really. Meet me afterwards and I can explain.'

'That little welcome home seemed pretty self-explanatory to me.'

'Nessa, please. At least give me five minutes. After this. Five minutes.'

'OK,' she said eventually.

'Thank you.' I squeezed her arm, then braced myself for the task ahead.

Dennis listened carefully as I outlined my considerations with regard to the ecological impact. 'The upshot,' I said, 'is that I think the existing plan is wrong for all the following reasons.' I handed over the photocopied pages: the list of alternative sites and the breakdown of incurred costs that altering our proposal would take. 'I think, having done the research, that these are by far the better options in terms of our new, added USP, which is that of responsible, community-friendly development.' I gestured towards the table. 'Vanessa has been out with me. She's seen these creatures in the flesh, and the strength of feeling about them. She's in agreement that the best way forward is either one of the two alternative options. I know there will be penalties, I know we'll have to sell the existing site, but I believe that I could swing Vallance Equity round to the same way of thinking.'

'Bloody hell,' said Dennis, studying the figures. 'That's some change you're proposing. It's going to cost twenty per cent of the total budget.'

He had not, I noted hopefully, dismissed it all out of hand. 'But if you look at column three, you'll see there is very little in the final figures.'

Dennis turned to Vanessa. 'Ditch the whole thing, eh? You really think we should move the whole development to a different site?'

She looked at him, and then she turned slowly to me. Her eyes were cold. 'No,' she said. 'I think we should go ahead with what we've got.'

Liza

I saw a whale today, one of the last of the season. She came right up to the boat with her calf and then sat there starboard side, close enough for me to see the pattern on her tail fluke, close enough to see her calf, half protected under her belly. The customers were thrilled—they squealed, took pictures and said it was an experience that had changed their lives. But I couldn't smile. I wanted to shout at the whale to take her baby far from here. I kept remembering that other calf, washed up on the shore, covered with tarpaulin. I didn't want the mother to trust us like she did.

I'd really thought that, after everything I'd been through, I would spot someone like Mike a mile off. And the knowledge that I'd failed to do so gnawed away at me. For several days during that first week, while he and his girlfriend remained in the hotel, it had been an effort to get myself out of bed. Then he had gone. And somehow that didn't make it any better.

Hannah had told me, a little defiantly, that Mike had paid her for her photographs, and before I could say a word she had announced that she was donating the money to the National Parks. She had spoken to them, she said, and there was enough to buy another dolphin stretcher and some over.

She seemed low. She had stopped asking about the New Zealand trip and now spent a lot of time in her room. When I asked if anything was the matter, she told me, very politely, that she was fine, in a way that let me know my presence wasn't wanted.

The demolition of the Bullen place went ahead. Overnight, wire fencing went up round it, contractors came and clawed it to pieces. Less than seventy-two hours later there was nothing left but earth where the old house and sheds had been. To add to the despondent mood, the skies were unusually grey and soulless, and guest numbers had fallen.

Kathleen seemed oddly reconciled to our fate. I didn't understand why she was so willing to let Mike off the hook, and she didn't enlighten me. Night after night I lay awake listening to the sea and wondering how long I would still be able to hear that sound before Hannah and I were forced to pack our bags and move on.

Eventually, the council officers announced that there would be a planning inquiry. I couldn't see that this inquiry would pay any more than lip service to our views. And, besides, it had become an issue that divided the town: there were those who accused us whalechasers of dramatising the whales' plight; a greater number who didn't seem to care much one way or the other; and some who pointed out that what we did was an intrusion in itself. It was hard to refute that, especially when we were faced with the fact that other boats, with less rigorous codes of behaviour, increasingly treated our waters as their own. The café owners and boutique managers had an interest in a bigger, busier town and, while it sounds unlikely, I had some sympathy for them. We all had to earn a living.

Then there were the whalechasers, the fishermen, and those who simply enjoyed the presence of the dolphins and the whales, and others who didn't want to see our quiet bay become loud and lively. But it felt as if we were the quieter of the voices. It felt as if we were unlikely to be heard.

LET ME TELL YOU something about humpbacks. The first time I saw one I was a child of eight. I was on holiday, out fishing with my aunt Kathleen and my mother. Kathleen had been carefully explaining the different flies in her little fabric roll and attaching them to her line when, not ten feet from us, making no sound except the gentle breaking of the waters, a huge black and white head surfaced. My heart was thumping so hard that I thought the terrifying creature would hear it.

'Aunt Kathleen,' I whispered. My mother was asleep, her mouth slightly open. I remember wondering, fleetingly, whether it was preferable to be asleep when you were killed so you wouldn't know what had happened. 'Wh-what's that?' I honestly thought we were about to be eaten. I could see what I thought were its teeth and its huge, assessing eye. This creature appeared to be weighing us up, as if we were some tempting seaborne morsel.

But my aunt just glanced behind her, then turned back to her bait. 'That, sweetie, is a humpback. It's just being nosy. It'll go soon enough.' And, minutes later, the head slid back beneath the waves and the whale was gone.

And this is what I love about them: despite their fearsome appearance, they are benign creatures. They come to look, and then they go. If they don't like you, their signals are pretty clear, and if they think the dolphins are getting a little too much attention from our passengers, they will occasionally come partway into the bay and jealously divert them.

Kathleen once told me she suspected I felt such a bond with the whales because they are solitary creatures. There is no lasting male-female bond. The male plays no parenting role to speak of, but the females are admirable mothers. I have seen a humpback risk beaching itself to nudge her baby into deeper water. I have heard their songs of love and loss breaking into the silence of the deepest parts of the ocean, and I have cried with them.

After Letty died, I thought I would never be happy again. There is nothing redemptive, no lessons of value that the loss of a child can teach you. Every time you think you might have moved forward an inch, the bleak, overwhelming pain swells back, like a tidal wave, to drown you again.

If you blame yourself for that child's death, the days when you get your head above water are even fewer. In the weeks after we got here I was so lost that I had nothing to give Hannah. There was no relief from Letty's absence, not from the moment I woke or during my nightmare-filled sleep. I saw the sea as my one opportunity for release.

Kathleen is no fool. She must have guessed my intentions when I expressed interest in that boat. My depression insulated me from the idea that I might be transparent. One afternoon, when the two of us dropped anchor round the heads, she secured *Ishmael*, turned away and said, 'Go on, then. Jump. That's what you're planning, isn't it?'

I had thought I was numb to feeling, but it was as if she had kicked me in the stomach. She turned back and fixed me with a gimlet stare. 'I don't want to have to lie to your daughter about what happened to her mother. If that little girl discovers you didn't love her enough to stay here for her, it will finish her off. So, if you're going to do it, do it now while I turn my back.'

I let out a coughing sound then. I couldn't speak. I found myself shaking my head, as if I was telling her, telling myself, even, that I wasn't going to do what she had predicted. That somehow I was making a decision to live.

It was then that we saw them. Seven whales, their bodies slick with seawater as they rose and fell around Kathleen's boat. There was a kind of graceful rhythm to their movements, a flowing continuity that told us of their journey. Each emerged briefly, then vanished below the waves.

As a spectacle, then, it diverted me from the most despairing thoughts I have ever had. But later, when we returned to Whale Jetty and I took my poor living, grieving child in my arms, I saw that there had been a message in what I had seen. It was to do with life, death and cycles, perhaps the knowledge that everything will pass. One day I will be reunited with my Letty again, although I no longer expect to choose when that will be.

Since that day, I had never had a problem with finding the humpbacks. I just seemed to know where they were. I followed my nose, and nine times out of ten they would show for me.

But towards the end of winter something odd happened. At first it was the slapping. When a whale is sending a warning, either to humans or other whales, it engages in 'the peduncle slap', thrashing the water with the flukes of its tail, sending out a noise that reverberates for miles. Suddenly I seemed to see it in all of the few that surfaced. Then, at least two weeks earlier than they should have done, the whales disappeared. Soon, both the *Moby*s had switched to dolphin trips around the bay.

Then some of the dolphins seemed to disappear too. Before long, mine was the only boat still going out every day, more in hope than expectation. I couldn't believe so many sea creatures would just leave us, that they would change the behaviour of centuries at whim.

ON A FINE spring day John John rang to say Mr Gaines had suffered a heart attack. My aunt Kathleen was a tough woman. They didn't call her Shark Lady for nothing. It was the first time I had ever seen her cry.

Mike

Monica's guest bedroom was not remotely geared up for guests, and was a bedroom only in that it contained a camp bed. 'I'll clear you a space,' she had promised, when I had tentatively mentioned moving in. But in Monica's world that didn't mean clearing some fourteen boxes, but just shifting a bin bag or two so that there was room for the camp bed to open out on the floor.

There I lay, night after night, surrounded by the detritus of my sister's life, with the springs digging through the thin foam mattress into my back, as, like some penitent, I considered the mess I had made.

I had an ex-fiancée whose hatred of me was exceeded only by her determination to propel the new hotel I didn't want into existence. I had no home, since she had informed me in a typed letter that the very least she expected was that I should allow her to buy out my half.

I had a dead-man-walking role at work, where I was no longer consulted on any of the remaining deals. At the moment Vanessa had contradicted me at the Silver Bay project meeting, my authority had been fatally undermined. Dennis ignored me. Worst of all, I sat in at the meetings with Vallance, read the copied-in documentation and watched the slow but steady progress of the Silver Bay project. I knew that Dennis was only holding me in position because if he lost such a key member of his team at this crucial moment Vallance would look twice.

I also knew that to survive professionally beyond this deal I had to sharpen up. But I was immobilised, paralysed by indecision and guilt.

One thing was clear: Vanessa had released me at the moment she had said she wanted the development to go ahead. Every last atom of love was gone from her eyes and I had been sobered by the depth of her enmity.

'Bloody hell. You can't blame her.' Monica handed me a glass of wine. I had got through quite a lot that month—in fact, I was drunk much of the time. Not that anyone would have guessed. I was a subtle drunk.

'I don't blame her,' I said. 'I know it's all down to me.'

'My brother the serial shagger, eh?'

'I'm not a serial shagger.'

'Snogger.' Monica giggled. 'Serial snogger, then.'

I couldn't help laughing too. It sounded so ridiculous.

'There,' she said, pointing her cigarette at me. She was cross-legged on the rug. 'You can't have loved her that much or you'd be devastated.'

'You have no heart,' I accused. But perhaps my sister was right. I felt bad, admittedly, and guilty, but I was not sure I liked the elements of my character that had revealed themselves to me recently. 'What can I do, Monica? How can I stop it happening?'

'Why does it matter?' she asked.

'Because it just does.' I stared around the tiny, chaotic flat, where the sound of traffic penetrated the walls, and felt homesick.

'Mikey, you'll lose your job if it doesn't go ahead. What the hell went on out there? You went out as Billy Big Shot and came back a bloody mess.'

So I told her everything. It took me two hours and several more glasses of wine, but I told Monica about Kathleen and the hotel, Hannah, Liza and the whalechasers, and as I spoke, their faces came alive to me and I felt as if I were back there with just the sound of the sea in my ears and the salt breeze on my skin. And when I got to the part where I had watched the thin, blonde figure recede into my rearview mirror, I understood. 'I'm in love,' I said. I sat back, dazed, against the sofa. 'God. I'm in love.'

'Hallelujah!' said my sister, stubbing out her cigarette. 'Can I go to bed now? I've been waiting for you to work that out since you got here.'

WHEN DENNIS BEAKER yawned, I knew it was a tactic he used to effect when someone was attempting to say something he didn't want to hear.

He leaned back now, in his leather chair, and yawned so widely that I could count the fillings in his upper jaw. 'Sorry, Mike. What did you say?'

I stood in front of him, and said evenly, 'I'm giving notice.'

Dennis's yawn stopped abruptly. He looked at me from under lowered brows, then leaned forward. 'Don't be ridiculous, Mikey boy,' he said.

'I'm hoping you'll let me go immediately. I'm happy to forgo my salary.'

He looked irritated, as if I were trying something on. 'Is this about money? You'll get a salary review in January.'

'It's not money.'

He let his gaze travel around the room as if he were considering something. Finally, it settled on me. 'Oh, sit down, for God's sake.'

I sat, fighting the urge to pull off my tie and loosen my collar. Dennis studied his hands. Waiting, thinking.

'Look, Dennis, I'm sorry about Vanessa,' I said, at last, into the silence. 'I never wanted to hurt her.'

His demeanour changed then, his expression softening briefly. 'She'll get over it,' he said. 'She'll find someone better. I should be madder at you, given that she's my daughter, but I'm well aware that Tina's a minx.' He let out a huge sigh and chucked his pen across the desk at me. 'Bloody hell, Mike. How has it come to this?'

I caught the pen and placed it back on the desk. 'I can't be part of this development, Dennis. I told you. We'll be . . . ruining people's lives.'

'It's a ruddy hotel, Mike, not a nuclear-waste plant.'

'Might as well be, for the effect it's going to have.'

I could tell he couldn't quite believe what he was hearing. He shook his head. 'You know we're too far down the road to back up now.'

'We're not. We'd earmarked two other viable sites.'

'They're more expensive.'

'Not if we offset the costs of the S94. I've been through it.'

'Well, it's going ahead, whether you like it or not.' He was apologetic, not bullish, and I saw now that this was about Vanessa. He could forgive me, but to undermine his daughter publicly was asking too much. 'I'm sorry, Mike.'

I shook my head regretfully. 'Then I have to quit.' I rose from my chair and held out my hand. 'I'm really sorry, Dennis.'

When he didn't shake my hand, I walked towards the door.

His voice, lifted in exasperation, followed me: 'This is effing ridiculous. You can't ruin a bloody good career for a few fish.'

I hesitated by the door. 'I'm sorry,' I said.

As I opened it, he spoke again. 'Go if you have to, but you're not going to fight me on this, Mike. You'll never get a job anywhere decent again.' He nodded, to make sure I'd got the message. 'You know what I can do.'

'I know.' More than most, I knew.

We stared at each other.

'Oh, *bollocks*.' Dennis stepped forward and enveloped me in a bear hug.

I MET MONICA in a bar a short walk from her newspaper's offices. She had nipped out for a drink, but said she'd be returning to her desk until late that evening, trying to follow up a story about farming fraud and EU subsidies. 'I hate stories that involve finance,' she muttered. 'You spend weeks trying to understand the figures, and when you run it nobody cares because there's no human interest in it.'

'Want me to help?' I said. 'I can find my way across a spreadsheet.'

She seemed a little taken aback. 'I might.' Her face lit up with a brief smile. 'If I get stuck I'll bring some home, and you can take a look.'

I had to admit that one of the unexpected benefits of my collapsed personal life was that my sister and I had discovered, to our mutual surprise, that we liked each other. Now I understood that insecurity lay beneath the sarcasm, and that at least some of her ambition stemmed from having an older brother who appeared to have scaled the career ladder effortlessly.

'Did you bring the pictures?'

I reached into my pocket and handed over the little paper folder. She began to flick through them. 'I've been thinking about this, and the best hope you have is in publicity. You reckon Vallance are nervous of bad publicity so what you have to do is get one spokesman to oppose the scheme, and then work on two levels, local and national.'

'Meaning what?'

'On the local level, leaflets, posters, newspapers. Try to create a ground-swell of opposition. On the national level, you need well-placed features that might get you some telly coverage. Maybe use some new research. Isn't there a whale-conservation society who can help you?'

I began to scribble some of this down. 'Whale-conservation society,' I murmured. 'Dolphins too?'

Monica held up one of the pictures of Liza that Hannah had taken. She was tilting her head, smiling directly at the camera, the way she often smiled at her daughter—brimful of warmth and love.

'That her?'

I nodded, temporarily silenced.

'She's pretty. Make her the figurehead of the campaign. I could probably get her a feature or two. Put her and the old lady together and you've got a better chance. Did you say there were old newspaper reports about the aunt?'

'I think I can get them off the Internet.'

'If she hasn't been written about for years it might make a piece. First you need a press release, something to send out to all the news organisa-tions with your contact details. And then, bruv, you need to get tough.'

'Me? I was asking how *they* could do it.'

'You're not helping?'

'Well, I'll do what I can from here.'

My sister's face was suffused with disappointment.

The barman asked if either of us wanted a refill, and for a minute she appeared not to have heard him. Then she glanced at her watch and declined. 'And he doesn't want one either,' she added, nodding at me.

'I don't?'

'You said you loved her,' she said accusingly, when he had gone.

'Doesn't mean she loves me,' I said, taking the last swig of my drink. 'In fact, I have it on fairly good authority that she hates my guts.'

My sister raised her eyebrows, sat back on the bar stool and folded her arms. 'Mikey, what the hell are you sitting here for?'

'Because I'm a stupid bloke who can't make a decision to save his life?'

My sister shook her head. 'Oh, no,' she said, and grinned. 'You made a decision. You're just too stupid to realise it.'

I BOOKED THE FIRST available seat on a flight to Sydney, packed a suitcase of essentials, and my sister drove me to the airport.

'This is a good thing,' she said, straightening my jacket, almost fondly, as we stood outside at the drop-off point. 'Really. A good thing.'

'She won't talk to me,' I said.

'Then for once in your life, Mikey, you're going to have to work at it.'

During that flight I kept trying to think of what I would say when I saw her, but every conversation opener was inadequate. In fact, my presence would be inadequate. I had not done what I had promised Kathleen I would do, which was to stop the development. Despite my feelings for Liza, I was still the duplicitous pig she had identified: if Tina had not sent that incriminating text, would I have split with Vanessa?

Sitting on that flight, headed east, I discovered before the end of the first in-flight movie that I had no idea what I was doing. Few people in the town would welcome me. I was not even sure where I would stay.

Some thirty hours later, I got out of the rental car that had driven me to Silver Bay, stood up in the bright sunlight, and fought an almost overwhelming urge to climb back into the car and drive back to the airport.

I KNOCKED three times on the back door before I caught sight of the note: *Lance/Yoshi: Help yourselves, we are at the hospital. Back soon. Please write down what you take in the book. L.*

I held it for a minute, then looked down to the jetty. There were no boats except *Ishmael*, and as it was only a quarter past ten in the morning, it was possible that Liza and Kathleen would be gone for some hours. I walked to MacIver's Seafood Bar and Grill and ordered a coffee.

'Hey, are you that guy from the development company?' The owner, a large man in a grubby apron, was staring at me.

'Yes,' I said. 'I've just come in for a quiet coffee. If you want to pick a fight about the plans, I'll leave, if you don't mind.'

'You won't get a fight from me, mate,' he said. 'I'm looking forward to it. Glad of the extra business. Not everyone's against it, you know, no matter what the papers are saying. Strewth, I reckon the whale guys make a big deal about these old whales. Those big fish have been swimming past this bay for a million years and a few little jet-bikes ain't going to make any difference to that. Oh, sure, they might quiet off for a while, but they'll be back.'

'Quiet off?'

He jerked a thumb towards the jetty. 'Oh, they're all moaning, saying they've already gone. Like the fish know what's coming. I ask you!'

'Who's gone?' I was having trouble keeping up with the conversation.

'The whales. There's none showing. Now the boats are just going round the bay to let folks see the dolphins. I don't reckon it makes a big difference to their profits. They can do two dolphin trips in the time it takes to do one whale trip. I don't know what they're complaining about.'

I sat there for a while, digesting this. Then I turned to him. 'You wouldn't serve me a drink, would you?' I had a feeling that the next conversation I had would require of me rather more Dutch courage.

IT TOOK ME almost an hour to make it back up the coast road to the Silver Bay Hotel. Normally it would have taken twenty to walk. But the jet lag had combined unhappily with the several large Scotches that Del had pressed on me, and it was difficult to maintain a straight line. A few times I sat down on my case and thought hard about how best to continue my journey. The hotel was there, within spitting distance, but somehow kept moving away from me, like a mirage in the desert. I kept a tight hold of my wallet, holding it out in front of me so that I could keep an eye on it at all times. My parents had always impressed upon me the need to hang on to your wallet when in a strange country.

When I made it to the hotel I felt an almost euphoric sense of achievement, tempered only by the fact that I could no longer remember why it had been so important to get there. Then, suddenly immeasurably weary, I decided I needed a lie-down. The wooden benches were too narrow and the sand, at this end of the beach, was pebbly. I could just make out the Whalechasers Museum a short distance away and stumbled towards it. I would grab forty winks in there, and when I woke I would remember what the hell I was meant to be doing here.

I WOKE TO THE SOUND of shouting. At first it had been part of my dream—I was on an aeroplane, and the stewardess was trying to wake everybody up. Gradually, I became aware that even as the stewardess evaporated, the shouting was louder and her grip on my arm was uncomfortably tight.

'Let go,' I murmured. 'I don't want any peanuts.'

But then as my eyes opened I realised I knew the face. Standing above me, her yellow oilskin flapping like the wings of some great bird, was Liza McCullen. And she was shouting at me: 'I don't believe it! Like, this is all we need—Mike bloody Dormer turning up here drunk.'

I closed my eyes again, feeling a strange calm descend on me. And, just before I did, I could have sworn I saw Kathleen smiling behind her.

Kathleen

He told me I should 'step up'. He told me he had discussed it with his sister, who knew about such things, and that I could be the main focus of a feature on 'The Shark Lady Trying to Save the Whales'. I told him I didn't want to stir all that up again and that I certainly didn't want to feature in any newspapers.

He looked at me like I was insane. 'It would bring a lot of helpful publicity,' he said. 'Kathleen, I told you I would fix this, and I'm doing my best.'

Mike had had three days to recover. He had come back to save us, he had announced, when we stumbled across him in the Whalechasers Museum. It's hard to take a man seriously, I'd told him afterwards, when he's lying drunk on the floor. He appeared to have taken this to heart.

'Mike, I'm touched you saw fit to come back to help us. But I've told you, I don't want to dredge up all that Shark Lady business again.'

'Liza, then,' he said. She had been doing her best to ignore him.

'Liza what?' she said, not looking up from the paper.

'You'd make a great figurehead for the campaign. There aren't many female skippers. You know a lot about whales. You're'—here he had the grace to cough and flush—'you're a good-looking woman and—'

'No,' she said abruptly. 'I don't want Hannah exposed to . . . all that.'

'I don't mind,' said Hannah. 'I'd like to be in the paper.'

'It's the only way to stop the development,' Mike said. 'You have to galvanise as much support as you can. Once people know what's—'

'No.'

He stared at her. 'I thought you'd do anything for the whales?'

'Don't you dare tell me what I should be doing for the whales.' Liza folded up her newspaper and slammed it down on the kitchen table. 'If it hadn't been for you we wouldn't be in this bloody mess.'

'You really believe that?' he interrupted. 'You really think this area would have been untouched for ever?'

'No—but we would have had more time . . .' Her voice trailed away.

'What do you mean, "more time"?'

The kitchen went quiet. Hannah glanced up, then down at her homework. Liza looked at me and shook her head, a delicate, discreet movement. Mike caught it and I saw it register on his face as disappointment.

'Look,' he said, finally. 'You two are the best chance we've got to stop this development, but you have to cut me a little slack.'

'No,' said Liza. 'You might as well get this straight, Mike. Neither Hannah nor I will appear in any publicity.'

With that, she got up and left the kitchen. Hannah followed her mother.

'Right,' Mike said. 'On with Plan B, then.' He gave me a lopsided grin and flipped a new sheet of paper. 'I just have to work out what Plan B is.'

I DISCOVERED pretty quickly that Mike had given up everything to come back to Silver Bay. He admitted he no longer had a job, or a girlfriend, or apparently even an address. 'I can pay, though,' he said, when he asked for his old room back. 'I don't need to worry about money.'

He seemed oddly changed by his time away. The slickness had disappeared and a new uncertainty had crept in. He also drank more, so I took pains to remark on it, which brought him up short. 'Is it that bad?' he asked.

'Perfectly understandable,' I said, 'as a short-term measure.'

He got the picture. I found the new Mike Dormer rather more endearing. It was one of the reasons I had allowed him to stay.

Perhaps because she was so distracted by the plight of the whales and—although she would not admit it—Mike's return, I persuaded Liza to agree to Hannah having sailing lessons. I took her to the first, with her friend, Lara, at Salamander Bay, and when I saw her out on the water I realised, with a start, that it couldn't have been the first time she had negotiated her way alone in a dinghy. She confessed afterwards, with a grin, that I was right, and we agreed that it was probably best not to tell her mother.

'Do you think she'll let me take out *Hannah's Glory*?' she said, as we drove home. 'When the teachers say I'm good enough?'

'I don't know, sweetie. I think we should just take it one step at a time.'

I slowed down to say g'day to old Mr Henderson, returning on his bicycle from the fish market. When I turned back to Hannah she was staring out of the window. 'Can you change the name of a boat?' she said.

'It can be done. Why?'

'I'm going to call mine *Darling Letty*.'

I braked hard and pulled the car over, raising a hand in apology to the van that had had to brake suddenly behind me.

For a moment neither of us spoke, and then Hannah's eyes widened. 'Can't I even say her name?' she cried.

I turned in my seat and stroked her cheek. 'Sweetie, you can say whatever you like. I'm sorry. You just gave me a start.'

'She's my sister,' she said, her eyes filling with tears. 'She was *my sister*. And I want to be allowed to talk about her sometimes. I thought if my boat had her name I could say it whenever I wanted.'

I stared at my great-niece and wished there was something, anything, I could say that would alleviate what I now knew she had been hiding.

When we got home, I pulled out the drawer where I kept the picture of Liza with her two little girls. The edges are a little uneven, where I'd cut that man out. Liza thought the only way to protect them all was to bury Letty, I knew. It was the only way she could continue to live.

But they couldn't bury Letty then, and they couldn't bury her now. And trying to pretend otherwise was no kind of living at all.

EVERY AFTERNOON I visited Nino Gaines. I brushed his hair, brought him freshly laundered pyjamas and even gave him a shave—not out of sentiment, you understand, but because there wasn't anyone else to do it.

I had to come. I reckoned he hated it in there by himself, his strong old body hooked up to bleeping monitors and tubes that fed him God only knows what. Nino was built for the outdoors. I tried not to see him as he was now: somehow diminished.

His family were happy for me to stay. They brought photographs, in case he opened his eyes, and music, in case he could hear. The doctors said that his brain was working fine. I talked to him about the planning inquiry, and about Mike and the hours he spent on the telephone, doing what he could to stop the development. I told him about my sneaking affection for the young man, despite what he had brought to bear on us.

And I told him about my niece, who seemed so rattled by Mike Dormer's reappearance that she didn't know what to do with herself. She ignored Mike at every meal, but scolded her daughter if she did the same. She swore she had no feelings for him, and when I told her she couldn't see what was in front of her face she had the temerity to use the words 'pot and kettle' at me.

But Nino Gaines said nothing, did nothing, just let me pour my troubles into him as if he hadn't a care in the world.

IT RAINED all afternoon, and by nightfall it had turned into a storm. It was what my father would have called an old-fashioned storm—no-nonsense, biblical weather with thunderclaps that made your teeth rattle and sparked lightning strikes out at sea. When I got back from the hospital I closed the shutters, built up the log fire and Liza, Hannah and I sat in front of the television, Hannah glued to some programme she liked, Liza and I locked in our own thoughts. At around a quarter past six, I heard noise in the hall, and stepped out to find Yoshi, Lance and Greg shedding their oilskins, bringing with them the cold damp air, their skin shining with rain.

'You all right if we stop with you for a bit, Kathleen? Thought we'd have a drink before we set off home.' Lance apologised for the puddle his feet had left on the floor.

'You've been out all this time in this weather? Are you mad?'

'Someone didn't check the weather reports,' said Yoshi, glancing at Lance. 'We thought we'd head round the coast towards Kagoorie Island, in case there were any whales round there, and it came on awful sudden.'

'It's OK, we didn't have any passengers,' said Greg.

'You'd better come in and sit down,' I said. I was pleased to have them there. The hotel had been empty lately and their presence was reassuring.

'Did you find any?' Liza put down her newspaper.

'Not a sign.' Yoshi fumbled in her pocket and brought out a comb. 'No dolphins today, either. If they go we're all in trouble.'

Greg had sat down next to Liza. Then his eyes narrowed. 'What the hell is he doing here?' he said sharply.

Mike stood in the doorway, holding a sheaf of papers, a little taken aback to find so many people in the lounge.

'Paying his way, Greg, just like anyone else.' I hadn't told Greg about Mike's return. I'd figured that it was none of his business.

Mike walked over to me. 'The phone lines appear to have gone down,' he said quietly. 'I can't get an Internet connection.'

'They often do in heavy rain,' I said. 'Sit tight, and they'll be back later.'

'Are you trying to ruin some more businesses?' Greg snarled.

'Leave it, Greg,' Liza snapped.

'Why are you defending him? How can you even have him sit here, given what he's done?' Greg glared at Mike.

'I'm not defending him.'

'I'm trying to clear up the mess,' said Mike. 'OK? I'm no longer attached to Beaker Holdings. I want to get the development stopped.'

Greg looked at me. 'How do you know he's not a plant? His company must know there's opposition brewing. What's to stop them sending him here to suss out what's going on?'

Mike took a step towards him. 'Are you calling me a liar?'

I held my breath, feeling the atmosphere start to spin.

'Yes, I'm calling you a liar. And howsabout cheating, stinking—'

It was Greg who threw the first punch, his left fist slicing through the air to catch Mike a glancing blow to the side of his head. He stumbled and Greg swung his fist again, but Lance stepped between them. Mike squared up immediately, fists raised. 'Back off!' Lance shouted, pushing Mike backwards, inadvertently knocking over a side table.

My heart was thumping so hard I felt almost dizzy.

Mike lunged forward. 'You bastard—'

'Stop it! You're pathetic, the pair of you.' Liza, on her feet between them, threw up her hands. 'Get out! You hear me?' She was pushing at Greg, trying to eject him from the living room.

'What the hell did *I* do?' he yelled, as she and Lance manoeuvred him towards the kitchen.

'I don't have to take this crap from you!' Mike shouted.

It was only when they were in separate rooms that my breathing slowed.

'Jesus Christ,' said Lance, stepping back into the room. Mike began mopping at his cheekbone with a handkerchief. I could hear the sound of my niece and Greg engaged in a shouting match in the kitchen.

It was then I noticed Hannah. She was huddled in a corner of the settee, clutching Milly. 'Sweetie,' I said, trying to make my own voice steady, 'it's OK. It's just the storm making everyone cranky.'

'They're not going to fight again, are they?' Her brown eyes were wide with fear. 'Please don't let them fight.'

Mike knelt down beside her, horrified by the effect on her of what had happened. 'Hannah, it's OK,' he said. 'It's nothing to be frightened of. I'm sorry. I just lost my temper for a moment, but it was nothing serious.'

She didn't look convinced, and recoiled from him. 'I'm not stupid,' she whispered, her face both furious and fearful.

We all looked at each other.

'Look,' he said, 'I'll show you.' As I held her to me, he stood up and went towards the kitchen. 'Greg?' he called. He disappeared. A second later they both appeared in the doorway, followed by Liza. 'Look,' Mike said, holding out a hand—I could tell that that gesture half killed him, 'we're mates.'

'Yeah,' said Greg, as he took the hand and shook it, 'nothing to be frightened of. Sorry, love.'

She looked at her mother, and Liza's smile seemed to reassure her.

'I'll be headed off now, said Greg. 'And, Liza,' he said to her meaningfully, 'you know where I am.'

I could tell she wanted to say something but the telephone started to ring. She strode past him into the hall to answer it.

'Kathleen. Hannah.' Greg was deflated now. 'I'm real sorry . . .'

Suddenly Liza was back in the room, her oilskin already half on. 'That was Tom,' she said. 'He says there's ghost nets drifting into the bay.'

Mike

The room was a blur of activity. I stood in the midst of it, wanting to ask what a ghost net was, but it was as if they were marching to a drumbeat I couldn't hear.

Yoshi already had her jacket on. 'Has someone rung the coastguard?'

Lance had a mobile phone pressed to his ear. 'Signal's down.'

'You stay here, lovey,' said Liza to Hannah.

'No,' said Hannah, her previous fragility forgotten. 'I want to help.'

Liza's face was stern. 'No. You stay here. It's not safe. When the lines are back up, field the calls. Ring the National Parks, the whales and dolphins people, anyone you can think of. Get them to send out as many people as they can, OK? We're going to need as many people as possible.'

Hannah seemed mollified. 'OK.'

Kathleen came back into the room, oilskin on, a large torch under her arm. 'I've put the wetsuits in the car. Has everyone got cutters?'

Greg pulled his woollen hat low over his head. 'I've got a spare pair in my lockup. I'll run down and get them. Lance, give us a lift down.'

I looked at Liza, feeling useless. 'What can I do?' I said. I wanted to talk to her in private, to apologise for my stupidity.

'Stay here,' she said, glancing at Hannah. 'Best that there's someone in the house. And don't let the dog out.'

'OK, let's go,' said Kathleen. 'We'll keep in touch by radio.'

As they trooped out, Hannah explained that ghost nets were vast fishing nets, some many miles long, with floats at the top and weights at the bottom. Labelled 'walls of death', they were now illegal in Australian waters, but as a result many had been dumped overboard or had torn away from their ships and floated along until, weighed down by the sea creatures they had trapped and killed, they sank to the seabed. She bit her lip. 'I hope our dolphins'll be OK.'

'I'm sure your mum and the others will do everything they can to make sure they're fine,' I said. 'Come on—haven't you got some calls to make?'

The lines were back up, the mobile signals restored. I made myself a cup of tea while I listened to Hannah leaving messages on answerphones and occasionally talking to someone. She was astonishingly poised, I thought, for an eleven-year-old.

Outside, the thunder and lightning had moved on, but the rain beat down mercilessly. I put another couple of logs on the fire, watching Milly's eyes flicker from me to the door and back again.

'You get them?' I said, when Hannah came in.

'Most of them,' she said. 'I think the coastguard must be out already. I wish I was helping.' She peered out wistfully through the rain-spattered window. 'There are loads of boats in the bay with their lights on.'

Then I heard a shrill sound from upstairs—my mobile phone. 'Back in a sec,' I said, and leapt upstairs, wondering fleetingly if it was Liza. She might have tried to call the hotel while Hannah was on the telephone.

But the little screen on my phone told a different story. I gazed at the name, then flipped the button. 'Hello? Vanessa?'

'Mike.'

I had no idea what to say.

'I heard you quit,' she said. She sounded as if she might be next door.

I sat down on the leather chair. 'A week ago. I—ah—didn't work any notice.' It already felt another lifetime ago.

'I've been off,' she said. 'I didn't know. Dad didn't tell me. I didn't want to go in with you and—and her still there.'

I took a deep breath. 'I'm so sorry, Ness.'

There was silence. I felt the hurt in it, and was crushed.

'It was stupid and—and you deserved better. But you should know that it was only once and I regretted it more than I can say. Really.'

More silence. I guessed she was digesting this.

'Did Dad make you go? I never meant you to lose your job. I just—'

'It wasn't your dad,' I said. 'It was my decision. I thought it would be . . . best, given . . .' I was distracted by Milly barking. 'In fact, he asked me to stay.'

'I'm glad,' she said. 'It's been worrying me.'

Milly sounded as if she was at the front door. I wondered if I should go down but I knew that if she kept barking I wouldn't hear a word Vanessa said. And it was important to me that we squared this. 'Vanessa, I—'

'What's that noise?'

'The dog,' I said absently.

'You don't have a dog,' she said. 'Where are you?'

'I'm in Australia,' I said.

'Australia?' she said weakly.

'I had to come back,' I said. 'I told you I thought this development was a mistake, Ness, and I'm here to try to put it right. I've got to go—there's things going on here—and I'm sorry, OK? I'm sorry for everything.' I switched off my phone and ran downstairs. Milly was hurling herself at the front door, barking feverishly.

'Hannah?' I said, sticking my head round the kitchen door, hoping she might tell me what was going on.

But she was not in the kitchen or the living room. She was not in her bedroom, or any of the other rooms upstairs. Neither was her jacket.

I stared at the empty peg, then at the dog, who was still barking, glancing round at me as if I should be doing something. My heart sank.

'Oh Christ,' I said, and grabbed an oilskin jacket. Then I fumbled for the lead and attached it to Milly's collar. 'OK, girl,' I said, opening the door. 'Show me where she's gone.'

THE RAIN BORE down in solid unforgiving sheets, sending rivers over my feet as I splashed down the coast path after Milly. It saturated my jeans and shoes within seconds. Only my upper half was dry, protected by the oilskin.

Milly strained at the lead. 'Steady!' I shouted, but the word was carried away on the wind. I ran through the dark and in the bay, as I drew closer, I could see the lights of the boats, maybe a hundred feet apart, bobbing as they struggled against the waves.

'Hannah!' I yelled.

Milly skidded to a halt by the lockups where some of the whalechasers stored their gear. Several doors were open, as if the crews had been in a hurry to get out onto the water, and Milly scrabbled into one.

'Hannah?' I yelled. The rain thrummed dully on the flat roof and fell in ceaseless streams through cracks in the guttering. A low-wattage bulb hung from the middle of the ceiling, and I could just make out the framed licence on the wall. Greg Donohoe. This was Greg's lockup. I remembered a snatched conversation I had once heard about a little boat that was out of bounds. A boat that lived in Greg's lockup.

'Oh no,' I said, and grabbed a torch as Milly, perhaps coming to the same conclusion, bolted for the waterfront.

I ran, my fingers locked round the dog's lead, trying to fight rising panic. As I drew close to the sea, heavy waves crashed onto the beach, clawing and pounding at the shore. Perhaps half a mile out in the bay, boats bobbed and engines whined, trying to maintain position. I could see that even the experienced crews were struggling in that water.

I ran on towards the jetty, the thin beam of the torch scanning the ground in front of me, and found two men pushing a small motorboat towards the sea. 'There's a child, a girl—' I gasped. 'I think she's gone out on the water.'

'What?' One of the men stepped forward, and I recognised him as a dog-walker I'd met before. 'I can't hear you, mate.'

'A girl. I think she might have taken a dinghy out. She's only a kid.'

The two men looked at each other, then at the boat. 'Grab a jacket,' one shouted. I couldn't think where to leave Milly, so I shoved her into the boat and helped them push it out onto the water.

'Hannah McCullen,' I yelled, as the engine roared into life. 'Little girl from the hotel.' The other man gestured to me to point the torch out to sea. As I grabbed the side with my free hand, trying to hang on, he took his own light and hooked it onto the front of the boat.

'See anything?' one of the men yelled. I shook my head. I was shivering now, which made it hard to keep Milly wedged safely between my legs. I tied her lead to the side rail—I had to focus on finding Hannah.

'Got to watch out for the nets,' one shouted. 'If we get the propeller caught up we're really stuck.'

I worked out their plan—to do a sweep of the bay taking in all of the boats we could see, making sure Hannah's was not among them. I sat braced against the side, stomach lurching, as we negotiated the waves, my torch's beam showing nothing but the dark, churning waters beneath us. We drew closer to the other boats and it seemed that half of Silver Bay had turned out in huge cruisers and little motorboats. I caught sight of bodies in wet-suits, others in oilskins handing down shears.

'It's a bugger of a size,' yelled one of the men. I assumed he was talking about the ghost net, but I couldn't see it.

As we headed for the mouth of the bay, I became aware of the ghost nets. We passed between one of the *Moby*s and another cruiser and, with the greater illumination their lights shed, I glimpsed what looked like a tangled web, just visible at the top of the floodlit waves. In it I could see unidentifiable shapes, and struggled to work out what it was I was seeing.

Then Milly barked, great anxious gulps, and I heard screaming.

The dog sprang up, straining at her lead. I swung my torch and shouted to the men, 'Cut the engine!' As it stalled, I could hear Hannah—a terrified shriek. I saw, briefly illuminated by my weak beam, a little boat rocking dangerously, a small figure clinging to its side. The men started the engine and steered towards my pointing arm.

'Hannah!' I shouted, and the motorboat swung towards her. The boat's light was on her then, and I could see her face contorted with fear.

'The nets are caught up in my rudder. I can't move,' she screamed.

'It's OK, sweetheart. We're coming.' I turned as I felt the engine slow beneath me. 'We've got to get closer!' I yelled to the men.

'I can't go any nearer,' one yelled. 'We'll get stuck in the nets ourselves.'

Hannah's scream as a huge swell hit galvanised me. 'I'll get her,' I shouted, kicking off my shoes.

The other man handed me a pair of cutters. 'Just watch you don't get caught in the net yourself,' he shouted. 'I'll try to keep the light on you.'

The force and cold of the sea struck me like a blow. I gasped as a wave crashed over me. I fought my way to the surface and looped the cutters round my wrist, and then, as another wave hit me, began to swim.

She can have been only thirty or forty feet away, but that swim was the most arduous I have ever undertaken. The current pulled me away from her, but I stuck my head down and ploughed towards where I thought she was.

I was about ten feet away when I saw that she was wearing a life jacket, for which I thanked God. 'Hannah!' I yelled. 'You'll have to swim.'

And then, as the beam of the motorboat swung round and the swell lifted the net wrapped round Hannah's rudder, I saw something I shall never forget: caught up in the fine filaments of the tangled net, visible only for the briefest moment, the bodies of fish, seabirds and other creatures. I saw a baby turtle, a huge gull—its feathers half torn away—and worse, near the surface, a live dolphin, its body bound tight in netting. And Hannah, hanging over the edge, had seen it too. As I reached for the side of the boat, she was sobbing, lost to me, paralysed by what she now knew to be beneath her.

'Hannah!' I pleaded. 'You've got to swim. Come on.' I couldn't climb up to her: there was nothing for me to hang on to.

Then, over the rain and my yelling I caught her wail of despair: '*Brolly!* You've got to get her out! You've got to!'

'Hannah, we have to get to the boat!' I shouted.

But she was near-hysterical. 'Cut her free! Please, Mike. Cut her free!'

There wasn't any time to debate. I took a deep breath and, when the light swung round again, I grasped the cutters and ducked under the water.

The most surprising thing was the silence after the noise and wind and rain. The looming shape of the trapped dolphin swayed into view and I lunged for it with the cutters, trying to keep a purchase as the surprising weight of the ghost net pulled it away. I felt the nylon filaments give. The dolphin twisted, perhaps frightened out of its deathly torpor by this new threat. Then, as the light swooped upon us, suddenly I had cut through the last of the net and the dolphin had fled into the murky dark.

I broke the surface, retching in relief. 'Hannah!' I shouted, holding up the cutters. At last, she slipped over the edge of the boat and into my arms.

SHE SAID NOTHING during the trip back to shore. I held her close to me as we bucked and dipped across the waves, and the looks I exchanged with the two men told me everything I needed to know about how lucky we had been.

Liza was already running towards us when we arrived at the jetty. She didn't even see me, so desperate was she to grab her daughter to her.

'I'm sorry, Mum,' Hannah was crying, her frozen, bloodless arms wound tightly round her mother's neck. 'I just wanted to help them.'

'I know you did, darling. I know . . .'

Liza grabbed the blanket that was held towards her, wrapped her daughter in it and rocked her gently on her haunches. 'Oh, Hannah,' she kept saying, and what I heard in her broken voice nearly felled me.

'I'm so sorry, Liza,' I said. I was shaking, despite the blanket someone had placed round my own shoulders. 'I was only upstairs five minutes and—'

She shook her head mutely, and I grasped that I had sabotaged my last chance with Liza, and what my lack of watchfulness had almost cost her.

I felt something catch in my chest and dropped my head. Then Kathleen appeared. 'We'd better get you back,' she said, laying a hand on my back.

'I'm sorry,' I said again, into the blackness, hoping that Liza would hear me. Then I turned and walked slowly up the path towards the hotel.

It was almost one in the morning before I began to feel warm again. Kathleen had forbidden me the steaming bath I craved, but had plied me with hot tea. She had built up the fire in the fireplace in my room and, as I shivered under several duvets, she brought up a concoction of her own, which included hot lemon, honey, something spicy and brandy.

'How's Hannah?' I asked.

'Sleeping,' she said. 'Little mite's exhausted. But she's OK.'

'She was . . . pretty shocked by what she saw.'

Kathleen's face was briefly grim. 'Not a sight I'd wish on anyone,' she said, 'but we did what we could. They freed a whale, you know. And they're still going. What that net would have taken if the boys hadn't spotted it . . .'

I saw again that murky water, those floating bodies, and tried, as I had for the past hours, to push it all away.

'Kathleen,' I said quietly. 'I'm so sorry—'

But she cut me off. 'You need rest,' she said firmly. 'Really. Burrow down and get some sleep.' And, finally, weary to my bones, I obeyed.

WHEN I HEARD the noise, I could not be sure whether I had been asleep for hours or minutes. I propped myself on an elbow, blinking into the dark. For a moment I couldn't remember where I was, and then the dying red embers of the fire reminded me. I sat upright, my eyes adjusting.

Someone was standing by my bed.

'Wha—'

Liza placed a finger on my lips. 'Don't say anything,' she murmured.

I wondered, briefly, whether I was still dreaming. In the warm darkness, I could smell the sea on her, feel the faint grittiness of the salt on her skin as her hand met mine. And then, as she moved closer, I could feel her breath. She slid wordlessly into the bed beside me, her limbs still chilled and damp from the night air. Her fingers traced my face and I felt the shocking, numbing softness of her lips on mine. She kissed me with a ferocity that incapacitated me. Then, my thoughts jumbling, I stopped her. I took her face in my hands, trying to see her. 'Liza,' I said. 'I don't understand.'

She paused. 'Thank you,' she whispered. 'Thank you for bringing my daughter back to me.'

For weeks I had imagined this, had thought of myself making tender love to this sad girl, kissing away her melancholy. But here was someone I had not anticipated. She was electric. Every fibre of her body pulsed with energy, greedy, encompassing, alive. Is this a reaction to the shock of the evening? I wanted to ask. I recalled Kathleen's words, that Liza took the death of sea creatures hard. 'And then, twice a year, that poor fool thinks he's got a chance.'

I made to speak, but as Liza's lips melted into me, as her skin warmed and then burnt fiercely against mine, and I finally felt heat grow within me, I was incapable of speech, or of thinking anything at all.

WHEN I WOKE, the bed was empty. Even before I was awake enough to think with any clarity, I realised I had known that would be the case.

She had let me see into her soul and allowed me to be the man I had always wanted to be with her, the man I had waited all my life to become. Strong, certain, filled with passion. Someone who could protect her, cherish her, bring her joy. I was unsure whether to feel elation at what I had been given or sorrow that it had already been taken from me.

It was several minutes before I saw that Liza was sitting in the leather chair. She was in her jeans, and her knees were pulled up to her chin, her arms wrapped round them. I glanced at my watch. It was a quarter past five.

'Good morning,' I said quietly.

She turned slowly. Her eyes met mine, and I observed that wherever her thoughts were they were far from me. How could that be? I wondered, when I felt as if her body was etched on my own.

'Mike,' she said, 'you say you know about publicity.'

I stumbled mentally, trying to keep up. 'Uh-huh,' I said.

'What if someone who had done something really bad owned up to it? That would generate publicity, wouldn't it?'

I ran a hand through my hair. 'Sorry,' I began. 'I don't follow . . .'

'I'll tell you how Letty died,' she said, her voice soft, but as clear as a bell, 'and you can tell me who that will save.'

PART THREE

Liza

Pills to help me sleep. Nitrazepam—Mogadon, by its commercial name. Perfectly legitimate, perfectly understandable, given my history of postnatal depression. The doctor had been happy to give them to me. He had known me for some time. I stood in the car park of the pharmacy gazing at the bottle in my hand. Sleeping pills. Takers of life, in the wrong circumstances.

When I began my life in Australia—my real life, rather than the period in which I had merely existed—Kathleen persuaded me to see her doctor and ask for something to help me sleep. I was still plagued with nightmares. In sleep I would see Letty's terrified face, hear her screaming my name, and I prayed for oblivion. The first remedy the Australian doctor offered was these pills, albeit under a different name. When I registered what they were, I took a faltering step towards him and passed out cold.

I NEVER FELT the lack of a father: my mother was enough parent for anyone. She shepherded and chivvied me, scolded and adored me, and I never felt the lack of anything. I sensed that my lot was a good one.

There is no good age at which to lose your mother, but my seventeen-year-old self was spectacularly ill-prepared to face life alone. My mum's cancer was shockingly efficient. I saw her appetite for life disappear, buried in morphine and confusion, and I sat at home alone, staring at the pitiless bills. She died one dark, painful November night; I was with her, and told her that I would be fine, that I knew I was loved. 'There's money in my blue bag,' she told me hoarsely, in one of her last moments of lucidity. 'Use it to go to Kathleen. She'll look after you.' But when I looked, there was not enough to get me to Scotland, let alone Australia. I suspect pride kept me from telling Kathleen of my plight. I left school and got a job stacking shelves, then discovered that this would not keep me in my mother's house.

My life became chaotic. I lived in a squat in Victoria and worked as a barmaid. For a while I was a Goth, and when I was twenty-one I got pregnant by one of the many men who passed through the squat. A giant of a man whose last name I never knew but who stroked my hair and called me 'baby'.

Once I realised I was pregnant, everything changed. I don't know if it was hormones, or just the inheritance of my mother's good sense, but a self-preservation instinct took over. I stripped my hair of its violent dyes, got a job working as a mother's help and, after Hannah was born, I was employed by friends of that family in a picture-framing shop. They were happy for me to work until half past one when I had to pick Hannah up from nursery. I wrote to Kathleen occasionally, and sent her photographs, and she always wrote back promptly, enclosing money 'to buy something for the baby', telling me she was proud of me for the life I had created for myself.

But I was lonely. I was lucky, I knew, to live with a family who were prepared to tolerate me and a baby, but I used to watch them as they sat round the kitchen table, joking with each other, and I wanted the same for my beaming, affectionate toddler. I wanted Hannah to have a father who would love her and swing her round by her hands in a garden.

I had soon found that men were not interested in women with babies.

They didn't see the charms of my beautiful, fair-haired girl, just the restrictions she imposed on me. So, when Steven Villiers bumped into me outside the supermarket and not only did not eye Hannah like she was something infectious but also offered to push the buggy for me on the short walk home, my life, as I had created it, changed for ever.

Steven had a kind of inbuilt authority, one of those people who make you stand back without quite understanding why. He was surprisingly old never to have married—a fact he put down to never having met the right person—and lived with his mother in a beautiful house at Virginia Water in Surrey.

Given his background, his assets, I was unsure what he saw in me. I wore clothes from charity shops. I had nothing to offer. Now, when I look at photographs from that period, I know better. I was beautiful. I had a kind of unworldliness that men found appealing.

The first time I went to bed with him I lay in his arms and I told him of my life, while he held me close and told me I was safe. There is something remarkably seductive, if you have been alone and vulnerable, in hearing you are safe. He said he was meant to be with me, that he thought I was his mission. I was so grateful that I saw nothing worrying in that statement.

Six weeks after we met, Steven asked me to marry him. I moved in with him and his mother. He took me shopping and bought me clothes more fitting for his fiancée. I took a new pride in my housekeeping skills, slowly adapting under the terse tutelage of my prospective mother-in-law. There were hiccups, but Hannah and I soon learned how to live under that roof.

Then, some four months later, I discovered I was pregnant. Initially Steven was delighted. Letty was born on April 16, and I thanked God, as Hannah and Steven cooed over her, that I finally had a family of my own.

It wasn't until several months after Letty's birth that I realised Steven hardly noticed Hannah. Until then I had told myself he loved her, and if Hannah frustrated him with her two-year-old tantrums and her faddiness about food, was it any surprise that he sent her to bed? I tell myself now that I should have grasped earlier that my daughter's increasing silence was not solely the result of adapting to a new sibling. I should have seen that Steven and his mother had become harsher with her.

That woman never forgave me for saddling her son—her senior manager with prospects—with a child who wasn't his. Then, after Letty was born I could not meet her standards of discipline and routine: as toys spread across the floors and our beds remained unmade until the afternoon, she discovered she could say and do whatever she liked. Once, before it got too bad, I dared to ask Steven whether we might find somewhere of our own, but the look he gave me was withering. 'You can barely get those girls dressed,' he said, 'let alone run a house. Do you think you'd last five minutes without my mother?'

The first time he hurt me we were upstairs and the girls were crying, fighting over some toy. I had been so distracted by them that I had forgotten the iron, which was burning through his shirt. He had come into the room, furious at the noise, yelled at the girls, and then, when he saw the shirt, he cuffed me, as if I were a dog. He apologised later, blaming work stress but once he had crossed the line, it was easier to cross it again.

Our wedding was no longer spoken of, and there were times when almost anything I did prompted a fist or a hard hand. Hannah learned that the better she behaved the less likely she was to be scolded. I learned that it was best not to offer an opinion, answer back or draw attention to yourself, and that wearing long sleeves stopped the mothers at the nursery from remarking on the bruises.

Then one day I looked at Hannah's face when he hit her, hard, for not taking her shoes off before stepping on the pale green hall carpet, and my resolve returned. I began to stash money. I would ask for an amount to buy a coat for Letty then buy something from the charity shop, pocketing the difference. I squirrelled away money from the grocery shopping. They suspected nothing.

By then I hated him. I saw his coldness, his arrogance, his blind ambition. I saw his determination to ensure my elder daughter knew she was a second-class citizen in his house, even at the tender age of six. But seeing the truth of my situation did not help me—I could leave with Hannah, I thought, and they would barely care. But they would never hand over Letty. In one argument, when I had threatened to leave with both the girls, he had laughed at me. 'What kind of judge is going to let you look after my daughter?' he said. 'Look at your history—squats and goodness knows what—your lack of education or prospects, and then look at what she'll get with me. You wouldn't have a hope.'

What kept me going was the money mounting up in the lining of my coat, and the hours I spent plotting escape.

They were creatures of habit. Every Tuesday and Thursday Steven's mother would play bridge, and on Thursday and Friday evenings Steven 'went to his club'—a euphemism for another woman. I cherished those Thursday evenings, when I knew I had a few hours alone with the girls.

Then, one Thursday, Steven came back early and found the letter I was writing to Kathleen, telling her what he had done to me. When his initial rage was spent, I suspect he told his mother I was never to be left alone, for after that, whenever I was in the house, so was one of them.

I bided my time. I just needed to get to Kathleen. I could work out everything from there. Steven knew only that I had a distant aunt. He had no idea where she lived. But by the time I had worked out a plan and a date for its execution, I was so nervous that I was surprised they couldn't see it.

'Your daughter needs a haircut,' Steven said, that morning. 'We're having a family photograph taken for my council election leaflet on Saturday. I've got a meeting tonight, but I'll be home before Mother goes out.'

I barely remember that day now, except that it rained heavily, and that the girls, stuck indoors, squabbled. It was the holidays, and Hannah being at home had irritated Steven's mother so much that she'd got one of her 'headaches'.

While she slept, I packed two holdalls with the bare essentials so that a cursory glance in the children's drawers would not suggest we had gone. At one point Hannah came up to see what I was doing.

'Are we going on holiday?' she asked.

'Something like that. A little adventure,' I whispered. 'Go downstairs now, Hannah, and don't say anything to Letty. It's very important.'

Hannah didn't need telling twice: she left my room and, as silently as I could, I put the bags under the bed in the spare room.

Steven was late that evening, and his mother grew increasingly agitated. 'He's going to make me late for bridge,' she said bad-temperedly, staring out at the wet driveway. 'I really can't wait any longer. Tell Steven I had to go.'

As her car left the drive, I ran upstairs and grabbed the sleeping pills from their hiding-place in the wardrobe. Downstairs again, while the girls watched a video, I broke several capsules into a glass, then added some wine, stirred and tasted it. The drug was undetectable.

I would have several hours before his mother came home. Several hours in which to get to nearby Heathrow in his car. To board a plane.

As I heard Steven's car pull up in the drive, I tried to quell the butterflies in my stomach. I had never before prayed for him to come home sooner rather than later. The smile I had on my face as his key turned in the lock was as close to genuine as I had worn in years.

'IT'S ALL RIGHT,' Mike said, his eyes kind. 'It's all right.'

My breath was coming in deep jags, tears streaming down my face. 'I can't—' I shook my head. My chest was so tight I could barely breathe.

I felt his arms surround me. 'You don't have to say anything,' he murmured. 'You don't have to tell me anything.' He held me without saying anything, his face pressed to mine so tightly that his skin must have absorbed my tears.

'Mum?'

Hannah stood in the doorway, still in her nightdress, looking from me to Mike and back again. I pulled away from Mike and wiped my eyes. My beautiful daughter, my beautiful, frightened, brave, living daughter.

'Why are you crying?' she whispered.

I wanted to tell her, but for years I haven't spoken about Letty in front of her. For years, not knowing how much she remembered, I'd tried to shield her from the memory of that awful night.

'Hannah—' My voice stopped in my throat.

Mike's voice cut across the room, quiet and firm: 'We're talking about Letty, Hannah,' he said gently. And as she stepped forward to take his outstretched fingers, my heart broke, overwhelmed not by the pain, or the memory of my poor lost daughter, but by the presence of so much love. Then, my hand pressed to my mouth, I had to run from the room.

Hannah

My mother didn't talk for almost two weeks after we came here. She just lay in her bed, like someone dead. My aunt Kathleen looked after me, getting me to explain what had happened, holding me when I couldn't stop crying. She got Lara round, and helped us bake cakes together, as if we were cooking up a friendship. As if she was trying to find me a substitute for Letty. And when I asked her what was going on with my mum, why she wouldn't come down and be with me, Auntie K said: 'You and your mum have suffered something unimaginable, Hannah, and she's not coping with it quite as well as you are. We have to give her time.'

One day I think she must have decided Mum had had enough time. 'Your Mum and I are going to have a little chat,' she told me. 'You and Lara stay here with Yoshi and mind the dog.' They went out on Auntie K's boat, and when they got back Mum climbed out onto Whale Jetty, walked down to me and held me. I felt like it was the first time she'd actually seen me for ages. 'I'm really sorry, Mum,' I said, as the tears started.

Her voice didn't sound the same. 'Nothing to be sorry for, lovey. You did everything right. It was me who got it all wrong.'

But I knew that if Letty and I hadn't had that argument in front of Steven . . .

if Letty hadn't said that thing about not wanting to go on holiday . . . Suddenly I missed Letty so badly. I couldn't believe she wasn't alive any more. 'I want her to be here,' I cried.

I felt a big sob catch in Mum's chest. She squeezed me tight. 'Me too, lovey,' she said softly. 'Me too.'

Mum had told me not to say anything. But I'd been so excited at the thought of me, Mum and Letty going somewhere, 'I didn't mean to tell her,' I whispered. Then my mother took my shoulders. 'Your sister's death was not your fault, OK?' Her voice was fierce, but her eyes were kind. 'Not one iota of this was your fault, Hannah.'

A couple of weeks later, after I'd had my tea, we had a service for Letty. Out at sea. Just me, Mum, Auntie K and Milly. We went out on *Ishmael* to what Auntie K said was the prettiest spot in the whole of Australia, and while the dolphins bobbed around and the sun shone red Auntie K gave thanks for Letty's life and said that even though we were on the other side of the world it was perfectly obvious to her where Letty's spirit was.

That was one of the last times we ever spoke about Letty.

I have two photographs of her in my drawer and if I didn't look at them every night I wouldn't remember how her face was, how her missing tooth looked when she smiled, the way she stroked her nose with her finger when she sucked her thumb, how she used to feel when she slept with me.

There are some things I'd like to forget. Like that night when Steven came home. He smelt of drink, but Mum had poured him a glass of wine anyway. As she served up the supper, I saw her watching him out of the corner of her eye.

And then Letty and I had a stupid fight about crayons, because we both wanted the same green one, and I won because I was bigger and Letty started to cry and said she didn't want to go away, and Steven said, 'Go where?' And he looked at Mum and they stared at each other for a few seconds. Then he went upstairs, and I heard him pulling out all the drawers. When he came down his face was so angry that I hid under the table and pulled Letty with me. I heard him shouting, 'Where are the passports?' and his voice had gone all slurry and I shut my eyes really tight and there was lots of banging and Mum fell on the floor and hit her head and his hands reached under the table and he picked up Letty, who was screaming and screaming, and he said she'd be going anywhere over his dead body, and his voice sounded like he was under water or something. I tried to grab Letty's hand but he pushed me really hard.

And then, as Mum woke up, I heard the sound of his car going down the drive, all the gravel spraying up, and Mum started crying, 'Oh my God, oh my God,' and she didn't even notice that her face was bleeding and I held on to her because I was scared of where he'd taken Letty.

I don't know how long we sat there. Mum held me close and said, 'They'll be back soon,' but I wasn't sure she believed it. I was afraid because I guessed that when Steven came back he was going to be really angry.

I think it was a few hours later that the phone rang. Mum was still sitting, shaking, on the floor, and I picked up the receiver and it was Granny Villiers. She said, 'Put your mother on, please,' like I was a stranger. And then Mum kept saying, 'What have I done? What have I done?'

When it started to get light, I remember Mum waking me up. I'd fallen asleep on the floor and I was cold and stiff. She said that we had to go now. I said, 'What about Letty?' and she said there had been an accident, that Steven had had a car crash and Letty was dead in the hospital, and it was all her fault, and her teeth were chattering.

I can't remember much after that—just being in a taxi, and then an aeroplane. I remember my aunt Kathleen standing at the airport barrier and hugging me like she knew me, and telling me that everything was going to be all right. And all the time I wanted to say to Mum, 'We should have brought Letty with us, not left her all those miles away so that we couldn't put flowers on her grave and let her know we still loved her.' But I didn't say anything. Because for a long, long time, my mum couldn't say anything at all.

THIS WAS WHAT I told Mike, on the morning I saw him with his arms round Mum in his bedroom. This was what I told him, after she'd gone, even though I've never been able to tell that story to anyone, not even Auntie K, not with everything in it. But I told him, because I got the feeling that somehow things had changed, and that Mum would think it was OK.

Mike

As the rest of Silver Bay slept late the following day, and the waters stilled under a clear blue sky, several miles away, in a gently humming room at the Port Summer Hospital, Nino Gaines woke up.

Kathleen had been sitting at the end of his bed. She had gone straight there explaining afterwards that she had wanted to tell her oldest friend a little of what had happened that momentous night. As dawn broke, exhaustion caught up with her and she had dozed for a while, then sat reading the previous day's newspaper, occasionally aloud when she found something that might interest him. In this case, it was a report about a man they both knew who had set up a restaurant. 'Be a bloody disaster,' he croaked. So weary was she from the fright of Hannah's disappearance and the horror of the ghost nets that Kathleen Whittier Mostyn read on for another two sentences before she realised what she'd heard.

He was frail, and a little disorientated, but he was indubitably Nino Gaines, and for that the whole Silver Bay community was grateful. The doctors gave him a raft of examinations, and finally pronounced him surprisingly well for a man of his age who had been unconscious for so many days. Kathleen was allowed to sit at the end of his bed throughout, as long as she didn't raise his blood pressure.

'Been raising my bloody blood pressure for more than fifty years,' he told the nurses, in front of her. 'Fat lot of good it's done me.' And Kathleen beamed. She has not stopped beaming since.

A LUCKY FEW know their purpose in life from an early age. I finally learned mine on a clear dawn at the start of an Australian spring, when an eleven-year-old girl trusted me with a secret. From that moment, I understood that all my energy would be given to her protection and that of her mother.

After they had told me about Letty, Liza had feared I would see her differently—at worst, as a murderer. I had found her in her room, sitting in a chair, her face a mask of misery. I knelt down and put my arms round her, saying nothing, trusting in my presence to say it for me.

A long time later, I understood why she had told me. 'I don't think you should do it,' I said. 'You're punishing yourself for something that wasn't your fault. How could you know he'd react like that? How could you know he'd crash the car? You were a battered woman, for God's sake. You could say you were temporarily insane.'

'I've got to do it.' Her eyes, although swollen with tears, were clear with determination. 'I as good as killed my own daughter. I may have killed her father too. I'll give myself up, and use the publicity to tell them what's going on out here.'

'It might be a disastrous wasted gesture. You'll probably go to jail.'

'You think I don't know that?'

'How will Hannah cope without you? Hasn't she lost enough already?'

She blew her nose. 'Better she loses me for a few years while she's still got Kathleen. Then we can start again. And maybe someone will listen. What other chance have we got against the development?'

And there she had it.

She held my hands. 'Mike, for years I've lived a half-life, full of fear. Hannah can't leave Australia. The moment they see her passport, they'll catch up with us. She can't even leave Silver Bay—it's the only place I feel sure we're out of the way. I don't want Hannah to grow up like this. I want her to be able to go where she wants, see who she wants to see.' She leaned forward. 'It's like living with ghost nets,' she said. 'What I did, Letty, Steven . . . It may be thousands of miles away but it's all out there, waiting to pull me down.' She pushed her hair behind her ear and I caught sight of a little white scar. 'If the development goes ahead, we'll have to move on,' she said. 'And wherever we go, it will all be drifting silently behind us.' She swallowed. 'So here it is. If I hand myself in, I'll give Hannah her freedom and bring some attention to the whales.' She smiled at me tentatively. 'And I'll be free. You've got to understand, Mike, that I need to be free of this too. As far as I can ever be.'

I stared at her. 'Do me a favour,' I said, reaching for her again. 'Don't do anything until I've spoken to someone.'

THE FOLLOWING EVENING, I called my sister. Forcing her to agree not to say anything to anyone, I told her, with as much detail as I could remember, what Liza had told me. 'Do you think it would be a story?'

'Are you kidding, Mike? The news desk would wet themselves,' she said.

'If we do this, Monica, I need it to be as sympathetic as possible to her case. I need people to understand how she ended up in such a position. If you knew her . . . if you knew what kind of person she is . . .'

'You want *me* to write it?' My sister sounded incredulous.

'I don't trust anyone else.'

There was a short silence.

'Thanks, Mike . . . I reckon I could make it sympathetic. I'll have a chat with the lawyer here—no names, of course. I don't want to write anything that might jeopardise any case that comes to court.'

I stared at the receiver, hearing in those words the unwelcome truth of Liza's situation. 'And you think . . . she could highlight the cause?'

'If she made it clear that the reason she was coming forward now was not just to put things right but to protect a load of baby whales, people might be well disposed towards her. But I can't guarantee what'll happen to her once it's all in the open. It's not going to look good that she ran away.'

'She had to take steps to protect Hannah.'

'But even if I make her sound like a bloody angel she could still end up in prison. Especially if the ex-partner died too. If the prosecution can prove that she gave him those pills knowing he'd been drinking, knowing he would get in his car, well, I hate to say this, but that sounds like manslaughter at best. But spell out his name for me again. I'll see what I can find out and get back to you.'

THE OBJECTIONS presented to the public inquiry were widely predicted to be disregarded. The newspapers began to talk of 'when' the new development went up, rather than 'if'. And, as though to prove as much, hoardings rose round the demolition site promising 'Two-, three- and four-bedroom holiday homes, part of a unique recreational experience'. I read the phrases I had proposed and felt sick. The gleaming, twelve-foot-high hoardings highlighted the shabbiness of the Silver Bay Hotel. It stood as a silent sentinel to a lost age, when a hotel had been somewhere to escape to, not a unique investment opportunity.

One morning, while I watched yet another people-mover pull up with a group of unidentified people, all of whom got out and walked around with clipboards talking into phones, I turned to find Kathleen beside me.

'So, when do we need to start packing?' she said, looking straight ahead.

My stomach lurched. What could I say? Yoshi was in contact with the whales and dolphins organisations, who were compiling a report on the disruptive effect of sound on cetaceans. We had a petition with almost 1,700 signatures. We had a website that scored several hundred hits a day and attracted messages of support from all over the globe. We had other whale-watching communities sending letters of objection to the council. After school Hannah sat emailing other schools, trying to get other children involved. I spent hours on the telephone, trying to persuade local townspeople to go against it. None of it seemed to make any difference.

'It's not over yet.' I was trying to convince myself as much as anything.

HANNAH'S GLORY had gone down that night, swamped by the tall waves, its rudder entangled in the ghost nets. Nobody talked about the little boat, once its resting place on the seabed had been established. It was too easy to imagine Hannah out there with it.

Then, apropos of nothing, Liza had announced over breakfast that she was going to find Hannah a boat.

'What?'

'I think you're old enough. I've asked Peter Sawyer to keep an eye out for one. But if I ever catch you going out on the water without permission that will be it. No more boat, ever.'

Hannah leapt from her place at the table and threw her arms round her mother's neck. 'I'll never go anywhere without telling you,' she said. 'Oh, thank you, Mum.'

Liza tried to make her face stern. 'I'm trusting you.'

Hannah nodded, eyes shining. 'Can I call Lara and tell her?' she said.

'You'll see her at school in half an hour.'

'*Please.*' Her mother's hesitation was all the confirmation she needed. We heard her feet skipping joyfully down the hallway, then her high-pitched exclamations on the phone.

Liza looked down at her breakfast, as if embarrassed by her *volte face*. Kathleen and I stared at her. It is possible that my mouth had dropped open.

'She lives by the sea. Besides,' said Liza, her eyes briefly meeting mine, 'it's only sensible. I might not always be here to watch out for her.'

LIZA AND I had not talked about 'us'. Several weeks in I assumed there was an 'us', even though by unspoken agreement we displayed no affection in front of Kathleen, Hannah or the whalechasers. The southern migration had begun and sometimes, in the day, I would go out on a trip with her. I liked the lilt in her voice when she told stories about the whales, the affectionate way she rubbed Milly's ears as she steered, and the way she was at ease with every part of the boat. The protest, ironically, had brought passengers morning and afternoon, but every time I went out with her it might have been just ourselves for all the notice I took of anyone else.

I also felt an overwhelming urge to protect Hannah, and I understood why Liza would have given up everything to keep her safe. Hannah knew about her mother and me and said nothing. But the way she grinned at me conspiratorially left me choked with pride at her tacit approval. I wanted to stay in her life, if Liza would let me.

We had not mentioned love, but I carried it in a cloud around me like sea mist. The lifting in Liza's manner, her ready smiles, told me she felt it too. Most nights she would pad silently down the corridor to my room, and in the dimness I would peel back my bed covers and let her in. When she touched my face with her fingertips, her expression slightly disbelieving, I knew it mirrored my own. I don't know if Kathleen knew what was going on. In any case, she was preoccupied with Nino Gaines, getting him out of hospital and helping to restore his health.

One night, when we lay talking quietly, she told me that having a child brought the most love and the most fear anyone could feel.

'I'll help take care of Hannah,' I said. 'If you want.'

I could hear her breathing. When she spoke there was a catch in her voice. 'I don't want Hannah to lose anyone else. I don't want her to get attached to you and then, a few years down the line, for you to realise it's too much for you. The waiting, I mean.' She paused. 'I won't blame you,' she continued quietly, 'if you want to leave when I do. You've been . . . a good friend to us.'

'I'm not going anywhere,' I said. And with those words a new atmosphere settled around us in the dark. I hadn't even thought about what I was going to say, but it was out there: a true reflection of what I felt.

Her voice broke: 'Hannah will need as many friends as she can get.'

I ached for her, wishing that, somehow, I could take that pain for her.

'You don't have to do it,' I said, for the hundredth time.

She silenced me with a kiss. 'I know you find it hard to understand, but I feel like I'm taking control for the first time in my life.' I pictured her brave smile in the darkness. 'I'm at the helm.'

MY SISTER RANG at a quarter past three that morning. She'd never been any good with time differences. Liza stirred as I fumbled for my phone.

'OK, you want the good news or the bad?'

'I don't know,' I said, half asleep. 'Whatever.'

'The good news is I've found Steven Villiers, and he's still alive. The old woman is dead, which helps, as there are fewer people who can corroborate his side of things.'

She paused as I digested this, trying to force the relief I wanted to feel.

'The bad news, Mike, is that he's a councillor. A respected member of his community. Married, two children. Round Table, charitable efforts, you name it. A councillor with parliamentary ambitions. Every single newspaper report he features in has him shaking hands with some police chief or handing over a cheque to a good cause. None of that is going to make your girlfriend's case any easier at all.'

Liza

Mike worked night and day to stop the development. Some nights he worked so late I thought he'd make himself ill. Everyone he telephoned he warned of noise and pollution levels. He explained how business would be drawn away from local bars, restaurants and small hotels. He showed where the profits from this hotel would go, and it was not into Silver Bay. I think he thought that if he could stop it by other means I wouldn't go to England and somehow everything would be all right. When I told him I'd go anyway, he told me I was a masochist.

He was trying to haul together a protest for when the architectural model went on view at the Blue Shoals Hotel, a short distance from Silver Bay. He was finding it hard going: many people saw the new hotel as a given now and were already planning ways to capitalise on its presence. Even among those who didn't want it you couldn't guarantee action.

Hannah was Mike's greatest support. She and Lara had created new petitions, rallied their classmates, even been on local radio talking about the different personalities of the bay's dolphins. Mike had set her up with an email account so that she could alert all the whale and dolphin societies she had found on the Internet. It had focused her attention away from her shock over the ghost nets. She seemed more confident, enthusiastic, determined.

As SOON AS I COULD I told my daughter. One warm Friday afternoon after school I bought her an ice-cream and we sat at the end of Whale Jetty, while Milly drooled hopefully on our shoulders. The solicitor had told me that if I went back to England there would be a court case and I'd have to explain what had happened. I told Hannah that it was likely she would be asked, too, and would have to tell them everything, just as she had told Mike.

'Will I have to go back and live with Steven?' she asked.

Even the mention of his name made me go cold. 'No, lovey. You'll stay with Kathleen. She's your closest blood relative after me.'

'Will you go to prison?' she asked.

I told her it was possible. But I added that the solicitor had told me that if I was lucky I might get a short sentence, or even a suspended one.

The important thing, I told Hannah, forcing a smile, was that once it was over we would be free to get on with our lives. She would be able to go where she wanted. 'Hey,' I said, holding her shoulders, 'you might even be able to go to New Zealand. That school trip you were talking about.'

The depth of her horror shocked me. 'I don't want to go to New Zealand,' she said, her face crumpling. 'I want you to stay with me.' There was nothing but fear and desperation in her eyes and I hated myself for putting them there. 'Everybody leaves me,' she whispered.

She cried for a while, and I held her tight, trying not to cry with her. The truth was that the prospect of being separated from my daughter made me feel ill. When I held her now it was no longer pleasurable, but as if I was trying to imprint her on myself, preparing for when I would not have the privilege of holding her close to me. I closed my eyes, breathing in the smell of her hair. 'It might feel bad now, but it's going to get better,' I told her. 'We can write to each other and speak on the phone and we'll be together again before you know it.'

She sniffed and wiped her eyes with the ball of her palm.

'And, most importantly, whenever I talk about Letty, I'll make sure to talk about the whales. And the dolphins.'

'You think that would stop the hotel?'

'It might. And that way her life and death might mean something good.'

We sat there, staring out over the water, mulling over what I had said, but Hannah didn't tell me what I knew to be true: that I was wrong, that nothing good could ever emerge from Letty's death.

KATHLEEN WAS NOT one of society's great party-givers. In fact, it would be fair to say that, despite her trade, she was one of the least outgoing people I knew, happier alone in her kitchen than making small talk with guests. So, it was a bit of a surprise when she announced that when Nino Gaines came out of hospital she was going to throw a celebration at the hotel.

'Lance, you've no need to be catching flies. It's about time we had something to celebrate in this sorry little hole,' she said, as the whalechasers were stunned momentarily into silence at the bleached table.

Three days later, on an afternoon warm enough to hint of the summer to come, we were sitting out under canopies when Kathleen's car pulled up in front of the hotel and Frank helped his father out.

'Welcome back!' we all shouted, and Hannah ran to hug him. He was the closest person she'd ever had to a grandfather.

He had lost weight and he was frail, a little unsteady on his stick. He held onto the open car door with one hand, squinting at us. 'This sorry parade of humanity the best you could get to welcome me, Kate?'

'Ungrateful old sod,' she said, hauling out his bag.

'You get to sit near me, Mr Gaines,' said Hannah, holding his free hand as he made his way slowly up the path. 'It's a special chair.'

'Hasn't got a bedpan in the bottom, has it?' he said, and Hannah giggled.

'I meant it's got all the cushions.'

'Ah, that's all right, then,' he said.

He winked at me and I stepped forward to hug him.

It was a glorious afternoon. The crews had taken time off and, by tacit agreement, no one discussed the development. We drank and watched Hannah, Lara and Milly tear up and down the sand. Mike sat beside me and, periodically, I felt his hand reach for mine under the table.

Look at me, I mused. Look at Hannah, Kathleen and Nino, at the whale crews, who had, over the years, given me more friendship and support than many people's blood relatives would. Whatever happened, even though there would always be someone missing at the heart of it, I had a family.

'Where's Greg?' Hannah asked. 'He said he'd be here by now.'

'He was being mysterious this morning,' said Kathleen. 'I saw him at the fish market. He said he was on a mission.'

'Yeah? What was her name?'

Before any of us could say anything, the whine of Greg's truck could be heard and, as if on cue, he drove slowly up to the front of the hotel. 'Sorry to interrupt,' he said, climbing out of the cab. He looked uncommonly pleased with himself. 'I just thought you should all know—you might want to swing by my lockup in half an hour. Got something to show you.'

'We're having a party, in case you hadn't noticed.' Kathleen placed her hands on her hips. 'And you were meant to be here two hours ago.'

'I'm real sorry, Kathleen, but this is important. Good to see you back, Mr Gaines. I'll be glad to crack open a couple of stubbies with you later.' He tipped his cap and, with a definite swagger, headed back to his truck.

'He been on the amber fluid again?' Nino stared after him.

Yoshi and Lance were exchanging a glance. They knew something, but it was obvious they weren't going to let us in on it.

WE DIDN'T HAVE long to wait. Nino stayed up at the hotel with Hannah, but the rest of us ambled down the sea path, enjoying the sun and watching, with mild surprise, a crowd swell outside Greg's lockup. There were reporters and photographers, I noticed. Greg was standing in front, smoking a cigarette, as if he was waiting to ensure that everyone was there. His truck was not outside.

Finally, he spat out his cigarette and ground it into the dirt with his heel. Then, he slid his key into the padlock, opened the doors and flicked on the light inside his lockup. As we stared into the interior, he whipped a tarpaulin off the back of his truck to reveal an enormous tiger shark, its eye still clear, its mouth slightly open, revealing angled, pointed teeth. There was a gasp.

'Went out fishing early this morning,' he said to the reporters. 'Just to the mouth of the bay, like. I thought I had a blue marlin at first—but look at the bugger I hauled in! Dragged me round the cockpit like you wouldn't believe. Tony, back it up!' he called, to the man in the cab. As he stepped aside, the truck reversed out into the daylight and a few cameras clicked.

'I've called you guys out because we've not had tigers this close before and I want to tell everyone in the bay to keep their kids out of the water. You can't trust these monsters not to come in.' He slapped the shark appreciatively. 'I brought it in to the market and the guys there identified it and weighed it. I'm told it's not the only one that's been seen in our waters.'

Yoshi stepped forward. 'Tiger sharks,' she said, 'are known as the dustbins of the sea. This one may have been attracted into the bay by the ghost net and the dead creatures attached to it. There's a good chance this big guy wasn't alone. The sharks feed on anything, fish, turtles, humans . . .' She let that word dangle long enough for people to glance at each other nervously.

'We need shark nets,' called someone in the crowd.

'How are you going to have shark nets in a bay full of dolphins?' said Greg, sharply. 'They trap whales too.'

'Sharks are smart,' said Yoshi. 'If you check out the figures, shark-death rates stay around the same whether the beaches have nets or not.'

'I reckon you're making something out of nothing.' I recognised one of the hoteliers. He wouldn't be happy, I knew, about this sort of publicity just as the spring season was about to take off. 'Everyone knows you're more likely statistically to be hit by lightning than killed by a shark.'

'Fine, Alf,' Greg said. 'You go swimming, then. I just thought it was my duty to let you guys know what's out there. Meanwhile, we'll alert the coastguard if we see any others in the bay, and the fishermen will do the same.'

There was a murmur of concern. Several people turned away, and others moved closer to the truck, wanting to touch the shark. Then Kathleen stepped forward and stared at the dead creature.

'Shark, eh?' she said, frowning, her arms firmly crossed.

'You'd know,' said Greg, as he hoisted it up on the winch so that the photographers could get a better picture.

'Where did you say you—'

'This, gentlemen,' Greg said, gesturing towards Kathleen, 'is the world-famous Shark Lady of Silver Bay, Kathleen Whittier Mostyn. This lady here caught an even bigger shark some half a century ago. Biggest grey nurse shark ever caught in New South Wales, wasn't it, Kathleen?'

Kathleen stared silently at him. She knew she'd been set up, but Greg rattled on regardless: 'So, gentlemen, you see? Once again Silver Bay has a shark population. The wildlife people will be delighted, but I do want to warn our good citizens not to take part in any kind of watersports without great caution while the threat of shark attack exists.'

The press gathered around Kathleen, their notepads and microphones in front of her. Several flashbulbs went off. After the horror of the ghost nets, the local newspapers had their second good front-page story in a fortnight.

'I thought you didn't get sharks and dolphins in the same place,' Mike said, as he and I strolled back to the hotel. The afternoon was clear and bright, the sea glinting benignly. Ahead I could make out Hannah and Lara collapsing, giggling, onto the sand. On days like this, I could convince myself that the world I inhabited was a good one.

'Sometimes I think the whole planet is topsy-turvy,' I said, glancing up at him. I wanted to kiss him, then—I wanted to kiss him most of the time.

'DON'T GO,' said Mike, that night after the party. He was standing in the bathroom brushing his teeth, and I had walked in behind him to get a glass of water. 'Don't do this. I've been thinking about it, and it's madness.' The rigidity of his back told me the tension I thought I had seen in his face that evening had not been imagined.

I sighed. 'Mike, I don't want to go through all this now,' I said. I wanted to enjoy the day for what it was, to savour it and go to bed in peace.

'Nothing's going to stop the development,' he said, pausing to spit out toothpaste. 'When Dennis Beaker sees money, nothing stops him. You're about to ruin your own life, and Hannah's, for no reason. She's safe and happy here. And you're happy—the happiest I've ever seen you. We could be a couple and stay here and . . . see how things go. Why risk all that for something you might not be able to pull off?'

'Mike, we've been through this a million times. And I'm too tired to talk now.' I was irritated that he was speaking the truth.

'Every time I mention it, you say the same thing. We're all tired, Liza. It's the human condition. It's not just you that your decision affects. Hannah barely leaves your side. She was glued to you this evening.'

I glared at him. 'I don't need you to tell me anything about my daughter, thank you very much.' I hated him for seeing Hannah's fear.

'Well, someone's got to talk to you. You haven't even discussed it with Kathleen because you know she'll say the same as I have. Have you thought about what prison really means? Being locked up twenty-three hours a day and labelled a child-killer by other inmates? You think you could survive that?'

'I'm not talking about this now,' I said, moving towards the door.

'If you can't cope with me saying those words, how are you going to cope with it in court? From the police? From people who want to hurt you?'

'Why are you doing this to me?'

'Because I don't think you've thought it through. You know what? I think you're determined to punish yourself for Letty's death. You feel the need to atone for it by sacrificing yourself. But you've already paid for what happened, Liza. You need to think about this. You need to know that by—'

'*You* need to butt out of my business.'

'—that by going through with this, you'll take Hannah down with you.'

My blood ran cold. I couldn't believe he would attack me like that. If his words hadn't sunk into me, like a knife, I probably wouldn't have said what I did: 'Who the hell landed us in this situation, Mike? You ask yourself that the next time you start judging me. If Hannah and I end up spending years apart, you ask yourself whose bloody fault it really is.'

Mike, his face grey, held up his hand. 'You're right,' he said. 'I'm sorry.'

And I understood, with a painful lurch, the truth of it: that he hadn't meant to hurt me. He just couldn't bear the thought of losing me.

Mike

We no longer discussed Liza's plans. I worked harder, partly because that was the only way I could think of to stop her, and partly because I found it increasingly painful to be with her. I couldn't look at her, touch her, kiss her, without thinking of how it would feel to be without her.

Kathleen evidently knew now what she planned—they had had a conversation—and her way of dealing with it was merely to plough on, being practical. I hadn't talked to her about it—I didn't feel it was my place—but I saw her paying extra attention to Hannah, making plans for treats, and I knew she was engaged in her own form of preparation. Nino Gaines came by most days now, and while Hannah was at school the two could often be found at the kitchen table, reading the newspaper and listening to what they both called the wireless. I was glad that Kathleen would not face this alone.

Liza had forgiven me for my outburst. She was gentle with me, occasionally running a finger down the side of my face with sympathetic eyes. At night she was increasingly passionate, as if she, too, was determined to glean every last bit of happiness from what remained of our time together. Sometimes I had to tell her I couldn't—I felt so sad and angry about what would soon take place. She never commented. She would just rest her face against the back of my neck and the two of us would lie in the darkness, each knowing the other was awake, neither knowing what to say.

Several times she had asked when my sister was likely to do the interview. She tried to make her enquiries sound casual, but I knew she needed to know exactly how much time she had left. I tried several times to reach Monica, but always I got her voicemail.

Despite my best efforts, I hadn't managed to get a protest demonstration going on the day the architectural model went on display. The owner of the Blue Shoals Hotel rang to tell me that, sympathetic as he was to what I was doing, he 'didn't want any aggro' as there was a christening party in the back room that lunchtime. I didn't feel I could ruin a family's special day, so I called it off. Kathleen had laughed drily when I told her, and said some revolutionary I would have made. I didn't like to tell her that only a handful of people had shown interest in joining the demonstration, as it was.

Liza was out on *Ishmael*, and Hannah was at school, so after I'd tried and failed to continue the fight from my desk, I had headed down to the Blue Shoals. There, in the foyer, flanked by screens that illustrated projected visitor numbers and benefits for the community, the model of the development sat in a Perspex case. It was exactly as I had pictured it. Its four buildings were situated elegantly round a series of courtyards and swimming-pools. The watersports area, which jutted far into the bay, was punctuated by little plastic boats and even two waterskiers. Whale Jetty was lined with expensive white yachts and catamarans. The sand was white and the buildings gleamed with whitewash and glass. It looked, I had to admit, like a little stretch of Paradise. Then I saw that Kathleen's hotel and the Whalechasers Museum no longer existed.

'Looks pretty good, doesn't it?'

I glanced up to see Mr Reilly, from the council's planning department, gazing into the Perspex case. 'Different when you see it in three-D,' he observed. 'Brings it to life.'

'It's a mistake,' I said. 'It's going to be a disaster for the area.'

Mr Reilly, deflated slightly, straightened up. 'You surprise me, Mike, given how hard you fought for this place.'

'Then I saw what you would lose,' I said.

'I don't believe we'll lose too much.'

'Just your whales and dolphins.'

'You're being a little dramatic, mate. The coastguards have had a clamp-down on those disco boats. There's been none here for over ten days now. And there's no evidence that building on shore is going to stress the animals. Beaker have promised to put some pretty tough regulations in place. I don't really understand why you're so opposed to it.'

I took a deep breath and gestured towards the model. 'Mr Reilly, tell me what you see when you look at this,' I said.

He shoved his hands into his pockets. 'I see life in an area that's pretty short on it. I see a new bus and a brick-built library for the school, and I see commerce. I see opportunities.' He smiled wryly at me. 'You should know, Mike. It was you who got me to see those things.'

'I'll tell you what I see,' I said. 'I see men who've had a beer too many skidding too fast round the bay in motorboats. I see dolphins injured by rudders. I see disco boats trying to catch passing trade and disorientated whales beaching themselves on that pristine white shore. I see what remains of the humpback migration moving many miles from here, and the people who relied on them losing their jobs.' I pointed at the model. 'And I see a bloody great hole where a family-run hotel that has existed seventy-odd years should be.'

'There's no reason why the Silver Bay Hotel can't exist quite happily alongside the new development. You can't expect them to include every local building on the model.'

We were silent for a minute. An elderly couple stood in the doorway of the hotel, glancing nervously at us. I realised I had been shouting. 'I gotta tell you, mate, you've surprised me. That's some about-turn,' Reilly said. But his voice was not unfriendly. 'Tell me something, Mike. You're against the development now, but you must have seen the advantages once. When you came to me all those months ago, what did *you* see when you looked at this plan?'

I looked at this thing, at this unstoppable force, and my heart felt like lead. 'Money,' I said. 'I saw money.'

WHEN I GOT BACK, Hannah was in my room, sitting at the computer. The window was open and a light breeze passed from the window to the door. Bright sunlight streamed in onto the white-painted floorboards. I rarely shut my door now—there had been no guests for weeks, and Kathleen behaved as though I lived there.

'Mike!' Hannah exclaimed. She spun round on the chair, beckoning me closer, and showed me an email from someone in Hawaii, who had fought off a similar development. 'She's going to send us details of the organisations who helped her,' she said.

'That's great,' I said, trying to sound positive. 'Good work.'

'Me and Lara have been emailing everyone. I mean *everyone*. Someone from the *South Bay Examiner* rang and wants to take our picture because of the petitions!' She grinned. 'I've made a list of everything we did today— it's in the blue file in the corner. I've got Hockey Club now, but I'll carry on when I get back. Are you still coming out with me and Mum?'

'Hmm?' I was thinking about Mr Reilly. The planning inquiry would close in three days' time, he'd told me as he left the Blue Shoals. But he'd added that nothing had been submitted that was persuasive enough to change the panel's mind.

'Mum said we could all go out, the three of us, on *Ishmael*—remember?'

'Oh,' I said, trying to smile. 'Sure.'

She pulled on her school cardigan and thrust a newspaper at me. 'Did you see Aunt Kathleen's picture with the shark? She's raging. She says she's going to have Greg's guts for garters.'

The headline said: SHARK LADY WARNS OF TIGER'S RETURN. Underneath it, the photographer had caught Kathleen, her own expression almost as baleful as the dead shark's. Beside it was the picture of her as a seventeen-year-old. Poor Kathleen. She was right: she'd be haunted by that shark.

I watched Hannah gather her things and, with a cheery wave, she was off down the stairs. She seemed to have blocked out her mother's imminent departure. Perhaps, like me, she was hoping for divine intervention.

It was then that my mobile phone rang.

'Monica?' I checked my watch. It had to be nearly two o'clock in the morning in England.

'How's it going?' said Vanessa.

My first fleeting thought was: Where the hell is my sister? My second was irritation. Vanessa would know very well that my opposition to the plans was coming to nothing.

'I'm fine,' I said.

'I hear you're still in Australia,' she said.

'Still playing Canute,' I said, 'against the unstoppable tide.'

'Dad's got a cuttings file,' she said, 'all the pieces you've placed about opposition to the development. He throws things at it daily.'

'Why are you telling me?'

'To let you know that what you're doing is not totally in vain.'

'But it's not stopping him.'

There was a brief silence. 'No,' she conceded. 'It's not.'

Outside a flock of parakeets had landed in a tree.

'Tina left.'

So what? I wanted to say. Instead I closed my eyes. I felt so tired.

'I miss you,' said Vanessa.

I still said nothing.

'I've never known you like this before, Mike. You're stronger than I thought . . . I've been thinking'—she took a breath—'I can get him to stop. I know he'll listen to me.'

The world seemed briefly to stop turning. 'What?'

'If it means that much to you, I'll stop it. But I'm asking you—please—let's give it another try.'

My breath stalled briefly in my chest. 'You and me?'

'We were a good team, weren't we?' She was uncertain, pleading. 'And we can be even better now. You hurt me, Mike, I'm not going to deny that. But Dad says Tina was a troublemaker, and I don't think you'd deceive me intentionally. So . . . so I guess I don't want to lose what we had.'

When I spoke, my mouth, suddenly dry, stuck on the words: 'You're saying that if I come back to you, you'll stop the development?'

'That's putting it very baldly. It's not a *quid pro quo*, Mike. But I'm hardly likely to go to all that trouble for someone I don't care about. Is it so hideous a prospect? Us giving it another go?'

I shook my head, trying to clear my thoughts.

'Vanessa, you've really . . . surprised me. Look—I've got to go out now, but let me ring you later. OK? I'll ring you later this morning. Your time.'

I ended the call and sat, my ears ringing. I had nowhere to go. Vanessa Beaker was the only person in the whole world capable of stopping the development.

IN THE END I made excuses. I told them I had a headache and I had to return some calls. That I had used two excuses where one would have been adequate immediately alerted Liza to the truth: that some other reason lay behind my decision not to go on our planned outing. As Hannah pleaded with me to change my mind, her mother eyed me but said nothing.

'I'll see you both when you get back,' I said, trying to sound casual.

I needed to think.

I waved at the boat as the engines powered up and it bounded away from me, then I began the longest afternoon of my life. I walked down the coast road, over the dunes, and lost myself for a couple of hours, not sure where I was headed, not really noticing my surroundings. I walked and I thought, and every possible solution felt ruinous.

I, Michael Dormer, a man renowned for his ability to weigh up the pros and cons of any situation and hit the right answer, now found that whichever way I turned the options made me want to sink to my knees, like a small boy, and howl.

I WAS BACK on Whale Jetty when they returned. It must have looked as if I hadn't been away. I had allowed myself a couple of beers, and sat there, watching *Ishmael* come round the headland. Its swimming nets were stretched across the boom, where Hannah must have been allowed to sit in the water to see the dolphins. As they came closer, I could see her treading sure-footed on the deck in her swimsuit and shorts. Milly was standing up at the helm in front of Liza, anticipating the return home. They looked beautiful and joyous and, in other circumstances, the sight of them out on the water would have made my heart sing.

Hannah waved when she saw me, a huge windscreen-wiper of a wave that shifted her weight from one foot to the other.

'We saw Brolly!' she was shouting. As they grew closer, she yelled louder, to be heard above the noise of the engine. 'She was fine. No cuts or anything. It wasn't her in the nets, Mike. And guess what! She was with her baby!' She was beaming—they both were—Liza with a mother's pleasure at her daughter's joy. I stood up, wishing suddenly that I had gone with them, that I could have shared a simple outing full of small happinesses.

'I couldn't believe it when I saw her,' said Hannah, jumping onto the jetty as her mother manoeuvred slowly in and began to secure the boat.

'There. You see? Sometimes good things happen,' Liza said, her face pink with the effort of tying the knots. 'If we have faith.'

I didn't answer her. I suspected Hannah's illuminated smile had made my decision for me, and I was no longer sure that she was right.

THE FOLLOWING MORNING, when Liza returned from the school run I was waiting for her in the car park.

'Hey, gorgeous,' she called, as she reversed in. I had chosen to sleep alone the previous night, and in her smile was the relief of seeing me after what had felt like a day's separation. 'You're a sight for sore eyes.' She climbed out of the car and closed the door behind her.

'Walk with me,' I said.

She blinked and looked at me suspiciously. 'What's up?'

I forced my face into the most neutral expression I could manage. 'I've got some news. I'm going to stop the development. I've—I've spoken to someone behind it, and I think I can persuade them to go elsewhere.'

She lifted a hand to her brow, the better to see my face. 'But—how?' A smile was playing on her lips, as if she daren't give it full vent until she knew what I was saying to be true.

'I don't want you to say anything to anyone until I've made sure. I'm going back to London.'

'London?' The half-smile vanished.

'So you don't need to go anywhere, Liza,' I said slowly.

'You know the development's only half of it now, Mike. I need a clean slate. I need to stop running.'

'Then do it when Hannah's older. Tell the authorities when she doesn't need you so much. It'll keep.'

She stood there and I watched every thought I had had flicker across her face, like clouds scudding across the sky. 'What's going on, Mike?'

'I'm going to make sure you're safe,' I said, 'and that Hannah gets to grow up with her mother.'

She stared at me for a long time, her eyes questioning. 'Are you coming back? When you've done this thing?'

'Probably not,' I said.

There it was, out in the open.

'I thought you wanted . . . I thought you wanted to be with us?'

I said nothing. There was nothing I could say.

'You're not answering my question.'

'I need you to trust me,' I said.

I saw her jaw tighten. I knew she wanted to ask me how I could do this when I had told her I loved her. I knew she wanted to ask me to stay. But she wanted to stay with her daughter more.

'Why won't you trust me enough to talk to me?' she said.

Because I can't make you choose, I told her silently. *But I can carry that burden for you.* 'Do you always ask so many questions?' I said jokingly. I stepped forward and held her, and knew that my heart was broken.

GIVEN THE MOMENTOUS nature of what was about to happen, of what had already happened, my final conversation that day was almost anticlimactic.

'Vanessa?'

She had picked up on the second ring.

'Mike . . .' She let out a long breath. 'I wasn't sure when you'd call.' She sounded unsure of herself. I wondered how long she had been waiting. I had promised to call several hours previously, but had sat in my room, staring at the phone, my fingers refusing to hit the keys. 'Mike?'

'You still want me?'

'Do you want me?'

I closed my eyes. 'We've been through a lot,' I said. 'We've hurt each other. But I'll give it a go. I really will give it a go.'

I was almost relieved when she didn't say anything.

'When's your flight home?' she said.

Monica

When Mike rang me and told me this story . . . I can't lie, my first thought was not, as he put it, how do we protect her? It was too good a story: the battered girlfriend of a political wannabe who fled the country after accidentally killing their child. It had everything: violent crime, long-buried secrets, a dead child, a beautiful blonde. It even had whales and dolphins.

Except it didn't add up. After I'd called Mike to tell him that I'd located the guy, I'd looked again at all the cuttings. I cross-checked that information with every database I could find. And it still didn't add up.

I guessed Mike was royally pissed off with me—he'd left increasingly strident messages on my voicemail about the interview. But I couldn't ring him back, not until this made sense. And I couldn't tell him what I was going to do: I was worried he'd tell me not to. But I know when something odd's going on, and my blood was up. So, on my one weekday off, I headed to Surrey, caught a cab from the station, and shortly after ten I was standing outside a large house in Virginia Water.

'Nice place,' the cabbie said, peering at it through the windscreen.

I soon saw that I wouldn't be able to check out the house as I'd planned: it was surrounded by high hedges, and was so far from the road that I would have drawn attention to myself walking up the long drive. Instead I stood at the bottom of the drive, half hidden by a tree, outside a five-bar gate.

It was a big mock-Tudor affair, with leaded windows. The lawns and flowerbeds were tidy enough to suggest a gardener's vigilant attention. Five or six bedrooms, I thought, staring at it from the roadside. At least three bathrooms. A Volvo estate stood in the drive, and pricey wooden play equipment in the damp garden. I shivered. There was something cold about that house. Mike had told me what had gone on inside it, and I couldn't help but imagine that young woman looking out at the drive as she tried to plot her escape.

Several cars drove by, their occupants turning to stare at me as they passed. It was not the kind of area where people tended to walk, so I stuck out like a sore thumb. As I was considering where to move to, I caught sight of a woman walking past an upstairs window: probably the wife. I wondered what he had told her about his previous life. I wondered whether he treated her well. Then I thought of what Liza had told my brother and wondered whether love had blinded him to the possibility that she was lying to him. How else to explain such huge holes in what she had described?

As I considered what to do next, a girl in a thick blue jumper and jeans came round the side of the house. She might have left the door open; from inside I could just hear the dull murmur of the radio, then the sound of a baby crying and being pacified. As I ducked back, she walked towards me, to the end of the drive, and made to pick up the post from the mailbox. I stepped from behind the tree, trying to look as if I had just been passing.

'Hello there. Is Mr Villiers in?' I asked. 'His office told me he'd be working from home today.' I don't know why I lied. I thought perhaps if I could keep her talking I might find out a little more about him.

'He's in London,' she said. 'He's always in London on Thursday nights.'

'Oh,' I said. 'I must have got it wrong. He's still at the bank, right?'

'Yes.'

She pulled the letters from the box and leafed through them. Then she looked at me. 'I can give you his number, if you like.'

I glanced at my notebook. 'I have it, but thank you. I'll ring his office. Thank you.' I smiled, in a friendly, businesslike way, as if it were of no importance. I would go into the village and have a coffee. I could always come back, once I had worked out the best way to proceed. ''Bye then.'

''Bye.'

The girl stood in front of me, not really paying me any attention, and pushed her hair back behind her ear. Then, as she began to walk slowly towards the house, I noticed she had a pronounced limp.

I've heard that expression: the world just fell away. I hate cliché. Yet that was the only phrase that echoed through my head.

'Excuse me!' I called, not caring who heard me. 'Excuse me!'

She turned round and limped back towards me. 'What?' she said, head tilted to one side. It was then that I saw it. And, for a moment, everything stopped.

'What . . . what's your name?' I asked.

Kathleen

I was making lunch for Hannah when I heard the door slam. That isn't unusual in this house, not with a dog, a near-teenager and guests who leave the sea wind to close doors. But the ferocity with which my ancient portal hit the frame, then the agitated thumping of Mike leaping up several steps at a time made me curse gently. The door to his room banged noisily behind him too, sending a shudder through the house.

'We're not in need of demolition just yet,' I yelled at the ceiling, wiping my hands on my apron.

We had the radio on so at first I couldn't make out what he was yelling, but we both paused at the commotion in his room.

'You think he's having another fight with someone?' said Hannah.

'You get on with your homework, Miss,' I said, but I turned off the radio. This is an old house, wood-built, so from the kitchen you can hear a lot of movement upstairs. Mike dragged the chair back from his desk. 'Monica?' he was yelling into his phone. 'Send it now. Send it *now.*'

Hannah and I exchanged a glance.

'That's his sister,' she said quietly. And I thought, That's the journalist, and my peaceable mood dissolved.

I was making a cheese omelette, and whisked the eggs furiously, trying to lose the dark thread of my thoughts. It was several minutes before I noticed that since Mike's shout there had been no noise at all from upstairs. There was a quality to the silence that made me curious.

I walked to the doorway. 'Mike?' I called up the stairs. 'Everything OK?'

'Kathleen,' he said, and his voice was tremulous. 'I think you'd better come up here.'

As I entered the room he told me to sit on the bed. In truth, he was so unlike himself, that it was a couple of seconds before I agreed to do so. He squatted in front of me, like someone about to propose. Then he said those two little words, and as I heard them I felt the colour drain from my face.

'What kind of joke is this?' I asked, when my voice returned to me.

He stood up and scanned down a load of messages on his computer. Then a little box opened on his screen and there she was. Unbelievably. In full colour. Staring at us with an incomprehension that matched my own.

'This is the picture Monica took today. It looks like her, right?'

My mouth hung open and I was unable to tear my eyes away from that face. And then he told me what his sister had told him.

'Hannah,' I croaked. 'You've got to get Hannah.'

But Hannah must have become curious about what was going on upstairs because she was already in the doorway.

'Hannah, sweetheart,' I said, 'I need you to look at something. I need you to tell me whether this— this looks like . . .'

'*Letty.*' Hannah moved closer to the screen, lifted a finger and traced her sister's nose. '*Letty.*'

'She's alive, sweetheart,' I said, as the tears came and I felt Mike's hand on my shoulder. 'God save us, she's alive.' My thoughts were in turmoil, my heart numbed by the sight of that child, whom I'd never known but whose life and death had hung over this house.

Hannah was the only one of us not crying. 'I knew,' she said, a smile

breaking across her face. 'I knew she couldn't be dead. She never felt dead.'
She turned back to the image again. It was as if she was staring into a
mirror. It's hard to believe now that I could have doubted it.

'Those bastards,' Mike was saying, forgetting Hannah's presence. 'How
can they have kept the truth from her for all those years? How could they do
that to her? How could they do that to the *child*?'

The size of their deception had hit me too, and the language that
emerged from my mouth I haven't heard since I was a wartime barmaid.
'That yellow-bellied, rat-eating son of a rabid dog! That . . . sh—'

'Shark?' suggested Mike, raising an eyebrow.

'Shark,' I affirmed, glancing at Hannah. 'Yes. Shark. I'd sure love to gut
him like one.'

Then Hannah spoke again. 'I still have a sister,' she announced, and the
simple delight in her voice stopped us both. 'Look!' And as Hannah placed
her own face beside that oversized image, so that we could both take in the
reality of that statement, Mike and I turned to each other.

'Liza,' we said, in unison.

WE DIDN'T KNOW how to tell her. She was out on the boat and this news
was too huge, too shocking, to tell her over the radio. Yet we couldn't wait
for her to come in. In the end we borrowed Sam Grady's cutter. With me at
the tiller, we sailed out past the bay to Break Nose Island. The breeze was
light, the seas gentle, and within minutes we were accompanied by pods of
dolphins, the joyful arcs of their bodies echoing the mood on our boat.
'They know!' Hannah said, laughing. 'They've come because they know!'
For once I didn't put her straight. Who was I to say how life worked?

And there she was, coming back in, standing at the helm with Milly
beside her. She had a full boat, largely Taiwanese. The tourists leaned over
the front rails, curious as to why we had approached, some still clutching
their cameras, then snapping madly as they saw the dolphins in our wake.

She spotted us and steered towards us. 'What's up?' she yelled, as we
pulled alongside. When she saw the three of us crammed into the little boat,
she knew we couldn't be there for any ordinary reason.

I looked at Mike, who nodded at me, and I began to shout, but before I
had even said the words, the tears were streaming down my face. 'She's
alive, Liza. Letty's alive.'

Liza looked from me to Mike and back again. Above us, two gulls
wheeled and cried, mocking what I had said.

'It's true! Letty's alive! Mike's sister has seen her.' I waved the picture that Mike had printed off, but the breeze whipped it round my hand and she was too far off to see it.

The colour had drained from her face. 'What do you mean?'

Struggling to keep my balance, I unfurled the picture and held it above my head, in two hands, like a banner. 'Look!' I shouted. 'Look! They lied to you. She never died in the car crash. Letty's alive!'

The tourists, who had been listening intently, hushed, and a few of the Taiwanese, perhaps sensing the enormity of the occasion, began a spontaneous round of applause.

MIKE SAID HE'D never realised how much he loved his sister till that day. In a three-hour conversation, as Liza sat pressed up to him, still pale with shock, she told him how she had arranged to meet Steven Villiers at his office and told him she was following up a story about a respected councillor who had deliberately told his girlfriend that her daughter was dead in order to separate them. A councillor who had systematically beaten his girlfriend until she left in fear of her life.

The shocking thing was how easily the Villiers man had caved in. He went quiet, then said, 'What do you want?' He had married, you see, and had two young sons, and Monica thought that this was a conversation he had probably expected for some time. They struck a deal: restore the child to her mother, and this would remain a family matter. He agreed a little too readily; she had the impression that it wasn't the happiest of families.

He had known where Liza was for years—through a private investigator, probably. The irony was that he had wanted her to stay away from him as much as she had wanted to stay away. He said his mother had told Liza the child was dead, partly because at that point they thought it might be true, and partly out of spite. Then, when they discovered that Liza had disappeared, they'd decided it might be useful to let her believe it, an easy way to have her out of their lives. Villiers had the grace, Monica said, to look a little ashamed. He wanted proper access, he said. Monica told him he could have as much as his daughter wanted.

Then, accompanied by a lawyer, and with a child psychologist at the ready, they went to the house to tell Letty she was going on holiday. It was quick. We worried later that it was too quick, given the shock that the girl experienced on being told that her mother had not abandoned her, after all. But Monica admitted that she'd been afraid Villiers would change his mind.

There were so many lies that Letty would have to learn to disbelieve. Mike's sister said she was a bright kid, that she wanted to know everything. It was night-time there now, and they were letting her sleep, but in the morning—our evening—Monica would ring us and Liza would be able to speak to her.

I SAW THE LIGHT on in the Whalechasers Museum as I let Milly out for her last walk of the night, and I guessed who it might be. I don't bother locking the museum half the time and Milly would let us know if strangers headed up here when they shouldn't. Liza and Hannah were upstairs making their telephone call, so I grabbed a couple of beers and went out there. He was probably feeling like I was, a bit of a spare part.

Besides, I was curious about what Liza had told me the previous day, before her whole world had changed again—about the possibility that the development might not go ahead. It was nothing certain, she said, and she was not meant to tell anyone until it was confirmed. Then she said that Mike would be leaving for good tomorrow and after that she wouldn't say much at all.

He was sitting on one of *Maui II*'s rotten timbers, his shoulders stooped, as if he were carrying a great weight. Given what he had achieved, it seemed an odd stance. Milly shot in past me, wagging her way to him, and he glanced up. 'Oh. Hi,' he said.

'Thought you might like this.' I held out a beer to him. As he took it I sat down on the chair a few feet away and cracked one open myself.

We sat and drank in companionable silence. The barn doors were open, and through them, in the near dark, we could see the shoreline, the distant lights of fishermen's boats preparing for their night's work.

'Thank you,' I said, quietly. 'For everything. I don't understand how you've done it all, but thank you.'

His head dropped then, and I knew something was wrong. I sat and waited. I've been around long enough to know you catch a hell of a lot more fish by keeping still and quiet.

'I don't want to leave,' he said, raising his head again, 'but it's the only way I can stop the development. There was a choice . . . I want you to know this, Kathleen. Whatever you might hear in the future, it's important she knows she was loved.' His eyes were burning into me. 'I don't want you to think badly of me,' he said, choking, 'but I made a promise . . .'

'You really can't tell me what any of this is about?'

He shook his head. I didn't like to push him. Call me old-fashioned, but I think a man becomes physically uncomfortable if you make him talk too much about what he's feeling.

'Mike,' I said finally, 'She'll be OK. She'll have her girls.'

He stood up and walked slowly around the barn. I realised then how sorry I was that he was going. Whatever wrongs he had done us, he had put right in spades and then some. I'm no great romantic—Lord knows, Nino Gaines could tell you that—but when it came to him and Liza I had hoped for a happy ending. I knew now that he was a decent human being.

He stopped in front of my Shark Lady picture. I raised myself out of my chair and walked over to join him.

There I was, smiling into that camera, my seventeen-year-old bathing-suited self preparing to pursue me through the rest of my days.

'I'll let you into a secret,' I said. 'I never caught that ruddy shark.'

That got him. He faced me.

'Nope,' I said. 'My dad's partner caught it. Told me it would look better on the hotel, give us more publicity, if it came from me. I hated lying. Hate it still. But I understand something now. If it hadn't happened, this hotel would never have survived the first five years.' I turned the picture to the wall. 'Sometimes,' I said, 'a lie is the way of least pain for everyone.'

I placed my hand on Mike Dormer's arm, and waited until he felt able to look at me again. He nodded towards the door, as if we should go.

'You know something? I've never seen a tiger shark in this bay. Never,' I said, stepping out into the dark.

'Greg has,' he said, as he made to close the doors behind us.

'You're not listening,' said the Shark Lady.

Mike

I couldn't fill my two suitcases, and the empty space within them was so great that I could almost have fitted one inside the other. Somehow, during my time here, I had shed half of my wardrobe so that all I wore now, day after day, was one of my two pairs of jeans, perhaps a T-shirt and shorts if it was a really warm day.

I was not taking my oilskin: somehow it was too bound up with being here. I didn't pack the jumper I had lent Liza one night when we had sat out by ourselves until 2 a.m., and which I secretly hoped she might want to keep. I had left my laptop in the living room for Hannah, knowing it would be of more use to her. Besides, I couldn't bear to separate Hannah and Liza from that pixellated image. They both sat in front of it for hours, talking, comparing Letty's and Hannah's faces, considering the myriad different ways in which they had changed and not changed.

Liza was out on *Ishmael*—her last trip before they all, too, left for the airport. I had hardly seen her since the previous day and wondered whether a quiet exit with no goodbyes might be the best thing for both of us. At least they would be occupied: this afternoon they would finish doing up Letty's room. Hannah had been allowed the day off school, and they had spent the previous evening painting the room and filling it with the kinds of things a nine-year-old girl might like, and arranging Letty's dolphins. Hannah was up there now, pinning up posters.

I watched all this from a distance, half removed from their happiness, too consumed with my own loss. They might miss me a little, but they had a far greater prize to contemplate, and a whole new life ahead. What was I going back to? To a woman I was not sure I could love in a city that now stifled me.

I thought of having to pick up the pieces of my old life, shoehorning myself into a new job in an anonymous office block. I thought of Dennis, who would doubtless convince me to return—and what was the alternative? I thought of Vanessa's smile, her perfume and high-heeled shoes, our smart apartment, the trappings of our former life, and knew, with a sick feeling, that it meant nothing. Every last atom of me wanted to be here.

The worst of it was that I still liked Vanessa. I still cared about her happiness. And I cared about my own integrity. For those reasons alone it was important that if she held true to her promise I should hold true to mine. Those were the words I would repeat to myself silently several hundred times a day. Then I would visualise the months ahead, of lying awake at night, with Liza's face haunting me, of making love to someone whose body did not instinctively fit my own.

Come on, I told myself sternly, as I walked briskly to the hire car to drive it round to the front of the hotel. Liza had her girls, and I was about to secure their future. I reversed into a space, then sat staring at the dashboard.

My flight was not due until the following morning, but I decided I had to leave now. I would drive to the city and book a room in a hotel for the night.

It meant that I would not see my sister, that I would not witness the reunion, but I knew Monica would understand. If I stayed an hour longer, I might not be able to do the thing I had promised.

As I got out of the car, I heard a familiar whine. Greg's pick-up skidded into the driveway. He climbed out, pulling the brim of his cap over his eyes. 'I heard the news about the little one. Unbelievable. Unbe*liev*able.'

'News travels fast,' I said. But it was a platitude—Hannah had run to the jetty the previous evening, to tell every one of the whalechasers.

He pulled a packet of cigarettes from his pocket and lit one. 'Good on you, mate. I can't pretend I like you but, strewth, I can't argue with some-one who brings children back from the dead, eh?'

'Thanks,' I said.

I went inside to fetch my cases and when I carried them out, Greg was still leaning against his pick-up. 'Going somewhere?'

'London,' I said, swinging the luggage into the open boot.

A slight pause. 'Not coming back?'

'No.'

His face actually lit up. He was as transparent as a child. 'Not coming back. Well, now, that's a shame. For you, I mean. I always thought you were an odd one, mate, and now I know I'm right.'

'Quite the psychologist,' I said. I wished he would get lost.

'Best to stick where you fit in, eh? And I'm sure Liza will get over it. She'll be a whole lot happier now I reckon. And I'll make sure she has enough . . . attention.'

For a moment, the gloves were off. It was as well that Kathleen emerged from the house. 'Mike!' she called, her voice indignant. 'What are you doing with your cases? I thought you weren't going till tomorrow?'

I went towards her. 'I'm—waiting for a call. Then I think I'll head off.'

'You can't leave now,' she said, her hands on her hips. 'You haven't said goodbye to anyone. Hell, I was going to do you a little party tonight. You not even going to hang on till Liza gets back?'

'That's really kind of you, Kathleen, but I think it's best if I go.'

She stared at me, and I wasn't sure whether it was sympathy or frustra-tion in her face. 'You really can't hang on? Just till after lunch?'

I held out a hand. 'Thanks for everything, Kathleen,' I said. 'If any calls come here for me this afternoon will you give them my mobile number? I'll phone you as soon as I know for certain about the development.'

I found it difficult to meet her eyes. Then she hugged me. 'You call me,' she said. 'You don't get to disappear just like that. Doesn't have to be about the ruddy development.'

I walked to my car before the pain in her voice could change my mind.

I HAD TO DRIVE slowly down the coast road because there seemed to be something in both of my eyes and I couldn't see straight. When I got to Whale Jetty I found myself hoping that I might see *Ishmael* coming into the bay, that I might, one last time, see the thin figure, the hair blowing under the cap, steering in, the dog beside her. But there was only the glinting water.

I hadn't even been able to write her a letter: telling her what I felt would have meant telling her the truth, and I couldn't do that. You've done the right thing, I told myself, heading back to the coast road. For once in your life, you've done a good thing.

I HAD BEEN on the highway for only twenty minutes when my mobile rang. I pulled onto the hard shoulder and rummaged in my jacket pocket.

'Mike? Paul Reilly. This is a courtesy call, really. I thought you should be the first to know that the development isn't going ahead.'

She'd done it. I let out a long sigh, not sure whether it was with relief that Vanessa had done as she'd said, or resignation that I had to keep my side of the bargain.

'Well,' I said, 'I know we differ on this, but I'm glad.'

'Can't see it myself. I thought that development would have been a real asset to this area. Pretty unusual for someone to pull the plug so late in the day. I mean, they were after putting the foundations down this week.' His voice lifted in resignation. 'But you can't argue with the money men.'

'Beaker will have done their research,' I said. 'If they thought Bundaberg had the better margins, then—'

'Beaker? It wasn't Beaker. It was the venture capitalists. They pulled the plug unless the site was changed.'

'Sorry—what did you say? I don't understand.'

'They got antsy about the shark, apparently. They heard about all the newspaper reports and took fright.' He sighed. 'I guess from their point of view it's going to be pretty hard to sell watersports holidays to people if they think there are sharks but, really, I think they got it all out of proportion. Seems British people hear the word "shark" and all reason goes out the window.'

Why would Vanessa go to Vallance first? I wondered.

'You've surprised me, Mr Reilly,' I said, my mind working. 'Thanks for the call. But if you'll excuse me, I need to speak to someone.'

I reached into my briefcase for my laptop, realising too late that it wasn't there. Then I wrenched the car back onto the highway and accelerated hard to the next exit.

'DENNIS?'

'Michael? I wondered how long it would be before you rang, you old bastard. Rung to gloat, have you?'

'You know that's not my style.' I had to wedge my phone between ear and shoulder as I negotiated the roundabout into Silver Bay.

'No—what do you want? Calling to beg for your old job back?'

I ignored him. 'So where's it going?'

'Bundaberg. We're using the same model. Heaps better tax breaks. To be honest, you did us a favour.'

There was nobody outside the hotel. I walked through the front door and into the deserted lounge, my phone pressed to my ear, and made for my laptop. It was still where I'd left it.

'*I* did you a favour?'

'Freaking the VCs out, your lobbyist bombarding them with shark tales.'

'My *lobbyist*?' This was weird.

'I have to admit you did a good job, sending all those newspaper reports about sharks. I was pissed off at first—we had to work four days and nights just to keep Vallance on board—but, now I think about it, we wouldn't have made any money in shark-infested waters. Much better off up the coast. So, who was it? More importantly, how much did you pay them? I know professional agitators don't come cheap.'

He hadn't mentioned Vanessa. I'd opened my computer. I glanced down the record of emails sent, trying to work out what had happened.

'So, what's your next move, Mike?' he was saying. 'You know, I made good on my promise. No one will touch you in the City—'

I found the emails that had been sent to Vallance. I opened one and began to read.

'—that said, boyo, if you're desperate, I might be able to find a small opening. To do you a favour.'

Dear Sir, it began. I am writing to let you know of the risk of shark attack at the Silver Bay development . . . I began to laugh. She had done what I had failed to do. She had done what I had thought was impossible.

'Mike?'

'Dennis,' I said, still laughing, 'your professional agitator, your over-priced lobbyist, your reverser of multi-million-pound developments, is an eleven-year-old girl.'

I HAD ONE more call to make and walked outside as I wanted privacy. I stood for a moment before I dialled, breathing in the undisturbed scents that had been there for half a century, and would now remain, if lucky, for half a century more. But I didn't feel any sense of peace. Not yet.

'So, you did it, then,' I said.

'Mike,' she said. 'Yes. You heard. I told you I would.'

She began to talk about how she had booked a table for the night of my return at a restaurant that it was near-impossible for mere mortals to enter. 'We're eating at eight thirty. That should give you plenty of time for—'

'How? How did you persuade your dad to turn everything round?'

'Oh, I can twist Dad round my little finger. You know that.'

'Must have been hard, though, with Vallance so far down the line.'

'Well, I just . . .' She sounded irritated. 'I went over the reasons you and I had discussed and by the end of it he saw sense. He listens to me, Mike, and we had the alternatives ready, as you know. Do you want picking up?'

'I'm not coming, Ness.'

'What?'

'I just checked the emails that went to Vallance from our end, and I guess when you rang me you must have known for, oh, two or three days at least that the development was to be shifted. So, you thought, I'll capitalise on this little opportunity and make myself out to be the great saviour. Earn Mike's undying gratitude.'

'It wasn't like that.'

'Did you think I wouldn't find out that it wasn't down to you?'

There was a long silence.

'I thought . . . I thought that by the time you found out we'd be happy and it wouldn't matter any more.'

'Our whole relationship would have been based on a lie.'

'Oh, you're a fine one to talk about lies. You're the one who did *me* a wrong, if you remember.'

'Which is why I'm not coming back. Good luck, Vanessa,' I said icily.

My ears were ringing when I flipped my phone shut. I stared at it for a moment, then I hurled it as hard as I could into the sea. I felt such extreme emotion erupting inside me that it was all I could do not to roar.

'*God!*' I shouted, wanting to punch something. Wanting to turn cartwheels.

'I'm not sure he'll hear you,' came a male voice from behind me. I spun round to see Kathleen sitting at the end of the whalechasers' table with Nino Gaines, watching me calmly.

'That was a very nice phone, you know,' Kathleen told Nino. 'This generation is so wasteful. They're all the same.'

'Emotional too. We didn't do all that yelling in my day,' said Nino.

I took a step towards them. 'My room,' I said, trying to slow my breathing. 'Any chance . . . any chance I can keep it a little longer?'

'Reckon you'll have to check your books, Kate,' Nino told her.

'I'll see if it's still available. We'll be getting busier now . . .'

I stood there, my heart-rate slowing, grateful for the two gently mocking old people before me, and for the sun, the benign glinting blue of the bay, the prospect of creatures dancing joyfully, unseen beneath the water. For the thought of a carefree young woman in a battered old cap out chasing whales.

Kathleen motioned to me to sit down and pushed a beer towards me.

I loved this beer, I thought, as I lowered the cold bottle from my lips. I loved this hotel, this little bay. I was unable quite to grasp the magnitude of what had happened. I would stay here for as long as they would have me. The thought filled me with the closest thing to contentment I have yet known. I leaned back in my seat and the three of us sat in silence.

'Greg never caught that shark, did he?' I said, at last.

Kathleen Whittier Mostyn, legendary Shark Lady, laughed, and when she turned to face me there was a steely glint in her eye. 'One thing I've learned in my seventy-odd years, Mike. If a shark wants to bite you, as far as I'm concerned, you do whatever the hell you have to just to stay alive.'

Hannah

It takes three hours to drive from Silver Bay to Sydney airport, another twenty minutes to find a parking space, and on top of that, in our case, four lots of fifteen minutes' stopping time for me to be sick out of the back door with nerves. My tummy still gets me—it was like that every time I went out on a whale-watching trip. Auntie K told me that it didn't matter—I heard her telling the others she'd brought four kitchen rolls in expectation—and Mike had set off an hour early, thanks to her warnings.

There were five of us in Mr Gaines's seven-seater—Mike, Mum, Mr Gaines, Auntie K and me. A convoy of trucks, trailing bits of net and lines and probably smelling of fish, all pretending not to be there, was following us. Every time we stopped they stopped too, but none of them got out. No one had wanted to come too close, knowing what my mum was like about her privacy, but everyone had wanted to be there. My mum didn't care. To be honest, I don't think she'd have noticed if the Queen of England had turned up to watch. For twenty-four hours she had hardly spoken, just stared at her watch and calculated. If Mike hadn't stopped her, I think she'd have moved into the arrivals lounge two days ago and waited there.

We got there fifteen minutes before the flight arrived. At least twenty more, Mike calculated, for baggage and Passport Control. And for every single one of them, there Mum stood, her hands gripping the rail, while we tried to make conversation around her, eyes on the gate.

Finally, just as I thought I might be sick again, the first trickle of passengers from flight QA2032 came through. We stared in silence, each of us straining to see the distant figures through the swinging doors. What if she didn't come? Worse, what if she came and we didn't recognise her?

And suddenly there she was. My sister, with Mum's blonde hair and a crooked nose like mine, holding tightly to Mike's sister's hand. She was wearing blue jeans and a pink hooded top, and walked with a limp. Mike's sister saw us and waved. She said something to Letty, and Letty nodded, her face towards us, and they began to walk faster.

We were all crying then, even before they had reached the barrier. My mother had begun to shake. Aunt Kathleen was saying, 'Thank God, oh, thank God,' into a handkerchief and even Mike was gulping. But I was smiling as well as crying because everything was going to be all right.

And as Letty got close Mum ducked under the barrier and started to run. She and my sister locked eyes and it was as if they were magnets, as if there was nothing in the world that could stop them moving towards each other. My mother grabbed her and Letty was sobbing and I pushed through then, and held on to them too, wrapped in arms and kisses and tears.

The sound that came from my mother, as she rocked my sister in her arms, was both terrifying and glorious and spoke of all the love and pain in the world. It echoed through the great arrivals hall and sounded, Aunt Kathleen said afterwards, exactly like the song of a humpback whale.

EPILOGUE

My name is Kathleen Whittier Gaines and I'm a seventy-six-year-old bride. Even to say those words makes me wince with the silliness of it all. Yes, he caught me in the end. He told me if he was going to pop his clogs he'd like to do it knowing I was nearby, and I figured that was not a lot to ask of a woman, not when she knew she had been loved by a man most of her life.

I don't live in the hotel any more. Not full time, anyway. Nino said he had to be near his vines, and I told him I wasn't going to spend the rest of my days inland. So we split our week between our two houses, and this arrangement suits us both fine.

Mike and Liza live in the hotel, which is probably a little smarter and a little more welcoming than it was when I ran it alone. Every now and then Mike gets ideas about making more money, and I disagree, and the rest of them nod and smile and wait quietly for him to blow himself out.

Nino bought the old Bullen land. A wedding present for me, he said. A bit of security for the girls. He and Mike have ideas for the space. They occasionally go down together, but when it comes down to it, neither of them seems like they actually want to do anything.

Down the coast road, the southern migration is shaping up just fine. There are reports every day of pods, mothers and babies, and passenger numbers are pretty well what they were at the same time last year. The whalechasers come and go, the occasional new face replacing the old. Yoshi went back to Townsville to study whale conservation, promising to return, and Lance often talks about visiting her, but I doubt he will. Greg is courting a twenty-four-year-old barmaid. He spends less time at the hotel, anyhow, and I can see that suits Mike fine.

And Letty thrives. She and Hannah hang on to each other as if it was five days they were separated, not five years. Several times I've found them sharing a bed, and made to move them, but Liza says not to bother. 'They'll want space from each other soon enough.' She says, looking at them entwined. There's such a lightness in her voice that I can't believe she's the same woman.

The first few weeks were strange. We tiptoed around Letty, afraid that this strange series of events would leave her shattered. For a long time she stayed glued to her mother, as if afraid that she would be ripped apart from her again. She was better once her father had called: he told her he was happy for her to stay here, and would allow all decisions to be hers.

And there it ends. Mike's sister, true to her word, never printed her story. Mike says it's actually a love story—not about him and Liza, although you only have to look at them laughing together to know that that's the case—but about Liza and her daughters. Sometimes, if he's teasing me, he says it's about me and Nino. I tell him I don't see it that way. Look out at the sea for long enough, at its beauties and terrors, and you'll have all the stories you need—of love and danger, and about what life lands in your nets. And the fact that sometimes it's not your hand on the tiller, and you can do no more than trust that it'll all work out OK.

Almost every day now, if Liza doesn't have too many trips booked, they head out together on *Ishmael* to see the whales still making their way back to their feeding grounds. At first I thought it was Liza's way of binding them together, but soon I realised that they were as drawn to it as she was. The girls like to watch the humpbacks disappear and enjoy the thought that there's a whole life beneath that they cannot see. Songs being sung into an abyss and lost for ever, relationships being forged, babies being nurtured and loved. At first Mike laughed at them for being fanciful, but now he shrugs and admits: what the hell does any of us know?

And I watch the four of them now, running down Whale Jetty in the sunshine, and I think that this story is about an elusive balance; about a truth we all struggle with whenever we're blessed enough to be visited by those creatures or, indeed, whenever we open our hearts—that sometimes you can damage something wonderful merely through proximity.

And that sometimes, Mike adds firmly, you don't have a choice. Not if you want to really live.

JOJO MOYES

Born: London, August 1969
R & R: riding in the Essex countryside
Comfort read: Enid Bagnold's *National Velvet*

Jojo Moyes was 40,000 words into a new novel and had just finished a hectic promotional tour of Australia with her husband and their young family, when the inspiration for *Silver Bay* struck her. 'The children had been so good and we felt we should splash out and end with a holiday before coming home. We were out there in the middle of the Australian winter and we had to think of something we could do with two young children and a baby that didn't involve flying again. We had already done something like eleven flights in three weeks! I went online and found a place a few hours north of Sydney, where one of the things on offer was whale watching.

'The first time we went out, the seas were rough and we were in a small boat that creaked every time it hit a big wave. My daughter started crying almost immediately, the baby needed feeding and my other son fell asleep with his head on the table and had to be propped up so that he didn't fall and hurt himself. It was hilarious! As it turned out, I was the only one of us who made it up onto the top deck to see the whales, so nobody else got the whale-watching bug quite like I did. Whales are very benign creatures. They're curious and faithful and jealous, and they mourn and behave erratically when they are grieving. They do show lots of similarities with human behaviour.'

Jojo was also intrigued by the different kinds of people who were involved in whale watching. 'You'd meet enthusiasts dedicated to the whales, dolphins and conservation, but you'd also find a whole variety of young people, such as students, working on the big tourist boats: a disparate community who wouldn't necessarily fit together in any other situation. I chatted to them quite a lot, and they tended to hang out together at night, which gave me the idea of Kathleen's hotel and how these people would congregate outside in the evenings, talking and drinking.'

Was Kathleen based on anybody Jojo met in Australia? 'Funnily enough, she was inspired by a photograph I saw in our hotel. On the walls there were pictures of the area back in the twenties. And there was this sepia photograph of a teenage girl holding up a huge game fish. It was such an incongruous image, because you certainly wouldn't expect to see a young woman struggling with a game fish back in those days. She gave me the opening to *Silver Bay*, and from the moment I started writing her I knew her. Kathleen's the kind of older woman I just love and I hope I'll become.'

Jojo Moyes began to invent short stories as a child, but stopped in her teens when her diary was stolen by somebody who mockingly repeated chunks of it at her and put her off writing anything for ten years. At university, however, she contributed articles to the student newspaper, which led her to a career in journalism and, after stints on various smaller publications, a job on the *Independent*'s newsdesk. 'I loved working as a journalist, but after I'd had my daughter, eight years ago, the little voice that kept telling me I wanted to write fiction just got louder.'

She completed three novels before her first published book, *Sheltering Rain*, became a best seller and gave her the confidence to become a full-time novelist. Her second, *Foreign Fruit*, won the 2004 Romantic Novelist of the Year Award. *Silver Bay* is Jojo's fifth novel, and there's a sixth book on its way. 'I'm unbelievably lucky to be able to do what I really want to do and also see a lot of my family. But the biggest stress in my life is not having enough time to plot and write my books, so twice a year I shut myself away in a quiet room in a health farm for three days. I must be the only person who doesn't arrive home looking healthy, but I know that I'm much easier to live with afterwards!'

SONG OF THE SOUTHERN SEAS

In an incredible display of power, an adult humpback male propels its body out of the sea with just a few beats of its flukes, or tail.

The annual winter migration of humpback whales from the cold of Antarctica to warmer seas, such as those around the Great Barrier Reef, happens very much as it is described in *Silver Bay*. Female humpbacks and their young, as they head back to southern waters, may be temporarily accompanied by a male who is termed an 'escort'.

Some scientists now believe that the song of the male humpback—in which sound patterns are repeated for up to fifteen minutes or more—may well be a means of communicating with the vulnerable female and her calf.

LOSING

NICCI FRENCH

YOU

Nina Landry's fortieth birthday begins in a mood of cheerful anticipation, as she prepares to jet off for some winter sun with her two children and new boyfriend. But, as noon arrives, and yet another call to her daughter's mobile goes unanswered, unease fills her mind and the day turns into a fear-filled race against time.

Sometimes I still felt that I had fetched up on the edge of the world. The wintry light slanting onto the flat, colourless landscape; the moan of the wind, the shriek of sea birds and the melancholy boom of the foghorn far out at sea all sent a shiver through me. But I stamped my feet on the ground to warm them and told myself that in a few hours I would be far away.

Rick Blythe dropped the spanner and straightened up from the open bonnet of my car. His unshaven face was raw from the cold northeasterly that whipped over us, and his pale blue eyes were watering. His dark curls were damp and lay flat on his head. He blew on his whitened fingers and tried to flash me his boyish smile, but I could see it was an effort.

'Rick,' I said, 'it's kind of you, but you don't need to do this. It was just a rattle in the engine and I thought something had come loose. I can take it to the garage after we get back from holiday.'

His wife, Karen, came out of the front door with three mugs of coffee on a tray. She was almost as tall as Rick, big-boned but thin. Sometimes she looked striking, and then I could understand why the pair of them had got together, but too often she seemed gaunt and unfinished, as if she hadn't paid proper attention to herself. Her brown hair was peppered with grey, and pulled into a hasty bun, her skin was bracketed with worry lines. She had the bossy abruptness of someone who was fundamentally shy, and her manner usually swung between sprightly sarcasm and barely suppressed anger.

'White no sugar, right? How's it going, then? All sorted?'

Rick grimaced at her in exasperation, then down at the ground on which lay the battery from my car and a couple of other parts.

'You said when you came back that it would only take a couple of minutes. That was before ten.' She glanced ostentatiously at the watch on her wrist. 'You've been out here for nearly three-quarters of an hour.'

'I know,' said Rick, wryly.

'Nina's got a plane to catch.' She cast me an amused smile that said, *Men*.

'It's all right,' I said. 'I've done most of the packing for me and Jackson, and Charlie promised she'd be ready by the time I was back.'

Rick's head disappeared beneath the bonnet again. There was the sound of several sharp taps and a mumbled curse. It seemed funny but I bit my lip to forestall even the tiniest hint of a smile. I pulled off my gloves to pick up my coffee mug and wrapped my fingers round it, grateful for the warmth, the curl of steam that licked at my cold face.

'Christmas in the sunshine instead of this endless cold grey drizzle,' said Karen, and pulled her quilted jacket more closely round her. 'What time does your plane go?'

'Not until six. I'm picking Christian up on the way to Heathrow.'

I said it casually, but felt a small prickle of nervous happiness in my chest: Christian and I had been friends for nearly eighteen years, lovers for just a few months, and now, for two weeks, the four of us would all be together in the Florida Keys. We would be a family unit, going on trips, making plans, collecting shared stories that we could retell later, even eating breakfast together. Except Charlie, my daughter, never ate breakfast: she acted as though toast was immoral. I hoped she would behave herself.

'I think Christmas should be cancelled,' Karen was saying. 'Eamonn has a kind of ideological objection to it anyway, and is always trying to make us celebrate the winter solstice instead, stand round a bonfire at midnight like witches. Rick tries to make us play board games and Charades and Wink Murder, even though you can't play Wink Murder with just three people, and I . . .' She raised her eyebrows. 'I'm the one who drinks too much and burns the turkey.'

Rick came round to the driver's door, leaned in and turned the key in the ignition. 'Right,' he said. There was a hasty splutter, then silence. He pulled a face that was a caricature of confusion and distress. This was what he did in life. He helped people, he fixed things; he was unflappably, charmingly capable. People turned to him, just as I had this morning.

'At least you've solved the rattle,' said Karen, gaily, and gave a small, explosive snort.

'What?' said Rick, with a glance at her that she pretended not to see.

'The car won't rattle if you can't switch it on.'

His face went a scary shade of crimson. He looked at his watch and I cast a surreptitious glance to it as well.

'Shall we just call the garage?' I suggested. 'Or the AA? I'm a member.'

'Well,' began Rick. 'It might just be—'

'Don't be ridiculous,' said Karen. 'You've got nothing on today, have you? Just working on your boat. Though God knows why on the first day of your holiday. You can't just take Nina's car apart and leave it like that. She's got to get to the—'

'I *know*. How old is this car, anyway?' Rick stared at the rusty little Rover as if it was one of his more hopeless pupils.

'About ten years,' I said. 'It was already quite old when I got it.'

Rick gave a grunt as if the car's age was to blame for the situation.

'Can't you work backwards?' said Karen. 'At least you could get it back to the way it was when Nina drove it here.'

'What do you think I'm doing?' Rick asked, with effortful calm.

'Don't worry, Nina,' Karen said reassuringly.

'I'm not worried,' I said, and it was true. I knew that in a few hours, even if I had to get a taxi to Heathrow, we'd be in the air, far from the pinched, icy days of English winter. I imagined sitting beside Christian and gazing out of the window as London became an intricate grid of orange and white lights.

For thirty-eight years, I had lived in a city where I could go a whole day without seeing the horizon. Here, on Sandling Island, it was all horizon: the miles of marshes, the saltings, the grey, wrinkled sea. Now it was mid-morning and from where I stood—facing west towards the mainland—I could see only the glistening mud flats with their narrow, oozing ditches of water where waders were walking with high-stepping delicate legs. It was low tide. Little boats tipped at a steep angle to show their blistered, slimy hulls; their halyards chinked and chimed in the wind. From my own house, a bit further round to the southeast, I could make out the sea and sometimes, when I woke in the morning and opened my eyes on its grey, shifting expanse, I still wondered how on earth I'd landed up there.

It was Rory who had wanted to come, who for years of our marriage had dreamed of leaving London, giving up his job as a solicitor and running a restaurant instead. At first, it had just been a daydream, an if-only that I didn't really share, but bit by bit it had taken on the harder edge of an obsession, until at last he'd found premises on Sandling Island and dragged his reluctant family with him to begin a new life. It was only sixty miles from London but, rimmed as it was by the tidal estuary and facing out to open sea, it had the feel of a different world, gripped by weather and seasons; full of wild spaces, loneliness, the strange call of sea birds and sighing winds. It was even cut off from the mainland every so often, when the highest of high tides covered the causeway. From my bedroom, I could hear the waters lapping at the shingle shore, the foghorns booming out at sea. Sometimes, when the island was wrapped in the darkness of night, I could scarcely bear the sense of solitude.

Yet I was the one who had fallen half in love with Sandling Island while Rory had been driven mad by it. Somewhere, the dream had gone wrong. There was an argument with a supplier about the ovens, cash failed to flow and the restaurant had never even opened. As he found himself trapped by the fantasy he'd held for so long, Rory no longer knew what he was for or even who he was. Eventually the only way out was to run away.

'Sorry.' I turned my attention back to Karen, who was saying something.

'It's your birthday, isn't it?' she repeated.

'That's right.'

'And not just any birthday.'

'Forty,' I said reluctantly. 'It's one of the ones you're not supposed to be happy about. How did you know?'

She gave a shrug. 'Everyone knows everything about everyone round here. Happy birthday, anyway.'

'Thanks.'

'Do you really mind about it?'

'I'm not sure. A friend of mine once told me—'

'I minded,' she said. 'I looked at myself in the mirror, and I thought, That's you now. No escape. Nothing turns out the way you expect, does it?'

'I think I'm getting there,' said Rick. 'Give me my coffee, will you?'

He had a streak of black grease on his jaw that rather suited him, and a rip in his jacket. I watched as he took a large gulp of coffee.

I had a list in my mind that I kept adding to: pack swimming stuff, goggles and sun cream; remember the Christmas presents, including the snorkel and flippers I'd bought for Christian, who was a marine biologist yet lived many miles from the coast; some dollars; books for the plane; packs of cards. Leave out the dog food and instructions for Renata . . .

'I've been wanting to ask,' Rick moved closer to me and spoke in a low tone, 'how's Charlie doing now, Nina? Are things better?'

'I think so,' I said cautiously. 'You can't really tell. At least, I can't with Charlie. She's quite private, you know.'

'She's a teenager,' said Rick. 'Teenagers are meant to be private. Especially with their parents. Look at Eamonn, for Christ's sake.'

'What's this?' Karen moved in closer, a flicker of interest in her eyes.

'Charlie's had a rough time at school,' I said. I didn't want to talk about this because it was Charlie's story, not mine. I didn't want to discuss it lightly. I imagined Charlie's pale, truculent face behind the turbulent fall of her reddish hair. 'Rick found out about it. He talked to the girls who were bullying her, and to their parents. And to me. He was very helpful.'

'Girls can be cruel,' said Karen, with a sweeping sympathy.

'She was at a sleepover at one of their houses last night,' I said. 'Tam's. Maybe that's a breakthrough. I haven't seen Charlie yet. It would be a good way to end the term.'

'She'll be fine, you know,' said Rick, putting down his mug and reluctantly picking up the spanner once more. 'Being bullied is horrible. Sometimes I think we forget how undermining it can be. Especially if we're teachers, because we come to take it for granted, don't you think? But Charlie's resilient. Very bright, with a mind of her own. I always enjoy having her in my class. You should be proud of her.'

I smiled gratefully at him.

'She's got all those piercings, hasn't she?'

'For God's sake, Karen, what on earth has that got to do with anything?' Rick tweaked a knob with his spanner.

'I just thought that maybe she got picked on because she seems different.'

'Different? Have you seen Amelia Ronson recently? She's had her right eye half sewn together, and talking of different, look at our own son . . . Oh, speak of the devil.'

A baroque figure had appeared on the doorstep, wrapped in a bottle-green trench coat that almost reached the ground, bare grubby feet poking out beneath it. Eamonn had a face so pale it looked like a mask, a mask that was pierced with rings in several places. His eyes were Rick's eyes, but sad. His mane of tangled matt-black hair had green streaks in it. His fingernails were painted black and he had a swirling tattoo on his right forearm. He always appeared unwashed, hung over, drugged-up and ferociously glum, though when he smiled, he looked sweet and lost, younger than his seventeen years. I knew from Rick that he was a problem child, an all-out Goth on a small island that regarded him with suspicion or hilarity; a loner; a bright lad who felt he didn't belong. I also knew that he and his parents could hardly manage to get through a minute together without arguing. But

I'd always got on with him. He liked talking to me about funny little number problems he'd come across in books—after all, I am an ex-accountant masquerading as a maths teacher—and about God (or the lack of any God). And he liked being around me in case Charlie walked through the door. Mothers notice these things.

Karen looked at her watch. 'Do you know what time it is?' she said.

'No,' said Eamonn.

'It's gone half past ten,' she said.

'Low tide's in ten minutes,' Eamonn said, as if it was the most logical response. He wrinkled his face in distaste. 'We're surrounded by putrid-smelling mud.'

'I thought you might have got up and gone out.'

'How do you know I didn't?'

'That'll be the day,' said Rick, from somewhere inside my engine.

'Hello, Eamonn,' I said brightly, trying to forestall another argument.

'Happy birthday.' He gave an abrupt half-bow.

'Everyone really does know.' I laughed.

'Charlie told me,' he said.

'Have you seen her recently?' I began, but then my mobile sang in my pocket, an irritating jangle, and I turned away. My ex-husband was already in mid-sentence by the time I brought the phone to my ear, and it took me a few seconds to separate the stream of sounds into recognisable words.

'. . . and if I'd known, fuck it, that you'd turn out to be the kind of mother who'd take my children away from me at Christmas and fly off with a man who hardly knows them to the other side of—'

'Rory, Rory, hold on . . .' I walked a few steps down the driveway.

'Just because I went off the rails a bit, does that mean I've forfeited the right to see them and they're growing up so quickly my little children only of course they're not so little any more and now there's this Christian and soon they'll stop thinking of me as their father that's what you want isn't it—'

'What's up?' I hated the way my voice took on a calming tone, as if I was murmuring to a scared horse, all the while wanting to slide a bridle over its head. I knew what his face was like when he was ranting, screwed up in wretched anger, an unnerving replica of Charlie when she was upset. I knew there were tears in his eyes and that he'd been drinking. 'You've known for weeks we were going away. You said it was fine. We discussed it.'

'At least you could have let me see them before they go,' he said. 'Just for a bit, to say happy Christmas.'

'That's not possible,' I said. I heard a crunching on the gravel behind me and turned to find Karen making exaggerated semaphores with her arms and mouthing incomprehensible words at me. Behind her, my car's engine coughed and rasped, then stuttered into life. I held up a finger, signifying I'd only be a few seconds, making a pathetic attempt to suggest to the eagerly eavesdropping Karen that I was in a perfectly civilised discussion. 'We're leaving in an hour or so for the airport.'

'I'm speaking about principle. You know that word? Principle? The principle of a father seeing his daughter.'

'You've got a son as well,' I said. I had always hated the way he was besotted with Charlie and often seemed barely to notice eleven-year-old Jackson, who adored him.

'Of a father seeing his children. That's what I'm speaking about.' His voice broke up.

'You're on your mobile. You're not driving, are you?' Drink-driving was what I meant but didn't say.

'I got your solicitor's letter.'

I was wary now. I'd asked my solicitor, Sally, who was also a close friend, to write a letter to his solicitor. It had been the first step on an unpleasant road. The letter warned that if his behaviour with Jackson and Charlie didn't become more rational I would be forced to seek a restraining order. I'd done it after their last visit, when he'd got drunk and knocked Jackson over. The children hadn't told me about it until I'd insisted on knowing how the bruise on Jackson's shoulder had come about.

'You just want to take them away,' Rory said.

'I don't,' I said hopelessly.

'It's Christmas and I won't see them.'

'I've got to go. I'll ring you from home in a few minutes. Have a strong coffee or something and I'll call you.' I clicked the phone off, then blinked and hoped it might look as if it was just the wind in my face.

'Oh dear,' said Karen. 'Upset?'

'He's fine.' I felt my pity flare into protectiveness before Karen's blatant curiosity. 'I mean, no.'

'Christmas can be difficult for the absent father, can't it?'

'I guess.'

'And, after all, Rory was always rather . . . volatile,' she said at last, with heavy-handed tact. 'Like Charlie,' she added. 'Not like you and Jackson. You're always so polite and methodical.'

I turned with relief to my now nicely chugging car. 'That's fantastic, Rick. Thanks so much.'

'Don't mention it.'

'Now go and work on your boat,' I said. I stood on tiptoe and gave him a kiss on both cold, stubbly, grease-stained cheeks. 'I'm going to collect Jackson and finish the packing. 'Bye, Karen.' I kissed her too, missing her cheek and landing on her nose. 'Thanks for the coffee. Take care, Eamonn.'

I got into the car, pulled the door shut and wound down the window.

'Happy Christmas,' I called, as I reversed down the drive. I waved, then swung into the narrow lane. 'And new year.'

I put it into gear and drew away, free. The car rattled happily as I went.

As soon as I had turned inland and was out of sight, I pulled over, tugged my mobile out of my back pocket and phoned Christian. The engine was still running, and the heating system blew warm air onto my hands. Outside, gusts of wind blew twigs and tin cans along the road. He didn't answer his land line, so I tried his mobile but only got his voicemail.

'It's just me,' I said into it. 'And I don't really know why I'm calling.'

I had first met Christian at university when I was in the third year of my degree in maths. He was a graduate in marine biology. I was going out with Rory by then and I used to spend every weekend in London with him. We were planning our future together, and university already felt like part of my past. I liked Christian and his circle of friends, but because he was of the world I was preparing to leave, I don't remember him very well. I've tried, but he's a blur. We had a drink together a few times. I think I once went to his house and had a meal with lots of other people there. He says we danced together more than once; he swears he once put his arm around me when we were in a pub. Though we promised to keep in touch, we hadn't really. He sent me a postcard from Mexico several years ago, and it took me a few seconds to work out who 'Christian', signed with an inky flourish, actually was. Two years ago I heard from a mutual acquaintance that the relationship he'd been in had broken up and I thought then of getting in touch, but I never did. I sent him a change-of-address card when we moved to Sandling Island, but assumed it would never reach him.

Six months ago, he called me out of the blue to say he was going to be in East Anglia for a conference, and maybe we could meet. I almost made an excuse. Rory had left in a maelstrom of tears and smashed dreams, and I felt lonely, bewildered and reclusive. I had already had a forlorn, short-lived fling, and I knew it wasn't the answer to anything. Certainly not to loneliness. All I really wanted was to spend time with the children, and work on the house and the small, nettle-filled garden. I was trying to create a tiny haven for us, filled with the smell of fresh paint and baking, and I didn't really want to make an effort for a half-remembered stranger.

In the end, I arranged to meet him because I couldn't think of a reason not to quickly enough. I told him as much at the end of that first meeting, because even by then—two and a half hours in—I wanted to be honest with him. I felt I could trust him. He didn't seem to be trying to impress me or pretend in any way to be someone he wasn't. Had he always been like that, I wondered—and why hadn't I noticed?

He was still slim, still boyish-looking, but his unruly hair was shorter and streaked with grey, and there were crow's-feet round his eyes. I tried to fit this fortyish face with the smooth, eager one from the past, and I could feel him doing the same with me. Our ghosts were with us. We walked along the sea wall, with the lovely light of an early spring evening gradually thickening into dusk, and we talked. He told me the names of the birds that glided on the currents although, as an islander, I was the one who should have known. But that became part of the flirtatious joke. He came back and had a glass of wine at my house; he played a computer game with Jackson (and lost), and when he met Charlie, who burst into the room with mud on her shoes and a dangerous glint in her eyes, he was friendly without being sycophantic or matey. He rang me almost as soon as he had left the house. He told me he was crossing the causeway and the water was nearly over the road, and would I invite him for dinner the next day? He would bring the pudding and the wine, and what did the children like to eat?

Now, having left the message, I put down my phone and set off once more towards the centre of town, past the shops and the church, the garage, past the building that had been going to be Rory's seafood restaurant, with its 'To Let' sign swinging above its blank windows. I felt a sudden twinge of guilt. I'd dropped Jackson off with his best friend, Ryan, just after breakfast and had promised to collect him very soon. 'Soon' is an elastic concept but I'd heard Ryan's mother, Bonnie, talk about Christmas shopping and the day was advancing. I got to Ryan's house in just a few minutes—practically everywhere on Sandling Island was a few minutes' drive from everywhere else—and knocked on the door.

I was carried inside on a wave of apologies.

'I'm so very sorry,' I said to Bonnie. 'You were going out. I've sabotaged your day.'

'It's no problem,' she said, with a smile.

That made it even worse. Even though we'd been on the island for less than two years and I still felt I was finding my feet, Bonnie was one of the people I had decided would be a friend. She was in the same position as I was—bringing up a young son alone—and she was doing it with uncomplaining cheerfulness. She had short hair, red cheeks and was quite large. It wouldn't take very much make-up to turn her into a circus clown.

'But you said something about Christmas shopping?'

'That's right. I have a rule: all Christmas shopping has to be done in one day. And this is the day.'

'Or, in fact, half a day, in this case,' I said anxiously.

'Three-quarters of a day. It's not eleven yet. Ryan and I are heading into town and we'll be back in about six hours, laden like packhorses.'

'So I'd better say happy Christmas,' I said, 'and a happy new year and everything.'

'That's right,' said Bonnie. 'You're flying off. That's the way to turn forty. I'm so sorry we won't get to see you over the holiday. But let's meet up properly in the new year.'

I said I'd like that. Then I went to retrieve Jackson from where I'd left him, in front of a computer game with Ryan, who grunted but barely looked up as we gave Bonnie a Christmas-and-new-year hug and went out.

Once back in the car, Jackson retrieved another miniature computer game from his pocket and started to play. I glanced across at his serious face, the tip of a pink tongue sticking out in ferocious concentration, and didn't attempt conversation. I was going over my mental list again: passports, tickets, credit cards. If I got to the airport with those items, two children and one nearly new boyfriend, nothing else mattered.

I took the scenic route home. Instead of snaking through the back streets, I drove down the main street, imaginatively named The Street, wound to the left to reach the beach and turned right past the deserted caravan site, the closed-up beach huts, and the boat-maker's yard, which was now full of boats pulled up for the winter.

Our house was in a motley line of cottages that lined The Saltings, just across the road from the boatyard and mooring jetties. They were odd, ill-sorted and squeezed in at strange angles as if each had had to be fitted into a space slightly too small for it. Ours was probably the oddest of all. It was made of clapboard and looked more than anything like a square wooden boat that had been dragged onto land, turned upside-down and unconvincingly disguised with a grey-slate roof. It had been hard to sell because it was damp and the rooms were poky, but Rory and I had fallen in love with it immediately. From our bedroom windows we could see mud and sea and beyond that nothing except sky.

As Jackson and I approached the door, we heard a desperate scratching, whimpering and groaning from inside.

'Stop that, Sludge,' I shouted, as I fiddled with the key in the lock. The door opened and a black apparition flew at us.

The time between our arrival on the island and Rory leaving had been a disaster of unpaid bills and half-finished building work, then more bills. His sole contribution to the household in that terrible period had been to give in to the entreaties of Charlie and Jackson over many years for a dog. He obtained a labrador that looked like an oversized mole, christened her Sludge, left her with me and departed. When he walked out, I couldn't believe it. I literally couldn't compute in my brain how he could be somewhere else, away from the children.

However, it quickly became all too clear that Sludge would never leave us. As we came in and she went through her emotional welcome home, Jackson asked for the hundredth time why we couldn't take her with us on holiday and I said because she's a dog, and he said that we should get her a pet passport and I said that pet passports took a lot of time and money, and I didn't even know if they had them for the States.

Charlie and I had had an animated discussion on the phone the previous evening. I had said that I wasn't sure it was such a good idea for her to be out the night before we went away. She had hardened her voice in a way I knew well, and asked why. I said there was a lot to do and she said she could do it when she got back. It never became an argument because really I felt relieved, and she knew it, that her enemies were, perhaps, becoming her friends. So when she said that she could come back early and feed Sludge, put the washing out, tidy her room and do her packing, I didn't say anything sarcastic. She had said she would do her paper round, too, on her way home. There was plenty of time. And she was right. There *was* plenty of time.

I hadn't fed Sludge this morning because Jackson or Charlie liked to do that. And Sludge had done what Sludge always did when she hadn't been fed: she found something else to eat. In this case it was a box of porridge oats. Oats and fragments of box were scattered through the living room. I took a deep breath. This was the first day of the holidays: nothing could make me angry. At least she hadn't eaten the mail, which had been pushed through the door in my absence—it was mostly birthday cards, as far as I could see.

I put them to one side to open later, picked up the fragments of box, then took out the vacuum cleaner and in a few minutes the room was as it had been. Jackson fed Sludge, not that she needed much feeding now.

Nor was I angry when I went into the kitchen and found the clothes still in the washing machine. If Charlie hadn't fed Sludge, it was hardly likely that she would have hung out the washing. I bundled the clothes we needed for our holiday into the dryer and turned the dial to forty minutes.

It was just about certain that Charlie wouldn't have tidied her bedroom or packed either. I went upstairs and gave her room a glance. I knew that the bed hadn't been slept in but it looked as if it had been, then jumped on. Clothes lay on the carpet where they had been dropped, along with a belt, an empty violin case, a fake tigerskin rug, pencils, a broken ruler, scissors, a pair of flip-flops, CDs with no cases, CD cases with no CDs, a couple of teen magazines, the top half of a pair of pyjamas and three bath towels. Charlie seemed to prefer using a clean towel after each bath or shower, though not to the extent of putting the dirty ones in the washing basket. Since she had had this new bedroom she had been firmly private about it. I didn't even clean it. We had an agreement that I would leave her to order it as she wished, so long as she tidied up in the rest of the house. She hadn't exactly kept her end of the bargain, but I had kept mine.

In the past, Charlie had always been open with me about all her fears and problems, until sometimes I felt heavy with the weight of her confessions. That had changed, as it had to, as she changed and grew. It wasn't that I believed she had important secrets to keep from me. I knew that she needed a door she could lock and a space she could call her own. Sometimes I felt excluded, but I couldn't separate that feeling from all of my emotions at watching my only daughter become a woman; someone separate from me with her own life.

So I didn't do any clearing up or any of her packing. I looked at my watch. It wasn't on my wrist. Where was it? On the floor next to my bed? At that moment a sheep emerged from Charlie's ridiculous sheep clock and bleated the hour. Eleven o'clock. No rush. I left the room—except that I took her flip-flops off the floor to pack, because she would probably forget them and I'd end up having to buy new ones. I carried them to my bedroom and tossed them into my suitcase.

Walking downstairs I almost collided with Jackson who was looking through the camcorder Rory had bought for us a year ago. I'd never even got it out of the box. I'd planned to take it to Florida and had already packed it, but Jackson can sniff out electronic equipment just as Charlie can sniff out chocolate.

'What are you doing?' I asked.

'Filming,' he said. 'It's brilliant.'

'That was meant for the holiday,' I said. 'I charged it up specially.'

'I'll charge it up again,' he said, proceeding on his way, leaving me on the stairs with my mouth open.

I knew that once Jackson had attached himself to something technological, it required major surgery to detach him from it. But right now, I had other things on my mind. Eleven. Charlie deserved a lie-in at the end of what had been a difficult, tiring term at school but she had a paper round to do, she had packing, she had a holiday to prepare for. I picked up the phone from the low table at the bottom of the stairs and dialled her mobile. I was immediately connected to her voicemail but that didn't tell me much. There were several dead zones on Sandling Island where mobile phones lost their signal. Charlie might have switched off her phone or left it in a drawer in her room or she might have been on her paper round already. I made a mental note to call her a few minutes later.

I remembered the unopened mail and decided that, before anything else, I would have a cup of coffee and look at the cards and intriguing little parcels that lay on the kitchen table. I put the kettle on, ground some coffee beans, pulled out the white porcelain cup and saucer that Rory had given me this time last year. I remembered opening it, sitting at this very table. I was turning thirty-nine, still married, and we had been starting out on a new adventure together. Now I was forty and single, with the wreck of my marriage behind me. But because of Christian, I felt younger than I had for a long time, more attractive, energetic and hopeful. Falling in love does that.

The kettle boiled and I poured the water over the coffee grounds, then opened the first card, from an old schoolfriend. There were about a dozen cards in all, and three presents: a pair of earrings, a book of cartoons about getting older, and a CD by a sultry female singer I'd never heard of. I nearly didn't bother with the large brown envelope at the bottom of the pile, because I assumed it contained a brochure. As I ran my finger under the gummed flap, I saw a glossy sheet inside, and I drew it out carefully. It was an A4 photograph of Jackson and Charlie, with 'Happy Fortieth Birthday' written in Charlie's handwriting along the top and their signatures underneath.

I smiled at the faces: there was Jackson, rather solemn and self-conscious, his neat dark hair with its widow's peak, his brown eyes gazing directly into the camera. Charlie stood beside him, her copper hair in a glorious tangle, her wide red mouth flashing a smile that dimpled one cheek, her blue-green eyes in her pale freckled face.

'Jackson!' I called upstairs. 'This is lovely!'

'What?' came his voice.

'The photo. It arrived in the post.'

'It was Charlie's idea. She said it was more exciting to get things by post.'

'It's really good,' I said. 'Who took it?'

He put his head round the kitchen door. 'Oh, I dunno. Some friend of Charlie's when you weren't here at the weekend.'

'On Sunday?'

'Yeah. I can't remember her name, though.'

'Thanks. I'll always treasure it.'

He wandered off once more, as if he hadn't heard.

Later I would frame it but for the time being I pinned it to the fridge door with a magnet. What to do now?

First, I put the bag with the snorkel, the flippers, our bathing suits and towels into the boot of the car, to get them out of the way. I put the dollars I'd ordered from the bank into my wallet. I wrote a note for the milkman, cancelling the milk, rolled it up and put it into the neck of an empty bottle outside the front door. I washed the dishes and swept the kitchen floor, because I wanted Renata to arrive at a tidy house. I stripped the sheets off our beds and threw them into the kitchen to deal with.

At eleven thirteen, by the clock on the oven, I rang Charlie again, and once more got a message.

I decided I would wash my hair before she got home—she's the only person I know who can single-handedly empty a water tank with one shower—and was halfway through rinsing off the conditioner when I heard a knock at the door. I groaned. The knock sounded again, louder this time. Charlie, I thought. She's lost her keys again. I stepped out of the shower, pulled on a ratty grey dressing gown and ran downstairs, rubbing my hair as I went. I opened the door starting to say something like 'The prodigal daughter returns,' but stopped, because it wasn't Charlie.

I could see at least a dozen faces at the door. Several people were singing loudly. I felt a flash of horror of the kind you experience when you know you're about to have an accident and there's nothing you can do to prevent it, when you have elbowed the vase off the shelf and it hasn't yet hit the floor. I was the victim of a surprise birthday party.

At the front was Joel, head and shoulders taller than anyone else, dressed in jeans and a heavy green jacket. He was smiling at me apologetically. At least he wasn't singing. He'd promised never to come to the house again, yet there he was and there—right behind him was his wife Alix. And, as if that wasn't bad enough, there was the vicar. He was certainly singing. He was leading it, as if he was in church. Behind me, Sludge was moaning in panic. She was never much of a guard dog.

'Happy birthday to you-ou-ou-ou!' they finished.

'Surprise,' said Joel.

For one moment, I thought I would slam the door in their faces and lock it. But I couldn't. These were my neighbours, my fellow islanders, my friends. I changed my expression of dazed shock into a smile.

'Charlie arranged it,' piped up Ashleigh, Charlie's best friend. She was dressed in a black velvet coat over a small, flouncy green skirt. Her face was glossy and fresh: full red lips, arched brows and smooth, peachy skin. Tendrils of dark hair snaked down her neck.

'Oh, did she?' I said. 'Is that why she's not here?'

'She said eleven, but we thought that was a bit early.'

'Eleven fifteen seems a bit early for a party to me,' I said weakly.

'Not when it's your birthday!'

'Anyway, I think we can be certain it really is a surprise,' said Alix, drily, as I tugged the belt of the dressing gown tighter and tried to look nonchalant.

'Let us in, then, Nina. We're getting cold out here,' said a man brandishing a bottle of champagne. Had I met him before? I couldn't place him, or the woman his arm was wrapped round.

'I'm packing,' I said. 'I'm leaving in a couple of hours.'

The man pulled the cork from the bottle and a spume of smoke and froth oozed over its neck. I stood back as the group advanced over the threshold like a small army. Someone thrust a bunch of flowers into my hands.

As I was about to shut the door on us all, I saw more people coming round the corner, carrying bottles and parcels: Carol from the primary school and her husband; Ashleigh's mother; the nice woman who's a solicitor, Joanna or Josephine or something. Behind her Rick and Karen and, trailing them, Eamonn.

'Make yourselves at home,' I said, although most of them already had. Alix was shaking crisps into one of my serving dishes and the vicar had dug out glasses for the champagne. 'Can you answer the door for me? I'm going to get some clothes on.'

'Take a drink up with you,' someone called.

'I can't,' I said. 'It's not even midday and, anyway, I'm driving later.'

'I'll make you some coffee,' said Joel.

'Thanks,' I said.

'Go and change. I know where everything is. Sorry to be dressed like this. I've got some work to do afterwards.'

'It doesn't matter,' I said, meaning that it didn't matter how he dressed, it didn't matter whether he had work to do. He didn't need to tell me about his life.

I escaped upstairs and put my head round Jackson's door. He was sitting on his bed, in an immaculately tidy room, filming his feet.

'There's a horde of people downstairs,' I said, in a hiss.

Jackson aimed the camcorder at my face. 'Charlie said something about it. She told me not to tell you.'

'Yes, I can see that. Where is Charlie? Has she prepared something else?'

'Dunno.'

I heard the sound of more knocking on the front door and Sludge barking. The swell of voices and laughter from downstairs grew louder.

'Please stop filming me,' I said.

He put the camcorder down on his bed. 'She'll be here soon. You know what she's like. She only did it because she thought you'd be pleased.'

I went to my room and rang Charlie's number again.

'Where are you?' I said, leaving a message. 'Charlie, this is getting ridiculous. Come home now. There are dozens of people drinking downstairs, thanks to you, and we're leaving for Florida soon. You haven't even packed and—oh, never mind, just come home.'

I pulled on the jeans and top I planned to travel in and brushed my hair in front of the mirror, then tied it, still damp, in a loose bun. I put on some earrings Christian had sent me days before as an early present. Then I knelt in front of my suitcase and rifled through its contents. Had I packed enough books? I wondered. I could always get more at the airport. I wished we were there now, just the four of us, loitering together in the timeless, placeless limbo before departure, buying things we didn't need. On an impulse, I called Christian again on his mobile. This time he was there.

'Hi,' I said softly. 'Me again. That's all I'm ringing to say, really. And I'm looking forward to seeing you.'

'Me you too,' he said. 'Where are you? You sound like you're calling from the pub.'

'I'll tell you about it later.'

'Don't be late.'

'I won't. Unless I can't find Charlie.'

'What does that mean?'

'Never mind. We'll be there.'

I stood for a moment at the window. The tide was advancing now, creeping up the mud flats. Far out at sea, boats floated free at their buoys. It was misty, a fine gauze hanging over everything, but I could still see the shapes of the old hulks and, beyond them, the stocky concrete pillboxes built as a defence against invasion during the war. Soldiers would have hidden inside and poked their rifles out of the narrow slits to prevent the Germans coming ashore. So much effort, so much concrete, but the Germans never came and here they were, still waiting, cracked, immovable, half toppled on the sands.

On the way downstairs, I had to push through a group of young people. I didn't recognise any of them and they didn't seem to recognise me.

'Hello,' I said. 'I'm Nina.' Blank faces. 'Charlie's mother.'

'Is Charlie in her room?' The youth who spoke was tall and skinny, with a shock of black hair and eyes that were green in the subdued light of the stairwell. Everything about him seemed a bit undone: the laces on his heavy boots were trailing, his shirt was half unbuttoned, his sleeves frayed.

'No,' I said. 'Only Jackson. Where *is* Charlie, anyway? You haven't seen her?'

He shrugged. 'Typical Charlie, to be late at her own party.'

'My party, theoretically. If you do hear from her . . .'

But they were gone and I proceeded downstairs to where the party had become an independent noisy organism. I stood and looked at it, feeling like an impostor in my own home. They were crammed into the tiny kitchen and the living room beyond. I saw Karen speaking to Alix, gesturing largely with one hand, pausing only to drain her wineglass, then refill it from the bottle she was holding. Karen was the receptionist at Alix's GP surgery in the town. Rick was in conversation with Bill, probably about boats. Rick was a senior science teacher at Charlie's school, a few miles from the one I taught at, but his passions were sailing, kayaking and windsurfing, anything out on the water. He taught them during the summer. And Bill worked at a boatyard. His face was like carved dark wood, from years of toil in the sun and wind.

There was a cluster of people round the fridge, and Eamonn was sitting on the rocking chair by the window. He was wearing a black T-shirt with widely flared sleeves, black fingerless gloves and wide black trousers that came down over high black boots. His hair was tied back in a beautiful green and black ponytail. He looked ready for a night out in some sleazy London club and didn't seem to notice that he was sitting in a kitchen surrounded by middle-aged men and women, talking about Christmas presents and traffic congestion. I felt a kind of admiration for him. Sludge was wedged beneath him, whining pitifully. I bent down and scooped up the pile of dirty sheets on which he was resting his boots.

'You don't know where Charlie is, do you?'

'Isn't she here?' he asked.

'She's disappeared on me. Unless there's some extra surprise she's arranged.' I turned and searched among the crowd. 'Ashleigh! You have to tell me now. Has Charlie got some secret plan? Is that why she's not here?'

Ashleigh shrugged. 'She didn't say anything to me, Nina. Honestly. She just said come to your birthday party at eleven, and don't smoke.'

'So you haven't heard anything from her?'

'Hang on.' She pulled out a pink phone the size of a matchbox and jabbed at it with casual expertise. 'No,' she said, after a few seconds. 'Sorry.'

'Happy birthday, gorgeous Nina,' said a portly man, ambushing me from the side and giving me and the laundry a bear hug. 'Bet you didn't expect to see me here, did you?'

'No,' I said truthfully. 'I didn't. Did Charlie—'

'Yup. Lovely girl, your daughter. Growing up, isn't she?' He winked.

'Will you excuse me for a minute?'

I wriggled free and crossed the room to the washing machine, pushed in the sheets and selected quick wash.

As I stood up, there was another knock at the door. I squeezed my way though the crowd to get to it.

A woman with untidy hair and a flushed face was standing on the step. I had been so destabilised by the shock of the party that for a few seconds I didn't speak, even though I had been expecting her.

'Nina, what's going on? It was today I was meant to arrive, wasn't it?'

Renata was my cousin, or a sort of cousin. I'd known her all my life without really knowing her, and now she was here to look after Sludge while we went to Florida. Or that was the excuse. She had just been left by her husband, having tried and failed for ten years to have children, and she had spent the last two months crying, unable to get out of bed. I'd thought maybe our house on Sandling Island, so far from her own where she'd been humiliated and abandoned, might do her some good. She had clearly put on her country clothes: green Wellingtons, sensible trousers, a waxed jacket that looked brand new with a scarf tucked tidily into it. But it was as if she was acting a part. Her face was a bit puffy and her smile was too bright and brave. I hugged her, kissed her icy red cheeks. 'How lovely to see you. Come in out of the cold. It's the right day. Sorry. It's all a bit mad, but we'll be gone soon and so will all of them.'

'I'll get my luggage, shall I?'

'Do you mind if I leave you to it? I'll put the door on the latch.'

I edged back into the house. Someone pushed a glass of wine into my hand and I put it down on the nearest shelf. Then I called Charlie's mobile again. Surely she wouldn't still be at the sleepover if she'd arranged all of this? I made out Alix in the living room, and reluctantly made my way over to her. 'Sorry to butt in,' I said. 'I don't know where Charlie is. Was she still at your house when you left?'

She frowned, then replied with brittle politeness, 'I don't think so—but that's what these teenage sleepovers are like. You don't know who's there, unless you happen to bump into them in the bathroom. You just hope that they clear up the mess when it's all over.'

'So you didn't see her leave?'

'I'm afraid not. Have you lost her?' She made Charlie sound like a bunch of keys.

'Is Tam still at your house?'

Tam was Alix and Joel's daughter: petite, blonde, demure—beloved of all teachers, and Charlie's most persistent persecutor in and out of school.

'I'm not sure.' Alix gave her chilly smile. 'But you know how it is with teenagers, they—'

'Can you give me her mobile number, please? Charlie's not answering hers. I'm getting a bit anxious. We're meant to be leaving for a holiday in a couple of hours.'

I punched in the number as she said it and listened to the ringing sound. The voicemail picked it up and I left a message, asking Tam to ring me back at once and leaving both my numbers.

Renata came downstairs. She had taken off her jacket and scarf, brushed her hair and put on some lipstick. She was making an effort. 'Tell me who everyone is, then,' she said.

'I don't know who half of them are. Charlie invited them as a surprise.' I looked round the room. 'That's Joanna—or Josephine. She's a solicitor. She lives in a lovely house to the north of the island. That's Carrie. She taught Jackson last year and he liked her. That's Karen.'

'The woman who's a bit the worse for wear?'

'Yes. I think she'd already had quite a bit by the time she arrived. She's a medical secretary, and she's married to a teacher at Charlie's school, Rick, but I can't see him at the moment. No—there. Tall, rather good-looking, curly dark hair. Her son, Eamonn, is the one who's walked straight out of a scary movie. I think he's all right, though. That's Bill—you might bump into him because he works at a boatyard across the road. I'll introduce you to him in a bit if you want. And that girl who's smoking and thinks I can't see is Ashleigh, Charlie's best friend.'

'Who's that? He was trying to catch your eye. He looks nice.'

'That's Joel. He's a tree surgeon.'

I half turned away to blush. When I first met Joel, he had been separated from Alix for much of the year, by her choice and not his, and I had not long ago been left by Rory. We knew each other because of our daughters. He was the opposite of Rory in almost every way: capable, steady, practical. We'd drunk wine together, told each other our life stories, swapped confidences, become maudlin, sad and weepy together. We had tried to comfort each other, and had slept together a few times, although it had never been about desire. For me it had felt too much like two drowning swimmers clutching at each other. I suppose I had wanted to know that I was still capable of attracting a man, but very quickly I felt guilty for allowing Joel to fall in love with me. I'd quickly broken it off and then a few weeks later Alix had taken Joel back. I thought it had all been kept secret but it had become apparent that Joel had told his wife everything.

The phone rang in my pocket.

'Excuse me,' I said to Renata. 'Hello. Nina here.'

'This is Tam.' Her voice was wary. 'You said I should ring you.'

'Yes, thanks. I wanted to know if Charlie was still there.'

'Charlie? No. She left ages ago.'

Something tightened in my chest. 'What time did she go?'

I heard Tam talking to someone else: 'Jenna, what time did Charlie go? Do you reckon? Yeah, we think about nine thirty. Maybe before that. She had to do the paper round and then get things ready for your—um, you're having it now, right?'

'Yes,' I said.

'She was going to bake a cake or something. Or buy it.'

'How did she seem?'

'Fine,' said Tam, breezily.

'So there was nothing . . .' But I stopped. I didn't know what I wanted to ask. 'Thanks, Tam,' I said, and rang off.

'Not there?' asked Renata.

I shook my head, then made my way out into the back garden and, standing in the lee of the wall to shelter from the vicious wind, dialled again. 'Christian?'

'Hi again.'

'Sorry. Listen. I don't know where Charlie is. I'm sure it's fine, but I thought I ought to warn you that we might be running late.'

'You don't know where she is?'

'I know it's nothing to worry about,' I said, to damp down the immediate concern in his voice. 'She's probably had a flat tyre on her paper round or she's rescuing a stray cat or . . . well, you know Charlie. She's very impulsive. I'll call you as soon as she turns up.'

Back in the house, the party showed no sign of coming to a close. Karen was halfway up the stairs now, swaying gently and trying to open another bottle of wine. Beneath her, Renata was being introduced to Sludge by Jackson, who still had the camcorder round his neck. Only Rick, coming downstairs with his thick coat on, was making his way to the door.

'Escaping to your beloved boat at last?' I said to him. 'I don't blame you.'

'The light starts to fail so early,' he said. 'This was a terrible idea of Charlie's, wasn't it? If I see her, I'll give her an earful.'

'Just tell her to come home. I'm going to chuck everyone out now. I've got things to do. Pack. Find my daughter. Catch a plane.'

'Right. Well, then, I'll say—'

He never got the chance to finish. There was a yowl, and then a flying mass made up of black dog, a human figure or two and a terrible smashing of glass. Pieces fell and shattered on the hard floor. Sludge shot past me and up the stairs, and on the floor in front of us lay Karen and Renata, surrounded by a sudden silence.

'Wow,' said Jackson, and started to pull the camcorder into position until I slapped down his arm.

'Well,' said Renata, getting up slowly, glancing from side to side as if she had wandered by mistake into a staged farce. 'Well.'

Karen, however, did not move, not at first. She had fallen from halfway up the staircase, and now lay at its foot, a smashed bottle beside her and her arm twisted unnaturally at her side. I squatted down and smelt the alcohol on her breath. At least she was breathing.

'Fuck,' said Rick. 'Now what?'

All I could think was that I had to get hold of Charlie and that none of this was going to get in my way.

'Joel!' I shouted, springing up. 'Can you find Alix? There's been an accident. Are you all right, Karen?'

'I don't think anything's—'

'Good. Right, everyone, sorry about all this, but I think you'd better go.'

Alix hurried into the hall. Professional, concerned, she was a different person from the baleful presence she'd been earlier. She bent over Karen, who was now her patient. 'Let's see,' she said. Karen was blearily opening her eyes and trying to shift into an upright position. She gave a shout of pain.

Alix looked up at me as if I were nominally in charge. 'She's broken her arm,' she said, 'and there's a nasty gash on her shoulder that needs attention before she loses more blood. I think we'd better call an ambulance.'

'Shit,' said Rick. 'Are you sure it's broken? It might just be—'

'It's broken. Look.'

'Ow! That's agony! The dog jumped on me.'

'You jumped on the dog,' said Jackson, indignantly. 'You fell like a tree.'

'Call the ambulance, Rick,' I said. 'I've got to find Charlie. Renata, can you get rid of everyone?'

'But—'

I ran upstairs, away from the noise, the mess and the confusion. I saw the clock radio by my bed. Eleven thirty-six. For a few seconds I stood by the window, staring out at the sea that was drawing closer all the time, at the grey sky, the grey water, the grey light falling in wide shafts.

I lifted the phone. 'Christian? It's me again . . . Yes . . . No, no, she hasn't. Listen, I'm very sorry about this but you'll have to make your own way to Heathrow. I'll join you there . . . Yes, once Charlie's come home. Bye.'

I took a deep breath and walked downstairs. Alix was talking on the phone in an authoritative tone. She had taken control. For just a tiny fraction of a second I resented this, then told myself not to be so bloody stupid. Karen was lying on the floor covered with one of our blankets. The shoulder of her blouse was dark with blood.

Alix put down the phone and addressed Rick decisively: 'You have to drive Karen to the hospital,' she said. 'I'll come with you. Joel can follow behind us.'

'But the ambulance . . .' said Rick. He seemed dazed, as if he was finding it hard to take in the seriousness of what had occurred. He seemed to want to pretend that this was a normal Saturday, that he could carry on with the weekend he had planned.

'It'll take too long,' said Alix, in a tone that permitted no disagreement. 'I'm concerned about shock and loss of blood. We must go at once.' She turned to me. 'Sorry to spoil your party.'

That was pure Alix. In the middle of a crisis, she was still able to aim a jab at me. Clearly her feelings about me and her husband were still raw.

'Is there anything I can do?' I said.

Alix asked if they could take the blanket with them. Since it was wrapped round Karen and possibly preventing her falling into shock, I wasn't about to refuse. It was a grim conclusion to what had been an awkward social occasion. Karen was half led, half carried out to her car by her husband and Joel. She was laid on the back seat, then Rick and Alix drove away.

Joel gave me a constrained hug. 'Sorry,' he said. He looked round to see if anybody was within earshot. 'Alix is still a bit funny about us.'

'That's all in the past,' I said, wishing he would leave.

'You're going away for Christmas,' he said 'With your new, er . . .'

'Joel,' I said. 'You're meant to be following Alix.'

'I know the way,' he said. 'So.' He paused. 'Have a really good holiday. And happy Christmas.' He gave me a peck on the cheek.

'You've got to go, Joel. And I've got so much to do.'

He still hovered as if he was trying to think of a pretext to stay. 'So if I don't see you—'

'Go,' I said, almost pushing him into the car.

I watched him drive away but I wasn't really seeing anything. I was thinking. Should I dial 999? Was it enough of an emergency?

When I got back into the house I opened a cupboard and fumbled for the phone book. Eventually, I found a whole page of police numbers. There were numbers for recruitment, a drugs-crackdown hot line, a gay and lesbian helpline, victim support . . . I ran my thumbnail down the page and found the number for the service desk for Sandling Island.

Unbelievably, the party was still going on, so I retreated with the phone into the utility room off the kitchen, and shut the door behind me. A female voice answered and I realised I hadn't considered what I was going to say.

'This may sound stupid,' I said. 'I think my daughter may be missing.'

The woman stopped me right there and took my name and address, then Charlie's full name and age. She didn't sound impressed by my answers.

'How long has your daughter been missing?'

'It's difficult to put it like that. She was staying with a friend last night, but she was due back a couple of hours ago and . . .'

'A couple of hours? And she's fifteen years old? I'd give it a bit longer.'

'Hang on,' I said. 'I know it doesn't sound like much time but we're due to go away on holiday. We're supposed to be leaving before one and it's gone twenty to twelve now. She's excited about it. She had to get back to pack her things. And she organised a party for me this morning but she didn't turn up at it. Why would that be? Something's happened.'

'She's probably been held up.'

'Of course she's been held up,' I said. 'The question is, what has held her up? What if it's something serious?'

We were locked in a battle of wills. I didn't know who this woman was but I could tell she wanted me to go away and wait for the problem to sort itself out. But I wasn't going to go away. I argued and insisted, and ended the conversation only when the woman had agreed that the officer would be with me in a few minutes. Now I had to wait for him to arrive. What did I do in the meantime? I had to finish my packing. I could throw out the last of my so-called guests. No. All that could wait. Charlie was all that mattered. Was there anything productive I could do before the police came?

I opened the door and went back into the kitchen. A teenager I didn't recognise was opening my fridge. She looked round at me unconcernedly.

'The newsagent's on The Street,' I said. 'Do you know what it's called?'

She paused, a carton of orange juice in her hand. 'Walton's,' she said, and poured juice into a glass.

I found the name in the phone book and rang it. 'Hello,' I said, when a woman answered. 'Mrs Walton?'

'No,' said the woman. 'But this is Walton's.'

'My name is Nina Landry. I'm Charlotte's mother. Did she do her paper round this morning?'

'I think so.'

'Didn't you see her?'

'Gerry,' the woman shouted, 'who did the papers this morning?'

I heard a voice say something I couldn't make out.

'Yes,' said the woman. 'She did them.'

'What time did she get there?'

'That was before I arrive. Probably between nine and nine thirty. That's when she usually comes.'

'Thanks.' I rang off. Was this good or bad news? She had been around, but that was hours ago. Suddenly it became clear. My ex-husband. I dialled his number. A woman answered.

'Hello, is Rory there?'

'Who's this?'

'I'm Nina.' There was a pause. Further explanation was called for. 'His ex-partner.'

'Yes, Nina. I know all about you. I'm Tina.'

Tina. At his flat. Answering his phone. Knowing all about me. I hadn't heard anything about a Tina. Where had she come from? When? I grimaced into the phone, happy to know that Rory had found someone else as well, but also feeling strange that both of us had moved on so quickly.

'Is Rory there?'

'He's out.'

Tina seemed to want to talk but I rang off and dialled Rory's mobile.

'Hi, Nina,' he said.

'Rory, is there something I should know?'

'I think there's rather a lot you should know. Is there anything particular you had in mind?'

I steadied myself. 'You were talking about seeing Charlie earlier.'

'I was talking about seeing the children, about missing the children. Are you ringing to apologise? Because all I want to say is that I know we've got our differences, but I really hoped you'd keep the children out of it.'

'Rory, if you knew the lengths I've gone to to do that. Is Charlie with you?'

'Would it be a problem if she was?'

'Don't mess about. We're meant to be leaving for the airport in a few minutes. If you've picked her up, then—'

'Then what?'

Slow, deep breath. 'Just drop her back. We're in a desperate rush.'

'But I haven't picked her up.'

'She's really not there?'

'Are you saying I'm lying?'

'I don't understand this,' I said. 'I've already called the police and an officer is on his way. So if—'

'What the hell are you accusing me of?' Rory said, his voice turning angry. 'I'm her father. What's going on? Where is she?'

'I don't know. I hope it's nothing—well, it's bound to turn out to be nothing. Probably she'll just turn up.'

'But you've called the police?'

'I thought it was sensible.'

'Right. I'll be over. I'm coming now.'

'No, Rory. Please—'

It was too late. He had hung up.

With no compunction or shame, I went round the house emptying it of people. I shooed some teenagers off the stairs, I told the vicar how nice it was to see him but that I was about to leave. I woke Eamonn up from the sofa. But I found time to ask them all about Charlie. If they saw her, tell her to ring me. It was urgent.

Jackson and a friend were wandering around, the camcorder still recording. I pulled the friend away, reunited him with his mother and wished them a happy Christmas as I steered them firmly out into the street. I saw on my mobile phone that it was eleven minutes to twelve. In an hour or so we were meant to be heading for the A12.

At the gate, I turned and held Jackson tightly by his shoulders. 'Listen,' I said. 'Charlie's missing. At least, she's not here. And though I'm sure it will be fine, it's a bit odd. Do you have any idea where she might be?'

He shook his head mutely.

'If she doesn't turn up soon, we're not going to get that plane.'

'We'll be able to get another one later, though, won't we, Mum?' His eyes filled with tears and he wrenched himself away from me and kicked at a stone.

'The important thing is to find Charlie.'

'Yeah,' he mumbled. Then, 'She'll be all right, won't she?'

'Yes,' I said.

In the house, Renata was clearing glasses of surfaces and stacking the dishwasher, not briskly but with a lethargic sadness that made me want to scream. The party had barely started before I'd ended it, yet there was an extraordinary mess everywhere—bowls of crisps, saucers with cigarettes stubbed out in them, blood in the hall, a smashed bottle by the front door.

'Right, Nina,' she said, picking up a bowl. 'You can leave all of this to me. I'll put all those flowers in water for a start.' I saw that she was hobbling a bit, presumably from her collision with Sludge and Karen.

'No,' I said. 'I'm sorry, and I know this isn't what you came for, but here's what I want you to do, Renata. Can you take Jackson and Sludge and walk through the town? Ask if anyone's seen Charlie. Jackson will point people out, won't you, my darling?'

'Oh,' said Renata. 'Yes, of course. I'll just get my jacket on . . .'

'Have you got a mobile?'

'Yes.'

'Call me if there's any news.'

'Are you staying here?'

'The police are coming.'

'Oh.' Her face became grave. She glanced at Jackson and pulled her features into unconvincing cheeriness. 'Right, then. Let's be off. Lead on, Macduff.'

'What?' said Jackson.

At any other time, I would have laughed at the sight of Sludge racing down the road with her demented crab-like gait, red tongue lolling and ears turned inside out, pulling Renata after her in a stiff-legged run, Jackson jogging behind them, looking like a troll in his oversized skiing jacket.

I went back into the house. Where were the police? The timer-clock on the oven told me it was eleven fifty-three. I picked up a small bunch of flowers and put my face into the satin cool of their petals, thinking furiously. She'd left the sleepover at between nine and nine thirty and I knew she'd gone straight to the newsagent's . . .

The bell rang and I ran to the door.

'Nina Landry?'

The man who stood there was short and stout, and he wore a uniform that was slightly too tight. He had short brown hair and jug ears. His face was weathered and inappropriately cheerful. 'PC Mahoney,' he said.

'Come in,' I said. 'Mind the broken glass.'

We walked through the living room, which looked like a crime scene, and into the chaos of the kitchen. I pulled out a chair for him, then sat down myself at the littered table. PC Mahoney took out a notebook and a pen, licked his finger and flipped over several pages. He wrote the date at the top of a clean page, then glanced at his watch and wrote the time: 11.54, I read upside-down.

'Let me take a few details. Your daughter's full name and age?'

'I already gave it,' I said. 'To the woman at the police station.'

'Please,' he said.

'Charlotte Landry Oates. Landry after me and Oates after her father.'

'Is Mr Oates here?'

'He doesn't live with us,' I said, and watched the expression on his face become shrewd as I said it. 'He left at the start of the year.' I didn't wait for his next question. 'Charlie's fifteen. She was born on the 3rd of February.'

'So she's nearly sixteen.'

'Yes, but—'

'And when did she go missing? The duty officer said it was just an hour or so ago.'

'I don't know exactly. She was at a sleepover, and then she did her paper round. I was out, doing errands, and I expected her to be here when I got back, which was later than I'd thought because I rang up a friend to look at my car and then—oh, the point is, she wasn't here when I got back.'

'And that would have been when?'

I remembered Karen telling Eamonn, as he shuffled out of their house in his bare feet and trench coat, that it was gone half past ten. And when I'd gone into Charlie's room her sheep clock had sounded the hour.

'It must have been about eleven. She wasn't here and that was odd because we're going on holiday. *Were* going on holiday. I don't think we'll make it now. We needed to leave at one or one thirty at the latest, and she was going to come home and pack. Plus she arranged this party for me. It makes no sense. She was so excited.'

'Where are you going for your holiday?'

'Florida,' I said impatiently.

'Nice. Just the three of you?'

'Four. My boyfriend is coming as well.'

'New boyfriend?'

'Quite, why does that—'

'Does your daughter get on with him?'

'Yes. I mean, there've been . . . but yes, basically.'

'Mmm. Does Charlotte have a mobile phone?'

'I've been ringing it. No answer. I've rung the friend she was with last night. I've rung the newsagent's to check she did the paper round. I've spoken to her best friend. Nobody knows where she's got to.'

I wanted him to tell me it was nothing to worry about, and when he did I felt frustrated because I knew he was wrong. 'I know Charlie,' I said. 'I *know* this isn't in character. Something's wrong. We have to find her.'

'Ms Landry,' he said kindly, 'I understand what teenagers are like. I've got one myself. They go missing all the time. You wouldn't believe how often they're reported missing and then they turn up a few hours later, or the next day. Have you had an argument recently?'

'No.'

That wasn't strictly true, of course. I rarely lose my temper, but Charlie quarrels with everyone, whether they participate or not. She has a strictly confrontational attitude towards the world. She challenges people, she glowers, she squabbles, she storms out of rooms and slams doors. But like Rory, or like Rory used to be, she's quick to anger and quick to apologise or forgive, generous and contrite to a fault, never bearing grudges. She argued with me yesterday, and the day before that, about whether she and Ashleigh could go to London for a concert on a school day, about borrowing my shoes without asking and breaking the heel . . . But those were small tiffs, the daily stuff of Charlie's life.

'No,' I repeated. 'We hadn't argued.'

'Boyfriend trouble?' he asked.

'No,' I said. 'Charlie doesn't have a boyfriend.'

'As far as you know,' said PC Mahoney, smiling humorously at me.

'She would have told me,' I said. 'She tells me things.' For she did. She'd told me about the boys who'd asked her out; she'd confessed about getting horribly drunk on Bacardi Breezers at Ashleigh's house; she'd asked my advice about spots and period pains, talked about how she felt stifled by her father's overprotectiveness. 'Look, this is all irrelevant.'

'How about at school? Was she happy? Any trouble with her peer group?'

'Nothing that would have made her run away from home.'

'There was trouble, then?'

'She was bullied for a bit,' I said. 'She was the new girl and didn't fit in. You know how vicious girls can be in a group. But that's all stopped now.'

'Mmmm.' He stood up suddenly, tucking his notebook back into his pocket. 'Let's pay a visit to Charlotte's bedroom.'

'What for?'

'Upstairs, is it?'

He was already on his way, and I followed him.

'I've already looked. There's nothing to see.'

'This one?'

'Yes.'

PC Mahoney stood in the doorway, gazing in at the catastrophe of Charlie's room.

'Not very tidy, is it?' he remarked mildly, stooping to pick up a Chinese wrap that lay at his feet, like a bright, wounded bird, and place it carefully on the unmade bed. He frowned at the havoc, stepped further into the room, his substantial frame making the space seem smaller and darker. His thick black boots moved softly across the carpet and I could almost hear Charlie's voice hissing, 'Get him out!' There was an empty beer can next to the wastepaper basket and he touched it with his foot as if it was evidence.

'Is anything missing?'

I gazed around in despair. I opened the wardrobe and peered inside at Charlie's clothes, a mixture of exotic and grungy. I closed the door. 'I don't think so,' I said cautiously.

'Nothing she would have taken with her if she was thinking of staying somewhere else?'

'I don't know.' I glanced around the frenetic jumble again.

'Her mobile, for instance.'

'She had that with her last night, so of course it's not here.' I looked at the desk. Her computer was turned off. I picked up a shoebox. Inside, there was a pair of long, jangly earrings, a strip of four passport photographs of her and Ashleigh, an inky rubber, a bottle of clear nail varnish and several hairbands. I put the box down and stared at the desk. Clearasil, deodorant, CDs . . . Suddenly I saw it. Saw what wasn't there.

'Her washbag,' I said. 'It's blue with lighter blue patterns on it. I can't see it. Or her make-up bag. It's pink. Maybe it's in one of her bags. That's odd.'

I started picking up all the garments on the floor to make sure nothing was hidden beneath. I held up a pair of pyjama bottoms and frowned at them, suddenly breathless.

'What?' asked PC Mahoney.

'She wears these with a nightshirt. Where's the nightshirt?'

'There's a simple explanation, Ms Landry. These are all items she would have taken to a sleepover.'

'She didn't.'

'She didn't take them, you mean? You're sure?'

'Absolutely sure. She wasn't going to stay over. She just went round there for a party. Then Tam suggested she stay over, and she called me to say she wasn't coming home but she'd be back the following morning. I know she didn't have her things because we talked about it. I even offered to bring them round to her, but she laughed and said she'd clean her teeth with her finger and change her clothes when she got back. I don't think she had her purse with her. Just her phone.'

'There you are, then. Ms Landry, I know it must be very distressing but we see things like this all the time.'

I sat on the bed and rubbed my eyes. 'I don't understand. Like what? What are you saying?'

'For some reason Charlotte has gone to stay somewhere else for a while. I'm sure she'll be back soon. It sounds as if she's got a lot on her plate at the moment. Her father has left, you have a new boyfriend, she's had problems at school . . .'

'No. She was happy. It's not right, it can't be. There's some other explanation. She wouldn't.' I closed my eyes and tried to think. The evidence was incontrovertible. At some point, Charlie had come home, taken her things and gone again. I couldn't argue with that, yet at the same time I remembered that yesterday, before she'd gone out, she had been carefree and affectionate with me. We had talked eagerly about Florida. We'd discussed what she would pack. She had even been nice about Christian, kissing my cheek, saying that she supposed he was all right, really. 'She would have told me if something was wrong. I know she would.'

'Teenagers have secrets, Ms Landry. My wife often says that—'

'So what's going to happen now?'

'As soon as you hear from her, get in touch with us.'

'No, I mean what are *you* going to do?'

'We'll put her on our lists, keep an eye out—you can come down to the police station later and make a statement.'

'That's it? That's all?'

'She's probably quite all right, just needs time to think things through.'

I looked at his unconcerned face. 'I'm afraid I don't agree with you. If she's run away, that's because something happened to make her do so. And presumably it's the job of the police to think about the bad scenarios as well as the good ones. We can't just wait and see. We have to find her.'

The phone rang loudly and I started up off the bed.

'That's probably her right now,' said PC Mahoney.

I ran downstairs two at a time and picked up the receiver, my heart thudding with hope. 'Yes?'

'Nina, it's Rick. I wanted to apologise for the rumpus we caused earlier.'

'It doesn't matter,' I said. 'I hope Karen's all right.'

'Has Charlie turned up?'

'No,' I said. 'She hasn't.'

'I'm so sorry. And your holiday . . . I wish there was something I could do, but I'm stuck at the hospital. Have you thought of calling the police?'

'They're here now. And they think—they think she's run away,' I continued reluctantly. 'It doesn't make sense, Rick. I don't think Charlie would do that. She seemed fine yesterday.'

'I'm sorry I can't be much help,' he said. 'I'm in the middle of things here. All I'd say, as a teacher—as Charlie's teacher—is that teenagers often don't behave in the ways you'd expect.'

'That's what the police officer says, too. He doesn't think there's anything to worry about.'

'I'm sure there isn't.'

'Thanks, Rick. I've got to go now. She might ring and I've got to keep the line clear.' I remembered where he was calling from. 'How is Karen?'

'The doctor's seeing her now.'

'I'm so sorry.'

'That's all right,' he said. 'I'd better go. Let me know when Charlie gets back. She will, you know.'

I put the phone down and turned to PC Mahoney as he came downstairs. 'Not her?'

'No. You're going?'

'I'm sure she'll come walking in through that door right as rain . . .'

'And if she doesn't?' I said dully.

'I'll send a patrol car round the island now, to look out for her. Perhaps you could give me a recent photograph?'

'Yes. Yes, of course. Look, here.'

I pulled the photograph they had sent me for my birthday off the fridge—Charlie and Jackson, smiling at me, their eyes bright in their young and lovely faces. 'This was taken a few days ago.'

'Thank you.' He studied it for a few seconds. 'Pretty girl. Well, as I said . . .'

I opened the door for him. I could hear the wind in the masts of the boats in the yard and a few drops of rain splattered against my face. I closed the door after him and leaned against it, dizzy with the unreality of what was happening. My beloved, tempestuous, impulsive Charlie, had run away from home. From me. I took deep, steady breaths then went into the kitchen and splashed water on my face. 'Right,' I said.

I dialled Christian's mobile.

'I'm on the M25. Where are you?' he said.

'Charlie's run away.'

'What? Charlie has? But why?'

'I can't talk now. We're not coming. Go without us, Christian. I'll be in touch. I'm so sorry.' There was silence on the line. 'Hello? Are you there?'

'Yes, I'm here. Nina, listen. I'm sure it'll be all right, but I'll come back and help you look. It's going to be all right.'

'You're breaking up,' I said, and ended the call.

I hadn't eaten anything all day and suddenly felt terribly hungry. I found some breakfast cereal in a cupboard and ate it in handfuls, without milk. I filled the kettle with water, and when it boiled I made some coffee.

I had woken into a new world, a world that was cold and harsh and entirely different from anything I had ever imagined for myself, and I had to think about it with clarity. I was now a woman whose daughter, aged fifteen, had run away. There was somewhere else she would rather be, perhaps someone else she would rather be with. Anywhere but here.

I poured the coffee and sipped it slowly. This was the first time that I hadn't known where my daughter was. I had to decide what to do. I picked up the phone and called Renata's mobile.

'Nobody's seen anything of her,' she said, 'but—'

'I know,' I said, interrupting her. 'You can come back now. I'll tell you about it.' I hung up.

The policeman had made Charlie's departure seem like just another of those things that happen as children grow up, like birthday parties and Brownies. According to that view, I could get on with my life, with a few regrets and sniffles, and wait for my daughter to be in touch. I only had to articulate that to myself to realise how impossible it was. I tried to think what other mothers would do. Where did I start? I reached for the pad that I kept on the table for shopping lists. It had a pen attached to it by a Velcro strip. I ripped it off and doodled as I tried to order my thoughts.

The worst possibility was that Charlie had upped and gone alone, hitched a lift, left with no plans and no destination, just heading away. I thought of her standing by a road, thumbing a lift, getting into a stranger's car, and felt a stinging in my eyes.

What was more likely, though, was that she would be with a friend, or that a friend would know of her plans. If I could find someone to put me in touch with Charlie, I could talk to her and she could tell me what had gone wrong between us. Charlie's decision to leave today, before going on holiday, must have been sudden or she would definitely have taken her purse and washbag to Tam's. My daughter was a wonderfully strange and chaotic girl, but would even she organise a surprise party for her mother on the day she was going to run away from home?

Now a thought occurred to me. Could something have happened at the sleepover to provoke this crisis? I couldn't think of a scenario that made sense but it was clear I had to start there. I reached for the phone book, then remembered I didn't need to: Joel's home number was on my mobile. Another life, another story. I clicked on it and rang the number but it was engaged. A voice asked me to leave a message but I couldn't say what was needed to a machine. Rather than wait, I decided to drive over—their house was only a couple of minutes away.

I left a scrawled note to Renata and got into the car. I drove along the front and turned right into Flat Lane, which led inland, and eventually pulled up outside Alix and Joel's whitewashed, thatched cottage, a tasteful anomaly in a road of terraced houses.

I rapped hard with the heavy, wrought-iron knocker. Alix opened the door with the phone at her ear, gave me a look of puzzlement and gestured me inside. I hovered on the threshold while she continued with her conversation, which sounded like a routine discussion with someone at her practice. I took a deep breath and tapped her shoulder. She frowned. Was I really telling her to get off the phone, as if she were a garrulous teenager?

Yes, I was. 'It's urgent,' I mouthed at her.

'Sorry, Ros,' she said. 'I'll have to call you back. There seems to be some sort of emergency.'

Alix put a sarcastic emphasis on the word 'seems' but she hung up. 'Karen's not too bad,' she said. 'I just got back from the hospital. She's had some stitches and the break in the arm was quite nasty. She'll have to stay for the night at least. Rick's stuck there with her, poor man—'

'It's not about that,' I said. 'Charlie's missing.'

Alix looked at me quizzically. 'Missing?'

I gave her a run-down of the events of the morning. There was a moment when I had the temptation to let go, to howl, put my arms round Alix and ask for comfort and help. But a glance at her sceptical, detached expression made me take control again. This wasn't the right shoulder to cry on. And this wasn't the time to collapse. 'I'll need to talk to Tam,' I said.

She looked at me for a second. Everything that was important in our relationship was unsaid, lying deep and cold under the surface politeness. We both knew this, both knew that the other knew. I had had an affair—no, a brief fling—with Joel, although at the time they weren't living together and I wasn't sure if that counted as betrayal or not. We'd never mentioned it, but it was in every glance we exchanged, every word we spoke.

And then, as if in a weird act of revenge, Alix's daughter had bullied and tormented my daughter until Charlie had dreaded setting foot in school. Alix was certainly aware of that. I knew that Rick had called her into school and talked to her about it, but I never discovered how she had responded, whether she'd been defensive, appalled, disbelieving or secretly pleased. We'd never mentioned that, either, and we probably never would.

In another life, I thought, as I stood inside the front door, we could have been friends. But all I could think now was that her daughter had made mine suffer and now my daughter had disappeared. We were never going to be friends and I didn't feel like pretending that we were.

'You've already talked to Tam,' Alix said. 'On the phone.'

'I need to talk to her properly, in person.'

Alix didn't move. 'She's having a shower. Jenna's still here as well.'

'I can talk to them both. Can you call them down, or shall I go up?'

'I'll call them.' She went upstairs and I heard her rapping at a door, then the muffled rise and fall of voices.

'They're on their way,' she said, walking downstairs. 'You'd better come into the kitchen. Coffee? Tea?'

'No, thank you.'

She led me through and gestured to a chair. Stainless-steel surfaces gleamed above stone tiles. All the domestic appliances—espresso machine, food processor, toaster, juicer—stood in a line. There was a Christmas cactus on the table, next to a large bowl of satsumas. I could see it was a lovely room but it felt implacable and coldly efficient. Alix sat opposite me: clearly, she had no intention of leaving me alone with Tam and Jenna.

Bullies come in all shapes and sizes. Tam was at least a head shorter than me, with a tiny face, large eyes and mouth and a cascade of dark blonde hair. She came into the kitchen all washed, curled and pampered, wearing a brightly coloured smock-top and blue jeans. Everything about her glowed. I felt a stab of fury and had to take a deep, calming breath. Behind Tam, her friend Jenna was large, clumsy and anxious.

'Mum said you wanted to talk to us.'

'That's right. Charlie's disappeared.' An expression I couldn't read flickered across her face as I made myself say: 'It looks like she's run away.'

Jenna gave a little gasp.

'Run away? Charlie?' Tam frowned.

'Listen,' I said. 'I know what happened between you and Charlie last term. I'm not interested in any of that right now. I want to find out where she's gone and I want you to tell me anything that might help. You were the last people I know saw her. Was there a quarrel last night? Did she say anything that seems odd to you now?'

'No,' said Tam.

'That's all you've got to say—*no*?'

'She was all right,' Tam said, with stubborn sulkiness. 'There wasn't a quarrel, she didn't say anything odd.'

'Tam, I don't care if there was. I just want to know about it. I need a clue.'

'I think Tam is saying she doesn't have a clue to give you,' said Alix. 'Is that right, Tam?'

'Right. Nothing happened.'

'She was excited about going on holiday,' said Jenna, pulling strands of long brown hair over her face and looking embarrassed.

'Did she seem troubled?'

'Not really.'

'What did you do?'

'Talked, watched a movie, ate pizza . . . you know.'

'Did she phone anyone, send a text, anything like that?' I asked Tam.

'Probably. I didn't notice. I wasn't watching her all the time, you know.'

'So, what did you talk about?'

'We just talked. Stuff, you know. Nothing, really.'

'What time did you all go to sleep?'

'About one,' said Tam, at the same time as Jenna said, with a furtive giggle, 'We didn't really sleep much.'

'You didn't really sleep much but she set off around nine to do the paper round. Was she exhausted?'

'She seemed all right,' said Tam, looking away. 'I'm sure she'll turn up. Have you asked Ashleigh?'

'Of course I've asked Ashleigh. I've asked the newsagent, I've asked her father, I've abandoned the holiday and I've called the police.'

'The police?' Jenna's voice was high with distress.

'Yes.'

'Will they come and see us?'

'I've no idea. Why?' I looked at her closely. 'Is there a problem?'

'I think that's enough,' said Alix. 'I know you're distressed, Nina, but—'

'I'm not *distressed*, I am scared. Your daughter made my daughter's life a misery for months. Last night Charlie was here and now she's run away. It doesn't take a genius to make the connection. Something happened.'

'Tam says it didn't.'

'It didn't,' repeated Tam, in a high, indignant voice.

'I don't believe her. I want to know what they did to Charlie last night.'

'That's enough. I think you'd better leave now.'

'Was Suzie at the sleepover as well?' I asked.

'Yes, why?'

'Just wondering. She lives in the pink house near the church, doesn't she?'

'I don't know what you're trying to achieve,' said Alix, frostily, 'but if you think you'll do any good by making wild accusations, you're mistaken.'

I stood up. 'I'll do whatever I can to find Charlie. Listen, if you two think of anything—*anything*—you have to get in touch.' I saw a Post-it pad and pen lying on the counter. I scribbled down my mobile and land-line numbers. 'There. Just call me.'

They nodded mutely.

'I can see myself out,' I said to Alix, as she rose from the table.

But she followed me to the door and shut it firmly behind me.

SUZIE WAS A LANGUID girl who scarcely spoke but always wore a half-smile. Charlie had told me she was powerful at school, precisely because of her inscrutable passivity.

I knocked on the door of her house and Suzie's mother opened it, wearing an old track suit and washing-up gloves. Behind her, there was the sound of a TV at full volume and, over that, children fighting.

'Hello?' she said, then, turning her head, shouted, 'Shut up, you boys. Sorry. It's Nina, isn't it? Charlotte's mother.' And she frowned at me. Like Alix, Suzie's mother—whose name I couldn't remember—had been informed that her daughter was part of the group who had bullied Charlie. I'd imagined that one of the mothers might have contacted me to say sorry or to talk over what had happened, but no one had.

'Sorry to bother you, but may I have a word with Suzie, please? Charlie's disappeared and I wondered if Suzie could help me.'

Suzie's mother stayed solidly in the doorway. 'Why would she know?'

Would I react like this, I thought, if Suzie had gone missing, with an aggrieved sense of my own blamelessness? I hoped not. I hoped I would lay aside all hostility and help in whatever way I could. 'Is she there?'

'She went out,' said Suzie's mother.

'Where?'

Even as I asked, we both saw Suzie meandering along the road towards us, and by her side an equally stringy and unhasty boy, carrying her bag.

'May I have a quick word?' I said, as she approached. 'About Charlie.'

Suzie stared at me as if she couldn't understand anything I was saying to her. The lanky youth shifted his weight from foot to foot.

'It's getting cold,' said her mother. 'You'd better come into the hall.'

So the four of us stood wedged together in the narrow hallway, among the Wellington boots and coats.

'Charlie's disappeared,' I said again. 'I was hoping you might be able to tell me whether anything happened to upset her last night.'

Suzie shrugged. 'She was fine.' She slid her ironic smile across to the youth and he smiled back.

'Tam and Jenna said—'

'You've been to see them and now you're here too?' said the mother. She peeled off her washing-up gloves as if preparing for a fight. 'Did they say something I should know about?'

'Not at all, they couldn't really help, but—'

'They couldn't help but you come here making all your old accusations about Suzie. I know there was a falling-out last term, but you can't go around making out that your daughter's a victim and mine's a bully.'

'I don't care what happened last term, I'm just trying to find my daughter.' I drew a deep breath. 'She's run away.'

'Run away? That's different from going missing, isn't it?'

'I—'

'If you ask me, you're trying to shift responsibility for this from where it should be onto my daughter. And we all know where it should be.'

I turned away from her and tried to meet Suzie's gaze.

'Please, Suzie,' I said. 'Something happened, didn't it? I'm not trying to get you into trouble, I just have to find Charlie. Please.'

She looked at me and half opened her mouth to speak.

'Out,' said her mother. 'And don't come bothering us again, do you hear?'

Suzie took the boy's hand and said, 'Let's go to my room, shall we?'

The door slammed.

SLUDGE LAY UNDER the kitchen table covered in sticky estuary mud, so I knew Renata and Jackson were back, and I called to them as I checked for messages on the answering machine. There was only one, from Rory, saying, 'Hello, *hello*. Nina! Will you pick up?'

'Jackson's crying in his room,' said Renata, as she came downstairs.

I went to find him. He was sitting on his bed, still in his jacket and boots, which had left muddy tracks across the carpet, and tears were streaked down his cheeks. He looked thoroughly forlorn and suddenly much younger than eleven. I picked up his cold hands and blew on them to warm them.

I told him about the police, about Charlie's missing things, and the inescapable conclusion that she had chosen to run away, although I had no idea why. I put my arm round his tense shoulders, pulled him close to me and said it was rotten for him that we were missing going to Florida, but that we would go as soon as everything was sorted. Which I was sure would be very soon. I said that for a while—until Charlie was found—I was going to be busy. I told him I was relying on him to help me.

I said all these things—I heard my calm, authoritative voice speaking and saw myself as I stroked his dark hair back from his forehead—but only a tiny part of me was there with my son. My brain was making lists and running through options. I was looking back over the past days to find anything, a single word or scrap of conversation, that might lead me in the right direction.

'So what shall I do to help?' he asked, in a wobbly voice.

'Think,' I said. I kissed his forehead. 'Think of anything she said to you. Anything you heard her say to anyone else.' I hesitated for a second. 'Anything your dad said to her, or she said about him to you, for instance.'

'Dad? Why Dad?'

'No real reason.'

'And that's all I can do, just think?'

'For now,' I said. 'And don't use the phone in case she's trying to call.'

I left him. Downstairs Renata was back at the clearing-up. I could hear the chink of glasses, the busy tapping of her feet across the tiles, cupboard doors opening and closing. I stood at the top of the stairs, my hand on the banisters, and felt suspended in an eerie sadness. Then I turned sharply and went into Charlie's bedroom. I sat on her bed and picked up her clothes, pressing my face into the soft folds that smelt of her, musky and sweet. I closed my eyes and let myself imagine that she was with me, in the room, standing there with her lanky-legged slouch, her dishevelled mane of hair, her bold gaze . . . 'Stop it,' I said, out loud, and stood up.

I prowled round the room once more. I sat at her desk and picked up the notebooks: an English exercise book, a red French book, filled with irregular verbs, accompanied by one of Charlie's doodlings. She doodles on everything. She'll sit at breakfast and draw spirals over the newspaper headlines and absent-mindedly ink out the teeth of politicians. She's defaced my address book. Her school books are covered in jaunty little designs or bold, crosshatched words. When she was little, she used to draw stick men running along the wallpaper above our bed, or trail indelible pens along the sofas and armchairs. Lately, she had taken to drawing on herself.

I picked up a notebook full of scraps of messages, presumably passed round during classes. 'Give me some chewing gum!' it said. 'I'm bored,' and 'Can u come tonite?' Then a spiral-bound notebook, in which there was a sketchily drawn picture of a face with a sharp nose and a mass of scribbled-in hair, and underneath, in Charlie's scrawl: *I think he likes me!*

I flipped over the pages, and this time she had written: 'I *know* he likes me.' And 'I think I'll wear my pink skirt.' Then just a few meaningless insignia, as if she had been trying out a new pen.

I put down the notebook and pulled open Charlie's drawers, which were crammed full of notepads, playing cards, postcards, bits of wrapping paper, loose pens and pencils. And then I found an elaborate doodle, which, on closer inspection, seemed to be made out of interlaced letter Js.

It reminded me of something. I flicked back through the last notebook until I got to the page I was looking for. 'I think I'll wear my pink skirt.' And those swirling inscriptions . . . They weren't just meaningless scrawls.

I phoned Ashleigh.

'Has she turned up?'

'No,' I said. 'Who's J?'

'What?'

'I've been looking through some of Charlie's stuff and I saw the letter J written several times. I don't know if it means anything.'

There was a silence.

'Ashleigh,' I said, 'I'm not going to be cross with anybody about this, not with Charlie, not with you. Maybe all of this is nothing. But if you know anything you really ought to tell me. Just in case.'

Another silence.

'Ashleigh?'

'He's a friend. Jay.'

'What does it stand for?'

'No,' said Ashleigh. 'That's his name. J-A-Y.'

'Who is he? A boyfriend?'

Another pause. It felt as if Ashleigh was sitting there with a lawyer at her ear, advising her to say nothing that might incriminate her.

'I don't know,' she said. 'I can't really . . . He's a friend.'

'Where can I reach him?'

'I don't know his number.'

'What's his second name? Where does he live?'

Another pause. 'Birche. His dad's a farmer. The one over near that big old empty building.'

'The Malting?'

'That's right.'

'Is there any chance she might be with him?'

'I don't know.'

'Did she talk about Jay when you spoke to her yesterday?'

'Not really. You know.'

This was becoming ridiculous. I couldn't tell whether Ashleigh was being so uncommunicative because she had something to hide or because she was fifteen years old. I told her I'd be back in touch and rang off.

I tried to think if I might know any friends of the Birche family but nobody sprang to mind. Clearly it would have to be a cold call. I found the number in the phone book and dialled it, and a man answered.

'Is that Mr Birche?'

'Who's that?' the voice said abruptly, as if he was shouting at me across the island with a megaphone.

'My name is Nina Landry. Is this Mr Birche?'

'What do you want?'

I took that as a yes. 'You don't know me, but I think your son, Jay, may be a friend of my daughter. I was hoping I could talk to him.'

'He's not here.'

I felt a spasm of excitement. Had they gone together? Could it possibly be as easy as that?

'This will sound strange but I really need to talk to him. It's important.'

'I don't know when he'll be back. He went out this morning to some sort of birthday party.'

I felt a disappointment so keen that it was physical, a wave of nausea passing through me. So Jay must have been one of the teenagers in my house. He had been there and she hadn't. What did that mean? A row?

'What's this about? Has he done anything wrong?'

'No, no, nothing like that. But it's an emergency. I'm trying to find my daughter and I thought your son might be able to tell me where she is.'

I could tell he was thinking, Is this woman mad? Is she to be trusted?

'He's probably in town with friends. He hangs around the café or that dreadful coffee place. But I've got his mobile number somewhere here.'

I heard paper rustling and then he came back on the line and read me the number. I thanked him effusively and rang off. But when I dialled it there was just a message. I left my number and asked Jay to call at once. But I knew I couldn't sit and wait—he might have left his phone at home.

I met Renata downstairs. She was sitting holding the newspaper with a dazed expression on her face. She clearly wasn't reading it and when she saw me she put it down, and looked up at me questioningly.

'No,' I said. 'There's no word. But it does now seem clear that . . .' I swallowed hard. 'That Charlie has gone missing of her own accord. There are things missing from her room: her washbag and make-up bag, and her favourite nightshirt. So it looks, well, it does look like she's run away.'

I held up my hand to ward off Renata's questions and expressions of appalled sympathy. 'I'm going out to try to find a friend of hers.' I was going to leave it at that but then I stopped. 'Jackson's in a bit of a state. I'm sorry, but could you do something with him to take his mind off things?'

Renata looked panicky. 'Of course, anything. But what shall I do? I'm not really used to children.'

'I don't know,' I said. 'Mechanical things are usually a good idea. He was messing around with our new camcorder. Perhaps you could ask him to recharge it and get rid of all the rubbish he was filming this morning.'

Renata nodded and turned to go upstairs. I pulled the front door open and found myself standing face to face with Eamonn, his hand raised to knock. He looked white and peaky.

'Ms Landry, um, Nina. Mum and Dad are still at the hospital, they'll be there for ages, they said. I just wanted to know about Charlie. Has she come back yet?'

'No, she hasn't, and I can't stop now, Eamonn.'

'But—'

'If you think of anything, Eamonn, or hear anything, let me know, will you? I'm going to dash now.' A thought struck me. 'You don't happen to know Jay Birche, do you?'

His face flamed and an odd little smirk twisted his lips. 'Him? He's a turd. Little private-school idiot.'

I was taken aback by Eamonn's outburst. 'Live and let live, eh? Listen, I might come and talk to you later.'

'Is he with Charlie, then?'

'I don't know. It doesn't look like it.'

As I drove off, my mobile rang. It was Rory.

'Any news?' he asked.

'Some things are missing from her bedroom.'

'So she's staying with someone?'

'I don't know.'

'Did you two have a row, Nina?'

'No.'

'I hear you talked to Tina.'

I was at a loss for a moment. Then I remembered whom he was talking about. 'Oh, yes.'

'I was meaning to tell you about her.'

'Rory, this isn't really the time.'

'She's been a rock for me.'

'Rory . . .'

I drew the car in beside the café opposite the library. As soon as I stopped, there was a tap on the window. I lowered it and saw a dark uniform.

'Excuse me, madam,' said a familiar voice, 'are you aware that it's an offence to use a mobile phone while driving?'

It was the policeman. Mahoney.

'Got to go,' I said to Rory, and then pleadingly to Mahoney, 'Oh God, I'm sorry. I'm still searching for my daughter. I've been on the phone solidly. That was my husband. I'm really sorry.'

'Have you heard anything?' Mahoney said.

'I'm looking for someone now who might know.'

'And you're on a yellow line,' he said.

'I'll be five minutes. And please tell me if you hear anything at all.'

I ran towards the café and looked through the window. Two old men at one table, eggs and bacon and a cloud of cigarette smoke. At another a young woman was sitting with a toddler. This was hopeless. Jay could be anywhere. I walked along the street to Beans, where you can read newspapers and drink about twenty-seven different kinds of coffee, and went inside. In one corner a group of teenage boys was sitting round a table. I walked over to them. 'Is one of you Jay Birche?'

A boy looked up. I immediately recognised him from the surprise party. He was about seventeen, dark hair, pale, stubbly skin, grey eyes that were almost green, clothes worn in layers as if he'd just got out of bed and pulled on whatever was at hand. He had about him a slouchy, unkempt beauty that reminded me at once of Charlie.

'I'm Charlie's mother.'

He raised his eyebrows but didn't move from his place.

'Can we have a word? In private?'

He half grimaced at his companions, as if to say, 'Old people, what can you do?' then got up and followed me outside.

'I'm Nina,' I said. 'We've not met but Ashleigh told me you're a friend of Charlie's. Is that true?'

'What's the problem?' he said.

'She's disappeared,' I said. 'We were meant to fly to the States this afternoon but she never came home. I don't know where she is. I wondered if you knew.'

'I haven't seen her today,' he said. 'I thought she'd be at your party, but you know Charlie. She's not the most reliable person in the world, is she?'

'You haven't any idea where she might have gone?'

'No.'

'You don't go to school on the island?'

At this his expression broke into a half-smile. 'I'm at the high school.'

The private school on the estuary by Hemsleigh; that made sense. Farmer's son. Farmers were in a different social league from most other people. They didn't send their children to the local schools. I wondered where he and Charlie had met. 'I'm worried,' I said. 'She's disappeared. She's taken some of her things with her. It's like she prepared it.'

'I haven't seen her and I think I'd know if she was going to run off. You shouldn't worry about her. Parents always worry too—'

I interrupted him: 'So, are you her boyfriend?'

'I'm sorry?'

At that moment my phone rang. 'Hang on,' I said, and answered it.

It was Renata. 'You need to come back,' she said. 'There's something you need to see.'

'Can't you tell me?'

'It's hard to explain. I'm not sure I'm right. But if I am, you need to see it.'

'I'll be there in two minutes,' I said, and turned to Jay. 'I've got to go. Something's up. May I call you on your mobile? Your father gave me your number.'

'I guess. Good luck,' he called after me, as I ran back to my car.

There was a parking ticket on the windscreen. I looked at it: 12.26. I scrunched it up and threw it onto the back seat, then drove home, ignoring the speed camera that flashed at me on The Street.

'What is it?' I said, as I burst through the door. 'Tell me. Renata, this had better be important.'

Renata called upstairs for Jackson. 'Your mum's here. Come on down now. Quickly.'

My son bounded down, two steps at a time. The camcorder bounced round his neck and his face was hectic with tiredness and excitement.

'Let me find the right place,' he said, pressing rewind and watching as images jerked incomprehensibly backwards. 'Yeah, here. Look, Mum.'

I stood behind him and squinted at the small screen. A blur of grey-green colour moved along it. The upstairs carpet.

'Fast-forward, Jackson,' said Renata.

'No, it's here.'

The camera had reached Charlie's bedroom door. It swung up to the sign that said KNOCK FIRST! in big block letters, then bobbed down again as the door was pushed open, presumably by Jackson. It moved in and out of focus round Charlie's room. To the window, the strewn bed, the half-open wardrobe, the sheep clock. I watched the familiar objects slide past, all the things that I'd been sifting through . . .

'There,' said Renata.

The nightshirt, held in a blurred freeze-frame, lay on the floor. I could even half make out what was written across it, and supply the rest: 'Please do not sell this woman anything.' I'd bought it for her last summer. She'd worn it the night before last. The camcorder moved on.

'Hang on, look,' said Renata, pressed against me behind Jackson.

The camera swung over something pink and Jackson pressed pause. Out of focus, and only half in view, but indisputably Charlie's make-up bag.

'We looked for the washbag as well, and the purse, but there's nothing else. We've gone through all of it,' said Jackson.

'Several times,' said Renata. 'It doesn't mean they weren't there, just that Jackson didn't film them. Lucky he didn't delete it all, wasn't it? It was the nightshirt that did it.'

'Go back a bit,' I said. 'Yes, stop there.'

The sheep clock told me it was 11.17, and the small screen on the camcorder had the same time in the bottom corner. It must have been just when the first guests were about to show up. I pressed my fists into my eyeballs and tried to think. So, the things that had gone missing were still there when I came back from Rick and Karen's. She'd taken them later. Was that it? She hadn't come back after her paper round, while I was still out—

she had sneaked into the house a couple of hours later, when the party she'd organised was under way, when I was there, already worrying about her, phoning her mobile, pestering her friends. But how had I not seen her? Unless she'd climbed into her room through the window, in which case she would have had help. Jay, I thought. I'd seen him going upstairs. Or Ashleigh. Or someone I didn't know about yet.

'Nina?'

'Yes?' I was startled. I had forgotten that Renata and Jackson were there, waiting for me to speak.

'It's very odd, isn't it?'

'Jackson, did you move anything in Charlie's room when you went in there? Think carefully.'

'I didn't touch anything, honestly.'

I ran upstairs, two at a time, and into Charlie's room. Restlessly, I walked round it, touching the shelves and the bed, as if to convince myself they were real. I pulled open the top drawer of the chest next to Charlie's bed. Everything I saw felt like a jab of memory. A few foreign coins she had kept, a broken wristwatch she had never thrown away, a daisy chain of coloured paperclips, the container of antibiotics for her impetigo. There was a ceramic plate—the first thing she had ever brought back from secondary school. I picked up the pink plastic bottle of her make-up remover, sniffed it and the familiar astringent odour stung my nostrils.

Downstairs I dialled the number for the police station; asked to speak to Mahoney. I was told he was expected back in a few minutes and they'd make sure he called me. I put the phone down and stared at it. I didn't want to sit, doing nothing while scary images slid through my mind.

'Can I make you some tea?' asked Renata. 'Or something to eat?'

'No,' I said, picking up the camcorder. 'I've got to go to the police station.'

'Can I come with you?' Jackson plucked at my sleeve.

'No.'

'Mum—Mummy—please can I come? Please?'

'All right, then,' I said, abruptly changing my mind. 'Renata, I'm on my mobile. Call me if there's anything.'

I took Jackson's hand in mine and we ran to the police station. It was quicker than driving. Our feet smacked against the icy road and the cold wind blew in from the east, whipping our hair onto our cheeks, making our ears ache. I tugged Jackson past houses with windows strung with Christmas lights or illuminated with baubled Christmas trees. In the distance the grey sea lay beneath the grey sky. You couldn't see the sun at all.

'Is PC Mahoney here yet?' I asked, as we clattered breathlessly into the station.

'Excuse me?' The woman at the desk looked at us both suspiciously.

'I'm Nina Landry—I called. I have to see him at once.'

'He just got in. I gave him your message and—'

'In there?' I took Jackson's cold fingers again and marched him across to the door, knocked firmly and opened it before anyone had a chance to reply. Mahoney was standing near the window that overlooked the car park at the back, with a polystyrene coffee cup in his hand. He looked chilly and tired. Tinsel hung along the walls, a tiny fake Christmas tree stood on top of the filing cabinet in the corner, and on the desk were two framed photographs: of him with a curly-headed woman I assumed was his wife, and of a girl who must be the teenager he'd talked about . . . about Charlie's age.

He looked at me in surprise.

'I've got something to show you,' I said. 'Jackson, go ahead.'

Jackson started fiddling with the camcorder. His hands were shaking. I put a hand on top of his silky head and watched as Charlie's door swung open on the small, smeary screen in front of us.

'Look at this,' I said. 'Hold it there, Jackson.' I gestured at the miniature screen. 'That's her nightshirt. Her nightshirt that's not there any more. Go forward, Jackson. There. That's her make-up bag.'

'Ms Landry—'

'Don't you see? Look, it's eleven seventeen. Go back, Jackson, show him the clock. There. It makes everything different. We'd assumed she came back after the sleepover or the newspaper round, took her stuff and then ran away. But she didn't. She waited until I was at home and then she came back. But how did I not see her?'

'Sit down, please. Would your son like to wait outside with—'

'No.' Jackson settled himself in my lap, as if he was six not eleven, and I wrapped my arms round his solid body and put my chin on his head. 'Well done,' I whispered into his ear, and he leaned more heavily against me.

'Either she came back or someone came back for her,' said Mahoney, slowly. He rubbed his eyes with both fists.

'Yes, yes, that's true. That's possible.'

'Now.' He sat at the desk opposite us, picked up a pen, pulled a pad of paper towards him and thought for a moment. 'We know this film was taken at eleven seventeen.' He wrote down the time and frowned at it. 'Charlie, or someone on her behalf, took her things away after that, but before we went into the room at, let me see, five to twelve.'

'Yes.'

'And you were in the house all that time?'

'Yes, I was. I got back at about eleven with Jackson and didn't leave again until after you left, when I visited one of Charlie's friends.'

'Who else came to your house between eleven fifteen and before twelve?'

'Oh God, a whole crowd of people. There was the party. You know about that. So, there was me and Jackson . . .' I put my fingers to my temples and tried to picture the first group at the door this morning. 'Joel Frazer and his wife, Alix Dawes—Dr Dawes. And then Ashleigh Stevens and her mother. Ashleigh's Charlie's best friend. And the vicar, Tom something.'

'Reverend Drake.'

'Right, and there was a man I'd never even met before, with his wife or partner. And Carol Lowell from the primary school, with her husband, and Rick and Karen Blythe. They left early—Karen had an accident. She was drunk and broke her arm.'

'Quite a party,' he said glumly.

'Dr Dawes went with Rick and Karen to the hospital, Joel followed. Oh, and Rick and Karen's son Eamonn was there. He's in love with Charlie, I think, but I'm pretty sure she'd never look at him. Joanna or Josephine, the solicitor who lives in that grand house. And then, well, lots of people whose names I don't know and some I probably never even saw. Other people let them in, and it was a party that kind of went on without me. I was upstairs a lot of the time. I wasn't really in the mood—I was worrying about packing and wondering where Charlie was.'

'I see,' said Mahoney, fiddling with his pen and staring helplessly at the list of names. 'I see.'

'Then there was Jay,' I continued. 'Jay Birche, but I didn't know that then. I tracked him down at Beans, the coffee shop. Ashleigh told me his name.'

'You have been busy,' he said drily, but he wrote down the name, then underlined it.

'He lives at the big farm near the marshes. I didn't know Charlie knew him but obviously she does. He was with a load of other teenagers, and I've no idea who they are, although some of their faces were a bit familiar.' I came to a halt at last. 'What does it mean?' I asked, in a low voice.

'I know Mr Birche,' said Mahoney. 'This Jay, his son, was he Charlie's boyfriend?'

LOSING YOU | 341

Not so long ago, I had been vehemently denying that Charlie had a boyfriend, insisting that I would have known. Now I stared at Mahoney across Jackson's head. 'Maybe.'

'What was your daughter wearing when you last saw her?'

I could see her now, as vividly as if she was standing at the door and looking back at me. I had the strangest sensation that I could reach out to that memory and pull her back, stop her walking away from me into the gusty winter night. 'She was wearing faded blue jeans, a leather belt with an ornate buckle, a bright pink T-shirt, scoop-necked and long-sleeved. A black, scuffed-leather bomber jacket that belonged to her father. Flat suede boots with beads on them. And she had a scarf thing—blue, pink and silver, with sequins; she sometimes ties it round her hair, but when she left it was round her neck. A small leather shoulder bag . . .'

'That's probably enough,' he said gently, and I looked away. I wasn't going to cry; I mustn't. I could cry later, when Charlie was safe again.

He tapped his pen on his pad. 'All I can say to you is what I said before. You should go home and wait by the phone. There's a patrol car keeping an eye out for her. From what we now know, it seems possible that your daughter is not acting alone. I know it's hard, but I've dealt with more cases like this than you'd believe, and the youngsters usually come home.'

'Something's wrong,' I said.

'You don't know that.'

'Every minute counts, that's what I keep thinking. We've got to find her now. It's so cold outside.'

JACKSON LET ME hold his hand again as we walked home but we didn't talk. My mobile rang several times and each time I answered it with a terrible lurch of hope. First it was my friend Caroline, but I cut her short saying I'd call her when I could; then Rory saying he was nearly there; then Christian, at a standstill on the M25 because of an accident. I was curt with each of them. I didn't want to talk to anyone unless it was Charlie or someone who could tell me how to find her. Everything else was noise, an irrelevant hiss and rumble from a world to which I no longer felt connected.

'Mum, Mum.' Jackson was saying something, tugging at my hand.

'Mmm?'

'Why's she here?'

I looked up and saw, walking very fast towards our house from the opposite direction, Alix. Stranger still, she was gripping Tam's upper arm, pulling her forcibly along. Tam was half stumbling; her head was down, hair flapping in the wind. Behind them came Jenna in an ungainly jog, openly crying. We met at the gate.

'There's something you have to know,' said Alix, her face stern and pinched. 'Can we come in?'

I opened the door, noticing that the key shook in my hand. Sludge hurled herself at us as we entered, but I didn't touch her, just told Jackson to throw a few sticks for her in the back garden.

Renata was on the phone, but she shook her head at me and quickly ended the call, saying to the caller we would ring if there was any news.

We went into the kitchen. I didn't take off my jacket and didn't offer tea or coffee, just gestured at the chairs.

'Tell me,' I said.

'Tam,' said Alix. It was an order.

Tam looked up at last. Her eyes were red. 'We didn't mean anything,' she began, and beside her Jenna stifled a sob. 'It was meant to be a bit of fun. Last night, about one o'clock maybe, after we'd watched the film, we—' She looked at her hands, then back at me, and finished the sentence in a rush. 'We put vodka in Charlie's orange juice. It wasn't that much, but she drank it more quickly than we'd expected, all in one go.'

'Was she drunk?'

'Yes,' said Tam.

'How drunk?'

'Kind of floppy and quiet at first.'

'Was she sick?'

'Yeah,' mumbled Tam.

'After she vomited, she passed out,' said Alix, quietly but clearly, looking straight into my eyes. There was still enough space in my teeming brain to admire the way she was making no excuses for her daughter or herself. After all, she had been the adult in charge. 'As far as I can tell, she was unconscious for a while, but then she came to and vomited again. Is that right?'

'Yes,' said Tam, tonelessly.

Jenna snuffled again and put her face into her hands. 'We didn't know it would be like that. It was just a laugh. But then she got ill. At first, we couldn't wake her up and when we lifted up her eyelids, her eyeballs just rolled back and she made this groaning noise. It was horrible. We got so frightened.'

'We were asleep in bed,' said Alix, quietly. 'I had no idea. I should have suspected something was up when I found they'd opened the bedroom windows and washed the sheets.'

I forced myself to concentrate on the stark facts: 'She was sick and she passed out and then she was sick again. What time was that?'

'Three or four in the morning,' said Tam. 'I didn't look at the time. But she got better,' she added. 'We told her how sorry we were.'

'We made her have a shower,' added Jenna. 'And Tam gave her some extra-strong coffee and she drank it and I made some toast for her but she wouldn't have that.'

'She still left at nine to do her paper round?'

'Something like that.'

'What did she say?'

'She said I was weak and Tam was vicious,' said Jenna. 'She said she was sorry for us because we had such manky little lives that spiking someone's drink was our idea of fun.'

That sounded like my Charlie. 'And then she left. On her bike?'

'I think so.'

'And you haven't seen or heard from her since?'

Jenna covered her face with her hands and said, in a muffled sob, 'It'll be all right, won't it? We didn't mean anything to happen. We would never have done it if we'd known, Ms Landry, you have to believe that—'

'Shut up,' said Tam. 'Just shut up.'

'I thought you should know immediately,' said Alix.

'I've got to ring the hospital,' I said. 'She might be there.'

'I'll do that. I know people there. Is there a phone in the living room?'

'Yes.'

'You two can go home now,' said Alix, to Tam and Jenna. 'Get Joel and tell him what's happened.'

'But, Mum—'

'Tell your father,' she said. 'And you, Jenna, you'd better tell your parents as well. If you don't, I will.'

The girls left, and I saw them walking down the road several yards apart, their feet dragging against the pavement.

I could hear the rise and fall of Alix's voice from the living room, then a pause while she waited. Outside in the garden, Jackson watched while Sludge charged around wildly with a stick in her jaws. My hands were clenched in my lap. I opened them out and stared at my ringless fingers. Charlie's hands were whiter and smoother than mine, her fingers long and elegant. She wore a glass thumb ring and round her wrist a thin leather bracelet. I hadn't told Mahoney that.

'Nothing,' said Alix, coming into the room. 'So that's good news.'

'Is it?' I said. 'The problem is—*one* of the problems is—that I've stopped being able to tell what's good news and what's bad and what things mean.' I halted. 'For instance, I've looked through Charlie's room. She seems to have taken her washbag and her nightshirt, the things that were lying on the floor. But then I opened her drawer and there were other possessions—like her antibiotics—that were just as important.'

Alix nodded in recognition. 'Yes,' she said. 'She was very self-conscious about her impetigo. She asked how quickly the rash would go.'

I looked at her sharply. Alix was so super-discreet about her work as a GP that it was a shock to hear even so guarded a comment as that. 'You don't know something, do you?' I asked. 'Did she tell you anything? I mean, that might throw any light on why she would run away?'

Alix's expression hardened. 'If I did, I would tell you, or the police.'

I paused. Clearly there was no point in pressing her. 'But do you see?' I said. 'Isn't it strange?'

'I don't know,' said Alix, uneasily. 'I suppose so. But if you were running away, you wouldn't be thinking very clearly, would you?'

'It's as if . . . as if she could only take the things she could see. But to forget her medication . . . Or take her make-up bag but not the make-up remover. Maybe it means she sent somebody to get the stuff for her, somebody who didn't know where everything was.'

'I'm going to make you something to eat now.'

'No. I've got to go. I'll let you know if anything . . .'

It was a sentence I couldn't complete. Images swirled in my mind and I made myself focus on the tasks ahead.

'Renata?' I called up the stairs.

There was a muffled groan, then silence. I ran up the steps, two at a time, and knocked on my bedroom door.

'Yes,' came her faint voice, and I pushed open the door.

She'd closed the curtains and at first I couldn't see her. Gradually I made out a humped shape in the bed, and shook it gently. 'Renata?'

'Whassit?'

I pulled the duvet back. She was fully dressed under it, and half sat up. 'I don't feel very well,' she said. I could see she had been crying. Her mascara had run in smudgy streaks down her cheeks. 'I'm very sorry, Nina. Maybe

I ought to leave. I'm no use to you—I'm just in your way.'

'You can't leave,' I said. 'You have to stay here and make sure Jackson's all right. I'm going out to look again. Up you get. Make yourself some coffee, help yourself to food. Keep an eye on Jackson. I'll call you.'

I didn't wait for a reply, but ran downstairs again. Alix followed me out of the house, looking awkward. She began to say something but I got into the car and drove away, not knowing where I was going.

For the moment I had done with rationality. Now I had the wild idea of searching randomly. I drove along The Street, quickly passing the shops, the bowling green and the playing fields and then I was in open farmland— on a country road that bisects the island. After a few hundred yards I turned right onto a road that leads to the sea. At the end there is a youth camp where children come in the summer to play football and canoe. But now it was deserted. I parked in front of Reception, a green wooden hut. I had thought of asking if anybody had seen Charlie but the car park was empty, the hut door padlocked. A cat peered at me suspiciously and a couple of seagulls stalked round the bins, steadying themselves in the breeze with their huge wings. Was it worth walking along the sea wall? I decided I was better off staying in the car. I turned round and drove back to the main road, then right, heading for the less populated end of Sandling Island.

On my left I saw a sign for Birche Farm. Jay. If someone had helped Charlie, Jay was an obvious candidate, but would he help her and not go with her? Was there someone else she hadn't told me about?

The road narrowed into a lane and then into a rough parking area. It was hard to believe that in the summer there was often a jam even to get into it but now only two cars were there. Dog-walkers. I stopped, got out and ran across the rough grass that led to the sea wall. In the distance I could make out an elderly couple and a white-haired woman, two small dogs scampering and yapping at their feet. They turned as I ran up to them.

'I'm looking for my daughter,' I said. 'Have you seen anybody?'

They shook their heads.

'We just got here,' said the woman. 'There's a man picking cockles on the sand. I didn't see nobody else.'

The tide was still quite low, and the water between the island and Frattenham on the mainland was just a hundred yards or so wide. I was standing on the easternmost tip of the island, and from it I could see along the path a mile to the north and almost as far in the other direction, to the southwest, until it disappeared from view round the gentle curve of the sea wall. North, I could only see one figure, the cockle-picker, on the sands. Southwest, there was nobody, just a crane in the distance, where the sea wall was being repaired, but even that was still and unused at the weekend.

As I turned back towards the car, I passed the three old people again. 'She's a fifteen-year-old called Charlotte,' I said. 'If you see her, ask her to call home.'

They didn't speak.

On the way back, the grey sky started to break up and widening patches of blue appeared. An idea occurred to me, and I turned right onto the road that led to the mainland. The island is almost flat, except for a few hillocks, bumps and sandbars, and one prominent reminder of its ancient past, a grass-covered barrow or burial site, chosen because of its vantage point.

I parked the car and made my way up the slope. The mound gave a view of much of the island and across to the mainland. I could see the town to the far west and I let my gaze follow the line of the coast, past the caravan park, then a mile of marshland and grass until it reached the causeway, which stood well clear of the water now that the tide was still only halfway in. Once there had been a path round the whole island but there had been a winter of terrible storms ten years ago and the sea wall had collapsed under the onslaught. I turned, clockwise. The far end of the island was difficult to make out in the haze of the winter day and the south side I couldn't see at all, hidden as it was by lines of pine trees.

I took a deep breath and felt the cold sun on my face. Either my daughter had passed across that causeway and was gone, or she was somewhere within my gaze on this island. But where? I remembered a recent walk along the sea wall with Charlie and Sludge, on just such a day as this, bright, windy and cold. I remembered her wild eyes looking at me, her hair blowing across her face. I closed my eyes and prayed to the God in whom I didn't believe: Give me my daughter back. Give that moment back to me. I'll do anything. I'll go to hell for all eternity if you make my daughter safe.

And I remembered her in the impossibly distant heat of last August. I had gone to collect her one late Friday afternoon when she had been—what was it? Kayaking? Windsurfing? I had seen her from a distance with a group of people her own age who were too far away to identify. But I could recognise Charlie's profile anywhere. At that moment I had thought, She's becoming a woman. She has friends I don't know anything about. At the time it had made me feel happy, complicatedly happy. I remembered how I had seen her throw back her head and laugh. I could hear that lovely, carefree sound again now as I stood on the barrow in the icy winter silence: a peal of mirth so clear and fresh that I stared wildly around as if Charlie would suddenly be standing in front of me and I could run to her and put my arms round her. Of course, no one was there, nothing. I was alone.

I wondered if I should go home and wait for the phone to ring. But there was one more thing. I ran back to the car.

As I reached it my mobile rang. Once more, I felt a wave of hope, quickly followed by despair. It wouldn't be Charlie. I knew that.

'Yes?'

'It's me. Rory. I'm nearly there.'

'No Charlie yet. Listen. When you come, wait with Jackson. Cheer him up. Keep him occupied. I'll be back soon. There's something I've got to do.'

'I'm here to find my daughter, not to baby-sit my son.' He was practically shouting down the phone.

'I know. Look, I'll call later.' I cut him off before he could say anything else, then I drove back the way I had come, and turned at last onto the main leg of The Street, where most of the shops were. I drew up outside Walton's, the newsagent's, leapt out and went inside the shop.

'Hello,' I said, pressing up against the counter, ignoring other customers. 'I'm Charlie's mother. I phoned earlier to ask about her newspaper round.'

'Hold on a minute,' said the woman behind the counter. She was counting ten-pence coins into a small plastic bag.

'No. I can't hold on. It's important.'

The woman carefully sealed the little bag. 'How can I help you?' she said, chilly disapproval in her voice.

'I have to know who's on Charlie's paper round. At once.'

'What for?'

'Oh, for God's sake. She's missing. I've got to have those names.'

'We don't just give out customers' names to anyone, you know.'

'Why not? You're not a doctor or a priest.'

'There's no need for that tone.'

'Sorry. Sorry. Sorry. I'm doing this wrong. It's because I'm worried. So please—*please*—can you give me those names?'

'I'll have to ask my husband.'

I gritted my teeth to stop myself howling in her face. 'All right.' But she didn't move. 'Is he in the back?'

'He's out on a delivery. I'll ask him when he returns. It shouldn't be long.'

'But I need the names *now*!'

'I'm afraid you'll have to be patient. Excuse me, I've got work to do.'

She went into the back of the shop, the bead curtains parting to let her through. In despair, I banged the bell on the counter, but she didn't reappear.

So I left the shop, barging past customers, stumbling out like a drunken woman. I could feel fear rising in me inexorably, and I knew that if I let it, it would engulf me. I stood outside the door and closed my eyes. In the darkness, I searched for a way forward, a pinprick of light that I could follow. 'Where are you?' I whispered. 'Where are you, my darling?'

'Here. This is what you were after.'

My eyes snapped open and the world loomed back into view. 'Joel. What are you—'

'The names you were after.' He held up a sheet of paper.

'Were you in the shop? I didn't see you—how did you get them?'

'I know Janet. It's a matter of asking her in the right way.' He handed me the sheet. 'Tam told me what happened last night.' He put his hands on my shoulders and gazed at me. 'I'm so terribly sorry, Nina. And ashamed.'

'Never mind that now.'

Together, we looked at the list. There were nineteen names, with titles of newspapers and addresses next to them. Unfortunately, they were scattered through the east side of town and out towards the coast.

'Which route would Charlie have taken? Which one is Pleshey Road?'

He frowned. 'We need a map for this. Hold on, Nina.'

Once more he headed back into the shop, but this time returned empty-handed. 'No maps in stock,' he said. 'We'll have to draw our own. Let's go in here.' Holding me by the arm, he drew me into the coffee shop next door.

'Sit down,' he said.

I sat at the table next to the window, still buttoned up in my jacket and perched on the edge of the seat, ready to jump up at any time. Joel turned over the sheet with Charlie's paper round on it to give him a blank space, then pulled a pen out of his overall pocket. He handed it to me. 'Get started on this. I'll get us coffee.'

'I don't want coffee.'

'It's going to be all right, Nina. I'm going to help you. You're not alone.'

Then I knew Joel was still in love with me, that Alix was right to be jealous. But I didn't care, if it meant he would help me. 'Thank you,' I said.

He smiled down at me, laying his large hand on the crown of my head for a moment, and was gone. I drew the approximate shape of the island, like a clumsy boot, its toes facing out to open sea, sketching in The Street, running from the causeway towards the south coast, then veering inland.

'Drink this. Here, let me.' He took the pen. 'This one's Low Road, and Barrow Road goes here. Pleshey Road's the small one that connects East Lane and Lost Road. Approximately like this.'

'Right.'

'Now look.' He drew the pen in a wavering line down a pattern of roads. 'Charlie'd probably have gone this way, starting on Tippet Row, up Cairn Way, then East Lane, Pleshey Road and ending up at Martin Vine's house at the far end of Lost Road, here. It's the obvious route.'

'Right,' I said. I stood up and took the piece of paper. 'Thanks, Joel.'

'You haven't touched your coffee. Anyway, I'm coming with you. We'll find Charlie.'

I didn't have time for niceties. 'I hope so. And I'm grateful.'

'You don't need to be. I feel responsible, and . . .' He stopped himself.

I pushed at the door and the wind stung our cheeks as we stepped outside. Joel linked his arm through mine and pulled me close to him.

'Where do you think you two are off to?' Alix was standing in front of us, a hat pulled down over her head and her eyes bright in the cold wind. 'I saw your truck and wondered where you were.'

'We're trying to find Charlie, that's all. We're going to follow her newspaper round,' Joel said.

'We are, are we?'

I didn't have time for this, but Alix laid her hand on Joel's arm. 'You promised to take Tam into town for her Christmas shopping.'

'Do you really think Tam deserves to go shopping? Anyway, I'm not taking her. This is an emergency. And I'm going to help Nina.'

'No. I'm going with Nina,' said Alix. 'You're staying here.'

'I don't think so.'

For an awful few seconds they stared at each other, but the winner of the battle of wills was never in doubt. She turned to me. 'Come on, Nina—it would be better if we went in my car. I'll drive and you can direct me.'

At any other time I would have left them there, tied up in the bitterness of their marital discord. Not now. I shrugged at Joel and turned away, leaving him disconsolate in the road. Alix and I hurried down the street towards her car, the sheet of paper fluttering in my hand. I climbed in and sat in the passenger seat, leaning forward anxiously, seat belt undone. After I'd given her the address of where we were going first, neither of us spoke.

When we arrived at the seventh address on Charlie's list (23 East Lane, the *Daily Mail*), I leapt out and rang the bell, then heard it sing a clanky little tune deep in the house. I heard footsteps and the door was pulled open.

The young woman who stood there was holding a tiny baby, its red, wrinkled face peering out of a white blanket. A smell of washing and baking wafted from the kitchen. Life was going on.

'Mrs Gordon?' I said. 'My name is Nina Landry and I just wanted to ask if you received your *Mail* this morning?'

'My *Mail*?'

'Your newspaper. Did you get it all right?'

'Yes. It's here. I haven't read it yet, though. No time. We only came back from the hospital a few—'

'Thank you,' I said, and stepped away from the door, hearing her voice following me down the path.

Next was Sue Furlong, whom I knew vaguely because her black labrador was Sludge's sister. As I knocked at the door, I could hear the dog barking frantically inside. But no one came. I pushed open the letterbox and peered through it. There, on the mat, lay her chewed newspaper, beside a pile of mail.

The Gunners (Honey Hall) had received their *Guardian*; Bob Hutchings on East Lane his *East Anglian Daily Times*. Down Pleshey Road, Meg Lee had her paper. She'd even glimpsed Charlie as she cycled up the short drive. The teenage son of the Dunnes didn't know if his parents had received theirs, but I pressed him. He sighed, then went into the kitchen and came back to tell me it was there on the table.

The houses were more scattered after that. Alix and I drove onto the coastal road that led along the crumbling sea wall. We didn't speak. The tide was drawing steadily nearer, and the long grass in the distance shimmered like a mirage in the chill breeze. It was probably not more than half a mile, but the flat road stretched ahead of us and we seemed to be getting nowhere, stranded in a monotony of oozing mud flats. I tried not to think of how we were probably wasting our time, going in the wrong direction, further away from the truth, further away from Charlie.

At last we bumped down the drive to the Wigmores' ramshackle cottage with its sagging roof and stained, ancient walls. Small white lights festooned the tree at the front door. I knocked, and after a while an elderly man came to the door, wearing an apron. His face was whiskery and shiny and he was annoyed at being interrupted. 'What is it?' he said.

'Did you get your paper this morning?' I asked.

'Eh?'

'Your newspaper, did you get it?'

'My paper? I'm making the Christmas cake.'

'Sorry?'

'That's all very well.'

I exchanged a dispirited glance with Alix.

'Did you get your paper today, Mr Wigmore?' she enunciated loudly, clearly, and he scowled.

'I can hear as well as you and I got it all right, but it was missing the sports. I like my sports pages on a Saturday.'

'Thanks,' I said, backing away, past the ancient tractor, the pile of wire netting and old doors.

The next house was half a mile further on, a red-brick town house that looked built for a residential road in a northern town.

As she parked, Alix said, in the same voice she had used to Mr Wigmore, as if she were teaching elocution, 'You weren't the first, you know.'

'What's that?'

'I said, you weren't the first.' It was almost a shout. 'With Joel.'

'Oh,' I said. I opened my door and swung out my legs. 'I didn't know.'

'He likes women. Usually younger than you, though.'

'I'm sorry,' I said, although it wasn't true. I didn't care about what had happened between me and Joel, and I didn't care if there had been others before me. I knew that later these things would mean something again— unless, of course . . . My mind shuddered to a halt right there.

As we approached the door, Alix hesitated. 'Is there a point in this?' she said. 'I mean, Charlie delivered the papers. Is this telling us anything?'

'I don't know,' I said. 'We're retracing her steps. Someone might have talked to her. What else can I do?'

Alix nodded and rang the bell, then rang again.

A woman wearing a blue housecoat answered the door. 'Yes?'

I glanced down at the piece of paper. 'Hello. It's Mrs Benson, isn't it? I was wondering if you got your newspaper this morning.'

She looked puzzled. 'My paper? Sometimes it comes late on a Saturday, so I don't usually get too bothered. Have you brought it?' she said.

'No,' I said.

'I thought you were bringing it. Will you tell them at the shop?'

'You mean the paper wasn't delivered?'

'No.'

'You're really sure. You're absolutely sure?'

Mrs Benson seemed confused. 'It makes a noise when it comes. I hear the flap of the letterbox. I get it from the mat here.'

I made myself thank Mrs Benson, and we hastened back to the road. The ground felt unsteady beneath my feet. We got back into the car.

'What now?' asked Alix.

'Now we know that the paper was delivered to Mr Wigmore but not to Mrs Benson.'

Alix and I stared at each other, thinking furiously. I felt that, if I let myself, I would faint. But I had to be calm and think clearly. It helped to talk. It helped to have cold, rational Alix there. 'If you're fifteen years old and you're going to run away from home on the day you're meant to be going on holiday,' I began, 'you might skip your paper round, because that is the least of your worries. Or, if you're feeling some peculiar sense of obligation, you might do your paper round and then leave home. But what doesn't make sense is to do part of your paper round and run away.'

'Could she have had an accident?'

'You checked the hospital.'

'She might . . .' She paused, not wanting to say the words. 'She might still be there—between the houses.'

We got out of the car again and together we began to stumble along the tarmac road, looking carefully to either side. There were some car-tyre tracks but I saw no sign of bicycle tyres. On the left side of the road there was a ditch and some small bushes, twisted by the wind. Beyond them rough grass dipped down and led towards the mud of the estuary. On the right-hand side there was a hedgerow and some trees marking the boundary of a large field that had just been ploughed.

'We'll look as far as the Wigmores' house and then—' I stopped because I didn't know what to say. And then what? I couldn't bear that thought now. Leave it for later.

There are a lot of things on an empty road when you walk it slowly, staring at every inch. Remnants of damp leaves, a cigarette packet, a torn shopping bag, a soggy tissue, a sodden newspaper, a polystyrene container with some unrecognisable remnant of food stuck to it . . .

'What are you looking for now? Lost something?'

It was Mr Wigmore, with a strange tweed hat on his grey head.

I didn't have time to explain properly. I waved a hand in his direction and said, 'My daughter. She delivered the paper to you but not to the Bensons. I need to find her.'

'She never delivered the paper to me.'

I straightened up. 'But you said—'

'She never delivered it,' he repeated. 'I collected it myself. I thought you understood. It didn't arrive so in the end I had to go and get it. But it didn't have the sports section.'

'Why didn't you tell us it hadn't been delivered?'

'You asked if I'd got my paper. I did get it. I got it myself.'

'All right, all right,' I said. 'My mistake.'

Mr Wigmore walked off, muttering to himself.

'We're looking in the wrong place,' I said to Alix. 'It's between Mr Wigmore's house and the Dunnes' that she disappeared.' I took her by the sleeve and pulled her, half running, back to the car.

Once more, we retraced our route and stopped by the side of the road, just beyond Mr Wigmore's shabby cottage. Once more, we trudged along the road, not knowing what we were looking for. The day deepened. The light was changing and thickening. The tide was coming in.

Something caught my eye. A newspaper. I shouted at Alix, who was ahead of me and ran back. It was a copy of the *Daily Mail*, spattered with mud, lying in the grass, half hidden. I picked it up and a magazine wrapped in polythene fell to the ground, along with a clutch of advertising cards. I showed it to Alix.

'That may explain it,' she said. 'Charlie must have dropped Mrs Benson's paper without realising. On a windy day like this, newspapers could easily have blown from under her arm.'

'Maybe,' I said.

I knelt down and looked closely at the ground. At the edge of the road where the tarmac ended, it was muddy, messy. 'Alix,' I said, 'does the ground look churned up here?'

'I don't know,' she said. 'It's pretty muddy everywhere. There's been a lot of rain.'

'I know, I know,' I said. 'But this is all we've got. This spot. Before we move on, can we make a circle about twenty yards round it and look very carefully?'

There was just the tiniest hint of a pause. I was a person about whom Alix had mixed feelings—to put it mildly—and she was a busy doctor on a free day. There must have been a million things she would rather have been doing. I could see a silent, internal sign of resignation. 'All right,' she said.

Alix had walking boots on so I pointed her into the thicker undergrowth.

'Just look in that direction. I'll do the same across the road.'

I looked at every twig, every loose stalk, but there was nothing. I walked off the road on the coast side. Twenty yards through that long, rough grass was quite a long way. How was I going to search it? With my fingertips? Was there any point? As I was pondering this I heard my name shouted. I turned but I couldn't see Alix. She was on the other side of the hedge. I spotted a gap, which had allowed her through.

'Are you all right?' I cried.

'Come here quickly.'

I couldn't move. My skin went hot. I gulped and thought I might vomit. And then, slowly, I made myself walk, one foot in front of the other, as if I had never done it before. I had to step precariously over the ditch and through the gap into the field. Alix was standing there, gesturing. Half leaning against the hedge and hidden from the road, was Charlie's bicycle. On top of it was the bright orange bag in which she carried the newspapers.

'You mustn't touch it,' Alix said. 'We must call the police. Now.'

'Yes,' I said. 'Police.'

She took a mobile phone from her jacket pocket, held it for a moment and then dropped it. She picked it up. Her hands were trembling. 'I'm sorry,' she said. 'It's stupid. I can't.'

'That's all right.' I took the phone and punched in the digits.

ALIX WANTED TO WAIT in the car, but I couldn't be inside. I paced up and down the road, tipped my head back to see the sullen sky then faced out towards the expanse of grey, inhospitable water. The sea was spreading and the island was shrinking. Alix was beside me, her face raw with cold.

From half a mile away the police car, with its glowing orange stripes came trundling towards us like a toy. Alix and I stood awkwardly, almost embarrassed with each other, waiting for it to pull up.

There were no pleasantries when PC Mahoney got out. We had met too often today for that. 'Where is it?' he said.

I nodded at the gap in the hedge. 'And in case you're wondering,' I said, 'I'm absolutely sure that it's Charlie's bike, and that's the bag she uses for delivering the papers.'

He walked through but we didn't follow. We knew without being told that we shouldn't trample over the scene.

I could picture Mahoney in the field, standing and staring. When he walked back through the gap to us he seemed puzzled. 'Is there any possibility that she could have loaned the bicycle to a friend?'

At that moment I had to control my emotions. Shouting at a policeman would make a bad situation worse. 'No,' I said, with exaggerated calm. 'We're sure. We talked to the woman at the newsagent's. Charlie arrived, collected the papers and set off.'

I described how we had followed her route and what we had found out. He again seemed baffled as I told our story and I had to stop myself saying that we were only doing what he should have been doing. When I had finished he nodded, told us to wait a moment, then returned to his car and spoke on his radio. At times he was silent, nodding. He said goodbye, or over and out, whatever people say on radios, then sat there for a few seconds before joining us.

'I talked to the boss,' he said. 'This is more than I can handle. There'll be people coming over from the mainland.'

'But what do we do now?'

'I'd like you to sit in your car. I've got to secure the scene. It's important that nothing is disturbed.'

That was the thing with Mahoney. Now that we were facing the sickening possibility that something *had* happened to Charlie, it made him feel safe to fall back on a narrow form of procedure that would use up precious time.

He opened the boot of his police car and returned with a pile of traffic cones. With a great show of solemnity he arranged them in a half-oval shape on the road adjacent to the gap in the hedge. Then he went back to the car and returned with what looked like a bundle of canes and a giant roll of tape, and disappeared through the gap. When, eventually, he emerged into view, we saw he was unwinding the tape and connecting the cones to form a barrier round the area where the bike and the bag were lying.

I walked over to Alix. 'Do you think this is necessary?' I hissed. 'It's not as if there's a crowd of people likely to disturb the crime scene.'

She looked across at Mahoney, who was now sitting on the driving seat of his car with the door open and his feet resting on the road. He seemed to be filling in a form. 'I'm sure it's required,' she said. 'And the important thing is that people are coming who know how to deal with things like this. They'll sort it out quickly, I'm sure of it.'

I didn't share Alix's faith in the authorities. I walked over to the car. Mahoney was scribbling busily in large, almost childlike handwriting.

'I'm sorry,' I said, 'but nothing seems to be happening. Nothing!' And I waved at the empty road and the empty sky. My voice was cracked.

'I told you, Ms Landry, officers are on their way.'

'But look at what we've found. Not only is my daughter gone but her bike had been hidden behind a hedge. Which suggests that somebody put it there. Which suggests that she is with someone against her will. In which case, the situation is terribly, terribly urgent. Do you agree with that?'

'Ms Landry, if there was anything I could do, this moment, that would help find your daughter, I would do it. What we have to do is wait for the officers to arrive. It's their job now.'

'You should have called them earlier.'

'Ms Landry—' he began, but I interrupted him.

'Don't say it. Don't say anything. How long will they be?'

'Not long. No more than half an hour.'

I looked at the time on my mobile. It was twenty minutes to two. How long is not long? Oh, they were a long time. Each second was an agony of trying not to think and thinking all the time, of trying not to see her face and seeing it all the time, hearing her voice call out for me and I couldn't help her. I could feel the seconds ticking by, turning into minutes. I felt I was burning up with the need to act.

A quarter to two. I phoned home and talked to Renata, who said there was nothing to report. I talked to Jackson and tried to sound reassuring, but halfway through he started weeping and there was nothing I could say to comfort him. I reminded him he had to write down anything he could think of that Charlie had said to him recently, or that he had overheard.

I called Jay, said that I very much needed to meet him and that as soon as I was free I would call. He sounded jumpy, but agreed to stay on the island. I rang Ashleigh and said I needed her to help me by calling all of her and Charlie's friends and mobilising them. I wanted them to contact other people, who should in turn get involved in the search for Charlie. I wanted to cast the net as wide as possible. Perhaps someone could offer a lead.

Ten to two. What now? I had nothing to busy myself with, and the horizon was empty. My gloveless hands were freezing, my fingers numb.

A tractor passed, and a woman on her bike, her hair tied back in a scarf and her coat billowing around her. Mahoney sat stolidly in his car. The police from the mainland still didn't come. It was five to two.

I turned to Alix. 'You should go now,' I said.

She looked awkward. 'You know, I'm sorry . . . it's just that . . .'

'Absolutely,' I said.

'You've got my number?'

'Yes.'

'If there's anything at all I can do . . .'

'You've done a lot already,' I said.

'I'm sure Charlie will . . .' Alix began, and stopped, because what could she possibly be sure about? What comfort could she offer? She gave a helpless shrug, then drove away. I watched the car dwindle, then disappear.

I walked across to Mahoney. He asked if I would like to sit in his car, to keep out of the cold, but I thanked him and said I preferred to stay outside. I walked back and forth. I stared at the empty road, the horizon wavering and warping in the winter light. The sun was dipping towards the sea, and the waters rose and swelled, spray riffling off the grey surface.

Like a dot, a car appeared, driving towards us. I held my breath as it came closer. It wasn't a marked police car. There were no flashing blue lights or sirens. I could make out two people inside as it pulled up behind Mahoney's.

A youngish woman and an older man got out and I watched intently: these were the people who were supposed to find Charlie. The man was tall and stringy. He had a balding, shiny head and a neat grey beard.

'Ms Landry?' he said, as he came towards me, holding out his hand and giving me a vigorous shake. Grey eyes, with deep wrinkles radiating out from them as if he'd smiled a lot through his life; corrugated wrinkles on his high forehead, as if he'd frowned a lot; brackets round his mouth that gave him a lugubrious air. His lived-in, furrowed face gave me a feeling of hope.

'Yes,' I said. 'Nina Landry. My daughter—'

'I'm Detective Inspector Hammill. This is Detective Constable Andrea Beck.'

The woman was shorter than me, and boxy. She had thick, light brown hair in a high ponytail, with a fringe that fell below her eyebrows, making her blink continuously, which irritated me. She, too, shook my hand, smiling sympathetically at me as she pressed my fingers.

'Thank God you're here,' I said, pulling away my hand and stepping back. 'Something terrible's happened to my daughter.'

'In a minute a constable will arrive to secure the site,' said DI Hammill. 'Then we will go with you to the police station and you can tell us everything you know.'

'I've told everything already. Twice. It's all written down. But that's her bike over there. Look. She's in danger and you've got to find her now. What about sniffer dogs or helicopters or something? Not just more words, for Christ's sake.'

'We're here to help, Ms Landry. I know how very anxious you must be. Here's Constable Fenton now.'

Obviously there was a proper way to do everything: there were rules and appropriate procedures. The detective inspector talked to Mahoney and the detective constable talked to the constable, who looked hardly older than Charlie. They walked over to the bike and studied it. And I stamped my feet and rubbed my hands and damped down the great howl rising in my chest.

'Right, Ms Landry. Forensics will be arriving in a few minutes, but Constable Fenton's staying here to wait for them and we'll go to the station. You haven't got your car with you, have you?'

'My car? No. It's—I came with a friend who's gone home.'

DC Beck drove slowly, as if minding the speed limits. DI Hammill sat beside her, frowning in thought. Every so often he tapped a rhythm on his knee with his large, bony fingers.

I hunched forward in my seat. 'Will you send lots of people out looking?' I was thinking of those television documentaries, police in a long line, each one at arm's length from the next, heads down, searching for clues.

'Well, now, Ms Landry, or can I call you Nina? Nina, first we have to assess—' began DC Beck.

'*Assess?* What do you mean "assess"? Don't you get it? You don't need to assess anything, you need to do something. Charlie's not run away, she's not at a friend's house, she's not in a hospital. Her bike's lying in a field halfway along her newspaper route. Assess?'

DC Beck slid a worried glance to DI Hammill, who continued to stare imperturbably out of the window. 'Nina . . .' she began.

'Don't speak to me like a child. I know my daughter and I know something terrible is happening to her right now. *Now*. At this very minute—while you're minding the speed limit and talking about assessing the situation. I know something else too. I've read enough newspapers and I've watched enough television. It's the first few minutes that count, isn't it?'

'Every situation is different. Your daughter isn't a young child.'

'I'm right, though. If you don't find the missing person quickly then the chances of a *favourable outcome* decrease dramatically, don't they?'

'Yes, they do,' said DI Hammill, suddenly.

'Thank you.'

'We'll do everything we can to find Charlie,' he said. 'First, we have to ask for your help. All right?'

'All right. Just get her to drive a bit faster, will you?'

AT THE STATION, I was shown into the room I'd been in with Mahoney before. The same tinsel, the same smiling photo of him and his wife, of his teenage daughter. But now there was another photograph as well: the one I'd given him earlier, of Charlie and Jackson standing together and smiling. I stared at it for a few seconds, then turned away.

It was stale and warm in the room, and my hands started to throb as the feeling returned to them. DI Hammill asked questions and DC Beck took notes. They insisted on exact times. I could hear the scratch of the pen on paper, the rustle as pages were turned, the hum of the radiator.

I had said these words too many times before. They were starting to sound unreal, with the tinny resonance of a performance. The events of the day had become a story I was telling to a captive audience.

I described everything: not just the chronology of the day, but the context surrounding it. I told them about Charlie's father, about my affair with Christian and Charlie's initial disapproval of it, about her hard time at school. I described Charlie's character and my relationship with my daughter as honestly as I could. I told them about Jay. At the same time, I was filled with a new, cold terror. It was as if I had, for those few moments, half given up on Charlie. By letting go of the urgent sense that I could rescue her if only I tried hard enough and loved strongly enough, I felt I was allowing her to slip further from me. She was somewhere out there, in the cold and the wind and the inhospitable wilderness, and I was sitting in that warm little room, reciting the precise events that had led to her disappearance and describing her character and behaviour as if that had anything to do with this sudden loss, this fall through a crack in the world.

'So she could be anywhere,' I said finally.

I heard the break in my voice. She could be anywhere, with anyone, as far from here as five hours could take her; as inexorably and eternally far from me as it was possible to be. I made myself think it, and it was as if my own heart almost stopped beating while I did so. In my mind, I glimpsed a series of freeze-frames: Charlie raped, Charlie tortured, Charlie screaming, Charlie dying. And once more I heard her cry out for me, calling me 'Mummy' the way she never did nowadays. I gripped the table. 'Is that all?' I asked. My voice was strong and steady now, someone else's voice.

'You've been very helpful,' said DI Hammill. He looked up at the clock on the wall. Twenty to three. 'It hasn't been much more than five hours since your daughter was last seen. It's still most likely that she's safe and well and that she'll be contacting you.'

'I was trying to make myself believe that as well, until we found the bike. If Charlie were an eight-year-old, you wouldn't be here evaluating the situation. There'd be helicopters and roadblocks . . .'

'An eight-year-old is different from a fifteen-year-old,' said Hammill.

'What else could have happened apart from her being snatched?'

DI Hammill sat back in his chair. 'An abduction of the kind you're describing is extremely rare. Teenagers running off is relatively common. In this instance, she might have encountered someone she knew, abandoned her bike and departed with him or her. It might have been a decision made on the spur of the moment.' He paused. 'An obvious possibility is that it was whoever collected the things from her bedroom.'

'Why didn't she do it herself?'

'She might have been nervous about encountering you. I'm sorry. That's a painful thing to say but it may be true.'

'There was a party going on at the house,' I protested. 'Charlie knew that.'

'She might have asked the person because she knew they were going to be at the party. This is the sort of possibility we need to eliminate.'

'The problem with this way of thinking is that by the time you're convinced that she's genuinely missing, it may be too late.'

DI Hammill looked at me gravely. 'We're not going to waste time,' he said. 'As soon as this conversation is over, we'll be contacting the people whose names you've given us and ascertaining your daughter's state of mind over the past days.'

'Then we'd better get the conversation over with, hadn't we?'

'Indeed.' DI Hammill was writing as he spoke. 'We'll keep you constantly informed.' He took his wallet from his jacket and produced a card. 'My mobile number. Call me any time. And now we'll drive you home.'

'No, no,' I said. 'Please, get on with your work. It's just as quick for me to walk.'

'I insist,' he said, and nodded at PC Mahoney.

The constable picked up the car keys and led me to the car park behind the station. He had to turn the car round and drive left and right along residential streets and left onto The Street to reach the front of the police station and then to the seafront and along to my house. He pulled in and leaned across to open my door. 'Just ring us if you need any information.'

'You must keep me informed,' I said. 'Please let me know if you find out anything at all. Anything. Even if it's . . .'

'You're in good hands,' Mahoney said.

I got out and he began the two-minute drive back to the police station. We should both have been charged with wasting police time. I walked up the short path and put my key into the door. As I did so, I felt a hand on my shoulder. Before I turned I knew. I just knew. 'Rory,' I said wearily.

'Are you going to ask me in?' he said.

He looked different from when I had last seen him. His coppery hair was cut shorter, he was unshaven and the skin beneath his eyes was dark, as if he had missed a night's sleep. He was wearing a leather coat and blue jeans. I breathed deeply. He was Charlie and Jackson's father. But now, when I looked at him, I could believe he had done something to Charlie. I didn't trust him.

'Rory, I know all that's happened between us. God knows, there were faults on my side as well. But if this is something you've done to get at me, or if it's a kind of joke or if you know something, just tell me, I implore you. Tell me and I promise I won't do anything. I'll try to protect you . . .'

'Nina,' he said, 'how can you think that?'

'And if it turns out that you were involved in some way, I swear that I'll make sure you go down for it.'

'We've started well, haven't we? Our daughter's missing and you're accusing me. I'm here to help. I came to help as soon as I could and I don't see why I should stand here and listen to you insulting me. It's freezing. Can we please go in?'

I turned the key in the door and opened it. Rory pushed past me. Within seconds Jackson ran to his father and pressed his face into his stomach, sniffling, while Sludge jumped wildly up at them. Meanwhile Renata was sitting in the corner of the room with one foot on a stool. She explained to me that she had been holding Sludge on the lead when the dog had seen another labrador and leapt forward, pulling her over.

'It's my ankle,' she said. 'Now I can't put my weight on it.'

I apologised profusely on behalf of my dog—or, rather, strictly speaking, Rory's dog—then retreated to the kitchen to make tea. I filled the kettle and switched it on. After a few seconds I touched the surface with my fingers. It was still cold. What proportion of our lives do we spend waiting? For kettles to boil. For lifts to arrive. For people to answer a phone. To see Charlie.

I made myself consider the situation. The professionals had taken over. What I ought to do, as a good citizen, was wait for the police to apply their specialised skills. There was nothing for me to do now. By the time I had felt the kettle once more and found it was lukewarm, I had dispensed with that defeatist nonsense. I had to do something. Anything.

I thought of some advice I had once heard for when you've lost your keys while walking home in the dark. You should look under a lamp-post, not because they are any more likely to be there than anywhere else, but because if they happen to be there, it's the only place you'll be able to see them.

I needed to think rationally. What were the possibilities? Where were the lamp-posts? I had to act on the assumption that Charlie was still on the island, still alive . . .

RORY HAD THIS IDEA that if he gave Sludge something of Charlie's to smell she'd act like a sniffer dog and trace her from that. I collected an unwashed T-shirt from the floor of her room, and when I pressed it against my face I could smell our daughter's sweat, deodorant and perfume. We went downstairs and Rory gave it to Sludge. She dribbled over it dutifully and ran round the kitchen holding it in her jaws, thinking it was a game. When Rory tried to take it back, it ripped.

'We're ready, I think,' said Rory. He put on his coat and picked up the lead.

'Take Jackson,' I said.

'Right. Jackson, Sludge, let's go. We'll take the car down to the beach and walk from there.'

'May I lie on your bed again for a while?' asked Renata, as they closed the door. 'I don't feel too good. Unless, of course, you need me.'

'Sure.' I wanted her out of the way now.

The phone rang and I picked it up. 'Yes?'

'Nina.' It was Ashleigh. 'I did what you said and rang lots of people and they're ringing people now.'

'Thank you,' I said wearily.

'The thing is, Carrie, who was staying over last night, has a sister in the year below us. She told Carrie she thinks she saw Charlie this morning.'

'When? Where?'

'She's rather vague about it. I didn't know whether to bother you with it. Shall I give you her mobile number? Her name's Laura.'

'Thanks, yes.'

She read it out and I wrote it down, repeating it to make sure I'd got it right. I put down the phone and immediately rang the number. 'Laura?'

'Yes.'

'This is Nina Landry, Charlie's mother.'

'Charlie? Oh, right, Charlie.'

'Ashleigh told me that Carrie said you saw her this morning.'

'Right.'

'What time was that, Laura, and where? It's very important.'

'Is Charlie in trouble?'

'What time was it?'

'I dunno, really. I'd had breakfast.'

I squeezed the phone hard in my hand and tried to keep calm. 'What time did you have breakfast? Nine? Ten?'

'Maybe. Between that. No, I know, it was nearer half past nine. I thought I saw Charlie. It might have been someone else, but I think it was her. We were at the top of the long hill. Lost Road or something funny like that. She was at the bottom. She had a bike and she was talking to someone in a car.'

'Listen, Laura, did you see who she was talking to?'

'No.'

'What colour was the car?'

'Red,' she said. 'Or maybe blue. It wasn't white. Definitely.'

'Red or blue?'

'Or that silvery colour all cars are.'

'But you think it was Charlie?'

'I didn't think so at the time, but when Ashleigh called Carrie and then Carrie told me, I thought I remembered.'

'Did Carrie see it too?'

'No. She was talking about something. She wasn't paying attention. Maybe it was someone older that Charlie was talking to. They had their head out of the window. They didn't look young.'

'Man or woman?'

'You're asking too many questions. I don't remember. Maybe a man. It was a long way off. I didn't know I was meant to be keeping an eye out or I'd have noticed more. You don't notice things if you're not trying to.'

'OK, listen to me. I'm going to give you a number to call. You want to speak to Detective Inspector Hammill, and tell him what you've just told me. Do you hear?'

'Detective Inspector Hammill,' she repeated.

'This moment. Do you promise?'

'Yeah, all right.'

'Everything you remember, tell him. Don't wait. If he's busy, hold on.'

She promised and wrote down the number as I dictated it but I was doubtful of her managing it, so I phoned DI Hammill and gave him her details. There. Let him do some detecting.

I WENT INTO Charlie's bedroom again, my head buzzing. Charlie talking to a man. It seemed like important information, but even when I was talking to Laura I had thought of a snag. After my day of driving around, I had a map of Sandling Island inside my head and I could picture exactly where Charlie had been when Laura saw her, and it was at the beginning of her paper round. Whoever this man was and whatever their conversation had been about, Charlie had gone on to deliver half a dozen more newspapers. So who had he been?

The sheep clock told me it was twenty past three. In a couple of hours or so we should have been boarding the plane to Florida. I sat on the floor and once more stared around. Perhaps I would find, amid the clutter of her teenage life, some sign. I began with the desk drawers. One by one I opened them and tipped out their contents.

A light bulb, a tiny velvet cushion in the shape of a heart, several coloured crayons of various lengths, pencil sharpeners, certificates for swimming and hurdle-jumping, an empty perfume bottle, several tangled necklaces, last year's birthday cards from friends—I looked through each one—dried-up Pritt Sticks, her old mobile phone, a half-full pack of Marlboro Lights, a small torch that didn't work, scented candles that had never been lit, hairbands, a thin white wristband with the message 'Make Poverty History', a bright cotton scarf with an inkstain at one fringed end.

I rifled through the possessions on her desk once more, then stopped abruptly. The laptop Rory and I had given her on her last birthday.

I pulled out her chair and sat down. I turned it on with a ping and waited for it to load up. Like her room, her virtual desktop was in a state of total disorganisation but there was an MSN icon and what I really wanted was to go through her emails. I knew Charlie used Hotmail, and I assumed her user name was Charlie, but I didn't have a clue what her password was. I tried 'Charlie' and 'Charlie1', 'Charlie2', 'Charlie3', 'Charlie4'. I tried 'Landry' and 'Oates' and 'Landry Oates'. I tried the road we'd lived on in London (Wiltshire), then 'Sludge', then the name of her beloved rabbit, who had died when she was eight, 'Bertie'. Despairingly, I keyed in several of the bands or singers I knew she liked.

I nearly gave up. Then I remembered that a year or two earlier Charlie had wanted to give herself a middle name: Sydney, of all things. I tried that. And I was in.

There weren't very many emails, once I had discounted the junk mail, but there were enough for me to get a glimpse into her private world. For a start, there were several messages from her father. If I hadn't known who Rory was I might have thought they were from a boyfriend, for in them he told Charlie how beautiful she was, how special, how he would always love her.

There were a couple from Ashleigh, in text language so I could barely decipher their meanings. 'LOL & CU l8er?' said one. Another sent her the entire text of the song 'My Favourite Things'.

There was one message from Eamonn saying simply, 'Parents suck. This is the piece I told you about', followed by an article on some musician.

And just one brief message from Jay: 'My phone's buggered, so this is to say you should meet me in our usual place at 2. I'll bring the stuff. Jxxxx.' What stuff? What place? I put my head in my hands and closed my eyes.

I heard the door slam downstairs and Sludge's muffled barking, and rose to my feet, closing the laptop as I did so.

'Sludge wouldn't stay out,' called Jackson, as I went downstairs. 'She kept whimpering and dragging at the lead to come home.'

'Where's Dad?'

'He had to go and fetch the car where we'd left it. He'll be here soon.'

Jackson's eyes glittered and his cheeks were flushed. 'Mum? You know you asked me to make that list?'

It took me a few seconds to remember the instructions I'd given him while I was waiting for the police. 'Yes. Did you?'

'Shall I get it? It's not very long. Really, it only says a few words. It says, have you looked at her computer?'

'I've just been looking at her messages.'

'And have you looked at her diary?'

'What diary?'

'You know. In her schoolbag. That's where she usually keeps it.'

'Her bag?' I hadn't come across that. 'Where is it?'

'I saw her put it in the downstairs toilet yesterday when she came in.'

It was there, under her old coat. While Jackson watched, I pulled the bag down from the hook and opened it at once. In the front pocket was a little spiral-bound diary. I leafed through it. At the beginning of the year she'd put in almost everything: the dates that terms began or ended, coming weekends with Rory, visits to the dentist, appointments with friends, parties, concerts. But gradually the pages became blanker. Occasional initials were put against dates with question marks. Phone numbers were jotted in corners. Autumn and winter were scarcely marked except, I noticed, the occasional small cross in the top left-hand corner of a day.

There was a cross against Monday, July 26, Friday, August 20, then September 16, October 13, November 9. That was all. I gazed at the crosses, frowning, turning the pages between them. They came approximately every month, and struck by a thought I counted the days between each cross: twenty-five, twenty-seven, twenty-seven, twenty-seven. Charlie's periods. Of course. An icy trickle ran down my spine and I turned to December again. Nothing. No cross. There were—I did the sum—thirty-nine days between the last cross on November 9 and today, Saturday, December 18. Perhaps it didn't mean anything, or perhaps it meant that Charlie had missed her period and was anxious she was pregnant. Perhaps it meant that she *was* pregnant.

I closed the diary and stared blankly at Jackson.

'What is it, Mum?' he asked.

'Nothing,' I replied. 'I think your dad's coming in. Why don't you run and ask him to make you one of his famous toasted-cheese sandwiches?'

'Will you have one too?'

'I've got a phone call to make.'

I ran upstairs to avoid Rory and went into my bedroom. Renata was lying in bed staring blankly at the ceiling. I snatched up the phone and rang Hammill's number. It was engaged. I couldn't leave this as a message, so I rang the station, asked for Detective Constable Beck and was put through.

'This is Nina Landry,' I began. 'My daughter may be pregnant, or think she is.'

'How do you—'

'In her diary,' I said shortly. 'Did you follow up Laura's sighting?'

'I believe she's talking to DI Hammill now.'

'No other news, then?' I asked, knowing the answer.

'We're proceeding. We'll let you know as soon as we find anything. I've got a daughter of my own and I can imagine how desperate you must—'

'Right.' I slammed down the phone, closed the curtains in case Renata wanted to sleep, and left the room, shutting the door behind me.

Rory and Jackson were in the kitchen. Rory looked terrible, peaky and red-eyed. He was talking nineteen to the dozen to Jackson, who was gazing at him anxiously.

'I need to talk to you,' I said to Rory. 'Alone. Jackson, darling, can you wait in your room for a bit?'

He stared at me for a few moments, then wandered disconsolately out of the kitchen. We heard him trudging heavily up the stairs.

'I've been looking through her diary,' I said. 'And the thing is—'

The phone rang in the living room again and I ran to it.

'Nina? This is DI Hammill.'

Hope blasted through me, and I could hardly stand up straight. 'Yes?'

'No news yet, I'm afraid, but we're very anxious to talk to your husband as soon as possible. Has he arrived yet?'

I called Rory, who came through and took the receiver. His face was chalky; there were beads of perspiration on his upper lip and forehead.

'Yes,' he was saying. 'Right. Of course.' He put down the phone and turned to me. 'I've got to go to the police station. They want me to make a statement.' He gave a twisted little smile. 'Funny how they make a man feel guilty for being a father. It's just off Miller Street, right?'

My insides were churning. 'Right.'

He hesitated, and I waited without speaking.

'See you, then,' he said.

As soon as he closed the door, I took my mobile from its charger and dialled. I waited and a young voice answered: 'Yes?'

'Jay? It's Nina.'

'Have you found her yet?'

'No.'

'The police called. They want to talk to me.' He sounded scared. But, then, Rory was scared of the police too.

'They're talking to everyone,' I said. 'Everyone who knows Charlie well. I wondered if I could come and see you.'

'If you like.' He paused. 'I want to help.'

'Good. I'll come to the farm, shall I?'

'OK.' Another slight pause. 'Don't tell my dad what it's about, though. I'll wait by the barns. You don't need to go all the way to the house.'

'All right. I'll fetch my car and be with you in ten minutes.'

FIRST I HAD to sort out Jackson. Rory was at the police station, and it was clear that I couldn't leave Jackson with Renata any more. She needed looking after herself. I didn't want to take him with me, to hear about Charlie's sex life, but I didn't want to leave him alone. He was eleven years old and very frightened.

I rang Bonnie's house, in case she had come home early from her Christmas shopping, but there was only an answering machine. It was nearly Christmas. Everyone was out, shopping, collecting Christmas trees, waiting in airports for their flights to the sun . . .

I went to Jackson's bedroom. He was standing by the window, looking out at the sea. His shoulders were hunched and when he turned to me his face was pale and stunned.

'Honey, I've got to go out and I think you should come with me. Grab your jacket, will you?'

Wordlessly, he followed me downstairs and pushed his arms into it.

'We've got to get my car. I left it by the newsagent's.'

He nodded and we left. The wind was like iron. The sky had turned white and low. As if snow might fall. I held on to Jackson's cold hand and hurried him along. Occasionally I said things like 'It's all right, darling,' and 'We'll find her.' I remembered that he hadn't had anything to eat.

In The Street I took him into the bakery.

'Do you want a cheese roll or a ham roll?'

'Don't mind.'

They were only a pound. I bought one of each. I tried to remember when I had last eaten and couldn't. Outside the bakery, I handed the cheese roll to Jackson, then I peeled back the polythene from the other and took a bite. It didn't taste of anything, but I just needed to get something into my body so I wouldn't faint. I took Jackson's free hand and stepped over the road towards the car. Somewhere close there was a screech of brakes and tyres, and I swung round, Jackson behind me, and saw the grey bonnet of a car that had come to a halt inches in front of us. Steam was rising through the grille as if the car itself was angry. I couldn't see the driver because of the reflections on the windscreen, but the vehicle was familiar. I walked round and was greeted by Rick's shocked face.

He wound down the window. 'I . . . er . . . Are you all right?' he said, looking shaken.

As if I hadn't put him through enough already today. 'I'm so sorry,' I said. 'I walked out without looking. It's completely my fault.'

I asked him if he could pull in to the kerb. I said I needed to talk. He restarted his stalled car and parked outside the bakery.

'How's Karen?' I asked when he'd brought the vehicle to a halt.

'She's fast asleep,' he said. 'They gave her some strong medication. She needs to rest. She was drunk at your house. I'm sorry.'

'It doesn't matter.'

'Yes, it does.'

'Is she in the hospital?'

'Yes. They didn't want her to be moved. It'll be a couple of days at least.'

'Is anyone with her?'

'Eamonn said he'd pop in. For what it's worth. Children, eh?'

'What are you doing now?' I asked.

'Nothing much,' he said. 'I've got a couple of fairly unimportant things to get on with. I might as well pass the time. But what am I thinking, going on like this? Have you heard anything about Charlie?'

'She's still missing,' I said.

'What? Are you sure she hasn't gone off with a friend? I'm afraid she's that age.'

'That's what I thought at first. But we found her bike and her bag. She'd been delivering papers.'

'Oh my God,' Rick said. He stared at me, shocked. 'That's awful. Have you called the police?'

'Yes, of course. They've started interviewing people. I'm not sure they've got the proper sense of urgency.'

'I'm so sorry,' he said. 'I've been taken up with Karen. But if there's anything at all I can do, Nina, you know you only have to ask.'

A thought struck me. I glanced down at Jackson, who was gnawing his cheese roll and looking bored. He knew Rick well and was comfortable with him. 'There is something,' I said. 'I've got to go and talk to someone who knows Charlie. It's desperately urgent. Could you take Jackson for a few minutes while I do it?'

'Oh . . .' said Rick. He glanced at his watch—nearly a quarter to four. I could see he was already regretting his impulsive offer. At any other time, on any other day, I would have let him off but I was merciless.

'Please, Rick. It would be the most enormous help.'

'I, um . . .'

'Give me your mobile number and I'll ring you as soon as I've seen this er, this person. It'll be twenty minutes, half an hour tops. You know I wouldn't ask unless it was important.'

Rick gave a sigh. My car. My party. And now my son.

'All right,' he said. 'Come on, Jackson. Out of the cold with you.'

Jackson hopped into the back seat quite cheerfully. He was probably glad to be away from me. I tapped the number of Rick's mobile into my phone and they drove away. I could see Jackson talking and making gestures and Rick looking stoical, his face blank.

I found my car outside the newsagent's and got in. But before I started it, I sat for a few moments, settling my thoughts. Then I turned the key in the ignition. The engine hiccupped and stalled. I tried again. This time the hiccup was brief.

'No,' I said. 'Please don't.'

I turned the key again and there was a faint click. Then nothing. The car was not going to start.

I picked up my mobile. Rory was still at the police station; Renata was weeping in my bed; Christian was stuck on the M25, probably for the rest of his life; Bonnie was out shopping; Rick was with my son. My heart sank. Maybe I should try Joel: he'd come, unless it was Alix who answered.

Then I had another thought, and dialled.

'Hi.'

'Jay, it's Nina. Listen, I'm in town, just near the newsagent's, and was about to drive over to you but my car won't start. I don't suppose there's any chance of you coming here? Do you drive?'

'A motorbike,' he said.

'Can you come, then?'

'Why not?' he said. 'Give me a minute or so.'

'Thanks.'

Another wait. I sat in the wretched car and drummed my fingers on the steering wheel. I turned the key in the lock a couple more times and heard the dead click. Then, coming down the road towards me, I saw Tom, the vicar. He was carrying a large shopping bag and seemed to be talking to himself. Or maybe he was talking to God. He stopped by the car and I opened the door.

'Hello, Nina. I thought you'd be in Florida by now.'

'Change of plan,' I said wearily. I couldn't tell the story again.

'Is something up with your car?'

'Yes. When I most need it, it won't start.'

'Shall I have a look?' He put his shopping bag on the passenger seat, leaned across me, and pulled the lever that opened the bonnet. He tugged off his gloves and bent over the engine, a look of pleasure on his face. Men and cars, I thought.

Then I heard a motorbike, which pulled up beside my car. Tom stood upright as a figure climbed off. A black helmet covered his head and face, and he lifted it off. I opened the door.

'Hello,' said Jay.

'Do you want to sit in the car?' I said. 'I've got something important to ask you. Things are looking serious. Bad.'

'Bad,' he repeated. 'Bad with Charlie?'

'Yes.'

He looked at me and then at Tom, whose head was back under the bonnet.

'Can we talk somewhere else? I feel kind of exposed. Especially with him there.' He gave a sudden grin. 'Why don't you hop on the back? I'll take us somewhere private.'

'On your bike?'

'Why not? Unless you're scared.'

It sounded like a challenge. I looked at his thin, pale face; the green-grey eyes. This boy—or young man—was Charlie's secret life. He might know something, or everything, of what had happened. He might be an ordinary teenager or he might be violent and disturbed.

'Nothing scares me now, except what's happened to my daughter,' I said, shrugging, and climbed out of the car, slamming the door behind me. 'But not too far. I don't have time.' I turned to the vicar, who was trying but failing to hide his curiosity. 'Tom,' I said. 'I don't have time to explain but I've got to go now. It's been very kind of you to try to help.'

'But I've hardly begun. I tell you what, if you leave me the car key, I'll tinker a bit more. I like mending things.'

'If you're sure.' I pulled the key off the key ring and passed it to him, then turned back to Jay. 'Let's go, then.'

'There's a spare helmet in there,' he said, pointing behind the seat. I took it out and put it on, adjusting the chin-strap and pulling down the visor. I swung my leg up and over and straddled the seat behind him.

'Put your feet on those bars,' he said. 'And put your arms round my waist.' I did. 'Go with the bike,' he instructed. 'Relax.'

The next minute we were roaring along The Street, so fast that the road melted to a grey river beneath me and the houses blurred. As we accelerated round the corner and headed east, we seemed almost to be lying flat against the surface, like our own shadow. Then the bike straightened again; the world righted itself. Past the boatyards and the caravan site, past the beach where dinghies were turned turtle on the sand, past the beach huts. Houses petering out, the road narrowing.

I held on to Jay, leaned as the bike leaned. Charlie had done this, I thought. She had put her arms round this young man's waist, laid her cheek against the black leather of his jacket as the world ripped by. Then she had come home to me and said nothing about it.

'This'll do,' he said, and we stopped on a track that led down to the shoreline. In front of us was a lonely wilderness of scrubland, marshes and dykes, leading to the open sea. It felt as though we were the only people in this flat grey world in which you couldn't tell where water ended and sky began. I pulled off the helmet and swung myself down.

'You didn't do badly,' he said, pulling off his own helmet.

'Charlie is missing,' I said. 'It's getting worse with every minute that passes. The police are asking questions but I can't sit at home, so I'm going to ask you questions that no mother should ever ask her daughter's boyfriend. It doesn't matter what you say. I'm not going to judge you. I don't care what you two got up to together. I want to find Charlie. That's all.'

He gazed out to sea impassively and I stared at his face, looking for some kind of sign. A small tremor passed over it, like wind across water.

'I want to help find her,' he said. 'Of course I do. I'm sure she'll turn up. There'll be a reason. People don't just disappear.'

'First off, you have to tell me if there's anything you know that could help me. Do you know where she is?'

'No.' His eyes were steady.

'You swear it.'

'If you like. I swear.'

'All right, are you Charlie's boyfriend?'

'You could call it that.'

'How long has it been going on?'

'About four, five months. Since the summer.'

'Why didn't she tell me?'

'I don't know. It was between us. We liked it secret. Things change when they're public. Adults think they can tell you what to do, they think they can remember what it's like to be young. We didn't want that.'

'Was it serious?'

'Serious?'

'Yes. Do you love her? Does she love you?'

'We don't say "love".'

'What do you say?'

His face flamed. 'Stuff,' he said. 'You know.'

'Don't piss around, Jay. Don't you understand she might be in terrible danger? Did she tell you anything secret, anything that might be a clue?'

He ground the toe of his biker's boot into the ground. 'This is weird. She talked about her father a bit.'

'Go on.'

'She didn't like it, the way he doted on her so much. She said it wasn't fair on Jackson and it gave her the creeps. She didn't like to discuss it with you because . . . well, you know, you're her mother, it would be too weird.'

'But nothing specific?' I said.

'Like . . .?'

'Like he was sexually abusing her,' I said, loud and clear. 'For instance.'

He winced. 'No. But she did tell me she thought all older men were perverts.'

'Why? Why did she think that?'

'I don't know. At the time, it just seemed like one of her wild statements. You know what she's like.'

'Were you having sex?'

He mumbled something.

'I know you were, Jay, but I need you to tell me because Charlie was scared she was pregnant. She'd missed her period.'

It was as if I'd slapped him. 'What? We didn't . . . we haven't had sex,' he mumbled.

'I don't believe you.'

'That's up to you.' He raised his chin and glared at me. 'It's true.' He clenched his fists and, for a moment, I thought he would hit me. 'Whatever else we've done together, I haven't had sex with your daughter. OK?'

'Do you promise?'

'Promise, swear, cross my heart and hope to die. If I was lying, I'd still promise I was telling the truth, wouldn't I? She wanted to go on the pill first.'

I thought of Alix, Charlie's doctor. 'So is she on the pill?'

'She didn't say.'

Maybe those crosses in the diary meant something different, I thought. Perhaps I was on the wrong track. 'But if you're telling me the truth, why did she think she was pregnant?'

'You'd have to ask her that. Sorry, sorry, I didn't mean that. Maybe . . .'

'Maybe what?'

'*I don't know.*'

'Tell me. Tell me what you're thinking.'

'She had a one-night stand a few weeks ago.'

'Who with?'

'I don't know. She didn't say. She just said she'd done something she regretted and hated herself for it and would I forgive her.'

'And you did?'

'It was like her revenge.'

'You mean you'd done the same?'

'That's really not your business, is it?'

'When did she do this?'

'A few weeks ago.' He thought for a moment. 'Towards the end of last month. I don't know the exact date. I was away in France on my exchange. She told me when I got back.'

I was making calculations in my head. The last cross in her diary had been on November 9, so Charlie's one-night stand had been about two weeks after that. Which would make her almost a couple of weeks late with her period now.

'What else don't I know?' I asked despairingly. 'If I didn't know about you, there might be all sorts of other things I didn't know as well. I thought I knew her inside out and suddenly she's like a stranger to me.'

'She says she's close to you,' said Jay. 'She says you let her be who she is. Not like her dad. She was going to tell you about us when you were in Florida. That's what she said.'

'I just want to find her,' I said. 'If you've done anything to her, I swear—'

'No.'

'Where did you two meet?'

'All sorts of places. On the mainland. Sometimes at my place when no one was there, and in Dad's barns. Or the hulks, though we haven't been there for a week or so. Too cold in this weather.'

'You mean those old boats near the point?'

'Yeah. Nobody goes there, they're too creepy. But me and Charlie like them that way.'

He smiled, and my skin prickled. I felt as cold as ice, and scared.

The hulks were a collection of houseboats and barges that had seen better days. It had been many years since the boats had been lived in by artists and sixties' hippies. Now, the paint had peeled from the hulls and the gangways had collapsed as the boats tipped from their moorings towards the green-grey mud on which they stood. Vandals had done the rest, thrown stones through the windows, ripped off steering wheels and torn out beds and tables, painted graffiti on the decks. I'd walked past them a few times with Sludge, but even on a summer day they gave me the shivers.

'Take me there now,' I said. 'If they're a hiding place for you and Charlie, she might have gone there.'

'You won't find anything. You're wasting your time.'

'Then let's get it over with.'

I pulled on the helmet and fastened the chin-strap. Still he didn't move. I stared at him. 'Is there something you're not telling me?'

'Course not.'

Without another word, he put on his helmet and started the bike. I climbed on behind.

THE LAST TIME I had walked past the hulks it had been with Christian, in early October. A sharp autumn day. The tide had been low then and there'd been dozens of noisy, cheerful gulls perched on the smashed decks. Now, the tide was high and vicious little waves riffled round the hulls. The wind hummed along the ripped planks. There must have been eight or nine.

'Which boat did you and Charlie go to, Jay?' I asked, as I dismounted.

He jerked his head. 'That one there.'

He was indicating one of the smaller wooden boats, which had to be reached by climbing over a larger boat nearer the shore; in its better days it had obviously been bottle-green. In the gloom I could see that the trap door leading to the cabin had been ripped from its hinges.

I dropped the helmet beside the bike. 'You go first.'

'You want to go inside?'

'Why do you think we're here?'

He placed his own helmet on the seat of his bike. 'If this is what you want.'

We had to walk along a gangway to get to the first boat. The wood was slimy and broken, and several times I thought we would slither into the shallow water that was lapping over the mud flats. I clambered onto the deck after Jay and made my way across to the other side, avoiding broken plant pots and a bent, rusted bicycle wheel. We climbed onto the wooden boat.

'Charlie?' I called, as I climbed across. 'Charlie, are you there?'

My voice bounced off all the grimy surfaces, winding its way down into the boat's dismal interior.

I called again, louder, then made my way across to the cabin's splintered entrance and turned round to lower myself down the narrow ladder that led into the cabin. The air was cold and clammy, and everything inside seemed greasy, ancient, abandoned. The mattresses lying across the benches had foam spilling from their split surfaces; a blanket lay on the floor.

Jay, peering in from the deck, gave a little grimace. 'It was OK here,' he said. 'Especially in the summer. We brought beer. Charlie even brought hot chocolate in a flask sometimes.'

So that was where my flask had gone.

I pushed open the door into a foul-smelling toilet. I pulled open the cupboard doors. 'Charlie?' I called again, although I knew she wasn't there.

'I want to see all the others,' I said.

'You what?'

'Now we're here I want to look inside the others. It'll only take a minute.'

When we came back outside, the search didn't look entirely possible. The next boat along had tipped over and brought its neighbour down with it. The two were splayed over in the mud and rising water, their gangways shattered.

'You can't get into those,' said Jay.

'Charlie could have walked across the mud.'

'There'd be tracks.'

'The tide would have worn them away.'

'There's nothing there,' said Jay. 'They're broken and rotten. Who would come here?'

'You came here.'

I walked on. The next boat was a huge barge that looked as if it had been rebuilt by a madman. A junkyard of chaotic objects—planks, tin baths, paint pots, sheets of corrugated iron, a car tyre—had been nailed and bolted to its upper level. The gangplank was rickety and swayed when I stepped onto it.

'It doesn't look safe,' said Jay.

'You're the teenager,' I said. 'I should be the one saying that to you.'

I stretched my arms out like a tightrope walker and teetered across. Once I was on the deck I found a half-open doorway, which led into the darkness below. I saw the slow, shifting glint of stagnant water and there was a smell of seaweed and decay. I took a deep breath and eased myself down a few steps, looked around and saw that there was nothing I needed to bother with. I climbed back up quickly, gasping in the cold air as if I had been under water.

'I'll have to go soon,' said Jay, shifting uneasily.

'I'm almost done,' I said, when I was back on land. The last of the hulks was almost respectable by comparison with its neighbours. Whoever had converted it into a houseboat, a generation or two ago, had done a skilful job. The windows were smashed and the roof was falling in, but enough survived to suggest what had drawn people here to the far side of the island. With a storm raging outside, this boat would have been a cosy refuge.

As I drew closer to its gangplank, I stopped. 'Look,' I said, pointing at the dirty gangplank. 'Someone's been here.'

Jay seemed doubtful. 'Maybe,' he said. 'People come with their dogs.'

I began to shout Charlie's name and that there was nothing to worry about, but it was lost in the wind. Nobody apart from Jay could have heard anything.

'I'll just walk across and check it out,' I said. 'Then you can drop me back.'

I went across the gangplank and stood on the deck looking for a way inside. It wasn't very nautical, more like a dinky wooden shack built on top of the barge. I walked round it until I found the door, then turned the brass handle and it opened inwards. I stepped inside and then felt many things at the same time. It was as if I had stepped off a precipice. Tears prickled behind my eyes. My whole body was very hot, then ice cold, then hot again.

Because what I saw in that cabin, projecting out of the shadows, was the naked foot and leg of a girl. I took several deep breaths. Don't cry. Don't be sick. This was the last thing I could do for my baby, for Charlie.

'Charlie,' I said faintly, but I knew it was hopeless. There was a white, waxy stillness to the foot and the leg that was as dead as the wood it was lying on. I turned away. Then I swallowed and made myself turn round and look at the foot with its grubby sole. I moved closer, feeling my eyes grow accustomed to the darkness.

And then, once again, a jolt and the feeling that the floor had disappeared beneath me. I stood and stared at the body.

With entire calmness, I walked back out onto the deck, took my phone from my pocket and clicked the number of the police station. A voice answered. I didn't know who it was. It didn't matter.

'This is Nina Landry. I'm at the hulks on the southeast of the island. I've found the body of a young girl.'

The voice said something. Static in my ear.

'No,' I said. 'No. It's not my daughter. It's someone else. She has white skin and straight dark hair and is about Charlie's age. I don't recognise her. I'm going to stay here now and wait until you come.'

There was a blue milk crate on the deck and I sat down on it and spoke to the God in whom I don't believe and I said sorry to him and implored him for forgiveness. Because at the moment I had looked down at that girl's face with her blank dead eyes, I had felt a rush of happiness that it wasn't Charlie. I thought of another mother somewhere. Had she been doing what I had been doing? Had she been searching for her daughter?

As the tide rose steadily, slapping against the hull of the boat where I sat, the light was failing. They only had to come from the station and would be here very soon, a few minutes at most. The flat, bleak landscape around me was shrouded in an indeterminate grey; all colours had faded and it was scarcely possible to make out where the sea ended and the solid ground began. I wondered what the dead girl's name was, and who had left her there. A cold, ghastly dread settled on me as I thought of her puffy face and blue lips. Someone had strangled her.

Jay was trying to light a cigarette. He had his back turned to the wind and his fingers were cupped round the flame of each match he struck. Was his hand trembling? I watched him for a few seconds, then stood up and called his name. He didn't hear: the wind wiped away my words. Eventually I left the deck and crossed the gangplank towards him. I called his name sharply.

He spun round, tossed away another spent match and tucked the unlit cigarette behind his ear. 'Are you done?'

'I've found something.'

His face changed: his green eyes seemed to darken, the muscles round his mouth to tighten. 'To do with Charlie?'

'I've found a body,' I said bluntly.

He lifted a hand to cover his mouth but stopped it halfway, and stood for a moment, frozen. I waited, not taking my eyes off his face.

'Is it Charlie?' he asked at last, in a voice that broke, so he started the question a young man and ended it still a boy.

'No.'

His hand made it to his mouth. He closed his eyes and I noticed his long lashes. Then he sprang into activity, fumbling urgently at his jacket for his phone with quivering fingers. 'We've got to call the police.'

'I've called them,' I said. 'They'll be here any minute. Before they arrive, I want you to come and see if you know her.'

'You want me to . . . No, I can't do that. I want to go now. I've done everything I can. This isn't right.'

'Just one quick look.' I held him by the forearm and tugged him towards the gangplank. 'I'll go first. You follow.'

'I want to go home,' he said. 'I want to help find Charlie, but this is sick.'

'Wait till I'm across before you get on, otherwise we'll both fall in.' I walked steadily across, arms akimbo, and at the other side turned to him.

Jay mounted the plank. His face was screwed up as if he was about to cry and his eyes looked like black holes in his pale face.

'Here,' I said briskly, reaching out to him. 'Just a few more inches.'

He put his thin, cold hand into mine. I yanked him towards me and he clambered onto the deck.

'She's in here,' I said. I pulled my sleeve over my hand, pushed the cabin door and went in. I heard Jay behind me, his breathing coming in great gasps. I crouched beside the girl and saw that there were dark red marks on her throat, like violent bruises.

There was a noise behind me, like a door creaking open after decades of disuse, and a shadow fell over her empty face. Jay was bent double in the opening to the cabin, one hand pressed into his stomach. His mouth was half open and out of it came a strange, rusty groaning.

'Do you know her? Jay?'

'No,' he managed, then turned away and ran back across the deck. I heard vomiting. I took a last look at the girl, her long white legs, her uncurled hand, dark hair and open eyes staring through me, and held my breath.

I went out into the icy air to join Jay, who was crouched by the side of the boat, staring out to sea.

'Here,' I said, handing him a tissue from my pocket. He took it and pressed it to his mouth.

'I've never seen a dead body before.'

'You're quite sure you didn't know her?'

He closed his eyes. 'Yes.'

'Here are the police, anyway. Two cars. They'll want to talk to you as well. You'd better ring your parents, tell them what's happening.'

'Yeah,' he said, but made no move.

I stood by the gangplank and raised my hands as the cars approached, their headlights cutting into the gathering darkness. 'This way,' I called as DI Hammill got out, followed by Andrea Beck and, from the second car, Mahoney and a small, balding man who was already pulling on white gloves.

They walked towards me in the grey winter dusk, four figures in thick jackets and stout shoes who cast an air of grim, professional seriousness. No one said anything. DI Hammill walked calmly across the gangplank, upright and unwavering; DC Beck tottered more uncertainly behind him. They both wore white plastic covers on their feet.

'Will you two wait on the shore, please?' Hammill asked. 'I'll be with you shortly.'

In the distance I saw another set of headlights making its way towards us. All four police officers were on the deck now.

I opened my mobile, and selected a number, watching the scene in front of me all the while. 'Ashleigh?'

'Nina? Have you found her?'

'No, but—'

'What can have happened?' she said, in a wail. 'Did you talk to Laura?'

'Yes. Listen, I need to ask you something. A few weeks ago, towards the end of November, you and Charlie went to a party. Jay was away on an exchange and the two of you went together. Remember?'

'I think so. I wouldn't know about the date, though.'

'Whose party was it?'

'Rosie's. Rosie and her older brother, Graham. They live next door but one to the pub on Sheldrake Road.'

'Who was Charlie with that evening?'

A shadow fell across me. Jay was standing beside me, listening. I half turned away from him, but was conscious of him there.

'You mean, like, a boy?'

'Yes. Tell me. Ashleigh, I swear this doesn't matter to me, not a scrap. I just want—I *need*—to know who Charlie might have been with.'

'I think there was someone,' she mumbled. 'But I don't know who. Charlie didn't say. I'd tell you if I did know, honestly. You have to believe me. But the thing is, I wasn't with her most of the time. I'd had a bit to drink, and then it was very crowded and dark, with these strobe lights and a disco. Lots of dancing and people jostling each other and laughing and shouting things at each other. Charlie kind of disappeared on me. But she was all upset afterwards. Really upset, crying and stuff. She never cries. I'm the one who cries and she comforts me. She had to go and wash her face and try to get calm before you came to collect us.'

'What did she tell you?'

DI Hammill had reappeared on the deck.

'She said she'd gone and ruined everything. I pestered her to tell me more, but she went all silent and scowly. I thought she'd tell me in her own time, if she wanted.'

'So who'd know?'

'Maybe Graham. Rosie's brother. He was sniggering about it a few days later, and said something about her taste in men getting weirder, or something, and Charlie turned on him. I thought she was going to hit him. What's it about?' said Ashleigh. 'Why do you want to know?'

'She didn't say she was worried about anything in particular, did she?'

'I don't think so.' Her voice rose in panic. 'I don't know. She's my best friend. I've let her down. I should know how to find her and I don't.'

'No,' I said wearily. 'You shouldn't feel like that.'

'She'll be all right, though, won't she? Nina?'

'Yes,' I said. My voice cracked, so I said it again, louder and firmer. 'Yes. Thanks. And you're being very helpful.'

I watched as DI Hammill walked towards me, then started removing the plastic bags from his feet.

'Well?' I asked, as he stood up.

He ignored me and turned to Jay. 'You're Charlotte's boyfriend?'

Jay nodded. His face was blotchy and scared. There were tears in his eyes.

'The constable there'—he nodded at Mahoney, who was now coming towards us—'will take you to the station to make a statement. All right?'

Jay nodded again.

'Have you called your parents?'

He shook his head.

'Why don't you do that at once?' he said. 'Tell them to come to the station and meet you there. They'll be present while you give the statement.'

Then he turned towards me. 'Come with me,' he said, and walked to his car. As we approached it, we were joined by Andrea Beck, who leaned towards DI Hammill and whispered something in his ear. I heard, 'Brampton Ford,' and saw Hammill nod. I repeated the name to myself for later: Brampton Ford. I'd never heard it.

'What?' I said. 'Who is it? Who's the girl?'

'We'll talk in the car,' Beck said. 'It's cold. You've had a shock.'

Had I? Was I in shock? I thought of my behaviour. Was it affecting my ability to do what I could for Charlie? That was all I cared about.

'I'm fine,' I said, but she opened the back passenger door for me. I got in and she closed it. Hammill sat beside me with Beck in the driver's seat in front. There was a pause.

'What the hell were you doing there?' Hammill asked, a new, hard tone in his voice.

'What do you mean?' I asked. 'There's the body of a young girl over there. What does it matter why I was there?'

Another pause. 'Ms Landry. Your daughter is missing. We're conducting an urgent search for her. Now a girl of about your daughter's age has been found, and you are the person who found her. That seems strange to me. I'm starting to wonder whether you're telling me everything you know. If you're not, I need to warn you that that would be taken very seriously indeed.'

'Of course I am,' I said. 'This is my daughter we're talking about, as well as another poor girl who is someone else's daughter. I've been the one trying to get the police involved when they weren't interested. I'm the one who found this body. I'm doing what you should have done. How dare you accuse me of concealing anything?'

'But that's my point,' said Hammill. 'How did you come to find it? What are you doing here?'

So I told them how I had contacted Jay and what we had talked about. 'I think it's a place where young people come and hang out,' I said. 'There aren't all that many places to get away from people without going to the mainland. As soon as I saw the hulks, it seemed the natural place for someone to hide. Or hide a body, as it turned out.'

'I don't believe this,' said Hammill. 'There are colleagues I know who would lock you up for what you're doing. Haven't you thought you might be making things worse for Charlie? You're talking to witnesses who should be talking to us. You're contaminating the scene. That body in there may be our best chance of finding your daughter and you walked all round it.'

'But the only reason you've even got a crime scene here,' I said, incredulously, 'is because I found it. What I feel is that we're wasting time sitting about. Don't you understand how it feels to be sitting here in this warm car talking and just watching the tide come in, when all the time Charlie may in danger?' I pointed at the watch on Andrea Beck's wrist. 'Look, it's well after four. It's almost completely dark. It's freezing cold. Charlie's been gone for hours. Every minute counts now, every second.'

I stopped suddenly and waited for them to respond.

DI Hammill stared out of the window. His eyes narrowed as if he was looking for something in the gloom. 'I'll be frank with you, Ms Landry. In cases such as this, when a girl has disappeared, we talk to friends, and we check the records for local sex offenders. But, guided by statistical probability, what we do overwhelmingly is talk to boyfriends and, even more important than that, we talk to the family.'

'I know that,' I said. 'That's why you're talking to Rory.'

'He's at the station,' said Hammill. 'He's giving a statement as we speak.'

'As long as it doesn't stop you searching elsewhere,' I said.

'We want a full statement from you as well,' he said.

'I've given a statement. I've given two. There's nothing more I can tell you except this: my daughter's in danger and we've got to find her, and by taking another statement from me, you're letting the clock tick by and it's stupid. It's wrong. You've got to find Charlie!'

'Let's go, Andrea,' said DI Hammill. The young woman turned the key and the car rumbled away.

I pulled my mobile out of my pocket and dialled. 'Hello,' I said, when Rick answered. 'It's me, Nina.'

'Any news? Jackson and I were just—'

'No,' I said shortly. 'Listen, I can't fetch Jackson just now. I've got to go to the police station again.'

'What for?'

I was going to mention the body, then realised it would demand explanation and another telling of my story. 'Another statement,' I said. 'I'll be quick but I won't be picking Jackson up for a bit.'

'But—'

'I really am grateful,' I said. 'Can I speak to Jackson?'

'Mummy?' His voice was small and hopeful. 'Have you got Charlie yet?'

I swallowed hard and gripped the phone. 'Not yet, darling. I won't be long. Either Dad or I will come and fetch you from Rick's soon, all right?'

'Dad's got my Game Boy in his car. I left it when we—'

I cut him off in plaintive midstream. 'We'll bring it.'

'I want it now. I'm bored here and I want my Game Boy.'

'This isn't the right time, Jackson. You're going to have to be patient. I'll get your Game Boy, then I'll come and get you soon.'

'Promise?'

'Promise.'

'Children,' said Beck, as we drew up outside the police station.

I glared at her back, curled my fists in my lap and tried to think only of the things I would have to do as soon as I left there. The first was to track down Rosie's brother and find out who Charlie had been with at the party. I frowned, forcing myself to concentrate, blocking out the terror, erasing the image of the dead girl from my mind. One step at a time, I told myself.

The light thickened outside. A flake of snow fell on my cheek. Behind us, Mahoney was also drawing up. Jay got out of the car. He seemed to have grown thinner and younger in the past hour.

'This way,' said Beck. 'Ms Landry? You're going to have to wait in here for a few minutes until we're ready for you. Have you got anything to read?'

'Are you insane?'

'I know you're upset but there's no need—'

Just then, Rory was shown out of a small side room, a uniformed police officer at his side. If Jay had grown younger, Rory had grown older. He was creased with exhaustion. His hair stuck up in greasy peaks. He was dragging his coat along the floor and walked with a shuffling step.

'This way, sir,' said the police officer, pointing to the toilets.

'What's going on?' I asked.

'They're making me feel guilty because I'm her father. What kind of world are we living in?' he said. 'You believe me, don't you, Nina?'

I looked at his angry face. I thought of the creepy messages he'd sent Charlie. I couldn't think of anything to say.

'Sir,' said the officer, holding open the toilet door.

'Nina?'

'I need something from your car,' I said politely. 'Jackson's Game Boy. He left it in there.'

'Did you even hear what I said?'

'Keys,' I said.

'Our daughter's missing, they're treating me like a criminal and you're going on about Jackson's Game Boy?'

'This way, Ms Landry,' said Beck.

'Just coming,' I said. 'Go ahead and I'll be with you in a minute.'

She sighed and went into the small waiting room. I glimpsed two chairs, and a low table with a large box of tissues on it. Probably a lot of weeping went on in this station. 'Give me your keys,' I said, holding out my hand to Rory. 'You're parked outside, right?'

'I'll get it later.'

'But—'

'I'll fucking get it later,' he shouted, his face crimson with rage. He dropped his coat on the floor and shuffled through into the toilets. I picked it up, pulled out the keys, and walked out of the station. It was heaving with activity, radios crackling, phones ringing, and nobody noticed me go. If I was going to have to wait, I could at least fulfil my promise to Jackson.

I'd spotted Rory's car when we arrived, parked a few yards down the road, one wheel on the kerb. I unlocked the driver's door and peered into the familiar messy interior. No Game Boy. I felt under the seats.

'Ms Landry.'

Beck had followed me. I ignored her, wriggled out of the car and unlocked the boot. There was the usual stuff—a spare tyre, a Wellington boot, a coil of rope, a couple of spanners, a hessian sack. And a flash of colour in the corner. I reached over to investigate it.

For a moment I thought I would be sick. I was feverish, icy, clammy. I bent double, seeing the ground loom queasily towards me. Then the world righted itself and I was standing upright again, holding Charlie's scarf.

It was pale blue, pink and silver, with tiny sequins sewn into it. I had bought it for her when we were on holiday in Italy, eighteen months ago, and she'd fallen in love with it. She wore it all the time, round her neck, tying back her hair . . . She'd been wearing it when she walked out of the door last night, smiling back at me over her shoulder.

I plucked up the hessian sack and there, underneath it, was her leather shoulder bag. I lifted it up with trembling fingers.

'Ms Landry,' said Beck, crossly, 'can you come with me, please? DI Hammill is asking for you and he's—'

I wheeled round, holding the scarf and bag, and started to run. I think I may have been shouting something, but I don't know. I saw startled faces as I sped up the steps, into the station, past the reception desk. I hurtled up the corridor and threw open the door of the small interview room. Rory was sitting on one side of the desk, DI Hammill on the other. As if in slow motion, I saw the cup of coffee jump out of Rory's hand and slop in wide splashes round his chair. I saw his startled face as I brandished the scarf. I saw him half rise, and his mouth was open to say something but I took two strides across the space that separated us and, raising my fists, banged him violently back into his seat, the bag bumping against his chest. Then I leaned towards him and shouted, 'Where is she?'

I felt myself being pulled back as if I were taking part in a pub brawl. I tried to wrestle free but I was forced down onto a chair. I was breathing heavily. Everything around me was like a red fog. Gradually I made myself calm down. 'I'm fine,' I said. 'You can let me go.'

'What's the meaning of this?'

It was DI Hammill, astonished and angry.

'That,' I said, pointing at the scarf and bag on the desk. 'I went to get my son's Game Boy from the car. Charlie's scarf and her bag were in the boot. She had them with her when she went to the sleepover yesterday. It's Rory.'

Hammill and Beck both looked at him. His skin had turned beyond white to an awful blue, like that of a corpse.

'Mr Oates,' said Hammill, in a quiet voice, 'do this scarf and this bag belong to your daughter?'

Rory dabbed at his lips with his tongue. 'I'm sorry, Nina.' He looked back at DI Hammill. 'Yes,' he said. 'They're Charlie's.'

'Did you get them from her today?'

'Yes.'

'Where is she?'

'I don't know.' He put his face on the desk and started to weep, a snotty, wet howling in the silence of the room.

I felt a pain growing inside my chest and spreading through my body.

'Mr Oates,' said Hammill, 'I want to give you another chance. I'm not sure that you recognise the seriousness of the situation.'

'I do,' he said miserably, raising his face from the desk. 'Oh God, I do.'

'Do you admit to seeing your daughter today?' asked Hammill.

'Yes.'

'Has she been in your car?'

'Yes.'

'What the—' I began, but Hammill quickly shut me up.

'Stay out of this, Ms Landry. Try to restrain yourself.' He picked up a chair and moved it closer to the desk at which Rory was sitting. 'Mr Oates, where did you see your daughter? And when?'

Rory gave me another glance. 'Nina is taking our children on holiday,' he said. 'I was in the area this morning. I drove over because I wanted to see them for a moment and say goodbye.'

'You mean,' I said, in a quiet, almost strangled voice, 'that when we talked on the phone this morning, you were on the island?'

Rory continued as if I hadn't spoken. 'When I drove into the town I met Charlie. She was doing her paper round. She sat in the car and we talked for a couple of minutes. She'd been on a sleepover and she left some things with me to save her the trouble of carrying them. In fact, it didn't look safe to me, carrying her shoulder bag as well as the bag of newspapers. And she looked a bit rough. I was going to drop them at the house later.'

'What time was this?' asked DI Hammill.

'About a quarter to ten, something like that. It wasn't for long,' he added.

'And where? Exactly.'

'On Lost Road. It must have been fairly near the beginning of her paper round. Her bag was still quite full.'

'What was her mood?'

'She was surprised to see me, but we had a fairly normal conversation. She mentioned the holiday, that she was looking forward to it.'

'Did she say anything else? Did she mention plans for the day?'

'No. She said she had to get on with her paper round.'

'Mr Oates,' said Hammill, a hard edge to his voice now. 'Why on earth didn't you tell us this before?'

Rory's face had a sullen, expressionless quality that I remembered from the worst of the days before he left. 'It didn't seem relevant,' he said. 'I didn't have any new information to give. I met Charlie before she disappeared, obviously. And people saw her after that.'

'This is our daughter you're talking about!' I said, aghast. 'Are you drunk? Is that it?'

Rory glanced at me and turned back to Hammill, as if in exasperation. 'No,' he said evenly. 'I'm not drunk.'

I looked at Hammill. 'You don't believe this rubbish, do you?'

Hammill's entire face furrowed. 'Mr Oates, I'm inclined to agree with your ex-wife. I cannot understand why you didn't tell us this.'

'It didn't make any difference,' Rory mumbled.

'It *did* make a difference, though,' said Beck. 'One witness told us that she saw Charlie talking to a man while she was doing her paper round. We've been searching for this man. It now seems that he was you.'

'You need to explain yourself,' said Hammill.

Rory crossed his arms hard over his chest, as if he were shutting the rest of the world out. 'I'm not sure if this is the time or the place, but Nina has probably said things about me to you. She's certainly said them to me over the phone today. She's clearly suspected me of having something to do with Charlotte running off. That's the opinion she has of me.'

'So?' asked Hammill, bluntly.

'I've had some business difficulties recently,' said Rory. And Nina has used these problems as a weapon to separate me from my children. She's been threatening me with a restraining order to stop me seeing Charlie and Jackson. When I came to see them this morning, I was breaking our agreement. I couldn't stop myself. I had to see them before they went away. I was worried that if Nina found out, she would start proceedings against me. I'm sorry, I panicked. I didn't think it would do any harm.'

'Hang on a minute,' I said. 'There's something wrong.' I pointed a finger at Rory. 'You talked to me at half past ten, asking if you could see Charlie. I remember Karen telling Eamonn that was the time just before you rang. But you're telling us you saw Charlie at about a quarter to ten.'

'Mr Oates?' said Hammill. His face was stern, grim.

'I was upset,' Rory mumbled. 'Everything felt wrong. Charlie didn't really seem to care that I'd driven all that way to see her. She was just excited about going on holiday with Nina and this new boyfriend. I wanted to see her for more than a few snatched minutes in my car. I wanted to see her properly, and Jackson, like a family.'

'What were you doing between approximately ten and half past?' asked Beck. I'd almost forgotten she was in the room with us.

'I had some beer in the car,' said Rory. 'I drove to the causeway and I was going to go home but then I stopped at the lay-by and walked along the marshes and had a bit of a drink. I was thinking. What? Don't look at me like that. It's true. I know what it sounds like, but it's true.'

'Where's Charlie? Where is she?'

'I love her,' he shouted. 'She's my daughter, for fuck's sake.'

'Stop this, both of you,' said Hammill. 'This is a mess. It's my fault for having you in the room together.'

'What are you talking about?' My voice cracked. 'If I hadn't found Charlie's things in Rory's car, you'd be wasting your time with him lying to you. If he's not going to admit the truth, you've got to get a move on.'

'No,' said Hammill. 'Wait. There's a lot we need to get straight. I'm not clear about the involvement of you and that young man, the boyfriend, in the finding of the body. And it seems to me that there is a good deal that needs to be established about the involvement of Mr Oates. I agree that we need a full account of his movements this morning. But I also need to know more about the dispute over the children.'

'No,' I said. 'That's a diversion. I've told you all you need to know about that. Of course you need to know Rory's full story. And you need to find out if she was pregnant.' I saw the spasm of shock on Rory's face. 'And who by. You don't need to speak to me. Everything I know I've told you. Just find Charlie. It's urgent. Please.'

'Excuse me, Ms Landry,' said Hammill, 'but for now I'd like you to leave me to decide what's urgent. At the moment the danger is to be distracted by a clue which may be irrelevant or misleading. What's important is to get the whole picture clear. So, what I propose to do is to take a detailed statement from Mr Oates here.' He looked at Rory sharply. 'Because there is a possibility of charges being brought against you, we will now be interviewing you under caution. I have to give you certain warnings and the interview will be tape-recorded. You are not under arrest, you are free to leave the interview or seek legal advice at any time. Do you understand?'

'Yes,' said Rory.

'Do you wish legal representation?'

There was a pause. Was it possible that Rory was going to hold up the proceedings while a solicitor was rustled up from somewhere?

'No,' Rory said finally. 'I just want to help.'

Hammill turned to me. 'I want you to wait outside until we have finished with Mr Oates.'

He nodded at Beck, who escorted me out and along the corridor into the office, where a WPC was talking on the phone. Beck asked me if she could get me tea or coffee.

'Coffee, please.'

It was from a percolator in the corner of the office, so it came instantly. I added milk from the little plastic tub, then tore open two packets of sugar and emptied them into the cup. Beck said she would join me again in a minute, then left. I saw that a young uniformed constable was standing outside the room, presumably to keep an eye on me.

I gulped the coffee, which seared my mouth. I was grateful for the jolt that the pain gave me. It helped to clear my mind.

I wasn't sure what to make of Rory, whether he was criminally stupid or guilty of something monstrous. But now he was with the police and there was nothing more I could do. I had to consider other possibilities.

Beck had whispered something into Hammill's ear as she came from the boat where the dead girl lay. Brampton Ford. What was it? A place?

I made up my mind. I swilled back the last of the coffee, stood up and crossed to the window. I tried to pull it open but it was locked. I thought of the young constable standing outside the room, and of Beck returning any minute, and I pulled open the door.

'Can I help you?' the constable asked.

'Where are the toilets?'

'Just down there, to the left.'

'Thanks.'

I went inside the toilet area, had a pee, swilled cold water over my face and wiped it dry with paper towels. Then I walked past the desk once more, trying to appear relaxed. No sign of Beck. I nodded and smiled at the officer on duty, who was on the phone.

'Back soon,' I mouthed at him, and tapped meaninglessly at my wrist, where my watch should have been. He glanced at me, then away again.

I walked out into the street, into the cold dusk. I didn't run until I turned the corner, out of sight of the station, then I sprinted as fast as I could to Sheldrake Road.

Ashleigh had said that Rosie and Graham lived next door but one to the pub that was at the far end of Sheldrake Road. I had a stitch in my side and my legs felt heavy when I arrived at the Barrow Arms, which had a huge inflated reindeer outside the front door. The lights inside were all on and I could hear laughter through the closed doors.

Next door but one was a pink, pebbledashed house. The curtains were drawn and lights were on, upstairs and down. That was a good sign.

I rang the doorbell and stood, panting, as I waited for someone to answer.

'Hello?' The fattest man I'd ever seen stood in the doorway.

I tried to smile at him. 'Sorry to bother you,' I said. 'Could I speak to Graham or Rosie?'

'Rosie's not here. Graham's around. Who shall I say it is?'

'He won't know me. I'm Nina Landry. Tell him I'm Charlie's mother. Charlie Landry Oates, and I need his help. It's urgent. Really urgent.'

Slowly he turned his bulk on the patterned carpet. 'Graham,' he called up the stairs. 'A lady to see you. She says it's urgent.' Over his shoulder he asked me to come in and I followed him down the hallway and into a warm living room where a bar fire glowed in the corner. On every shelf, there were massed armies of tiny, brightly painted warriors and strange creatures.

'Graham and I painted them together,' he said, following my gaze. I had the awful feeling that he was settling down for a conversation. 'After his mother died. It was something to take his mind off things. There's three different armies there. Over two thousand of them.'

'Amazing,' I said. 'Is Graham coming?'

'He doesn't play with them now. Hardly even talks to me. They get like that as they grow up. He's on his way down. Get you a cup of tea?'

'I'm all right. No tea, thanks. I won't be a moment.'

'Hi, you wanted to talk to me?'

The young man was tall and slim, with the brown eyes of his father, who might once have resembled him before he became fat.

'I'm Charlie Landry Oates's mother, Nina.'

'Yes?'

'She came to a party here.'

'Yeah, that one time.' He cast an amused, contemptuous glance at his father. 'You were away.'

'A party? You should have told me,' his father said.

'We cleared up, didn't we?'

'Yes, but—'

'Can I ask you one thing?' I interrupted. 'Then I'll go.'

'Right. This lady doesn't want to hear you complaining. She's come to talk to me.'

'Do you want me to leave?' asked his father.

'It doesn't matter,' I said.

'Yes,' said Graham.

His father struggled to his feet. 'I'll leave you two together, then.'

'Thanks.'

'Right,' said Graham. 'That's him out of the way.'

'I want to know who Charlie was with that evening.'

'You mean who she got off with?'

'Yes.' I gritted my teeth. 'That's what I mean.'

'Why would you ask me something like that? And why would you think I'd tell you? It was a party. People were with other people.' He gave a shrug.

'Charlie's missing,' I said. 'She's in danger.'

'Missing? I wouldn't worry too much. I'm sure she can look after herself.'

I thought about kneeing him hard in the groin to wipe the smile off his face. 'The police are involved. She's in danger and every minute counts. Whoever she was with at your party might know something. So, tell me.'

'Right, right.' He raised his hands in mock surrender. 'But tell her I tried to stop you. If you really want to know, it was that Goth boy. The teacher's kid. You know. Eamonn. The one with the ponytail and black nails.'

'Eamonn and Charlie? You're sure?'

'Oh, yes.' He gave a horrible suppressed snigger. 'Quite sure.'

I closed my eyes. I saw Eamonn's face at the surprise party as he asked after Charlie. His expression, which I'd read as one of furtive supplication but now saw as something different. Lust? Triumph? Fear?

'Thanks,' I managed. 'Say goodbye to your father, will you?'

I shut the front door and walked back down the street.

Eamonn. He was a clever, lonely boy flooded by dark, troubled thoughts. I'd always liked him, felt sorry for him, but now, with no difficulty at all, I could imagine him as someone who would harm my daughter. Him, Rory, Jay . . . My mobile rang in my pocket. I pulled it out and looked at the number. I guessed Hammill or Beck was wondering where I was, ordering me to report back to the station, like a schoolgirl caught truanting. I let it ring. There were two messages and I listened to them both. The first was from Jackson, who must have left it before I talked to him in the police car, and the second from Christian, saying the traffic was still crawling along and it would probably take him another couple of hours before he could be with me. He told me he loved me.

I had to find Eamonn. I didn't have his mobile number, nor did I know any of his friends. I'd have to ring Rick. The screen on my mobile flashed a low-battery warning, then went blank. I pressed the on button and nothing happened. It was dead. I'd have to go there.

Sheldrake Road wasn't far from Karen and Rick's house, although as I jogged along the unlit street, gasping for breath, it felt impossibly far. I raced past Miller Street and onto The Saltings; the road ran along the shoreline. On my left there were houses with lights glowing through drawn curtains, smoke rising out of chimneys, on my right the dark water. The tide was nearly up now. I could hear little waves lapping against the shingle.

The lights were still on in Rick's house, but when I rang the doorbell and banged furiously with the knocker, no one came. I banged again, then stood back and yelled their names. My voice echoed over the water behind me. There was no response.

I stood outside in the icy darkness, thinking. If I couldn't find Eamonn, I had to concentrate on finding out who the dead girl was. I turned and walked along the seafront, past the restaurant that never was, past the boatyard, and to my front door. In the gloom, I fumbled the key into the lock, and as I pulled the door open Sludge shot forward and banged into my leg. She jumped up, putting her paws on my chest, all shining eyes.

As I brought her inside I switched on the light and saw an envelope on the mat. I tore it open. It was my car key with a note from Tom the vicar: *Dear Nina, The terminals just needed a wipe. Buy me a drink some time. Cheers! Tom.* I took that to mean that my car was functioning.

In the kitchen I plugged my phone into its charger and a little digital plug on the screen winked at me.

I found a road atlas and looked up Brampton Ford. It was a village a few miles inland. So the dead girl was from nearby. I had an idea. I ran upstairs and opened the door to my own bedroom. It was dark but I couldn't hear Renata's breathing and neither was there a submerged hump in the bed. I turned on the light and saw she had gone. I found a scribbled note on the pillow: *I was only in the way. I'll be in touch. R.*

In Charlie's bedroom I sat at the laptop and went to Google. I typed 'Brampton Ford'. It was hopeless. There were a quarter of a million entries. It turned out that there was even a Brampton Ford in Australia with a squash team in the third division of a league in New South Wales.

Charlie had been good at searches. What would she have done? What would the sort of information I needed consist of? Nobody knew yet that the girl was dead . . . So I added the words 'girl' and 'missing' and pressed search again. I knew instantly that I had found what I was looking for: *Local schoolgirl, Olivia Mullen, 16, has been missing since . . .* I clicked on the link. It was a series of short items on a news report from the southeast of England. *Local schoolgirl, Olivia Mullen, 16, has been missing since December 12, when she failed to return from a shopping expedition at the Coulsdon Green centre. At a press conference, her parents, Steven and Linda Mullen, made an emotional appeal for information . . .*

Olivia Mullen. It provoked a distant, elusive memory. Livia Mullen. Livvie Mullen. Liv Mullen. I knew that name. I went through my memory, looking for it as if it were a book in a library, saying it aloud to myself. I was sure I had never heard her name spoken. So I had seen it printed. No, not printed. Written. In handwriting. Where would I have seen a girl's name written out by hand? I made an effort of searching my memory that was almost physical, that hurt, as if I were pushing my hand into a tiny dark space for something that was just out of reach. It was on a letter or a postcard. I was sure of it. No problem. Charlie's bedroom was now my special sphere of knowledge. I was the world expert. Charlie kept her letters in the bottom two right-hand drawers of her desk.

I pulled them all out, and tipped them onto the floor in a large pile. One by one I scanned them for names, moving them to another pile when I had found no mention of Liv or Livia or Olivia. There were names I knew and names I had never heard of. How had Charlie made time for all these people? The pile shrank and then I was at the end and I almost howled. I had found nothing. But I was right. I knew I was right.

I started pulling out the other drawers and tipping the contents onto the floor. I rummaged through them, looking for a letter or a card I might have missed but there was nothing. In this one respect, Charlie had been organised. She might have lived in chaos but it was an organised chaos. The letters and cards she received went into those drawers and nowhere else.

Except for one other place. Charlie had spent much of the last few months working on her coursework for her art GCSE. This consisted of a bulky scrapbook full of drawings, text and pictures. There were images downloaded from the Internet, cut from magazines. And postcards. I sat at Charlie's desk and began to flick through, ripping out postcards and checking the text on the back.

And then I saw it. A picture of a row of beach huts, in pastel colours: blues, yellows, greens and pinks. I recognised it immediately. A cross had been drawn on one of the huts, and the single word 'Remember?' written perkily beside it. I peeled off the card and turned it over. That was it. She wrote in a large, beautifully formed handwriting: *And being blown over in the wind? And the wettest wet suit in the world. Sorry for silence. Computer down. Yeah, you're right. Gonna finish it. Don't know why I ever let it start. See soon. Luv Liv.*

That was what I'd remembered. The funny salutation, like a tongue twister from the Dr Seuss books I used to read to Charlie: *Luv Liv.* I stared at the words until they blurred. *Gonna finish it. Don't know why I ever let it start.* What did that mean? Finish what? Finish with whom? Was I right to connect the Liv of the postcard with the Olivia I had seen lying in the abandoned hulk? Was I just looking at clouds and seeing shapes in my imagination? I put the thought away. I felt instinctively certain that Liv was Olivia Mullen, and that Olivia Mullen was the girl I had found dead in one of the hulks—where Charlie used to go with Jay.

Perhaps Olivia had gone there to finish 'it', whatever 'it' was. Who had she met there? And now Charlie had disappeared too and . . . The thought rose in my throat, choking me. I jumped up and ran downstairs, catching my foot halfway in my hurry and twisting my ankle. I felt a sharp, searing pain. When I reached the phone I dialled the number for the police station. A woman answered and I said I would like to speak to DI Hammill or DC Beck, at once. To do with the dead girl, I added, to make them hurry.

In less than thirty seconds, Beck was on the phone.

'It's Nina,' I said.

'Nina—Ms Landry—would you please come to the station immediately,' she said, trying to inject authority into her voice. 'DI Hammill is not at all pleased that you disappeared. Well, actually, I've never seen him so furious. I'd hate to be in your shoes right now. He's talking about an—'

'Never mind all of that now. I have some important information for you. Charlie was a friend of Olivia Mullen.'

'Olivia Mullen? But how do you know? What makes you think—'

'I don't have time to explain. I know who the dead girl is and I know that Charlie knew her. There's a postcard I've just found.'

'But—'

I heard a voice and the rattle of the receiver being seized. 'Is that her? Let me take it. Give it to me now.' Beck was right. DI Hammill sounded very cross indeed. 'Ms Landry, I am warning you that if you don't come to the police station this instant there will be serious consequences.'

'Shut up!' I shouted over him. 'Charlie knew Olivia Mullen. There's a postcard from Olivia to her. And it has a picture of beach huts on it. That may be important.'

'Ms Landry.' He was shouting too. 'Your behaviour is inappropriate and it may be dangerous. You may be putting your daughter at greater risk because of it.'

'Did you hear? They knew each other—'

'*Ms Landry!* I'm sending a police car to collect you. Do you understand? And if you're not there . . .'

I put the phone down. I shut my eyes and pressed my fingers to my temples, trying to think. Olivia and Charlie were friends. Yet I didn't think I'd ever heard Charlie speak about her and I'd never seen her myself. Who would tell me? Ashleigh? I dialled her mobile.

'Hello, Ash—'

'Did Charlie know someone called Olivia Mullen?'

'What? I don't know. Maybe, but you know Charlie has all these different compartments in her life and she kind of keeps them separate—'

I cut her off, and stood holding the receiver, keeping the police calls at bay. Who would know? A nasty little thought sneaked into my brain. Olivia's parents, of course. Steven and Linda Mullen. Two people who had been waiting for their daughter, as I had. But had they been told yet? I couldn't call them . . . Yes, I could. I could do anything, however terrible, if it helped me find Charlie. I could save my guilt and my pity for later.

I dialled 118118 and an operator asked me what number I was looking for. 'Mullen,' I said. 'Steven Mullen, from Brampton Ford.'

There was a pause. Then: 'I have the number here. Shall I put you through?'

'Yes,' I said. My heart was thumping loudly.

An automated voice came on, giving me the number and saying that the remainder of the call would cost nine pence a minute. Then there was a ringing tone. Then there was a voice.

'Yes?' The woman sounded breathless. I knew at once it was the mother, and that she hadn't heard yet. I knew she was sitting, waiting for the phone to ring, and every time it rang she would snatch it up and think it might be Olivia. I knew exactly the sickening dread and choking hope she was feeling. I knew all that and still I pressed on. 'Is that Linda Mullen?'

'Speaking.'

'Mrs Mullen, this is Detective Constable Andrea Beck,' I said.

'Olivia?' The question came out in a gasp.

'There's no news as yet,' I said. 'I just wanted to ask you a question.'

'Yes?' This time the voice was flat and dull.

'Do you know if she ever went to Sandling Island?'

'Sandling Island? Yes, she did. I think I told that other detective she—'

'That's fine. It's just something we're checking. Can you tell me why she was there, and when? The exact dates, please?'

'She went on a five-day windsurfing course.'

Charlie had done the windsurfing course. I remembered her at the end of each day, her hair streaked and bleached by sun, sand and salt, her skin gritty and golden.

'She had a wonderful time, made friends with some other teenagers there. She came back all tanned and glowing. She wanted to go again next year.' There was a tiny sob at the end of the line. 'Um, sorry—when? Hang on, I've got my diary here, I can check the dates.' There was a rustling of pages. 'Here: Monday the 9th through to Friday August the 13th.'

'Thank you,' I said.

'Why? Is there something you've found?'

'One last thing: did she ever mention a girl called Charlie. Charlotte Landry Oates?'

'Charlie? Yes, she really liked her. There's a postcard from . . . Hold on. There's someone at the door. I won't be a minute. I'll just see who it is.'

Now I could hear her feet clipping across a tiled floor, her breath still coming down the line. There was the sound of a door opening. 'Hello,' she said, to whoever was there. Then her voice changed. 'What? What is it?'

I banged the phone down and pressed my forehead against the wall. I felt sick with shame. But I had no time for that. The police would be here at any minute. I picked up the car key and my charging mobile, and ran out of the door, banging it shut behind me.

As I ran, my ankle throbbed and my head throbbed and the wind howled against my sore eyes, which were straining in the gloom to see where I was going. I tried to think. Ideas, thoughts, bounced around in my head. Charlie and Olivia had met at a windsurfing course last summer. Who had taught them? Well, among other people, Joel. Bloody Joel. The man who'd held me in his arms and told me he loved me.

I ran up The Street to my car, praying it would work. A police car passed and I put my head down, hoping they wouldn't see me. Music and light spilled out from the pub. I reached the car, fumbled the key into the door, flung myself into the driver's seat. There was a newspaper on the front passenger seat folded up in a roll. It must have been left by Tom the vicar because in a white space he had written *SERVICE ME!* I think he meant the car. I put the key into the ignition and turned it. The engine coughed, rasped, then started. One day I'd buy the vicar his drink.

I plugged in my mobile, then swung the car out and accelerated along the road, turning right into Lee Close, left on The Street, then into Flat Lane.

I screeched to a halt outside Joel's house, leapt from the car and hobbled up to the front door, where I leaned on the bell, banging with my other fist. When the door swung open, I almost fell into the hall, stumbling upright to see Alix staring at me in a kind of angry astonishment. I could see Tam's frightened face through the banisters.

'Where's Joel?' I shouted into Alix's face.

'What on earth—' I saw her eyes narrow, her face pinch. 'He's at the back. He's just come in and is about to take a shower. Why—'

I barged past her, my shoes slapping on the floor. 'Joel?' I yelled.

'Nina!' He came out of the utility room, still in his work clothes, although his shirt was half unbuttoned and his boots were off. 'What on earth . . .?'

'Olivia Mullen,' I said, advancing on him with Alix behind me. 'Did you teach her windsurfing in the summer?'

'Hang on.' He put one hand on my shoulder to steady me and I twitched it off. 'Calm down and tell me what's going on. You haven't found Charlie?'

'I don't have time for all of that. Olivia Mullen. I think her friends called her Liv. She was knocking around with Charlie.'

'I don't remember her.'

'You must do. She was there from August the 9th to the 13th.'

He thought for a moment. 'For what it's worth, I was off that week.'

'You weren't,' said Alix, coldly, from behind him.

'I was.'

'Where were you, then?' said Alix. 'Off with some woman?'

'Mum?'

Tam was standing in the doorway. Her eyes were red and her face was puffy.

'Don't worry,' said Alix, not turning. 'I'll be with you in a minute. Wait upstairs.'

'I don't believe you,' I said. I glared at Joel and his eyes were cold and steady on me.

'I don't care what you believe,' he said. 'It happens to be the truth. What's this Olivia got to do with Charlie disappearing anyway, and what makes you think that I'm in any way involved? I'd like you to come out with it.'

For a moment his face was taut with anger, then his expression softened. He took a step forward so his face was just a few inches above mine. 'Look, Nina, I know how desperate you are about Charlie. It's every parent's nightmare, and if there's any way I can help you, I will, but you should know who your friends are.' Alix gave a loud snort behind us but I paid no attention. 'I'm your friend,' he continued. 'And you can trust me—'

'Right. Give me that,' I said, pointing at the large wooden mallet that was protruding from his toolbag.

'What on earth do you want it for?'

'Never mind,' I said, and bent to pick it up. Its heaviness surprised me.

'She's gone mad,' said Alix.

'Maybe. Maybe not. I need a powerful torch, too.'

'There's one in the bag,' said Joel. 'Here.'

'I'm calling the police,' said Alix.

I walked past them and out of the front door, carrying the mallet in one hand and the torch in the other. I was huge and strong with despair.

I climbed into my car, and as I was about to pull away, the passenger door opened.

'Nina.'

'I don't have time,' I said.

He got in and shut the door. 'I'll come with you, then.'

I shrugged and moved off, out of the corner of my eye seeing him wince at the sudden speed.

'I don't know Olivia Mullen, whoever she is. You have to believe me, Nina. And how can you not believe me, after all the things we—'

'No more, Joel. I'm through with people's promises, and I'm through with trust. It doesn't matter what you say.'

There was a brief silence.

'Where are we going?'

'Not far.'

I turned onto The Saltings and drove past my house. A thought occurred to me. 'If you weren't teaching that week, who would have taught her?'

'In the summer there are dozens of people teaching sailing, kayaking and windsurfing. Some of them belong to the yacht club. Some are just students hired for the summer. Some instructors come with their groups. Then people from the island help out as well, even if it's only for a day or so. Me, of course. Bill usually, but then boats are his business. Rick, though it's become a bit of an issue that Eamonn always refuses to join in. Tom occasionally, and some of the kids think it's a hoot when they find out he's the vicar. Even Alix has been known to rig a dinghy or two on weekends off. If you want to find the one who taught this girl, I wouldn't know where to start. We could go to the yacht club when it opens tomorrow morning, but it would be a long business.'

'I can't wait till tomorrow morning.'

Everything that was familiar now looked strange. The moon was low in the dark sky and I could see the first scattering of stars above the inky, shifting water. I used to love Sandling Island at night: the silence, the smell of salt and mud, the chime of halyards and the forlorn cry of birds. Now it terrified me.

I rounded the corner, past the boatyard, and arrived at the sandy beach. I drew to a halt and climbed out, dragging the mallet.

'Bring the torch,' I called to Joel, over my shoulder.

'Nina, what are you doing? Wait. Let's talk about this. Nina!'

Joel was behind me, slipping on the soft sand in his big boots. I ignored him and marched towards the beach huts, my ankle sending stabbing pains up my leg. They stood in the gloom like a row of sentinel boxes. They weren't like the pastel pictures in Olivia's postcard. Many were run-down, with peeling paint and rusty locks. They were numbered, as if in a residential street. There weren't that many—twenty or thirty, perhaps.

I started with number one, a green hut with curtains at its windows. After a cursory push to make sure the door was locked, I lifted the wooden mallet to one side, like a cricket bat, and swung it violently. There was a satisfying crash, a splintering sound, and the door caved in.

'Nina! What the hell . . .'

'Torch. Shine it inside.'

Joel turned it on. I saw his face glowing eerily in its light, then the beam turned on the interior of number one. It was all put away neatly for winter, everything in its proper place, not a thing awry.

'You can't—'

'I can do anything. Charlie might have been in there.'

I stepped out, picked up the mallet again, and walked the few steps to number two, which had seen better days. It was a faded red, and someone had patched up its holes with rusting corrugated iron. I swung the mallet again. This time, I aimed wrong and missed, spinning with it, and feeling the force of the blow wrench my shoulder almost from its socket. The mallet glanced off the side of the door, leaving an ugly welt in the wood.

'Are you planning to break into all these huts?'

'That's the general idea.'

'There's no point in me talking about things like criminal damage or breaking and entering?'

'No.'

'Here,' said Joel. He laid the torch on the ground, its beam pointing at the door. 'Give it to me.'

'No.'

He put his hand on the handle, and for a brief moment, we struggled. I saw him in the torchlight, his face a luminous whitish-green and his mouth and eyes black holes. Then he wrenched it from my grip.

'Stand back.' He lifted the mallet and with one efficient blow on the lock, sent the door swinging open.

I picked up the torch and peered inside. It was a mess—old towels, plastic bottles and crisp packets on the floor, baggy swimming trunks and a stained T-shirt flung across a chair—but nothing sinister. What was I expecting? Charlie tied and gagged, waiting for me there?

'Number three?' asked Joel. I nodded, and he chopped into that door. There was a faint smile on his face as the wood splintered. 'Don't tell Alix,' he said. 'I don't think she'd be very understanding.'

I didn't reply. I had no words left for anything except the task in hand. I could only pick up the torch and shine it into each unfamiliar interior, stare in on the intimate details of some stranger's life, turn away again.

Joel got into a rhythm, smashing a door and moving on. I followed. The waves licked the beach; the torch threw long, quivering shadows against the rippled surface of the sand and the sea. The ripped doors of the huts banged uselessly in the wind. The world was as unreal as a nightmare.

'That's all,' said Joel at last. 'Are we done?'

'Yes,' I said blankly. 'I'll drop you back.'

The idea of the beach huts had seemed like an inspiration, a brilliant deduction, which would end with Charlie back in my arms. Now I realised it had simply been a last act of useless despair.

We got into the car and I started to drive. 'I won't say anything about all the damage to the huts,' Joel said.

'I will,' I said. 'I'll be seeing the police in a minute. I'll tell them.'

'Don't,' he said. 'They'll assume it was vandals. It'll all come off insurance anyway.'

'Joel,' I said. 'I don't care.'

There was more silence. Silence and darkness outside, and beyond that the sea. All hope had gone, really, and I felt now I needed activity to stop myself thinking about the horror of what the rest of my life would be. I saw my mobile phone blinking up at me as it charged.

'Could you phone Rick for me?' I said. 'The number's on the phone.'

'Sure. I know it anyway,' said Joel, punching it in. He put the phone to his ear. 'Hi, Rick, it's Joel. I'm with Nina . . . No, nothing yet . . . I know. Any word about Karen? . . . Right. Well, let me know if you hear anything.' He looked at me. 'What do you want to tell him?'

'Tell him I'll be along in a few minutes to pick Jackson up.' I remembered something else. Did it matter any more? Well, what else did I have to do? 'Ask him for Eamonn's mobile number. There's a pen in the glove compartment.'

Joel wrote the number on the rolled-up newspaper. The rest of the short journey took place in silence. I pulled up outside his house.

'I hope things are all right with Alix,' I said.

'Not too good,' he said. 'As you saw.'

'I've probably made it worse.'

'I'm not sure that's possible, just at the moment.' He opened the passenger door, then paused. 'Nina, I'm not sure if I've ever told you how much—'

'Joel,' I said, stopping him. 'This is not the time for it. I've got to go.'

He got out, shut the door and walked slowly up the path to his house. I put the little light on above the rearview mirror so that I could read Eamonn's phone number and dial it. It was answered after several rings.

'Eamonn? It's Nina. Where are you?'

He didn't seem sure. I heard him ask someone the address. I heard the someone say it slowly and clearly, as if to a deaf person. It was Grendell Road, just round the corner on the way out of town. 'Don't worry,' I said. 'I heard. I'll be there in a minute or two. Meet me outside.'

I was there in less than a minute and when I arrived I could see that the front door to number fourteen was ajar. As I shut the car door, I could see the outline of a person standing to the right of the porch. I pushed open the gate and walked up the gravel path. 'Eamonn?' I said.

'Yeah.' He stepped out of the shadows. From inside I could hear voices and music that I could feel under my feet. As I approached, I realised I hadn't thought of what I wanted from him, what I needed to know. He took a last drag of his cigarette and tossed it aside. His eyes looked different from when I had seen him last, the pupils dilated.

I brought up my right hand and slapped him hard. I felt so very, very angry. About his silence, his evasions, but also his being here, with music and friends and dope on this night of all nights, for laying his hands on my daughter, for loving her but not being out on the marshes howling her name, for being young and thoughtless, safe and alive. He hardly reacted.

'I know that you and Charlie had sex. Why the hell didn't you tell me?'

'How could I have told you?' he said.

'For Chrissake, Charlie's missing, Eamonn. Missing. Gone. That's the only thing that matters. I needed to know. And hours ago, not now.'

'It's not got anything to do with Charlie going,' he said. 'Why should I have told you? I promised Charlie it would always be a secret and that I'd never tell anyone. It was just something that happened,' he muttered, his face screwed up. 'It happened, and then she was sorry and I . . . I didn't mention it because it wasn't relevant to anything.'

'Who are you to judge that?' I said, my voice raised. 'The police will be talking to you soon. I'd guess they'll be suspicious of a boy who had recently slept with the missing girl and said nothing about it.'

'I'm sorry,' he said, shuffling from one foot to another. 'You know how much I like Charlie. I love her, if you want to know. She's different. But she doesn't love me. She thinks I'm a weirdo.'

He turned abruptly and kicked the wall of the house several times; little chips of mortar flew off his massive black boot. When he turned back to me tears were rolling down his face.

'You'll need to pull yourself together before you're interviewed. But before that, I want to ask you a couple of questions. 'Do you know where Charlie is?'

'No.'

'Who knew about you and Charlie?'

'Nobody,' he said. 'It was a secret.'

'That's not true, for a start,' I said. 'There were other people at the party. They knew.'

'They didn't really know,' said Eamonn. 'And I didn't talk about it. Maybe there were rumours.' There was a pause. 'Like I said, I think Charlie felt sorry for me. I knew that even at the time. And she was a bit drunk. That's a bit pathetic, isn't it? I was a bit angry when she told me it had been a mistake. But it was what I expected in a way. It seemed too good to be true.'

'Did your parents know?'

'My dad found out.'

I felt a terrible plummeting sense of misery that was almost physical, as if my stomach had been pummelled. Did everyone know more about my daughter than I did? Rick should have told me. He owed me that. That was what I needed. Honesty, not someone mending the rattle in my car.

'What did he say?'

'He said what he always says, which is basically that I'm a piece of shit and that I'm not worth anything. Which is probably about right.'

That was my cue to say something reassuring and nurturing but I didn't have time. 'Do you know a girl called Olivia Mullen?'

'Who's she?'

'I think Charlie got to know her over the summer. They learned to windsurf together.'

'I didn't know anything of that bit of her life,' Eamonn said. 'I don't get to the beach much, as you can see. That's another of my dad's gripes with me. Why can't I do outdoor things like other teenagers? Like he does?'

'All right,' I said. 'You'd better get yourself some coffee, or whatever you need to clear your head, because you're going to have a difficult couple of days. I'm driving to your house now to get Jackson. Do you want a lift?'

'No,' he said. 'I don't.'

'If you remember anything else, call me on my mobile. You've got my number now.'

'All right. The police haven't found anything, then?'

'No,' I said, as I walked away. 'They've found nothing at all.'

As I turned round in Grendell Road and drove back onto The Street I felt like a shell of a person. I would be able to drive and talk and do things but inside there was nothing. All there was to do now was to collect Jackson and then go back to the police station to face the music. Wasting police time. Criminal damage. There was probably plenty more. As I turned towards Rick and Karen's house I could see the lights on the mainland. Everywhere there were homes for which this had been just another day.

I turned right along the seafront and pulled up outside their house. The lights were still on. I knocked at the door and Rick opened it and I saw Jackson behind him. I thought, What would a normal person with real, human emotions say at this moment? They would express regret and gratitude. 'I'm so sorry,' I said. 'I'm really grateful to you for looking after Jackson. Especially after everything that's happened to Karen.'

'That's no problem, Nina. Jackson and I have had a rare old time, haven't we, big guy?'

Jackson didn't answer. He was leaning on me, clutching my hand, rubbing himself against me, something he would do only if he was very,

very tired. It almost made me feel human.

'I'm sorry,' I said. 'I came earlier but you were out.'

'We went to do some shopping,' he said. 'Your son's good company.' His face shifted to that look of useless concern I had become used to. 'Any word of Charlie?'

I shook my head. 'I heard about her and your son,' I said.

There was a long pause. I tried to make out the expressions that flickered across his face: surprise, contempt, anger. He looked like a stranger.

'Rick? You should have told me at least.'

He rubbed his face and when he turned to me again it was simply tired. 'Maybe you're right, Nina. God knows, I thought about it then because I was worried and, of course, I thought about it again today and wondered if it was relevant. I honestly don't think it is. The boy's a disaster zone, Nina. He always has been. I was furious with him at the time. But even then . . . It was just a mess, a typical bloody teenage mess. I thought Charlie might have told you. Did you have no idea?'

'No. But I'm discovering that there was a lot she didn't tell me.'

'I'm sorry. So sorry about everything.' He put a hand on my shoulder and squeezed it. Jackson tugged at my hand, trying to pull me away.

'I know,' I said. 'I don't mean to blame you. I've spent the day shouting at people.'

'That's all right,' said Rick. 'You know I'll do anything I can to help you.'

I said wearily, 'There's nothing left. You've done too much already. I'll give you some rest. Come on, Jackson. We'll go home. Thanks, Rick.'

'She'll turn up,' Rick said. 'I'm sure of it.'

'I guess so,' I said. 'You've never come across an Olivia Mullen, have you? Charlie got to know her over the summer.'

Rick looked thoughtful and shook his head. 'It doesn't ring a bell,' he said. 'But there are so many people who come to the beach in the summer. It's hard to keep track. Who is she?'

'That's what I'm trying to find out. Joel said the same about her. Nobody seems to have met her except Charlie. Anyway, thanks for everything.'

'That's all right, my love,' said Rick. 'Go home and get a good night's sleep. You look as if you need it. Things will be all right, Nina.'

I thought that for the first time in that frenzied day, with his wife's injury and the visit to the hospital, he seemed calm, composed. Perhaps it was a relief to have Karen away for a night. He closed the door and I walked to the car with my arm round Jackson. I held him as close as I could, feeling his warm body against mine. I opened the front passenger door for him. He took the newspaper that was lying there and put it on his lap.

I switched on the engine and drove away. 'What did you do with Rick?' I asked.

'Played on the computer.'

'And then you went out?'

'Yeah.'

I imagined Rick taking Jackson for a treat, like the uncle my son didn't have. 'Did he buy you anything nice?'

'No, nothing. Just a booklet he needed. He was looking for it in all his drawers and then he said we might as well buy another.'

'Oh, right,' I said. 'We're home.'

I opened the door and the light inside the car came on. Jackson looked down at the paper on his lap. 'What's this?' he said.

'The local paper. The vicar left it. He fixed the car. First Rick tried to fix it when there was nothing wrong with it, and then the vicar fixed it when it wouldn't start. People have been trying to fix things all day.'

'I mean why's her picture in the paper?' asked Jackson.

He held it up. On the front page there was a photograph of a girl, smiling at the camera. She had dark brown hair and looked happy and young. The headline read, *MISSING GIRL, 16*, and in smaller letters, *Police Hunt*. I looked at the caption and saw what I expected: *16-year-old schoolgirl, Olivia Mullen, missing since last week.*

I put my hand on Jackson's. 'It's very sad,' I said. 'Her body was found here today.'

'She's the girl who took the photo.'

'What photo?'

'The one of me and Charlie. The one she sent in the post.'

The one I'd given to the police. My head spun. I leaned towards him in the half-darkness and gripped his arm. 'She was with you and Charlie last week?'

'You were saying who was she, and I didn't know, but it was her. Now I remember. She was nice. Giggly.' He jerked away from me. 'What d'you mean, her body? Is she dead? What's she got to do with Charlie going?'

'I've got to think,' I said. 'Don't say anything. Wait.'

I turned on the car's interior light and scanned the story. Olivia had disappeared last Sunday. She had told her parents that she was going shopping with a friend; they had neither seen nor heard from her since.

Did this change anything? Aware of Jackson huddled beside me, tired and scared, I gazed out at the sea, almost invisible in the dark, and tried to clear my brain of everything but the necessary information. I had the feeling that I knew all I needed to know but hadn't been able to connect the pieces.

Olivia Mullen had come to see Charlie on the morning of Sunday, December 12. I knew that from the date print-out on the photograph. I even knew the time: 11:07. According to the paper, that was the day she had gone missing. So she had visited my daughter and then she had disappeared. And she had said she was going to 'finish it'.

A story about Olivia's disappearance had been published this morning in the paper that Charlie was delivering, and Charlie had also disappeared. The two linked facts whirled in my brain. What else did I know? I knew Charlie had been bullied and yesterday night had had her juice spiked by her so-called friends. I knew that she had a boyfriend, but had kept it secret for months, creeping out to assignations with him on the hulks. I knew she'd had a fling with Eamonn, that Eamonn had told his father.

I knew that someone had come into my house while the abortive party had been going on and taken things that belonged to Charlie, but that it couldn't have been Charlie. This was after the bicycle had been abandoned halfway through the paper round. Could it have been as a decoy? To make it look as if Charlie had run away when she'd done no such thing? Whoever had done it had perhaps only done it for show. They had taken only things that were visible, things whose absence would be noticed. I knew that Olivia and Charlie had met in the summer on a course that Joel had taught on. But so had dozens of others.

Something had crept into my brain, a tiny wisp, like fog. What? I stared at the darkly glinting sea and tried to catch it. Yes: something about so many people coming to the beach that it was hard to keep track . . . Who'd said that?

'I never said the beach,' I whispered aloud. 'I never said Liv was connected to the beach.'

Think. Think. Joel had said that many people from the island taught windsurfing, kayaking and sailing in the summer: himself, Alix, Rick, Bill, Tom . . . I remembered Rick's calm look, the sudden sense of composed purpose. Why would Rick be calm? What was his purpose?

The waves licked at the shingle a few feet away, a soft shucking sound. They gave me my answer: calm because the tide was rising to the full flood and my time to find Charlie had all but run out.

'Jackson, what did Rick get when you went out with him?'

'What?'

'Tell me what he got. You said a booklet.'

I knew what he was going to say and he said it. 'For the tides. When it's high and low.'

I tore open the car's glove compartment and pulled out a pile of maps, service records—and a tide table. I opened it and followed with a finger the tides for today, Saturday, December 18. Low tide was at 10.40 a.m.; high tide was at 4.22 a.m. and 5.13 p.m. Beside the day's times was a dotted black line, signifying that today's tide was a relatively high one. I glanced at my mobile: 16.58.

Rick had left Charlie just before low tide, and had spent the whole day—with Karen at the hospital, with Jackson, of all people—being hampered from getting back to her. But now, when the tide was up and there were only fifteen minutes before it was at its highest, he had relaxed.

I pulled out my mobile and punched in the number of the police station. A familiar voice answered. 'This is—' I began, but then, with a start, I disconnected. Because now I was thinking with complete clarity. I knew what would happen. The detectives would bring Rick in and he would spend hours giving a statement, admitting nothing. And all the while the sea would be doing his work for him . . . To call the police would be finally to lose any chance of finding Charlie.

I turned to Jackson, took a deep breath and made my voice calm, reassuring. 'A change of plan, honey. You're going to have to wait for me in the house.'

'No,' he said, his voice high with hysteria. 'I won't. I'll run away. I'll follow you. You can't leave me again. It's not fair.'

For a desperate stupid moment, I thought of taking him with me. He could hide on the back seat. He could stay quiet. He might fall asleep. Then, somewhere out of my reverie, I saw two figures walking down the road, an adult and a child. The adult was laden with shopping bags, shuffling towards me. I saw that they had come from the bus-stop. And then I recognised them: Bonnie and Ryan.

'Bonnie,' I called, opening the door.

She recognised me and smiled. 'We're all done,' she said. 'It took us five hours and we hardly had time to eat but we've got presents for everyone, haven't we, Ryan? In fact we were so busy examining them we missed our stop.' Then her expression changed. 'Aren't you supposed to be on your way to Florida by now? Nina, you look terrible.'

'No time,' I said. 'An emergency. The biggest emergency. You've got to take Jackson again. I'm so sorry. Charlie's missing.'

'Missing?'

'No time. Take Jackson. I'll phone. Jackson, out. Quick.'

'But—' said Jackson.

'Great!' said Ryan.

'Right,' said Bonnie immediately, dragging Jackson out by his forearms. Then she looked at me. 'Go.'

I sped away as she slammed the car door, driving back in the direction I'd just come from. When I was a few yards from Rick's house, I drew to a halt. I switched off my headlights but kept the engine running.

And I waited, praying that I wasn't too late, praying that I hadn't got it wrong, praying that I had and that in a nightmare of fear I had simply concocted a Gothic tale that had no roots in the truth. This was my gamble, my one last throw of the dice. I was risking the life of my daughter on the chance I was right. I believed that Rick had taken Charlie, hidden her somewhere that would be covered by the tide, which was now almost at its height. And I was staking everything on the hope that he was still at his house and that he would now go to her and I would be able to follow him. If I was wrong, I would have the whole of the rest of my life to dwell upon these moments, replay them and know what I should have done if I could have looked down upon the story from a distance. But it was all I had.

I don't know how many minutes I sat there. Maybe very few. There was a movement, the front door opened and he emerged. I clenched the steering wheel with both fists. He carried a sack over his shoulder that looked like the kind of nylon bag that sailors use. He walked over to his car, slung the bag into the back, and started the engine. I waited as he drew off and disappeared round the bend, his taillights red. I memorised his number plate and the back of his old grey Volvo in case I lost him, although there was no one on the roads this winter evening. They were all inside, with their Christmas trees, their televisions and their log fires.

The road turned right and I could see Rick ahead. I followed at a distance, praying he wouldn't notice my car in his rearview mirror. We crossed The Street, then took the right turn that led to the barrow, where he turned left, onto Lost Road. I slowed the car and turned off the headlights. Now I could barely make out the road in front of me and several times the car bumped against the verge, once tipping sharply sideways. I shuddered at the thought of sliding into a ditch.

I leaned forward, concentrating, making sure that I could still see the pair of red lights. Now, on my right, there was farmland and I could occasionally make out, between the trees, the lights from Birche Farm. On my left were empty stretches of marshland. In the distance was the sea, the moon casting a wavering yellow path over its waters.

The road veered to the left, past a couple of houses. The red taillights followed it, going gradually down a shallow slope, and now, against all my instincts, I stopped. I couldn't risk Rick seeing me. He reached the coastal road and the car stopped at the junction. To the right was Charlie's newspaper route, which dwindled to a track, then a boggy path. To the left, the road ran along the low, subsiding cliffs, then turned inland again.

I watched, leaning over the wheel, ready to move forward. 'Hold on, Charlie, my darling. I'm coming to get you. Just hold on.' I don't know if I spoke out loud or not. Her name throbbed in my blood.

The two taillights disappeared and instead I could see the glow of headlights in the mist ahead of the car. Rick had turned left. My eyes were accustomed to the dark now and I could see the shadow of the road ahead of me. I reached the junction, turned left and saw, once more, the taillights. It was impossible to judge their distance from me. There were still some streaks of light behind the clouds but soon it would be entirely dark. Where was Rick heading? The direction in which he was driving along the coast would eventually lead to the causeway to the mainland but I was almost sure that the road didn't reach that far. It petered out into marshland.

The lights had vanished. I stopped the car, blinked, rubbed my eyes and stared into the darkness. There was nothing now but grey behind the clouds, and along the horizon, lights from houses on the mainland. The car's lights could have been hidden by a dip in the road. He might have turned off again. He might have stopped and switched off his lights. Was it possible that he had spotted my car and was waiting for me? Waiting was the safest option, but also potentially the most disastrous. If the lights didn't reappear, I might have lost Rick completely. No. I had to continue and take the risk. I rolled down the window and the wind off the estuary blew wetly and noisily into my face.

I started to move forward slowly and stared ahead so hard that my eyes ached with the effort. I wanted to switch on the headlights and accelerate with as much power as I could, but I was sure that if I did so I would lose any chance of finding Charlie.

The silvery sheen of Rick's car loomed out of the darkness and, even at that crawling speed, I nearly ran into it. I braked and felt the scrape of gravel under my tyres, switched off the engine and sat still. There was no sign of any movement. I picked up my mobile and found the police station number. When it was answered I didn't ask to be put through to anyone. I just said as calmly as I could, 'This is Nina Landry. I have found my daughter but she is in great danger. Come immediately to the end of Lost Road. Turn left where it meets the coast road and drive as far as you can. Where the road ends, you'll find two cars. We're there. Come at once. It is urgent. Life and death. Send an ambulance.'

I ended the call. Was there anything in the car I could use? I remembered a possibility. I opened the glove compartment and was almost blinded by the light that came on. Inside there was a road map, the car manual and a small torch. I tried the torch, pointing down at my feet, and a thin beam illuminated my trainers. Thank God. I slipped it into my pocket.

Trying to avoid making even the smallest noise, I opened the car door. The light came on inside and I quickly stepped out and shut the door. The light stayed on. I cursed silently. He might not hear anything but that light would be visible for miles. I opened the door an inch, then slammed it. The light vanished. I was in darkness again but damage had been done.

I tiptoed round Rick's car. Empty. He had gone. Trying to think of anything else from my car I could use, I edged my way back to the boot and opened it. Another light came on, but hidden under the lid. I almost laughed, almost cried, to see the luggage I had packed for the airport, long ago, many years ago, when we had been going on holiday. Something heavy, something solid . . . To one side there was the long black plastic bag containing the car jack. I pulled at the drawstring and tugged out a long steel handle. That would do. I pushed down the lid and looked around.

Think, Nina, think. Which direction had he taken? He had moved across the road and parked on the right-hand side. Surely he had gone in that direction over the grass, the marshland and the mud flats that led to the mouth of the estuary. I didn't know this landscape well but I had walked it with Sludge on blustery windy days and I knew there were no buildings, scarcely even a bush to shelter behind. Nowhere for a living person to be imprisoned . . .

I started off into the darkness. The flicker of light, when it came, was brief and faint, a wavering firefly, sometimes obscured, by grasses or ferns, sometimes disappearing altogether but always returning. It was real.

I held the torch below my knees, pointing it at the ground. Around me was rough grass but I was on a narrow path. I couldn't see any of my surroundings, but I could feel the path carrying me towards the light. Bent forward, I walked as quickly as I could. My posture was agonising but I had no choice. After a few minutes I switched off the thin light. I was almost on top of him. The torch he had been carrying was now on the ground and he was squatting to one side doing something I couldn't make out. I crouched down, hoping that the scrub around me would provide some concealment.

He had placed his torch so that it threw a pool of light towards him. I put the jack handle into the same hand as the torch and felt the ground. It was gravelly, even sandy. And wet. We were right by the water. I could feel the high tide round my feet. And what was that, just beyond us in the rising waters? I squinted and saw the dimmest, most shadowy of shapes against the cloudy sky. It was solid with straight lines. But there were no buildings out there on the sand and mud . . .

I rummaged through my memory. I made myself look back to those awful winter days after Rory had left, wandering the remote paths of Sandling Island with Sludge in the stinging northerly gales. I thought and remembered and suddenly I knew. It was one of the pillboxes left over from the war.

With that I realised with absolute clarity what I must do and that I must do it immediately. As it was, there was almost no hope . . . I took the steel handle back into my right hand and held it firmly. The important thing now was not to think. I needed to feel and act. I stood and took a few steps forward, and as I approached him I brought my right arm back.

From his crouching position Rick looked round as I swung the metal bar into his head, catching him above his left eye. There was a ringing crunch as the metal bar met his skull and he folded up on the ground.

I turned away, dropped the bar, and shone my torch out over the sea. Its frail light skewed on the small inky waves and then, as I raised it higher, picked out the looming shape of the pillbox. I ran towards it, splashing through the icy water that rose to my knees and then my thighs, slowing me down. The shocking cold almost took my breath away. My jeans clung to me, my feet sank into the muddy sand, salt water stung my face and made my eyes weep. 'Charlie!' I shouted as I waded forward, cursing the thickness of my sodden jacket. 'I'm here. Wait, darling, just wait.' For I had the sense that every fraction of a second counted. The world could fracture at any moment.

My voice rolled out over the sea. There was no answer. I flung myself the last few yards, holding the torch high above me so it didn't get wet, searching the darkness for the opening, which I could hardly make out. I reached out my free hand and found the wall at last, rough and gritty under my fingers. I followed it with the torch's beam until I found the entrance, and fought through the rapidly rising waters to get to it. The pillbox, which had once stood on the cliffs and now lay in a wreck at their base, was tipped askew, so that its small doorway was tilted slightly upwards. The tide, temporarily held back by the pillbox's walls, was gushing in rapidly.

I shone my torch into the interior. And there was nothing. Nothing but water, rolling at the door and calmer further in.

'Charlie!' I called, in a voice that cracked apart. 'Charlie!'

And then the torchlight touched on a shadow, a blur the shape of a water lily. I shone my torch directly on it and heard my breath catch in my throat, for it was a tiny island of flesh in the flood, like the belly of an upturned fish. A mouth open like a gill, pursed for oxygen.

With painful slowness, I inserted myself into the pillbox's small opening, feeling rough stone against my hands and face, salt in my mouth. The sea came up above my waist and then, as I moved forward, up to my neck. I dared not make any rough movement, for fear of splashing water into that tiny, pitiful mouth. I shuffled towards my daughter, one hand holding the torch high, the other reaching out to touch her.

And at last my fingers found the stretched stem of her neck and the tangle of hair. 'It's all right, dear heart,' I whispered. 'I'll get you out.'

Her eyes stared at me blindly. Her lips gasped at the remaining air.

I needed to put the torch down. I stared frantically around the clammy space until I saw a shallow nook, where the stone had crumbled. I crammed the torch into it, its light now shining horizontally so that I could no longer see Charlie at all. I put my arms round her waist, under the water, and pulled. She rose an inch or so, heavy and unresponsive as a corpse, then jerked to a stop. She was tied down, but I couldn't tell with what, or to where.

I sank beneath the surface, my jacket opening. I opened my eyes but could see nothing except the brackish swirl of the sea. I groped with my hands and found that her ankles were tied with something rough, thick and strong. A rope. I followed it to where it stopped, knotted to something heavy and cold. I tore at the thick knot with my fingers, trying to wriggle it free, but I knew I couldn't. Not in time. My lungs were aching now. I had seconds—Charlie had seconds.

I rose again, gasping. I pulled off my bulky, sodden jacket, bundled it up into a thick parcel and plunged down once more. I blew air out of my lungs so I could stay submerged while I put my hands round Charlie's calves and pushed her up until the rope went tight. I forced the folded jacket under her dangling, booted feet, pushing it into a shape that would accommodate her weight, not tip her off if she shifted. At least I'd gained a minute or so.

Once more I surfaced. I reached for the torch and shone it into my own face. 'Wait,' I said. 'Don't move. Stand tall. Breathe. I'll be back in a few seconds. I swear to you that I'm going to save you.'

Her eyes widened. Out of her mouth came a long, bubbling mew. It wasn't a human sound.

I turned away, pulled myself out of the hole, and waded back through the waves and the ripping wind. Past Rick, whose splayed body was now lapped at by the waves, and to my car. As I ran, my eyes scanned the land for headlights. Surely the police would arrive soon. But the road was dark.

I threw open the boot and the light came on, dazzling me. Leaning in, I unzipped the nylon sports bag and drew out Christian's Christmas present, wrapped in silver paper. I put my torch into my mouth because I needed both hands now, then turned back to the sea and ran, tearing off the paper as I went, fumbling at the packaging inside. A snorkel and mask. I yanked them free, dropping the rest into the mud. I took the torch from my mouth, held it in my free hand, and, brandishing the snorkel in the other, launched myself through the tide towards Charlie, both arms raised.

Into the small opening. The torch was dying. Its beam flickered. But it found the half-open lips of my child. With one hand, I inserted the snorkel between them, making sure the mouthpiece fitted securely. I pushed the mask over her face and pulled the strap round the back of her head.

'Hold on to it with your teeth, Charlie,' I said, my voice loud and steady. 'Grip it and breathe. If the water comes above your face, don't panic. You can still breathe. Now I'm going to get something to cut you free.'

Easy to say, but I had no knife, no scissors, no blade. Then I thought of someone who might have something. I left Charlie alone once more, in that terrible flooded darkness, and waded to the shore.

Rick's body was half in the water now, half out. His sail-bag was still roped over his shoulder and I had to half roll him over to pull it free. His body was heavy and limp, and my hands came away sticky with his blood. The bag had a drawstring top, pulled tight shut, and I had to jiggle it open with my numb, clumsy fingers. Inside, I found a towel, a change of clothes and odd bits and pieces to do with his boat—a couple of cleats, a few lengths of thin nylon rope, a spanner, a pair of rowlocks, pliers—perhaps I could use those to ease the knot free. Secateurs: they might do. And what was this? I held it up to the last rays of the torch: an army knife.

I took the pliers, the knife and the secateurs and returned to the pillbox.

As I reached it, the moon emerged from behind a cloud and cast a faint, silvery light over the surging water.

I pulled myself through the entrance and found myself floundering for a foothold. I was almost out of my depth now and had to stand on tiptoe at the higher edge to breathe properly. I managed to hold the torch above my head and shone its wavering light around the deathly space. Nothing. Charlie had gone. A howl rose in my throat but I pushed it down, staring at the place she had been. And there I saw a small tube rising just a few inches above the water. My daughter was under it. Was she breathing?

My torch gave a last few flickers and went out. I let it drop with a muted splash. I was in darkness. I pushed the pliers into my jeans' tight wet pocket, gripped the secateurs between my teeth and blindly opened the knife's largest blade. One deep breath and I sank under the water, free hand stretched out. I found Charlie's body. Her arms tied and bound behind her back. I felt for the rope round her ankles and, facing downwards, like a diver, clutched it with my left hand. I started sawing at the rope with the knife. I needed to breathe but I couldn't stop. The rope was soaked and thick, the knife was small and blunt. My lungs were shrivelling, scorching with pain. A spasm jolted my body and I let go and rose up into the air, retching and gasping, nearly losing the secateurs. But I took them in my hand, opened them at the ready, and put the knife into my mouth.

Down again. The rope. My fingers found the groove where I'd been cutting. I snipped at it with the secateurs, sometimes missing and snapping them closed on water. I let the ache build in my lungs again, filling each cubic millimetre with solid pain. I imagined the threads breaking, one by one. Just a few more cuts, surely, but it took so long, so agonisingly long, and my body was about to explode. All the while, Charlie hung above me, swaying with the waves.

When I thought I could bear it no longer, the rope gave a tremor and snapped. My body floated upwards and I heaved against Charlie as I rose to the surface, pushing her head into the air, grappling with her weight. She lolled against me, and I couldn't hold her properly because I was now out of my depth. Her head tipped back in the water as I thrashed by her side. Violently gulping air, I put my hands on either side of her head, over her ears, and lay on my back, towing her the short distance towards the entrance. She was unresponsive. Her legs bumped against mine under the water.

At the doorway, I tried to haul myself backwards, one arm wrapped round her torso, but I couldn't get a grip on her clothes or her clammy skin. Several times I almost let her go, back into the flooding darkness. The concrete scraped at my face and I felt blood gush down my cheek and neck. I tumbled over the submerged threshold, back into open sea, and dragged her after me, hooking my hands under her armpits. Her eyes were closed now.

'You're OK, you're OK,' I was shouting, as I towed her to the shore, hauling her past Rick and up onto the dry sand, where we collapsed in a heap. I struggled to my knees. In the moonlight, her face and lips were grey. Her slack mouth was gaping open, her flesh cold as the sand she lay on.

I gathered Charlie's body to me, pressing my face into her neck and holding her head to my ear to feel or hear her breath. But there was only the steady, rumbling wash of the sea behind me, and the fretful moan of the wind. I pinched her nostrils between my thumb and forefinger and put my mouth to hers. I blew once, twice. I tried to remember what I knew of first aid. I pumped down on her chest several times, then breathed air into her mouth once more. Again, then again.

'Don't go, my lovely,' I said. 'Stay with us now.'

Suddenly, a tiny bubble of air and a gurgle came from her colourless lips. Then a choking sound. I hauled her into a sitting position. With her arms tied behind her and her head lolling forward, she vomited. I held her against me and pressed my lips to her forehead. A terrible, agonising hope opened its wings inside me, stopping my breath and knocking my heart against my ribs. I felt her body tremble and wrapped my arms round her as tightly as I could, rubbing her back, trying to press my living warmth into her. If only there were blankets in the car, or clothes.

I remembered Rick's bag. I laid Charlie on the ground, sprinted down the sand and grabbed it, stumbling back to where she lay. I shook out the contents and found a small metal spanner, which I twisted into the knot that bound her arms. I wriggled it free and unwound the rope, feeling the deep welts it had left on her wrists. I tugged off her jacket, snatched up a large towel and sweatshirt, and wrapped them round her, then put the nylon bag round her. I took the bulky, layered weight of her in my arms again and cradled her to me while I tried to lift her up.

'Come on, Charlie,' I gasped, into the coarse salt coils of her hair. 'You're safe, my bravest darling.' I slung one of her limp arms round my shoulder. 'I've got you now, the ambulance is on its way and I'm going to carry you to the car.'

Charlie's eyes opened and she looked at me. Then she looked past me. Her mouth opened but no sound came. I saw a widening of her eyes and felt an explosion of pain so great and so sudden that I could see it, flashing white and then in bursts of blue and red, and I could hear it too, ringing in my ears. I saw the ground move up and then slimy mud was against my cheeks, in my mouth.

I rolled over and felt the pain in my left leg, flowing down to the foot, up through my thigh and into my body. As I turned, I saw Rick. He was on his knees. Even in the darkness I could see that his face was covered with filth and blood. I realised that he had crawled towards me from behind and had struck my right knee with something, which had made me collapse, and now he was raising it to strike me again, on my head this time. I realised I had dropped Charlie and I thought, All this has been for nothing. The police will get here too late. While I was thinking all that, I raised my right arm to ward off the blow and there was another explosion of light and sound. I cried out again, but I snatched with my left hand and gripped the metal bar he was wielding.

Rick was far bigger and stronger than me, but I thought of Charlie and I held the bar and knew that I would never release it until I was dead, and then he would have to prise my fingers from it. My right arm was hot with pain but I clawed at his face with my right hand. I heard a scream from somewhere close. I had been pulling the metal bar but then, suddenly, instead of trying to wrench it free he pushed it down on my neck, and I began to choke. I pushed and twisted with all my last strength, I scratched at his face but he was staring down at me. I was losing consciousness and then I heard a sound, felt it as much as heard it, of something heavy hitting the earth, and his weight on me was gone.

It was several seconds before I could see. There was a shape in front of my eyes, which gradually I made out as Charlie, pale as a corpse. She was holding a piece of concrete from the disintegrating pillbox and she let it drop and stood there, looking through me with dead eyes. She swayed like a tree that was about to fall. I glanced around. There was no sign of Rick.

I cried out my daughter's name and got to my feet. I knew there was pain and damage in my arm and leg but it felt like a distant memory. I held her close in my arms; we were both trembling violently, with cold and fear. I looked into her eyes. 'Charlie,' I said loudly. 'Can you hear me?'

She didn't answer. Her eyes were rolling as if she was drugged or desperate for sleep. I remembered Rick. Where had he gone? Was there a chance he could come for us again, out of the darkness?

Then I saw him. He had rolled down into the water and I could see the shape of his body pushed this way and that by the tide, which was now at its height. He was lying on his back with one of his legs deep in the soft, gluey mud. I thought he was unconscious, but then his eyes flickered open and he looked up at me, lifting his head as far as he could. Waves swept over him, making him choke, but he couldn't move.

My first thought was to stand there and watch him die, but the idea made me nauseous. I laid Charlie gently on the ground and stood up, whimpering with pain. The world rocked around me and lights were exploding inside my skull. I dragged myself to a few paces from where he lay. I took a tentative step onto the mud to see if it would hold my weight. But my leg sank straight to the knee. It was only by grabbing on to a rough bush that I could drag myself free. The pain in the other leg made me howl. I couldn't reach him.

With my numb, fumbling fingers, I undid my belt and pulled it free from the loops of my jeans. 'Catch hold of this and pull,' I said. I held the buckle and tossed the leather belt across the gap separating us. He lifted a hand feebly but missed. I tried again and this time he had it. He wrapped the leather round his hand. I hauled as hard as I could and felt a gradual shifting of his weight towards me. A small part of me was aghast as I tried to save the life of the man who had tried to kill my daughter.

All of a sudden, his weight shifted back again. I felt it in the tightening of the belt, I heard it in the sucking sound beneath us. The tide was going out at last, drawing the debris of the muddy shore with it. And drawing Rick away too. For one moment, we stared at each other, then I let go. The belt curled towards him and he slid back, drawn by the steady tug of the tide. The waves washed over his face until I could no longer make it out.

I looked round. Charlie was slumped on the ground and her eyes were shut again. I hobbled over to her, cradled her in my arms and put two fingers against her neck where a pulse should have been, but they were too numb to feel anything. As I sat there, I felt my last reserves of strength ebbing away. I just wanted to curl up with my daughter and close my eyes at last.

'No, you don't, Nina,' I snarled, snapping open my eyelids.

I grasped Charlie and pulled her into a sitting position just in front of me, between my open legs. I started bumping us both towards the car, which was so near, yet so infinitely far away. If I could get into the warmth . . .

I saw it first as a path of light that shone past the pair of us and onto the black water. I stopped and turned my head. Over the horizon, a yellow beam fanned out, then narrowed again as the car came over the hill. Another set of headlights followed, then a third. Blue lights flashed.

I put my chin on top of Charlie's head and rocked her. 'They're here to save us,' I said. I cleared her matted hair off her face and tucked it behind her ears, then picked up her cold hands and rubbed them between my own. The lights were nearly on us now. I heard doors opening, voices shouting.

They came over the hill, silhouetted figures behind the torches that shone down, pinning us in a dazzling brightness. I put a hand over Charlie's eyes to protect them, even though she lay unmoving in my lap, and I looked out onto the landscape of our blind struggle. Tomorrow, the winter light would return all of it to normal: placid blue-green sea, shingle and sand where wading birds would lift their long legs in the shallows. I saw no sign of Rick. I stared at the sea, and saw nothing but its heaving, glinting surface.

Then they were there with us, stretchers lowered, blankets unrolled, voices talking into radios, a sense of controlled urgency. There were calm voices in my ear, warm hands on my freezing limbs, something soft wrapped round me. Someone called me by my name. My eyes were burning. My arms were empty. I called out for my daughter.

I saw a face looming towards me. 'Just relax now. Don't try to talk.'

I was on a stretcher, being carried over the rough ground, and I lay on my back, feeling as if I was a bit of detritus tugged by the tide. I wanted to close my eyes, but couldn't. I stared up at the white moon sailing serenely on.

'Rick,' I said, raising my voice against the throb of pain in my knee, leg, head, heart. 'In the water. Help.'

In the agony of not knowing if Charlie was alive or dead, I had to try to save the man who'd nearly killed us both, to hang on to the last shreds of my humanity.

'What's this?' A sharp voice cutting through the hubbub: DI Hammill. I put a hand out and clutched his arm.

'He's out there, drowning,' I said.

I was aware of orders being shouted, people running. Shafts of light slid over me. At the centre of all the activity, I raised my head to see Charlie's still figure being slid on a stretcher through the open doors of the ambulance. Someone pushed me down onto my stretcher.

'My daughter,' I said. 'I need to see her.'

'You'll see her,' said a voice. 'We need to check you're OK. But if you keep shifting around we'll drop you.'

I lay back and suddenly I saw the stars. The Plough. The Great Bear. I was feeling woozy, drifting off to sleep, when I heard shouts of 'Shut the door' and 'Watch out'. The sky had gone and my eyes were dazzled by bright lights. It was suddenly warmer. I saw green uniforms moving around me. The stretcher was put down. A woman's face came close to mine. A nice face, short red hair, green overalls. 'I'm Claire,' she said, talking to me in the overloud voice that's used for the very young, the very old or the very badly hurt. 'We need to check you out. How are you feeling, Nina?'

'How's Charlie? What are they doing to her?'

'She's here,' said the woman. 'She's being looked after.'

I howled because she had run her hands down my leg. I heard different voices shouting, but it was difficult to penetrate the fog of fear and pain that surrounded me. Doors were slammed. There was a jolt, and I realised I was in the ambulance and that we were driving away.

'Charlie,' I cried. 'Where is she? What's happening?'

I made myself twist round and saw two other figures in green overalls bent over the stretcher across from me. 'Is she dead?' I whispered.

'Nina.' Claire came close to me so that I could see her brown eyes. 'Your daughter has got very cold. Her core temperature has fallen drastically. We've got to get it up. We're doing all we can.'

The sympathy in her eyes struck terror into me. 'Get Rory,' I said. 'At once. Get her father.'

There were shouts from around Charlie. 'I can't get a BP reading!' someone said.

The interior of the ambulance was taking shape, coming into focus. I could see Beck by the rear doors, swaying with the vehicle's movement. I looked again at the stretcher across from me, but couldn't see Charlie. She was still surrounded by crouching figures.

'What's happening?' I shouted. 'Someone's got to tell me.'

One of the figures turned round. He was a young man, with sandy hair and pale skin. 'Your daughter is severely hypothermic,' he said. 'We're warming her up.'

I struggled to get off the stretcher. 'Let me help,' I said. 'I'll—'

'Save your strength,' he said. 'We'll do everything possible. You need to look after yourself,' he added gently. 'Now let Claire deal with you.'

I heard a tearing sound and felt something burning along my leg: my clothes were being cut off. I was lifted and twisted. Pain flowed through me like a deep, fast river. 'I'm all right,' I whispered. 'But please can I . . .'

Suddenly the motion of the ambulance ceased.

'What's happening? Are we there?'

'The causeway's covered by the tide. We're seeing if we can get through.'

'Can I talk to Ms Landry?' said Beck.

'We need to do some checks,' Claire said. 'And she may be in shock.'

'It's very important.'

Claire turned to me. 'Can you manage a few questions?'

'No! I want to see Charlie! What's happening to her?'

Claire moved across to the huddle round my daughter. There was some murmuring and then she was back, crouching by my side. 'They're still monitoring her temperature. We just have to wait.'

'How serious is it? I have to know. Please tell me.'

She looked uncertain. Her eyes flickered as if she wanted to avoid my gaze. 'They're doing their best.'

The ambulance started up again. I thought of going through so much, of pulling my daughter from the icy water, then losing her. I saw the two police offices' faces close to me. Like figures from long, long ago.

'Call Rory,' I said once more. 'Immediately.'

'He's being driven straight to the hospital.'

'Can you talk a little?' said Beck.

Her face was coming in and out of focus. 'What for? It's all over.'

'Did he get away?' said Beck.

'What?'

'The man who took your daughter.'

'He's in the water,' I said. 'I tried to get him out. Couldn't. I had to save Charlie.'

'The water?' said Beck. 'When we left, the officers were trying to retrieve Mr Blythe's body. But what about the perpetrator? Did he fall in the water?'

I felt as if the whole world was going fuzzy around me. 'Rick did it,' I said. 'There was nobody else.'

'Are you sure?' said Beck.

'Of course,' I said. 'What have I been saying? What did I say on the phone?' I looked at her, but at the side of my vision I could see one of the figures standing back from Charlie and saying something to his colleague.

'What are they doing to Charlie?' My voice came out in a screech.

Claire pushed her way past Beck, sat next to me and took my hand. 'Nina,' she said, looking into my eyes.

The world tipped and roared; my blood cascaded down my veins; my heart pounded in my chest. I knew what she was going to say and I waited for the words I'd been dreading ever since Charlie had disappeared. 'Yes?'

'We're nearly there. Try to remain calm. She's a resilient young woman.'

I raised my hands to my face and in my own private darkness I let myself think of the way Charlie's body had felt: slack, cold and dead. I just wanted her to know that she wasn't alone any more.

I felt the creaking of the ambulance as it swung through the curves. There was a hand on my forehead and dimly, distantly, I heard voices but it seemed impossible to make out their meaning. I thought I made out the words 'losing her', but everything was jumbled and I was sinking into the darkness behind my eyes.

I could feel the ambulance slowing and making a turn. The surface of the road was rougher, then smoother. I could see lights outside. The doors were pushed open and there was a rush of cold air. There were people with trolleys, two of them, and now things were happening quickly. As Charlie was bundled out on her stretcher, I said weakly, 'I want to go with her.'

'You'll see her,' said the sandy-haired man, covering me with several blankets. 'But she needs attention. And so do you.'

As I was lifted out, I looked for Charlie but she was already gone. I was wheeled past several police officers, through flapping doors and into a curtained-off cubicle where a nurse followed me with a clipboard and immediately started to ask questions. It was so bureaucratic it almost made me scream. She wanted my name and address and date of birth.

'I'm not ill,' I said, though the words came out in a slur and I'm not sure she understood them. 'Just tired, cold. Is Rory here?'

She asked if I was allergic to anything, if I was on any medication, if I had eaten in the last four hours.

'I don't want to be operated on,' I said. 'I withhold my permission.'

'Ms Landry,' she said, very sternly, 'your daughter is being looked after. It does nobody any good if you don't let us look after you as well. For a start, I need to take your temperature—'

'I need the toilet,' I said. 'Now.'

'Someone can bring you a bedpan.'

'No, thank you. I can manage quite well on my own.'

'I don't think that's a very good idea,' she said, with such forbidding grimness that on any other day I would probably have obeyed her. But how could I rest until I knew that Charlie was all right?

So I levered myself into a sitting position, my head woozy and aching, swung my feet to the floor, then gathered the blanket that covered my almost naked body and stood up. Astonishing pain shot up my injured leg and through my whole body. My head spun so disastrously that I had to hold on to the trolley for support while the ground tipped and the walls fell towards me. I thought I would be sick, and for a few moments I simply stood there, looking down at my bare, filthy feet on the shabby lino.

'Where is it?' I said, when I could speak.

'Just down the corridor on the left. Shall I help you?'

'No. I can manage. I'm fine.'

I clutched the blanket round me and shuffled towards the Ladies. Beck was standing by the desk, speaking to a doctor, and beyond her, near the door, were two policemen. I turned away and limped into the toilet, locking the door behind me. For a moment, I leaned against the wall and shut my eyes. The world felt infinitely strange and unreal.

I let the blanket slither to the floor and lowered myself painfully onto the lavatory. Then, using my hands to pull myself up, I got to my feet and moved across to the basin. I lifted my face and, in the mirror, met my reflection. I almost shrieked at the stranger staring back at me. She had wild snakes of damp black hair, bloodshot eyes, a violet bruise flowering across her scratched and muddy cheeks and swelling her nose. She looked old.

Charlie mustn't see me like this. I turned on the tap and, when the water was running warm, pulled a paper towel from the dispenser and soaked it, then gingerly wiped away some of the mud and blood. I cupped my hands and splashed water over my face, then bent down and twisted sideways so that water ran over my hair, which was thick with sand and grit. When I stood upright again, I didn't look much better, but there was nothing more I could do except squeeze water from my hair and push it behind my ears.

I wrapped myself once more in my blanket, then eased open the door. There was no sign of my stern nurse, so I shuffled out and looked around. There was a flurry of movement at the far end of the corridor—a young man in white overalls coming out, a nurse pushing a trolley going in—and I guessed that was where Charlie lay.

It seemed to take me a long, hard time to get there.

As I reached the door, it opened, and DI Hammill came out. I saw the startled expression on his face as I reeled past him like a drunken boxer, my breath coming in gasps. He reached out to stop me, then halted and let me pass. I saw his face, and I saw the figures in white coats standing beside Charlie's metal bed, as in a dream. She was surrounded by machines, with a white sheet and several thick blankets pulled up over her body, a needle taped to her thin arm and her face so pale and small on the pillow.

I staggered across and bent over her. I took her cold hand in mine and held it to my cheek. 'Charlie?' I said. 'It's me. I'm here.'

'What are you doing here?' said a voice. 'Who let you in here?'

'I'm her mother,' I said.

'I know who you are.'

'How is she?'

The doctor gave me an exasperated smile. 'She was severely hypothermic. But her core temperature is rising. She's a fighter. She's not fully responsive yet but . . .'

Charlie's eyes half opened. 'Mummy?' she whispered.

'I'm here,' I said. 'You're safe now.'

Her eyelids started to close again. Her fingers relaxed in mine. Just as I thought she was asleep, she mumbled, 'Happy birthday.'

'It's been different, I'll give you that,' I said. 'Next year, I'd like to do something a bit quieter. Hey, you're wearing my bloody watch. So that's where it was. I needed it today.'

A muffled sound came from her, then just regular breathing. She was asleep. I thought of when she was a baby. Sometimes I would creep up in the middle of the night, lean over her cot and listen for her breath. And even nudge her to wake her up, to make sure she was still alive. But this time I needed only to touch her to reassure myself. I stroked her matted hair and closed my eyes. I had expected joy from this moment, but what I felt instead was a peace such as I'd never experienced before. The nearest equivalent was that mysteriously beautiful moment after giving birth, when the struggle is over and there's nothing left that you have to do.

'I thought I'd find you here,' a voice said, from behind me. I opened my eyes again and smiled blearily up at the stern nurse, who led me back along the corridor the way I had come, a firm grip on my upper arm.

At the end of the corridor I saw a small huddled group: DI Hammill, Beck—and Rory. They were too far away for us to speak to each other, but Rory was evidently aghast at the sight of me and for the second time that day started crying. He ran towards me and gave me a hug, but stepped back when he felt me flinch.

'Sorry,' he said. 'Sorry. You look . . . but Charlie's going to be all right, isn't she? She's going to make it.' Tears streamed down his face.

'Yes. She's pulling through,' I said. 'I thought I'd lost her, Rory.'

'We,' he said. 'We'd lost her. We. You and me. I should have been there too,' he said. 'And I would have been. If I hadn't been in custody. I hope you can see that I was telling the truth.'

'You weren't . . .' I started to say, then stopped. It didn't matter. Nothing mattered. Charlie was safe. Doctors and nurses watched over her.

'You should go and see her,' I said. 'They'll probably let you sit by her bed. It might be good to talk to her, even if she's asleep.'

'I'm sorry,' he said. 'I didn't mean—'

'We never do,' I said. 'I'm sorry too. Sorry for everything. But she's alive, she's all right. Can you do something for me? Phone Jackson. He's at Bonnie's house. The number is—'

'I can get the number.'

'I need to see him,' I said. 'He's had a terrible day.'

'I'll call him now,' he said. 'And I'll come and see you later. If you want.'

I didn't reply. I didn't know if I wanted him to come and see me. All I wanted now was to hug Jackson and tell him I was proud of him, then turn my face to the wall and close my eyes.

Rory gave his characteristic helpless shrug and walked away, leaving me, the two detectives and, I could see from her name tag, Nurse Steph Bowles.

'Did you find Rick?' I asked Hammill and Beck.

'It took a while,' said DI Hammill. 'They weren't able to revive him.'

'I tried to save him,' I said.

'Why?' said Beck.

'Perhaps I wanted him to live so that he could think about what he had done,' I said, then started to shiver violently.

'We need to go,' said Nurse Bowles, with a bossy solicitude that I was grateful for. 'You're in no fit state for questions. We need to get you into bed.' She waved at a porter walking towards us with an empty wheelchair.

I was wheeled along, with Steph Bowles ahead and the detectives following. We went into a small room, where I was lifted into a narrow bed and had thin, pale blue blankets piled on top of me. Hammill and Beck hovered awkwardly, waiting to be given permission to ask more questions.

'I'm going to leave you for a few minutes,' said Steph Bowles. 'I'll be back with the doctor. Be quick,' she murmured to DI Hammill as she left.

'Rick's wife's here,' I said.

'What?'

'Karen. His wife. She was injured this morning. She's in a bed somewhere here. You'll have to go and tell her what's happened.'

Hammill sounded dazed. 'She's here? I don't understand.'

'She had an accident,' I said. 'She had too much to drink this morning, fell over and broke her arm. Rick had to bring her here. They kept her in.'

'How do you know about it?'

'It happened in my house,' I said. 'That was the thing. Rick needed to get back to Charlie, if only to kill her. But suddenly he had to take Karen to hospital and stay with her. Then, when he got back onto the island, I met him and gave him Jackson to look after.'

'What?' said Beck.

'It's almost funny, isn't it?' I said. 'He had one of my children and I gave him the other to look after.' I thought for a moment. 'But there's more. I can see now why he came to my house for the party. It makes sense. He had Charlie, he was probably panicking, and wondering what to do next. Then I phoned him, asking if he'd take a look at my car.' I gave a little laugh. 'Maybe if it hadn't been for the rattle in my car, Charlie would be dead now. It was a kind of alibi for him. Because it would seem as though she went missing when Rick was with me. And then he must have remembered he was going to my house anyway, for the surprise birthday party that Charlie had organised. If he could do anything to make it look as though Charlie had run away, a serious police investigation would be delayed until he had killed her and disposed of the body.'

As if a photograph had been put in front of my eyes, I remembered seeing Rick coming down the stairs. Coming down, as I now realised, with a few things grabbed from Charlie's room to make it look as if she had left in a hurry. 'He stole those things from her room,' I said. 'And, if he had been lucky, we might not have looked for Charlie properly for a day or two and he could have done it and dealt with her and got rid of Olivia Mullen's body and never been caught.'

DI Hammill shook his head. 'But I don't understand how Olivia Mullen is connected with your daughter. The style of assault is different,' he continued. 'There is no link between Olivia and Rick Blythe.'

It was all so tiring. By now, Hammill and Beck were like two annoying wasps buzzing around keeping me from sleep. I just wanted to swat them.

'Rick knew Olivia Mullen,' I said to Hammill. 'He taught her windsurfing in the summer and they had a relationship, a fling nobody must know about—he was a teacher, for God's sake, and she was only a teenager. Charlie knew Liv, she knew about the relationship and knew Liv had been on her way to see Rick to break off their affair. I'm sure she will have seen Liv's photo in the paper this morning and realised what had happened. Then she met Rick on her paper round, said something and he panicked and grabbed her. If you wait until tomorrow, Charlie will be able to tell you.'

'Right,' said Steph Bowles, coming into the ward. 'Dr Marker is on her way to see you. She'll be here in a few minutes.'

Hammill and Beck made an awkward exit. Steph Bowles turned back to me. A watch hung from her breast pocket. I saw that it was past six o'clock.

'We would be taking off now,' I said. 'I was going to Florida today.'

'Oh.' She picked up a chart and looked at it, tutting.

'And it's my birthday.'

'Many happy returns,' she said, popping the cold tip of a thermometer under my tongue. 'I'll get you some more blankets in a minute. Tea and blankets.' After a while, she removed the thermometer, frowned, looked at me as if I'd done something wrong, and wrote on the chart.

'I'm forty today. I had a birthday party,' I continued, although I wasn't really talking to anyone. My voice was fuzzy, but I needed to keep awake. I needed to see Jackson, my little boy who'd been wandering around all day like a lost soul. 'Charlie gave me a party. It was a surprise party.'

Steph Bowles wasn't interested. She only wanted to know about my temperature, blood pressure and heartbeat. She wanted to put me back together again. I closed my eyes and the room swung round in my skull.

'It wasn't a success,' I went on. 'Surprise parties rarely are. They're good in theory, but—well, anyway, that's when it all started . . .'

I opened my eyes and Steph Bowles was gone. I was talking to myself. It didn't matter. 'I wonder where Christian is,' I muttered. 'He's been stuck on the M25 all day . . .'

'Ms Landry,' said a voice. 'I'm Dr Marker. How are you feeling?'

She was slim and blonde in her white coat, a stethoscope round her neck.

'Not at my very best,' I said.

'Here.' She sat beside me on the bed and held my wrist between her two fingers, feeling my pulse. She looked at my chart, put her stethoscope to my chest, then ran her fingers down my leg, probing my knee and finding the pain there. She took my foot in the palm of her hand and rotated it to see where the ankle was injured. She pressed her fingertips against the cuts and bruises on my temple and cheek while I tried not to cry out.

'I think you'll get away without stitches. This must hurt.'

'A bit,' I croaked.

'The nurse is bringing a bowl. Cold?'

'To my bones. But it's getting a bit better.'

'Dizzy?'

'Just tired, I think.'

'How's your memory? Do you know what day it is?'

'It's Saturday, December the 18th, of course,' I said. 'Because it's my fortieth birthday. Never to be forgot.' Her face swam in and out of focus.

'Good. How many fingers am I holding up?'

'Three.'

'Fine.' She stood up. 'You need warmth and rest, but I think that's all. You've been concussed so we need to keep an eye on that.'

'Tea,' said Steph Bowles, putting a large green mug on the table beside me. 'And I've got a nightgown for you. Let me help you with it.'

Dr Marker left. With surprising gentleness, the nurse half raised me and, as if I was a tiny child, pulled the thin nightgown over my head, then tugged it down my sore, chilly body. She pulled the sheet and all the blankets back over me and withdrew. I lay back and gulped the tepid, milky tea.

Then I heard Bonnie's voice. 'Can he just go in?'

And another voice saying, 'Mum?'

Jackson stood in the doorway, a small figure wrapped in a quilted red anorak so much too big for him that it came down almost to his knees and both his hands were hidden. He stared at me with beetle brows.

'Hello, my hero,' I said. I put down my mug and held out my arms, but he didn't move.

'What's happened to your face?'

'It's only a bruise. Come here and let me tell you how proud I am of you.'

'It's all blue and lopsided.' He wore an expression of faint embarrassment.

I grinned at him, my heart galloping with bruised tenderness. 'Soon it'll be yellow and lopsided instead, then I'll look even weirder. Are you all right?'

'Bonnie gave me hot chocolate with marshmallows in it. Where's Charlie? Is she alive?'

'Yes.'

'Can I see her, then?'

'I think she's sleeping. Why don't you wait until tomorrow?'

'I want to see her.' His voice quavered, then righted itself. 'Bonnie can take me. She's waiting by the lift.'

'All right, then. Can I have a hug before you go?'

He edged forward. 'Where was Charlie, anyway? Did she run away?'

'No.'

'Are we going to Florida?'

'Not today.'

'Can we go another time?'

'Yes.'

There was a pause. He sat down by the bed and I put a hand into his sleeve, found his small, warm fingers. He didn't taken them away, and I felt him soften gradually. After a few moments, he said, 'Sludge will be going mad all by herself. She'll have chewed half the house down.'

'I expect so.'

'But you won't be angry with her?'

'No. I won't be angry.'

'Will you have to stay in bed for ages?'

'Of course not. I'm just a bit tired.'

'Bonnie said I'd have to look after you.'

'Nonsense.'

'That's good. It's Christmas in six days and a bit less than six hours. I'm starving.'

'In a bit Dad can take you to the café and buy you something.'

'Do they do chips?'

'Probably.'

'Shall I go and see Charlie now?'

'Go on, then. Don't stay too long, though. She needs rest, remember.'

'Do you promise you'll still be here?'

'I'm not going anywhere.'

He wriggled off the chair, gingerly planted a kiss on my bruised face, then turned to go. I lay back with my eyes closed, then heard Steph Bowles return. I felt a rummaging in bed, then there was something against my feet.

'A hot-water bottle,' I said sleepily.

'Don't shout about it,' Nurse Bowles said, 'or everyone will want one.'

I didn't reply, or even open my eyes. She switched off the overhead light and left and I was alone. I let myself go, as if I were on a boat, releasing the painter and letting myself be carried out to sea . . .

'HELLO.'

I didn't know if I had been asleep, if any time had passed. I opened my eyes. They hurt in the harsh light of the hospital room. A middle-aged man was standing by my bed, holding a clipboard. He looked tired.

'Are you a doctor? I've just seen a doctor and she said I was all right.'

'I'm Dr Siegel. I'm sorry if I woke you. I need to check on you. You were hit on the head so I'm afraid you'll be woken regularly all night. Just to make sure you're not unconscious. I've just seen your daughter.'

'You have? How is she?

'She's not too bad,' he said. 'But mainly, I'd say she's very lucky to have you. You can tell her that tomorrow.'

'I don't think I will,' I said. 'She's had enough to put up with.'

Dr Siegel frowned. 'I'm meant to check your comprehension and responses. How do they seem to you?'

'Not too bad,' I said. 'I don't know.'

He grunted and wrote on the clipboard. 'You live on Sandling Island.'

'Yes.'

'I've never been there. I work just a few miles away and I keep meaning to go, to walk along the coastal path. Would you recommend it?'

'Not today,' I said. 'I think I've fallen out of love with it.'

'Everything will seem different in the morning. Let me see if I can find a pulse.' He took my wrist in his left hand. 'Happy birthday, by the way.'

'What?'

'It says on the clipboard,' he said. 'Forty years young.'

'Yes. It wasn't much of a celebration, though.'

Dr Siegel placed the clipboard back on the end of the bed and touched my hand gently. It felt very consoling. 'I'll see you tomorrow. Try to sleep. You did well.' Then he went, switching off the light as he left.

As my eyes grew accustomed to the dark, I saw for the first time that there was a small window in my room. From the bed, I couldn't see much out of it. I lay gazing out at the dark night sky. Was there a moon out there? Were there stars? Just a few miles away the flooding tide must be going down now, the waves ebbing, sucking up the pieces of driftwood, the broken shells and the litter. Out on that desolate waste of mud and shingle, underneath the subsiding cliffs, was the pillbox, the sea seeping out, only to return once more by dawn. The body had been dragged from the black waters, the blood had been washed away. The winter sun would hang on the horizon, and everything would look the same as it always had, peaceful, vast and undisturbed.

I turned on my side and pressed my face into the pillow. I took a long deep breath and, at last, I began to cry. I was here; Charlie was here; Jackson was here. And the morning would come to us all.

NICCI GERRARD

Born: Worcestershire, June 1958
Marital status: Married to Sean for 16 years
Favourite city: Venice

Who or what always puts a smile on your face?
We have just given in to five years of pressure from the children to get a dog—a black labrador puppy called Maisie. She's ludicrous, clumsy, greedy, grubby, eager, unconditional, absolutely without dignity or guile. It makes me feel cheerful just to think of her.

Have you ever had any other jobs apart from writing?
As a student I picked starwberries and hops, worked in a library, was a waitress, sold jewellery on the Ponte Vecchio in Florence, taught English. Later, I worked with emotionally disturbed children, taught briefly in an American university, was a freelance reviewer, a magazine editor, a literary editor, a feature writer. But now I just write, which was all I ever wanted to do anyway.

What is your greatest fear?
Something happening to one of the children.

How would you like to be remembered?
Giggling.

Have you ever done something you've really regretted?
Yes.

How do you spoil yourself?
Lying in a hot bath with the door locked and not answering when someone shouts for me.

What makes you angry?
Bullying.

What's your worst vice?
I nag my family. I have no patience. I'm obsessive and a binger.

What are you proudest of?
The fact that almost every evening we sit down together round the kitchen table, all six of us, and eat and talk and argue.

One wish: what would it be?
That all my children have long, good, full, thinking, loving lives.

SEAN FRENCH

Born: Bristol, May 1959
Favourite city: London
Home (with Nicci): Suffolk

Who or what always puts a smile on your face?
Laurel and Hardy attempting to deliver a piano or to fix the radio aerial on their roof.

Have you ever had any jobs apart from writing?
I haven't had that many jobs. I was a stagehand in the first West End production of *Jesus Christ Superstar* (which caused a profound aversion to the works of Andrew Lloyd Webber). I've been a cleaner in a Swedish hospital and had a few editing jobs, but that's about it. The last time I worked in an office, Margaret Thatcher was prime minister.

What is your greatest fear?
Violence.

How would you like to be remembered?
As someone who is still alive.

Have you ever done something you've really regretted?
Almost every day. But, funnily enough, my real regrets are for the things I didn't do.

How do you spoil yourself?
I always think it's important to reward myself with alcohol for the achievement of having reached the end of the day.

What makes you angry?
People who don't put CDs back in their cases.

What's your worst vice?
In 1972, I bought *Yessongs*, the triple live album by Yes. And I still listen to it occasionally when Nicci is out of the house. Also, I used to play *Tetris* on my Game Boy so obsessively that I would see shapes when I closed my eyes to go to sleep.

What you proudest of?
This question brings out my superstitious side. I'm sure that if I said—for example—my children, they would instantly be struck by lightning. So I'm going to take the Fifth on that one.

One wish: what would it be?
I'd like to know the place where I'll die, and then I'd never go there.

CLIVE CUSSLER
TREASURE OF KHAN

The massive freak wave on Lake Baikal
that almost kills marine expert Dirk Pitt
seems like a rogue act of nature. But, when
his research vessel is attacked as well, Dirk
suspects a more sinister cause.

From the frigid lakes of Siberia to the Gobi
Desert, he encounters intrigue, adventure
and danger all the way, as he unearths clues
to a mysterious treasure from Xanadu.

1

Arik Temur peered into the darkness and tilted his head towards the side rail as the sound of oars dipping through water grew louder. When the noise closed to within a few feet, he slouched back into the shadows, pulling his head down low. This time the intruders would be welcomed aboard warmly, he thought with grim anticipation.

The slapping of the oars ceased, and a wooden clunk told him the small boat had pulled alongside. The midnight moon was a slim crescent, but crystal clear skies amplified the starlight, bathing the ship in a cottony luminance. Temur watched as a dark figure climbed over the stern rail, followed by another, then another, until nearly a dozen men stood on the deck. The intruders wore brightly coloured silk garments under tunics of leather armour which rustled as they moved. But it was the glint of their razor-sharp *katanas*, single-edged duelling swords, that caught his eye.

With the trap set and the bait taken, the Mongol commander turned to a boy at his side and nodded. The boy began ringing the heavy bronze bell he cradled in his arms, its metallic din shattering the still night air. The invaders froze in their tracks. Then a hidden mass of thirty armed soldiers sprang silently from the shadows. They flung themselves at the invaders, thrusting their spears with deadly fury. Half the boarders were killed instantly. The rest were quickly overpowered, and within seconds all lay dead or dying on the ship's deck. All, that is, except a lone, standing dervish.

Clad in an embroidered red silk robe with baggy trousers tucked into bearskin boots, he was clearly no peasant soldier. With devastating speed and accuracy, he turned and ran right into the defenders, dropping a group of three to the deck with a flash of his sword, and nearly cutting one man in two.

Temur jumped to his feet and unsheathed his own sword, then leapt forward. The swordsman saw Temur charge at him and deftly parried a spear thrust aside before whirling round and plunging his sword into the path of the oncoming warrior. The Mongol commander calmly sidestepped the blade and, as it whisked by, thrust his own sword into the attacker's side. The invader stiffened as the blade tore through his rib cage and bisected his heart. He bowed weakly at Temur as his eyes rolled back, then he fell over dead.

The defenders let out a cheer that echoed across the harbour, letting the rest of the Mongol fleet know that this night the guerrillas had failed.

As the dead were unceremoniously dumped over the side, Temur was approached by the ship's captain, a stern Korean named Yon.

'A fine battle,' Yon said without empathy, 'but how many more attacks on my ship must I endure? My ship and crew were to have been back in Pusan by now. The invasion is turning into a debacle.'

'The land offensive will regain momentum once the South of the Yangtze Fleet arrives,' Temur replied testily. 'Conquest shall be ours.'

The captain walked away, shaking his head, and Temur cursed under his breath. Relying on a Korean ship and crew and an army of Chinese foot soldiers was like having his hands tied behind his back. Land a division of Mongol cavalry, and he knew the island nation would be subdued in a week.

Grudgingly he admitted the validity of the captain's words. The invasion had indeed started on a shaky footing. When Kublai, emperor of China and Khan of Khans of the Mongol Empire, had requested tribute from Japan and been rebuffed, it was only natural to send an invasion fleet to subdue their insolence. But the fleet sent in 1274 was much too small, and a severe gale had decimated it before a secure beach-head could be established.

Now, seven years later, the same mistake would not be made. Kublai Khan had called for a massive invasion force, combining elements of the Korean Eastern Fleet with the main battle group from China, the South of the Yangtze Fleet. Over 150,000 Chinese and Mongol soldiers would converge on the Japanese island of Kyushu to overrun the ragtag warlords defending the country. The Eastern Fleet sailing from Korea had arrived first, and tried landing forces north of Hakata Bay, but in the face of spirited Japanese defence they were forced to pull back and wait for the second fleet to arrive.

Their confidence growing, the Japanese warriors had taken the fight to the Mongol fleet. Brazen raiding parties in small boats would sneak into the harbour at night and assault the Mongol ships at anchor. The gruesome discovery of decapitated bodies told the story of yet another attack by samurai, who took the heads of their victims as war trophies. The fleet began tying their ships together for protective safety. Temur's ploy of mooring his ship apart from the others at the edge of the bay had worked as anticipated, enticing a Japanese boarding party to their death.

The late-night attacks dampened the fading morale of the invading forces. After nearly three months provisions were low, and dysentery was cropping up across the fleet. But Temur knew that the arrival of the South of the Yangtze ships would swiftly turn the tables. If only they would arrive.

The next morning broke sunny and clear, with a stiff breeze from the south. On the stern of his *mugun*, a giant troopship, Captain Yon surveyed the Korean fleet—nearly 900 vessels of assorted shapes and sizes stretching across Hakata Bay. It was an impressive sight.

At half past three in the afternoon, a call rang out from a lookout, and soon excited cries and the banging of drums thundered across the harbour. Out to sea, the first dots of the southern invasion force appeared on the horizon. Hour by hour, the dots multiplied and grew larger until the entire sea seemed to be a mass of dark wooden ships with blood-red sails. All night and well into the following day, squadron after squadron of Chinese junks approached the Japanese coast—more than 3,000 ships carrying 100,000 additional soldiers—and assembled in and around Hakata Bay.

Behind the defences of their stone sea wall, the Japanese looked on in horror and despair. Even the most fearless samurai recognised that there was little likelihood they would survive an assault from the massive fleet.

But a thousand miles to the south, another even more powerful force was brewing. In the warm waters of the western Pacific, a percolating mix of wind, sea and rain was welding into a wicked mass of energy. The storm moved northwards, growing in intensity, then it shifted northeast towards the southern islands of Japan.

Standing off Kyushu, the Mongol forces were focused only on conquest. Oblivious to the approaching tempest, the joint fleets assembled for a combined invasion. In Captain Yon's squadron, signal flags were exchanged.

'We are ordered to join the deployments to the south,' Yon reported to Temur. 'Preliminary ground forces have secured a harbour for unloading the troops. We are to follow the Yangtze Fleet out of Hakata Bay and prepare to land our soldiers as reinforcements.'

'It will be a relief to have my soldiers on dry land again,' Temur replied.

'You shall have your chance to fight soon enough,' Yon muttered, turning away to oversee the retrieval of his ship's stone anchor.

As they followed the main body of the fleet southwards along the coast, Yon stared at the blackening horizon. A single cloud seemed to grow larger and larger until it shaded the entire sky. As darkness fell, the wind and seas began to seethe, and rain slapped against the ship. Yon recognised the signs of an approaching squall and repositioned the *mugun* further offshore. Some of the less experienced Chinese captains attempted to put troops ashore in the maelstrom, though most remained at anchor a short distance away. Few believed that another typhoon could strike and damage the fleet as in 1274.

But the typhoon rolled closer. Soon after dawn the sky turned black and the storm reared up with its full might. Torrential rains blew horizontally, the water pellets bursting with enough force to shred the sails of the fleet. Waves crashed to shore in thunderous blows that could be heard miles away.

On Kyushu, a ten-foot wall of storm surge pounded over the shoreline, inundating Japanese homes, villages and defence works and drowning hundreds. In inland areas, a continuous deluge overflowed rivers and flooded valleys. Flash floods and mud slides buried whole villages in seconds.

But the maelstrom on shore paled in comparison to the fury felt by the Mongol fleet at sea. Mammoth waves were blown high by the storm's wrath. Rolling mountains of water belted the invasion fleet, capsizing vessels or smashing them against the rocks. Aboard the Korean *mugun*, Temur and his men clung on desperately as Yon expertly guided his ship through the teeth of the storm. It wasn't until a forty-foot wave suddenly appeared out of the gloom that the salty captain turned pale.

The huge wall of water bore down on them with a thunderous roar, burying the ship in a froth of sea and foam. For several seconds, the *mugun* disappeared under the raging sea, and by rights it should have broken to pieces under the wave's pounding. But the tough little vessel held together, and as the giant wave rolled past, she rose like an apparition from the deep.

Temur was tossed across the deck during the submersion and barely managed to cling to a ladder rung. As the ship resurfaced, he gasped for air and was distraught to see that the masts had been torn off. Behind him, a sharp cry rang out in the water off the stern. He realised with horror that Yon and five Korean seamen, along with a handful of his own men, had been swept off the deck. A chorus of panicked cries pierced the air and Temur caught sight of the captain and the men struggling nearby in the water. He could only watch helplessly as a large wave carried them from his sight.

Without masts and crew, the ship was at the mercy of the storm. After hours of pitching and wallowing, the wind died down and the pelting rain ceased. For a moment the sun broke clear, and Temur thought the storm had ended. But it was just the eye of the typhoon passing over, offering a brief reprieve from the assault. Temur found two Korean sailors belowdecks and forced them to help man the ship. As the wind picked up and the rain returned, they all took turns tying themselves to the rudder and battling the waves.

Not knowing their position or the direction in which they sailed, and buffeted by gusts of over ninety miles per hour, the men bravely focused on keeping the ship afloat. Several times they approached landfall, inching past islands, rocks and shoals, unseen in the gloom. Miraculously, the ship blew clear, the men aboard never realising how close they came to death.

No such luck had befallen the rest of the Mongol invasion force. Nearly the entire Yangtze Fleet was destroyed. The cries of the dying had long since stopped echoing over the shrieks of the wind. The few who crawled ashore alive were quickly cut up by marauding bands of samurai roving the shoreline. It was a crushing defeat for Kublai Khan, and showed the rest of the world that the forces of the great empire were far from invincible.

ABOARD THE KOREAN troopship, Temur and the surviving crew had no idea of the devastation suffered by the invasion fleet.

'We must rejoin the fleet,' Temur told his men. 'The emperor is expecting victory and we must fulfil our duty.'

But there was no telling where they were, and no one aboard was capable of navigating the vessel. The two Korean sailors who survived the storm were a cook and a ship's carpenter, neither possessing navigation skills.

Temur conferred with the carpenter. 'The land of Japan must be to the east of us,' he said. 'Construct a new mast and sails, and we shall use the sun and stars to guide us east until we relocate the invasion fleet.'

The carpenter argued that the ship was not seaworthy. 'She is battered and leaky. We must sail northwest, to Korea, to save ourselves,' he cried.

But Temur would have none of it. A temporary mast was constructed and makeshift sails raised. With fresh determination, the Mongol soldier-turned-sailor guided the waylaid ship towards the eastern horizon, anxious to put ashore and rejoin the battle.

Two days passed, and all Temur and his men could see was blue water. Then another, less intense storm crept up on them from the southwest. For five days the troopship battled high winds and heavy rains. The new mast and sails were again lost overboard to the gales, while leaks kept the carpenter working round the clock. More disconcertingly, the entire rudder broke free of the ship, taking with it two of Temur's soldiers.

When it seemed that the ship could bear no more, the second storm passed. But as the weather eased, the men aboard grew more anxious than ever. Land had not been sighted in a week and food supplies were dwindling. The ship was adrift with no bearings and little means to guide the way.

The hours drifted into days, the days into weeks. Their provisions depleted, the feeble crew caught fish for food and collected rainwater for drinking. As they floated aimlessly over a flat sea, Temur looked over his emaciated soldiers with a feeling of dishonour. Rather than die in battle, their fate was to starve on an empty ocean far from home.

As the men around him dozed in the midday sun, a sudden clamour erupted on the portside deck. 'It's a bird!' someone cried. 'Try to kill it.'

Temur lurched to his feet to see a trio of men attempting to surround a large, dark-billed seagull. One of the men grabbed a wooden mallet and flung it at the bird. With a squawk of indignation, the gull sidestepped the mallet, then flapped its wings and rose lazily into the sky. While the men cursed, Temur studied the gull as it melted into the horizon. Squinting at the far line of blue where the water met the sky, he suddenly blinked. His eyes had registered a small green lump on the horizon. Then a sweet, slightly flowery fragrance wafted through his nostrils.

'There is land before us,' he shouted in a parched voice, pointing towards the path of the gull. 'Let every man who is able help guide us to it.'

The exhausted crew staggered to life. A large deck-support beam was sawn loose and manhandled over the stern, where, secured with ropes, it acted as a crude rudder. While three men wrestled the beam to steer the ship, the remaining men used brooms, boards and even sabres as makeshift oars. Slowly the distant spot grew larger, until a shimmering emerald island materialised, complete with a broad, towering mountain peak.

Approaching the shoreline, they found a large, crescent-shaped cove and paddled the vessel towards a sandy beach. When the barnacle-encrusted hull ground to a halt a few feet from shore, Temur grabbed his sword and staggered ashore with five men to search for food and fresh water. Following the sound of rushing water, they cut through a thicket of tall ferns and found a freshwater lagoon, fed by a waterfall that rushed down a rocky ledge. Temur and his men happily plunged into the lagoon and gulped down mouthfuls of the cool water.

Their enjoyment was short-lived. A sudden pounding broke the air—the boom of the signal drum aboard the *mugun*, thumping out a cry to battle.

Temur sprang to his feet. 'Back to the ship. At once.'

He bounded ahead through the jungle until he finally burst onto the beach. The veteran soldier's eyes scanned the surrounding waters and immediately spotted the source of the alarm.

Midway across the cove, a narrow canoe was moving swiftly towards the grounded ship. Seated inside, a half-dozen shirtless men rhythmically muscled spade-shaped wooden paddles through the water. The men's skin was coloured a deep bronze, and most had curly black hair.

'Your orders, sir?' asked the frail soldier who had been banging the drum.

Temur knew that a harem of old maids could defeat his exhausted crew. 'Arm with spears,' he ordered. 'Defensive line behind me on the beach.'

The ragged force lined up behind him with the few remaining spears still aboard. He knew they would die fighting for him if necessary.

The canoe made its way directly towards the men on the beach. When the bow scraped the sand, the occupants jumped out and stood beside their craft. The parties eyed each other suspiciously for several seconds, then one of the men from the canoe crossed the sand and stood before Temur. He had long white hair wrapped with a bark strip into a ponytail. His brown eyes sparkled, and he smiled broadly at the Mongol, displaying crooked white teeth. In a melodic language, he spoke rapidly, offering what seemed to be a nonthreatening greeting. Then he returned to the canoe and reached inside.

Temur tightened his grip on the samurai sword he now wore at his belt and gave his men a look of caution. But he relaxed when the old man stood up holding a fat thirty-pound yellowfin tuna. The other natives brought out other fish and shellfish in reed baskets, and placed them at the feet of Temur's men. The famished soldiers anxiously waited for approval from the Mongol leader, then voraciously attacked the food, smiling thanks to the native hosts.

Mutual trust having been gained, the natives pointed into the jungle and motioned for the shipwrecked men to follow. Reluctantly leaving their ship, Temur and his men followed the natives to a small clearing containing several dozen thatched huts. A larger hut with a high roof served as the home of the village chief, who was none other than the white-haired man.

A feast was hastily prepared and the Asian warriors were welcomed with great honour. The ship, clothes and weapons of the strangers were evidence of great knowledge, and the men were prized surreptitiously as new allies against potential enemy combatants. The warriors were simply glad to be alive and welcomed the generous offers of food, housing and female companionship that the friendly villagers extended.

Over the next few weeks the men took up residence in the village, gradually assimilating into the community. Only Temur had reservations, thoughts of his wife and four children playing in his mind. But when the storm-ravaged *mugun* finally sank in the cove, Temur gave up hope of returning home, and resigned himself to the life of a castaway.

THE YEARS TRICKLED BY, and Temur and his men learned the lyrical native tongue of the island community. The Mongol commander often enjoyed swapping adventure tales with the white-haired chief. Mahu, as he was called, spoke of how his ancestors had sailed an epic voyage across the great sea just a few generations before. The island had called to them, he said, with a rumble and a billow of smoke from the mountain top, a sign of welcome from the gods to come and prosper.

Temur chuckled at the thought of these primitive natives, who barely traversed to neighbouring islands in small canoes, crossing the great ocean. 'I would like to see one of these majestic sailing ships,' he told the old man.

'I will take you to one,' Mahu replied indignantly. 'See for yourself.'

Amused, Temur took the chief up on his offer. After a two-day trek across the island, he was beginning to regret his curiosity when the weathered jungle path they followed suddenly opened onto a small, sandy beach.

The old man pointed towards the far end, where a pair of large tree trunks lay perpendicular to the shore. Suddenly Temur realised that they were more than just dead wood; they were the support frames for a massive raft.

The Mongol warrior ran towards the half-buried object, not believing his eyes. The ancient sailing craft was a double-hulled design, with a flat deck supported by the two large logs. Over sixty feet long, it carried only a single mast, which had rotted away. But though the plank deck had disintegrated, Temur could see that the massive support timbers looked sturdy.

'You shall return me to my home and emperor,' he muttered wistfully.

With a native crew working under the direction of the Korean ship's carpenter, Temur set about refitting the old sailing vessel. Deck planking was cut from nearby hardwood trees. A reed sail was woven and fitted to the replacement mast, cut from a young tree near the beach. In a few short weeks, the ocean voyager was made ready to ply the waves again.

Temur knew that most of his old crew would be afraid to risk their lives again in a daring sea voyage. Many of them now had wives and children on the island. When he asked for volunteers, just three stepped forward, along with old Mahu. It would be barely enough to sail the old craft, but Temur accepted the decision of those who elected to stay. Provisions were stocked, then the men waited until Mahu declared that the time was right.

'The goddess Hina will offer us safe passage to the west now,' he finally told Temur a week later, when the winds shifted direction. 'Let us be away.'

Loaded with plenty of water, dried fish and fruit, the ship set sail. Fair skies and calm seas greeted the men each day for a fortnight as they sailed with the wind. Only an occasional squall tested the boat's sturdiness. All the while, Mahu calmly issued the sailing orders while constantly tracking the sun and stars. Studying the clouds on the horizon several days later, he noticed an unusual clustering to the southwest.

'Land to the south, two days' sailing,' he proclaimed.

Relief and excitement flowed through the crew at the prospect of reaching land again. But what lands were they approaching?

The next morning a dot appeared on the horizon, and it grew larger with each passing hour. It was not land, however, but another sailing vessel, an Arab merchant ship, crossing their path. The trader drew alongside the catamaran and dropped its sails as a thin, dark-skinned man in a brightly coloured robe shouted a greeting from the rail.

The vessel was from Zanzibar, its captain a jovial Muslim merchant who had traded goods with the court of the Great Khan. The ship was bound for Shanghai with a cargo of ivory, gold and spices, to be traded for fine Chinese porcelain and silk. Temur's crew and Mahu were welcomed aboard, and they watched sadly as their canoe was cut loose, left to drift the Pacific alone.

When they landed at Shanghai, news of the soldiers' return thirteen years after the aborted invasion of Japan spread like wildfire. Representatives from the government whisked Temur and his men up to the Imperial City at Ta-tu for a briefing with the emperor. Temur learned from his escorts that the invasion of Japan had been an unmitigated disaster, the typhoon having wiped out over 2,000 ships and nearly 100,000 men. Though Kublai Khan had wished to attempt a third invasion, his advisers had wisely quelled the notion. In the ten years since the Mongol Empire had defeated the Song Dynasty and united China under a single rule, its dominance had been shattered.

Arriving in the Imperial City, Temur and his men were escorted into the emperor's private chambers. Though Temur had seen Kublai Khan many times in earlier years, he was shocked at the sight of the fat, bloated man before him now, stretched out on a padded chaise longue and clad in yards of silk robing. Despondent over the recent death of his favourite wife and the loss of his second son, Kublai had turned to food and drink for solace.

'Commander Temur, you have returned from a considerable absence to resume your duty,' the Khan stated in a raspy voice.

'As the emperor commands,' Temur replied, bowing deeply.

'Tell of your voyages, and the island on which you were shipwrecked.'

Carved chairs were brought for them, as Temur described the typhoon that blew his ship away from the Japanese mainland and their subsequent luck at landing on the island and being welcomed by its inhabitants. Introducing Mahu, he told of the old man's aid in sailing back to China.

'A remarkable journey,' Kublai lauded. 'This island was rich and fertile?'

'Exceedingly. The soil is bountiful, and, with a temperate climate subject to much rainfall, an abundance of wild and cultivated plants flourish there.'

'Congratulations, my emperor,' said a wrinkled man with a long white beard standing at the Khan's side. 'You have added new lands to the empire.'

'You left a garrison behind?' Kublai asked. 'It is under Mongol rule?'

Temur silently cursed the Confucian adviser's ploy to fabricate glory for the emperor. 'Yes,' he lied. 'A small contingent rules the land in your name.' He looked at the old village chief Mahu with shame, but the old man simply nodded back, understanding the politics of the empire.

Kublai gazed into the distance. 'I should like to see this wondrous place, this land where the sun first shines on my empire,' he whispered dreamily.

'Yes, it is a paradise on earth. As beautiful as any lands under the reign.'

'You know the route back, Temur?'

'I do not know the ways of navigation at sea, but Mahu can read the sun and the stars. He could find the way back to his home, I believe.'

'You have served the empire well, Temur. Your loyalty to the empire shall be well rewarded,' Kublai gasped.

Temur bowed again. 'Thank you, my emperor.' A pair of palace guards suddenly materialised and escorted them out of the chamber.

As Temur exited the palace grounds, he felt saddened that the great Kublai Khan was now a tired and ancient shell of the visionary emperor he once was. Suddenly he noticed that Mahu was not by his side, and realised that the old villager had remained behind in the emperor's chamber. Temur waited several hours for the chief to emerge, then gave up and went home to his village and family. He never saw the old man again.

JUST TWO MONTHS later, the death of the great emperor was announced. Kublai Khan had finally succumbed to the ravages of age and alcoholism. An elaborate ceremony to honour his life was held in Ta-tu, the city now known as Beijing. Afterwards a solemn procession toting the coffin of the Great Khan in an ornate carriage marched slowly north into Mongolia and

Kublai's homeland. At a secret spot in the Khentii Mountains, the coffin was laid to rest with a cortege of animals, concubines and riches from across the empire. To disguise the site and ensure a peaceful afterlife, the burial region was trampled with horses. Labourers tasked with digging the tomb were executed, and the procession commanders sworn to secrecy under penalty of death. In a few short years, the burial site of the Mongol leader was lost to history, and the memory of Kublai Khan cast to the winds that whip tirelessly down the slopes of the forested mountain range.

A THOUSAND MILES to the south, a large four-masted junk slipped out of its dock at Shanghai before dawn and drifted down the Yellow River towards the Pacific Ocean. With the Yuan Empire still in mourning, the vessel didn't fly its usual state banners, and, in fact, carried no identifying flags at all. At the helm an old, dark-skinned man with flowing white hair stood next to the captain, pointing to the rising sun. In a strange tongue, he directed the path of the majestic vessel as it set sail for a distant and uncharted destination.

2

Shangdu, China, August 4, 1937

Muffled booms echoed in the distance. Leigh Hunt stood up from a freshly dug trench and set his trowel atop a mud-brick wall. The British Museum's field archaeologist was dressed for the part, in long khaki trousers and matching shirt. Instead of the classic pith helmet, he wore a battered fedora to shield his head from the sun. Through tired hazel eyes, he peered east down a wide valley towards the source of the noise. For the first time, small puffs of smoke could be seen on the horizon.

'Tsendyn, it would appear that the artillery is moving closer,' he said nonchalantly in the direction of the trench.

A short, broad-shouldered man with Mongolian features climbed quietly out of the pit. He was wearing a thin woollen shirt with a red sash round his waist. Beyond him in the trench a crew of Chinese labourers continued to dig through the dry soil with heavy spades and hand trowels.

'Peking is falling,' said the Mongolian. 'Already the refugees are fleeing.' He pointed towards a dirt track a mile away, where half a dozen ox-drawn carts toted the life possessions of several Chinese families escaping to the west. 'We must abandon the excavation, sir, before the Japanese are upon us.'

Hunt instinctively felt for the revolver holstered at his hip. China was imploding under the juggernaut of Japanese military might. Ever since they seized Manchuria in 1931, Japan's military leaders had set their sights on colonising China. Six years of thrusts and parries finally erupted in the summer of 1937 when the Japanese Imperial Army invaded northern China.

Hunt listened to the crack of the approaching artillery that signalled the loss of Peking and he knew that the Chinese were in trouble. The capital city of Nanking would be next.

'Have the coolies cease all excavations at noon,' he said. 'We'll secure the artefacts and complete the documentation this afternoon, then join in the caravan heading west.' Glancing at the road, he noted a ragtag band of Chinese Nationalist soldiers filtering into the evacuation route.

'You will leave for Nanking tomorrow?' Tsendyn asked.

'There's no sense in flying to Nanking under these hostile conditions. Assuming the plane shows up, I intend to take the most important artefacts and fly north to Ulaanbaatar. You'll have to manage the remaining items, equipment and supplies with the pack train, I'm afraid. I'll wait for you in Ulaanbaatar before catching the Trans-Siberian railway west.'

Tsendyn surveyed the maze of trenches. 'It is unfortunate we must leave now. We have nearly finished excavating the Pavilion of Great Harmony.'

'It's a bloody shame,' Hunt said, shaking his head in anger.

This was his third summer on the grounds of Shangdu, excavating the remains of the royal summer palace built in 1260. Staring at a barren hillside dotted with mounds of fresh dirt, Hunt found it difficult to imagine the grandeur of the palace and grounds that once stood here.

Built on a huge mound at the centre of a walled city, the original palace had been surrounded by a forest of transplanted trees and lapis lazuli stone paths, which lent a magical blue hue to the estate. Exquisite gardens and fountains wove through the government buildings and residences that encircled the imperial palace, or 'Pavilion of Great Harmony'. Constructed of green marble and stone, gilded and inlaid with glazed tiles, the palace was used primarily as a summer residence by the emperor to escape the heat of Peking, and Shangdu quickly developed into a scientific and cultural hub, a haven for scholars both foreign and domestic.

Centuries of abandonment, neglect and looting had reduced the palace to little more than scattered rubble in a barren landscape. Xanadu, the romantic name of Shangdu popularised by the Samuel Taylor Coleridge poem, existed now only in the imagination.

Since excavations had begun three years before, Hunt had pieced together the boundaries of the Palace of Great Harmony, identifying a grand hall, a kitchen and a dining hall. An assortment of bronze and porcelain artefacts were recovered from the earth, and the British Museum would be pleased with them, but to Hunt's disappointment there were no dazzling discoveries that would make his name.

'I've kept you from your family long enough, Tsendyn,' Hunt told his assistant. 'I doubt the Russians will allow the Japanese to pussyfoot around in Mongolia, so you should be safe from this craziness.'

The Mongol smiled. 'My wife shall welcome my return.'

Behind them, a commotion erupted from one of the excavation trenches. A Chinese labourer popped his head over the edge, his jaws jabbering.

'What is it?' Hunt said, setting down his tea.

'He says he's found some lacquered wood,' Tsendyn replied.

Both men walked to the edge and peered down. The labourer excitedly pointed his trowel towards the ground, where a flat, square, yellow object the size of a serving platter was exposed through the dirt.

'Tsendyn, you handle it,' Hunt barked, waving away the other labourers.

The Mongolian jumped into the trench and began scraping the dirt away carefully with a trowel and brush. Hunt retrieved a notebook and pencil and began sketching. As the dirt and dust fell away, he could see that the object was a yellow lacquered wooden box, delicately painted with images of animals and trees. A wolf was depicted on the lid. Tsendyn brushed the dirt from its base, and gently placed the box on a flat stone outside the trench.

Hunt studied the box before taking it in his hands. Something heavy was inside, which shifted as he lifted the box. With his thumbs, he could feel a seam midway round the shallow sides and gently tried to separate the lid. The box, sealed for centuries, protested at first, then slowly opened. Tsendyn and the labourers all leaned in to see what was inside.

Two objects were nestled in the box and Hunt removed them for all to see. A spotted animal skin, coloured black and yellow in the pattern of a cheetah, was rolled up like a scroll, the ends tied together with leather straps. The other item was a bronze tube, aged a deep green colour, sealed at one end but with a removable cap at the other.

Hunt set down the cheetah skin and examined the bronze tube. The image of a dragon stretched along its length, the tail of the imaginary beast curled round the end of the tube like a coil of rope.

'Go ahead, open it up,' Tsendyn urged.

Hunt prised off the end cap and carefully tipped out the contents. It was a rolled-up bolt of silk, dyed a pale blue. Tsendyn shook clean a nearby blanket and spread it across the ground at Hunt's feet. With trembling hands the archaeologist unfurled the silk roll to its full length of nearly five feet.

A picturesque landscape scene was painted on the silk, portraying a mountain top with deep valleys, gorges and streams. Along the left border was a sizable section of text which Hunt recognised as Uighur script, a Mongolian written language adopted from early Turkic settlers to the Asian Steppes. On the right margin was a sequence of smaller images, depicting a harem of women, herds of horses, camels and other animals, and a contingent of armed soldiers surrounding several wooden chests. The landscape portion of the painting was bare of life except for a single Bactrian camel draped with a saddlecloth inscribed with two words. Oddly, the camel was shedding oversized tears that fell to the ground.

As he studied the silk painting, a band of sweat formed across Hunt's forehead. He felt his heart thumping loudly in his chest.

'Tsendyn . . . Tsendyn,' he muttered, nearly afraid to ask. 'It is Uighur script. Can you read what it says?'

The Mongol assistant's eyes widened as he, too, grasped the meaning of the image. 'The wording on the left is a physical description of the mountainous region in the painting,' he stuttered. ' "At home atop Mount Burkhan Khaldun, nestled in the Khentii Mountains, our emperor sleeps. The Onon River quenches his thirst, between the valleys of the doomed." '

'And the inscription on the camel?' Hunt whispered.

'*Temujin khagan,*' Tsendyn replied in a hushed tone of reverence.

'Temujin,' Hunt repeated, as if in a trance. They had made an astounding discovery—the weeping camel, the offerings depicted on the side, the description of the locale. Then there was the name on the camel's back. Temujin. It was the birth name of a tribal boy who became the world's greatest conqueror. History would remember him by his royally appointed moniker: Genghis Khan. The ancient silk painting before them could be nothing other than a diagram of the hidden burial site of Genghis Khan.

Hunt collapsed to his knees. The grave of Genghis Khan was one of the most sought-after archaeological sites in history. Genghis died in AD 1227 at the height of his power, and was known to have been buried near his birthplace in the Khentii Mountains. In the Mongol tradition, he was buried secretly with forty concubines and untold riches, the grave site carefully concealed after interment. But a decade or so later, so the legend went, the grave site was located when a Bactrian pack camel, known to be the mother of a camel interred with the great leader, was found weeping at a spot in the Khentii Mountains. The camel's owner realised it was crying for its lost son buried beneath its feet. Yet the fable ended there, the secret kept by the herder, and the grave of Genghis Khan left undisturbed. Now the legend was whisked to life in the silk painting before Hunt's eyes.

'This is a most sacred find,' Tsendyn whispered. 'It will lead us to the tomb of the Great Khan.'

'Yes,' Hunt gasped, imagining the fame that would sweep his way if he led the discovery of Genghis Khan's grave.

Suddenly fearful of exposing the significance of the silk to the Chinese labourers, Hunt hastily rerolled the fabric into the tube and replaced it in the lacquered box with the cheetah skin. He wrapped the box in a cloth and secured it in a large leather satchel, which he kept with him the rest of the day.

Finding no other artefacts in the earth where the box had been found, Hunt called a halt to the dig. With equipment and artefacts loaded onto a trio of wooden carts and the Chinese labourers paid and dismissed, Hunt retired to his tent after dinner and packed up his belongings. That night he slept fitfully, cognisant of the dangers around him for the first time. Rising groggily at day-break, he was relieved to find the satchel safe and sound under his cot.

Tsendyn was cooking goat meat over an open fire. 'Good morning, sir.' Smiling, he handed Hunt a cup of steaming tea. 'All the equipment is packed, and the mules are hitched to the carts. We can depart at your desire.'

'Jolly good. Stow my tent, if you would, and take mind of that satchel under the cot,' Hunt said, and he watched the sunrise as he enjoyed his tea.

The first distant artillery shell sounded an hour later as the remaining excavation party rolled away from the site aboard three mule-drawn wagons. They made their way to a large meadow at the edge of Duolun and waited. A faint buzz broke the air, and the archaeologist watched as a tiny silver speck grew larger against the clouds as it approached the makeshift airfield.

With a gentle touch, the pilot circled the Fokker F.VIIb trimotor in a wide, low turn, then set the noisy plane down onto the turf. The motors had barely gurgled to a stop when the fuselage door burst open and out jumped two men in worn leather jackets.

'Hunt? I'm Randy Schodt,' said the pilot in greeting. He was a tall man with a rugged yet friendly face who spoke with an American accent. 'My brother Dave and I are here to fly you to Nanking, or so the contract says.'

'What's a pair of Yanks doing way out here?' Hunt asked.

'Been flying for the Chinese Ministry of Railroads, supporting rail extensions on the Peking–Shanghai line,' Randy explained. 'Though work came to a halt with the unpleasantness caused by these Japanese folks.'

'I have a change in destination,' said Hunt. 'I need to fly to Ulaanbaatar.'

'Mongolia?' Randy scratched his head. 'Well, as long as we're headed away from the Nippon Army, I guess it's OK with me.'

With the brothers' help, Hunt supervised the loading of the more important artefacts and tools into the fuselage of the Fokker, which bore the name *Blessed Betty* beneath the pilot's window. When the crates had nearly filled the interior, Hunt carefully placed his satchel on the front passenger's seat.

'That will be a hundred and fifty miles less than the flight to Nanking,' said Randy Schodt, spreading out a map. 'But we'll need return mileage, which exceeds what your British Museum people contracted me to fly.'

Hunt handed the pilot a written request for the route change. 'You have my authorisation, and the museum will honour the additional expense.'

'Sure they will; they don't want your artefacts to end up in the Tokyo Museum,' Schodt said, laughing. Sticking the note in his pocket, he added, 'Since we'll be flying over the Gobi Desert, you're lucky the *Blessed Betty* has extra fuel tanks. Whenever you're ready.'

Hunt walked over to where Tsendyn stood with the two remaining carts still packed with equipment and artefacts. 'Tsendyn, we have had a difficult but fruitful expedition,' he said. 'You have been invaluable to its success.'

'It has been my honour. You have done a great service to my country and heritage. My heirs shall be particularly grateful.'

'Take the remaining equipment and artefacts to Nanking. A representative from the British Museum will meet you and arrange shipment of the items to London. I will wait for you in Ulaanbaatar.'

'I look forward to the next search with great anticipation,' Tsendyn replied, shaking the archaeologist's hand.

'Farewell, my friend.'

Hunt climbed aboard the loaded Fokker as the plane's three engines roared to life. Tsendyn stood and watched as the big plane lumbered into the air, then swung northwest towards the Mongolian border.

Not until the aircraft had completely vanished from sight did Tsendyn reach into the pocket of his coat for a reassuring touch. The bolt of silk was still there, as it had been since the early hours of the night before.

IT WAS TWO HOURS into the flight when Hunt reached for the satchel and pulled out the lacquered box, drawn to touch the silk painting one more time. With the box in his hands, he felt the weight of the bronze tube rolling around inside. Yet something didn't feel right. Prising off the lid, he found the cheetah skin tightly rolled up and stuffed to one side, as it had been before. But picking up the bronze tube, he noticed it felt heavier than he remembered. With a shaking hand, he quickly pulled off the cap and released an outpouring of sand onto his lap. The silk scroll had vanished.

His eyes bulged at the sudden realisation that he'd been duped. The shock quickly turned to anger and he began screaming at the pilots.

'Turn back! Turn the airplane around! We must return at once,' he cried.

But his plea fell on deaf ears. In the cockpit, the two pilots suddenly had something more troubling of their own to contend with.

THE MITSUBISHI G3M bomber, known in the west as a Nell, was on a reconnaissance mission. With their easy conquest of Manchuria and successful advance into northern China, the Japanese had sharpened their sights on the seaports and coal mines of Siberia, and were probing the defensive lines of that barren country in preparation for an outright northern offensive.

The Nell had come up empty on its foray into eastern Mongolia, finding no sign of Russian troop deployments or runway construction.

'Nothing but sand out here,' the Nell's copilot, a youthful lieutenant named Miyabe, said with a yawn. 'I don't know why the wing commander is excited over this real estate.'

'As a buffer to the more valuable territory to the north, I suspect,' Captain Nobuji Negishi replied. 'I just hope we get repositioned to the front when the invasion occurs. We're missing all the fun in Shanghai.'

As Miyabe stared at the flat ground beneath the plane, he saw a glint of sunlight out of the corner of his eye. Squinting, he tracked its source.

'Sir, an aircraft ahead and slightly below us,' he said, pointing.

Negishi peered ahead and quickly spotted the Fokker trimotor. 'She's crossing our path,' he exclaimed. 'At last, a chance for battle.'

'But sir, that's not a combat plane,' Miyabe said, observing the markings on the Fokker. 'Our orders are to engage only military aircraft.'

'The flight poses a risk,' Negishi insisted. 'Besides, it will be good target practice, Lieutenant.' It was a rare chance for an easy kill and he wasn't about to pass it by. 'Ready with the forward guns,' he ordered.

Negishi swung the bomber round in a wide arc and approached the trimotor from the side. The Mitsubishi was nearly twice as fast as the Fokker, which didn't stand a chance. The Japanese turret gunner squeezed a round from his 7.7mm machine gun and the Fokker's right wing engine disintegrated.

A plume of smoke burst from the engine as Randy Schodt shut down the fuel line before the motor caught fire. Jockeying the remaining two engines, he fought to keep the Fokker airborne, but a well-placed shot by the Mitsubishi's topside gunner severed the *Blessed Betty*'s elevator controls.

Without the ability to control altitude, the wounded trimotor began a flat descent towards the ground. Amazingly, the airplane held its balance, gliding downwards, its nose bent just a fraction forward. Shutting down the remaining engines just before impact, Randy felt the left wing tip clip the ground first, throwing the plane into a clumsy cartwheel.

The Schodt brothers were killed instantly. Hunt survived the crash, but his back was broken and his left leg nearly severed. For two days he painfully clung to life in the jumbled wreckage. With his last ounce of strength, he pulled the lacquered box to his chest and cursed his sudden turn of luck. As his final breath left him, he had no idea that, still clutched within his arms, he held the clue to the most magnificent treasure the world would ever see.

3

Lake Baikal, Siberia, June 2, 2007

The still waters of the world's deepest lake radiate the deep translucent blue of a polished sapphire. Fed by cold, ancient streams, free of silt and sediments, Lake Baikal possesses remarkably clear waters. On a calm day, a silver coin can be seen from the surface at a hundred-foot depth.

Surrounded by craggy, snowcapped peaks to the north and dense taiga forests of birch, larch and pine to the south, the 'blue pearl of Siberia' curves in a crescent shape from south to north just above the border with Mongolia. Four hundred miles long and more than a mile deep in some spots, the lake holds a fifth of all the fresh water on the planet. A few small fishing villages dot its shore, with Irkutsk, a modestly hip city of half a million Siberian residents in the south, the only significant centre of population.

Theresa Hollema glanced up from a laptop computer and briefly admired the purple mountains at the edge of the lake, their peaks grazed by cotton-wool clouds. The Dutch geophysicist delighted in the clear blue skies that so seldom graced her home outside Amsterdam.

'It is an agreeable day on the lake, no?' asked Tatiana Borjin. Although she spoke in the gruff, emotionless manner endemic to Russians speaking English, the woman was, in fact, Mongolian. With long black hair, bronze skin and almond-shaped eyes, she possessed a natural and robust beauty. But there was a deep intensity behind her dark eyes, which seemed to take everything in life with harsh seriousness.

'I had no idea that Siberia was so beautiful,' Theresa replied. 'The lake is breathtaking. So calm and peaceful.'

'She is calm at the moment, but sudden winds from the southwest can burst on the lake with the force of a hurricane. The graveyards are filled with fishermen who failed to respect the fierce natural forces of Baikal.'

A chill ran up Theresa's spine. The locals seemed to speak constantly of the spirit of the lake. Baikal's pristine waters were a proud cultural resource to the Siberians, and protecting the lake from pollutants had fostered an environmental movement that had grown globally. She just hoped that a Greenpeace rubber-boat armada would not appear to assail their presence.

At least her involvement was relatively harmless, she convinced herself. Her employer, Royal Dutch Shell, had been contracted to survey a section of the lake for reported oil seeps. The company was trying to cosy up to the owners of some exploratory Siberian oil fields in hope of landing more significant business. Theresa had never heard of the Avarga Oil Consortium before travelling to Siberia, but she knew that there were many oil companies clamouring in the Russian marketplace.

'They're obviously not pumping their revenues into R & D,' she joked to the two Shell technicians who joined her on the leased survey boat.

'Clever how they designed her to resemble a decrepit fishing boat,' cracked Jim Wofford, a tall, friendly geophysicist from Arkansas.

The twenty-eight-foot boat looked like it should have been scuttled years earlier. Paint was peeling everywhere and the vessel reeked of wood rot and dead fish. Theresa noted with unease that the bilge pump ran continuously.

'We do not possess our own sea vessels,' Tatiana said without apology. She was Avarga Oil's representative and sole interface with the Shell team.

Wofford smiled. 'That's all right, for what it lacks in space it makes up for in discomfort.'

'True, but I bet there's some caviar hiding aboard someplace,' replied Wofford's partner, Dave Roy. Lake Baikal, he knew, was home to enormous sturgeon that could carry up to twenty pounds of caviar.

'Caviar? With your beer tastes?' Theresa chided. She was lending a hand as Roy and Wofford lugged their equipment onto the cramped stern deck.

'As a matter of fact, the two make an excellent combination,' Roy replied with mock seriousness. 'The sodium content of caviar produces a hydration craving that is perfectly fulfilled by a malt-based beverage.'

'In other words, it's a good excuse to drink more beer,' Wofford added.

'I give up.' Theresa laughed. 'Far be it from me to argue with an alcoholic.'

Tatiana looked on without amusement, then nodded towards the boat's dour-faced captain, whose bulbous nose was tinted red from a steady consumption of vodka. Ducking into the small wheelhouse, he fired up the boat's smoky diesel engine and they chugged away from their berth at the fishing and tourist village of Listvyanka, on the lake's southwest shore.

Tatiana unrolled a map of the lake. 'We shall survey here, at Peschanaya Bay,' she told the geologists, pointing to an area north of the town. 'There have been numerous oil slicks reported by the fishermen in this area, which would seem to indicate a hydrocarbon seepage.'

'You're not going to take us into deep water, are you?' Wofford asked.

'I understand the limitations of the equipment available to us,' Tatiana replied. 'Our research objective is focused on four locations in the south of Lake Baikal that are near the shoreline, presumably in shallow water.'

'Are all the sites on the western shoreline?' Theresa asked.

'Only the Peschanaya Bay site. The other three are on the eastern shore.'

The old fishing boat motored past the docks of Listvyanka and turned north, hugging the craggy western shore. Deep taiga forests marched down to the shoreline in a carpet of green, interspersed with meadows of thick grass. It was difficult for Theresa to picture the stark bitterness of the region in winter, when a layer of ice four feet thick covered the lake.

Bright and analytical, the petroleum engineer had chosen her career less for the intellectual challenge than for the opportunity to travel. Working in a man's field proved to be no setback, as Theresa's vivacious personality easily broke down barriers with men who weren't already attracted to her athletic build, dark hair and walnut eyes.

Forty miles north of Listvyanka, the captain nosed the boat's prow into the shallow bay called Peschanaya.

Tatiana turned to Theresa. 'We will start here,' she announced.

Roy and Wofford lowered the sonar towfish over the stern as Theresa plugged a GPS antenna into the sonar's computer.

Tatiana glanced at a Fathometer and shouted, 'Depth, thirty metres.'

'Not too deep, that's good,' Theresa said as the boat moved forward again, towing the sensor thirty metres behind.

Slowly they swept back and forth across the bay, studying the sonar monitor for lake-bed features that might indicate a hydrocarbon seep.

As they reached the northern edge of the bay, the captain swung the boat round and aligned it for the last survey lane. Towards the centre of the lake Theresa noticed a large, dirty-grey ship sailing north. It appeared to be some sort of research vessel, with an old-style helicopter wedged on the stern deck. She noted that the ship's mast was flying both a Russian and an American flag. Probably a joint scientific study, she mused. Geophysicists, microbiologists and environmental scientists migrated from around the world to study the lake and its unique flora and fauna.

Twenty minutes later they were at the bay's southern edge. 'That wraps it up for the opening act of today's programme,' Wofford said. 'Where next?'

'We will cross the lake to a position here,' Tatiana said, tapping the map with a slender finger. 'Thirty-five kilometres southeast.'

'Might as well leave the sonar in the water so we can get a look at the water depths as we cross over,' Theresa said.

'No problem,' Wofford said, but as he casually watched the monitor, a quizzical expression appeared on his face. 'That's odd,' he muttered.

Roy leaned over and studied the monitor. The shadowy image of the lake bottom had gone haywire. 'Towfish bouncing off the bottom?' he asked.

'No,' Wofford replied. 'She's riding forty metres above the lake floor.'

The interference continued for several more seconds, then abruptly ceased.

'Maybe one of those giant sturgeon tried to take a bite out of our towfish,' Wofford joked, relieved that the equipment was working properly again.

But his words were followed by a low, deep rumble, which echoed across the water for almost half a minute. Lower pitched than a clap of thunder, the sound had an odd muffled quality to it.

'Some sort of construction?' Theresa asked.

'Maybe,' Roy replied, glancing at the sonar monitor again. 'But whatever it is, I just wish it would stop messing with our equipment.'

TEN MILES TO THE NORTH, Rudi Gunn walked onto the bridge wing of the grey-hulled Russian research vessel *Vereshchagin* and looked up at the azure sky. Removing a pair of horn-rimmed glasses, he peered upwards again. 'Sounds like thunder, but there's hardly a cloud in the sky,' he muttered.

A hearty laugh erupted at his words, flowing from a portly man with black hair and matching beard. Dr Alexander Sarghov, a geophysicist from the Russian Academy of Sciences Limnological Institute, resembled a circus bear, his large frame softened by a jovial demeanour and twinkling eyes. 'You Westerners are very amusing,' he said in heavily accented English.

'You'll have to excuse Rudi,' answered a warm, deep voice from the opposite side of the bridge. 'He's never lived in an earthquake zone.'

The green opaline eyes of Dirk Pitt, head of the National Underwater and Marine Agency, sparkled with mirth as he stood up from a bank of video monitors and stretched his six-foot-three frame. Though more than two decades of undersea adventures had exacted a toll on his rugged body, he still had a lean and fit form. Just a few wrinkles round the eyes and a growing tussle of grey at the temples indicated a wavering battle with age.

'An earthquake?' Gunn speculated. The deputy director of NUMA stared out from the bridge in wonder. 'I've only been in one or two, but those were felt and not heard.'

'There is a great deal of tectonic activity under Lake Baikal,' Sarghov said. 'Earthquakes occur frequently in this region.'

'I hope they don't disrupt our data collection,' Gunn said.

The *Vereshchagin* was engaged in a joint Russian–American scientific survey of Lake Baikal's uncharted current flows. The Russians provided the ship and crew, while the Americans provided high-tech sonobuoys and monitoring equipment, which would be used to paint a three-dimensional image of the lake and its currents. The great depth of Lake Baikal was known to create unique water-circulation patterns that often behaved unpredictably. Tales of swirling vortexes and fishing boats getting pulled underwater by their nets were common among the local lakeside communities.

Starting at the northern tip of the lake, the scientific team had deployed dozens of tiny sensors, packed in orange-coloured pods that were ballasted to drift at varying depths. The pods relayed data to a series of fixed underwater transponders, and computers onboard the *Vereshchagin* processed that data. Gunn glanced at the bank of monitors in front of him, then focused on one of them. The image resembled a pack of orange marbles floating in a bowl of blue ice cream. Suddenly a vertical string of the orange balls jumped rapidly towards the top edge of the screen.

'Whoa!' he blurted. 'Either one of our transponders is going weird or there's a significant disturbance at the bottom of the lake.'

Pitt and Sarghov turned and studied the monitor.

'The current is uplifting, at a dramatic rate,' Sarghov said with a raised brow. 'It's difficult to believe the earthquake could produce that effect.'

'Perhaps not the earthquake itself,' Pitt said, 'but a side effect. A submarine landslide set off by a minor quake might create that sort of uplift.'

Pitt was right. Though seismologists would later determine that the quake's epicentre was near the lake's northern shore, it had created a devastating effect 2,000 feet beneath the surface, midway down the western flank, near Olkhon Island. Directly off the island's eastern shore, the lake floor dropped like an elevator down a steep slope which ran to the deepest part of the lake.

Seismic studies had revealed dozens of fault lines beneath the lake floor, including one at Olkhon Island. The shock waves of the earthquake, which measured 6.7 on the Richter scale, caused a movement of less than three millimetres, but it was sufficient to shear off a chunk of alluvial sediment nearly twenty metres thick. The mountain of rock, sediment and mud slid down a subterranean ravine like an avalanche, building momentum as it went before colliding with the lake bottom at a depth of 1,500 metres.

In seconds, a million cubic metres of sediment was dumped on the lake floor. The landslide's muffled rumble quickly fell away, but a violent energy was unleashed. The sediment displaced a great mass of water, driving it first to the bottom ahead of the landslide then squeezing it up to the surface.

The submarine landslide had fallen in a southerly direction off Olkhon Island, and that was the direction in which the upsurge of water, ten feet high, began to move. At sea, the rolling wave would be labelled a tsunami, but in the confines of a freshwater lake it was called a seiche wave. As it pushed into shallower depths, the upswell squeezed higher, increasing the size and speed of the surface wave. To those in its path, it would be a liquid wall of death.

On the bridge of the *Vereshchagin*, Pitt and Gunn tracked the development of the killer wave with growing alarm.

'It's a rolling wave, all right,' Gunn reported grimly. 'The sensors are getting kicked up almost five metres as it passes.'

Pitt nodded. 'How fast is she moving, Rudi?'

Gunn toggled the computer mouse and drew a line between two pods, measuring their distance apart. 'Based on the spikes in the sensors, it looks to be travelling at about a hundred and twenty-five miles per hour.'

'Which will put it upon us in about fifty minutes,' Pitt calculated, his mind racing. 'Dr Sarghov, I suggest you have the captain issue an immediate emergency warning to all vessels on the lake. And contact the authorities on shore to evacuate all residents at risk to flooding. There's no time to lose.'

Sarghov beat a path to the ship's radio and issued the warning himself. The radio hummed with chatter as people called back for confirmation. Though Pitt didn't speak Russian, he could tell by the tone of scepticism in their voices that many thought Sarghov was either drunk or crazy.

The normally jovial scientist turned red and spat obvious obscenities into the microphone. 'Idiot fishermen! They're calling me a fool!' he cursed.

But when a fishing boat in the protected cove of Aya Bay barely survived capsizing as the fringe of the wave passed by, and its captain hysterically reported the event, the warnings were heeded. Pitt scanned the horizon with binoculars and could make out half a dozen fishing boats motoring towards the safety of Listvyanka, along with a small freighter and a hydrofoil ferry.

'I guess you got their attention, Alex,' Pitt said.

'Yes,' Sarghov replied with some relief. 'The Listvyanka Police Department has issued alerts to all stations around the lake and is going door to door to evacuate risky areas. We've done all we can do.'

As the *Vereshchagin* turned towards Listvyanka, Gunn eyed the map of Lake Baikal, rubbing his finger across the lower toe of the lake, which angled to the west. 'If the wave holds its southerly track, we should be positioned away from its primary force,' he remarked.

'That's what I'm banking on,' Pitt replied.

The *Vereshchagin*'s captain, a quiet, steady man named Ian Kharitonov, gripped the ship's wheel and silently urged his vessel to sail faster. He periodically took sneak peeks to the north, looking for signs of the wave.

Pitt studied the ship's radar, noting a stationary object lying ten miles to the southeast of their position. 'Apparently, someone still didn't get the word,' he said, motioning towards the radar target.

'The fool probably has his radio turned off,' Sarghov muttered, grabbing the radio microphone again. Hailing the vessel several times brought only silence. He shook his head. 'Their ignorance will mean their death,' he said.

His anguish was broken by a loud thumping noise which rattled the windows of the bridge. Skimming low above the water, a small helicopter swooped towards the *Vereshchagin*'s bridge before suddenly pulling up and hovering off the starboard wing. It was a Kamov Ka-26, an old Soviet civilian aircraft sporting a seal from the Limnological Institute on its fuselage. The elderly helicopter dipped closer to the boat as its cigar-chomping pilot tossed a genial wave towards the men on the bridge.

'Have released all of the survey pods. Permission to park this whirlybird before surf's up,' crackled the deep voice of Al Giordino over the radio.

Sarghov looked aghast at the movements of the helicopter. 'That is a valuable asset of the institute,' he said hoarsely to Pitt.

'Don't worry, Alex,' Pitt said, suppressing a grin. 'Al could fly a 747 through a doughnut hole. But if it's all the same to you, I'd like to fly by that wayward fishing boat first and try and alert them.'

Sarghov looked into Pitt's calm eyes and nodded.

Pitt reached for the radio microphone. 'Al, go ahead and set her down on the pad, but keep her wound up. We've got an emergency call to make.'

'Roger,' the radio squawked. The helicopter immediately rose and slipped to the rear of the ship, where it set down on a rickety helipad.

'Rudi, keep us advised of the wave's progress over the radio,' Pitt directed. 'We'll take the chopper to shore after we head off the fishing boat.'

'Aye, aye,' Gunn responded as Pitt dashed out of the bridge.

Sprinting to the rear of the ship, Pitt ducked down a level to his cabin, emerging seconds later with a red duffle bag flung over his shoulder. Up on the open stern deck, he edged past a bulbous white decompression chamber and climbed a narrow flight of steps onto the helipad.

As Pitt sprinted to the right of the Kamov's cockpit, the passenger door popped open and a young Russian technician jumped to the deck. Nodding at Pitt to take his seat, he handed the tall American his radio headset, then scrambled off the platform. Pitt climbed in, glancing towards his old friend in the pilot's seat as he slammed the door shut.

Albert Giordino hardly cut the figure of a suave aviator. The stocky Italian with jackhammer arms stood nearly a foot shorter than Pitt. A shock of unruly black hair curled round his head, while an ever-present cigar protruded from a hard face that hadn't seen a razor in days. His mahogany brown eyes glistened with intelligence and a hint of the sardonic wit that sparkled at even the most trying of times. The director of underwater technology for NUMA was more at home piloting a submersible, but had acquired a silken touch with most types of aircraft as well.

'I heard the distress warning. You want to go track that roller as it pounds Listvyanka?' Giordino asked through his headset.

'We've got a social call to make first. Head southeast, and I'll fill you in.'

'LOOKS LIKE WE'VE got some company,' Wofford said, pointing off the fishing boat's stern towards the horizon.

All eyes turned skyward as the stubby silver helicopter roared up to the small boat, then hovered off the port beam. The ebony-haired figure in the passenger's seat was waving a microphone towards the window.

'He's trying to call us on the radio,' Wofford observed. 'Do you have your ears on, Captain?'

Tatiana translated to the annoyed captain, who grabbed a radio microphone from the wheelhouse and held it up towards the helicopter while slicing his free hand horizontally across the front of his throat.

'He says his radio is not operating,' Tatiana said, reporting the obvious.

'Now why does that not surprise me?' Roy said, rolling his eyes.

'It looks like they want us to turn around,' Theresa said, interpreting new motions from the copilot. 'I think they're trying to warn us.'

'The helicopter is from the Limnological Institute,' Tatiana noted. 'We're probably intruding on an experiment of theirs.' Shooing her arms at the helicopter, she yelled, '*Otbyt, otbyt* . . . Go away.'

GIORDINO PEERED OUT through the cockpit windshield and grinned in amusement. 'Apparently, they don't like what we're selling,' he remarked.

Pitt shook his head in frustration. 'Their captain is either short on brains or long on undistilled vodka,' he said. 'You're going to have to put me on the deck. That old rust-bucket won't stand a chance against a thirty-foot wave.'

Giordino knew it would be futile to question the wisdom of the request or protest the danger to Pitt. With a steady hand on the controls, he inched the helicopter in a tight circle round the boat, searching for a spot he could touch down. But the old vessel would not cooperate. A tall wooden mast ran up from the wheelhouse a dozen feet, shielding the boat like a lance.

'I can't get in tight enough with that mast,' Giordino said. 'You'd have to swim it or risk a twenty-foot drop without breaking a leg.

Pitt surveyed the derelict boat with its crowd of occupants staring up in confusion. 'I'm not ready for a swim just yet,' he said through the headset. 'But if you can put me on that mast, I'll do my best fireman's imitation.'

Giordino pulled the Kamov up, then inched forward until its passenger door was directly above the mast. 'With the boat rocking, I'll have to take just a quick dip to get you down,' he said. 'Sure you can climb up again?'

'I'm not planning on coming back,' Pitt replied matter-of-factly. 'Give me a second, and I'll guide you down.'

Pitt took off his headset, then reached down and pulled out the red duffle bag at his feet. He opened the cockpit door to a rush of air from the rotors, tossed the bag onto the wheelhouse roof, then dangled his feet out of the door. The mast swung back and forth from the rocking motion of the boat, but when it slowed between swells, Pitt dropped his palm to Giordino. The pilot instantly dipped the helicopter and, in a flash, Pitt was out of the door.

Giordino immediately lifted the helicopter up and away from the boat. Through the side window, he could see Pitt sliding down the mast.

Rudi Gunn's voice burst into his ears. '*Vereshchagin* to airborne unit, over.'

'What's up, Rudi?'

'Just giving you a status on the wave. It's now travelling at a hundred and thirty-five miles per hour, with a wave height cresting at thirty-four feet.'

'What's the current ETA?'

'For your approximate position, eighteen minutes. Suggest you stand by for emergency relief.'

Eighteen minutes. It was nowhere near enough time for the fishing boat to reach safe haven. With a gnawing dread, Giordino realised that he might have just given his old friend a death warrant by dropping him to her decks.

PITT GRABBED his duffle bag and climbed down a stepladder to the deck of the dilapidated boat, where a group of people stared at him with open mouths.

'*Privet.*' He grinned disarmingly. 'Anyone here speak English?'

'What is the meaning of this intrusion?' Tatiana demanded. Behind her, the fishing boat's captain launched a tirade in his native tongue.

'Comrade, tell your captain that if he ever wants to hoist another vodka, he had better turn this tub towards Listvyanka right now,' Pitt barked.

'What's the trouble?' Theresa asked, trying to thaw the tension.

'An underwater landslide has triggered a freak wave near Olkhon Island. A thirty-foot wall of water is bearing down on us as we speak. Emergency warnings were broadcast, but your captain was incapable of hearing them.'

Tatiana looked ashen as she spoke rapidly to the captain. He nodded without saying a word, then climbed into the wheelhouse. Seconds later, the boat's old motor whined in protest as the throttle was pushed to its stops and the bow eased round towards Listvyanka.

Theresa approached Pitt with a nervous smile and a handshake. 'Thank you for flying out to warn us,' she said. 'That was a dangerous way to come aboard.' She had a warm honesty that reminded Pitt of his wife Loren and he decided that he liked the Dutch woman.

'Yes, we are grateful for the alert,' Tatiana said in a warmer tone than before. 'How much time do we have before the wave reaches us?'

Pitt glanced at his orange-faced Doxa dive watch. 'Less than fifteen minutes, based on the rate it was travelling when I left the *Vereshchagin*.'

'We'll never make it to Listvyanka,' Tatiana quietly assessed.

'The lake broadens at the southern end, which will dissipate the wave. The closer we get to shore, the smaller the wave we'll have to navigate,' Pitt explained. 'But we'd better prepare for a wild ride. Life jackets on, everyone. Anything you don't want lost over the side should be secured to the deck.'

Roy and Wofford quickly tied down their survey equipment, with Theresa lending a hand. Tatiana rummaged around in the wheelhouse for a few minutes, then returned with an armful of aged life jackets.

'There are only four aboard,' she announced. 'The captain refuses to wear one, but we are still short a jacket,' she said.

'Not to worry, I brought my own,' Pitt replied.

While the others fastened their life jackets, Pitt kicked off his shoes and outer clothes and slid into a neoprene dry suit he pulled from his duffle bag.

'What's that noise?' Theresa asked.

An almost imperceptible rumble echoed lightly across the lake, then grew ever so slightly louder. Pitt realised that the wave must have increased speed—and power—as it raced towards them.

'There it is!' Roy yelled, pointing up the lake.

'It's huge,' Theresa gasped, shocked at the sight.

The wave wasn't a cresting white-capped breaker but an oddly smooth cylinder of water that rolled from shore to shore like a giant rolling pin. Everyone froze and stared in awe at the surreal image. Everyone but Pitt.

'Tatiana, tell the captain to turn the bow into the wave,' he ordered.

As the captain swung the wheel, Pitt got Wofford to help him stretch an old fishing net across the deck, securing it to port and starboard stanchions.

'Everyone lie down and grab a tight hold of the net,' Pitt instructed. 'It will act as a cushion and hopefully keep everyone aboard.'

Roy sidled up to Pitt and whispered out of earshot of the others. 'A game effort, Mr Pitt, though we both know this old derelict isn't going to make it.'

'Never say die,' Pitt whispered back with an odd look of confidence.

The rumbling bellow of the moving water grew louder as the wave approached to within five miles. There would be just minutes to go before it struck. The occupants braced themselves for the worst, some praying silently while others contemplated death with grim determination. Against the roar of the water, nobody detected the sound of the approaching helicopter.

Suddenly Wofford looked up and blurted, 'What the heck—?'

All eyes darted towards the helicopter, barely a hundred yards off the port flank. Dangling beneath it on a twenty-foot cable was a white cylindrical object, which swayed just a few feet above the waves.

A broad grin spread over Pitt's face as he recognised the *Vereshchagin*'s decompression chamber twisting beneath the Kamov. Jumping to his feet, he waved at Giordino, who lowered the one-ton chamber onto the stern deck.

Pitt quickly unhooked the attached cable and gave a thumbs-up gesture towards the helicopter. Giordino immediately swung the helicopter away from the boat, settling in a hover a short distance away.

'Why did he dump that here?' Tatiana asked.

'That big ugly bobber is your ticket to safety,' Pitt replied. 'Everybody in!'

With the wave just a mile away, Pitt swung open the heavy circular door to the chamber. Theresa climbed in first, followed by Wofford and Roy, then Tatiana. Even the captain abandoned the wheel and scrambled in after them.

'Aren't you joining us?' Tatiana asked as Pitt began to close the door.

'It will be tight enough with five people in there. Besides, someone's got to seal the chamber,' he replied with a wink. 'There are blankets in the rear. Use them to protect your heads and bodies.'

The door clanged shut and Pitt twisted the locking mechanism. Then he reached into his duffle bag and removed his Dräger rebreather system. He quickly strapped on the equipment, stepped up onto the side gunwale and dropped over the side of the boat. Then the wave hit.

FROM HIS PERCH 200 feet in the air, Giordino looked on helplessly as the massive wave piled into the black fishing boat. Its throttle was still set at full, and the aged boat tried valiantly to climb the wall of water. But the rolling force of it overpowered the rotted hull timbers and the old wooden boat seemed to melt away, disappearing under the tall wave.

Giordino desperately scanned the surface for signs of Pitt or the decompression chamber. But as the waters calmed again, only the bow section could be seen floating on the surface. The old fishing boat had split in two from the force of the wave, and the stern deck, with the decompression chamber, had vanished. The black-hulled wreckage of the bow bobbed on the surface momentarily, then it too disappeared in a gurgle of bubbles.

WHEN PITT HIT the water, he kicked hard, attempting to swim away from the fishing boat into open water. An experienced body surfer since his childhood, he knew that diving under the approaching wave would let it roll over him with minimal surge. But he was a few seconds too late.

The seiche wave broke over him just as he cleared the surface. Rather than escape under the wave, he found himself being drawn up its face. The sensation was of riding an ascending elevator at high speed, and Pitt felt his stomach drop. His ears rang from the rush of the wave, but with the rebreather system on his back he was able to breathe normally through his faceplate, and a part of him actually enjoyed the ride. Trapped in the uplift, he realised there was no sense in fighting the overpowering force of water.

Suddenly he felt a leg break free, then a flash of light burst through his faceplate as his head broke the surface. He instantly realised that he had been pushed to the very top of the wave. Just inches away, the wave dropped over thirty feet in a vertical wall of water to the lake surface, and Pitt knew that if he fell over the precipice and the wave crested on top of him, he would be crushed to death under a mass of falling water.

Pivoting his body, he flung his arms through the water and kicked with all his might to swim over the top of the wave. But the rushing water continued to pull at his body, trying to suck him into the morass.

Then suddenly the grip released and the wave seemed to let go beneath him. He felt himself falling headfirst, which meant he had made it to the back of the wave. The elevator ride zipped down this time, but in a controlled free fall. In a froth of bubbles, Pitt found himself floating freely underwater.

Reorientating himself in the water, he eyed the shimmering lake surface twenty feet above him and kicked with tired legs until his head broke the water. Gazing towards the still-thundering rumble, he watched as the massive wave rolled rapidly towards its destructive rendezvous with the south shoreline. As the roar faded, Pitt's ears detected the rotor-thumping sound of a helicopter take its place. Turning in the water, he saw the Kamov making a beeline for him. There was no sign of the fishing boat.

Giordino brought the helicopter right alongside Pitt, who swam towards the passenger door. Climbing up the landing skid, he hauled himself through the open door and onto the passenger's seat.

'The fishing boat?' Pitt gasped.

'Didn't make it,' Giordino said. 'Snapped like a twig. Thought we'd lost the decompression chamber, too, but she shot to the surface a short time later.'

'Nice thinking, bringing the chamber over at the last minute.'

'Sorry I didn't have a chance to yank you out before the surf hit.'

'And spoil a good ride?' Pitt nodded at his good fortune in surviving the wave, then thought of the *Vereshchagin*. 'How did the institute ship fare?'

'The wave was down to fourteen feet near Listvyanka. The *Vereshchagin* rode it through without a hitch. She's on her way now to fish them out.'

Giordino slowed the Kamov as they reached the bobbing white chamber in the water below. 'Bet the air in that tank is getting a little foul,' he said.

'They'd need several more hours before any real danger of carbon dioxide poisoning,' Pitt replied. 'How long before the *Vereshchagin* arrives?'

'About an hour, but I'm afraid we can't hang around until then.' Giordino tapped a fuel dial that was heading low.

'Well, I'd better keep them company,' said Pitt, pulling on his faceplate.

Giordino started lowering the helicopter. 'You just can't get enough of the cold lake water, can you?'

PITT WAS SITTING atop the bobbing white chamber an hour later when the research ship pulled alongside. Giordino already had a large crane positioned over the side. The original transport cables were still attached to the decompression chamber, so Pitt just had to gather them together and slide them over the crane's hook. Then he straddled the chamber while it was hoisted onto the stern of the *Vereshchagin*. When its skids kissed the deck, Pitt jumped down and helped Gunn pull out Theresa and Tatiana, then the three men.

'Man, does that taste good,' Wofford said sucking in a deep breath of fresh air as he stepped out of the chamber.

The Russian captain, nursing a nasty gash to the forehead, climbed out last and staggered to the ship's rail, searching for his old fishing boat.

'You can tell him she was crushed by the wave,' Pitt said to Tatiana.

The captain shook his head and sobbed as Tatiana translated the news.

Amazingly there were no serious injuries, though the tumultuous ride had bruised and battered everyone.

'We couldn't believe it when you appeared after the wave passed,' Theresa marvelled at Pitt. 'How did you survive?'

'Sometimes, I'm just lucky,' he said, grinning.

'Thank you again,' she said, joined by a chorus of praise from the other survey crew members.

'Don't thank me,' Pitt said. 'Thank Al Giordino here.'

Giordino stepped over from the crane and bowed in mock appreciation. 'Hope the ride wasn't too rough in that tin can,' he said.

Theresa shook his hand gratefully. 'You saved our lives, Mr Giordino.'

'Please, call me Al,' the gruff Italian said, softening under her gaze.

'Now I know how that steel ball in a pinball machine feels,' Roy muttered.

'Say, you don't suppose they'd have any vodka aboard?' Wofford asked, rubbing his wrenched back.

'Does it rain in Seattle?' Gunn replied, overhearing the comment. 'Right this way, ladies and gentlemen. We'll have the ship's doctor check you over, then you can have a drink in the galley. Listvyanka's docks are chewed up, so we probably won't be able to put you to shore until tomorrow. We've heard of no reported fatalities, though, so the warning apparently did the trick.'

As dusk settled over the lake, the *Vereshchagin* steamed into the port of Listvyanka. The crew of the research ship lined the rails to observe the damage. The wave had shredded the smaller buildings that had stood along the water's edge. But most of the town and port had suffered minimal loss. The research ship dropped anchor in the dark a mile from the docks, which glistened under a battery of temporary lights. The hum of an old tractor drifted over the water as the townspeople began cleaning up.

In the ship's galley, Roy, Wofford and the fishing-boat captain sat in a corner drinking vodka with a Russian crewman. Pitt, Giordino and Sarghov sat across the room, finishing a dinner of baked sturgeon with Theresa and Tatiana. After the dishes were cleared, Sarghov poured a round of drinks.

'To your health,' Giordino said, toasting both ladies, his glass meeting a clink from Theresa's.

'Which is much improved on account of you,' Theresa replied, laughing.

'So tell me, what are a couple of gorgeous young ladies doing out hunting for oil on big, bad Lake Baikal?' Pitt asked after downing his glass.

'The Avarga Oil Consortium possesses oil and mining rights to territories east of the lake,' Tatiana replied.

'Lake Baikal has United Nations World Heritage status,' Sarghov said. 'How can you possibly expect to drill on the lake?'

Tatiana nodded. 'You are correct. We respect Baikal as sacred water, and if oil prospects are proven and deemed reachable, we would drill from the eastern territories at a high angle beneath the lake.'

'Makes sense,' Giordino stated. 'They angle-drill in the Gulf of Mexico all the time. But that still doesn't explain the presence of this lovely Dutch angel from Rotterdam,' he added, smiling broadly at Theresa.

Theresa blushed deeply. 'I'm actually from Amsterdam. My American coworkers and I work for Shell Oil. We're here at the request of Avarga Oil, exploring a joint-development opportunity for regional lands that show promise. We've already done survey work in Western Siberia, so it was natural for us to come here and perform the lake survey together.'

'Did you find any petroleum deposits before the wave struck?' Pitt asked.

'At the time we lost the boat, we had failed to survey any significant structural indications normally associated with hydrocarbon seeps.'

'Oil seeps?' Sarghov asked.

'Yes, a common if rather primitive means of locating petroleum deposits. Oil seeps show up as leakages from the sea floor that rise to the surface.'

'Fishermen have reported sightings of oil slicks on the lake where no surface traffic was evident,' Tatiana explained. 'We realise, of course, they could represent releases from small deposits that are not economical to drill.'

'A potentially costly venture, given the depths of the lake,' Pitt added.

'Speaking of ventures, Mr Pitt, what are you and your NUMA crew doing here aboard a Russian research ship?' Tatiana asked.

'We're guests of the Limnological Institute,' Pitt replied. 'A joint effort to study current patterns in the lake.'

'How did you become aware of the seiche wave before its appearance?'

'Sensor pods. We've got hundreds of them deployed in the lake, which measure the water temperature, pressure and so on. Rudi picked up the underwater landslide and the resulting seiche wave as it formed.'

'A fortunate thing for us, and many others, I imagine,' Theresa said.

'Can these sensor pods reveal where the quake originated?' asked Tatiana.

'If it occurred under the lake,' Pitt replied.

'The seismologists Rudi talked to placed the epicentre somewhere near the northwest corner of the lake,' Giordino said, glancing round the galley. 'Rudi said he'd pinpoint the exact location from the sensors. He's probably up in the bridge conversing with his computers as we speak.'

Tatiana downed the last of her drink, then glanced at her watch. 'It has been a trying day. I'm afraid I must turn in for the evening.'

'I'm with you,' Pitt said, suppressing a yawn. As Sarghov rose to join them, Pitt turned to Theresa and Giordino and smiled. 'I trust you two are waiting for the baked Alaska to be served?'

Giordino grinned back. 'Tales of the Netherlands await my hungry ears.'

PITT HAD BEEN ASLEEP for four hours when suddenly he sprang awake, his senses telling him something was wrong. He swung his feet to the floor and stood up but nearly fell over in the process. Rubbing the sleep from his eyes, he realised that the ship was listing to stern.

He dressed quickly, and climbed a stairwell to the deserted deck. The ship was strangely quiet as he walked uphill towards the bow. The silence finally registered. The ship's engines were shut down and only the hum of the auxiliary generator throbbed through the night air.

When he reached the bridge, he found it deserted. Scanning the bridge console, he found a red toggle switch marked TREVOGA. He flicked the switch, and the entire ship erupted in a clamour of warning bells.

Seconds later, the *Vereshchagin*'s captain charged onto the bridge like an angry bull. 'What is going on here?' he said. 'Where is Anatoly, the watch?'

'The ship is sinking,' Pitt said calmly. 'There was no watch on the bridge when I entered just a minute ago.'

The captain grimaced as he noticed the ship's list for the first time. 'We need power!' he cried, reaching for a phone to the engine room.

But as his hand gripped the receiver, the bridge suddenly went black. Mast lights, cabin lights, console displays—all went out as the power failed throughout the ship. Cursing, the captain found the emergency battery switch.

As the low-level lights flickered on, the *Vereshchagin*'s chief engineer burst onto the bridge. 'Captain, the hatches to the engine room have been chained shut,' he reported. 'It appears that the bilges have flooded and the lower deck is taking on water quickly at the stern.'

'You better prepare to abandon ship,' Pitt advised in a logical tone.

The captain knew it was unavoidable. With a grim look, he nodded at the chief engineer to pass the order.

Pitt made for the door, his mind churning over solutions to keep the ship afloat. The answer struck him just as he ran into Giordino and Gunn on the suddenly bustling middeck.

'Looks like we're about to get wet,' Giordino said without alarm.

'The engine room is locked and flooding,' Pitt replied. 'She's not going to stay afloat a whole lot longer.' He gazed down the sloping aft deck. 'How quickly can you get that whirlybird warmed up?'

'Consider it done,' Giordino replied, then sprinted towards the stern.

'Rudi, see that the survey team is safely on deck and near a lifeboat.

'What's up your sleeve?'

'An ace, I hope,' Pitt mused, then disappeared aft.

GUNN THREADED HIS WAY past the crowd of scientists and crewmen waiting to board the lifeboats, then dropped down a deck. Incoming water had risen above the deckhead at the far end of the passageway but sloshed only to ankle depth at the higher point where Gunn stood, close to the guest cabins.

The water swirled about Gunn's calves as he approached the first cabin, shared by Theresa and Tatiana, He shouted and pounded on the door, then turned the unlocked handle and pressed against it. Inside, the cabin was bare. Only the ruffled blankets on the twin bunks indicated the earlier presence of the two women. He closed the door and moved aft to the next cabin, shared by Roy and Wofford, the icy water stinging his thighs. Again he shouted and knocked on the door before forcing it open against the resistance of the water. The cabin was empty like the first.

Only the cabin of the fishing boat's captain remained unchecked, but the water outside that door was chest-high. Foregoing the opportunity to acquire hypothermia, Gunn turned and made his way up to the main deck as a third lifeboat was lowered into the water. Scanning what was now just a handful of crewmen left on deck, he saw no sign of the oil-survey team, or the fishing boat's captain. They must have made it off on the first two lifeboats, he thought with relief.

IVAN POPOVICH was asleep in his bunk, lost in a dream that he was fly-fishing on the Lena River, when a deep thumping noise jolted him awake. The ruddy-faced pilot of the Listvyanka hydrofoil ferry slithered into a heavy fur coat, staggered out of his cabin and climbed onto the ferry's stern deck.

He found himself facing a pair of blinding floodlights, and a blast of cold air that swirled about his body. The lights rose slowly off the deck, hovered for a moment, then turned and vanished. As the echo of the helicopter's rotors receded into the night air, Popovich was surprised to see a tall, dark-haired man standing before him, his white teeth exposed in a friendly smile.

'Good evening,' the stranger said calmly. 'Mind if I borrow your boat?'

THE HIGH-SPEED FERRY screamed across the bay, riding up on its twin forward hydrofoil blades for the brief journey to the *Vereshchagin*. Popovich span the ferry about as he killed the throttle, then idled just a few feet off the research ship's prow. Pitt watched the foundering vessel from the stern rail.

'Towline away,' came a shout from above.

Looking up, Pitt saw Giordino and Gunn near the *Vereshchagin*'s bow rail. A second later, they heaved a heavy rope line over the side and played it out to the water's edge. Popovich was on it instantly, backing his boat towards the dangling line until Pitt could manhandle the looped end aboard.

After securing the line round a capstan, Pitt gave Popovich the thumbs-up sign. 'Towline secured. Take us away, Ivan,' he yelled.

Popovich threw the diesel engines into gear and idled forward until the towline became taut, then he gently applied more throttle. As the ferry's propellers thrashed at the water, Popovich pushed the throttles to FULL.

On the stern, Pitt heard the engines whine, yet felt no forward momentum. But the ferry's twin 1,000-horsepower motors produced a blasting force of torque. Inch by inch, foot by foot, the *Vereshchagin* crept forward.

Wasting no effort, Popovich took the shortest path to shore. With agonising slowness, he ran the shallow-draft ferry towards a small rocky beach beside the damaged docks. The *Vereshchagin*'s stern sank lower and lower, but he kept charging forward until, just a few yards from shore, a muffled grinding sound affirmed that the research ship's hull had finally run aground.

In the ferry's cabin, Popovich shut down his overheated engines. A deathly still enveloped both vessels as the echo from the dying motors fell away. Then a loud cheer burst forth, first from the ship's crew who had landed the lifeboats ashore nearby, then from a crowd of villagers watching along the beachfront, and finally from the remaining men aboard the *Vereshchagin*. Popovich let go two blasts from an air horn in acknowledgment.

'My compliments on your skill at the helm, Captain,' Pitt said, when they were back on dry land.

'I couldn't bear the thought of seeing my old ship go down,' Popovich replied, staring at the *Vereshchagin* nostalgically. 'I started out scrubbing decks on that babushka. And Captain Kharitonov is an old friend.'

While local fishermen assisted in tying up the grounded ship, coffee and vodka were served in a local fish-packing plant that had been opened up. Pitt and Popovich were welcomed with a cheer and applause as they entered.

Captain Kharitonov thanked both men, and threw a bear hug round Popovich. 'You saved the *Vereshchagin*, my friend. I am most grateful.'

'I am glad to have been of help. It was Mr Pitt who wisely recognised the worth of using my ferry, however.'

'I hope next time I won't need to call on you in the middle of the night, Ivan,' Pitt said, glancing down at the slippers Popovich still wore on his feet. He turned to Kharitonov. 'Has all the crew been accounted for?'

The captain frowned. 'The bridge watchman Anatoly has not been seen. And Dr Sarghov is also missing. I had hoped he might be with you.'

'Alexander? No, I haven't seen him since we turned in after dinner.'

A subdued-looking Giordino and Gunn approached the group.

'That's not all who's missing,' Giordino said, overhearing the conversation. 'The entire oil-survey team has vanished. Not one made it into any of the lifeboats, and they were not in their cabins.'

'No one saw them leave the ship?' Pitt asked.

'No,' Giordino said, shaking his head. 'It's as if they never existed.'

4

When the sun crawled up the southeastern horizon several hours later, the precarious state of the *Vereshchagin* became apparent. The engine room, stern hold and lower-berth cabins were completely submerged, while water sloshed over nearly a third of the main deck.

Standing near the remains of a tourist kiosk, Pitt and Captain Kharitonov surveyed the grounded ship. Gazing at the waterline, Pitt noticed a smudge of red paint amidships that had rubbed off a dock or small boat.

'A salvage repair crew from Irkutsk will arrive tomorrow,' Kharitonov said grimly. 'I will have the crew activate the portable pumps, though I suppose there is little purpose until we can determine the cause of the damage.'

'More pressing is the disappearance of Alexander and the survey team,' Pitt replied. 'The flooded portion of the ship must be searched for bodies.'

The captain nodded. 'We will have to wait for a police dive team.'

'Maybe not, Captain,' Pitt said, nodding towards an approaching figure.

Al Giordino was marching along the waterfront towards them, toting a pair of red-handled bolt cutters. 'Found these at a garage sale in town,' he said.

'You? You will investigate the damage?' Kharitonov asked.

'Whoever tried to sink your vessel may have had an interest in halting our research project,' Pitt said. 'If so, I'd like to find out why.'

'It may not be safe,' Kharitonov cautioned.

'The only difficult part will be to convince Al to dive before breakfast,' Pitt said, trying to lighten the morbid task at hand.

GUNN JOINED PITT and Giordino as they motored up to the grounded ship in a borrowed Zodiac. They climbed the sloped deck to the forward hold, then Gunn lent a hand as the two men pulled on black dry suits and weight belts, and hooked up the lightweight rebreather systems.

As Gunn went to the bridge to check the computers, Pitt and Giordino waded into the water, then dropped down the starboard stairway, beyond the lower cabin level to the engine room. The water was as clear as a swimming pool, and Pitt's small headlight cut a bright white path through the gloom.

As the chief engineer had reported, the heavy steel door to the engine-room was sealed closed. An old rusty chain was wrapped round the latch and fastened to the bulkhead with a new-looking padlock.

Pitt turned and watched as Giordino cut a link of the chain as if cracking a walnut, the Italian's thick arms easily brandishing the bolt cutters. Pitt unwound the chain and pulled open the hatch, then stepped inside.

Though the *Vereshchagin* was over thirty years old, the engine room was spotless. No damage was evident to the deck and bulkheads, or to the engine itself. But a large steel-grated floor plate had been pulled up from the rear deck and left leaning against a tool bin. Peering inside the hole it had covered, Pitt recognised it as an opening to the bilge.

Pitt lowered himself through the hole and dropped four feet onto the curved steel plate of the ship's hull. Kneeling, he examined the compartment towards the stern. As far as his light could shine, the hull plates appeared smooth and intact. Spinning slowly round, he backed into a metal object, which turned out to be a squat valve rising a foot above a thick trailing pipe. Pitt placed his gloved hands on the valve and twisted it anticlockwise. The valve wouldn't budge. He tried turning it clockwise. The valve turned freely until Pitt pushed it to its stops. He glanced up at the open hatch. Giordino nodded back to him with a knowing look. It was as simple as that. The valve opened the ship's sea cock, which flooded the bilge—and, ultimately, the entire ship—if opened at sea. Somebody had disabled the bilge pumps, then sealed off access to the bay. An easy way to sink a ship in the middle of the night.

Pitt swam out of the bilge compartment and across the engine room. On the opposite side he found an identical floor plate in the deck. He yanked it off and climbed down, finding that the port seacock had also been opened. He closed the valve, and Giordino helped him back into the engine room.

Half their objective was complete. They had determined the cause of the flooding. But Sarghov, Anatoly and the oil-survey team were still missing.

Finding nothing in the other flooded compartments around the engine bay, they ascended the stairwell to the lower cabin berths. Pitt directed Giordino to check the portside cabins while he searched the starboard berths. Entering the first cabin, which he knew to be Sarghov's, Pitt was surprised to find that the contents of the room had remained largely in place. Only a few typed pages and sections of a local newspaper drifted lazily about the flooded cabin. A laptop computer sat open on a desk, and a foul-weather jacket, which Sarghov had with him at dinner, was draped over the desk chair. Not signs of a man who had planned to depart the ship, Pitt observed.

He exited Sarghov's cabin and quickly searched the next three cabins. The final starboard berth was the one that Gunn had been unable to reach when he searched for the oil-survey team. Pitt turned the latch and pushed the door open against the force of the water. Like the other cabins, its interior appeared orderly. Unlike the others, it still contained its occupant.

Stepping closer to the bunk, Pitt cautiously leaned over the corpse, illuminating it with his headlight beam. The open eyes of the surly fishing-boat captain stared up at him, confusion etched upon the dead man's face.

Pitt rubbed a finger across the fisherman's hairline. Two inches above his ear, a slight indentation creased the side of his head. Though the skin had not broken, it was obvious that a heavy blow had cracked the man's skull.

'IT'S GONE,' GUNN SPAT, his face flushed with anger. 'Someone yanked out our data-base hardware and disappeared with it. All our data, everything we've gathered in the last two weeks, it's all gone.' Fuming, he helped Pitt and Giordino out of their dry suits beneath the bridge.

'What about the back-up DVDs, Rudi?' Pitt asked.

'Missing too,' Gunn cried. 'I just don't understand. The research data would be of value only to the scientific community. We've shared everything with our Russian counterparts. Who would want to steal the information?'

'Don't feel bad. You still made out better than the old fisherman,' Pitt commented ruefully, then told Gunn of the discovery in the cabin.

'But why murder an old man?' Gunn gasped, shaking his head in disbelief. 'And what of the others? Were they abducted? Or did they leave willingly, after killing the fisherman and destroying our scientific data?'

The same questions percolated through Pitt's mind. But no answers.

BY MIDDAY, an overhead power line was tapped from shore and wired up to the *Vereshchagin*, providing electricity to the grounded ship and activating the bilge pumps. Slowly but surely, the submerged stern crept out of the water.

Listvyanka's residents continued the cleanup from the flood-ravaged waters. Word filtered in about the extensive destruction of property around the lake, but remarkably no loss of life was reported. The most costly damage was to the Baikalsk Paper Mill on the southern shore of the lake, and the Taishet–Nakhodka oil pipeline in the north.

Shortly after lunch, Listvyanka's police chief boarded the *Vereshchagin*, accompanied by two detectives from Irkutsk. The chief, a self-important bureaucrat, greeted Captain Kharitonov in a formal manner, and dismissed with a glance the three Americans who sat reconfiguring their computer equipment on the opposite side of the bridge. As Kharitonov relayed the story of the missing crewmen and the discovery of the dead fisherman in the flooded cabin below, a flash of anger crossed the chief's face.

'Nonsense,' he retorted. 'I knew Belikov well. He was a drunken old fisherman. Drank too much vodka and passed out. An unfortunate accident.'

'Then what about the disappearance of the two crewmen and the survey team we rescued?' Captain Kharitonov said with rising anger.

'Ah yes,' the police chief replied knowingly, 'the crew members who opened the sea cocks by mistake. They probably fled in embarrassment and will turn up eventually at one of our fine drinking houses.' Realising that the two Irkutsk detectives were not buying his rationale, he continued, 'It will, of course, be necessary to interview crew and passengers for an official account of the incident. Please request that they all return at once to the ship, where they will be confined until the completion of the investigation.'

When the lawmen had left the bridge, Kharitonov glumly announced the police chief's directions.

'They could have at least let us make a beer run first,' Giordino moaned.

'I knew I should have stayed in Washington,' Gunn grumbled.

'Washington is a miserable swamp in the summertime anyway,' Pitt countered, admiring the panoramic lake view from the bridge window.

A mile and a half away, at the far end of town, he could see an old black freighter docked at a pier, its cargo hold being picked at by a wharfside crane. A pair of binoculars dangled from a hook near the bridge window and Pitt pulled them to his eyes. Through the magnified lenses, he saw two large flat-bed trucks and a smaller enclosed truck parked on the dock adjacent to the ship. On a wooden pallet on one of the flat-bed trucks was a strange, vertically shaped object wrapped in a canvas tarp.

'Captain?' Pitt pointed out of the window. 'That black freighter. What do you know about her?'

Captain Kharitonov stepped over. 'The *Primoski*. A longtime scullion on Lake Baikal. Last I heard she was under short-term lease to an oil company. I do not know what for, probably to transport pipeline equipment.'

'An oil company,' Pitt repeated. 'Not Avarga Oil, by any chance?'

Kharitonov looked up. 'Now that I think about it, it was. Forgive a tired man for not recalling that earlier. Perhaps they know something of our oil-survey team.' He reached for the radio and issued a call to the *Primoski*.

A voice answered almost immediately and replied in short, clipped responses to the captain's questions.

'Al, take a look at this,' Pitt said.

Giordino ambled over and grabbed the binoculars. 'Being rather secretive with their cargo, wouldn't you say? Though I'm sure if we asked, they'd say it's nothing more than used tractor parts.'

Kharitonov's hearty voice interrupted as he hung up the radio microphone. 'I'm sorry, gentlemen. The captain of the *Primoski* reports that he has taken on no passengers, has not seen or heard from any oil-survey team or, in fact, was even aware of their activities on the lake.'

'Did he happen to reveal his ship's manifest?' Pitt asked.

'Why, yes,' Kharitonov replied. 'They are transporting agricultural equipment and tractor components from Irkutsk to Baikalskoe.'

THE ROOKIE POLICEMAN tasked with ensuring that no one left the ship that night quickly grew bored with his assignment, and his attention wandered. Distracted by the noises coming from a dockside bar, he failed to spot two men dressed in black as they slid a small Zodiac over the *Vereshchagin*'s stern rail, then dropped silently into the rubber boat.

Pitt and Giordino eased the Zodiac away from the *Vereshchagin*, keeping the research ship between them and the shore guard. Quickly melting into the night, they rowed to the end of the waterfront, where the *Primoski* sat at its berth. The trucks were still parked on the adjacent pier, loaded with their concealed cargo. A couple of men were studying a map spread across the fender of one of the trucks, but the ship appeared devoid of life.

Silently, Pitt and Giordino approached the ship's stern, drifting under the shadow of its high fantail. Pitt grabbed the stern mooring line, and used it to pull them alongside. As Giordino tied a line round a splintered pylon, Pitt climbed onto the dock and hid behind a pair of rusty oil drums. A second later, Giordino appeared behind him.

'Empty as a church on Monday,' he whispered, eyeing the silent ship.

'Yes, a little too peaceful,' Pitt replied, peering round the drums. There was a gangway at the far end that ran up to the ship's forward hold, but he noted that the freighter's side deck railing stood eight feet above the dock. 'Gangplank might be too grand an entrance,' he whispered. 'I think we can step over from this,' he said, pointing to one of the drums.

Pitt gingerly rolled the drum to the edge of the dock and climbed on top. Then he sprang off the drum and grabbed hold of the ship's lower side rail. He hung there for a second before swinging his body between the rails and onto the deck. It was a harder jump for the shorter Giordino, who nearly missed the rail and hung by one hand for a moment before Pitt jerked him aboard.

'Next time I take the elevator,' Giordino muttered.

Catching their breath in the shadows, they examined the silent freighter. It was small by oceangoing standards, with a central superstructure surrounded by open deck fore and aft. Near a hold on the stern deck there was a handful of metal containers. Pitt and Giordino crept across the deck and into the shadow of one of the containers, then peered into the open hold.

The deep bay was stacked at either end with bundles of small-diameter iron pipe. The centre of the hold was empty, but even in the darkness the scarred marks where the feet of some piece of equipment had stood could be seen etched into the deck. In the exact centre of the marks was a six-foot-diameter deck cap, sealing an access hole through the deck.

'Looks like a string hole for a North Sea drill ship,' Pitt whispered.

'And the drill pipe for it,' Giordino replied. 'But this ain't no drill ship.'

Pitt didn't stay to contemplate the point but moved quickly towards the portside passageway. Pressing himself against the bulkhead, he peeked round the corner. Still no sight of any shipboard inhabitants.

They crept forward, stopping at a cross-passageway that bisected the superstructure from beam to beam. The latch to a cabin door clicked behind them. Both men quickly turned into the side passage, out of sight of the opening door. A dimly illuminated open compartment beckoned on Pitt's left and he stepped into it, followed by Giordino, who closed the door behind them.

As they stood by the door listening for footsteps, their eyes scanned the room. They were in the ship's formal mess, which doubled as a conference room. Over an ornate Persian carpet, a polished mahogany table stretched across the room, surrounded by leather-backed chairs. At the opposite end, a set of double doors led to the ship's galley.

'Nice atmosphere to chow down fish soup,' Giordino muttered.

Pitt stepped closer to a series of maps pinned to one wall. They showed enlarged sections of Lake Baikal, with red circles drawn at various locations. A map of the lake's northern fringe showed a concentration of the circles, some overlapping the shore where an oil pipeline ran from west to east.

'Target drill sites?' Giordino asked.

'Probably. Won't make the green crowd too happy,' Pitt replied.

Giordino listened at the door as the footsteps descended a nearby stairwell. When the sound had faded away, he cracked the door slightly.

'No sign of anyone about,' he reported.

'It's the shore boat I want to get a look at,' Pitt whispered.

They inched the door open, and crept along the portside passageway to the open forward deck, which encompassed a split pair of recessed holds. Along the port rail near the bow sat a beat-up tender, stowed in a block cradle fixed to the deck. A nearby winch with cables still attached to the tender offered evidence that it had recently been deployed.

'She's in plain sight of the bridge,' Giordino said, nodding towards a fuzzy light that shone from the forward bridge window twenty feet above.

'But only if someone's looking that way,' Pitt replied, moving off.

While Giordino hung to the shadows, Pitt scurried across the open deck. He nearly sprinted as he reached the small boat, then ducked round its bow and knelt in its covering shadow. Peering up at the bridge, he saw two men talking. Neither paid the slightest attention to the ship's forward deck.

Pitt pulled out his penlight and held it against the hull of the shore boat. He flicked the switch on for a second. The tiny beam illuminated a battered wooden hull that was painted crimson—the same shade of red that had rubbed off against the side of the *Vereshchagin*.

As Pitt rose to his feet, something inside the tender caught his eye. Dropping his hand, he again flicked on the penlight, which revealed a worn baseball cap with a red emblem of a charging hog on the front. Pitt recognised the mascot of the University of Arkansas: it was Jim Wofford's hat. He had no doubt now that the *Primoski* was involved in the attempted sinking of the *Vereshchagin* and the disappearance of the crew.

Replacing the penlight, Pitt stood and glanced at the bridge again. The two figures were still engaged in conversation. Pitt crept round the tender's bow, then stopped in his tracks, sensing a nearby presence. But it was too late. A halogen flashlight burst on in his face and a screeching Russian cry of '*Ostanovka!*' split the air.

UNDER THE GLOW from the dock lights, a man emerged from the shadows and walked to within five feet of Pitt. He was young, slightly built, with oily black hair, and he was pointing a Yarygin PYa 9mm automatic pistol at Pitt's chest. The gunman had been sitting quietly in the forecastle behind the capstan, Pitt now realised, and must have caught sight of Pitt's penlight.

The guard pulled a radio to his lips with his left hand, and spoke into the transmitter. When a deep voice blared back through the handset, distracting the guard slightly, Pitt inched his left hand to the side rail and tightened his legs for a springing vault over the side. But that's as far as he got.

The muzzle flash flared with a simultaneous bark from the Yarygin as a baseball-sized chunk of teak splintered off the rail inches from his hand.

Pitt stood still as shouts erupted on the dock, and two men stormed up the gangway, each brandishing a Yarygin pistol. Pitt recognised the second man as the helmsman from the *Vereshchagin*, Anatoly. A third man emerged from the bridge companionway and approached with an authoritative air. Pitt could see a long scar running down his left cheek.

'I found this intruder hiding behind the tender,' the guard reported.

The man eyed Pitt briefly, then turned to the crewmen. 'Search the area for accomplices. And no more gunfire. We do not need the attention.'

While the two men searched the shadows. Pitt was led to the centre of the deck, where an overhead light illuminated the scene.

'Where is Alexander?' Pitt asked calmly. 'He told me to meet him here.'

Pitt didn't expect the bluff to work, but studied the man in charge for a reaction. A slight arch of the brow was all he offered.

'English?' he finally said without interest. 'You would be from the *Vereshchagin*. A pity you have lost your way.'

'But I have found those responsible for trying to sink her,' Pitt replied.

Under the dim lights, Pitt could see the man's face flush. He checked his anger as Anatoly and the other crewman approached, shaking their heads.

'No companions? Then put him in the container with the other one, and deposit them over the side where no one will find them,' the man hissed.

The guard stepped forward, thrust the barrel of his pistol into Pitt's ribs and nodded towards the portside passageway. Pitt grudgingly walked to the stern deck and was prodded towards one of the rusty cargo containers lining the rail. When the padlock was freed, he was shoved roughly through the double-doors into the container. Under the dim light he realised that he had fallen against a human form, lying crumpled on the container floor.

'Dirk, good of you to drop in,' rasped the voice of Alexander Sarghov.

GIORDINO HAD WATCHED the guard train his gun on Pitt and silently cursed. Without a weapon his options were limited. He decided to backtrack and skirt through the cross-passageway to the starboard side of the ship.

As he turned the corner he collided with a black-clad figure running from the opposite direction. The two men bounced off each other and fell flat on their backs. Quickly shaking off the blow, Giordino sprang to his feet and slammed the other man headfirst into the bulkhead. As he fell limp in Giordino's arms, the sound of footsteps resonated down the port deck. A glance to the forward deck revealed Pitt being escorted aft. He dragged the unconscious man into the conference room, noticing that the crewman was about his height. Giordino stripped off the man's black overalls, slipped them over his own clothes, and pulled on a dark woollen fishing cap that the man had been wearing. Then he stepped back into the corridor.

ANATOLY wrapped a pair of looped cable strands round the base of the steel cargo container. Another crew member climbed atop the metal box, pulled the cables together, and slid them over the hook that was dangling from a shipboard crane. Then he jumped down, and returned to the crane controls in a darkened corner a few yards away. Tapping his fingers on the lift lever, he elevated the boom until the cables went taut, then slowly raised the container off the deck. His eyes focused on the swinging container, he failed to notice a figure creep silently across the deck and approach from the side. He also failed to see the balled fist that materialised out of the darkness and struck him below his ear with the kinetic energy of a wrecking ball. Had he not blacked out from the fatal blow to his carotid artery, he would have looked into the face of Al Giordino as he was dragged from the controls and dumped on the deck.

Giordino took the man's place and quickly tested the controls. He pulled at a lever and watched as the boom rose, then he swung the container out over the ship's port side. As he had hoped, Anatoly and a second guard followed the path of the container and stood at the port rail to watch the impending drowning. When Anatoly waved at him to drop the boom. Giordino slowly swung the crane a few more feet away from the ship, waited until the container had swayed to its furthest point in the pendulum, then reversed the controls and jammed the boom back hard over the stern deck.

The container hung in midair for a split second, then its momentum shifted and the two-ton steel box came barrelling towards the men at the rail. The guard teetered back on his heels, and the container skimmed by just inches from his face. Anatoly tried to sidestep in the other direction, but took only a short step before the flying box was on top of him. A gurgled cry came from his crushed lungs as his body was tossed across the deck.

The dazed guard at the rail peered at the crane and cursed like a madman until he realised the man operating the boom was not his colleague. As he reached for his gun, Giordino whipped the lateral boom controls back to the right and the crane mechanism began marching again towards the port rail. Giordino ducked as the guard fired a shot. The bullet whizzed just above his head, but he kept his hands on the crane controls.

The swinging container now arced towards the port rail. Stepping into its path to fire his gun, the guard ducked low to let it pass over him. But as the container approached the gunman, Giordino yanked down on the elevation controls, lowering the boom to the deck.

The container struck the deck just ahead of the gunman, then toppled onto one side from the momentum, crushing his leg as he scrambled to get clear. The guard howled in agony. Giordino sprinted over and stepped on the man's wrist, grabbing the pistol that fell out of his grip. Then, taking aim at the padlock, he ripped off two shots, and threw open one of the doors. Pitt and Sarghov tumbled out like a pair of rolled dice.

'DON'T TELL ME, you spent a previous life as a carnival-ride operator?' Pitt said with a crooked smile as he staggered to his feet.

'Naw, just practising my bowling,' Giordino replied. 'If you boys are able, I suggest we vacate the premises posthaste.'

Pitt scanned the stern deck, noting the unconscious bodies lying there, then turned his gaze to Sarghov. The Russian scientist was moving slowly.

'I'll get the boat. Take Alex and get off down the stern line,' Pitt directed.

Giordino had barely nodded a reply when Pitt sprinted off towards the starboard rail. He climbed over the rail and sprang for the dock, landing in a self-cushioning ball. Then he sprinted back to the Zodiac as a drumbeat of footsteps tailed him down the dock. He leapt into the small boat, his prayers answered when the outboard engine fired on the first pull. Gunning the motor, he aimed the Zodiac at the freighter's stern and cut the throttle only when the rubber bow bounced off the steel transom. Directly overhead, he could see Sarghov clinging to the stern rope line with a tenuous grip.

Pitt stood up. 'Let go, Alex,' he urged.

He half caught the heavy Russian as he dropped into the boat. Above them, an automatic handgun barked, spraying shots about the ship and dock.

A second later, Giordino appeared on the stern line. He lowered himself hand over hand then dropped the last few feet. 'Exit stage left,' he urged.

Pitt was already gunning the throttle, steering the boat into the darkness.

RUDI GUNN RAN from the bridge when he saw the three men stagger aboard the *Vereshchagin*. 'Dr Sarghov . . . are you all right?' he asked, staring at the Russian's swollen face and bloodied clothes.

'I am fine. Please find the captain for me, if you would be so kind.'

Pitt shepherded Sarghov to the sick bay while Gunn roused the ship's doctor and Captain Kharitonov. Giordino located a bottle of vodka and poured a round of shots while the doctor examined the Russian scientist.

'That was a close call,' Sarghov declared, regaining colour as the vodka surged through his bloodstream. 'I am indebted to my friends from NUMA.'

'Do you know what became of Theresa and the others?' Giordino asked.

'No, we were separated once we boarded the ship.'

Kharitonov barged into the sick bay. 'Alexander, you are safe!' he bellowed.

'He has a sprained wrist and a number of contusions,' the doctor reported, applying a dressing to a cut on Sarghov's face.

'It is nothing,' Sarghov said, waving away the doctor. 'Listen, the Avarga Oil Consortium . . . there is no doubt they were responsible for sinking your ship. Your crewman Anatoly was working for them, and Tatiana too.'

'Anatoly? I hired him at the beginning of the project when my regular first officer fell ill with food poisoning. What treachery!' the captain cursed. 'I will call the authorities at once.'

The authorities, in the form of the chief of police and his young assistant, arrived nearly an hour later, with the two Irkutsk detectives. Sarghov retold his tale of abduction, while Pitt and Giordino added their escape from the freighter. The Irkutsk men gradually took over the interrogation.

It took nearly another hour to assemble a small contingent of local security forces. As the first light of dawn was breaking, they marched towards the freighter's berth. But they were too late. The dock was deserted. Methodically, the police searched the ship, but they found no crew or cargo, nor any shred of evidence to indicate where the three trucks had gone.

5

Captain Steve Howard scanned the glistening blue waters of the Persian Gulf through a scratched pair of binoculars. The waterway was often a bustling hive of freighters, tankers and warships, but today, apart from a small black drill ship trailing a mile or two off his stern, there was very little traffic. He turned to look at the prow of his own ship.

He needed the binoculars to obtain a clear view, for the *Marjan*'s forepeak stood nearly 800 feet away. The massive supertanker, classed as a 'very large crude carrier' and built to transport over two million barrels of oil, was en route to fill its cavernous holds with Saudi light crude.

'Coming up on Dhahran, sir,' said the tanker's executive officer, a soft-spoken African American from Houston named Jensen. 'Ras Tannurah is twenty-five miles ahead. Shall I disengage the autopilot?'

'Yes, let's go to manual and reduce speed at the ten-mile mark. Notify the berthing master that we'll be ready to take tugs in two hours.'

Steering past the city of Dhahran and its neighbouring port of Dammam, the tanker edged towards a thin peninsula which stretched into the Gulf from the north. Sprawled across it was the vast oil refinery of Ras Tannurah.

On the bridge of the *Marjan*, Howard focused on the half-dozen super-tankers moored in pairs to a fixed terminal called Sea Island. The mile-long terminal could feed up to eighteen supertankers at a time with a high-powered flow of crude oil pumped from huge storage tanks ashore. Unseen beneath the waves, a network of thirty-inch supply pipes fed the black liquid two miles across the floor of the Gulf to the deep-water filling station.

Howard watched a trio of tugboats approach his vessel. The *Marjan*'s pilot took control of the supertanker and eased it broadside to an empty berth at the end of the loading terminal, opposite a Greek tanker. As they waited for the tugs to push them in, Howard's eye was caught by the dirty white sail of an Arab dhow in the distance. The small boat was skirting the coastline, sailing north past the black drill ship that had tailed the *Marjan* earlier and was now anchored near the shoreline.

'Tugs are in position portside, sir,' interrupted the voice of the pilot.

Howard simply nodded, and soon the massive ship was pushed into its slot on the Sea Island terminal and secured. As the transfer lines began pumping black crude into the ship's storage tanks, Howard allowed himself to relax.

AT NEARLY MIDNIGHT, Howard woke from a short nap and stretched his legs with a stroll about the forward deck. The crude-oil loading was nearly complete, and the *Marjan* would easily meet its 3 a.m. departure schedule.

As he gazed at the lights twinkling along the Saudi shoreline, Howard was jolted by a sudden clanging sound, which echoed all along Sea Island terminal. Stepping to the side rail, he leaned out and looked along the quay.

Under the overhead lights, Howard could see the terminal pulsing back and forth against the sides of the tankers, hammering them like thunder. It didn't make sense, he thought. Sea Island was grounded into the seabed.

The banging grew louder. Howard gripped the rail and stared in shock as one after another of the four twenty-four-inch loading arms broke free of the ship, spewing crude oil in all directions.

The steel terminal rocked and swayed like a giant snake, battering itself against the ships. Alarm bells rang out as oil transfer lines were torn away by the rippling force, bathing the sides of the tankers in a sea of black. Then the lights of the terminal began to disappear in a slow succession. Howard realised with horror that the entire terminal was sinking beneath their feet.

For the first time, he noticed a deep rumble that seemed to emanate from far beneath his feet. The rumble grew for several seconds, then silenced. In its place came the desperate cries of men, running along the terminal.

A tumbling house of cards came to Howard's mind as the footings of the terminal gave way in succession and the mile-long island vanished under the waves. When he heard the cries of men in the water, his horror was replaced by fear for his ship's safety. He pulled a handheld radio from his belt.

'Cut the mooring lines!' he shouted into the radio, adrenaline surging through his body as he raced across the deck. 'Tell the chief . . . engineer . . . we need . . . full power . . . immediately,' he gasped.

Reaching the tanker's stern superstructure, he headed for the nearest stairwell and clambered up the eight levels to the bridge. As he staggered to the forward window, his worst fears were realised.

In front of the *Marjan*, eight other supertankers lay in paired tandems, divided minutes before by the Sea Island terminal. But now the terminal was gone, and the paired tankers were being drawn towards one another by their mooring lines, which were still attached to the sinking terminal.

'Emergency full astern,' Howard barked at his executive officer. 'What's the status of the mooring lines?'

'The stern lines are cut,' replied Jensen. 'But one bow line is still secure.'

'The *Ascona* is drawing onto us,' the helmsman exclaimed.

Howard turned towards the Greek-flagged supertanker berthed alongside. Originally moored sixty feet apart, the two ships were slowly moving laterally together as if drawn by a magnet.

The men on the *Marjan*'s bridge stared helplessly as the tanker's engines were brought up to high revs by the frantic engineer. Slowly, the huge ship began to creep backwards. The momentum slowed for a second as the bow mooring line drew taut, then suddenly it broke free and the ship resumed its rearward crawl. Along her starboard side, the *Ascona* drew closer.

'Starboard twenty,' Howard ordered the helmsman, hoping to angle the bow away from the drifting tanker. They had managed to back the *Marjan* 300 feet away from the sunken terminal, but it was not enough.

The *Marjan*'s bow was almost amidships of the *Ascona* when the two ships collided, but the rearward motion of Howard's ship had deflected much of the force at impact. For half a minute, the *Marjan*'s bow scraped along the other tanker's port rail, then at last the two ships were clear.

Suddenly a series of muffled explosions echoed across the Gulf.

'Sir, it's the refinery,' said the helmsman, pointing at the western shore.

An orange glow appeared on the horizon, growing like the rising sun as more explosions rocked across the water. Soon, thick plumes of black smoke mixed with the odour of burnt petroleum wafted over the ship.

'How could they do it?' the executive officer blurted. 'How could terrorists get explosives in there? It's one of the most secure facilities in the world.'

Howard shook his head. Jensen was right. The complex was guarded by a private army in a tight web of security. It must have been a masterful infiltration, he thought, to take out the Sea Island terminal as well.

Thankfully, his ship and crew were safe, and he intended to keep them that way. Once the search for survivors in the water was complete, he moved the tanker several miles out into the Gulf, where they circled slowly until dawn.

By daylight, as emergency response teams from around the region converged on the scene, the Ras Tannurah refinery was a smouldering ruin. The Sea Island terminal had vanished beneath the Gulf, and nearly a third of Saudi Arabia's oil-exporting capability was destroyed overnight. Yet terrorism was not to blame. Seismologists had already fingered the cause of the destruction. A massive earthquake, measuring 7.3 on the Richter scale, had rattled the Saudi Arabian coast. Its shock waves would ultimately ripple far beyond the Persian Gulf, shaking the globe for many months to come.

HANG ZHOU DREW a last puff from his cigarette, then flicked the butt over the rail. He watched in lazy curiosity as the glowing ember flittered to the black water below, half expecting the murky surface to ignite in a wall of flames, but the cigarette fizzled to a harmless demise.

The waters around the Chinese port of Ningbo had been contaminated by petroleum leaked from a steady stream of container ships, tankers and tramp freighters. Located in the Yangtze River Delta, not far from Shanghai, Ningbo was growing into one of China's largest seaports, in part owing to its deep-water channel, which allowed dockage for giant supertankers.

'Zhou!' barked a voice.

Zhou turned to see his supervisor, Qinglin, the overweight operations director for Terminal No. 3, high-stepping down the dock towards him.

'We've had a change in schedule,' Qinglin told the longshoreman. 'The *Akagisan Maru* has been delayed. So we're letting the *Jasmine Star* take her berth. She's due in at seven thirty. Make sure your crew is standing by.'

Zhou nodded. 'I'll pass the word,' he said.

Qinglin turned to walk away. But he stopped after two steps and slowly wheeled back round, his eyes widening. 'She's on fire,' he muttered.

Realising that his supervisor was looking past him, Zhou turned.

A dozen vessels were milling about in the harbour, huge container ships and supertankers overshadowing a handful of small cargo ships. One of the cargo ships trailed a plume of black smoke.

The smoke was billowing from the forward hold, obscuring most of the ship's rusting superstructure. Zhou turned his gaze towards the ship's prow, which cut a frothy white wake through the water.

'She's running fast . . . and heading towards the terminals,' he gasped.

'The fools!' Qinglin cursed, and sprinted towards the dock office.

Zhou stayed perched at the end of the container dock, watching as the burning ship steamed closer to shore. She appeared to be headed for the container terminal adjacent to Zhou's, but then she made a sweeping turn to port. As her path straightened out, Zhou could see that the ship was now headed towards Ningbo's main crude-oil offloading terminal on Cezi Island.

He scanned the length of the vessel but could see no crew. The flaming ship ploughed on, on a collision course with the docking terminal, a semi-floating ramp built on sectional pylons that ran 600 feet into the harbour.

The rusty derelict struck the end of the terminal, tearing through the wooden platform until it ground to a halt. Those who witnessed the collision let out a sigh of relief. But then a muffled blast erupted deep in the bowels of the ship, blowing the bow off in a wall of fire. In seconds, flames were everywhere, devouring the spilt crude oil that flooded around the ship and engulfing the harbour. The island was quickly clouded in thick black smoke.

Across the bay, Zhou stood in astonishment as the flames spread across the terminal complex. Staring at the blazing freighter, he grasped to comprehend what kind of suicidal maniac would destroy himself in such a rage.

IT WAS A STIFLING DAY in Beijing. A conflux of heat, smog and humidity doused the congested city in misery. Tempers flared as cars and bicycles jostled for position in the jammed boulevards. Children flocked to the city's lakes. Street vendors hawking chilled Coca-Colas made stellar profits.

The temperature was little cooler in the large, windowless meeting room of the Chinese Communist Party headquarters just west of the Forbidden City, where half a dozen humourless men sat at a scarred round table with the recently elected general secretary and president of China, Qian Fei. The minister of commerce, a balding man named Shinzhe, stood before them.

'Shinzhe, I approved the five-year plan for economic progress last November,' President Fei lectured in a belittling tone. 'You mean to tell me that a few "accidents" have rendered our objectives unfeasible?'

Shinzhe cleared his throat. 'Mr General Secretary, politburo members.' He nodded to the other bureaucrats. 'Just a few years ago, our country was a net exporter of crude oil. Today, more than half of our consumption is supplied by imports. Like it or not, we are captive to the economic and political forces surrounding the foreign petroleum market.'

'Yes, we are well aware of our growing energy appetite,' stated Fei.

'How severe is the shock?' another party member asked.

'The earthquake in Saudi Arabia will restrict their ability to ship us oil for months, though we can develop alternative suppliers. The fire at Ningbo is more damaging. Nearly a third of our imported oil flowed through that facility, which cannot be replaced quickly. We are facing drastic shortages and it may take a year before the current level of imports can be restored.'

'Minister Shinzhe, our factories are operating limited hours to conserve electricity, while workers have no power to cook their dinner at night. What is being done to solve these problems?' the president hissed.

Shinzhe took a deep breath. 'As you know, additional generators will go online shortly at the Three Gorges Dam hydroelectric development,' he said quietly. 'And six new coal- and gas-fired power plants are under construction. But obtaining sufficient fuel supplies for them is a problem. We have stepped up oil exploration in the South China Sea. And we are broadening supply relationships abroad. For example, we have recently completed successful negotiations to purchase fuel oil from Iran. However, the Ningbo Harbour damage physically limits the amount of oil we are able to bring in by sea.'

'What about the Russians?'

The white-haired foreign minister spoke. 'Our attempt to develop jointly a pipeline from the Siberian oil fields was rejected by the Russians in favour of a line to the Pacific that will supply Japan. We can boost rail shipments from Russia but that is not a long-term solution.'

'So our economic growth terminates and we all return to our cooperative farms in the provinces, where we can enjoy continuing blackouts,' Fei fumed.

The room fell silent. No one dared breathe in the face of the general secretary's ire. Then Shinzhe's assistant, a woman named Yee, cleared her throat.

'Excuse me, General Secretary, Minister Shinzhe,' she said, nodding to the two men. 'Today the ministry received a peculiar offer of energy assistance. I am sorry I didn't have the opportunity to brief you, Minister,' she said to Shinzhe. 'I didn't recognise the importance at the time.'

'What is the proposal?' Fei asked.

'It is an offer from an organisation in Mongolia to supply crude oil . . .'

'Mongolia?' Fei interrupted. 'There's no oil in Mongolia.'

'The offer is to supply one million barrels a day,' Yee continued. 'Delivery commencing within ninety days.'

'That's preposterous,' Shinzhe exclaimed, glaring at Yee.

'Perhaps,' Fei replied, a look of intrigue warming his face. 'It is worth investigating. What else does the proposal say?'

'Just the terms they demand in return,' Yee replied nervously. 'The price of the oil shall be set at the current market price and locked for three years. Also, exclusive use of the pipeline terminating at the port of Qinhuangdao shall be granted, and, further, the Chinese-controlled lands denoted Inner Mongolia shall be formally ceded back to the Mongolian government.'

Cries of outrage rocked through the room, but when Fei pound an ashtray on the table silence was restored.

'Find out if the offer is real, if the oil does, in fact, exist,' the president said quietly. 'Then we shall worry about negotiating an appropriate price. Tell me first, though. Who is making this contemptuous offer?'

'It is a small entity that is unknown to our ministry,' Yee answered. 'It is called the Avarga Oil Consortium.'

AFTER NEARLY TEN HOURS of jarring discomfort, the truck slowed. From the sudden alertness exhibited by the two guards sitting opposite her, Theresa knew they were arriving at their destination.

Wofford, who was nursing an injured leg, grimaced as they all flew off the hard bench after another encounter with a pothole. 'We might as well have flown, given the amount of time we've been airborne,' he complained.

Theresa smiled at the brave humour but offered no reply. The truck ground to a halt and the back doors were flung open, bathing them in a shock of bright sunlight. At the guards' nodding, Theresa and Roy helped Wofford from the truck, then stood absorbing their surroundings.

They were in the centre of a walled compound enclosing two buildings. The sky was blue, and the air was dry and dusty. Below in the distance was a rolling grass valley, while a grey-green mountain peak rose above the complex, which appeared to be dug into the pine-covered mountainside.

To their left, screened by a hedge, stood a low, industrial-looking brick building. At one end there were stables, and half a dozen horses milled about in an adjoining corral. At the other end was a large steel garage, which appeared to house a fleet of trucks and mechanical equipment.

'I thought the Taj Mahal was in India,' Roy said.

Theresa turned and studied the other building in the compound. It did bear a resemblance to the Indian landmark, albeit on a smaller scale. Thick columns fronted a gleaming white marble edifice which was built low to the ground. At its centre, a circular portico enveloped the main entrance and a bulbous white roof capped the entry hall, topped by a golden spire.

The landscape in front of the structure was equally palatial. A pair of canals flowed across the compound, feeding a large reflecting pool before disappearing under the building. Theresa could hear the rushing waters of a river, which presumably fed the canals some distance from the compound. Around the canals and the pool stretched a lush green ornamental garden.

Across the lawn, Theresa spied Tatiana and Anatoly conversing with a man who wore a holster on his side. The man nodded, then approached the back of the truck and said, 'This way,' in a thick accent.

Theresa and Roy each lent an arm to Wofford and followed the armed man as he marched towards the entrance to the opulent building. Flanking the carved wooden door was a pair of guards dressed in long embroidered silk coats and grasping sharp-pointed lances.

The door opened and they entered the domed foyer. A housekeeper led them down a side hallway to three guest rooms. One by one, Theresa, Roy and Wofford were escorted into the rooms, then locked in.

Theresa found a bowl of soup and a loaf of bread on a side table. After washing the grime from her face and hands, she sat down and devoured the food. Exhaustion overcoming her fears, she lay on the bed and fell asleep.

Three hours later, a hard knock at the door jolted her from a deep sleep.

'This way, please,' the housekeeper said.

Roy and Wofford were already waiting in the hallway. Theresa was surprised to see that Wofford's leg had been bandaged.

'The hospitality has taken a slight turn for the better,' he said, tapping his newly acquired wooden cane on the floor.

The three were led back to the foyer and down the main hallway to an expansive study. Shelves of leather-bound books lined the walls, punctuated by a fireplace at the far end and a bar along one side. The stuffed heads of deer, bighorn sheep, wolves and foxes leered at the visitors from their mounts on the walls. Tatiana stood in the middle of the room, next to a man who looked like he could have been mounted on the wall as well.

It was the grin, Theresa decided. He flashed sharp, pointy teeth like a shark's. The rest of his appearance was less imposing. He had a slight though muscular build, and was handsome in the classic Mongol sense, with high cheekbones, jet-black hair and almond-shaped eyes.

'It is good of you to join us,' Tatiana said in an emotionless tone. 'May I present Tolgoi Borjin, president of the Avarga Oil Consortium.'

'Pleased to meet you.' Wofford hobbled over and shook the man's hand. 'Now, would you mind telling us where we are and why the hell we're here?'

'My regrets for your hasty exit from Siberia,' Borjin said, ignoring Wofford's question. 'Tatiana tells me that your lives were in peril.'

'Indeed?' Theresa said, glancing warily at her former cabinmate.

'The forced departure was necessary for your security,' she explained. 'The environmental radicals of Baikal had tried to sink the institute's survey ship. It was best that we evacuated secretly, so as not to risk further attacks.'

'And what about Dr Sarghov, who was taken off the ship with us?'

'He was insistent on returning to the ship to alert the other institute members. I'm afraid we could no longer vouch for his safety.'

'So why haul us here?' Roy asked.

'We have abandoned the Lake Baikal project for the time being. But we will honour our contract with you through another project.'

'Has the company been notified?' Theresa asked, realising that her cell-phone was back on the *Vereshchagin*. 'I need to discuss this with them.'

'Regrettably, our microwave phone line is down at the moment. Once the service is restored, you will be free to make any calls you like.'

'Why are you locking us in our rooms like animals?'

'We have a number of sensitive research projects in development. I'm afraid we can't let outsiders wander round unsupervised.'

'And if we wish to leave right now?' Theresa probed.

'A driver will take you to Ulaanbaatar, where you can catch a flight to your home.' Borjin smiled, his sharp teeth glistening.

Theresa decided not to test the waters yet. 'What would you like us to do?'

Reams of folders were wheeled into the study, along with several laptop computers, all chock-full of geological assessments and seismic profiles.

'We wish to expand drilling operations into a new geographical region,' Borjin said. 'Tell us where the optimal drilling locations would be.' Saying nothing more, he left the room, Tatiana close behind.

'This is a load of bunk,' Roy muttered, slamming a file down on the table.

'Easy, big fella,' Wofford whispered, tilting his head towards the ceiling. 'We're on *Candid Camera*.'

Roy looked up. Mounted beside a deer's head was a tiny video camera.

Wofford picked up a map. 'Best we at least pretend to study the files,' he continued in a low voice, holding the map in front of his mouth.

Roy sat down and opened one of the laptops so the screen blocked his face. 'I don't like this. Let's not forget we were brought here at gunpoint.'

'I agree,' Theresa whispered. 'The whole story about trying to protect us at Lake Baikal is ludicrous. They may have killed Dr Sarghov, and the same fate could await us, after we've given them the information they want. We've got to find a way out of here.'

'The garage across the lawn was full of vehicles,' Roy said. 'If we could steal a truck, I'm sure we could find our way to Ulaanbaatar.'

Wofford adjusted his injured leg. 'Afraid I'm not up for any wind sprints or pole vaults,' he said. 'You two will need to try without me.'

'I've got an idea,' Roy said, eyeing a desk across the room. Making a show of looking for a lost pen, he stood and walked to the desk, where he grabbed a pencil from a round leather holder. Turning his back to the video camera, he scooped out a metal letter opener that was mixed in with the pencils, slid it up his sleeve and returned to the table.

'Tonight Theresa and I will check things out. Then tomorrow night we'll make our break. With the invalid in tow,' he added, grinning.

'I'd be much obliged,' Wofford said, nodding. 'Much obliged indeed.'

AT 2 A.M. ROY removed the letter opener from under his mattress and groped his way across the dark bedroom to the locked door. He felt along the door frame for the raised edges of three metal hinges. Sliding the letter opener into the top one, he prised out a long pin that held the interlocking hinge together. After removing the pins from the other two , he lifted the door and pulled it into the room as the deadbolt popped out of the opposite door frame. Roy then crept into the hallway and pulled the door back against the frame. He tiptoed to Theresa's room, unbolted the door and opened it.

She was waiting. 'You did it,' she whispered, running over to join him.

Roy flashed a thin smile, and they crept down the dim corridor towards the main foyer. When they reached the brightly lit entrance, Roy scurried over to a narrow window and peered outside. He turned back to Theresa and shook his head. The guards were still stationed outside the front door.

The foyer was at the base of an inverted T. The guest rooms had been to the left and the owner's private rooms were presumably to the right. So they crept instead down the wide main corridor, tiptoeing past the study, the dining hall and a pair of small meeting rooms. The corridor ended in a large, open conference room with floor-to-ceiling windows on three sides. Near the door was a stairwell down to a lower level. Roy motioned towards the stairs and Theresa followed him quietly. As she reached a turn in the stairwell, she looked up to face a huge portrait of a warrior seated on a horse, wearing a fur-trimmed coat, orange sash and the classic Mongol bowl helmet. His triumphant grin exposed sharpened teeth that reminded her of Borjin. She shuddered, and quickly moved on down the stairs.

They found themselves in a corridor with windows onto a courtyard.

'There must be a door to the courtyard here,' Roy whispered. 'If we can get out here, we ought to be able to sneak back to the garage.'

Theresa nodded. 'It's going to be a long way for Jim to hobble, but at least there aren't any guards here.'

They found an unlocked exit door at the end of the corridor. Theresa half expected an alarm to sound when the latch released, but all remained silent. They crept into the courtyard, which was illuminated by a few pathway lamps. Theresa shivered as a chill breeze blew through her light clothes.

They followed a slate path across the courtyard, and came to a domed stone structure which appeared to be a small chapel. Behind it they found a covered bay that had once been a corral. Enclosed by a low fence, it was crammed with half a dozen old wagons, their beds stacked with shovels, picks and empty crates. From beneath a canvas tarp poked the grimy front wheel of a motorcycle. At the back of the bay was a huge antique Rolls-Royce, layered with decades of dust and sitting on at least two flat tyres.

'Nothing here's going to get us to Ulaanbaatar,' Theresa lamented.

Roy nodded. 'The garage on the other side of the mansion will have to be our ticket.' He froze suddenly as a horse's whinny carried near on the breeze. 'Behind the wagon,' he whispered, pointing to the corral.

They crawled through the fence rails and slithered beneath the nearest wagon, then cautiously peeked out through the spokes of a wooden wheel.

Two men on horseback appeared from behind the stone building and stopped beside the corral. Theresa's heart nearly stopped when she saw that the horsemen were dressed in nearly the same garb as the warrior in the hall painting. Their orange silk tunics reflected gold under the courtyard lights. Baggy pants, thick-soled boots and a round spiked helmet completed their warrior appearance. The two men milled about for several minutes, then disappeared into the darkness amid a small thunder of hoofbeats.

'The night watchmen,' Roy whispered. 'We probably don't have much time before they make another pass.'

'OK. Let's try for the garage now. I don't want to meet those guys again.'

They scrambled through the fence and headed for the guest wing, but midway across the courtyard they heard a sharp cry and the clatter of hooves. Looking back, they saw the horses charging them. The two watchmen had obviously backtracked and seen Theresa and Roy sprint across the yard.

They froze in their tracks. One rider pulled his horse to a standstill, while the other continued galloping towards them. Roy flung Theresa out of harm's way and sidestepped the charging mount. But after regaining his balance, Roy didn't look for cover. He sprinted after the charging horse.

The animal galloped a few more yards, then wheeled round to make another charge. Its rider was shocked to find Roy standing in his path.

The seismic engineer grabbed at the reins dangling beneath the horse's chin and jerked them downwards. 'That's enough horseplay,' he muttered as he fought to restrain the horse, which was snorting out clouds of vapour.

'Nooooo!' The piercing cry came from Theresa's lips.

Glancing back, Roy detected a faint object whisking towards him. Suddenly his chest was squeezed in a vicelike grip, and a fire burned within. As he dropped to his knees, Theresa appeared and cradled his shoulders.

The arrow fired by the second horseman had penetrated Roy's chest and punctured his pulmonary artery. Theresa desperately tried to stem the flow of blood, but there was nothing she could do. She held him tight as the colour drained from his face. He gasped for air before his body began to sag. For a moment, his eyes turned bright, and Theresa thought he might hang on.

Then he looked at Theresa and gasped the words, 'Save yourself.'

His eyes closed and he was gone.

THE AEROFLOT TU-154 passenger jet from Irkutz banked slowly over the city of Ulaanbaatar before lining up on the main runway of Chinggis Khaan Airport for its final approach. Pitt looked out of the window and enjoyed an expansive vista of Mongolia's capital city under a cloudless sky.

The first impression was of a 1950s Eastern Bloc metropolis, complete with grey Soviet-style apartment buildings. Recent autonomy and a dose of economic growth had added colourful shops, restaurants and nightclubs. But the surrounding fields were still jammed with *gers*, muffin-shaped tents made of felt, the traditional homes of nomadic Mongolian herders.

As the jet's tyres screeched onto the runway, Pitt jabbed his elbow towards the seat next to him. Al Giordino opened his eyes and yawned.

'Welcome to Ulaanbaatar, which in Mongolian means "Red Hero",' Sarghov's jolly voice boomed from across the aisle.

The fat Russian was wedged into a tiny seat, his face still peppered with sticking plasters, and Pitt wondered how he could be so merry. When he saw the scientist slip a flask of vodka into a valise, he knew the answer.

The trio made their way through immigration, then collected their bags and took a cab to the Continental Hotel. Sarghov checked them in, and their luggage was taken up to the fourth floor. As they were enjoying a drink in the hotel restaurant, a wiry man in a red shirt walked up to their booth.

He greeted Sarghov with a laugh. 'Alexander, you old goat!'

'Corsov!' Sarghov exclaimed, standing and giving the smaller man a hug. 'Dirk, Al, this is Ivan Corsov, special attaché to the Russian embassy here in Ulaanbaatar. He's agreed to help us with the investigation of Avarga Oil.'

The four men shook hands and sat down to order lunch. After the usual pleasantries, the conversation turned serious.

'Alexander, what makes you think that the abducted oil workers were brought to Mongolia?' Corsov asked after he'd been brought up to date.

'We know the black freighter was leased by Avarga Oil, so we assumed they would return to their headquarters in Mongolia. Border security confirmed that three trucks matching the description of those seen at Listvyanka had crossed into Mongolia at Naushki. A formal request for assistance was sent to the Mongolian national police, but an Irkutsk police official warned me that assistance would not be swiftly forthcoming.'

'True. Russian influence isn't what it used to be,' Corsov said.

'What can you tell us about Avarga Oil, Ivan?'

Corsov spoke in a low voice. 'The Avarga Oil Consortium was one of the first private companies licensed by the newly autonomous Mongolian government in the early 1990s. Their publicly acknowledged holdings are a low-yielding oil field in the north near the Siberian border, a few exploratory wells in the Gobi, and exploration rights to land around Lake Baikal. But the company has also acquired oil and mineral rights to vast tracts of land throughout the country. And they have acquired outright ownership of thousands of acres of former state land spreading all across Mongolia. My sources tell me that Avarga paid a considerable sum to the Mongolian government for these rights, yet it would not appear to have the resources to do so.'

'There's always a bank somewhere that's willing to loan money,' Pitt said. 'Perhaps funds were fronted by outside mining interests.'

'I found no evidence of that. The land was bought with cash, the source of which is a mystery. And much of it is in regions with no known oil or mining geology. A large section goes through the Gobi Desert, for example.'

The waitress appeared and slid a plate of roast lamb in front of Corsov. The Russian stuffed a large piece of meat in his mouth, then continued.

'I found it interesting that the company's chairman does not appear to have any political clout or connections, and keeps a low profile in Xanadu.'

'Xanadu?' asked Pitt.

'The name of the chairman's residence and headquarters, about two hundred and fifty kilometres southeast of here.'

'Who exactly is the face behind Avarga Oil?'

'The company is registered to a man named Tolgoi Borjin. He has a younger sister and brother, but I could not discover their names. Public records indicate that Borjin was raised in a state commune in the Khentii province. His mother died at an early age and his father was a labourer and surveyor. The family has no visible presence in Ulaanbaatar's upper society, but rumour has it that they are self-proclaimed members of the Golden Clan.'

'Deep pockets, eh?' Giordino asked.

Corsov shook his head. 'It has nothing to do with wealth. The Golden Clan, according to the history books, were direct descendants of Chinggis.'

'Chinggis?' Giordino repeated.

'Accomplished tactician, conqueror, and perhaps the greatest leader of the medieval age,' Pitt interjected. 'Better known to the world as Genghis Khan.'

6

Theresa sat in the study, gazing blindly at a seismic report. A melancholy depression, tinged with anger, had gradually replaced her shock at Roy's brutal murder. Since that moment, she and Wofford had been under constant surveillance. She gazed across the study to the entrance, where two stone-faced guards stood staring back at her.

Wofford sat beside her with his injured leg propped on a chair, engrossed in a geological report. He seemed to be using the task at hand to conceal his emotions about Roy's death. 'We might as well give them the work they asked for,' he had told her. 'It might be the only thing that keeps us alive.'

Maybe he was right, she thought, trying to focus on the report.

'Take a look at this,' Wofford said, unrolling a computer print-out across the table. It showed a seismic section—a computer-enhanced image of sediment layers in a confined location. The chart was created by a seismic survey team that sent man-made shocks into the ground and recorded the sound reflections. He pointed to a bulbous shape near the bottom of the page.

'That looks like a classic, not to mention nicely sized, anticlinal trap,' said Theresa, referring to the dome-shaped layer of sediments before her.

'Nicely sized, indeed,' Wofford replied. 'It stretches nearly forty kilometres. And there are at least six others in the same region.'

'It certainly looks like the right conditions for a decent petroleum deposit. Six more, you say? That's a tremendous reserve potential.'

'Could be over ten billion barrels, just for one field. It's mind-boggling. But there's a hitch. All geographic references have been removed.'

'You mean we might be looking at the next North Sea oil fields and you don't know where they are located?'

'I haven't a clue.'

SARGHOV LOOKED UP from his cup of breakfast tea as Corsov entered the busy café. He stood and greeted his embassy friend, who smiled his toothy grin.

'Ivan, we were just discussing the investigation. Has there been any news on the official front?' Sarghov asked, as Corsov pulled a chair to the table.

'*Nyet*,' Corsov said, his face turning solemn. 'The national police have still not been assigned the case. I was wrong when I said that Avarga Oil has no influence within the government. A bribe is clearly in effect at some level. And I have some tragic news. A LUKOIL Russian oil-survey team was ambushed by men on horseback in the mountains north of here two days ago. Four men were brutally murdered for no apparent reason. A fifth man managed to escape, but when he returned to the scene with the local police, everything was gone—bodies, trucks, survey gear—all vanished.'

'Is there any link with Avarga Oil?' Giordino asked.

'We don't know. But it does seem an odd coincidence, you must agree.'

The table fell silent for a moment, then Giordino said thoughtfully, 'Every hour might count for Theresa and the others.'

'Our embassy is doing everything it can. We will find them, my friend.' Sarghov drained his tea. 'I'm afraid there is little more we can do for the moment. As it is, I must return to Irkutsk to file a report on the damage to the *Vereshchagin*. I have booked airline tickets for the three of us this afternoon.'

Pitt looked at Giordino, then turned to Sarghov. 'Actually, Alex, we have already made alternative travel plans,' he said.

'You are returning directly to the United States? I thought perhaps you would return to Siberia and collect your comrade Rudi first.'

Pitt's green eyes glimmered. 'No, Alex, we're not going to the United States, or Siberia, just yet,' he said, 'We're going to a place called Xanadu.'

CORSOV'S INTELLIGENCE NETWORK had come up trumps. A Foreign Ministry source had notified him of a pending Chinese state visit. But it was Corsov who had recognised it as a golden opportunity for Pitt and Giordino.

The Chinese minister of commerce was arriving at short notice, ostensibly to tour a solar-energy plant recently opened at the edge of the capital. Yet the bulk of his time was scheduled for a private visit with the head of Avarga Oil, at his secluded residence southeast of Ulaanbaatar.

'I can put you in the motorcade, which will get you past Borjin's front door. The rest will be up to you,' Corsov had told Pitt and Giordino.

He went on to explain that a formal reception was planned for the minister's arrival later in the day when a large welcoming escort from the Foreign Affairs Ministry would be in attendance. But tomorrow, when the delegation toured the solar energy plant and travelled to Avarga headquarters, only a small Mongolian security force would accompany the minister.

'So we are joining the Mongolian Secret Service?' Pitt asked.

Corsov nodded. 'Ordinary officers of the national police normally fill the roles. It took only a modest enticement to have you inserted as replacement security escorts. You will swap places with the real guards at the solar plant and follow the procession to Xanadu. Then, if you can prove that your friends are on site, we can prompt the Mongolian authorities to action.'

'Will do. What do we owe you for the bribes?'

'Anything you can share with me about Avarga Oil will more than repay the pittance spent,' Corsov replied. 'But there's one more thing,' he added with a smile. 'Try not to forget to keep the Chinese minister alive.'

'THAT'S OUR RIDE,' Pitt said, referring to a battered Russian-built UAZ four-wheel drive pulling up near the entrance of the solar-energy plant.

'I hope it's got a satellite radio and a nav system,' Giordino replied.

'I just hope it's got tyres manufactured this century,' Pitt muttered.

They had arrived at the plant an hour ahead of the Chinese minister's scheduled appearance, and flashed a pair of dummy ID cards provided by Corsov to the sleepy-eyed guard at the gate. Concealing themselves behind a large solar panel at the entrance, they had waited. Dressed in dark Chinese-tailored sports jackets and sunglasses, with black woollen beret-type hats on their heads, they easily passed for local security types from a distance.

They hadn't long to wait before the motorcade rolled through the gates. A trio of Toyota Land Cruisers had chauffeured the Chinese minister and his small cadre of assistants and security guards to the facility. They were led by a Mongol security escort driving a yellow UAZ four-wheel drive. The other UAZ, the one designated for Pitt's use, tailed the delegation.

Pitt watched now as two men casually got out of the last vehicle and disappeared into the field of solar panels as the welcoming committee greeted the Chinese minister. With the delegation preoccupied, Pitt and Giordino moved undetected to the car and took the guards' places in the front seats.

'Here's your nav system,' Pitt said, grabbing a map from the dashboard and tossing it at Giordino. The car didn't even have a radio.

In less than ten minutes, Commerce Minister Shinzhe had finished his tour of the plant, and was thanking his hosts and climbing back into his car.

'He's sure got ants in his pants,' Giordino said.

'Guess he's anxious to get to Xanadu.'

Pitt started the car and caught up with the third Toyota as it exited the facility. The caravan rumbled east out of Ulaanbaatar, curving past the Bayanzurkh Nuruu mountains, which gradually gave way to rolling grasslands.

After three hours they began ascending a cluster of pine-covered mountains. At a nondescript iron gate, they turned onto another road, which climbed several miles up a mountain before skirting a ridge and approaching a fast-moving river. Built off the river was an aqueduct, which the caravan followed round a tight bend and up to a high-walled compound. Two guards in bright silk tunics stood on either side of a massive iron gate in the wall.

As the vehicles slowed to a stop, Pitt contemplated their next move. 'We probably don't want to join the party for the grand entrance,' he said.

'Car problems?' Giordino asked.

'I was thinking a flat tyre.'

'Consider it done.'

Giordino slipped out of the passenger door, crawled beside the front tyre and removed the valve stem cap. Jamming a matchstick into the stem, he waited as air whistled out of the valve and the tyre deflated. Then he screwed the cap back on, and climbed back into the UAZ as the iron gate opened.

Pitt followed the line of cars, but at the gate he pointed out the flat tyre to a guard, who nodded, and motioned for Pitt to turn right once he was inside.

As they entered the compound, the spectacular marble residence was directly ahead. The procession was led by a pair of escorts on white horses.

'Any sign of Tatiana in the welcoming committee?' Pitt asked Giordino as he wheeled the car out of line and towards the building on the right.

'There's a woman on the porch, but I can't make out if it's her.'

Pitt guided the car towards the garage and drove through its open doors. A grease-stained mechanic in a red baseball cap came running over and Pitt pointed at the flat tyre. After examining Giordino's handiwork, he nodded and walked to the end of the bay to fetch a floor jack.

'Let's take a walk next door,' Pitt said, climbing out of the car.

The two men strolled nonchalantly out of the garage towards the brick building next door. They passed a large loading dock and walked through an adjacent glass door into the middle of a vast work bay. Test equipment and electronic circuit boards were scattered around several workbenches, being tinkered with by a pair of men in white antistatic lab coats. One of the men looked up at Pitt and Giordino suspiciously.

'*Stualét?*' Pitt asked, recalling the Russian word for 'toilet'.

The man studied Pitt for a moment, then pointed to a corridor that ran from the centre of the room. 'On the right,' he said in Russian.

Giordino led the way. 'Impressive language skills,' he said quietly.

'Just one of the five words I know in Russian,' Pitt replied. 'I recalled Corsov saying that most Mongolians know a smidgen of Russian.'

They moved slowly down the wide tiled corridor. On either side, large plate-glass windows revealed more labs and the occasional office. Only a handful of technicians appeared to be working there. Passing the toilets, they continued down the corridor until it ended at a thick metal door.

After glancing round the empty hallway, Pitt grabbed the handle and pushed on the heavy door. It swung slowly inwards, revealing a vast chamber with a ceiling that rose over thirty feet high. Row after row of conical rubber spikes protruded from the walls, ceiling and floor.

'An anechoic chamber,' he said.

'Built to absorb radio-frequency electromagnetic waves,' Giordino added. 'Usually used by defence contractors to test sophisticated electronics.'

'There's your sophisticated electronics,' Pitt said.

He pointed to the centre of the room, where a large platform stood on stilts above the rubber-spiked floor. A dozen tall metal cabinets were jammed onto the platform next to racks of computer equipment. In an open section in the middle, a long, tripod-like device hung from a gantry. Pitt and Giordino climbed across a catwalk that led from the door to the platform.

'What do you make of this?' Giordino asked.

'The cabinets look like commercial-grade radio transmitters. The computers must be used for data processing. And this . . .' He turned and examined the device dangling from the centre of the platform.

It consisted of three long tubes bound together and standing nearly ten feet high. The lower ends flared near the floor. The opposite ends sprouted a thick bundle of cables, which trailed overhead to the computer racks.

'They look like amplified transducers,' Pitt said, 'though bigger than any I've seen. Could be a beefed-up seismic-imaging system, for oil exploration.'

'Looks more advanced than any drill operation I've ever seen.'

Pitt glanced at what appeared to be an operating manual lying beside the equipment. Noting that it was written in German, he tore the first few pages out and stuffed them in his pocket.

'A little light reading material for the ride home?' Giordino asked.

'Some practice for my German verb conjugations.'

They recrossed the catwalk and exited the chamber, then walked back down the corridor at a fast clip. Nodding to a white-coated engineer in the work bay, they zipped through the exit door.

Outside, the winds had increased and were buffeting the compound with swirls of thick dust. Pitt and Giordino stepped back into the garage, finding the mechanic still wrestling with the front wheel. Pitt moved to the doorway and looked across the lawn towards the main residence. He could just make out the two Mongolian escorts talking casually on the porch. Two other men stood on either side of the doorway that led into the residence.

'If they didn't let our Mongol cohorts in the front door, then I don't think they are going to let us stroll right in,' he said.

'We'll have to find another entrance. If Theresa and the others are here, they would have to be somewhere in that building.' Giordino said, scanning the grounds around the residence. 'Let's go find the back door.'

Following a path round the perimeter wall, they made their way to the left side of the residence, but could see no other access to the building there. Ahead, the compound wall ended abruptly at a rocky precipice. They followed a small footpath that zigzagged steeply down to a narrow plateau, and made their way to the back of the building. They found that it was built up on a slight berm that rose above them, sided by a rock wall.

'Not many ways in and out of this joint, are there?' Giordino asked, eyeing the rock wall, which seemed to stretch the length of the building.

'I guess the fire marshal hasn't paid them a visit yet.'

They moved towards the centre of the house, hugging the stone wall so as to stay out of view of any windowed rooms above them. They shielded their faces with their hats to keep the blowing dust from stinging their eyes.

Reaching the edge of the courtyard, they crept behind a low hedge and immediately spotted an entry door, flanked by two silk-clad guards.

'Do you want to try your language skills with these two?' Giordino asked.

'If we keep behind those bushes and get to the back of that small stone building, we might be able to creep up and surprise them,' Pitt suggested.

Giordino nodded. When a thick swirl of dust kicked up, they sprinted towards the round stone structure in the middle of the courtyard. Skirting round the back, they ducked into the tunnel-like opening, and peered out. The guards were still standing beside the residence door, cowering slightly from the wind. Pitt and Giordino had made it across the courtyard unseen.

Or so they thought.

AFTER A BOUNCY three-hour trek across the mountains and steppes of Central Mongolia, Commerce Minister Shinzhe had been convinced that he was on a wild-goose chase. But when the caravan had rolled through the iron gates and into the stately compound, his angry scepticism had softened.

His host was waiting in front of his elegant residence. Dressed in a finely cut European suit, he bowed deeply as Shinzhe exited the vehicle. A translator at his side relayed his greetings in Mandarin.

'Welcome, Minister Shinzhe. I trust your journey was pleasant?'

'A delight to see the beautiful Mongolian countryside,' Shinzhe replied.

'May I present my sister Tatiana, our director of field operations?'

Tatiana bowed gracefully. Shinzhe smiled and introduced his entourage. He turned to admire the horsemen in warrior attire that ringed the driveway.

'I have heard much about the Mongol horse,' Shinzhe said. 'Do you breed horses, Mr Borjin?'

'Just a small stock for my security detail. In these parts, a Mongol horse can go where no vehicle can. My ancestors conquered half the world with the horse and bow, and I find they are still useful skills today. Please, let us escape this infernal wind and relax indoors.'

Borjin led the group through the front door and along the main hallway to the large room at the end. Its floor-to-ceiling windows normally offered an expansive view, but today most of the vista was obscured with swirling dust. Borjin invited his guests to sit at a formal mahogany table, and took a seat himself at one end, with his back to the wall. Behind him, a wide set of shelves displayed a medieval arsenal of spears, lances and swords.

Shinzhe looked from the weapons to the man who owned them and gave an involuntary shiver. Something about the oil executive's cold eyes hinted at a hidden brutality. As a cup of hot tea was placed before him, the minister tried to dispel his feelings and focus on the purpose of his visit.

'My government has gratefully received your proposal to supply a significant quantity of crude oil to our country,' he began. 'On behalf of the party, I have been asked to confirm the validity of the proposal and discuss the remuneration necessary to conclude an agreement.'

Borjin leaned back in his chair and laughed. 'Yes, of course. Why does Mongolia, a nation of ragtag peasants and shepherds, nemesis to Cathay for a thousand years, suddenly desire to assist our southern neighbour? Because you made us prisoners in our own land. You and the Russians barricaded us from the rest of the world for decades, leaving us in landlocked isolation. But Mongolia is a rich land, Minister Shinzhe. You didn't take the time or effort to appreciate that when you had the chance. Now, Western companies are clamouring to develop our mines, cut timber from our forests. But they are too late for the oil. For when nobody was interested in prospecting our lands, we made the effort ourselves, and now we shall reap the rewards.'

He nodded at Tatiana, who retrieved a map of Mongolia from a bureau and unrolled it in front of the minister. An irregular red oval was overlaid on a section near the southeast border with Chinese Inner Mongolia.

'The Temujin field. A natural basin that makes your ageing Daqing field look like a bowl of spit,' Borjin said, referring to China's largest oil field, which was in a state of decline. 'Our test wells indicate potential reserves of forty billion barrels of crude oil and fifty trillion cubic feet of natural gas.'

'I have heard nothing of such a find,' Shinzhe commented sceptically.

Borjin bared his teeth in a sharklike grin. 'Few people outside this room are aware of the find,' he said. 'My own government knows nothing of these reserves. How else do you think I was able to acquire the land rights to the entire region? A proprietary technology of ours helped pinpoint the windfall somewhat by accident. These are deep reserves, which explains in part why they were overlooked by previous exploration teams.'

The colour drained from Shinzhe's face as he considered the implications of this arrogant charlatan controlling such a vast oil field. 'Having oil in the ground is one thing,' he said soberly, 'but your offer suggests we could see crude oil flowing within ninety days. How is that possible?'

'It will take some doing on your part, but it is feasible,' Borjin replied.

He turned to Tatiana, who unrolled a second map, of Mongolia and northern China. A web of red lines crisscrossed the Chinese section of the map.

'The existing oil pipelines of China,' Borjin explained. 'Take a look at your recently completed northeast pipeline from Daqing to Beijing, with a spur from the port terminal at Qinhuangdao.'

Shinzhe studied the map, noting a small X along a stretch of pipeline that ran through Inner Mongolia.

'The X is forty kilometres from a nearly completed pipeline I am building to the border. You need only extend the pipeline from my termination to that spot on your Daqing line and the oil will begin to flow.'

'Forty kilometres of pipeline? That can't be completed in ninety days.'

Borjin stood up and paced around the table. 'I have taken the liberty of surveying the route and have the necessary pipe committed from a supplier. For additional consideration, I can also provide excavation equipment.'

'You have considered our needs well,' Shinzhe said with veiled contempt.

'As a good business partner should.' Borjin smiled. 'In return, my demands are simple. You will pay one hundred and forty-six thousand tugrik per barrel, or one hundred and twenty-five US dollars. You will accede the lands of southern Mongolia. And you will provide me with an exclusive pipeline to the port of Qinhuangdao and a facility for processing my excess supply of oil.'

As Shinzhe gasped at the demand, the Mongol turned and gazed out of the window, watching the swirling dust. A movement caught his eye. Two dark figures were sprinting across the courtyard. Borjin watched as they looped round the back of the sanctuary, then ducked inside the entrance.

A tightness gripped his throat as he turned to the minister. 'If you will excuse me for a moment, I must attend to an urgent matter.'

Before the minister could reply, Borjin strode briskly from the room.

THE WINDS HAD DIED down temporarily, forcing Pitt and Giordino to remain under cover in the stone entrance. Looking back towards the main chamber of the ancient stone edifice, they could see light flickering. Their curiosity piqued, the two men moved quietly down the wide, arched corridor.

Under the glow of a dozen burning torches and candles, they found that the chamber was a mausoleum. At the far end was a small wooden altar, with a white marble sarcophagus on either side. Though Pitt couldn't read the Cyrillic script carved on the top slabs, he guessed from the relative modernity of the casks that they were the tombs of Borjin's mother and father.

On a marble pedestal in the centre of the crypt stood another sarcophagus. Made of granite, with animals carved and painted on the top and sides, it appeared much older. At the head of the tomb, nine posts rose into the air, each dangling a shock of white fur.

'The illustrious Mr Borjin must be something of a blueblood,' Pitt said.

Giordino looked past the sarcophagus and noted an object lying beneath the altar. 'Looks like they're going to need another coffin in here,' he said.

Overlooked as they entered the chamber, the body both men now saw was stretched out on a bench beneath the altar, half covered in a blanket. Walking over, they were shocked to recognise the corpse. It was Roy.

'Theresa and Wofford *are* here . . .' Giordino said, his voice trailing off.

'Let's hope they haven't suffered the same fate,' Pitt said quietly.

As he pulled the blanket up to cover Roy's face, the chamber's stillness was broken by the clatter of boots on the stone floor. Two guards burst into the mausoleum, clutching wooden spears. Short knives hung in scabbards at their waists, and they carried small quivers and bows on their backs.

Giordino grabbed a small wooden bench by the altar and pitched it at the legs of the charging guards. The bench struck the nearer man's legs hard, and he stumbled to the floor, his spear rolling harmlessly to the side.

The second guard leapt over the bench and continued charging at Pitt, drawing back his spear for a lethal forward jab. With a quick thrust of his legs, Pitt sprang to one side. He tried to grab at the shaft of the spear, but missed, and as the guard barrelled past he swung the spear towards him. The side of the shaft whipped round and jammed Pitt on the shoulder.

Both men were thrown off-balance, the guard falling across the altar while Pitt was knocked towards the crypt. Pitt quickly rolled to his feet to face his attacker, who tightened his grip on the spear and prepared to charge again. Giordino was preoccupied with subduing the first guard, and in no position to help. Pitt's eyes darted about in search of a weapon.

Then he remembered the nine fur-tailed poles in their marble bases at the head of the tomb. He backed over to them and covertly gripped one behind his back with his right hand. When the guard was a few steps away, he quickly angled the eight-foot wooden pole in front of him. The blunt end of the pole struck the guard's stomach, driven forward by Pitt. He fell to one knee, sending the spear rattling across the polished floor. Ignoring Pitt, the guard desperately crawled towards the weapon before looking up in horror. The pole had been flipped round and now the marble base was swinging towards him. It struck his skull, knocking him out cold.

'No respect for a man's furnishings,' Giordino grumbled as the pole and marble base crashed to the floor. He was rubbing the back of his fist as he stood over the unconscious body of the first guard. 'What do you say we get out of this box before any more Royal Lancers show up?'

'Agreed.'

The two men ran to the archway, and peeked cautiously into the courtyard.

Two guards, clad in bright silk tunics and round metal helmets, still sat on their mounts near the residence door. Nearby, another horseman was combing the yard. Pitt and Giordino ducked out through the archway in the opposite direction under a dirty gust of wind. As they crept round the back of the mausoleum, they spotted half a dozen horsemen riding in their direction.

'Fine time for the cavalry to appear,' Giordino said.

'Just makes our exit route a little clearer,' Pitt replied.

They backtracked to the covered corral at the rear of the crypt, and ducked inside, winding through a maze of crates and wagons towards the opposite rail. Pitt had just slowed to eye the large antique car parked in the back when a whistling sound ripped past his ear, followed by a sharp twang.

'Incoming,' he yelled, ducking as another arrow whistled by.

Giordino was already crouching behind a wooden barrel when the arrow slammed into a support post, swiftly followed by another and another.

The galloping hoofbeats of the other patrol echoed above the wind as they raced to the scene. Within minutes, the air in the corral was filled with a flying maelstrom of razor-tipped arrows, but the gusting winds deflected their flight and hampered the horsemen's vision. Pitt and Giordino kept their attackers at bay by lobbing tools and field implements at them.

Suddenly the winds fell, leaving the two men exposed. They dived under a wagon, and half a dozen arrows buried their tips into the wood just inches above their heads. From the other side of the corral, gunfire erupted.

'D'you suppose they'd bite at a white handkerchief?' Giordino muttered.

'Not likely,' Pitt replied, thinking of Roy. An arrow smashed into the wagon wheel beside him and he instinctively rolled away from the impact. A thin, knobby protrusion struck him in the back. He twisted his head to find an object covered in a dirty canvas tarp sitting next to the wagon.

'The next cloud of dust, let's rush one of the horsemen on the fringe,' said Giordino. 'You grab the reins, I'll grab the rider; we've got ourselves a mount.'

'Risky,' Pitt replied, 'but probably our best chance.' Rolling onto his side to survey the perimeter, he accidentally kicked off a section of the tarp covering the object beside him.

Giordino saw a sudden glint in Pitt's eyes. 'A change of plans?' he asked.

'No,' Pitt replied. 'We'll just ride off on a horse of a different colour.'

THE WALL-MOUNTED RADIO popped with the receipt of a signal, followed by a gravelly voice. 'We have them surrounded behind the sanctuary. They arrived with the Chinese delegation, but are apparently Russian impostors.'

'I see,' Borjin replied in an irritated voice. 'Government agents or, more likely, spies from a Russian oil company. See that they don't leave the compound alive, but hold the gunfire until the delegation has departed.'

Borjin replaced the handset, then returned to the conference room. 'Excuse the interruption,' he said, taking a seat. 'A slight mishap has occurred with two of your escorts. I'm afraid they won't be able to join you on your return trip. I will, of course, provide replacements.'

Shinzhe nodded vaguely. 'And the gunshots?'

'A training exercise by my security guards. No reason to be alarmed.'

The minister stared blankly out of the window, his mind elsewhere. Then he slowly turned to face Borjin. 'Your offer is akin to blackmail and your demands are preposterous,' he said, his anger finally surfacing.

'My demands are non-negotiable. And perhaps they are not so preposterous for a country facing an economic meltdown,' Borjin hissed.

Shinzhe stared at his host with contempt.

'Minister Shinzhe, you must view it as a mutually beneficial transaction,' Borjin continued. 'China gets the oil it needs to keep its economy running, I get a long-term commitment as a major supplier, and the Mongolian Autonomous Region rejoins its rightful place as part of greater Mongolia.'

'Acceding sovereign territory is not an act taken lightly.'

'The region is little more than a rural dust bowl occupied by Mongol herders. I desire only to restore the lands that once belonged to our nation.'

'It is unusual for a private entity to interfere in territorial exchanges.'

'This is true. In fact, my government knows nothing of our accord. They will find it a pleasing political gift.' Borjin handed a thick leather binder to Shinzhe. 'I have worked up the necessary agreements for signature. It would please me to receive your country's acceptance at the earliest opportunity.'

'I report to the general secretary's council tomorrow afternoon. Your fixed position on the terms may negate an agreement, I must warn you.'

'So be it.' Borjin rose to his feet. 'I look forward to a long and fruitful relationship, Minister Shinzhe.' He bowed graciously, if insincerely.

Shinzhe rose and bowed stiffly in return, then left the room with his entourage. Borjin and Tatiana followed the Chinese delegation to the door and watched as they staggered through the howling dust storm to their cars.

As the taillights blinked past the gate, Borjin closed the door. 'The plum is ours for the taking,' he told Tatiana, walking back down the main hallway.

'Yes, thanks to our brother, the Chinese are in a desperate bind.'

'Temuge has been working miracles, hasn't he?'

'Although he nearly caused my death in Baikal,' she said irritably.

'An unforeseen side effect, the large wave. But you are safe now,' he said. 'And you must admit, the pipeline destruction in Siberia, setting fire to the Chinese port when a suitable fault line could not be found, and assembling the Persian Gulf team—it has all been most effective. After the next Middle East demonstration, the Chinese will be crawling to us on their knees.'

'And Temuge is proceeding to North America for the final strike?'

'They departed two days ago.'

Passing the conference room, he walked to the adjacent staircase, his sister following. Stopping at the head of the stairs, he looked up at the portrait of the ancient Mongol warrior that hung on the facing wall.

'We are well on our way to restoring the riches and glory of the Golden Clan,' he said. 'May the conquests of Chinggis begin again.'

BEHIND THE RESIDENCE, the head of security refastened a handheld radio to his belt. A bear-sized man by the name of Batbold, he had just received word that the Chinese delegation had left the compound.

The swirling dust obscured the interior of the corral, but there had been no sight of the two marauders for several minutes. They were surely dead, Batbold surmised. After three more volleys of rifle fire into the corral, he halted the shooting. He dismounted and led three other men on foot towards the corral. They were within ten feet of the fence when they heard a wooden crate being smashed inside. They froze, and a new sound emerged, a metallic whirring, followed by a movement behind one of the wagons.

'There!' he shouted, pointing towards the wagon. 'Aim and fire.'

As the guards raised their carbines to their shoulders, a wall of boxes erupted from the side of the corral, knocking out a section of the fence.

Wide-eyed, Batbold watched a faded red motorcycle with attached side-car racing straight towards him. The motorcycle appeared riderless, with a wooden crate propped on the seat, next to another crate atop the sidecar. In stunned confusion, Batbold stepped out of its path, and, as the motorcycle brushed by, Al Giordino popped up through the crate on the sidecar like a crazed jack-in-the-box. His hands gripped a square-bladed shovel, which he swung at Batbold. The blunt face of the blade struck the security chief on the side of his jaw with a hard smack, and he melted to the ground.

The three guards behind Batbold scattered in panic without firing a shot. One man slipped and fell, his legs run over by the sidecar's wheels. The second man dived to safety, while the third got whacked in the back of the head by Giordino's shovel, sending him sprawling.

Peeking through a slot in the crate draped over his shoulders, Pitt gunned the aged motorcycle away from the riflemen. Picking a gap in the archers' horses, he blasted towards it, trailing a cloud of black smoke.

'Keep down!' he shouted to Giordino.

An instant later, a flurry of arrows pinged into the sidecar and ripped into their makeshift armour. Pitt felt a stinging in his left thigh. As he had hoped, the riflemen behind him had held their fire for fear of shooting the archers. But the archers had no such qualms.

Deciding to lessen the fire, Pitt drove straight towards one of the horses. The startled beast reared on its hind legs and spun to the side, leaving its rider hanging on for dear life. Then the motorcycle was past the rearing horse and the archers, speeding away from the courtyard.

Giordino spun round in the sidecar and peeked over the edge of his protective crate. 'Still on our heels,' he shouted. 'I'm going to play toss with these guys. Let me know when we get to the ski jump.'

Before climbing aboard the motorcycle, Giordino had noticed a sack full of horseshoes hanging from the wagon and had tossed the bag into the sidecar. Popping out of the crate, he now began hurling horseshoes at their pursuers. He dazed two of the riders and disrupted the bow fire of several others.

Pitt raced the bike across the courtyard at full throttle. When he had rolled against the Czechoslovakian motorcycle in the corral, he figured it was a metal corpse. But the 1953 Jawa 500 OHC still had air in its tyres, a couple of gallons of stale gas in its tank and an engine that turned over freely. With the help of Giordino's horseshoes, they had opened up a comfortable lead.

Pitt suddenly swung the handlebars to one side. 'Fasten your seat belt, we're ready for takeoff,' he yelled.

Giordino ducked back into the sidecar and grabbed the handrail at the front. In his other hand, he gripped the last of the horseshoes. 'For luck,' he muttered, and wedged the horseshoe into the cowling of the sidecar.

At the back of the estate, where the yard dropped down a steep precipice, there was no perimeter wall. Pitt knew it might be suicidal, but there was no other avenue for escape. Blasting towards the edge of the yard, he braked slightly, then guided the motorcycle over the brink.

Pitt could feel his stomach drop as the ground disappeared from beneath their wheels. The first thirty feet were nearly vertical and they plunged through the air before the front wheel kissed the ground. The rest of the motorcycle struck hard, jarring the wooden crates off the driver and passenger.

Up on the ledge, several guards stood and fired at the fleeing motorcycle, cursing as it disappeared into a cloud of dust. Half a dozen horsemen led their mounts slowly down the steep incline, then continued the pursuit with speed.

Pitt and Giordino hung onto the motorcycle for dear life as it barrelled down the mountain. Gradually the incline lessened and the rocks, shrubs and scattered trees gave way to dry grass. Pitt feathered the throttle to maintain speed. The harsh wind blew into his face, limiting visibility.

'We still have a tail?' Pitt shouted.

Giordino nodded. Though the pursuers had long since been obscured by dust, he had stolen backward glances every few seconds and had observed the initial contingent of horsemen start their descent down the mountain.

Gritting his teeth, Pitt squeezed the throttle harder, holding tight as the old motorcycle roared into the swirling gloom.

7

Darkness settled quickly over the broad, rolling steppes. High clouds floating above the blowing dust blotted out the moon and stars, pitching the grasslands into an inky black. Only a tiny pinprick of light poked sporadically through the dry ground storm, accompanied by the constant rumble of a two-cylinder, four-stroke motor.

The aged motorcycle and sidecar groaned over every bump and rut but charged steadily across the hills at almost fifty miles per hour. Pitt's hand ached from holding the throttle at full, but he had to coax out every ounce of horsepower. Then the landscape started to change. The rolling hills softened, while the grass thinned. Pitt noted wryly that it had been a while since he had heard Giordino curse from the jolts. Soon the hills disappeared altogether and the turf gave way to hard gravel dotted with scrub brush.

They had entered the northern edge of the Gobi Desert, a vast former inland sea, more stony plain than billowy sand dune, which covers the lower third of Mongolia. The motorcycle picked up speed as its tyres met firmer ground, and they charged across the arid landscape for another hour. At last the engine began to hiccup, then it stuttered and coughed. Pitt coaxed the bike for another mile before the fuel tank ran bone dry and they coasted to a final stop. The winds had settled down, and a sprinkling of stars peeked through the dusty curtain overhead.

Giordino hopped out of the sidecar and stretched while Pitt examined the wound on his leg. An arrow had nicked the front of his shin before embedding itself in a cooling fin on the motor.

'Leg OK?' Giordino asked, noticing the wound.

'A near miss. Almost nailed me to the bike,' Pitt said, pulling a broken arrow shaft from the engine.

Giordino turned and gazed in the direction they had travelled. 'How far behind do you suppose they are?'

'Depends on their pace,' said Pitt. 'I'd guess we have a twenty-mile buffer. They couldn't run the horses faster than a trot for any length of time.'

'Hopefully they got saddlesore and threw in the towel.'

Pitt started walking back along their trail. A few hundred feet behind he found a hardened gravel gully. He returned to the bike, and he and Giordino rolled it back along the same path and pushed it down the gully as far as they could. Then they set about concealing it among a thick clump of tamarisk shrubs, brushing away the original tyre tracks along the way with a thick strand of scrub brush.

The two men cautiously scaled a nearby rocky edifice, stretched out on an indented ledge and slept intermittently. At dawn, after scanning the horizon for signs of their pursuers, they climbed back down to the desert floor.

'We go west,' Pitt said, pointing away from the rising sun. 'We'll have to come back later for Theresa and Jim. Somewhere in that direction is the Trans-Mongolian railway, which runs from Beijing to Ulaanbaatar. If we head west, we'll run into it eventually.'

'Eventually,' Giordino repeated slowly. 'Why does that sound like we don't have a clue how far that could be?'

Pitt shrugged. 'Because we don't,' he said, then started walking west.

THE TEMPERATURE BOUNDED over the 100-degree mark as the sun rose high in the sky, searing the rocky ground. The two men didn't dare shorten their sleeves or trousers, knowing that protection from the ultraviolet rays was more important than a slight improvement in comfort. They reluctantly kept their jackets as well, tying them round their waists for the chilly night ahead. Tearing a section of the lining out, they fashioned silk bandannas on their heads, which made them look like a pair of wayward pirates.

Pitt knew that conserving their strength was critical if they were to survive the desert heat. Every half hour or so, they would seek out a rock formation, and allow their bodies to cool in the shade. This was their second day without food or water. Strangely, their hunger pangs went away, but they were replaced by an unrelenting thirst.

'So at what point can we hope that Rudi calls in the coastguard?' Giordino asked, as they rested on a shaded slab of smooth sandstone.

'I told him to meet us in Ulaanbaatar at the end of the week. I'm afraid our mother hen won't miss us for another three days.'

'By which time we will have walked to Ulaanbaatar.'

Pitt grinned at the notion. Given a supply of water, he had no doubt the tough little Italian could walk to Ulaanbaatar carrying Pitt on his back. But without a source of water—and soon—all bets were off.

'DISAPPEARED? What do you mean they disappeared?' Borjin fumed, a vein protruding from the side of his neck. 'Your men tracked them into the desert!'

Though he physically towered over Borjin, the gruff head of security wilted under his boss's tirade. 'Their tracks simply vanished into the sand, sir,' Batbold said quietly. 'There was no indication that they were picked up by another vehicle. Their prospects for survival in the Gobi are nonexistent.'

Tatiana stood at the bar in the study, mixing a pair of vodka martinis. She asked, 'Were they spies for the Chinese?'

'I don't believe so,' Batbold replied. 'The two men apparently bribed their way onto the Mongolian state security escort. The Chinese delegation seemed not to notice their absence when the motorcade departed. And the men were not Chinese. Dr Gantumur at the laboratory claims that one of them spoke to him in Russian with an American accent.'

Tatiana looked up abruptly. 'What did they look like?' she stammered.

'One was tall and lean with black hair while the other was short and robust with dark curly hair.'

'Those sound like the men from NUMA,' Tatiana gasped. 'Dirk Pitt and Al Giordino. They were the ones who rescued us from the fishing boat on Baikal.'

'How did they track you here?' Borjin asked sternly.

'I don't know. Perhaps through the lease of the *Primoski*,' she replied, handing him a glass. 'They must be hunting for the oil-company employees.'

'You should never have brought them here in the first place,' he hissed.

'And if you hadn't killed the Germans before they had fully assessed the field data, we would not have needed further assistance.'

Borjin glared at his sister, refusing to admit the truth of her words. 'Then these oil people must be eliminated, too,' he said, his eyes raging. 'Have them accelerate the analysis, I wish them gone by the end of the week.'

'Do not worry, my brother. The Americans know nothing of our work. And they will not survive to talk anyway.'

'Perhaps you are right,' he replied, his temper cooling. 'These men of the sea are a long way from the water now.' He raised his glass. 'To their dusty demise,' he said, and sipped the martini.

Tatiana swallowed the rest of her drink, but silently wondered if the death of the Americans would come as predicted.

A COLD BREEZE nipped at their aching bodies as they trudged through the night, and they were forced to climb a series of low rolling hills in plummeting temperatures. As the first strands of daylight began lightening the eastern sky, the dark grey shapes of a nomad encampment became visible against the light-coloured floor of a bowl-shaped valley.

Pitt counted twenty-two *gers*. In the distance, the round Mongolian tents appeared larger than the ones they had seen in Ulaanbaatar and, oddly, there were no lights, lanterns or fires to be seen. The camp was pitch-black. Scattered around it, Pitt and Giordino could make out the dark shadows of animals, some in a fenced corral close to the *gers*, other roaming freely.

The two men were within a hundred yards of the camp when Pitt suddenly froze. Giordino caught Pitt's abrupt halt and followed suit.

'What gives?' he whispered to Pitt, straining to detect a danger.

'Those camels,' Pitt replied quietly. 'They're not moving.'

Giordino peered at a trio of fuzzy brown camels standing a few yards away, not moving a muscle. 'Maybe they're asleep,' he offered.

'No,' Pitt replied. 'There's no odour, either.'

He took a few steps forward, creeping up slowly until he stood alongside the three camels. Giordino looked on in shock as Pitt grabbed one of the animals round the neck and shoved. The camel keeled stiffly over onto its side. Like the rest of the herd, it was made of wood.

Feeling as though they were walking through a back-lot Hollywood film set, they made their way through the immobile herd and headed for the nearest *ger*. The circular felt tent was nearly a hundred feet across and stood over ten feet tall—more than double the standard size.

Pitt found a white-painted entry door, and rapped on the door frame. His knocking echoed with a deep resonance. Pitt placed his hand against the felt wall and pushed. The wall was backed by something solid.

'The big bad wolf couldn't blow this thing down,' he said.

Grabbing an edge of the wall covering, he ripped off a small section. Underneath the felt was a cold metal surface painted white.

'It's a storage tank,' Pitt said, touching the metal side.

'Water?'

'Or oil,' Pitt replied, eyeing the other phoney *gers* dotting the encampment.

Giordino picked up a small rock, and rapped it against the tank. A deep echo reverberated through the tank. 'She's empty,' he said. 'Why would some empty oil tanks in the middle of nowhere be disguised as a fake village?'

'We may not be far from the Chinese border,' Pitt said. 'Maybe someone is concerned about the Chinese stealing their oil?'

The men soon realised that there was no food or water to be found in the phoney village. All the *gers* were the same, masking empty metal tanks. Only at the very last tent did they find that the door actually opened, revealing a pumping station dug twenty feet into the ground. A maze of pipes led to the other storage tanks, fed from a single four-foot-diameter inlet pipe.

'An underground oil pipeline,' Pitt observed. 'May have something to do with the deal that our friends at Avarga Oil are cooking up with the Chinese.'

The two men fell silent again, disappointment damping their spirits. The rising sun was beginning to bake the sand-and-gravel floor. Tired from their all-night trek and weak from lack of food and water, the men bundled a pair of crude mattresses together from felt torn from one of the tanks, then lay down in the shade of the pumping house and slept.

The sun was dropping towards the western horizon when the two men awoke. The sleep had done little to restore their energy levels, and they departed in a lethargic state, willing their bodies forward with each step.

The winds kicked up again, jabbing and swirling in sporadic gusts as a prelude to the force to come. Both men had carried a thin section of felt from the storage tank, and now wrapped their heads and torsos in the fabric.

Pitt targeted a distant S-shaped ridge for a bearing as the sun slid away.

Time seemed to fade for Pitt, and consciousness nearly as well. He drifted along, then felt his eyes pop open, not sure if he had fallen asleep on his feet. How long he had been out, he had no idea, but at least Giordino was still trudging along beside him. After an hour or two, the winds started blowing hard from the northwest. The stars above quickly melted away in the dust, and Pitt's landmark ridge disappeared from view.

They staggered on until Pitt detected Giordino trip and fall down next to him. Pitt stopped and reached out to help his friend up. A burly hand grabbed Pitt's, yanking so hard that Pitt sprawled onto the ground beside Giordino. Lying there dazed, Pitt noticed that the blasting sand was no longer peppering his body. Giordino had apparently tripped over a rock piling, behind which lay an indented cove protected from the howling winds. With his last ounce of energy, Pitt unwrapped his felt cloth and draped it over both their heads for warmth, then lay back and closed his eyes.

Beneath the screeching desert sandstorm, both men fell unconscious.

GIORDINO WAS DREAMING. He dreamed that he was floating in a still pond of warm, tropical water. The water suddenly lapped at his face in a series of small hot waves. He jerked his head, but the warm moisture followed his motion. Then something about the dream became overly vivid. It was an odour, a very unpleasant one at that, and it finally spurred him awake.

He cocked open a heavy eyelid and bright sunshine stung his eyes, but he could squint enough to see a giant pink swab descend on him with a hot wipe across one cheek. Jerking his head away, he saw the pink swab roll behind a picket fence of large yellow teeth housed in a long snout. He stared past the snout into two chocolate-brown eyes shrouded behind long eyelashes.

The camel blinked curiously, then let out a short bellow and stepped back to nibble at a fringe of felt protruding from the sand.

Giordino struggled to sit up, and realised that a drift of sand a foot deep had piled up in the little cove during the night. He nudged the figure next to him, similarly buried under felt and sand. The felt rustled a bit then was thrown back, exposing the haggard, sunburnt face of Pitt. The sunken green eyes sparkled at seeing his friend alive.

'Another day in paradise,' he rasped through chapped lips.

They heaved their bodies upright and Giordino sneaked a hand into his pocket and nodded in reassurance, finding the horseshoe still there.

'We've got company,' he wheezed.

Pitt crawled weakly from under the blanket of sand and peered at the animal standing a few feet away. It was a Bactrian camel, as evidenced by the two humps on its back. 'The ship of the desert,' he said.

'Looks more like a tugboat. Do we eat him or ride him?'

Pitt was contemplating whether they had the strength to do either when a shrill whistle blared from behind a dune, and a small boy riding a dappled tan horse bobbed into view. When he saw the two haggard men, he froze.

'Hello.' Pitt smiled warmly at the boy. He climbed unsteadily to his feet as a pool of sand slid off his clothes. 'Can you help us?'

'You . . . talk English,' the boy stammered. 'I learn English at monastery,' he added proudly.

'We are lost,' Giordino said hoarsely. 'Can you share food or water?'

The boy slipped off his wooden saddle and produced a goatskin canteen filled with water. Pitt and Giordino took turns attacking the water.

'My name is Noyon,' the boy said. 'What is yours?'

'I am Dirk and this is Al. We are very happy to meet you, Noyon.'

'You are fools, Dirk and Al, to be in the Gobi without water or a mount,' he said sternly. His face softened, and he added, 'You come with me to my home, where you will be welcomed by my family. It is a short ride from here.'

The boy slipped off his horse and removed the small wooden saddle, then prodded Pitt and Giordino to climb aboard. Grabbing the reins, he led them north across the desert, the roped camel following behind.

After just a short distance, Noyon led them round a thick sandstone ridge. On the far side, a large herd of camels was foraging for grass on a stony plain. In the centre stood a lone *ger*, shrouded in dirty white canvas. An adjacent rope corral secured several stout brown horses. A rugged, clean-shaven man was saddling one of the horses when the small caravan rode up.

'Father, I found these men lost in the desert,' the boy said in his native tongue. 'They are from America.'

The man took one look at the bedraggled figures and came forward quickly to help them down off the horse. 'Secure the horse,' he barked at his son, then led the two men into his home.

Inside the tent, bright patterned carpets covered the dirt floor, melding with the vibrant floral weavings on its walls. Furniture was painted red, orange and blue, while the ceiling supports were yellow. In the centre of the *ger* was a hearth and cooking stove, attached to a metal stovepipe which rose through an opening in the ceiling. Three low beds were positioned round the walls.

Noyon's father led Pitt and Giordino to some stools near the hearth, where a slight woman with long black hair and cheerful eyes was tending a battered teapot. Seeing their exhausted state, she brought them damp towels to wash their face and hands, then set some strips of mutton to boil in a pot of water. When the meat was cooked, she served up a giant portion to each man, accompanied by a tray of dried cheeses.

After the meal, Noyon entered the *ger*. His father brought over a leather bag filled with home-fermented mare's milk, called *airag*, and filled three cups. He spoke quietly, looking Pitt and Giordino in the eye.

'My father, Tsengel, and my mother, Ariunaa, welcome you to their home,' the boy translated.

'We thank you for your hospitality. You saved our lives,' Pitt said, sampling the *airag* with a toast. It was like warm beer mixed with buttermilk.

'You were lucky my son found you. Tell me, what are you doing in the Gobi without provisions?' Tsengel asked through his son.

'We became separated from our tour group during a brief trip into the desert,' Giordino fibbed. 'We retraced our steps but got lost when the sandstorm struck last night.'

'How far are we from the nearest village?' Pitt asked.

'There is a settlement near the monastery about twenty kilometres from here. But enough questions for now,' Tsengel said. 'You must rest.'

Noyon led the men to two of the small beds, then went outside to tend the herd. Pitt lay back on the cushioned bed and fell into a deep sleep.

He and Giordino woke before dusk to the smell of mutton boiling. Feeling surprisingly refreshed, they went to stretch their legs outside the *ger* as Tsengel and Noyon returned from rounding up strays.

'You are looking fit now,' Tsengel said through his son.

'Feeling fit as well,' Pitt replied.

Back inside the *ger*, another meal of mutton and dried cheese awaited them, accompanied by noodles. The *airag* was poured in larger quantities.

'You have an impressive herd,' Giordino remarked. 'How many head?'

'One hundred and thirty camels and five horses,' Tsengel replied. 'A quarter the size of what we once owned on the other side of the border.'

'In Chinese Inner Mongolia?'

'Yes, the so-called autonomous region.' Anger glinted in Tsengel's eyes. 'It is no place for a simple herder any more. The Chinese keep commandeering the land, and we have been forced to drive our herds to the harshest portions of the desert. At least the herder is still respected here.'

Pitt took another sip of *airag* and said, 'Tsengel, we stumbled upon a strange sight in the desert before the sandstorm struck. It was an artificial village surrounded by wooden camels. Do you know the place?'

Tsengel gave a throaty guffaw. 'Ah, yes, the richest herdsmen in the Gobi. Only his mares don't produce a drop of milk.'

'Who built it?' Giordino asked.

'Many months ago, a large crew of men came with equipment, pipe and a digging machine. They dug tunnels that run for many kilometres. I was paid a small fee to direct their foreman to the nearest well. He told me they worked for an oil company in Ulaanbaatar, but were sworn not to tell anyone of their work. I have seen no one return since. It is just like the others.'

'Which others?' Pitt asked.

'There are three other such camps of metal *gers* located near the border.'

'Are there existing oil wells or oil drilling in the area?' Pitt asked.

Tsengel thought for a moment, then shook his head. 'No, none.'

'Why do you think they disguise the storage tanks and surround them with wooden livestock?'

'Who can say? I believe it is the work of powerful people, who wish to exploit the wealth of the desert in some way. Why do they disguise their efforts? Why else but to disguise their evil hearts.'

The *airag* had nearly finished Tsengel off. He rose uneasily to his feet and bid his guests and family good night. Staggering over to one of the beds, he collapsed onto the covers and was snoring loudly minutes later.

Despite the snoring, Pitt and Giordino slept soundly that night. Noyon had given up his bed and slept on pillows on the floor. At sunup they shared a breakfast of tea and noodles. Then, when Tsengel galloped off to tend his herd, Pitt and Giordino set off with Noyon for the monastery where he went for schooling three days a week. From there they would hop a ride with the supply truck that called regularly from Ulaanbaatar.

Pitt, Giordino and Noyon mounted three of Tsengel's stout horses and loped off towards the north.

'Your father is a good man,' Pitt said as he watched Tsengel's dusty trail disappear over the horizon.

'Yes, but he is sad to be away from the ground of his birth. It is a struggle here. I will help him when I am older. I will attend the university in Ulaan-baatar and become a doctor. Then I will buy him all the camels he desires.'

The horses plodded across a grainy plain, and it wasn't long before Pitt and Giordino found their backsides chafing from the wooden saddles.

'You sure there's not a bus-stop or airport round here?' Giordino groaned.

Noyon thoughtfully considered the question. 'No bus. But airplane, yes. I will take you to it.' He kicked his horse and galloped off towards a ridge to the east before Giordino could say another word.

'That's all we need, an extra side trip,' Pitt said.

'Maybe there's a Learjet on the other side of that ridge,' Giordino mused.

When they caught up with Noyon, he was waiting in the shadow of a rocky spire. As Pitt and Giordino approached, the boy smiled and nodded towards the back of the ridge behind him. A few of the rocks on the sandy incline were oddly shaped and seemed to reflect a faint silvery hue.

Pitt was intrigued. As he rode closer, he saw that they were not rocks but a pair of partially buried radial engines, one of which was attached to the blunt nose of an inverted fuselage. He dismounted and brushed away the sand from one of the buried cowlings, then looked up with amazement.

'It's not a Learjet,' he said to Giordino. 'It's a Fokker trimotor.'

THE FOKKER F.VIIB lay where she had crashed, undisturbed for over seventy years. The inverted plane's right wing and most of her fuselage were buried in the sand. Some distance behind, the port wing and engine lay hidden, crushed against the rocks that had torn them off during the forced landing.

'Must have been done in by a sandstorm,' Giordino speculated.

As Noyon watched from a respectful distance, Pitt and Giordino followed the sand-scrubbed belly of the fuselage aft until they found a slight lip on the side. Brushing away a few inches of sand, they could see it was the lower edge of the fuselage side door. Both men attacked the soft sand, scooping away a large hole in front of the door.

'Correction to the cause of crash,' Pitt said, running a hand across a seam of bullet holes stitched across the fuselage. 'They were shot down.'

'I wonder why?' Giordino mused, reaching for the door handle.

Noyon suddenly let out a slight wail. 'The elders say there are dead men inside. We must not disturb them.'

'We will respect the dead,' Pitt assured him. 'I shall see that they are given a proper burial so that their spirits may rest.'

Giordino gently tugged open the door. A jumbled mass of splintered wood, sand and broken pieces of porcelain tumbled out.

Pitt picked up a broken plate. It was glazed with a sapphire-blue peacock. 'Not your everyday dinnerware. At least five hundred years old, I'd wager.'

He crawled into the fuselage and waited a moment for his eyes to adjust to the dark interior. Shattered porcelain lay strewn across the floor in a carpet of blue-and-white shards. Only a few crates wedged near the tail had survived intact. Rows of wicker seats hung empty from the ceiling of the inverted aircraft. Ducking slightly, Pitt moved towards the intact crates at the tail section. The words ATTENTION: BRITISH MUSEUM had been stencilled along the sides. Pitt prised open the lid of a crate. Inside was a large porcelain bowl wrapped loosely in a cloth. As the debris on the floor seemed to confirm, the plane was carrying a cargo of antique ceramics.

Pitt moved towards the cockpit. Much of the cargo had been thrown forward when the plane crashed, creating a mountain of debris in the front of the cabin. Pitt spotted a dusty leather jacket lying amid some broken shards. He stooped to take a closer look, then froze in his tracks. In the dim light, he could see that the jacket was still occupied by its original owner.

The mummified remains of Leigh Hunt lay where he'd expired, decades earlier, in agonising pain from a broken back. His left arm cradled a yellow wooden box while his bony white right hand clutched a small notebook. A grimace was etched into Hunt's face, preserved by the dry desert air.

'Poor devil. He must have survived the crash, only to die later,' Pitt said in a hushed tone to Giordino, who stood watching at his shoulder.

With an uneasy reverence, he removed the wooden box and notebook from the skeletal grip, and handed the box to Giordino.

'I don't presume the pilots fared any better,' Pitt said, peering through the cutout in the forward bulkhead. The entire cockpit was filled with sand.

'It would take the better part of a day to excavate that,' Giordino said.

'Maybe on our next visit,' Pitt replied, climbing back out of the side door into the bright sunshine, followed by Giordino.

Noyon was pacing back and forth nervously. 'My friends, we must be on our way if I am not to be late for school,' he said.

Pitt slipped the notebook into his shirt pocket and closed the door of the plane while Giordino stuffed the wooden box into a leather saddlebag. They remounted the horses and trotted towards the monastery.

An hour later they crested a blunt ridge, exposing a narrow valley on the other side. At its midpoint was a splash of thick grass dotted with purple shrubs. Pitt noticed a cluster of small stone buildings, sided by a handful of white *gers*. A small herd of camels and goats were corralled nearby.

They threaded their way down to the edge of a compound, and tied up the horses. Three pagoda-shaped buildings stood opposite, their roofs layered in blue ceramic tiles. The central building appeared to be a temple. Stone dragons were mounted on its corner eaves, their long tails curving up the upturned roof. A small group of red-robed monks stood outside.

Noyon pointed to an elderly monk wearing thick glasses. 'That is Lama Santanai,' he said. 'He speaks English and will be glad to help you.' He bowed. 'Goodbye, Dirk. Goodbye, Al.'

'So long my friend,' Pitt replied. 'I hope that we shall meet again.'

'Yes, next time, you ride the camels.' The boy grinned, then hurried away.

Pitt and Giordino made their way across the compound. The lama with the thick glasses turned towards them as they approached. His brown eyes shone with warmth and intelligence.

'Welcome to our monastery,' he said in heavily accented English.

'Please excuse our intrusion,' Pitt said. 'We are anxious to return to Ulaanbaatar. We were hoping to catch a ride on your supply truck.'

The lama smiled. 'It shall be arranged. The truck arrives this afternoon.' He led them to one of the smaller buildings beside the temple. 'Please make yourselves comfortable in our storeroom. Then join us for our midday meal.'

'That is most kind,' Pitt replied.

The lama quietly turned and strode towards the temple, his loose red robe flapping in the breeze.

Pitt and Giordino climbed a short flight of steps and entered the storeroom, a narrow, windowless structure. Foodstuffs and blankets were stacked along the walls. At the back were several canvas cots.

'I think I'll take a nap until our ride shows up,' Giordino said, stretching out on one of the cots.

'I've got some reading to do,' Pitt replied, heading for the door.

Taking a seat on the front steps of the storeroom, he opened the field diary of Dr Leigh Hunt.

'HOW'S THE KISS-AND-TELL saga of our petrified archaeologist?'

Giordino had woken from his nap and joined Pitt on the porch.

'One that you won't believe,' Pitt said with a serious look in his eyes.

Giordino took a seat on the steps. 'What did you find?'

'Dr Hunt, his Mongolian assistant, and a team of labourers were excavating the remains of a vanished city in northern China named Shangdu, known mostly by its more romanticised Western name . . . Xanadu.'

'Did it really exist?'

'Most definitely. It was the summer palace of Kublai Khan. He built the joint about one hundred and twenty miles northwest of Beijing to get out of the summer heat. By the time Hunt came along, it was a pile of rock.'

'So the artefacts on the plane date from Kublai Khan's reign? They must be worth a fortune. That is, the ones not broken in the plane crash.'

'Possibly. Though Hunt himself was disappointed with the haul. Nothing of significance was uncovered until the very last day of the excavation. That's when your wooden box was dug up.'

Pitt had the open wooden box sitting on the porch. Inside was a bronze tube and a tightly rolled cheetah skin. He pulled out the animal skin first.

'Hunt made little mention of the cheetah skin, but look at this,' he said.

He lay out the fur, then flipped it over. On the underside was a series of eight paintings in boxed panels, showing a large Chinese junk sailing down a river, then at sea, then anchoring in a small bay. The final panel showed the ship on fire in the bay. A banner of a blue dog fluttered in flames from the ship's foremast. Flames and smoke consumed the land all around the bay.

'Seems to relay a voyage that ended in a firestorm,' Giordino said. 'There was no interpretation by the British archaeologist?'

'None. I wonder if he even saw the back of the skin before he died. It was the bronze tube he found noteworthy. Or, rather, the silk scroll apparently rolled up inside. Painted on it was a treasure map.'

'Do you suppose the scroll is still with Hunt on the plane?'

Pitt shook his head. 'Apparently, his assistant Tsendyn stole it.'

He handed the notebook to Giordino, and pointed to an entry for August 5, 1937. The entry ended midsentence, then resumed later in a shaky hand. Giordino noted that the dusty page was stained with drops of blood:

We have crashed in the desert, shot down by a Japanese warplane. Both pilots dead. I fear my back and legs are broken. Am unable to move. I pray we will be discovered soon. Pain is unbearable.

The last entry was in a crude scribble:

All hope is gone. My sincere regrets to the British Museum, and my love to my dear wife, Emily. God save our souls.

'Poor bugger,' Giordino said. 'That explains why he was lying atop the debris in the plane. He must have lain there several days before dying.'

'His pain must have been all the worse, knowing what he lost.'

'So what was the treasure on the silk map?'

'Hunt describes the silk scroll in an earlier entry, after its discovery. He was convinced that the map showed the final burial place of Genghis Khan.'

Giordino shook his head. 'Old Genghis has yet to be found. His tomb rates as one of the biggest archaeological mysteries on the planet.'

Pitt gazed at a cloud of dust on the horizon. Then it was his turn to shake his head. 'On the contrary,' he said quietly. 'His tomb has been found.'

Giordino stared at him with a blank look on his face.

'Hunt's assistant from Mongolia, Tsendyn. His last name is Borjin,' Pitt explained. 'And if I'm not mistaken, the tomb of Genghis Khan is sitting in Tolgoi Borjin's back yard.'

THE SUPPLY TRUCK arrived midafternoon, off-loading several crates of vegetables and dry goods into the storeroom. After helping the monks unload the truck, Pitt and Giordino prepared to depart.

The old lama spoke with the truck driver, then came over to where they waited. 'The driver welcomes your company in the cab,' he said. 'He says it will be a five-hour trip to Ulaanbaatar. Travel in wisdom and strength of spirit and you shall find what you seek.'

The lama bowed deeply, and Pitt and Giordino returned the gesture.

'Our sincere thanks for your hospitality,' Pitt said.

The two Americans climbed into the truck. The old Mongolian driver smiled broadly, showing several missing front teeth, then drove slowly out of the compound. The lama stood motionless until they were out of sight.

Pitt and Giordino sat silently as the truck bounced over the desert, both reflecting on the parting words of the lama.

'We have to go back,' Pitt finally muttered.

'To Xanadu?' Giordino asked.

'To Xanadu.'

8

The blue-spotted grouper cast a steely eye at the large figure swimming towards him. It moved too slowly to be a shark, and the neon-blue skin was too dazzling for a dolphin. Deciding it was neither friend nor foe, the grouper headed for another section of the reef to scour for food.

Summer Pitt paid scant attention to the big fish as it darted into the blue murk. Her focus was on a yellow nylon line stretched across the sea floor, which she followed like a marked trail. Her lithe body moved gracefully through the water, just a foot or two above the coral reef. She clasped a digital video camera, which she was using to document the reef as part of a NUMA project assessing the health of coral reefs in the Hawaiian Islands.

Summer kicked lazily along the track line to a sand gully, where a stainless-steel pin had been driven into the sea floor. A plastic card marked in grease pen was attached to the pin. She turned the card towards the camera, filming the designated line and waypoint. As she turned the camera off, something caught her eye. Kicking her yellow fins, she glided over to a small object protruding from the sand. A miniature face seemed to smile up at her. Summer picked it up and held it in front of her mask.

It was a tiny porcelain figurine of a maiden, wearing a flowing red robe, her black hair rolled high in a bun. Her plump cheeks were tinged with red like a cherub while the narrow eyes were unmistakably Asian.

A few yards away, silvery air bubbles caught Summer's attention. Another diver was kneeling on the edge of the reef taking a sediment sample. Summer swam over and held up the porcelain figure.

The bright green eyes of her brother Dirk glistened in curiosity as he studied the object. Lean and tall like the father he shared a name with, Dirk secured the sediment sample in a dive bag, and followed Summer to the gravelly patch where she had spotted the smiling face. The two of them swam in a wide circle round the sandbar, which ended abruptly in a gnarled bed of lava near the shore. A small patch of coral appeared in the middle of the sand field. Dirk noted that the coral stretched in a linear path for ten feet before disappearing under the sand, which appeared darker along a continuing line before meeting the lava wall.

Summer swam towards a small clump of coral, then waved Dirk over. He saw what appeared to be a rectangular stone nearly six feet across. He felt its hard, growth-encrusted edge with a gloved hand, and probed along its surface. Summer filmed a close-up with her video camera. The two divers then completed their circular sweep and kicked to the surface.

Their heads bobbed up in the sapphire-blue waters of a large cove near Keliuli Bay on the southwest shore of Hawaii's Big Island. A few hundred yards away, the surf crashed into a rocky shoreline, which rose steeply to encircle the cove in high cliffs of black lava.

Dirk swam to their small inflatable and bellied himself over the side. He unfastened his tank, then reached over the side and pulled his sister aboard.

'What do you make of that coral outcropping in the middle of the sand-bar?' she asked, barely catching her breath.

'It showed some linearity.'

'I thought so too. I'd like to excavate some of the sand around its fringes and see if there's anything there not devoured by the coral.' She pulled the porcelain figurine from her dive bag and studied it.

'You think you've got a shipwreck in the coral, eh?' Dirk chided, releasing the bowline and starting a small outboard motor.

'This had to come from somewhere,' she said, holding up the figurine.

Dirk gunned the throttle and the small boat leapt over the waves towards a ship moored in the distance. The NUMA research vessel was painted a bright turquoise, and as they approached from the stern, MARIANA EXPLORER could be read on the transom in black letters.

The rubber boat was winched onto the deck, and a muscular man with a thick moustache and steely blue eyes came to greet them.

Dirk held up the porcelain figure. 'Summer thinks she has a treasure wreck on her hands,' he said, grinning.

'Cultural treasure would be just as fine with me,' she added.

'What are the signs?' asked Jack Dahlgren, NUMA's technical director.

'Nothing obvious, but Summer did find an interesting stone object,' Dirk offered. 'We need to go look at the videotape.'

Dirk and Summer showered and dressed, then met Dahlgren in one of the research ship's laboratories. Dahlgren had hooked the video camera to a monitor and was replaying the images over the large screen. When the rectangular stone appeared, Dirk reached over and pressed the PAUSE button.

'I've seen something like that before,' he said, then sat down at an adjacent computer and began typing. 'It was at an underwater archaeology conference, from a paper presented on a wreck discovered in Malaysia.'

Dirk located a website containing a copy of the scientific paper, and scrolled through the photographs of the excavation. He stopped at an image of a rectangular piece of granite with two holes through the centre.

'Clear away the growth and I'd say you have a close match to the object in Summer's video,' Dahlgren asserted, comparing images.

'OK, I'll bite,' Summer said. 'What is it?'

'An anchor,' Dirk replied. 'Or, rather, the stone weight that fitted into a wooden grappling anchor in the days before lead and iron.'

'But what's it from?' Summer persisted. 'What kind of wreck did they excavate in Malaysia?'

Dirk scrolled down to a computerised drawing of a four-masted sailing ship. 'Would you believe, a thirteenth-century Chinese junk?'

OILY SMOKE spewed up by the holocaust a week before still choked the skies over the Persian Gulf. Even 180 miles away from Ras Tannurah, at Kharg Island, Iran's largest oil-export terminal, taking a breath of the thick, polluted air left the greasy taste of petroleum in one's mouth.

Dusk was approaching when a battered black drill ship flying the Indian flag chugged past the tankers lined up along the eastern terminal. Angling north, the drill ship turned and approached the island, mooring close to the bluffs at the tip of the northern coast. None of the oil workers ashore paid much attention to the old ship. But when night fell, she sprang to life, moving slowly back and forth before settling on a desired spot. Fore, aft and side thrusters were activated, gluing the ship to that spot despite wind and current. The crew assembled a short drill string beneath the derrick and lowered it through a moon pool. The end of the drill string didn't hold the usual roller-cone drill bit but a trio of cylinders bound in a tripod.

The tripod was lowered to the bottom, then the crew slowly disappeared and the ship grew quiet. Twenty minutes later, there was a loud but muffled clap on the surface. Fifty feet beneath the ship, a high-powered sound wave was blasted into the Gulf floor. The brief acoustic burst was directed at a marked fault line, and was followed by a second discharge, then a third, bombarding the fault with seismic waves until it fractured.

The rupture reverberated to the surface with a savage shake measuring 7.2 on the Richter scale. Since the Persian Gulf waters were too shallow for a tsunami to form, loss of life was minimal, with major damage limited to just a few Iranian coastal villages near the Gulf's tip. And to Kharg Island.

The tiny oil-pumping island shook as if a nuclear bomb had detonated beneath it. Dozens of oil storage tanks ruptured, spilling their black contents down the hillside and into the sea. The huge fixed oil terminal off the island's eastern shore broke into several free-floating pontoons, while the supertanker terminal on the western side disappeared altogether.

The small black drill ship didn't wait around to survey the damage, but steamed south, having single-handedly devastated Iranian oil exports, jolting the global petroleum market once again.

REPORTS OF THE DESTRUCTION at Kharg Island unleashed a fear-driven free-for-all in the teetering oil futures market, driving the price of sweet crude up to a stratospheric $150 per barrel. On Wall Street, the Dow headed in the opposite direction, with trading curbs halting activity after a massive sell-off erasing twenty per cent of the stock market's value in half a day.

At the White House, the president called an emergency meeting of his top security and economic advisers in the Cabinet Room. The president listened quietly as his chief economic adviser recounted a litany of disastrous consequences resulting from the oil shock.

'Isn't this price hike a knee-jerk reaction?' the president asked. 'After all, we don't import a drop of oil from Iran.'

'There is an element of panic, but the damage to Kharg Island disrupts the global supply of oil, which impacts the price in the US even if our imports remain steady. We are already seeing a shortfall in imports from the destruction at Ras Tannurah. The markets are on edge, especially as there are rumours that terrorists were responsible for the damage to both Gulf facilities.'

'Anything to that?' the president asked his national security adviser.

'None that we've ascertained,' the man replied. 'Evidence points to naturally occurring earthquakes, but I'll task Langley with a further look.'

'And let's make sure surveillance is boosted at our own oil terminals.'

'Consider it done, Mr President,' said the director of homeland security.

'I think a quick means to dampen public fears of an oil shortage, and perhaps boost confidence in the markets, would be to release some stocks from the Strategic Petroleum Reserve.' The suggestion came from Vice President James Sandecker, a retired admiral and former head of NUMA. He was a small man with blazing eyes and a fiery red beard.

'Write up a Presidential Order to that effect,' the president told an aide.

'Might be wise to promote conservation measures publicly, too, while privately twisting some arms,' Sandecker said. 'We can probably entice some of our other foreign suppliers to boost oil production.'

'But that will have almost no impact on the global markets,' the economic adviser warned. 'A major supply fix is what's needed and that will take months for Saudi Arabia and Iran to sort out. We are standing at the precipice of a prolonged economic depression.'

The dire assessment silenced the room. Finally, the president spoke.

'All right, gentlemen, I want to look at all options and every worst-case scenario. With the oil price holding at the current level, exactly how much time do we have before completely losing the economy?' he asked.

'Difficult to say,' the adviser replied nervously. 'Perhaps a month before we see the first major work stoppages and associated layoffs. Once the markets have digested this initial shock, the price pressure may abate. But another shock of any sort and we could have a global calamity on our hands.'

'Another shock,' the president said softly. 'God save us from that.'

THE PATCH OF SAND that had yielded Summer's porcelain figurine now looked like an underwater construction site. A sample test pit dug near the rocky outcropping had grown into a full-blown excavation after Dirk and Summer uncovered a large framing timber two feet under the sand. Additional test pits confirmed that an entire wreck was buried between the two coral reefs.

Beautiful blue-and-white porcelain plates and bowls, along with jade carvings, hinted at a wreck of Chinese origin. Portions of the ship's frame also correlated with the design of a large Chinese junk. To Summer's chagrin, the potential discovery of an early Chinese ship in Hawaiian waters had caused a sensation, and media representatives from around the world had descended on her like vultures. After a slate of interviews, she had been only too happy to slip on a tank and fins and escape underwater. Tossing her fins onto the deck at the end of the day, she was less than ecstatic to hear that she had yet another visitor who wanted to talk to her about the wreck.'

'Not another reporter,' Summer cursed.

She towelled her hair off, then made her way to the wardroom of the *Mariana Explorer*, where Dirk was having coffee with a dark-skinned Asian man wearing slacks and a navy polo shirt.

'Summer, come meet Dr Alfred Tong,' Dirk said, waving her over. 'Dr Tong is a conservator with the National Museum of Malaysia.'

Tong stood up and bowed, then shook Summer's outstretched hand. 'A pleasure to meet you, Miss Pitt,' he said, looking up into her grey eyes.

Summer tried hard not to stare at a prominent scar that ran down his left cheek, instead gazing at his intense brown eyes and jet-black hair.

'Thank goodness,' she said. 'I was expecting another TV reporter.'

Tong smiled and said in choppy English, 'I was attending a seminar at the University of Hawaii when I heard of your discovery. Your captain and brother were kind enough to invite me to visit the site.'

'The logistics were well timed,' Dirk explained. 'The *Explorer* happened to be in Hilo picking up supplies and will be returning later this evening.'

'What is your interest in the wreck?' Summer asked.

'We have a sizable collection of Southeast Asian artefacts in the museum. Though it is not my specific area of expertise, I have some knowledge of Yuan and Ming dynasty pottery, and thought I might offer assistance in identifying the age of the vessel through the artefacts you retrieved.'

'I'm afraid we've uncovered just a limited number of ceramic artefacts,' Summer replied. 'We sent a sample to the University of California for analysis, but I'd be happy to let you examine the remaining items.'

'Perhaps the context of the artefact finds will be useful. Can you share with me the condition and configuration of the wreck?'

Dirk unrolled a large chart, and they took seats at the table to examine it. It was a computer-aided plan of the wreck site. Sections of timber and artefacts were scattered in a horseshoe-shaped area next to the lava bed. Tong expressed surprise at the tiny amount of remains and artefacts documented.

'We've excavated nearly all the wreck's accessible portions,' Dirk said. Unfortunately, we are only seeing about ten per cent of the vessel.'

'The rest is under coral?' Tong asked.

'No, the wreck lies perpendicular to two reefs under a sandbar, with her nose to the shore,' Summer said. She pointed to the diagram, which showed two coral mounds on either side of the excavation field. 'This section of sand may be a natural channel cut through the reef aeons ago.'

'Then why are there not more remains visible?'

Summer pointed to a rocky bed at the closed end of the horseshoe. 'The rest of the wreck is under the lava. If the ship sank and was buried under sand before the lava flow arrived, then it may well be preserved intact.'

'Remarkable,' said Tong. 'And what have you identified of the ship?'

'Just a few thick timbers from the stern section. And the anchor stone, which is consistent with known Chinese design.'

'I am most interested to see what you have recovered,' Tong said.

Summer led them down a flight of stairs to a brightly illuminated laboratory. Racks of plastic bins lined the back bulkhead, all filled with various artefacts recovered from the wreck and now soaking in fresh water.

'Most of the items are fragments of the actual ship,' she explained. 'The cargo holds and living quarters must be under the lava. We did find a few everyday cooking utensils and a large pot'—she pointed to a rack—'but you will probably be most interested in these.' She pulled two trays off one of the racks and set them on a stainless-steel table.

Inside the trays were several plates, a bowl and many fragments of porcelain. Tong slipped on a pair of glasses and began examining the artefacts.

'Yes, very nice,' he muttered. 'The patterns and material are consistent with the product of the kilns at Jingdezhen and Jianyang.' He picked up a large teal-and-white plate with a pie-slice section missing and studied it intently. The image of a peacock strutted across the centre, while smaller images of a cheetah chasing a herd of deer circled the plate's perimeter.

'One of the lab conservators found a similar design in the data base used by Yuan royalty,' Dirk said.

'Yes, it is,' Tong muttered, then put the plate down and backtracked. 'Similar, that is, but surely not made for royalty. A close design used for trade, most likely,' he added. 'But I would agree that it is from the Yuan era.'

Summer smiled broadly and gave a happy wink to Dirk. 'Remarkable to think a ship of that era found its way to Hawaiian waters,' she said.

The door to the lab opened and in walked the *Mariana Explorer*'s captain. A towering, sandy-haired man, Bill Stenseth commanded the respect of the entire ship by his quiet intelligence and good-natured sense of fair play.

'Dahlgren has completed loading the fuel and supplies onto your floating hotel. Whenever you two are set to jump ship, we'll be on our way.'

'We're about finished, Captain. We'll get our things and join Jack.'

'You are still working on the wreck?' Tong asked.

'We have a final section of timber to uncover, which may be part of the rudder post,' Summer explained. 'The *Mariana Explorer* needs to continue a reef survey on the other side of the island, so Dirk, Jack Dahlgren and I will camp out on the barge for a few days to complete the excavation work.'

'I see,' Tong replied. 'Well, thank you for sharing the recovered artefacts with me. When I return to Malaysia, I will see if our museum's records can provide some additional information about the ceramics I have seen today.'

'Thank you for sharing your insights with us,' said Dirk. 'We're excited that you have confirmed our assessment of the ship's age and ancestry.'

Dirk and Summer threw together a few personal belongings and jumped onto the brown metal barge that was moored alongside the research vessel. Dahlgren was removing the ship's mooring lines. With a blast of the horn, Captain Stenseth backed the *Explorer* away and sped off towards Hilo.

'The good doctor seemed mighty interested in the plate our lab boys thought had royal markings, though he wasn't willing to bite,' Dirk said, as he watched the turquoise ship disappear round the jagged coastline.

'Professional jealousy,' Summer said, grinning. 'It's a royal ship, I know it.'

FIVE THOUSAND MILES to the east, Pitt and Giordino tramped into the lobby of the Continental Hotel in Ulaanbaatar looking like a pair of worn saddlebags. Their wrinkled clothes were laden in dust, which permeated their hair, skin and shoes. The hotel manager looked down his nose with disdain as the two stragglers approached the front desk with bleary eyes.

'Any messages for rooms 4024 or 4025?' Pitt asked.

The desk manager raised a brow in recognition, then briefly retreated to a small side room. 'One message and a delivery, sir,' he said, handing Pitt a slip of paper and a small box plastered with overnight-shipping labels.

Pitt took the message and handed the package to Giordino while stepping away from the desk. 'It's from Corsov,' he said quietly. 'He says he was called away to a Foreign Ministry conference in Irkutsk. He'll contact us in a few days when he gets back to town.'

'Very polite of him,' Giordino said sarcastically. He ripped open the package, revealing an old leather book and a heavy jar of vitamins. A small card fell out, which he picked up and handed to Pitt. 'From the wife?'

Pitt nodded, silently reading the handwritten note inside.

Your favourite book, and some extra vitamins to keep you healthy. Please use sparingly. Washington is a bore without you, so hurry home, my love. Loren

'A book and vitamins? Not very romantic of Mrs Pitt,' Giordino chided.

'Ah, but it is my favourite story. Always packs a wallop.' Pitt held up the leather-bound novel, displaying the spine to Giordino.

'Melville's *Moby-Dick*. A tasteful choice,' Giordino said.

Pitt opened the book and flipped through the pages until a cutout section revealed itself. Buried in the centre of the book was a Colt .45 automatic.

'I see she comes with a harpoon, Ahab,' Giordino whispered.

Pitt popped open the vitamin bottle, displaying a dozen .45 calibre rounds.

'Wouldn't a congresswoman get in a bit of trouble for shipping firearms around the world?' Giordino asked.

Pitt smiled, sealing the bottle. 'Only if she got caught.'

THE DOOR OPENED and a guard motioned for Theresa to step into the hallway. For two days she had been locked in the room with no explanation and no contact with anyone, save for when a tray of food was shoved inside. Though she knew nothing of the Chinese delegation's visit, she had heard the motorcade arrive and depart. Of greater mystery was the heavy gunfire that had erupted from the rear of the compound. She strained to peer through the tiny window at the back of her room but could see only swirling dust.

Now, walking out of her door, she was glad to see Wofford standing in the hall, leaning on his cane. He flashed her a warm smile.

'Vacation's over,' he said. 'Guess it's back to work.'

Borjin sat waiting for them in the study. 'Come sit, my friends,' he said, waving them over to the table. 'I hope you enjoyed your time off from work.'

'Sure,' Wofford said. 'Staring at four walls was most relaxing.'

Ignoring the comment, Borjin pointed to a fresh stack of seismic reports. 'Your work here is nearly complete,' he said. 'But there is urgency in the appropriate selection of well sites in this region.' He unfurled a topographic map of a section of the Chinese Gobi Desert near the Mongolian border.

'Aren't these sites located in China?' Wofford asked.

'Yes, they are,' Borjin replied matter-of-factly.

'You know that the potential reserves are rather deep?'

'We have the equipment to drill to the required depths,' Borjin snapped. 'I need two hundred high-producing wells in six months. Locate them.'

Theresa could see from the rising flush of red to Wofford's face that Borjin's arrogance had finally got to him. 'We can do that,' she blurted. Then stalling for time she added, 'It will take us about three or four days.'

'You have until tomorrow. My field manager will meet with you in the afternoon for a detailed briefing on your analysis.'

'Once completed, will we be free to return to Ulaanbaatar?' she asked.

'I will arrange a vehicle to transport you the following morning.'

'Then we better get down to work,' Theresa replied, grabbing the folder and spreading its contents across the table.

Borjin gave an untrusting grimace, then stood up and left the room.

'That was quite a show of cooperation,' Wofford whispered.

'I didn't want you to deck him and get us both killed.'

Wofford smiled sheepishly, realising how close she was to the mark.

Wary of the security camera, Theresa pulled a map out from the bottom of the file and casually flipped it over while scattering some other reports about. On the blank back side, she wrote *Ideas for Escape*, and jotted a few notes underneath. Wofford picked the chart up and studied Theresa's comments. While he was holding it up to his eyes, Theresa noticed that the map on the reverse side depicted Lake Baikal in Siberia.

'My word, look at that,' she said, pointing to the map.

A series of fault lines was marked on the map. Where one of them met the lake's northern shoreline, there was a red circle. A newly constructed oil pipeline was also marked, running just a mile or two north of the lake.

'You don't suppose they did something around the fault that triggered the seiche wave on the lake?' Theresa asked.

'Short of setting off a nuclear device, I don't see how,' Wofford replied.

Theresa found a similar map in the file. It was of the Alaskan coastline, from Anchorage down to British Columbia. Highlighted in yellow was the Trans-Alaska Pipeline, which carried crude oil from the rich Prudhoe Bay fields to the US domestic market. She pointed to a thick fault line marked on the map running just off the coastline. A red circle was drawn round a point on the fault, directly off the port of Valdez, where the pipeline ended.

They stared at the map in silent dread, wondering what Borjin had in store.

HIRAM YAEGER WOLFED down a grilled-chicken sandwich with green tea, then headed back to his lair on the tenth floor of the NUMA headquarters building in Washington, which he seldom left for long. The lanky computer whiz flaunted his nonconformity by wearing his long hair tied in a ponytail and dressing in jeans and cowboy boots. His skill had overshadowed his appearance, as indicated by the computer-resource centre he had built and managed from scratch. Within its data bases was the world's most exhaustive collection of research related to oceanography and underwater studies.

As Yaeger walked into his cavernous computer lab he saw a solid, slightly balding man sitting at the horseshoe-shaped console fronting the lab.

The man smiled. 'I can't believe it. I caught you away from the roost.'

'Unlike my beloved computers, I've still got to eat,' Yaeger replied. 'Good to see you, Phil,' he added, shaking hands. 'How are things in the gravel pit?'

'We're still pounding rocks,' said Dr Philip McCammon, head of NUMA's Department of Marine Geology, which was located in the building's basement. 'But I could use your assistance with some computing resources.'

'How can I help?' Yaeger asked.

'An associate at Langley has asked me to look at some seismic data. The CIA is interested in the two recent quakes in the Persian Gulf. They've arranged for the National Earthquake Information Center to transfer a copy of their global seismic activity record for the last five years.' McCammon handed Yaeger the contact information. 'One of my analysts has written a software program to evaluate the characteristics of the Gulf quakes, and check them against the global seismic data base for any other similar profiles.'

Yaeger nodded. 'Not a problem. I'll have Max pull in the data. Send up your program and we'll have some answers for you in the morning.'

'Thanks, Hiram.'

As McCammon headed towards the elevator, Yaeger turned to a keyboard and began typing in a string of commands. He stopped tapping when he noticed a multipage fax lying in his in-basket. He groaned when he spotted that it originated from the Continental Hotel in Ulaanbaatar.

'When it rains, it pours,' he muttered as he skimmed over the fax. Then he set it down and resumed his keystrokes.

PITT WAS AWAKE and dressed when an early-morning knock sounded on his hotel-room door. Opening it, he was relieved to find a smiling Al Giordino.

'I found this vagrant panhandling in the lobby,' Giordino said, jerking his thumb over his shoulder. 'I thought you might know what to do with him.'

A tired and dishevelled Rudi Gunn peeked behind the Italian's thick frame.

Pitt grinned. 'My long-lost deputy director,' he said. 'We thought you'd found yourself a nice babushka and taken up residence in Siberia.'

Gunn entered the room and fell into a chair. 'I was happy to leave, but I would have stayed had I known that there isn't a paved road in the whole of Mongolia. I feel like I hopped here on a pogo stick.'

'You were able to bring our search gear and dive equipment with you?'

'Yes, I got it all onto a truck that the institute loaned me. But Al tells me this nutcase at Xanadu is still holding the oil-survey team.'

'Roy is dead,' Pitt said. 'We can only presume the others are there.'

The telephone rang. Pitt answered, then activated the speakerphone.

Hiram Yaeger's easygoing voice boomed from the speaker. 'Greetings from Washington, where the local bureaucracy is beginning to suspect you had a hand in the breaking political news coming from your part of the world.'

The three men in the hotel room looked at each other blankly.

'We've been a little preoccupied,' Pitt said. 'What news?'

'China declared this morning that they are acceding Inner Mongolia to the country of Mongolia. China is playing it up as a friendly diplomatic gesture, but there's speculation that the deal involved an oil-trade agreement. Not that anyone thinks Mongolia holds much in the way of oil reserves.'

'That's exactly what it is about. I guess you could say Al and I were indeed a part of the negotiations,' Pitt said, glancing at Giordino. 'Hiram, were you able to track down any of the info that I faxed you?'

'I've dug up what I could. This guy Borjin is an enigma, and Avarga Oil operates in an almost clandestine fashion. There's no record of the company exporting oil from Mongolia. They operate only a handful of active wells.'

'So they're not pumping enough to make a dent in China's demand?'

'There's no evidence of it,' Yaeger said. 'But we uncovered some sizable contracts with a couple of Western oil-field equipment suppliers for specialised drilling and pipeline equipment, all shipped to Mongolia in the last three years. I haven't discovered how this Borjin obtained the resources.'

'Genghis Khan is picking up the tab,' Pitt replied.

'I don't get the joke.'

'It's true,' Giordino said. 'He's parked in the guy's back yard.'

While Giordino told Gunn and Yaeger about the tomb in Borjin's sanctuary and the discovery of Hunt's notebook in the crashed trimotor, Pitt pulled out a fax he had received back from a contact at Sotheby's in London.

'For eight years, the major auction houses have had a steady stream of consignments of major twelfth- and thirteenth-century Asian art and artefacts.'

'Loot buried with Genghis Khan?' Gunn asked.

'To the tune of over a hundred million dollars. The artefacts were consistent with the regions of Genghis Khan's conquests, and were consigned from a shadowy Malaysian firm called the Buryat Trading Company.'

'That's the company that purchased the tunnel borer!' Yaeger exclaimed.

'Small world, eh? Hiram, when we're finished perhaps you could take a closer look. And did you come up with anything for the German documents we found in Borjin's laboratory, near that three-legged tubular device?'

'Well, as you noted, they read like the first pages of a technical operator's manual. Operator's instructions for an acoustic seismic array, in fact.'

'Care to try that again in English?' Giordino asked.

'As you know, in oil exploration, seismic imagery relies on a mechanical explosive, such as dynamite, to send a shock wave into the earth,' Yaeger said. 'The refracted seismic waves are recorded and computer-modelled to create a subsurface image. Now, an eminent electrical engineer from the University of Heidelberg, Dr Friedrich von Wachter, has apparently eliminated the need for explosives by developing an acoustic array that transmits a high-frequency sound burst, which converts to seismic waves under the surface.'

'Our experience with survey sonar systems is that they don't provide adequate penetration to "see" very far beneath the surface,' Giordino stated.

'That's true. Most of the waves are easily refracted near the surface. But von Wachter's concentrated burst of sound waves ensures that a useful percentage can penetrate deeply. From the preliminary data in the manual, and your description of the tripod device, it looks as if the system von Wachter developed uses three rather large arrays to transmit the sound waves.'

'I'll bet that's how they found Genghis,' Pitt remarked. 'His tomb was supposedly buried in a hidden location in the Khentii mountains.'

'And they're obviously using it to hunt for oil,' Gunn added.

'A valuable technology that the oil companies would pay dearly for. Dr von Wachter must be a rich man,' Giordino said.

'I'm afraid he's a dead man. He and his team of engineers were killed in a landslide in Mongolia a year ago.'

'Why does that sound suspicious?' Giordino commented.

'Need I add that they were working for Avarga Oil at the time?'

'More blood on the hands of Borjin,' Pitt said without surprise.

'None of it adds up,' Giordino said. 'A seismic-survey team murdered, another abducted. Disguised storage facilities in the desert. All tied in to a system of underground pipelines. Yet no visible sign of output. Why?'

The room fell silent. Then a knowing look spread across Pitt's face.

'Because,' he said, 'they have been unable to drill where the oil is.'

'Borjin has probably greased enough wallets to drill anywhere he wants to in Mongolia,' Giordino countered.

'But suppose the oil isn't in Mongolia?'

'Of course,' Gunn said, the answer suddenly apparent. 'He's found oil in China, or Inner Mongolia to be precise. How did he convince the Chinese to turn the land over, that's what I'd like to know.'

'They're in a bad way,' Yaeger said. 'Because of the earthquakes in the Persian Gulf and the fire at their main oil-import terminal, China has lost more than half of its oil imports overnight. They're desperate.'

'It would explain the storage facilities by the border. They might already have some secret wells in Inner Mongolia pumping to one of the other sites,' Pitt speculated. 'The Chinese would only see the end product shipped from Mongolia and wouldn't know that the oil originated in their own back yard.'

'It might explain why Borjin abducted the oil-survey team from Baikal,' Giordino said. 'He probably needs their expertise to pinpoint the drill sites.'

'Maybe he'll release them, now that he's got his deal,' Gunn said.

'Not likely,' Pitt replied. 'They already murdered Roy and tried to kill us. No, I'm afraid they are as good as dead once Borjin has the information.'

'Have you contacted the local American embassy yet? We need to get the political forces working to save them,' Gunn said.

'Diplomacy ain't going to work in this case, Rudi,' Giordino said. 'Borjin is too well protected.'

'We've got to do something,' Gunn countered.

'We are,' Pitt said. 'We're going in after them. And you're coming too.'

A sick feeling struck Gunn in the stomach. 'I should have stayed in Siberia,' he muttered.

PHIL MCCAMMON ENTERED the NUMA computer centre just as Yaeger hung up the phone to Mongolia. On the opposite side of the console, the computerised image of a beautiful woman wearing a sheer white blouse and a pleated wool skirt turned towards the marine geologist and smiled.

'Good evening, Dr McCammon,' she said. 'Working late?'

'Uh, good evening, Max,' McCammon replied. He turned to Yaeger, and noted that he was dressed in the clothes he had worn the day before. 'Hello, Hiram. Long day?'

'Very,' Yaeger replied, suppressing a yawn. 'A late request from the boss yesterday kept us busy. We expected to see you hours ago.'

'Some unexpected meetings killed most of my day. Did you get a chance to retrieve the data from the National Earthquake Information Center?'

'Of course. Max can multitask with the best of them.'

A mirage of sorts, Max was in fact a holographic image that Yaeger had created as a user-friendly interface to his computer network. Modelled after Yaeger's wife but with the perpetual figure of a twenty-year-old, Max had become very real to Yaeger and others in the NUMA building who relied upon her artificial intelligence for solving complex problems.

'We ran your program early this morning,' Yaeger continued. 'Max, would you give us a verbal overview of your findings?'

'Certainly,' Max replied. 'I ran your program, which analysed the two recent earthquakes in the Persian Gulf, then filtered their key commonalities against the NEIC data base of global seismic activity for the last five years. Interestingly, both Gulf events were classified as extremely shallow earthquakes, as their epicentres were less than three kilometres beneath the surface. Most shallow-focus earthquakes are in the five- to fifteen-kilometre range.'

'That's a meaningful difference,' McCammon said. 'Anything else?'

'Both were tectonic quakes rather than volcanic in origin, and both measured over 7.0 on the Richter scale. It is a statistically significant anomaly for two quakes of that magnitude to strike in such close proximity.'

'Is there a large fault line in the area where the two earthquakes struck?' Yaeger asked.

'The Persian Gulf lies near the boundary of two tectonic plates, called the Arabian and Eurasian,' McCammon replied. 'Nearly all seismic activity takes place in narrow zones around the plate boundaries. So the two quakes in the Gulf were not extraordinary but for their proximity.'

Yaeger threw one last question. 'Max, when you ran Phil's filter program, did you match any other earthquakes to the same parameters?'

'Why, yes. It would be easier for me to show you graphically, so feast your eyes on the video board.'

A large white screen behind Max was suddenly illuminated with a colour map of the world. McCammon approached the map in curiosity. Two flashing red dots appeared in the Persian Gulf, marking the recent earthquakes. A few seconds later, a flurry of red dots erupted in an area of Northeast Asia, followed by a lone flashing dot slightly north of the others.

'Thirty-four seismic events from the NEIC's data matched the characteristics of the two sample earthquakes. The most recent occurred just over a week ago in Siberia,' Max said, pointing to the lone red dot.

Yaeger's bleary eyes widened in shock. 'And the others?'

'Primarily Mongolia. Fifteen in the mountains east of Ulaanbaatar, and another nineteen straddling the border with China in the south.'

Yaeger shook his head in disbelief, then turned to McCammon. 'Phil,' he said, 'I think you, me and Max are going to need some coffee.'

9

For Summer, boredom was beginning to set in. As she monitored the tension on the air lines snaking over the side of the barge, she found herself looking forward to getting back into the water and working the other end of the line. Standing up and stretching, she gazed seaward and caught sight of a black ship rounding Kahakahakea Point. She frowned as she watched the ship turn and aim its bow at the NUMA barge.

'Please, no more reporters,' she said aloud. But as she studied the ship, she realised that the approaching vessel, which was at least thirty years old and had clearly seen better days, was a drill ship. What was a drill ship doing in Hawaiian waters? There were no oil deposits here to speak of.

Summer watched as the old ship continued churning directly for her. When it closed to within a quarter of a mile, Summer glanced up at the makeshift flagpole over her barge's sleeping shack. A large red diver's flag with the cautionary white slash across the middle fluttered in the breeze.

'I've got divers in the water, you idiot,' she cursed as the ship continued its beeline track. She quickly walked to the shack, where a marine radio was mounted on the wall. Spinning the dial to channel 16, she spat into the microphone, 'Approaching drill ship, this is NUMA research barge. We have divers in the water. I repeat, divers in the water. Please stand off, over.'

There was no reply. With a greater urgency in her voice, she repeated the call. Again, there was no answer.

The drill ship was now only yards away. Summer returned to the rail and yelled at the ship while pointing to the dive flag. The ship started to turn, but, by its angle, Summer could see it was only preparing to pull alongside. She was surprised to see that there was no one on deck.

When its starboard rail hung just above the lower side rails of the barge the drill ship's multiple positioning thrusters were activated. The deserted ship stood perfectly still for a minute, then a half-dozen men, all tough-looking Asians, stormed out of a bulkhead door. As they began leaping onto the barge, Summer sprinted back to the shack and grabbed the radio.

'Mayday, mayday, this is—'

A pair of calloused hands reached into the shack and tore the radio off the wall. The man took a short step and hurled it over the side rail, watching it splash into the water. As he turned back towards Summer with a thin smile, she took a step towards him and let loose with a powerful kick to his groin.

The man fell to one knee in agony, his eyes bulging. Summer stepped back and delivered a kick to the side of the man's head. He crumpled to the deck.

Two of the other boarders charged Summer and grabbed her arms. She struggled, until one of the men pulled out a knife and held it to her throat, while the other man tied her hands and elbows together in front of her.

Gazing helplessly at the opposite end of the barge, Summer felt her stomach tighten. Two of the boarders had carried axes with them and were now using them to cut the mooring lines. A third man stood overseeing the work. His profile looked familiar, but it wasn't until he turned round and exposed the long scar on his left cheek that she recognised him as Dr Tong.

'There are no artefacts here, Tong,' she shouted, figuring he was no doctor but simply an artefact thief.

Ignoring Summer, Tong barked an order to the man she had kicked. The injured man limped to the shack, where the small portable generator was humming. As he had done with the radio, he hoisted the generator up in the air and shoved it over the side, silencing the gas motor. The man then set his sights on the two air compressors, searching for the kill switch.

'No!' Summer protested. 'There are men below on those air lines.'

Tong nodded to his minion. The man gave Summer a twisted smile and punched STOP. He then hobbled over and killed the second compressor.

'I hope your brother is a good swimmer,' Tong hissed.

A well of fury burned within Summer, but she said nothing. The two axemen finished cutting the bow anchor lines and walked back to Tong. The barge was now drifting freely, the current pushing it out to sea. The drill ship's helmsman had to bob and weave to keep from colliding with it.

'You—incapacitate the rubber boat,' Tong barked to one of the men hold-ing an axe. 'Everybody else, back on the ship.'

A small Zodiac was attached to the bow of the barge. With a few quick swings, the axe bearer cut loose the securing lines. He pulled a knife from his belt and stabbed it into the inflated craft in several spots, producing a loud rush of escaping air. Then he sent it over the side rail to the depths.

Summer witnessed little of the sabotage as the thug shoved her roughly to the rail. One of the men on the drill ship knelt down and reached over to help pull her onto the deck. She stretched up her arm but pretended to slip, and flung her right foot back, striking the knife holder in the nose with her heel. Hearing a muffled crunch, she ducked forward and was about to dive for the thin patch of water between the two vessels when a pair of hands grabbed the back of her shirt and she was flung sideways, falling hard on the deck of the barge. The same pair of hands jerked her to her feet.

'You will be going aboard,' Tong spat.

Before she could react, Tong's fist struck her on the side of the jaw. Her knees buckled, but she didn't pass out. She was yanked aboard the drill ship in a stupor and locked in a small storage room at the back of the wheelhouse.

It seemed to Summer that the whole world was spinning. Fighting a wave of nausea, she pulled herself up to a small porthole. Craning her neck, she saw the brown barge drifting out to sea, already a mile away. She fought to make out signs of Dirk and Jack aboard. But they were nowhere to be seen.

DIRK'S ARMS felt like spaghetti. The airlift had to be constantly wrestled into place against the push of the surrounding waters, the work made more stren-uous by the building currents of an outgoing tide. He glanced at his dive watch. Only fifteen minutes to go till the end of the shift. Progress was slow, but he had uncovered a rough timber the size and shape of a ship's rudder.

Following the ascent of his air bubbles as they rose to the surface, Dirk gazed again at the underside of the large black ship moored next to the barge. Another well-financed video-documentary team, he surmised.

He shook off the annoyance and refocused on driving the airlift into the fine sand. Pushing the lip towards a small mound, he noticed that no sand was being sucked up, then realised that the vibration and whooshing noise of the compressed air had ceased.

A few yards away, Dahlgren was driving his probe into the sand. Out of the corner of his eye, Dirk noticed him suddenly rise off the bottom. He looked over and saw that Dahlgren had let go of the probe and had his hands wrapped round his faceplate and air line. He was being yanked off the bottom like a puppet on a string.

Dirk had no time to react, for an instant later the airlift was ripped from his own hands, and he, too, was being jerked up off the sea floor.

'What the—?' The words fell away as he tried to draw a breath of air. The compressor supplying the air lines had been cut off, too. Like Dahlgren, he found himself grabbing hold of the air line to control his movements and not rip the connection from his dive helmet. But Dirk didn't panic. He knew he had to remain calm and think logically.

While working on surface-supplied air, all divers carried a small emergency bottle, or 'pony tank', which provided about ten minutes extra. Dirk reached under his left arm, and twisted the valve on the top of the tank. Immediately he drew in a breath of air through the regulator. After a couple of deep draws, he could feel his heart begin to slow its racing beat.

He looked across at Dahlgren, thirty feet away, and saw from the bubbles rising from his helmet that he was breathing emergency air as well. The airlift was gyrating in the water close behind him. The airlift pipe was being dragged by its outlet hose secured to the barge. The flexible hose would stretch under the drag of the water-filled tube, then spring back, whipping the tube through the water. Dirk waved, but Dahlgren was too busy pulling himself up the air line to see. A second later the tube burst forward, launching straight at Dahlgren. To Dirk's horror, the heavy tube struck the back of the Texan's head just beneath his dive helmet. Dahlgren's body went limp.

Dirk felt his heart race faster again. He noticed that the sea floor had dropped away beneath them and that they were being dragged out to sea. Why in blazes was the barge drifting, and where was Summer?

With a frantic determination, Dirk began reeling himself up the air line to close in on Dahlgren. He was within ten feet of him when the dancing airlift came rushing towards him, swinging past just out of arm's reach. The big tube swung towards Dahlgren, flexed a moment, then reversed direction. This time, Dirk caught hold of it as it swung by. He wrapped his legs round the violently jerking tube and shimmied up to the top, then pulled out his dive knife and began sawing through the thick rubber outlet hose. The heavy plastic tube snapped away with the last cut and sank to the depths.

Dirk turned his attention back to Dahlgren, who was being towed through the water by the line from his neck. His arms stinging, Dirk pulled himself up his own air line again until he was level with Dahlgren. He coiled the line round his waist, then swam over to his friend. Grabbing Dahlgren's buoyancy compensator, Dirk pulled himself up and peered into his face mask.

Dahlgren was unconscious, a small stream of bubbles floating out of his regulator. Clasping him with one hand, Dirk reached down, unbuckled both their weight belts, then reached up to his own buoyancy compensator and hit the button on the inflation hose. What little air was left in his pony bottle surged into his vest. It was enough to propel them to the top.

As soon as they broke the surface, Dirk twisted off his dive helmet and took great gulps of air. Then he grasped the manual inflation tube to Dahlgren's buoyancy compensator, opened the thumb valve and exhaled into it. In a few cycles, he had Dahlgren's vest fully inflated.

With his buddy mostly afloat, Dirk let go of him to grab his own air line again, pulling himself hand over hand towards the moving barge, his progress painfully slow. There was no sign of Summer or anyone else on the open deck. Something must have happened when the black ship came alongside. A renewed sense of urgency, mixed with anger, surged through his body, and he hauled himself up the last few feet of line to the barge.

Dirk yanked himself through the railing, then collapsed onto the deck. After a few seconds, he ripped off his dive gear. He shouted Summer's name, but was met with silence. He stood up, grabbed Dahlgren's air line and began reeling him in. The Texan had regained consciousness, and kicked his legs feebly. With his arms fatigued nearly to breaking point, Dirk pulled Dahlgren alongside the barge, then reached into the water and hoisted him aboard.

Dahlgren rolled onto the deck and clumsily pulled off his dive helmet. 'What in blazes happened down there?' he asked in a slurred voice.

'Before or after the airlift used your skull for batting practice?'

'So that was the sucker that hit me.'

'Lucky thing you hit your pony tank before the lights went out.'

'Thanks for not throwing me back,' Dahlgren smiled, his senses returning. 'So where's Summer? And why are we twenty miles from shore?'

'I don't know,' Dirk said solemnly. 'But I assume she's on board the ship we saw roll in.' He stared back towards the island. He could no longer see the cove but he knew the black ship was still there.

As Dahlgren rested, Dirk searched the barge. When he returned, Dahlgren could tell from his face that the news was not good.

'Radio is gone. Zodiac is gone. Generator is missing.'

'And we're drifting to China.'

Dirk nodded. He knew that once the *Mariana Explorer* returned to find the barge missing, a search-and-rescue operation would ensue. They had enough food and water for a week. But how much time did Summer have?

'We have to get back to land,' he said.

Dahlgren rapped a knuckle against the side of the shack. 'We could build a raft out of this,' he said. 'We've got some tools and plenty of rope.'

Dirk considered the idea without enthusiasm. 'It would take us a day to build, and we'd have a pretty tough job running it against the wind.' He felt sick with dread, wondering what kind of people had abducted her. Pacing the deck, he caught sight of Summer's surfboard atop the shack and felt an added pang of helplessness.

Then the light went on. It was right there in front of him.

A knowing beam crossed his face as he turned to Dahlgren. 'Not a raft, Jack,' he said with a confident smile. 'A catamaran.'

THE LAST PLACE in the world Rudi Gunn wanted to be was in a Russian-built truck bouncing over a rough dirt road. But that's where he found himself.

'The suspension on this thing must have been designed by the Marquis de Sade,' he complained as they rolled over a harsh bump.

Giordino grinned from behind the wheel. 'Relax,' he said. 'This is the smooth section of the highway.'

They had bounced on dirt tracks through the high steppes since midday, relying on Pitt and Giordino's collective memory to find their way to Borjin's compound. Familiar landmarks confirmed they were on the right route as they approached the small mountain range that housed the estate.

'Another hour, Rudi,' Pitt said, 'and your troubles will be over.'

Gunn had the distinct feeling that his troubles were just beginning. The follow-up phone call from Hiram Yaeger had added a new sense of urgency and gravity to their mission. Yaeger had told them about an odd series of earthquakes that had been occurring in northern Mongolia, all with epicentres relatively near the surface, just like the two quakes in the Persian Gulf, as well as the one at Lake Baikal that had created the seiche wave and ruptured an oil pipeline at the northern end of the lake. It seemed likely that the late Dr von Wachter's acoustic seismic array, a ten-foot hanging tripod like the one in Borjin's laboratory, had been used to trigger all the quakes.

Yaeger had spoken to NUMA's former boss, Vice President Sandecker, who still maintained a close relationship with the marine agency, and he promised to have the president convene a National Security Council special session if Pitt could prove that the quakes were linked to Borjin. Pitt had set off for Xanadu with Giordino and Gunn, hoping that with a little stealth, and a large dose of luck, they just might be able to free Theresa and Wofford at the same time as obtaining incriminating evidence against Borjin.

The dust-caked truck crested a small hill, then Giordino applied the brakes as they approached a side road. The smoothly grated lane, fronted by a small gate, signalled the entrance to Borjin's retreat.

'The happy trail to Xanadu,' Giordino announced.

Dusk was drawing near as he turned onto the side trail as it wound into the heart of the mountain range. After cresting a steep summit, Giordino slowed the truck, and all eyes kept a sharp lookout for wandering security patrols. When Pitt spotted the large pipe that fed the surging river water into the aqueduct, they knew they were within half a mile of the compound. Giordino pulled the truck into a strand of pine trees, then shut off the motor.

'What now?' Gunn asked nervously.

Pitt pulled out a Thermos flask. 'Relax and wait until dark,' he replied, pouring a round of coffees, 'when it's time for the bogeymen to come out.'

THE GREY AND WHITE herring gull flapped off the water with a loud squawk, angry at nearly being run over. The bird had never seen a sailing craft quite like it before. Nor had many people, for that matter.

Dirk's crackpot idea had been to construct a catamaran from his and Summer's surfboards, and the two men turned it into a workable design. The buoyant Fibreglass boards made for a perfect pair of pontoons. Dahlgren came up with the idea of using their sleeping cots as cross-members. Stripped of their fabric covering, two of the aluminium frames were laid crossways and secured to the boards with looped ropes, then sealed with duct tape. They took the third cot frame and rigged it into a mast supported by several guy lines. With the fabric from the three cots, they fashioned a sail, and within two hours they had created a bastardised version of a sailing cat.

'I wouldn't take her on the Sydney-to-Hobart yacht race, but I do believe she'll get us back to the Big Island,' Dirk said proudly.

The two men slipped back into their wet suits and attached a satchel of food and water to the mast, then launched the craft over the side. Cautiously climbing aboard, they checked its stability, then Dahlgren let loose a towline to the barge, which quickly floated away. When Dirk pulled the makeshift sail taut, the tiny little craft nearly jumped ahead through the waves under the force of its rectangular blue sail.

The little cat skimmed quickly along and held steady with the aid of a paddle that Dirk had rigged to the stern member as a rudder.

'You might want to rethink that Sydney-to-Hobart race, ol' buddy. She sails like a dream,' Dahlgren chided.

'True enough. Though I might want to pack a dry suit for that run.'

As they settled in for the ride, Dirk's thoughts returned to Summer. Just hang on, he silently willed her. Help is on the way.

TRAPPED IN THE TINY storeroom, Summer languished as time crawled. Having scoured the room unsuccessfully for anything that might aid an escape, there was little to do but sit and wonder about the fate of Dirk and Jack.

Around sundown, the storeroom door burst open and she was greeted by a bullnecked thug with crooked teeth. At his prodding, she followed him onto the bridge and over to a chart table, where Tong was examining a diagram. He looked up and gave her a condescending sneer.

'Miss Pitt. My divers have confirmed that your excavation was most thorough. And you did not lie. Most of the ship lies under the lava.'

He waited for a response, but Summer just gave him a cold stare, then raised her hands, still tied together at the wrist.

'Ah, yes. Very well, I suppose there is no place for you to run now.'

He nodded at Bull Neck. The underling pulled out a knife and quickly sliced through the ropes. Tong motioned for her to take a seat next to him.

'Yes,' Summer said. 'As we told you aboard the *Mariana Explorer*, which is due back any minute, we removed all accessible artefacts.'

Tong smiled at Summer, then leaned over and put his hand on her knee. 'My dear, we passed the *Mariana Explorer* outside Hilo. She should be near her destination of Leleiwi Point by now, on the opposite side of the island.'

Summer stared at Tong. 'Why is this wreck so important to you?'

'You really have no idea, do you?' he replied incredulously. Then he removed his hand from her knee and, nodding to the guard, strode to the bridge wing and disappeared down a flight of stairs.

A MILE AWAY, the low-riding catamaran skirted into the cove under a night sky. Dirk and Dahlgren resumed their prone positions on the surfboards and paddled along the high, rocky shoreline. The drill ship was within sight. Spotting a shallow ledge just above the water level, they grounded the boat beneath a near-vertical wall of lava.

The two men dismantled the mast and sail to improve their stealth profile, then sat and rested. They watched a dozen men scurrying about the derrick on the brightly illuminated stern deck, then lowering a tall tripod device into the water.

'Do you think they're actually trying to drill through the lava to get to the wreck?' Dahlgren asked.

'Can't imagine what they would expect to recover that way.'

The two men downed their supply of food and water and stretched their tired limbs. Slightly refortified, they were contemplating a plan of attack when a low-pitched rumble sounded from beneath the ship.

'What the Sam Hill was that?' Dahlgren drawled.

'Underwater explosion?' Dirk muttered. He looked at the water, anticipating a burst of spray and bubbles, but nothing appeared. 'Odd,' he said.

'How's about we take a closer look?' Dahlgren suggested.

They had started to drag the catamaran back into the water when a second muffled boom erupted. Like the first, it made no impact on the waters in the middle of the cove. Then a new, more thunderous noise began rumbling beneath their feet. The ground began shaking violently, and small chunks of debris began raining down from the steep cliff face above them.

'Watch out!' Dirk shouted, as a boulder broke free and slid towards them.

The two men barely dived out of the way as the rock rolled past them and splashed into the water.

The ground vibrated for several more seconds before fading away. A few frothy waves slapped violently against the cliff, then the waters fell calm.

Dahlgren stared at the drill ship. 'They created that earthquake,' he said matter-of-factly. 'They're trying to rip up the lava field to get to the wreck.'

'They can have it,' Dirk said, eyeing the lava wall warily. 'Let's find Summer and get out of here before they bring the island down on our heads.'

SUMMER WAS STILL SITTING at the wheelhouse chart table, under Bull Neck's malevolent gaze, when the first acoustic blast was triggered. Like Dirk, she assumed that it was some sort of explosion. The criminals must be trying to blast the lava off the wreck, she figured. They must believe there is something of great value in her holds. As Summer recalled Tong's interest in the porcelain plate, a second blast reverberated through the bridge.

She had to get off the ship. Once in the water, she could swim to shore, then hide in the rocks until the *Mariana Explorer* returned. Being on the bridge with just the helmsman and her brutish escort might be her best chance. The helmsman was little more than a boy, with a subservient look about him. Bull Neck, however, was clearly no stranger to violence.

Telling herself it was now or never, she rose slowly from the table and casually strode towards the front of the bridge as if stretching her legs and admiring the black view out of the window. Bull Neck immediately followed, stopping a few feet behind her. Summer lingered a moment, taking a deep breath, then turned towards the portside bridge wing. With a long stride, she paced towards the open door. The guard grunted at her to stop but she ignored him and nearly made it out of the door. The surprised thug jostled to catch up, placing a grimy hand on Summer's shoulder to stop her.

Anticipating his lunge, she reached up and grabbed the man's wrist with both her hands. Spinning to the side, she shoved his wrist up and jammed his open palm back towards the ground. Then she backed into the man a step and dropped to one knee. The thug hopped to the side, but Summer had him in a painful wristlock and could snap the bone with a flick of her hands. He tried to strike her with his free arm, but he lacked leverage. She rose to her feet and drove the man back with another twist to his hand. Gasping in agony, he flailed at Summer uselessly with his left arm. When the pain was too much, he staggered back, crashing into the forward console near the helm. As long as she maintained her grip, the burly thug was helpless.

A red light flashed on the console as something shuddered in the bowels of the ship. In his collision with the helm, Bull Neck had fallen against a button that deactivated the automatic ship thrusters. The shocked young helmsman backed away from the helm, chattering excitedly in Mongolian.

The ship's controls were all inscribed in Mandarin, but beneath the factory markings somebody had taped English translations. Summer glanced at the light and read the legend below: MANUAL THRUSTER CONTROL.

An idea chimed in her head. 'Slight change of plans,' she muttered to the uncomprehending helmsman. 'We're going for a little ride.'

Scanning the controls, she spotted a pair of dials marked PORT THRUSTER FORE and PORT THRUSTER AFT. Summer reached with her free hand and turned the dials to zero. Almost simultaneously, a third burst erupted beneath them as the acoustic array was triggered again, masking the sound of the changing thrusters. With luck, the crew might not notice that the ship was now moving laterally across the cove. In a few minutes it would collide with the lava cliffs. The ensuing confusion would give her ample opportunity to escape.

'Back off,' she barked at the helmsman, who had crept closer.

The young man jumped back from the helm, eyeing with fright the twisted look of agony on Bull Neck's face.

If she could just hold on a little longer, Summer thought, as her grip on the thug's hand grew weary. Nervously she waited for the impact of the ship's hull against lava. But a different sound issued from the doorway.

'What is this, now?' the voice grumbled.

Turning with dread, she saw that it was Tong. And in his hand, he held an automatic pistol aimed at her heart.

THEY HAD KICKED and paddled the mastless catamaran to within a hundred yards of the drill ship. As they scanned the decks for lookouts, Dahlgren suddenly leaned towards Dirk and whispered, 'Take a look at the bridge. Quick.'

Dirk glanced up at the ship's superstructure. Through the open side-wing door, he caught a glance of a tall person with flowing red hair.

'Summer.' A wave of relief fell over Dirk at seeing his sister still alive. 'Let's get aboard and find out what's going on.'

It was a task easier said than done. The ship's lowest deck was still ten feet above them. Hoping there might be a steel ladder on the stern, they were quietly paddling aft when the third detonation erupted below them. They had moved a few more feet down the ship's side when Dirk realised that the nearby side thrusters had fallen silent. Before he knew what was happening, the ship's side hull smacked into the catamaran with a bang, then jerked the craft up on a building wave of water. Sitting atop the side thrown high, Dirk could see that the catamaran was going to flip.

'Get off the board,' Dirk yelled at Dahlgren.

He was preparing to roll off the side himself when he caught sight of an unused mooring line looped over the side of the ship. With a desperate lunge, Dirk sprang up and off the twisting catamaran, barely grasping the rope with his left hand. Pulling his body round, he grabbed on with both hands, the line dropping taut under his weight to within a yard of the water.

He looked back to see the catamaran sucked under the advancing ship, and Dahlgren swimming like a madman in the cresting waves.

'Over here. I've got a line,' Dirk implored in a low voice.

Dahlgren fought his way frantically towards Dirk in the swirling water. When he finally got close, Dirk reached out, grabbed a handful of his wet suit and yanked with all his strength. He pulled him far enough out of the water that Dahlgren was able to hook an arm over the looped line. He hung for a minute, catching his breath, then he and Dirk proceeded to climb opposite sides of the loop, emerging undetected onto the deck a few yards apart. There was clearly something amiss in the wheelhouse, as the ship was on a collision course with the high wall of lava and nobody seemed to be aware of it.

'Let's move,' Dirk whispered. 'I have a feeling we've not got long.'

As they started to move forward, another deep rumble began to sound in the distance. This time, the noise came from the shore.

FIVE THOUSAND MILES away, the elevator doors opened on the tenth floor of the NUMA headquarters building and a sleepy-eyed Hiram Yaeger eased towards his computer room toting a Thermos of coffee. His eyes widened at the sight of Dr McCammon seated at the console, looking anxious.

'You got the jump on me again, Phil?' Yaeger asked.

'Sorry for the early intrusion. Something just came over the wire from the National Earthquake Information Center that looks important.'

He spread a seismogram across the table as Yaeger slid into a chair.

'A large quake struck the Big Island of Hawaii just moments ago,' said McCammon. 'A little over 7.0 magnitude. I just fed the data to Max. Hope you don't mind me taxing her talents while you were away,' he added.

Max was standing near a computer bank, looking deep in thought. She turned and smiled. 'Dr McCammon, I am delighted to assist you. It is a pleasure to work with a gentleman.' She tilted her nose in Yaeger's direction.

'Good morning to you, too, Max,' Yaeger said. 'Have you completed the analysis for Dr McCammon?'

'Yes,' Max nodded. 'The two foreshocks recorded before the quake appear to have originated near the surface, and show near identical signal characteristics to those preceding the quakes at Ras Tannurah and Kharg Island.'

Yaeger and McCammon looked at each other.

'I think it's time we contacted the White House,' Yaeger said.

SUMMER KEPT HER GRIP round Bull Neck's wrist, despite staring down the barrel of a Glock automatic pistol. Tong stood still in the doorway, assessing the situation. The helmsman stood on the other side of the bridge.

'The port thrusters are disabled,' he shouted at Tong. 'We will strike the rocks.' He pointed towards the lava cliffs materialising off the port beam.

As Tong looked out over the bridge wing, a pair of thick arms, clad in black neoprene rubber, reached out of the darkness and grabbed him round the torso. The Mongolian instinctively squeezed the trigger on his pistol, but the shot fired harmlessly through the bridge roof. Tong then turned to fight off his attacker by whipping the gun round as a club. But his assailant had already taken a step forward, pitching Tong off-balance. With a gyrating lift, the man swept Tong completely off his feet. He heaved him up and over the side railing, then let go. The stunned Mongolian let out a shriek as he fell, his scream ending with a loud splash as he struck the water.

On the bridge wing, Dahlgren turned to Summer and gave her a quick wink and a grin. An instant later, Dirk rushed onto the bridge.

'You're all right,' Summer gasped at the sight of the two men.

Dirk smiled. 'Alive but soggy.'

The reunion was cut short by a jarring crash that knocked everyone to the deck. The drill ship had smashed broadside into the lava cliff, and with a grinding screech the sharp volcanic rock sliced through the ship's hull. Sea water flooded in, quickly tilting the ship to a port list.

The young helmsman ran towards the starboard wing. Summer finally let go of Bull Neck's wrist, but the thug was in no mood to fight and fled through the port wing door. Outside, men's shouts competed with the rumbling.

'I had a feeling you had a hand in piloting the ship,' Dirk said with a grin.

'Desperate measures,' Summer replied.

'Company on the way,' Dahlgren said, peering off the bridge wing. Two flights down, a band of armed men was rushing towards the bridge.

'Can you handle a swim?' Dirk asked, heading for the starboard wing.

'A dip was actually on my agenda before you arrived,' Summer replied.

The threesome scrambled down to the lower deck. On the bow, several crewmen were preparing to lower a lifeboat, but Summer wasted no time in further encounters and climbed over the starboard rail, sliding down the ship's angled flank and into the water. Dirk and Dahlgren followed her in, and they quickly swam away from the ship.

The rumbling from the shoreline intensified until yet another, stronger earthquake rocked the ground, rattling the unstable sections of the lava cliff face. All along the cove, chunks of lava were jarred free, and a large spire of volcanic rock dropped onto the drill ship, slicing through the rear of the bridge and collapsing the deck. The base of the rock smashed into the port beam amidships. Panicked crewmen dived into the water as the lone lifeboat finally broke free of the bow.

A hundred yards away, Dirk, Summer and Dahlgren trod water while watching the old vessel tilt lower into the water. A few moments later, she rolled to her side, sliding off the rocks and disappearing under the waves.

'What did they hope to extract from the wreck?' Dirk asked.

'I was never able to find out,' Summer replied. 'But they were going to the extreme of ripping open the lava field to get to it.'

'While generating an earthquake in the process,' Dahlgren added.

The drone of an engine approached from up the coast, and a plane soon banked over the cove. It was a coastguard HC-130 Hercules turboprop, with its landing lights glaring brightly across the ocean's surface.

'That's a sight for sore eyes,' Summer said.

'I bet a cutter and some choppers are already on the way too,' Dirk said.

'Heck, we don't need a darn cutter to pick us up,' Dahlgren said, and chuckled. 'We've got our own rescue vehicle.'

He swam off towards a nearby object floating in the water, then returned a minute later. Behind him, he towed the mangled but still intact catamaran.

'The cat. It lives,' Dirk said in astonishment.

'My surfboard.' Summer declared with a frown. 'What's it doing here?'

'Sis,' Dirk said with a shrug, 'it's a long story.'

10

The hands of the clock had stopped. Or so it seemed to Theresa, as she glanced constantly at the ornate timepiece on the wall of Borjin's study. The pending attempt at escape was making her nervous.

Unbeknown to their captors, Theresa and Wofford had actually completed the drilling analysis hours before. They feigned continued work in the hope that their evening escort would be just one guard.

At nine o'clock, Tatiana entered the study, dressed in black slacks and a matching sweater. 'You have completed the analysis?' she asked bluntly.

'No,' Wofford replied, yawning. 'These additional profiles have impacted on our earlier assumptions. We need another three or four hours to make further adjustments in order to optimise the drilling prospects.'

Tatiana glanced at the clock. 'You may resume in the morning. I will expect you to complete the assessment and brief my brother at noon.'

'Then we will be driven to Ulaanbaatar?' Theresa asked.

'Of course,' Tatiana replied with a thin smile that bled insincerity.

Turning her back, she spoke briefly to the guard at the door, then vanished down the hallway towards her private quarters in the south wing.

Theresa and Wofford made a slow show of tidying up the work table, stalling for time as best they could. Then Wofford grabbed his cane and hobbled out of the door with Theresa, the guard following on their heels.

They walked down the empty corridor and through the foyer. When they were close to their rooms along the north hall, Wofford made his move.

By all appearances, it was simply a careless act. He poked his cane forward and a little out of line, tapping the ground in front of Theresa's right foot. She tripped on the cane and fell forward. Wofford staggered, then knelt down on his good leg. He looked over at Theresa, who was sprawled on the floor.

As Wofford had predicted, the guard proved himself more gentleman than barbarian, and reached down with both hands to help Theresa up. Wofford sprang like a cat, driving off his good leg, and swung his cane by the stock, catching the guard under the chin and popping his head back. The guard's eyes glazed over and he tumbled back to the ground.

Theresa and Wofford remained motionless, nervously waiting for a charge of guards down the corridor. But all remained quiet.

'You all right?' Wofford whispered, helping Theresa to her feet.

'I'm fine. Is he dead?' she asked, pointing at the guard.

'No, he's just resting.'

Wofford pulled out a drapery cord he had purloined from his room and bound the guard's hands and feet. With Theresa's help, he dragged the man along the polished floor and into the first of their rooms. He gagged the guard's mouth with a pillowcase, then closed the door and locked him inside.

'Are you ready to earn your pyromania stripes?' he asked Theresa.

She nodded nervously, and together they crept to the main foyer.

'Good luck,' he whispered, then slipped behind a side column to wait.

Theresa had insisted that she return to the study alone, having convinced Wofford that his lameness placed them both in jeopardy. Hugging one wall, she scurried down the main corridor. Then she ducked through the open door of the darkened study and felt her way across the familiar room.

When she reached the rear bookcase, she grabbed a stack of books at random, then knelt down and began tearing out pages. She crumpled the sheets into a small mound of kindling, and built a pyramid-shaped stack of books around it. Satisfied with her handiwork, she walked across the study to the table that held Borjin's cigar humidor and crystal decanter filled with cognac. She opened the humidor, feeling around inside until she found the box of matches that Wofford had discovered earlier. Then she grabbed the decanter and began pouring its contents around the room, dumping the last drops onto her paper pyramid. Finally she lit a match, and tossed it onto the cognac-soaked papers.

'Burn,' Theresa urged aloud. 'Burn this bloody prison down.'

MOVING IN SILENCE, the three black-rubber-skinned figures inched their way through the pine forest and up to the side of the aqueduct. A few yards away, the raging waters of the mountain river echoed across the hillside, but the clear water in the aqueduct swirled past at an easy current. It was no more than six feet deep, and they could probably have got by with snorkels, but they chose to use rebreathers in case they needed to stay under a bit longer. With a rebreather system, divers can breathe a contained supply of air recirculated with carbon-dioxide scrubbers without expelling visible bubbles.

'You gentlemen ready for a midnight swim?' Pitt asked.

'I'm ready for a warm bath and a glass of bourbon,' Gunn said.

Taking a final look around, Pitt pulled on his fins and mask and gently rolled into the aqueduct. Gunn splashed in a few seconds behind, then Giordino slipped in to follow from the tail position.

The gravity-induced water flow in the concrete channel was faster than he expected, so he shifted his feet forward and lay on his back. By lazily kicking his fins against the downward flow, he slowed to a walking pace. The aqueduct followed the winding course of the road, until the trees fell away and the channel straightened. A dim light shone ahead in the moonless night, and Pitt could just make out the top of the compound wall.

There were actually two lights, one mounted on the wall and another glowing from the interior of the guard hut, where a pair of duty guards sat chatting in front of a large video-monitor board. Live video feeds ran from a dozen cameras mounted around the perimeter. The grainy green nightvision images rarely captured more than the occasional wolf or gazelle.

Pitt purged a shot of air from his dry suit, sinking his body a few inches below the surface. As he glided closer to the compound wall, he flattened his feet and bent his knees to brace for a possible impact. He wasn't disappointed. As he whizzed past the lights on his right, his finned feet collided with a metal grate. He quickly kicked to one side, dropped to his knees and looked upstream. A black object loomed in front of him, and Pitt reached out and grabbed Gunn a second before he collided with the grate. Giordino stopped himself with his feet as Pitt had.

Feeling the way with his hands, Giordino grabbed the centre bar of the grate and pulled himself to the bottom. Attacking it with his hacksaw, he sliced through the rusted base of the bar in only a few dozen strokes. He cut through the adjacent bar with little additional effort. Then he bent both bars up and away from the grate, creating a narrow passageway.

Giordino grabbed Gunn's arm and guided him to the access hole. Gunn kicked his way through, twisting sideways to slip past the remaining bars. He turned and waited for Pitt and Giordino, then let the current pull him as far as the small footbridge. As he struggled to stop, an arm reached out of nowhere to yank him to the side.

'End of the line, Rudi,' he heard Pitt's voice whisper.

The steep sides of the aqueduct were slippery with algae, but the men used the bridge supports to pull themselves out. Then they stripped out of their dry suits and stashed them under the bridge footing.

Gunn unzipped his dive bag and pulled out his glasses, shoes and a small digital camera. Beside him, Pitt had retrieved his .45 and the two radios.

He clipped one onto his belt and handed the other to Gunn.

'Sorry we don't have enough weapons to go round,' Pitt said. 'You get in a bind, then give us a call.'

'Believe me, I'll be in and out of there before anyone can blink.'

Gunn's task was to sneak into the lab and photograph the seismic device, grabbing any documents he could along the way. Pitt and Giordino had the stickier objective of locating Theresa and Wofford.

'We'll try to rendezvous here, unless one of us doesn't make it out cleanly. Then we'll head for the garage and one of Borjin's vehicles.'

'Take this, Rudi,' Giordino said, handing Gunn a crowbar from his bag. 'In case the door is locked—or an overinquisitive lab rat gives you trouble.'

With a humourless grin, Gunn grabbed the crowbar and skulked off. Following Pitt's directions, he ran across the compound, dashing from shrub to shrub, then moved past the open garage, where the sound of tinkling tools told him that late-night mechanical duties were in progress, and on towards the adjacent laboratory.

After checking that there were no horse patrols around, he crept to the glass entry door and pushed. To his surprise, the door was unlocked and opened into the test bay. Gunn entered quickly, closing the door behind him. He grabbed a lab coat from a rack near the entrance and slipped it on as he walked briskly to the main corridor, which stretched the length of the building. To the three people still working in the adjacent offices at that late hour, he was just someone in a white lab coat, probably on the way to the bathroom.

Gunn quickly reached the thick door at the end of the hall. Heart pounding, he flipped the latch and shoved. The door swung open, revealing von Wachter's acoustic seismic device in the centre of the huge anechoic chamber.

'We're halfway home,' he muttered as he pulled out the digital camera, silently wondering how his colleagues were faring. At a large console he rummaged through some documents and papers until he found what appeared to be the operator's manual, a thick booklet clamped to a miniature stainless steel clipboard. Gunn stuffed the manual and clipboard into a zippered chest pocket on his jacket, then resumed his photography.

'IF YOU CAN PROVIDE a distraction from the front, then I should be able to slip round and surprise them from the side,' Pitt whispered, studying the two guards standing on either side of the main residence door.

'A visit from my pet monkey should do the trick,' Giordino replied, patting the heavy red pipe wrench dangling from his belt.

The two men moved quietly along one of the reflecting canals that flowed towards the house, advancing in short bursts. The guards stood leaning against the residence, accustomed to the uneventful grind of the night shift.

Pitt motioned for Giordino to stay put and give him five minutes to reposition himself. As Giordino hunkered down in a rosebed, Pitt silently looped his way round the grounds to the far side of the entrance, where he ducked behind a juniper bush. The guards stood just a few yards away, oblivious to his presence. He tightened his grip on the .45, and waited.

Giordino gave Pitt an extra minute before moving from the rose bed. He had noted that the wide columns supporting the portico roof offered a perfect blind spot from which to approach the porch. He inched sideways until a column blocked his view of the guards—and thus their view of him—then angled his way right up to the back of the column, less than twenty feet from the front door. Stepping casually from behind the column, he took aim at one of the guards, then flung the pipe wrench like a tomahawk.

Both guards saw the squat Italian step into view, but were too startled to react. They stared in disbelief as a red object tumbled through the air at them, smashing one of them in the chest and cracking his ribs. The guard fell to his knees, wheezing a moan of shock and pain. The other guard stepped to his partner's aid, but, seeing that he was not injured seriously, stood up and stumbled after Giordino, who had ducked back behind the column. The guard stopped when he detected footsteps behind him. He turned in time to see the butt of Pitt's .45 strike his temple.

Pitt managed to catch the guard before he collapsed to the ground, but the first guard had meanwhile staggered to his feet, armed with a short knife. Giordino dived towards him, deflecting the knife with his left arm, and beat his right fist into the side of the man's neck, knocking him senseless.

Pitt surveyed the compound. All appeared quiet. 'Let's get these guys out of sight,' he said, and dragged his unconscious victim towards some bushes.

Giordino followed suit, grabbing his guard by the collar and pulling him backwards. 'Hope the next shift change doesn't arrive soon,' he huffed.

'It may arrive sooner than you think,' Pitt said with a knowing wink.

THERESA WATCHED the tiny flames gobble up the torn pages, growing higher and brighter until it was clear that the fire would sustain itself. Grabbing a file containing samples of von Wachter's detailed imaging, she turned and bolted down the corridor, adrenaline pumping through her veins.

The escape plan was simple. They would hide off the foyer until the fire drew the response of the front-entry guards. Slipping outside, they would try to commandeer a vehicle in the ensuing chaos and make a break for it.

She slowed to a walk as she approached the foyer. Wofford stood where she had left him, beside a large fluted column. Theresa smiled, indicating with a nod that she had been successful. He looked back at her with dread in his eyes.

Then Tatiana stepped out from behind Wofford's shadow, waving a Makarov PM automatic pistol at his back. With a menacing smile, she hissed at Theresa. 'A beautiful evening for a walk, no?'

Theresa gasped as a chill ran down her spine. But she wasn't going to go down meekly. 'I couldn't sleep,' she bluffed. 'We are so close to finishing the analysis. I convinced the guard to let us retrieve some of the reports so that we could work in our rooms.' She held up the file under her arm.

'And where is the guard?' Tatiana asked sceptically.

'He is closing down the study,' Theresa replied.

A conveniently timed tumbling of books sounded from down the corridor, the work of the fire burning through a lower bookshelf. An inquisitive look crossed Tatiana's face and she turned to peek down the hall, keeping the gun pointed at Wofford. He glanced at Theresa, nodding slightly.

As if in a rehearsed move, Theresa flung her bundled papers at Tatiana's face while Wofford lunged for the pistol. With a quickness that surprised them both, Tatiana spun in a half circle, sidestepping Wofford's reach as the files bounced harmlessly off the back of her head. Spinning forward, she stepped towards Theresa and jammed the gun in her cheek.

'I should kill you for that,' she hissed while waving Wofford back with her other hand. 'What other tricks have you been up to.'

Prodding Theresa across the foyer with the muzzle of the gun, she led her to the front door and flung it open. 'Guards,' she barked. 'Come assist me.'

The two guards on the porch, dressed in Mongol warrior attire with their tin helmets pulled low, burst through the door and quickly sized up the situation. The first guard stepped towards Wofford and produced a hand-gun, which he jammed into the geophysicist's ribs. The second guard, a shorter man, stepped up to Theresa and grabbed her tightly by the arm.

'Take her,' Tatiana ordered, pulling the gun away from Theresa's face.

The guard obliged by roughly jerking her away from Tatiana. A wave of hopelessness fell over Theresa as she looked at Wofford with despair. Then the vicelike grip round her arm eased. In an unexpected move, the guard let go of Theresa's arm and suddenly grasped Tatiana by the wrist. With the flick of his powerful hand, he twisted Tatiana's wrist while applying a pincerlike squeeze to her hand. The gun slipped to the marble floor.

'What on earth are you doing?' Tatiana cried, cradling her bent wrist.

For the first time, she looked directly at the guard. His grin seemed famil-iar. She turned to the other guard, whose gun was now aimed at her. She looked at his face, and gasped at the penetrating green eyes that stared back.

'You!' she rasped. 'I thought you died in the desert.'

'Wishful thinking, perhaps,' Giordino replied, picking up the Makarov.

'Al, you came back,' Theresa gasped.

Giordino squeezed her hand. 'Sorry to rough you around on the way in.'

Theresa nodded her head in understanding and squeezed his hand back.

'I think it might be a good time to make an exit, before any real palace guards show up,' Giordino said, escorting Theresa towards the door.

'Wait,' she said. 'The seismic reports. We found evidence that they may try to disrupt tectonic fault zones in the Persian Gulf and Alaska.'

'This is absurd,' Tatiana declared.

'It's true,' Wofford said, helping Theresa to pick up the littered papers.

'They've already struck the Gulf successfully, I'm afraid,' Pitt said.

'The data should fit well with the photos Rudi is taking,' Giordino added.

Pitt saw the quizzical looks on Theresa and Wofford's faces. 'An acoustic seismic array sits in the lab across the way. Used to trigger earthquakes, we believe. It seems Alaska is next on the hit list.'

At that moment a deafeningly shrill sound pierced the hallway. The grow-ing blaze had finally triggered a smoke detector outside the study.

'We set fire to the study,' Theresa explained. 'Hoped to use it as a diver-sion for Jim and me to escape.'

'Maybe we still can,' Pitt replied, 'but let's not wait for the fire brigade.'

He led the group across the portico, then stopped at the outer support columns. The sound of galloping hooves to his right told him a patrol to the north of the residence had heard the alarm and was charging towards the entrance. Ahead and to his left, a commotion was erupting near the stables and security quarters as guards hurried towards the residence on foot.

Pitt motioned towards the rosebushes. 'Everybody get down flat. When they've entered the house, we'll move on,' he said quietly.

Theresa and Wofford dived to the ground. Giordino shoved Tatiana behind a budding bush, and clasped a hand over her mouth.

Pitt knelt down and pulled the handheld radio from his belt, then held it to his lips. 'Rudi, can you hear me?' he said quietly.

'I'm all ears,' came an equally hushed reply.

'We're on our way out, but there's a party starting up here. We'll have to meet up on the fly, in about five or ten minutes.'

'I'll wrap up and head towards the garage. Out.'

Pitt hit the ground as a trio of guards ran from the stables and into the residence, barely noticing that the entry guards were nowhere in sight.

The horse patrol, numbering eight men, was still fifty yards away but galloping fast. An uneasy feeling came over him as he watched the horsemen pull up hard on reaching the gravel drive. They fanned out at the edge of the portico, then stopped. Inside the residence, the alarm fell silent.

Suddenly a dozen floodlights mounted in the portico's rafters popped on in a blinding burst, spilling light onto the surrounding grounds. Clearly illuminated in the glare were the bodies of Pitt and the others in the rosebushes.

Pitt tightened his grip on the .45 and took aim at the nearest horseman. But he was chagrined to see that in addition to their lethal bows and arrows they all carried rifles, now aimed in their direction. Then the three guards who had rushed across the compound burst back onto the porch, their tunics blackened with smoke, and AK-74 assault rifles cradled in their arms.

Busting past the gunmen was a fourth man, dressed in a blue silk robe, who charged to the centre of the driveway and glared at Pitt and the others.

'I will have retribution for this,' Borjin growled.

Pitt rose slowly to his feet, the Colt held down at his side. He waited until Giordino jerked Tatiana to her feet and turned her towards her brother, the Makarov held clearly visible against her ear.

With all eyes on Tatiana, Pitt slowly raised the Colt until it was pointed at Borjin's midsection. With his left hand, he unobtrusively brushed the TRANSMIT button on his radio, hoping to clue Gunn in to their predicament.

Borjin gazed at his sister's peril with mild disinterest. When he studied Pitt and Giordino with a closer scrutiny, his eyes flared in recognition.

'You,' he cried, then regained his composure. 'You survived your ride in the desert to trespass on my property again? Why risk such foolishness?'

'We came to put an end to your earthquakes and your murdering rampage for oil,' Pitt replied. 'We came for our friends. And for Genghis.'

Pitt's mention of the Mongol warlord's name nearly sent a tremor through Borjin. 'Death will greet you first,' he spat, nodding at his guards.

'Perhaps. But you and your sister will accompany me on the journey.'

Borjin took a hard look at the rugged man who threatened him so boldly. 'My men will cut you down in an instant,' he threatened back. 'But I do not wish to see my sister die. Release her, and your friends are free to go.'

'No,' Theresa protested. 'You must let us all go free.'

'You are in no position to make demands,' Borjin replied. He pretended to pace back and forth, but Pitt could tell he was trying to remove himself from the field of fire. He stepped behind one of the guards, then halted.

The boom erupted like a sledgehammer striking iron. It came from the direction of the laboratory. Everyone froze in confusion as twenty seconds crept by, then a second boom erupted.

'It is von Wachter's device,' Tatiana shouted. 'Someone has activated—'

A third boom, like the crash of a temple gong, drowned her words.

GUNN HAD JUST LEFT the anechoic chamber with all the evidence he needed when his radio came to life. What he heard filled him with despair. But he couldn't just leave his friends to die. He stepped back into the chamber, thinking perhaps, just perhaps, he could turn Borjin's demon against its master.

He raced to the console, thankful that he had taken a few minutes earlier to joyride with the controls. Jumping into the operator's seat, he grabbed the mouse and scrolled down the screen, which showed a three-dimensional stratigraphic chart of the sediment layers beneath the lab. He was searching for an image he had seen earlier. As the tripod device ticked and hummed to follow the commands, Gunn frantically bounced the cursor about. Finally he spotted the stratum he was looking for. It was an odd jump in the sedimentary line, dividing two layers of sediment with a distinct cut. He guided the cursor to the crown of the cut and clicked the mouse. An illuminated cross hair began flashing over the indicated point as the tripod ticked again. Gunn rolled the cursor to the top of the screen and scrolled through a series of drop-down menus, sweat dripping off his forehead, until a window appeared showing the word AKTIVIEREN in bold letters in a flashing red box. Gunn mentally crossed his fingers and clicked the button.

At first, nothing happened. Then, with a flicker of lights, an explosive boom erupted from the inverted tip of the tripod. It felt as though a bolt of lightning had struck just inches away. The acoustic blast shook the building, nearly tossing Gunn from his chair. He staggered towards the door with his ears ringing, then stopped in dismay.

The anechoic chamber. It was designed to absorb sound waves. Even the concentrated blasts erupting from the acoustic array would be seriously diluted by the sound-deadening floor panels. His efforts were for naught.

Gunn jumped off the catwalk and vaulted over to the base of the tripod. He anticipated the next blast and covered his ears as a second acoustic burst was fired from the transducer tubes in a deafening bang. Then he frantically set about tearing at the foam floor panels beneath the device, which lifted off easily. Beneath the foam, the floor was tiled in lead plates as an extra sound deadener. Gunn grabbed the crowbar he had left on the table, quickly prised up one of the heavy tiles and muscled it aside. Then he dived down and ripped away three other lead plates, which together with the first had formed a square beneath the business end of the acoustic array.

Gunn stepped back just as the third acoustic blast fired. Jamming his palms to his ears, he looked down and saw that the device was now firing through the concrete foundations.

He tugged open the heavy door, half expecting to face a legion of armed guards. Instead, a small group of scientists, some in pyjamas, was swarming at the other end of the long hallway. As Gunn stepped through the chamber door, one of the scientists yelled, spurring the angry mob to charge towards him. Gunn rushed to the nearest office on his right and raced across the room to a small window that faced the compound grounds. He jabbed the blunt end of the crowbar into a corner of the window, shattering the glass, and dived out. He had barely hit the ground when the fourth and final blast emitted from the acoustic array, the impact much less violent to Gunn now that he was outside.

Gunn could hear a chorus of frantic yells through the broken window as the scientists rushed to deactivate the system. His rash gamble was finished. So too, he thought with dread, was his chance to save the lives his friends.

WHEN THE SOUND of the second blast echoed across the compound, Borjin ordered two of the mounted guards to go and investigate. They galloped away as a rumble echoed in the distance. The deep boom of a third seismic blast drowned out their pounding hoofbeats and the faraway rumble as well.

'You have brought friends?' Borjin sneered at Pitt.

'Enough to close you down for good,' Pitt replied.

'Then they shall die with you.'

A crash of shattering glass sounded from the laboratory, followed by the fourth detonation of the acoustic seismic array. Then all fell silent.

The sneer was still on Borjin's face when another distant rumble reverberated off the hills like thunder. This time, the rumble continued to resonate, with the growing intensity of an approaching avalanche. Outside the compound, a pack of wolves howled in mournful unison. The horses picked up the cue and began neighing in nervous anticipation of the pending cataclysm.

A thousand metres below the surface, a trio of condensed sound waves, fired from the three transducers, converged at the angled fracture targeted by Gunn. The sedimentary cut was, as he had hoped, an ancient fault. The first two blasts of the seismic array had struck the fault with only a minor pulse. The third blast, however, hit the unshielded ground at full power. Though the sediment held firm, the seismic waves rocked with a vibrating force that rattled the fault line. The fourth blast broke the camel's back.

The seismic vibrations beneath the Mongolian mountainside jolted the fracture, causing slips in both vertical and horizontal directions. The buckle was small, just a few inches spread across a quarter-mile rift, but because it was close to the surface the wave impact was dramatic.

When the shock waves reached the surface the ground began to shake back and forth. Then it seemed to break loose in all directions. One of the guards fell back onto the porch steps, his machine gun dropping at arm's length. Pitt dived to the ground, his smaller weapon giving him a sudden advantage. He zeroed in on the closest man still standing and squeezed the trigger. The man sprawled on the ground. Pitt swept his gun towards the second guard, who was on his knees, and fired three times as the guard let loose a return burst from his AK-74. Two of Pitt's three shots struck home, killing the guard instantly, while the machine gun's errant burst peppered the ground to Pitt's left.

Pitt immediately swung his muzzle towards the Mongolian tycoon, who had clambered up the steps at the first gunshot and was disappearing behind the door. The first guard scrambled after him, and had just reached the doorstep when Pitt fired once. Another shot rang out behind him, fired by Giordino. The shaking proved too great for either man to aim accurately, and the guard dived through the residence door unscathed.

At the other end of the driveway, the mounted guards had been of little concern. Whinnying with terror, the horses reared repeatedly, and their riders clutched the reins for dear life.

The violent shaking lasted for nearly a minute, making the prone observers feel as if their bodies were being tossed into the air. Across the compound, a lone alarm wailed feebly from inside the lab building.

And then it ended. The rumbling ceased, the shaking fell away, and an eerie calm fell over the blacked-out compound.

Gazing at the others, Pitt saw that Theresa and Wofford were unhurt, but a streak of red flowed down Giordino's left leg.

Giordino perused the wound with a look of minor inconvenience. 'Sorry, boss. Caught a ricochet from Machine Gun Kelly. No bones, though.'

Pitt nodded, then glanced at the horsemen, whose mounts were quieting. 'Take cover behind the support columns. Quick,' he directed. He had barely spoken the words when a rifleshot rang out from one of the horsemen.

Limping slightly, Giordino dragged Tatiana to the base of one column while Theresa and Wofford hunkered down behind the next. Pitt fired a round in the general direction of the shooter before scrambling behind a third column. He thought of Gunn and reached down for his radio, but it had been knocked off during the earthquake and lay somewhere in the dark.

'Lost the radio,' he said, cursing.

'I doubt Rudi can do anything more to help us,' Giordino muttered. 'I've only got five shots left,' he added.

Pitt had only a few rounds left as well. With Wofford and Giordino both hobbled, they couldn't move far in a hurry. Pitt looked to the open front door and decided that the residence might be the best option for a defensive stand.

He rose to one knee and prepared to lead the others towards the entrance when a shadow flashed by the doorway. In the faint light, Pitt detected what appeared to be the muzzle of a gun poking out.

Then a deep rumble echoed off the hillsides.

Pitt listened, and noted that it originated up the mountain rather than beneath the ground. The thundering noise grew louder until it matched the roar of a dozen 747 jumbo jets taking off.

A quarter of a mile upstream, the earthquake had triggered a deep chasm perpendicular to the riverbank. The raging river waters swirled in a confused vortex under the force of gravity. Near the mouth of the aqueduct, the entire river shifted laterally, staking a new course alongside the elevated dirt road. The river had rushed towards Borjin's compound before pooling in a large depression. A high berm, built as an equipment causeway between the road and the aqueduct, created an unintended dam within sight of the compound. The surging waters overflowed the depression, cutting a crack in the dirt wall that quickly expanded to its base. In a flash, the entire berm collapsed under its own weight, releasing a surging wall of water.

The icy black water burst towards the compound in a ten-foot-high wave. It gushed over the walls, crushing the front-entry guards as it ripped away the heavy iron gate, and breaching a large hole through the wall above the aqueduct. The two swells of water merged inside the compound and surged towards the residence in a six-foot-high rolling wave.

Pitt gazed at the approaching wall of water and knew they had no chance of outrunning it. 'Grab hold of the columns and hang on,' he shouted.

They barely had time to stretch their arms round the fluted marble before the deluge hit.

Following the path of least resistance, the wave rolled across the northern part of the compound and mostly bypassed the lab and garage. As Pitt had hoped, when the wave hit the residence the columns took the brunt of the impact, but his legs were still ripped off the ground and pulled towards the house. The icy water sucked the air out of his lungs and stung his skin like a thousand needles. When the tug of the water receded, Pitt pulled himself to his feet. At the adjacent column, he saw Giordino pull Tatiana up from under the water, the Mongolian woman coughing and spluttering. A second later, Theresa and Wofford emerged at the next column, gasping from the cold.

As he waded towards the others, Pitt noted the bodies of several guards floating about the driveway. He turned to find Theresa staring through glazed eyes, shivering uncontrollably in the freezing water.

'We need to get to dry ground,' Pitt said, looking around.

The diverted river had settled into two main channels through the compound. The primary flow ran from the front gate to the northern edge of the residence, which had begun to crumble under the force of the rushing waters, then cascaded over the cliff. A secondary flow swirled towards the lab, angled back to the residence's portico, then rejoined the main flow. Pitt quickly guided the group out of the deepest section of this secondary swirl.

Yelling echoed across the grounds as the scientists tried to prevent the waters from flooding the laboratory. Inside the garage, somebody shouted as a car was heard starting up. Further chaos ensued outside, as horses stampeded back and forth across the compound in nervous confusion.

Suddenly a vehicle came barrelling out through the garage doors with its lights ablaze, and ploughed through the surrounding water like a tank.

Pitt watched anxiously as the vehicle turned in their direction. The black water swirling about their ankles prevented a quick escape. Pitt calmly eyed the approaching vehicle, raised his .45 and took aim at the car's windshield.

The driver ignored the threat, charging forward as streams of water gushed off the front bumper and fender wells. As the car drew nearer, it drifted to one side, then started to slow. Pitt held his fire as the jet-black supercharged Range Rover cut a wide turn, then sloshed to a stop just a few yards in front of him. From the dark interior a familiar bespectacled face popped through the open window.

'Somebody call for a taxi?' Rudi Gunn asked with a grin.

11

'Nice shake, Rudi,' Giordino grunted from the back seat. 'But we could probably have done without the ice-water bath.'

Gunn had turned the Range Rover's heater up high. Theresa's shivering had abated, and she was helping Giordino to bandage his leg.

'I can't really take responsibility for the bonus elements of fire and flood,' Gunn replied with feigned humility.

Pitt, who stood leaning on the driver's window ledge, turned towards the laboratory and noticed for the first time a billow of smoke and flames pouring out of the windows. Somewhere in the building, a broken gas line had ignited, sending a fireball through the structure.

'Get out,' Tatiana hissed, regaining her feistiness. 'This is my brother's car.'

'I thought it a nice choice,' Gunn replied. 'Remind me to thank him for leaving the keys in the ignition.' He opened the door and started to get out. 'You want to drive?' he asked Pitt. 'I'll climb in the back with the wildcat.'

'No,' Pitt said. 'I'm going to make sure that our host doesn't disappear.'

'You can't last much longer in that icy water,' Gunn said, noting a shiver from Pitt. 'At least take my jacket,' he offered.

Pitt slipped off his own waterlogged garment and gratefully zipped up Gunn's dry jacket in its place. 'Thanks, Rudi,' he said. 'Now, get out of here. If I don't find you within an hour, then hightail it to Ulaanbaatar without me.'

THOUGH THE WORST of the flooding had subsided, there was still half a foot of water seeping though the residence when Pitt waded up the front steps.

The house was quiet, save for the distant sound of rushing water. The electricity had long since been extinguished, but a handful of emergency red lights dotted the ceiling. Pitt peered down the three separate hallways. He could see out through the open end of the northern corridor, where the river had washed away the end of the wing. Borjin couldn't escape that way unless he had a kayak and a death wish, Pitt thought, and slowly moved off along the main corridor, his feet numbed by the icy water.

A loud crash echoed from the side of the house as another chunk of the north wing crumbled under the river's surge. The whole residence shook, and Pitt knew there was a danger of the entire structure sliding down the mountain.

He moved quickly past a few side rooms, then hesitated as he reached the fire-blackened study. He could see the flood waters cascading down a stairwell just past the study entrance. And faint though they were, he could also see a pair of wet prints leading into the dry conference room beyond.

Cautiously he approached the conference-room door and peered inside. The moon had crept over the horizon and cast a bright silvery beam through the room's tall windows. Pitt strained to discern Borjin's presence, but all was still. He quietly stepped in, the muzzle of his Colt moving with his eyes.

Borjin's timing was impeccable. The Mongolian popped up from behind the end of the conference table while Pitt was facing the other end of the room. Too late, Pitt turned towards the movement as a loud twang erupted from the spot. Off-balance and wheeling round on numb feet, Pitt fired a single shot towards Borjin but missed wide, the bullet shattering the glass window behind him. Borjin's aim was to prove more accurate.

Pitt saw but a fleeting glimpse of the feathered arrow before it struck his chest, knocking him off his feet. Thrown to the floor, he caught a lasting image of Borjin standing with a crossbow cradled in his arms. The moonlight sparkled off his sharp teeth, which were bared in a satisfied, murderous grin.

AFTER SLOGGING the four-wheel drive through fallen bits of the entry wall, Gunn turned the Range Rover towards a small rise outside the compound. From the elevated perch, they had a perfect view of the disintegration below.

'I'd be happy if there's not a cinder left of that place,' Wofford remarked, eyeing the destruction with satisfaction.

'Seeing how we're a hundred and fifty miles from the nearest fire department, there is probably a pretty good chance of that,' Gunn replied.

'He shouldn't have gone back alone,' Giordino said, cursing.

'Nobody could have stopped him,' Gunn said. 'He'll be all right.'

But a strange feeling in his stomach said otherwise.

BORJIN PLACED the medieval crossbow back among his collection of antique weaponry, then stepped to the cracked window and took a hurried look outside at the growing pool of water accumulating in the courtyard. He gazed with distress at the stone sanctuary. The main edifice was still intact, but the arched entrance had been shaken to bits during the earthquake.

Ignoring Pitt's body on the opposite side of the room, Borjin rushed out of the conference room. As he moved down the adjacent stairwell, the cascading water surging at the back of his legs, he glanced up at the dark portrait of the great warrior khan. At the lower level, the rising water was waist-high, until he unbolted the side door, releasing an icy torrent into the courtyard. He stumbled across the flooded yard to the sanctuary. Stepping over a pile of fallen stones, he entered the torch-lit interior and was relieved to find only a few inches of water running across the built-up floor.

The tombs were undamaged, but large cracks stretched across the domed ceiling like a giant spider's web. The structure was in a perilous state. Borjin gazed at the centre tomb, considering how best to protect his prize possession.

'Your world is crumbling down around you, Borjin. And you with it.'

The Mongolian spun round, then froze. The spectre of Pitt standing on his feet across the room, the crossbow arrow protruding from his chest, was unearthly. Only the Colt .45 aimed at Borjin's chest dispelled any notion of supernatural rejuvenation.

Pitt edged towards one of the marble tombs at the side of the chamber, pointing at it with the barrel of his gun. 'Your father?' he asked.

Borjin silently nodded, trying to regain his composure.

'It was your father who stole the map of Genghis Khan's grave from a British archaeologist,' Pitt said, 'but that still wasn't enough to locate it.'

Borjin raised a brow. 'My father acquired information as to the general location. It required the use of additional technologies to find the grave site.'

'Von Wachter's acoustic seismic array.'

'Indeed. A prototype discovered the buried grave. Improvements to the instrument have proved remarkable, as you have witnessed. As a result, the people of Mongolia will revel in a new dawn of conquest. We will rise against the fools of the world and take our place in the pantheon of—'

Borjin's raving was interrupted by a deep rumble which echoed through the floor. The rumble grew and culminated in a loud crash, as the entire north wing of the residence broke free of its foundation and slid down the hillside.

The impact shook the grounds all round the estate. The mausoleum floor vibrated under the feet of the two men, throwing them off balance. Pitt grabbed hold of the tomb in order to keep his gun trained on Borjin.

Borjin fell to a knee, then his eyes widened as a sharp cracking sound rippled from overhead. He looked up to see a huge chunk of the ceiling come hurtling down beside him.

Pitt flattened himself against the side of the tomb as the rear of the sanctuary fell in on itself. Chunks of ceiling smacked the top of the tomb beside him, but none struck him directly. He waited for the dust to clear, then stood up. Through the stones of the collapsed rear wall, he could see clearly to the corral and the old car parked inside.

It took him a few moments to spot Borjin in the debris. Only his head and part of his torso were exposed from a mound of stones. Pitt walked near as Borjin's eyes fluttered open, dull and listless. A trickle of blood streamed from his mouth, and his neck seemed distorted.

'Why . . . why won't you die?' the Mongol stammered.

But he never heard the answer. A muted choke grumbled from his throat and his eyes glazed over. His body crushed by his own monument to conquest, Tolgoi Borjin died quickly in the shadow of Genghis Khan.

Pitt stared at the broken body without pity, then slowly lowered the Colt. He reached down and unzipped the large pocket on the front of his jacket, and peeked inside. The seismic array operator's manual with metal clipboard was right where Gunn had placed it. But it was now perforated by an arrow, which had penetrated every page and even dinged the metal clipboard.

Pitt walked over to Borjin and looked down at the lifeless body. 'Sometimes, I'm just lucky,' he said aloud, answering Borjin's final query.

The collapse of the northern wing had funnelled more water into the courtyard. It would be just a matter of time before the flood waters washed the sanctuary down the mountainside, too. Pitt turned to make his escape, but hesitated. He gazed again at the tomb of Genghis, and for an instant he wondered if he would be the last man to see it. Then it hit him. It was a crazy idea, he thought, and he couldn't help but grin.

'All right, old boy,' he muttered at the tomb. 'Let's see if you've got one more conquest left in you.'

THE FEELING was just returning to Pitt's feet with a painful tingle as he climbed through the back of the sanctuary and staggered over to the corral. He yanked several timbers off the wooden fence to clear an opening. Tossing boxes and crates aside, he ploughed a wide path through the junk and debris until he reached his objective, the dust-laden old car.

It was a 1921 Rolls-Royce Silver Ghost open tourer, and Pitt wondered briefly how such a grand automobile had ended up in Mongolia. But it didn't matter. What mattered was the silver-handled crank that protruded from the car's grimy snout. It gave him a small hope.

Praying that the engine block wasn't frozen solid, Pitt opened the driver's door and placed the gearshift in neutral, then he stepped to the front of the car. Leaning down, he grabbed the crank with both hands, and heaved.

'IT'S BEEN WELL over an hour,' Gunn remarked, looking glumly at his watch.

He and Giordino stood on the rise, watching the devastation below. The laboratory fire burned in a blazing tempest, consuming the entire building and adjacent garage, casting a yellow glow over the compound.

As they watched, a low rumble shook from below. No earthquake this time, they knew, but rather the erosive effects of the flooding waters. Then the northern end of the residence began toppling one wall at a time. The central part simply folded in on itself with a grinding crash, then slid down the mountain. In just a few seconds, the bulk of the structure was gone. Only a small section of the southern wing survived on a patch of dry ground.

Gunn and Giordino knew that no one in and around the residence could have survived. Neither man said a word, solemnly staring at the altered river roaring down the cliffside. Then Gunn's ears detected another sound.

'What's that?' he asked.

He pointed a finger towards the surviving chunk of the southern wing. The whirr of a high-revving engine rumbled from the hillside behind, with a sporadic cough and stutter. The roar grew louder until it was matched with a pair of dim lights that slowly crept over the hill.

The object appeared like a giant primordial bug crawling out of a hole in the ground. The two round lamps probed the night like a pair of large yellow eyes. A shiny metallic body followed, clouded by dirt and dust kicked up by its clawing rear appendages. The living beast even breathed vapour, a white cloud of smoke rising from its head.

A sharp gust of wind suddenly blew the smoke and dust away, and, under the light of the roaring blaze, Gunn and Giordino could see that it was no overgrown insect but the antique Rolls-Royce from the corral.

'Only one guy I know would be driving an old crate like that at a time like this,' Giordino shouted with a whoop.

Gunn jumped into the Range Rover and charged the car down the hill to the compound. They saw that the old Rolls had a chain stretched taut off the rear bumper, and was trying to pull something up the side of the hill.

Pitt threw a thankful wave towards the approaching Range Rover, then turned back to coaxing the old automobile forward. But the weight behind was too great, and the big car seemed to be losing the battle. What little coolant that had existed in the block and radiator had nearly all boiled away, and Pitt knew it wouldn't be long before the engine seized.

He saw Giordino appear and grab hold of the door post. With a wink and a smile, the stocky Italian threw his weight into pushing the car forward. Gunn, Wofford and Theresa took up spots around the vehicle and started pushing with all their might.

The extra manpower was just enough to propel the car in its last gasp. With a sudden lunge, the Rolls-Royce lurched forward. Thirty feet behind, a large block of granite teetered over the edge of the hill. Chugging forward to a safe, dry spot, Pitt killed the engine under a whoosh of white steam.

As the vapour cleared away, Pitt saw that he was surrounded by a dozen scientists and technicians, along with a guard or two, who had given up fighting the lab fire to investigate his appearance.

Fearing for his safety, Pitt gripped his .45 and cautiously climbed out of the Rolls. But he need not have worried.

At seeing that the sarcophagus of Genghis Khan had been rescued from the flood, the guards and scientists broke into a cheer and applauded him.

12

A crisp breeze rippled across the lower slopes of Burkhan Khaldun, snapping taut the multitude of blue-and-red Mongolian state flags fluttering high overhead. The largest of the flags, fifty feet wide, wavered above a huge granite mausoleum whose carved façade had been hastily completed by local craftsmen just days before.

A rush of excited whispers swirled through the crowd as the sound of marching boots drew near. A company of Mongolian Army soldiers appeared through the pines, the first in a long procession of military honour guards escorting the remains of Genghis Khan to his final resting place, nearly eight centuries after his original, secret funeral in this same region.

The Mongol warrior's body had lain in state in Ulaanbaatar for a week, drawing visits from over two million people. After a three-day funeral procession to his grave site in the Khentii Mountains, the ancient leader was being brought to a peaceful spot close to where he was said to have been born.

Pitt, Giordino and Gunn, with Theresa and Wofford alongside, sat in the front row of dignitaries, a few seats down from Mongolia's president. Pitt turned and winked at a young boy seated behind him as the procession drew near. Noyon and his parents, special guests of Pitt's, looked on with awe.

Amid splendour worthy of the greatest conqueror the world has ever known, Genghis Khan's body was carried on a mammoth wooden caisson painted bright yellow. A team of eight white stallions pulled the funeral cart, and the rescued granite tomb was now covered in fresh lotus blossoms.

A troupe of aged lamas wearing bright red robes and arched yellow hats quietly took up position in front of the tomb. Down the hill, a pair of monks blew into their *radongs*, enormous telescopic horns, which emitted a deep baritone hum that was heard all down the valley.

At the end of the service, the granite sarcophagus was rolled into the mausoleum, then sealed with a six-ton slab of polished stone lowered by a crane. Genghis Khan was at rest again in his beloved homeland mountains.

As the crowd began filtering out, the president of Mongolia approached Pitt's party with a small entourage. A short, elegant man of forty-five, the president spoke nearly flawless English.

'Mr Pitt, on behalf of the people of Mongolia I wish to thank you and your NUMA team for rescuing Genghis for all posterity.'

'A giant of history deserves to live for ever,' Pitt replied. 'Though it is a shame that the riches of the tomb have all been lost.'

'Yes, it is a tragedy that the treasures of Genghis were dispersed to collectors around the world simply to enrich Borjin's family. Perhaps our country will be able to buy back some of the antiquities from our new-found oil revenues. Thankfully, Borjin was unable to find the tomb of Kublai Khan, and his treasures still reside undisturbed somewhere beneath these hills.'

'Kublai Khan,' Pitt muttered, staring at the mausoleum. On its granite façade, a lone wolf had been engraved, the outline painted blue.

'Yes, that is the legend. Mr Pitt, I wish also to thank you personally for exposing Borjin's corrupt activities. I have initiated an investigation into my own government to determine the extent of his influence-peddling.'

'I hope that Tatiana is proving to be a cooperative witness.'

'Most assuredly,' the president replied with a furtive grin. Tatiana, he knew, was being held at a less-than-comfortable security site. 'With her help, and the continued assistance of your oil-industry companions'—he nodded towards Theresa and Wofford—'we shall be able to exploit the discovered oil reserves for the good of a new Mongolia.'

'That is good to know,' Pitt said. 'Mr President, I have one favour to ask of you. We discovered a plane crash in the Gobi Desert.'

'My director of antiquities has already informed me. We shall be sending a team to excavate the aircraft right away. The bodies of those aboard will be returned to their homes for proper burial.'

'They deserve that.'

'It was a pleasure, Mr Pitt,' the president said, as an aide tugged at his sleeve. He turned and started to walk away, then stopped. 'I almost forgot,' he said to Pitt. 'A gift from the people of Mongolia to you. I understand you have an appreciation for such objects.'

He pointed down the hill to a large flat-bed truck which had discreetly followed the funeral procession up the mountainside. A large covered object sat on the truck's bed. Pitt watched with curiosity as two workmen climbed up and pulled back the canvas covering. Underneath sat Borjin's Rolls-Royce.

'Should make for a nice restoration project at the weekends,' Wofford said, eyeing the decrepit car.

'My wife Loren will love that,' Pitt replied with a devious grin.

'I'd love to meet her sometime,' Theresa said.

'Next time you are in Washington. Though I take it you'll be working in Mongolia for some time to come.'

'The company gave us three weeks of paid leave for our ordeal. We're hoping to go home to rest and recuperate before Jim and I come back.'

From the look she gave Giordino and the tone in her voice, it was clear that the 'we' was not referring to Wofford.

'I don't suppose you could take it upon yourself to nurse a rabid old sea dog like Al back to health during that time,' Pitt offered.

'I was rather counting on it,' she said coyly.

Giordino, leaning on a crutch, smiled broadly. 'Thanks, boss. I've always wanted to see the Zuiderzee.'

As the friends parted company, Pitt strolled down the hill towards the flat-bed truck. Gunn joined him as he approached the old Rolls.

'The Mongolian energy minister just told me that the price of oil is down another ten dollars today,' Gunn said. 'Experts predict that the price will soon drop to levels below those seen before the Persian Gulf disruption. And it was lucky that Summer and Dirk stumbled upon Borjin's brother and the second seismic device in Hawaii. Or he stumbled upon them. Had the ship travelled on to Valdez and damaged the Alaska Pipeline as planned, there would have been real pandemonium.'

'It was the Chinese wreck Summer found,' Pitt said. 'It drew them there for some reason.' A faraway look crossed his face, then his green eyes sparkled in enlightenment.

'Not only were all the seismic devices destroyed,' Gunn continued, 'but Dr von Wachter's research data as well, in the laboratory building fire. There's nothing left for anyone to be able to resurrect the technology.'

'Is that a bad thing?'

'I suppose not. Though I'd feel better if I knew the knowledge was in our hands and not the likes of Borjin.'

'Just between you, me and the car,' Pitt said, 'I happen to know that the operator's manual you lifted from the lab survived the flood and fire.'

Pitt walked to the rear of the Rolls and opened a large leather trunk mounted to the car's luggage rack. Inside was the seismic array operator's manual, with the arrow still protruding from its cover.

Gunn let out a low whistle, then put his hands over his eyes and turned away. 'I never saw it,' he said, steering Pitt towards their rented SUV down the hill. 'So, it's back to Washington?'

Pitt stopped and stared at the mausoleum of Genghis Khan. Then he shook his head. 'No, Rudi, you go on ahead. I'll catch up in a few days.'

'You staying here a bit longer?'

'No,' Pitt replied, a faraway twinkle in his eyes. 'I'm going to hunt a wolf.'

THE TROPICAL SUN beat down on the *Mariana Explorer* as she entered the mouth of the now-familiar cove in Keliuli Bay. Ahead and to his left, Captain Bill Stenseth noted a red marker buoy bobbing on the surface. Seventy feet beneath it lay the remains of the Avarga Oil drill ship.

Seated at the chart table, Pitt was examining a coastal map of Hawaii. Beside it was the cheetah skin he had retrieved from the crashed Fokker. Pitt's children, Dirk and Summer, stood looking over their father's shoulder.

'So, this is the scene of the crime,' Pitt said, rising from the table and peering out of the window. He stretched his arms and yawned, tired from his recent flight from Ulaanbaatar to Honolulu.

Dirk smiled. 'The marker buoy is where Summer laid waste to the drill ship,' he said, pointing out of the window. 'The Chinese wreck site is almost in the dead centre of the cove.' He swung his arm to the right.

'The artefacts all date to at least the thirteenth century?' Pitt asked.

'Everything has indicated as much,' Summer replied. 'The ceramic pieces recovered date from the late Song to the early Yuan dynasties. And wood samples date to approximately 1280.'

'The geological records don't hurt either,' Dirk said. 'We checked the known history of volcanic eruptions on the Big Island. A lava sample from neighbouring Pohue Bay dates around seven hundred years old. If the lava flows that buried our ship were from that same eruption, and my money says they were, then our ship would have arrived no later than AD 1300.'

'Does it correlate with your cryptic cheetah skin?' Summer asked.

'That's impossible to date, but the voyage depicted shows some interesting similarities,' Pitt replied. 'The lead vessel is a mammoth junk, which seems to match the size of your wreck, based on the salvaged rudder. Unfortunately, there was no narrative accompanying the images. Only a few decipherable words, which translate as "A lasting voyage to paradise".'

Pitt sat down and studied the animal skin again. The series of drawings clearly showed a four-masted junk at sail with two smaller support ships. Several panels depicted a long ocean voyage terminating at a cluster of islands that lay in the same relative position as the largest of Hawaii's eight islands. The large junk was shown landing on the biggest island, anchoring near a cave at the base of a high cliff. The final panel was what most intrigued Pitt. It showed the moored ship near some crates at the base of the cliff. Fire and smoke enveloped the ship and the surrounding landscape. Pitt studied a flag burning on the ship's mast with particular interest.

'The volcanic eruption fits like a glove,' he said.

'And those crates,' Summer said. 'They must contain some sort of treasure or valuables. Tong, or Temuge Borjin, as you've said his real name is, knew something about the ship's cargo. That's why they were trying to open up the lava field with a directed earthquake.'

'I guess the laugh is on them,' Dirk said. 'If the drawing is correct, then the cargo was taken ashore and destroyed by the lava flows.'

'Was it destroyed?' Pitt asked with a wily grin.

'How could it have survived the lava flows?' Summer asked.

'I'd say it's worth a look. Let's go get wet and find out for sure.'

HALF AN HOUR LATER, the three divers converged on the bottom, less than twenty feet below, as close to the surf line as they could get. The crashing waves roiled the water with foam and silt, reducing the visibility to just a few feet. Summer saw her father nod at her then turn and head into the murk. She quickly followed, knowing her brother would take up the rear.

She had been following her father's trail of bubbles for twenty minutes when he disappeared into the dark waters ahead of her. She felt herself being carried close to a lava rise by a large wave. Turning to kick away, she was surprised by a second, more powerful wave, which slammed her back into the lava wall, her steel air tank grinding against the rock.

Unhurt by the collision, she remained pinned against the lava until the wave rolled past. She had started to move away when she noticed a dark patch in the rocks above her head. Pulling herself closer, she peered into a black tunnel that angled slightly upwards. She pulled out a flashlight and beamed it inside. The opening clearly travelled for some distance.

Her heart skipped a beat as she realised that this was what her father was searching for. She banged the flashlight against her dive tank. A metallic clanging echoed through the water.

Almost immediately Dirk appeared, and soon afterwards their father. Pitt playfully patted Summer on the head when he spotted the tunnel. Flicking on his own flashlight, he swam into the tunnel, his kids following behind.

Pitt had immediately recognised the opening as a lava tube, the result of a steady flow of hot lava cooling on the surface and creating an outer crust. The liquid centre ultimately flowed out, leaving a smooth, hollow tube, almost perfectly cylindrical, in this case about six feet in diameter.

Pitt followed the tube for thirty feet, noticing a gradual ascent on his depth gauge. The tube suddenly flared wide, and he found himself breaking the surface of a calm pool of water. Black walls of lava fell vertically to the water on three sides, but the fourth side opened to a rocky clearing. Pitt kicked towards the landing as Summer and Dirk surfaced near him. They all swam to the rocks and climbed out, then spat out their regulators.

'It's amazing,' Summer said. 'An underground cavern fed from a flooded lava tube. Though it could use a little air-conditioning.'

'It was probably a much deeper cave at one time, but became sealed off by the lava flows gushing down the mountainside,' Pitt said. 'It's a fluke that a lava tube happened to form at its entrance.'

Dirk flashed his light round the clearing. 'Summer, behind you,' he said.

She turned to see a man standing just a few feet away. She stifled a cry as she realised that the man wasn't real.

'A clay warrior?' Dirk asked.

Summer shone her light and noticed another figure nearby. They were both life-size soldiers, with painted uniforms and sculpted swords. She crept closer, and saw that each had braided hair and a stringy moustache.

Summer looked at her father quizzically. 'What are they doing here?'

Pitt stepped up to the two figures and noticed a small path between them, cut through the lava. 'I think they are guiding us to the answer,' he said.

Stepping between the clay sculptures, he followed the path, with Dirk and Summer in tow. The trail twisted round several walls of lava, then opened into a cavernous room. The walls were lined with an army of clay figures. Each wore a heavy necklace of gold or an amulet studded with gemstones. There was also an inner ring of sculptures, mostly carved figures of animals—deer, horses, falcons—in jade or gilded stone.

Interspersed with the sculptures were dozens of small lacquered cabinets and tables. On a large teak table, Summer noticed an elaborate place setting which shone under her light. The flatware and goblets were all cast in gold. Other tables held silver and gold ornaments, some adorned with Arabic lettering and literary Chinese script, and there were mirrors, boxes and art objects glistening with gems. But the sculptures and jewels didn't interest Pitt. He stared past them towards a raised stone platform in the centre of the chamber. On it stood a long, carved wooden box, painted yellow. Pitt stepped closer and shone his light on the lid. A stuffed cheetah, its teeth bared and a clawed paw scratching the air, seemed to hiss back at Pitt. He lowered the beam to the side of the box and smiled at the image. A large wolf, painted blue, was emblazoned across the surface.

'May I present the late emperor, Kublai Khan,' he said.

'Kublai Khan,' Summer whispered in reverence. 'It can't be.'

'I thought he was buried somewhere near Genghis,' Dirk said.

'According to legend. But the tale didn't seem to add up. Borjin located the grave of Genghis Khan with his seismic device, but didn't find Kublai. I suspect he may have found an empty tomb, or some other clue that Kublai was buried elsewhere. That's why his brother, your Dr Tong, sidestepped a mission to disrupt the Alaska Pipeline in order to visit a shipwreck.'

'I still don't see how that leads here,' Summer said.

'The story is in the cheetah skin. It was discovered at Shangdu, so it had an original link with Kublai. And the skin was unearthed with a silk map which purportedly showed the location of Genghis Khan's tomb. Borjin's father acquired the silk map, and Borjin himself admitted that it helped lead to the grave site. For some reason, the significance of the cheetah-skin paintings was overlooked when first found. The blue wolf was the trigger for me.'

'What blue wolf?' Summer asked.

Pitt pointed to the image on the wooden coffin. 'It was an emblem of the imperial khans, originated by Genghis. You can see a banner of a blue wolf flying on the mast of the burning junk in the last painting on the cheetah skin. It would be flown only in the presence of a khan. Your wreck, which matched the depiction of a royal vessel departing China on the panels, was dated fifty years after the death of Genghis, when Kublai ruled the empire. And died. The cheetah skin shows the final voyage of Kublai Khan.'

'But why was he brought to Hawaii?' Summer asked.

'His last years were difficult ones. Perhaps his "voyage to paradise" was a plan to spend eternity on a faraway shore.'

'Dad, how did you know his tomb survived the volcanic blast?'

'Whoever painted the cheetah skin had seen the tomb and treasures and had known they survived the lava flows, otherwise they would have been depicted in flames as well. I took a gamble on the entrance. The sea levels are higher than they were seven hundred years ago, so I figured the entrance might now be under water.'

'The treasures here must represent the riches accumulated during a lifetime of conquest,' Dirk exclaimed. 'It must be worth an untold fortune.'

'The Mongolian people were cheated out of Genghis Khan's treasure. It's only fitting they secure the riches of Kublai.'

The wonder of the hidden tomb played heavily on their inner thoughts as they roamed through the chamber's ancient treasures. Eventually, their lights running low, Pitt and Summer moved together towards the passageway. Dirk sidled up to his father as they took a last look around.

'First you save the tomb of Genghis. Now you discover Kublai Khan and the treasures of his empire,' he said with awe. 'That's one for the ages.'

Summer nodded in agreement. 'Dad, sometimes you are just amazing.'

Pitt reached his arms out wide and gave his kids an affectionate hug.

'No,' he replied with a broad grin. 'Sometimes, I'm just lucky.'

CLIVE CUSSLER

Born: July 15, 1931, California
Books published: 41
Website: www.numa.net

Clive Cussler once said of his lifelong fascination with underwater exploration: 'There aren't many thrills that parallel that of swimming through a shipwreck. I've always compared it to walking through a cemetery. You can sense and sometimes visualise the ghosts of the crew who lived on board and died without anyone to record their passing.'

In 1979, driven by his passion for marine archaeology, he founded the National Underwater and Maritime Agency (NUMA), a non-profit organisation whose objective is to preserve maritime and naval history through the discovery, survey and conservation of shipwreck artefacts. It is largely financed by the royalties from his books, and all significant expedition finds are given to deserving bodies such as museums and universities.

'You can sense and sometimes visualise the ghosts of the crew who lived and died without anyone to record their passing.'

Cussler coined the name NUMA in the early Dirk Pitt novels in which the fictional government agency first appeared. Headed by his intrepid hero, the fictional NUMA, which does the same kind of work as its real-life counterpart, employs many of the main characters, including Pitt's best buddy Al Giordino.

The *real* NUMA has, to date, discovered over sixty historically significant underwater wreck sites, including that of the *Hunley*, the first ever submarine to sink an enemy ship in battle during the American Civil War. In 2001, NUMA made its most exciting discovery: the wreck of the *Halifax*, better known as the fabled ghost ship, the *Mary Celeste*. In 1872 she was found sailing off the Azores with no one aboard, her captain and crew having inexplicably vanished. Almost 125 years later, NUMA recovered the wreck, covered by coral, from Rochelais Reef off the coast of Haiti.

The truth behind the sinking of the *Mary Celeste* and her missing crew may never be known, but through their ongoing work, Clive Cussler and NUMA are shedding light on many a maritime mystery, as well as increasing public appreciation of our ocean-going past and inspiring a new generation of sea lovers.